THE ONLY SIN

"Ellis keeps things fresh . . . and keeps readers hanging on every word."
—*The Chattanooga Times*

"Enchanting and well researched."
—*Booklist*

RICH IS BEST

"As much fun and even ultimately as moving as Julie Ellis's other bestsellers in the same vein . . . a solid and absorbing tale."—*The Pittsburg Press*

"Combines the appeal of a highly sympathetic character, the drama of her touching, troubled life, and the glamour of an inside look at the pursuits of the wealthy."—*Booklist*

GLORIOUS MORNING

"Ellis tells her story well."—*West Coast Review of Books*

"A warm and wonderful saga with a zesty, spirited heroine who won my heart from the very first page."—Cynthia Freeman

JULIE ELLIS

THE ONLY SIN

WORLDWIDE

TORONTO • NEW YORK • LONDON • PARIS
AMSTERDAM • STOCKHOLM • HAMBURG
ATHENS • MILAN • TOKYO • SYDNEY

THE ONLY SIN

Worldwide Library/July 1987

First published by Arbor House

Copyright © 1986 by Julie Ellis

ISBN 0-373-97039-0

For Helen and Alex Schulman
Marilyn and Melvin Satlof
Ira and Candy Meyers—and,
of course, "Miss Casey"

Acknowledgments

I would like to thank the staffs of the New York Historical Society, the Museum of the City of New York, the Broadcast Museum, the Jewish Division and the Genealogy Room of the New York Public Library, the Research Division of the Lincoln Center Library, the Mid-Manhattan Library, and Mr. Green of the Epiphany Branch of the New York Public Library.

I would also like to express my gratitude to the Steamship Society Library of the University of Baltimore, the Library of the British Museum, the Atlanta Public Library, the Atlanta Historical Society, the Amagansett Public Library.

My thanks to my daughter Susie for diligent research and copy-editing assistance, and to my son Richie, for his valued help in Xeroxing myriad notes and newspaper clippings and binding them in a workable research tool.

Hope is the only sin....

—BALZAC

1

ON THIS SUNLIT AFTERNOON of August 12, 1903, in the small, picturesque health spa of Marienbad the atmosphere was charged with happy anticipation. The streets had been scrubbed. The shop windows sparkled. The carriages gleamed. Although the season—which had begun officially on May 1— was now in its last weeks, everyone knew that the arrival of His Majesty, King Edward VII, would launch a special English season and revive the town's festive spirit.

Sixteen-year-old Lilli Landau stood at the window in her aunt's modest millinery shop on the main street, pretending to busy herself so that she would have a clear view of Edward's carriage as he passed by en route to the royal apartments at the Hotel Weimar, which stood high on a pine-clad hill overlooking the town. She watched impatiently for the royal carriage, her sea-green eyes and beautiful auburn hair attracting the glances of passersby.

This was not King Edward's first visit—as Prince of Wales, he had visited the Bohemian spa several times in the past; but this was his first appearance since ascending the throne. The townspeople were honored by his appearance. And the trades-people happily anticipated the inevitable surge of business during his stay.

For several days wealthy foreign ladies had been arriving, their enormous trunks stuffed with the finest gowns. This especially pleased the shopkeepers, who knew that these ladies would eventually grow bored and seek diversion in their wares. Each hoped that the king's lady of the moment would favor his or her shop, because then *every* female guest would follow suit.

Lilli's Aunt Sara was particularly fond of King Edward VII because of his friendship with Leo, Natty, and Alf Rothschild, which had begun in their school days at Trinity College, Cambridge, and was, rumor had it, extremely close; so close it created newspaper headlines and caused consternation among the court chamberlains. Aunt Sara loved telling how, as Prince of Wales, Edward VII had traveled through a terrible blizzard just to attend Leo's wedding in London.

Lilli knew that her mother and Aunt Sara had moved to Marienbad from Vienna four years before she was born. But only occasionally would Aunt Sara talk about life in Vienna:

"We grew up thinking we were Austrians who happened to follow the Jewish religion. We thought we were just like everybody else. We were simply closing our eyes to what we did not want to see. And then in 1882 papa and mama went to visit a cousin in Bratislava—thirty-five miles from Vienna. They never came back. They had been killed in an anti-Jewish riot."

A year later Sara's engagement to an Austrian university student was broken off when the young man's father discovered that Sara was Jewish. That evening the two sisters had packed all their belongings in a large black trunk and bought tickets for the next morning's train to Marienbad. There, twenty-one-year-old Sara planned to use their tiny inheritance to open up a shop that would support them. Sara felt guilty about taking her younger sister, Kathe, away so precipitously, but she knew she couldn't stay in Vienna any longer.

Just weeks before they left, the German-Austrian student fraternities had passed the Waidhofer Resolution, which held that "every son of a Jewish mother, every human being with Jewish blood in its veins, is born without honor and must therefore lack in every decent human feeling. Such a person cannot differentiate between what is pure and what is dirty. Ethically he is the lowest of the low...."

Even in Marienbad, where a beautiful synagogue was dedicated by the tiny Jewish community in 1884, there were those who resented the Jews among them. No Jew was allowed to be a member of the municipal council.

Sara vowed to keep their faith a secret. But while she hid it from the public, Aunt Sara acted proud to be a Jew in the privacy of their small flat above the shop. She lighted the sabbath candles. She and Lilli observed all the Jewish holidays—alone. "It's best this way," Aunt Sara would say. "The world is not yet ready to accept the Jews."

"THE ROYAL TRAIN has not come into the station yet!" A small boy's excited cry from the street brought Lilli back to the scene at hand.

As she gazed at the street, she wondered, as she always did in the season, if this year her father would be among the guests. Why was Aunt Sara so stubborn and secretive about him? "I never knew your father," she would say, her face tightening. "Your mother never mentioned his name. Except to say that he was of a titled English family."

At this moment Aunt Sara was in the small rear room of the shop, demonstrating the latest in her line of "secret" beauty creams to a prospective customer. Lilli fidgeted. Why didn't the king's procession appear? Once Aunt Sara emerged from the rear room, she would surely be banished from the window. Lilli knew that her aunt had listened too long to the old women of the town, who whispered about the king's habit of stopping off to buy some trinket from a pretty young girl and then insisting the purchase be delivered in person. She was determined that Lilli—her only surviving family—remain untouched until her marriage. Even for a king...

Of course, there were moments when Lilli adored the season—when the town suddenly became alive with the rush of rich and famous visitors from all over the world, fashionably gowned ladies and their escorts, gay and charming actors and actresses from Paris, London, and America. This season, due to his succession to the throne, Edward's entourage was expected to include such august personages as Prime Minister Balfour and Chancellor of the Exchequer Lloyd George. But the mood of the royal party would be more erotic than political. Queen Alexandra would *not* be part of the royal party. And

Edward's favorite of earlier years, the actress Lillie Langtry, was expected. The doctors who monitored the daily lives of those taking the cure—including His Majesty himself—wouldn't dare interfere with the stream of banquets, luncheons, and tea parties that livened the waking hours.

Lilli despised the season even while she adored it, because it was a reminder of her illegitimate birth. She had known from an early age—along with most of the natives of Marienbad—that she was the result of her pretty chambermaid mother's affair with a titled visitor to the spa. She would never forget the afternoon eleven years ago when she came home to discover her mother lying dead on the floor of the small flat above the shop. Her romantic mother, Kathe, had been convinced that the father of her child would return to claim his family. Each season mama had told Lilli that this was the year her father would return. Ultimately he did—with his wife.

As Lilli watched for the approach of the royal procession, she wondered again why Aunt Sara refused to talk to her about her father.

While Lilli loved her aunt, she was convinced Aunt Sara knew—and withheld—her father's identity. Lilli wove exciting fantasies about his rescuing her from her drab life, taking her to live in a castle in England.

"Don't expect too much of life and you won't be disappointed," Aunt Sara was fond of saying. But Lilli wouldn't accept that. Aunt Sara was forty-one, and she was only sixteen! *Someday she would escape from Marienbad.*

Lilli knew that their small circle of friends thought Aunt Sara spoiled her dreadfully. Aunt Sara had kept her in school beyond the normal time for those in their circumstances. She refused to allow Lilli to work as a "water girl" at the spa, or as a chambermaid at one of the hotels, lest Lilli's head be turned by some handsome young visitor to the spa—not even at the fine Hotel Weimar, where Sara's gentleman friend of fourteen years was a waiter.

The sound of a train whistle ricocheted through the streets. Lilli straightened to attention. The royal railroad car was pulling into the Marienbad station. Faces appeared at the windows in the flats across the way. Clerks in the shops gathered in the doorways. Within minutes a parade of carriages would pass the shop as King Edward VII and his party were transported to the multistoried Hotel Weimar, the jewel of Marienbad.

"Lilli—" Her smiling aunt emerged from the rear with the French lady who came each year to buy hats and Aunt Sara's beauty creams. "Will you please go with madame in her carriage to help with the parcels?"

"My pleasure," Lilli said, trying to hide her disappointment that she would miss the royal procession.

Lilli accompanied the French lady to her hotel. When the parcels had been deposited in madame's suite, she was sent downstairs to the carriage waiting to drive her back.

Upon returning, Lilli noticed another carriage in front of the shop. She sighed. Aunt Sara must be busy with yet another customer. With the English season in high gear, Lilli knew her presence would be in constant demand at the shop. While she and her aunt spoke fluent French in addition to their native German, Aunt Sara—despite her long association with George, the English waiter at the Weimar—felt insecure in English. She had insisted, when Lilli was not yet ten, that George teach her English so that she could interpret for the English ladies who came into the shop during the season, though there were some Englishwomen who enjoyed speaking French.

Walking into the shop, Lilli recognized the lady with her aunt was English, though they spoke in French. She always knew by the clothes. The English preferred simple dresses. The French, German, and Italian ladies adored ruffles and flounces, even for the early-morning promenades to the springs.

Aunt Sara admired the Englishwomen for their clothes and their beautiful complexions, which were no deterrent to the sale of the beauty creams for which Sara Landau was well known, not only in Marienbad but in the even more famous spa of Karlsbad, an hour and a half away by carriage.

Ever since she was twelve, Lilli had smoothed the delicately scented cream into her face every night. Once a week Aunt Sara provided a little "beauty treatment." Lilli delighted in these rituals, feeling like one of the pampered ladies who visited Marienbad in the season.

Now Lilli noticed that the charming English lady, appearing somewhere in her early thirties, was accompanied by a tall, handsome gentleman who looked ten years her junior. He sat on a small, tapestry-covered chair provided for waiting escorts. He wore white flannel trousers and a blue jacket, and on his lap he held a hard felt hat of the kind the English visitors—including King Edward—favored.

He brightened when he saw Lilli. While she busied herself at one corner of the shop, his eyes followed her. He lifted one hand to smooth his crop of unruly dark hair. What fascinating blue eyes, she thought, and promptly dropped her own before his smile.

Though she was at an age when the girls she had gone to school with were already preparing to marry, Lilli had been cloistered from male pursuit. When the proper time arrived, Aunt Sara maintained, Lilli would be allowed to walk out with young men. She would make a comfortable marriage. But whom would she marry? Lilli wondered. While Aunt Sara so carefully guarded their Jewishness, would she ever agree to her only niece's marriage to a young man who wasn't Jewish? And who in Marienbad would overlook her illegitimacy?

Aunt Sara was escorting the English lady into the small rear room to demonstrate her beauty creams. Instantly, her escort was on his feet. He moved toward Lilli. She pretended not to notice as she fussed with the aigrettes on a hat.

"*Pardonnez-moi,*" he said. "*Est-ce que vous parlez anglais?*"

"*Oui.* Yes."

"I'm Jacques Laval." He spoke English, but with an accent unlike those from London—softer, more melodic. "From the United States."

"I am Lilli Landau," she said in her highborn English, learned from George. "How exciting to live in the United States!"

Jacques smiled. "On occasion. At this moment it's most exciting to be in Marienbad." He reached for her hand and brought it to his lips. Lilli tingled with pleasure. This was like one of those beautiful operettas by Johann Strauss. "Could I persuade you to have supper with me at the Bellevue Café this evening?" His eyes rested momentarily on the door to the rear room. The English lady was too occupied with the discussion of beauty creams to hear them. "May I call for you at ten?"

"I'm not permitted." Color flooded her cheeks. She remembered her mother.... But her mother had been a dreaming, romantic girl. She was not. Defiance welled in her. "But I could meet you at the café. At ten."

"I'll languish until ten o'clock," he murmured.

At that moment the two women emerged from the rear room. Jacques quickly stepped away from Lilli and turned to his friend with a teasing smile. "Have you bought out the shop, Clarissa?"

The elegant woman laughed loudly, tossing her head back.

"Darling, two hats? The count can afford far greater extravagances."

So, the lady is a countess, Lilli thought. And married. Clearly not Jacques's sister. Everybody talked about the liaisons between the beautiful visiting ladies and the gentlemen who accompanied them. But Jacques Laval had asked *her* to have supper with him at the Bellevue Café, the restaurant at the edge of the woods! King Edward himself went to the café to hear the Wagnerian concerts whenever he was in Marienbad.

Tonight, when Aunt Sara fell asleep, she would sneak out of the house to go to the Bellevue to meet this handsome young gentleman from the United States. Nothing this romantic had *ever* happened to her.

Once they were alone in the shop again, it seemed to Lilli that her aunt inspected her with unusual sharpness. Could she have noticed Jacques's interest?

"Did you see the king in his carriage?" Lilli asked self-consciously.

"I was busy with my customer." Aunt Sara shrugged. "Why should I care that the king of England passes my shop?"

"I wish I could have seen him," Lilli said softly.

"Lilli! He's an old man already." Aunt Sara pretended to disapprove, though she always spoke fondly of the former Prince of Wales. "An old man who chases after young women."

"Aunt Sara," Lilli began cautiously, "could my father have come here with King Edward?" *Could he be in Marienbad at this moment?*

"Lilli, your father could be living next door, and I would not know." Exasperation crept into her voice. "When will you accept the fact that we'll never know?"

LATER, WHEN SHE WAS SURE her aunt was asleep, Lilli left the flat and hurried into the quiet dark night. She walked quickly through the sharp chill, drawing her blue wool cape snugly around her shoulders. Even in August, evenings in Marienbad were cool.

Most of the townspeople were asleep; but in the Hotel Weimar, situated above the town, lights appeared to glow from every window. The people of Marienbad used the new electricity only when it was absolutely necessary. In the less elegant hotels, guests were instructed not to turn on their electricity until 7:55 P.M.—and then only if needed. But the spa guests were wealthy and spendthrifts.

Though she had never been to the Bellevue Café, Lilli knew it was a festive place during the season. As she approached, she heard the gay strains of a Strauss waltz filling the air, blending with the fragrance of the pine forest.

Suddenly, Lilli was filled with misgivings. Perhaps she should not have come. It was wicked to disobey Aunt Sara, who was so good to her. And what would she say to Jacques Laval? She, who had never even gone for a walk alone with a young man...

"Lilli—" She spun around. "You are surely the most beautiful girl in Marienbad. In all Bohemia." Jacques stood before her, dressed in a dashing gray suit.

"I—I came as soon as I could." She *would* know what to say to him, she told herself with fresh confidence. And she would defend her virtue. If she had to.

Jacques led her inside the café. While a waiter guided them to a table, she took in the lively scene around them.

"You see those two girls there?" Jacques whispered, pointing to a pair of beautiful young ladies accompanied by fawning escorts. "They're Gaiety Girls from London. And that tall, raven-haired beauty at the next table is Maxine Elliott, a famous American actress."

After Jacques ordered for them, he began to talk about his life in the United States. He was of an old French family in New Orleans, though his maternal grandmother, he confided with a twinkle in his eyes, was the daughter of an Irish dockhand. Lilli was enthralled. Was she herself not the child of a chambermaid and a titled gentleman?

Jacques was the youngest child in the family. He had two brothers and two sisters. A rebel, he had run off from New Orleans to explore Europe. He was determined not to join his father in the practice of law.

Jacques told her colorful stories about his months in London and Paris. She sat wide-eyed while he described the new métro—the underground train—that was operating beneath the streets of Paris. While he admired London, he rhapsodized about the joys of living in Paris.

They ate "the specialty of the house" and sipped wine. After dessert, Lilli asked to be taken home. Jacques took her by carriage to her flat, kissed her goodnight—with a decorous distance between them—and asked her to meet him again the following evening.

Lilli met Jacques again the following evening, and then the evening after that. He understood that she was a "good" girl, she told herself with shaky confidence. But she was filled with frightening and exhilarating new emotions, and she wasn't sure how she would respond to Jacques's advances.

On the third evening, Jacques talked about going off to Australia to become a sheep rancher, and Lilli tried to hide her disappointment. How could she endure Marienbad while Jacques was off living an adventurous new life?

On the fourth evening that she was to meet Jacques at the café, Lilli realized at the last minute she had forgotten that this was the evening when George was free from his duties at the Hotel Weimar and called on her aunt. Whenever he visited, Aunt Sara entertained him in the small room at the rear of the shop—and Lilli's bedtime was delayed.

The evening was especially chilly for this time of year. Earlier, Aunt Sara had started a charcoal fire in the ceiling-high porcelain stove because the heat soothed George's rheumatism. Lilli sat on the edge of her bed, waiting impatiently for sounds of his departure. Only after he was gone and Aunt Sara asleep could she tiptoe from her room and down the stairs out into the street.

Her eyes never left her bedside clock. When *would* he leave? Jacques would be waiting for her at the café at ten. She must not be late.

Lilli would not let herself wonder how Jacques spent his time when he was not with her. She knew he was not here for the cure. He'd offhandedly mentioned spending evenings at the gambling tables. She tried not to dwell on images of him with the lovely countess Clarissa de Montaigne.

She heard the sound of a window being opened downstairs. The aromas from the stove were always unpleasant. George must have told Aunt Sara to let in some fresh air. Now, with the window open, she could hear their voices in the silence of the night. Lilli started as she heard her name. Had someone seen her at the Bellevue Café and told Aunt Sara?

She ran to the window of her room and cracked it open.

"George, I worry about her. You know how I worry. But to arrange a marriage to Sigmund? He must be forty years old."

"Forty-eight," George said. Lilli froze. Were they talking about her? She had met George's friend Sigmund. He was old and fat and always paid her exaggerated compliments that made her blush. "But he works hard. He's saved up money. He'll be a good husband. Lilli may never have an offer as good as this."

"Perhaps you're right. You are wise, George. Tomorrow I'll tell her the marriage has been arranged."

Lilli stared out the window, stunned. *How could Aunt Sara expect her to marry Sigmund?* The thought of spending her wedding night with a man three times her age, with a disgusting paunch and triple chins . . .

"With Lilli provided for, we can plan for ourselves," George continued happily. "You'll sell the shop. I'll quit my job at the hotel. We can be married. With our savings we'll buy a little house with a piece of land in the country. We'll open an inn like we've always dreamed about, Sara."

"I know we're doing right, George," Aunt Sara said uneasily, "but Lilli will not take well to this."

"She'll do as she's told," George said. "She'll marry Sigmund and give him a family. You've done your share for your sister and her child. Now it's time for you to live."

Lilli stood by the window, her thoughts in chaos. She would not marry George's friend. But how could she disobey Aunt Sara and stay with her, knowing she was keeping Aunt Sara from marrying George and living in the country? She could hear her aunt's voice now: *"George, I can't marry until I know Lilli has a husband who'll take care of her."* So many times she'd heard Aunt Sara say that. But not Sigmund—she couldn't marry him.

She'd always dreamed of leaving Marienbad behind her. Of living the kind of life her father lived. Every season, when the elegant ladies and gentlemen came to Marienbad, she told herself with pride and rebellion that she—the daughter of a titled English gentleman—should live as they did. Did her father have other children, who lived with him in a fine manor house somewhere in England and a mansion in London?

Someday she would live like that. It was her birthright.

IN THE BEDROOM of Clarissa's luxurious suite at the Hotel Weimar, Jacques sprawled against a mound of silken pillows on the French Empire bed and watched while she dressed for the evening's banquet in the royal apartments. Clarissa was invited each night, along with several other beautiful visitors to Marienbad, to be a guest of the king.

"Jacques, darling, fix my buttons, will you?"

"Clarissa," Jacques pouted, "you're neglecting me. We've been here ten days; but since the king arrived, you leave me alone night after night." He bent to kiss the nape of her neck, toying with the idea of keeping the king waiting this evening.

"Jacques..." His hand moved toward her breasts. After lovemaking, Clarissa always presented him with a token of her affection—usually jewelry, which he sold. Then he could amuse himself at the gambling tables in her absence. But four days ago he had discovered Lilli, who intrigued him more than the gambling tables. "Darling, Edward will be furious if I'm late."

"Damn Edward." It gave him a sense of power to have a rich and beautiful countess at his command. To be able to keep a king waiting. He undid the buttons she had so carefully fastened moments ago. For a thirty-four-year-old woman—eleven years his senior—Clarissa had a remarkable body.

He slid the dress from her shoulders and spun her around to face him. Clarissa closed her eyes and let her head fall back. Tonight the king would wait. Suddenly there was a frantic knock at the door.

"Who is it?" Clarissa called out, pulling her dress around her shoulders.

"Simone. Madame, the count is arriving!" Simone was agitated.

"Come in," she ordered, gesturing to Jacques to fasten her dress again. The door burst open. Clarissa's maid stood before them. "Simone, what is this nonsense? The count is not due to arrive for three weeks."

"He has just stepped out of a carriage in front of the hotel. François is with him." Jacques knew that François was the count's valet. "Madame, he will be in the rooms within ten minutes."

"Jacques," Clarissa said, "you must leave instantly." She turned to her maid. "Quickly, Simone. Pack for Monsieur Jacques."

"Clarissa!" Jacques was stunned. "What are you doing to me? Where will I stay tonight? There's not a hotel room to be had since the king arrived."

"Forgive me, Jacques. But you must be out of Marienbad tonight. You know how jealous the count is." She would not look at him as she spoke. "Simone, when you have finished packing, send Alphonse in a carriage to the Grand Hotel Pupp in Karlsbad." Clarissa found a piece of notepaper and a quill pen and began writing. "I'm known there, Jacques. They'll find a room for you." She finished the note and fumbled in her purse for money. "This will pay for your carriage, Jacques. Wait in town perhaps an hour. Go to the Bellevue," she said, and he stared sharply at her for an instant. But she couldn't know anything about his seeing Lilli. "Give Alphonse time to arrive in Karlsbad before you."

"Clarissa, I was to be with you here for three weeks longer. I've spent every cent of my savings on gambling tables when you left me alone these last three nights. I abandoned a well-paying position in London to come with you." The last was untrue, but Jacques was furious.

"Take this, then." She took off her diamond bracelet. "It will hold you until you find another job. But go quickly, Jacques." She reached to kiss him in sudden warmth. "I'll miss you, darling," she whispered. "You are a marvelous lover."

2

LILLI WAITED NERVOUSLY before the Bellevue Café. Tonight, luckily, George had left early, eager to tell Sigmund that the marriage had been arranged. As soon as her aunt had retired for the night, she had sneaked from the flat.

Where was Jacques? She had arrived early, she realized; but now it was well past the time when Jacques was to meet her. Was he already tired of her? Had he decided not to come to the Bellevue Café tonight?

She turned her head away from a pair of uniformed gentlemen clearly interested in her companionship. She could not wait any longer. Obviously Jacques did not plan to meet her. She started walking away from the café.

"Lilli, wait!" She turned, and saw Jacques stepping out of a carriage. He ran toward her. "Lilli, forgive me for being late. I was involved in a matter of business, which unfortunately did not work out as I had hoped." With a wry smile he led her inside the Bellevue.

Not until they were seated at what had become "their table" and had ordered did Jacques confide in her.

"My father has stopped sending me funds. He thinks in that way he'll bring me back to New Orleans and into his law firm. But my mother, bless her, gave me a diamond bracelet—one that once belonged to her own mother—to sell should I find myself in financial difficulties. I thought I had a customer this evening." He shrugged. "The lady changed her mind."

"Have you talked to a jeweler in town?" Lilli asked. She guessed that Jacques had been trying to sell the bracelet to the countess; then she scolded herself for harboring other thoughts.

Jacques grimaced. "A thief. He offered me one-twentieth of its value. But tonight I'm moving on to Karlsbad. The jeweler there, I'm told, is an honorable man."

"You're leaving Marienbad tonight?" What would she do without him? But was she not planning to leave herself? *She must leave.*

"It's time I moved on." He shrugged. "I've told you how I want to go to Australia to set up a sheep ranch. Since they've discovered a way to ship frozen meat to London, that's become a flourishing business. Though it's not being exploited the way it should. I plan to change that."

"How exciting to be traveling to strange places." Lilli's voice was wistful. "Australia must be halfway around the world."

"At least." Jacques laughed. His hand reached for hers. "It's a country for young people." He seemed to be deliberating as he studied her. "Why don't you come with me?"

Lilli looked at him in astonishment. "I—I couldn't." But her heart pounded at the prospect. Rushing off into an exciting new life...and with Jacques! Aunt Sara always said that God took a hand when life became desperate. Was God saying to her, "Go to Australia with Jacques"? But she remembered mama, and she knew she was too proud to give herself to a man who was not her husband.

As if reading her mind... "Lilli," Jacques said, "I mean for you to come with me as my wife. A man starting life on a new continent should have a wife." He smiled. "How could I bear to leave you behind? Lilli—I adore you. I want to spend the rest of my life making you happy. In Australia there are wonderful opportunities for us. We'll build a dynasty!"

"My aunt will forbid it." She trembled as she imagined taking Jacques home to Aunt Sara. A young man she had met only four days ago! But what was there for her here? "We'll have to run away," she said. Aunt Sara would be upset—but then she would sell the shop and go with George to live in the country.

"We'll go tonight to Karlsbad," Jacques said eagerly. "I have already arranged for accommodations at the Grand Hotel Pupp. In the morning we'll be married. The American consul in Karlsbad has the authority to do this. When you marry me, you become an American." He studied her for a moment. "Until we're married, Lilli, I will not take you for my wife."

Her smile was radiant. How understanding and tender Jacques was! Yes, she would marry him. She would become his American wife and go with him to settle in Australia.

"Jacques—there are things I must do. I must go to the flat for my clothes, and then leave a note for Aunt Sara. She won't find it until morning. I have to leave an explanation of some sort—" But then it occurred to her: What if Aunt Sara decided to look in her bedroom during the night?

Jacques shook his head. "Forget about going back to the flat. We'll buy new clothes for you in Karlsbad. There are fine shops on the Old Meadow there. Branches of shops from Old Bond Street in London and the rue de la Paix in Paris. I'll arrange with the waiter to have his young son take a message to your aunt early in the morning." Jacques glanced around the café and signaled their waiter, with whom he had established a friendly relationship. Everybody was drawn to Jacques, Lilli thought with pride. "You write out your message. We'll give it to Conrad, then take a carriage to Karlsbad." He lifted her hand to his lips. "My darling, within twelve hours you will be Mrs. Jacques Laval."

THOUGH JAQUES KISSED her in the carriage en route to Karlsbad with a disconcerting passion, his behavior in their rooms at the palatial Grand Hotel Pupp was exemplary. Lilli slept alone in the elegant bedroom. Jacques slept in the adjoining sitting room. In truth, she slept little. How could she sleep when her whole world had suddenly been turned upside down?

Quite early next morning, Jacques took her downstairs for breakfast at Pupp's Café-Salon. Most of the guests had not yet returned from sipping the waters and the hour's walk afterward that was part of the spa routine. *Kaffeemädchen*—coffee girls—served them eggs, ham, sausages, hot rolls and butter, jam, and coffee.

While they ate, Lilli imagined Aunt Sara reading her brief note that said she was being married and going off to live in Australia and would write. She had lied when she said they were taking the night train—last night—from Marienbad. But she wanted Aunt Sara to believe they were already en route to Paris. *Please, Aunt Sara, don't be terribly upset.*

"You'll wear the bracelet to the jewelry store," Jacques said. "We'll explain that it was a wedding gift from my mother, but that we prefer the cash. The jeweler will understand. And from there, we'll go to the American Consulate to be married."

In the jewelry store Lilli appeared the happy young bride while Jacques argued price with the jeweler. At last a deal was made. Lilli was shocked by the amount of money that passed from the jeweler's hands to Jacques's. Traveling halfway around the world would obviously require a fortune in itself.

Less than an hour later, standing together in the American Consulate, Lilli and Jacques were pronounced man and wife. Tears welled in her eyes—tears of happiness, but also tears of sorrow; she wished that Aunt Sara could be here with her today.

Jacques took her to the tree-lined Old Meadow, where he insisted on purchasing extravagant gowns for his bride. Mindful of their expensive journey, Lilli protested his generosity. Aunt Sara had instilled in her a respect and practicality regarding money, an attitude she suspected was lacking in her new husband. She couldn't forget that their entire fortune— until Jacques was launched in business—was the money received from the sale of his mother's diamond bracelet.

Over a sumptuous wedding luncheon, Jacques briefed her on the route they would travel to Australia, a journey of many weeks.

"We could go by way of the new Trans-Siberian Railroad to Shanghai and catch a boat there to Sydney. Or we could go by way of Egypt and the Suez. But I'm told that way we would encounter poor hotel facilities in addition to the language problem. So this way is best," he concluded cheerfully. "We'll connect with the Orient Express at Vienna and remain on that to Paris. From Paris we'll take the boat train to Le Havre. It's only five days by ocean steamship to New York." Lilli could barely contain her excitement. She had never seen a body of water larger than the river that ran through the center of Karlsbad. "We'll cross the United States by train in another five days—"

"Oh, Jacques," she said, "then we'll go to New Orleans to visit your family?" She imagined his two sisters and two brothers, his dignified father and lovely mother, the fine family estate in what Jacques called the Garden District. "Jacques, did you write your mother about us?" she asked, suddenly anxious. What if his family was upset that he had married her?

Jacques looked tense. "Don't worry, Lilli. I wrote my mother. But we won't be stopping in New Orleans. The trains we take travel far north of Louisiana. The Twentieth Century Limited to Chicago, and there we change to the California Limited. I have our itinerary carefully worked out." Lilli was disconcerted by his tone. Had she said something wrong? "In California we'll take another train up to San Francisco, darling," he continued, smiling now. "We'll sail from there for Australia. Five beautiful weeks on an oceangoing liner." Lilli relaxed. Whatever it was that had disturbed him had passed. "Lilli, think of it! You'll travel across two oceans!"

Dressed in a suit he'd bought earlier in the day at the Karlsbad branch of a fine shop from the rue de la Paix in Paris, Jacques escorted Lilli with obvious pride onto the special resort train that would carry them to Vienna.

Once in Vienna, they changed to the Orient Express, the internationally famous train composed entirely of drawing rooms, sleeping cars, and dining cars, which now traveled from Constantinople to Paris in sixty-seven hours and thirty-five minutes. Lilli gazed in awe at the huge blue, shining train, the bronze letters on the side proclaiming this the "Compagnie Internationale des Wagons-Lits, et des Grands Expresses Européens." Jacques led her into their private compartment, appointed in red plush upholstery.

Shortly after the train left, Lilli and Jacques went into the dining car, where they were immediately seated at a table covered with snow-white linen. The glassware sparkled. The silver had been polished to a mirror sheen. A bottle of claret sat on the table. Lilli listened while Jacques conferred with the brown-uniformed waiter about their dinner. Each day the menu offered the national dish of the country through which they were passing. The food and wine were superb. But tonight Jacques preferred not to linger over dinner. By the look in his eyes, the touch of his hand at her waist, Lilli knew he was impatient to consummate their marriage.

They returned to their compartment, which had been prepared for the night. Lilli was grateful when Jacques diplomatically announced he would retire briefly to the smoking lounge. She locked the compartment door and entered the adjoining *cabinet de toilette.*

Jacques himself had chosen the bridal nightwear. More suitable for an expensive French coquette, she thought as she slipped on the black chiffon and lace nightdress with its startling décolletage, and the sheer black negligee with its unexpectedly demure neckline.

She started at the light knock on the compartment door. Trembling, Lilli ran to unlock it. She did know a little about the wedding night, she told herself. She and her girlfriend Hilda had shared the confidences of another girlfriend who had recently been married. Panic swept through her. How could she lie in bed naked with a man? *To have him do what a husband did with his wife?* But Jacques would teach her. It would be wonderful.

"Lilli, you're beautiful." He pulled her to him. She tried not to stiffen at his touch. "My exquisite bride."

His mouth closed on hers, and she relaxed. Nothing mattered except being here with him. He found the buttons that closed the negligee and tossed it aside. Would Jacques be disappointed, she asked herself as he pulled off her nightdress. She so wanted to please him!

He swept her from her feet and gently placed her on a made-up berth. He sat on the edge, his hands following every curve of her body. She closed her eyes.

"Jacques, I love you." She cradled his head in her hands as his mouth moved from the valley between her breasts toward one taut nipple.

She welcomed the weight of him above her, crying out for only an instant when he entered her. Then her arms closed around him as they moved together....

She had asked Hilda, "How will I know what to do?"

She knew.

LILLI WAS AWED by her first sight of Paris: by the motorcars, rare in Marienbad; by the Bois de Boulogne; by the Eiffel Tower. Jacques took her for a sumptuous dinner at Maxim's. They stayed for the night at the elegant Hotel Mercedes at the rue de Presbourg.

Before they boarded the boat train for Le Havre, Lilli bought a postcard of the Eiffel Tower to send to Aunt Sara, and she felt a stab of fear. She was entrusting her life to someone she had known less than ten days. Aunt Sara must be so distressed. But she loved Jacques. He was her husband. If Aunt Sara could see them together, surely she would understand.

When they arrived at Le Havre, Lilli insisted—with some trepidation that Jacques might consider her too forward—that they seek out a modest pension for the two nights they must spend here before the sailing. She had been shaken by the cost of the Orient Express.

Jacques obtained passage to New York for them on an old French liner, *La Touraine*, which had once held the Blue Ribbon for speed across the Atlantic. The journey was calm and pleasant. Every morning they walked arm in arm around the deck while Jacques spun fanciful tales of their future in Australia. The passengers found Jacques charming, she noted with pride. He enchanted everyone he met.

They spent only a few hours in New York City. At 2:45 P.M. they boarded the crack Twentieth Century Limited. Five hours after boarding, they sat at a table for two in the attractive dining car, finished in Santiago mahogany. For one dollar and fifty cents each, they dined on tenderloin of beef, fresh mushrooms and grilled Spanish onions, green peas with mint, potatoes fondant. Jacques chose the plum pudding to accompany their coffee.

The next morning they were dressed and packed when the train pulled into the station in Chicago. They checked their luggage and went sightseeing, Lilli marveling, as she had in New York, at the buildings that climbed so high into the sky.

At eight o'clock that evening they boarded the California Limited, and almost immediately Jacques discovered a few fellow travelers eager to pass the time at a poker table. He won consistently, but Lilli worried. What if his luck ran out? How would they continue their journey? While Jacques played cards late into the night, Lilli devoured the American newspapers.

Not until they were aboard the ship bound for Sydney did Lilli tell Jacques that she was concerned about their reception in Australia. They were foreigners. Would they be welcome?

Jacques soothed her. "Lilli, my love, for you and me there'll be a warm welcome. We'll contribute to the country. The Australian government encourages the right kind of immigrants." He took her hand. "Imagine, Lilli, a country where two-thirds of the land has never been seen by a white man. The possibilities are endless."

A coldness closed in around Lilli as she was assaulted by images of threatening isolation. Would she ever see Aunt Sara—or Marienbad—again? Were she and Jacques destined to spend the rest of their lives on that strange, distant continent, more inhabited by primitive tribes than by civilized people?

3

THE FIVE WEEKS aboard the steamship bound for Sydney were calm and uneventful. Lilli reveled in Jacques's colorful stories of his years in New Orleans, pushing aside her anxieties about life in Australia.

As they approached their destination, however, she grew nervous again about what lay ahead. English was spoken in Australia, she remembered, so she and Jacques would have no difficulty with the language. But it was disconcerting to think of the distance between Australia and Europe. The differences. Even the calendar was reversed. When they arrived in Sydney, in early October, they would be greeted by early spring rather than the beginning of autumn.

She was worried, too, about their financial state. She suspected there were nights when Jacques left the gambling table poorer than when he had sat down. Their extensive travels had consumed a small fortune. Jacques was confident he would make immediate connections in Sydney. But suppose setting himself up in business was delayed? If need be, she could work. Of course, she dared not voice this to Jacques. He had come from a different world, where wives were idle ladies.

As soon as they were settled in Sydney, she would write Aunt Sara. And she would write Aunt Sara's friend, who operated the small shop next door. If Aunt Sara had already moved to the country, her friend would know where she was living.

The final few days aboard ship were restless ones for Lilli and Jacques, and they welcomed the captain's announcement at dinner one evening that on the following morning they would awaken to see the coastline of Australia.

With their luggage packed, they rushed up on deck at six in the morning. A winter sun had risen above the horizon. The air was cold, the wind sharp. A light salt spray whipped their faces.

Soon they saw the huge sandstone cliffs protecting the magnificent Sydney Harbor. "This is one of the finest harbors in the world," Jacques said with infinite respect. "There's no ship afloat that can't anchor here."

Enthralled, Lilli watched as the ship moved into the huge harbor. They stopped briefly at Watson's Bay, just inside the Heads—tall sandstone cliffs—for medical inspection, then sailed up to Neutral Bay.

Once through customs, they went directly to Petty's Hotel, recommended by a shipboard companion. Jacques made the necessary arrangements, and they were shown to their room. When they were alone, he looked around the small, unpretentious room and laughed. "It's not quite Maxim's of Paris, is it, Lilli, darling? Still, we have the public rooms at our disposal. And tomorrow morning I'll set out to investigate the local men's clubs. That's where I'll make my contacts."

A shipboard acquaintance had suggested that Jacques join the Union Club, one of the most prestigious and favored by the important merchants and wealthy commercial men of Sydney. Jacques and Lilli were convinced that one of these men would recognize his capabilities and be willing to back him in his venture.

"Jacques, let's unpack and go out for a walk about the city," Lilli said exuberantly. She was determined not to be as intimidated by Sydney as she had been by New York and Chicago. Marienbad had not prepared her for living in the midst of huge populations.

In high spirits they unpacked and headed for the streets of the city. Lilli clung to Jacques's arm as they walked among the bustling hordes. "Everybody seems to be in such a hurry," she said, laughing.

The streets of Sydney did make for a bustling scene. Hansom cabs, buses, carriages made their way over wood-block-paved roads. Horses' hooves clattered. The steam train moved noisily up and down Pitt Street. The cable tram, using double-deck cars, sped along King Street. Bicycles seemed popular, though Lilli suspected the hilly terrain would discourage most women cyclists.

With the end of the workday at 6:00 P.M., thousands jammed into horse buses and trams to go to the ferry wharves, where they pushed their way through the turnstiles to board the boats that would take them to their harborside homes in the new suburbs.

At the end of their first week in Sydney, Lilli began to be aware of a certain elegance and grace about the city. She admired the lovely parks; the charming shops; the narrow, winding cobblestone streets. The splendid harbor, with the bush—saltwater swamp oaks and mahoganies, tea trees and blueberry ashes—rising on the foreshores. But it was a lonely time for her, too, since she enjoyed new sights alone while Jacques was out in search of investors.

She began noticing how the dry weather affected her skin, and it occurred to her that the women of Sydney would benefit from Aunt Sara's creams. The thought reminded her of how much she missed her aunt. They had never been separated for more than a day. On her first night in Sydney, she had written Aunt Sara, but the fortnightly mail from Sydney to London required thirty-five days for delivery.

Lilli noticed, too, that the women of Sydney did not dress with the smartness of the visitors to Marienbad during the season. She had long been conscious of the difference in the attire worn by the visitors to the spa and by the women of Marienbad. In the clothes she made for the two of them, Aunt Sara copied the styles of the English ladies.

Each evening she and Jacques sat down to dinner together in the dining room, and he would tell her about his day. Most of the hotel guests were much older—mainly business people, he told her.

She became aware of one young couple who was obviously British, and she hoped that Jacques would cultivate their friendship. But he was quick to dismiss them as "poor contacts."

As the days passed, Lilli was dismayed by a change in Jacques's attitude. Now when he returned from his day in the city, he was taciturn or surly, and Lilli wondered what she had done wrong. Occasionally she glanced covertly about the dining room, her face hot in shame, to see if the other guests had noticed Jacques's sharpness with her.

Lying in his arms at night, she sought a reason for his behavior. Perhaps he was upset; he had expected to make fast business connections in Sydney. And he had to be worried about funds. But in bed his tension was forgotten.

At the end of their seventh week at Petty's Hotel, Lilli discovered the cost of a week's lodging for two, and she suspected that little remained from the sale of the bracelet and Jacques's poker winnings. Later, in their room, she timidly suggested that they move to one of the less expensive lodging houses near Wynyard Square.

Jacques stopped in the act of removing a shoe and glared at her. "We're not moving, Lilli! If I expect to make the proper contacts, we have to appear prosperous! We can't live in a cheap lodging house!"

"But, Jacques, if we would move to—"

"We're staying here." He slammed his shoe on the floor.

"Some of the lodging houses are very nice," she said quietly. While her life had been very modest in Marienbad, at least she had never feared for a roof over her head. "I saw a place right on Wynyard Square that—"

"No!" Jacques shouted. "I won't hear any more about leaving the hotel! You've been listening to all these 'new women' here in Sydney—that's why you're trying to tell me what to do." Everybody in Sydney talked about the improved status of women in the city. The university provided for the admission of women under the same terms as men. Women worked in the offices and shops. Since 1901, women had voted. And in Sydney the electorate had chosen a lady mayor. "Lilli, remember. I'm your husband. I make the decisions."

"I'm sorry, Jacques." Tears welled in her eyes. But she wasn't sorry. Why shouldn't a wife help her husband make decisions?

At the sight of her tears, Jacques's face softened. "Come along, darling. Let us forget this nonsense. We'll go out tonight. I had a bit of luck today at the club." Lilli tensed. "Yes, my love, I'll admit it—at poker. We'll go to the Tivoli to see Marie Lloyd."

She looked at him with reproach. How could he gamble when their funds were so low?

"It's Saturday night," she said quickly. "Why don't we go for a walk around town? I hear it's a lovely sight on Saturday nights." And no money spent.

"All right, we'll walk," he said. "Come give the old man a kiss."

Hand in hand they walked through the busy streets, where hundreds of brightly illuminated shops, thronged with customers, remained open until midnight. Workers, eager to spend part of their week's pay, lined up in the ornately furnished public houses. The sounds of laughter mingled with the music of pianolas and hurdy-gurdies.

"Tired?" Jacques asked.

"No." Her eyes were luminous. When Jacques was solicitous and caring like this, she forgot his dark side.

"Then, my darling, let's take a hansom over to the quay and look at the stars over the Pacific."

"We can walk," she said, mindful of the cost of a cab.

"No." Jacques was firm. His hand at her waist moved indecorously to her breast. "I want to make love to my wife."

Lilli's eyes widened. "In a hansom?"

"Darling," he chuckled, "you haven't lived until I've made love to you in a hansom."

ON MONDAY MORNING Jacques left the hotel as usual to go to the Union Club. Lately she had wondered whether perhaps Jacques should look for a job, but she didn't dare make the suggestion. Still, she reasoned, he might meet an investor when he went out to lunch at one of the hotels favored by the businessmen of Sydney. All the mercantile and professional men took time out for a three-course hot lunch in the middle of the day.

At midmorning, restless and troubled, Lilli left their hotel room and went downstairs. At the entrance to the street, she encountered the wife of the other young couple staying at Petty's Hotel.

"It looks as though it'll be a fine day for walking," the small, dark-haired girl said with a friendly, open smile.

"Yes," Lilli agreed, eager for conversation. "And I love to walk."

"I'm Frances Cohen from London." She held out her hand. "Charles and I are staying at the hotel while our house is being built."

"I'm Lilli Laval." She realized this was the first time she had introduced herself as Jacques's wife. "I'm from Marienbad, in Bohemia. My husband is from America. He hopes to become a sheep rancher."

As Lilli and Frances walked out into the busy street, Frances explained that she had been in Sydney for almost three months. She was homesick, she confessed, and lonely for her family in London. But here there was a wonderful business opportunity for her husband, and she was determined to adjust to her new life. Lilli confessed to missing her aunt even more than she had feared.

Each was elated at having found the other. Frances immediately began to plan a day of sightseeing for them.

"I'll show you Centennial Hall and the Marble Bar at the Adams Hotel—that's one of the sights of Sydney. And you must see the Chinese section." She paused and smiled at Lilli's look of alarm. "Someone told you it was a bad place—"

"Jacques told me it was dangerous."

"Most of the Chinese are fine people," Frances said. "A few run opium dens and gambling houses and have caused trouble in Sydney. But there are the larrikins—not 'yellow people'—who steal and rape and murder. Mostly they're working-class

boys and girls in their teens and out for no good. I have a cab-
inetmaker in the Chinese section who's a wonderful and skilled
old gentleman. I have to go there today—he's making something for me. I'm sure you'll love prowling about his shop.''

"If you say it's all right," Lilli said with a smile. She had
made her first friend in Sydney!

As Lilli and Frances explored the city, Frances confided that
she was about to open a small fabric shop. "I had to wheedle
Charles into letting me," she said. "But I made him see that I
would perish of homesickness if I had nothing to occupy me."
Lilli smiled; she, too, was homesick, but she hid it from
Jacques. "Even when the house is ready and Charles and I
move in, I'll keep the shop."

"My aunt ran a milliner's shop back in Marienbad." Lilli's
eyes were wistful. "I miss her so much."

"I'll open the shop the minute my merchandise arrives.
Everything else is ready." Frances's face glowed in anticipation. "Would you like to see the place? It's quite near."

"Oh, yes," Lilli said enthusiastically. Talking with Frances
about the shop brought Aunt Sara closer. "Let's go there now."

AT DINNER Lilli reported her day's adventure to Jacques. Immediately she sensed that he was dubious about her new
friendship.

"Her husband allows her to be a shopkeeper?" He frowned
in disapproval.

She smiled. "Women hold jobs these days. We are in the
twentieth century, darling." Had she not been a shop assistant
in Marienbad? Of course, the women Jacques knew led more
sheltered lives.

"What does this Cohen fellow do for a living?" he asked.

Lilli felt a guilty defiance at Jacques's condescending tone.
Why was he putting himself above Charles Cohen? "He's an
officer at one of the banks." Lilli knew she sounded defensive. "Frances says he's brilliant."

"A lot of Jews in Australia seem to be in banking." Jacques
shrugged.

Lilli stared at him, trembling. "Why do you think the Cohens are Jewish?" *Would Jacques be upset if he knew she was Jewish?* She had never thought to tell him.

"Their name. Cohen is a Jewish name." He seemed impatient at discussing the matter further. Lilli had hoped that the four of them could be friends. Why did he have this snobbish attitude? This was a side of him she had never seen.

"With all your gallivanting today," Jacques teased when their coffee arrived, "you won't be in the mood for a walk this evening."

"No, let's go for a walk." She wouldn't admit that her feet ached. It was always on their after-dinner walks that Jacques would tell her what had happened that day. Whenever he suggested an evening walk, she knew that afterward—in the privacy of their room—he would be the warm and adoring husband she loved. "Just let me go upstairs for my cape."

When they were out on the night streets, Jacques launched into a diatribe against the businessmen of Sydney.

"I can't understand their shortsightedness, Lilli. I show them figures. I answer every objection with logic. I'm meeting the cream of Sydney at the Union Club, at the Royal Exchange, in the best restaurants of the city."

"Jacques, we've been here only a few weeks," she soothed.

"You're right." He smiled. "I'll meet somebody tomorrow. I know it. Someone who'll see what fortunes can be made these days. Someday, Lilli, I'll drape you in diamonds. You'll have the finest house in Sydney. Every year we'll spend a month in Paris. Nobody can stand in our way. We have a world to conquer." His arm circled her waist. His eyes were amorous. "Enough walking. Let's go home."

EACH MORNING NOW Lilli went out with Frances. The fabrics Frances had ordered from London arrived. Together, the two girls prepared to open the shop for business.

"Lilli, you've been wonderful," Frances said on the night before the opening. "I don't know how I would have managed without you." She cast a worried glance about the prettily arranged shop. "Do you think the customers will wonder at all the emptiness? I didn't need so much space, but this was the only vacancy in this area. Charles said it was important to be on a good block."

"I think he's right," Lilli said. "And I can come in and help you tomorrow. I have nothing else to do, and it would be fun." She hoped Frances wouldn't feel obliged to offer to pay her.

"Would you?" Frances smiled in relief. "It would be moral support just to have you here."

Lilli said nothing to Jacques about spending so much time in Frances's shop, where business was slow and the two girls amused themselves by rearranging the bolts of fabric into colorful displays, or in redesigning the window. She was glad to be busy.

Waiting this morning while Frances returned to her room to collect letters she had forgotten to bring downstairs earlier, Lilli settled herself in a chair in a hotel lounge to read the *Morning Herald*. Turning the pages, she found her eyes riveted to a newspaper column by a woman journalist about a woman named Helena Rubinstein, who lived in Melbourne, which Jacques had told her was about 400 miles south of Sydney.

Fascinated, Lilli read about the Maison de Beauté Valaze operated by Helena Rubinstein, who not only made and sold beauty creams but gave "treatments." She remembered how Aunt Sara had demonstrated her creams for special ladies among her customers by giving them "small facials." That was what this Helena Rubinstein was doing in Melbourne. It was the first time a "house of beauty" had been offered in all of Australia, according to the article. Lilli had heard of such places only in Paris.

"Sorry, Lilli," Frances interrupted her. "I didn't mean to keep you waiting so long."

Lilli put down the paper. "Oh, don't be. I was enjoying the paper." She rose to her feet. "Let's go to the shop. We don't want to keep your customers waiting."

As TIME PASSED, Lilli became increasingly concerned about Jacques's finances. At the start of each week, she was certain this would be the last they could afford to stay at Petty's Hotel. *And where would they go without money?*

Jacques was alternately taciturn and sharp with her. She did not dare suggest again that they move, or that one of them consider looking for employment. She knew it would send him into a rage.

On the morning of their eleventh week in Sydney, Lilli covertly watched Jacques count the contents of his purse.

"Lilli, pay the clerk for our next week's lodging," he said casually, and handed her money. "And buy yourself a length of cloth from your friend's new shop," he added grandly. "You've told me your aunt taught you to sew."

"Thank you, Jacques." Her smile was that of an adoring bride, but her eyes were troubled as she watched him reach into a drawer and pull out his collection of cuff links and stickpins. Instinctively she knew that Jacques had handed over to her— for a week's lodging and a length of cloth from Frances's shop—all the money they owned in the world.

He kissed her and sauntered off as if he were the richest man on earth. Lilli had come to understand that special glint in his eyes. Jacques would sell his cuff links and stickpins, and he would use the proceeds to enter a poker game or to seek out a partner with gambling instincts at one of the numerous clubs about town for a game of billiards or dominoes, which were so popular with clubmen. His luck would determine whether they could remain at the hotel.

Cold and trembling, Lilli sat down at the edge of the bed, the money for the coming week's lodging—plus the sovereigns for her length of cloth—still clutched in her hand. How could she stop Jacques before they ran out of money? Perhaps there was a way. . . .

She reached for her cape, thrust the money into her purse for safekeeping, and hurried from the hotel room, stopping off to pay their coming week's lodging. Knowing that Frances had left for the shop, she walked swiftly through the springlike morning to join her friend.

"How nice to see you so bright and early," Frances said as Lilli came through the door. "Charles says I shouldn't bother to open at this hour, but I think, Suppose a customer does appear and I'm not here?"

"Frances, did you mean it when you said you don't need all this space for the fabric shop?"

"Lilli," Frances said fondly, "look around you." She pointed to one side of the shop, where the unused fixtures—bought as a package—sat on the floor.

"I have a proposition," Lilli said breathlessly. She would not let herself think about Jacques's reaction. "If you will let me use that space to set up a business for beauty creams, I'll pay you a commission on each jar that I sell, plus I'll help you make hats for a millinery department. I learned about that from Aunt Sara."

"Lilli, what a marvelous idea!" Frances threw her arms around her. "How long will it take you to have your beauty creams delivered?"

"I'll make them up myself. I told you—I used to help Aunt Sara. We used a formula her grandmother taught her." Lilli paused, trying to think clearly about the project ahead of her. "I don't have the equipment here to macerate flowers for scent—"

"Lilli," Frances said, laughing, "what are you talking about?"

"Maceration is the French process for producing scent from flowers. But I'm sure I can buy scent at an apothecary shop. It'll be more expensive," she conceded, "but later I can make my own. I'll need glycerin," she added. "It must be pure. Commercial glycerin is sometimes yellow and smells dreadful. I'll have to find an apothecary who can supply glycerin that has been purified by dilution with distilled water and boiled for forty-eight hours and filtered. . . ."

Frances was astonished. "You and your aunt did this?"

Lilli smiled. "Well, yes. I won't, for now. But all this, even bought from an apothecary, will cost only a few pence per jar." Aunt Sara always said she had to make the creams expensive or the rich ladies would think they were not good. "I'll need distilled water and oil—oh, and jars! I'll go right out and visit the apothecary shops here in the neighborhood."

"What scent will you use?" Frances asked.

"Rose," Lilli said. "Moss rose. Actually, moss rose is rose oil with traces of tincture of musk. It's a lovely scent. The fragrance is terribly important. Aunt Sara always says that the main ingredient of any beauty cream is hope."

"I must confess," Frances said, "I've never used any. Most of them smell so awful and feel so harsh. Mama used to tell me that some of them are even harmful to the skin."

"That's why the ladies who came to Marienbad always bought from us." Lilli nodded in pride. "Aunt Sara's secret formula doesn't use zinc oxide or carbolic acid. Her cream is soft and fluffy. I'm sure the ladies here in Sydney will love it. And they need it," she said enthusiastically. "Have you noticed how the sun and the wind have dried out their skin? I'll buy a bowl for mixing; and if I can find everything today, I'll make up a batch right away. I'll paste a label on each jar and paint a picture of a pretty pink moss rose on it. Like Aunt Sara and I did. I can print up a sign for the window and—" She hesitated. "If that's all right with you, Frances..."

Frances laughed. "Of course it is, silly. Half the window space will be yours. I can't wait to see this cream of yours. When will you be ready to sell?"

"Tomorrow morning." Lilli glowed. "Miss Lilli's Beauty Creams. What do you think? In a city of half a million people, how can I not sell a lot of jars?"

Lilli was nearly dizzy with newly discovered ambition. Jacques wove great dreams. While they waited for his dreams to come true, she would provide for them. Aunt Sara's beauty cream would be the means. Perhaps she would not earn enough to keep them at Petty's Hotel, but surely enough to pay for modest lodgings on Wynyard Square.

But how would she make Jacques understand that this was a practical way to solve the money problems? That it would be only temporary, until he made his "connections"?

She knew it wouldn't be easy.

4

WITH THE MONEY Jacques had given her to buy a length of cloth, Lilli was able to purchase the materials necessary to make up three dozen jars of cream. With infinite care she blended the water, the oil, the glycerin, the drops of this and that as required by her aunt's formula, until at last she was satisfied with the results. Now the essence must be added. Just the exact strength.

Frances watched Lilli in fascination, leaving her side only when an occasional customer came into the shop.

"It's all ready," Lilli declared finally as she pasted on the last handpainted label. She gazed in satisfaction at the pretty array of small jars.

"And what is it you have over here?" an inquisitive feminine voice inquired.

The two girls had been so absorbed in Lilli's labors, they hadn't noticed the arrival of a prospective customer. As trained by her aunt, Lilli glanced up with an ingratiating smile. "Miss Lilli's Beauty Creams, madame." Remembering Aunt Sara's approach to the ladies who had come into the shop in Marienbad, her voice dropped to a whisper. "They're made from a secret Viennese formula. I use them myself every night." She knew the porcelain loveliness of her own skin in comparison to the sun- and wind-punished skin of her potential customer was a good selling tool. Noticing the eager glow in the woman's eyes, she recalled Aunt Sara's words: *The secret ingredient in my creams is hope.* "Try the cream for four weeks," Lilli said, "and you'll be amazed at the difference in your appearance.

And wouldn't a jar of Miss Lilli's Cream make a lovely present for the ladies on your Christmas list?"

So impressed with Lilli was the customer, she bought not only two jars of Miss Lilli's Cream but also one of the hats Lilli had made for Frances. Aunt Sara had taught Lilli that ladies would pay well for beauty products; and here in Sydney, Jacques had told her, wages were high. She had set a price that had seemed daring, but her customer had displayed no objection.

"Lilli, you're wonderful!" Frances said after the woman had left. "I'll never learn to sell like you."

Lilli stared in delicious awe at the money she clutched in one hand. The first money she had earned entirely on her own.

"How am I going to tell Jacques?" she whispered.

Frances smiled. "You'll find a way."

Though Frances said nothing, Lilli suspected Frances agreed that Jacques ought to compromise and look for a job until he made his "business connection." Over lunch at the fine Café Monaco—Frances's suggestion—Lilli had confessed to being on a tight budget.

Frances didn't understand Jacques's high ambitions, Lilli told herself defensively. She loved to hear him talk about the exciting life he meant to provide for them—on his own, without help from his family back in the United States. She never doubted that one day Jacques would be rich and important. His ambitions were contagious.

Lilli arrived at the hotel to find a letter from her aunt awaiting her. Standing in the small lobby, she ripped open the envelope and pulled out the two pages filled with Sara's neat, precise handwriting. To her relief, Sara was brief in her chastisement of Lilli's impetuous marriage and wished her happiness.

"George and I will be married by the time this reaches you. I have sold the shop, and we're about to buy a small house on the other side of Karlsbad, which we'll open as an inn. I will send you the address as soon as we are in the house."

In the excitement of hearing from her aunt, Lilli had temporarily forgotten her fears of confessing her new venture to Jacques. But now, waiting in their room for him to return from his daily rounds, she tried to imagine how she would make him understand. These days it was considered respectable for married women to work. Particularly in Australia, so modern in its attitudes. There was even a minimum-wage law here!

They needed the money, on that he had to agree. What would they do at the end of the week if he was unlucky at the gambling tables? It would be too late to appeal to his family for help.

She ran to the door at the sound of a knock, an expectant conciliatory smile on her face.

"It's getting damnably hot," Jacques said as he came in. His face was tense; he didn't even kiss her. Clearly, he had not had a good day. Her throat tightened in anxiety. "I hate this reversing of the seasons," he said. "Back in America it's winter. It doesn't feel like almost Christmas when the weather is blazing hot like this."

Jacques tossed aside his jacket and began to unbutton his shirt, preparing to change before they went downstairs to dinner. Lilli always made sure there was a freshly washed and pressed shirt waiting for him.

"Darling"—she pretended not to notice his mood—"let's go for a walk down by the quay after dinner. It'll be cool there in the evening." Then she would tell Jacques about sharing the shop with Frances.

Jacques was irritable throughout dinner, then silent as they strolled along the quay in the comfortable night air. Instinct told Lilli this was not the time to confide in him about her new business. Instead she told him about the welcome letter from Sara.

He hardly seemed to hear her. He was worried because none of the prosperous businessmen in Sydney shared his enthusiasm for the future of the frozen-meat industry. How shortsighted of them, she thought indignantly. Jacques was so much younger than they were, but he had a wonderful head for business. Her face softened. Aunt Sara would appreciate that.

When Lilli and Jacques returned to their room and retired for the night, she waited for him to reach out for her in the darkness. But tonight he turned his back to her and went to sleep. Tomorrow night she would tell him, she promised herself guiltily. She wasn't deceiving him; she was just finding the right moment.

LILLI COULD TELL by the look on Jacques's face when he came home the following evening that it had been a special day.

"Lilli, it's happened!" He swooped her off her feet. "I've found an investor who understands what I'm trying to do!"

"Oh, Jacques, how marvelous!" She was filled with pride—relief—and guilt, for having doubted him. "Tell me all about it."

For the rest of the evening, Jacques talked of nothing but his "new connection." Lilli didn't dare ask how soon money might change hands, but she was ever conscious that they were without funds to pay for next week's board and lodging at the Petty. She was selling well at the shop—both she and Frances were amazed at the number of women who were coming in to buy the creams. She added up the money she had put away from sales. Not enough to pay their hotel bill for a week, even if business continued this well, but perhaps enough for a room at one of those pleasant little lodging houses near Wynyard Square. She stored that comforting thought away....

The next morning Jacques left the house in high spirits. When he returned in the evening, he was full of talk about the English gentleman who was arranging for him to meet with two associates the following day.

"Lilli, this is it," he said confidently. "It's like I always tell you. Success is all a matter of meeting the right people."

"Jacques, I'm so proud of you," she said. But she was anxious about paying their hotel bill—there were only four days left. She had been brought up to be practical; Jacques had not.

The following morning Lilli stopped at the apothecary shop while Frances went on ahead to open up. She already needed to replenish her stock. Today she bought not only essence of roses but essence of jasmine. Miss Lilli's Beauty Creams would now be offered in two fragrances.

On impulse, she stopped off at Wynyard Square to inquire about vacancies in a neat, well-kept, small boardinghouse. To her relief, the price was modest; if business continued as well as it had in the past three days, she would have enough money put aside to pay a week's rent for one of the smaller rooms available. Just in case Jacques saw no money from his new business associates right away.

Jacques returned to the hotel jubilant that evening, filled with news about his meeting with his prospective investor and two associates. His excitement was infectious; Lilli's imagination raced along with his as he predicted their rosy future.

"I'm sure I've sold them, Lilli. I gave them figures. I showed them the possible markets. I explained about the modern refrigeration methods. I showed them the profits to be made. They're having a meeting with their banker tonight. With any luck at all, we'll be drawing up the papers in twenty-four hours."

As she listened to Jacques, Lilli grew more anxious about her deception. *How* would she explain this to Jacques? Charles let Frances run her shop. Was it because of Jacques's New Orleans family that he was so opposed to women in trade? But she didn't have the heart to tell him tonight, when he was so happy about today's accomplishments.

Suddenly she realized that if Jacques were to be set up on a sheep ranch—or a "station," as a ranch was called in Australia—she would have to give up the shop, because they would be moving away from Sydney. And it would not be to a suburb like Darlinghurst, only fifteen minutes from General Post Office, where Frances and Charles were building a house. They would move to the unpopulated area where there was fine grazing land for sheep.

The thought saddened Lilli. She loved the shop, enjoyed talking to the ladies who came in to buy—or sometimes just to look. She loved making up the creams, feeling the velvet softness as she combined the ingredients. Lately she had caught herself imagining that she would one day have a "house of beauty" where she would give fine ladies her "beauty treatments"—as Aunt Sara had taught her. But it was too daring a thought—at least for now.

ONE DAY IN THE MIDDLE of a seemingly interminable heat wave, Lilli and Frances closed the shop at exactly 5:30—official closing time—instead of dawdling until six, which they usually did on the chance that a homeward-bound shopgirl or office clerk might stop by. Back at the hotel, they went to their respective rooms. Frances and Charles usually dined earlier than Lilli and Jacques, and Lilli suspected Jacques deliberately arranged it that way.

Letting herself into their room, she found Jacques sprawled across the bed, his jacket and shirt dropped carelessly across a chair, shoes and socks scattered around the room.

"You're early, Jacques."

"Those bastards!" He sat up, his face twisted in rage. "They've changed their minds. They're putting their money into some crazy invention their banker dug up. After practically telling me I had a deal!"

"Oh, Jacques . . ." She hurried to his side, her heart pounding as she reached for his hand. "Somebody else will come along."

"Damn it, Lilli. This seemed so sure." He looked like a lost little boy. "I expected any day to be opening up a company bank account."

Though Lilli was concerned for Jacques, she knew they were not as bad off as he thought. He didn't know that she was earning money now. She took a deep breath.

"Jacques, you're going to find the right men soon—I'm certain of it." She managed a shaky smile. "I've been waiting all week to tell you about *my* little adventure. I suppose it's silly, but I've been having such fun—"

"What adventure?" He looked irritated.

"You know how little I have to do, with us living here at the hotel, darling...." She paused. "Well, I've been spending a lot of time with Frances at the shop. You remember the money you gave me to buy a length of cloth? Frances told me to wait for her next delivery—and in the meantime, to have something to do, I used the money to make up some of those creams Aunt Sara used to sell to the ladies who visited Marienbad during the season. And, Jacques, you won't believe it, but Frances encouraged me to show them to her customers, and I sold them all and had to make up more."

Jacques flushed with anger. Lilli emptied the contents of her purse on the bed. He stared in amazement at the shillings, sovereigns, and pound notes.

"Lilli, I don't approve." He sounded stern, but she knew he was impressed. "But if you're enjoying yourself..."

"Just until you're set up in business," Lilli said. "If there's money coming in from the creams, then you'll be able to take the time to choose just the right connection." Jacques counted up their new bankroll and pocketed it. Lilli tensed. *What if he used it to gamble again?* "Jacques," she said, "just out of curiosity, I stopped by at one of those houses near Wynyard Square, and we have enough from the sale of my creams to pay for a week's lodging there. I'm tired of staying here. Can't we move over to the square? Let's go over tonight to make sure they have a room for us."

He looked at her for a long moment, his mouth set.

"All right." But his eyes were wary. "We'll move. I'm bored with the stuffy people staying here anyway."

THE NEXT MORNING Lilli and Jacques moved to the modest boardinghouse near Wynyard Square. Every night Lilli put a substantial chunk of the day's receipts into a wooden cigar box in her top bureau drawer, telling herself not to feel guilty for this subterfuge. After all, she was doing this for their own protection. . . .

From time to time she realized that Jacques had helped himself to more than his daily business expenses, and she was convinced he was using the money for gambling. On his lucky days he would come home in high spirits, talking mysteriously about a "new connection," and would whisk her off to an elegant dinner at the Paris House or Adolphe's Diner Parisien. Afterward, they would go to the Tivoli. Those were gay evenings, meant to be carefree—but Lilli couldn't help being concerned about Jacques's mercurial, mysterious moods.

Meanwhile, the shop was a blessing. Lilli loved working with Frances, and sales were brisk. Women who came in for fabrics or hats frequently bought Lilli's creams. Women who were drawn into the shop by the display of Lilli's creams were usually coaxed into buying one of Frances's hats.

When Lilli heard that Charles had encouraged Frances to invest in a small ad in the *Morning Herald*, she began to consider the idea for her beauty creams. She checked and rechecked her small financial reserve and decided to gamble. Together she and Frances could afford a much larger ad, one extolling the virtues of Miss Lilli's Beauty Creams along with Frances's merchandise.

The ad brought a flood of customers into the shop, all eager to test Lilli's creams. This was followed by a surge of mail orders from all over the state of New South Wales. The two girls were incredulous as each mail delivery brought additional orders. Lilli spent every waking hour making up the hundreds of jars of creams on order; writing charming, conciliatory notes to apologize for the delay in mailing back the creams and offering to return money to anyone who so desired it—but only a handful refused to wait.

At Charles's suggestion, she opened an account at his bank, and very quickly, it seemed, her balance grew into an impressive sum. Aunt Sara had never earned so much from the creams, she told herself with pride—but Aunt Sara had not lived in a city of a half-million people.

"Frances, I can't believe what's happening," Lilli said as they prepared to close one evening. After dinner she would return to work for another two hours in what Frances had affectionately dubbed her "laboratory"—a tiny screened-off area where Lilli prepared the creams. Jacques would sit and read the evening newspaper beside her so that she would not be alone.

"One little ad and all this business!" Frances's smile was wry. "You're providing something women are hungry for. The ad sold some fabrics and a few hats for me, but you're offering something new."

"When I've filled all the orders, I'll advertise again," Lilli said. "If business keeps up like this, Jacques and I will be able to afford to furnish a flat. We'll move out of the boardinghouse. Frances, we'll have a real home."

She imagined three rooms: a sitting room, a bedroom, and a kitchen. Though Jacques rarely complained, she knew he was tired of the bland food served at their boardinghouse. And lately he seemed pleased with the shop's success.

Lilli and Frances left the shop and joined the homeward-bound crowds. A few weeks before, Frances and Charles had moved into their charming little house in Darlinghurst; every evening after work they met on the street and traveled home together.

"I hope Jacques won't let you work too late tonight," Frances said. "You must be exhausted from being on your feet all day. You don't sit down for a moment."

Lilli laughed. "He'll pull me out at a respectable hour."

"Lilli..." Frances hesitated. "I haven't even told Charles yet, because I want to be sure before I do—but I think I'm pregnant."

"Frances!" Lilli stopped dead, her face alight with affection and tenderness. "Frances, I'm so happy for you!"

"Don't say a word to anybody yet." Frances giggled. "Charles *should* be the first to know."

"Oh, sure," Lilli teased. "I'll tell every customer who walks into the store."

"We hadn't planned to have a baby for at least three years," Frances said. "Anyhow, I won't be sure for at least another few days. I could just be late."

"Charles will be so happy if you are pregnant Frances," Lilli said. She'd often heard him say that as an only child himself, he looked forward to having at least two or three children.

"I hope." Frances was wistful. "Anyway, I'll be able to keep on with the shop until my fifth month if I wear a driving duster over my dresses. Actually, you'll be needing the extra space in the shop. You'll be able to open up a 'house of beauty' like you've been talking about. Lilli, in five years you'll be the most successful businesswoman in Sydney." She hugged Lilli, both of them oblivious to the rush of pedestrians around them bound for buses and trams and ferries.

JACQUES WAS ALTERNATELY ELATED and depressed about his encounters in the clubs around town. But he always wove for Lilli enticing visions of their future—"once I make my connection." Even though that day had not yet arrived, they were able to move out of the boardinghouse and into a modest flat of their own.

While Lilli enjoyed having a real home at last, she was now faced with the task of housecleaning and cooking in addition to the long hours at the shop. But she was young and strong, she told herself. She could handle the business and the flat.

When Frances approached her fourth month of pregnancy and Charles insisted she give up the shop, Lilli conceded she needed the extra space for her own business, and now she could afford to expand. At the same time she realized she needed to hire a salesgirl. She herself was too busy making up the creams, packing and shipping them, and handling correspondence.

Over dinner that night, Lilli told Jacques about Frances, and her plan to hire more help. He did not approve. "It's an awful extravagance. What happens if you have a bad month? Women won't go on forever buying those creams."

"But I can't make up the creams and fill the mail orders if I have to wait on customers," Lilli said. "The mail orders bring in most of the business." She paused—then, ignoring Jacques's annoyance, plunged ahead. "Jacques, do you suppose—just until you make your connection—that you could come in for a few hours each day to help me?"

"Have you lost your mind?" He pushed back his chair and rose to his feet. His color was high, his eyes dark with anger. "Since when does a man go into a little shop like yours to sell? It's insulting—how can you even think it?"

"Jacques, I didn't mean—"

"Besides, I don't have time," he said brusquely. "I have people to see every day." He glared at her as though she was an impudent stranger.

"Jacques, please—sit down and finish your supper." She should have known he would be upset. He didn't understand the world of small shopkeepers the way she did.

"Anyway, we'll soon be moving to a station far from here." He sat down again. "You'll be finished with this silly business of yours. I'm meeting with a very important man. He'll be arriving from London in about ten days. You've been so busy I haven't mentioned it. I've talked in great detail with his partner, who's most receptive. We agree on every point."

"Jacques, you should have told me." But, she thought, he probably had waited until he was sure about the deal so that he wouldn't disappoint her again. "I knew you'd find someone." That meant she'd have to give up the shop. . . . Would she be able to carry on a mail-order business from a sheep station?

"I suppose you'll want to go back to the shop tonight." Jacques made it sound as though she were bound for a festive social engagement.

"Just for an hour or so. I have some orders that should be ready to go out tomorrow morning."

"I'll take you there and then pick you up later," he said. "I'd like to stop by to discuss a few points of our shipping arrangements with my new associate. You won't mind being alone in the shop for an hour or two?"

"I don't mind. I'll lock the door and pack up the orders. If I get lonely, I'll play the phonograph to keep me company."

Frances had brought a phonograph into the shop, along with several Nellie Melba records.

They finished their supper in silence. When Lilli had washed the dishes and put them away, Jacques walked with her to the shop.

Standing in front of the shop, she watched him walk away, and prayed he would not be disappointed again.

JACQUES WAITED UNTIL Lilli had locked the door to the shop and waved to him. Now, whistling "Tell Me, Pretty Maiden," he looked down the dark cobbled street for a hansom. He had been worrying about how he would handle tonight. Lilli had made it easy for him.

He spied a hansom, summoned the driver to the curb, gave him instructions, and climbed inside. He leaned back, tense and restless. God, he was sick of the way they lived. The cheap little flat that Lilli thought was so grand. Never having enough money in his pockets. Scared to death to gamble because he had to worry about a roof over their heads. On his own he'd never had such worries. He'd never been scared.

He had let himself be trapped because Lilli made him so damn hot. He'd thought they'd come down here together and set the world on fire. Why couldn't those sons of bitches see the future in frozen lamb? Already there was some action, but not on the scale he envisioned. In two years a man could make himself a fortune! He could build a dynasty. They could live like royalty.

Within ten minutes the hansom deposited him before a brilliantly lighted mansion with a commanding view of the harbor. Leave it to Molly Bolton to buy one of the masterpieces of Sydney, he thought in admiration as he alighted from the cab. Leave it to her to have married a British millionaire who catered to her every whim.

She had been twenty then and dancing in a London music hall. Now she was close to forty, bored with her husband, and eager for diversion—especially in the bedroom. In ten days Lester Bolton—who had made his millions in the railroads—

would be in Sydney to expand his empire. With any luck at all, he'd prod Molly into persuading Lester to back him up in a sheep station.

As he approached the massive oak door, Molly herself pulled it wide in welcome. This was her domestic staff's evening off, as she had pointed out over lunch. In the muted light of the baronial hall, Molly—in a sheer black negligee and with her flaming hair falling loosely about her shoulders—seemed young and voluptuous. Only in the harsh light of day did one see that the years had dealt harshly with her beauty.

"You're late." She pretended to sulk as she drew him into the hallway. "I'm not sure I should entertain you, Jacques."

"There were complications." Molly knew about Lilli. "But nothing—no one—could keep me away tonight." He dropped his arm around her waist, his hand reaching toward her breast. He knew she was his tonight, and he knew that if he handled himself right, he might have found himself an investor.

"Let's not waste a moment." She pressed her ample hips against his. "There's a bottle of champagne waiting for us in my bedroom."

LILLI GAZED WISTFULLY around the shop. A pair of carpenters were putting up a partition so she would have a larger "laboratory." In one corner Frances, self-conscious in her blooming pregnancy, was explaining to Dorothy—Lilli's new helper—how to cut the fabrics that still remained in the shop and which ones Dorothy was to sell until the meager supply was exhausted. This would be Frances's last day as a shopkeeper. Lilli felt lonely just thinking about it.

"Lilli, don't look so sad," Frances said, but Lilli guessed she shared her feeling. "I know what you and I are going to do." Frances brightened. "We're leaving Dorothy in charge of the shop and going off to lunch at the Adams Café." The Adams Café was one of the finest restaurants in the city and catered to English visitors with a wide choice of imported fish. "You can't say no," Frances warned. "Not when it's my last day at the shop."

Lilli laughed. "You're right. I'd love to have lunch with you."

"I'm so glad the weather's turned cold," Frances said. "I can hide my big belly inside my cape."

Lilli felt a rush of tenderness for her dear friend and the child she carried. "I don't know why women should hide themselves when they're pregnant," Lilli said. "Every pregnant woman carries a small miracle." She felt a pang of envy.

"Come on, Lilli." Frances took her hand. "Let's leave now so we'll be there before the restaurant is crowded. I know just what I'm ordering. Charles says their Vancouver salmon is superb."

Lilli and Frances walked through the brisk noonday air to the Adams Café on George Street. Though it was early, Lilli noted that already a sprinkling of Sydney's leading merchants were seated at damask-covered tables in the large, well-lighted, comfortably heated room.

Suddenly she was ice-cold. She reached out a trembling hand to stop Frances. "Not here—"

Frances followed her gaze to the table across the room where Jacques sat with a tall, elaborately gowned woman. Lilli saw Jacques's hand reach across the table for the bejeweled hand of his companion. The same way he had reached for her hand across a table in the Bellevue Café. The same look in his eyes.

"Come, Lilli…" Frances tugged at her arm. "We'll go to the Monaco." And in a moment they were standing outside the Adams Café, shivering in the brilliant winter sunlight.

5

"I SHOULD HAVE KNOWN Jacques would be having lunch at the Adams." Lilli tried to sound casual as they walked away from the café. *Had Frances noticed the way Jacques reached for that woman's hand?* "It's his favorite place to talk business outside of his club."

"Charles says all the big business people in Sydney favor the Adams," Frances said.

What a good friend, Lilli thought. She didn't say business-*men.*

While Frances kept up a steady stream of chatter, Lilli grappled with the image of Jacques and his companion. She had to be twenty years older than he! Who was she? How long had Jacques been seeing her? Did she know Jacques was married? Humiliation colored her cheeks. She remembered the countess in Marienbad....

"Jacques told me he was having lunch with an associate of a very important man who's coming from London in a few days," Lilli said as they made their way through the noonday crowds. "Apparently she's very excited about Jacques's ideas for raising sheep for the frozen-food market."

"Oh, really? That's wonderful," Frances said. "Charles thinks that'll be important for Australia one day." But Lilli knew that Frances had already talked to Charles about the possibility of his bank's backing Jacques, and the bankers had not been interested.

Lilli tried to appear lighthearted once she and Frances had settled themselves at a table at the charming Monaco Café. But inwardly she continued to struggle with her suspicions. How

was she to go on living with Jacques if he had been unfaithful?
For an instant she closed her eyes, hoping to erase from her
mind the image of Jacques and that woman in the Adams Café.

"Lilli?" Frances's anxious voice brought her back.

She pretended to yawn. "I think last night is catching up with
me. I stayed up so late making a sachertorte for tonight's dinner. It's Jacques's favorite dessert." *Don't think about Jacques!*
She leaned forward, smiling tenderly. "When are Charles and
you going to settle on a name for the baby?"

In a show of celebrating their last business day together, Lilli
and Frances each ordered a glass of claret to accompany their
fish.

"You know, Lilli"—Frances leaned forward—"I wouldn't
dream of telling Charles, but I miss home more than ever now.
Mama and I have always been so close."

Lilli understood. More than ever she wished that Aunt Sara
were here in Sydney. All her life Aunt Sara had been there for
her. If she left Jacques, where would she go? Then she remembered the shop. She could support herself. She could live in the
back of the shop.

Tonight she would go back to the flat and pack her clothes.
She would find a hansom to take her to the shop. How could
she lie in the bed beside Jacques when she knew he had been
with that woman? Tomorrow she would tell Frances; she
couldn't bring herself to talk about it today.

Now Lilli was grateful that her work was so demanding. Next
week she would run another ad in the *Morning Herald* to bring
in more business.

Today Lilli delayed leaving the shop, letting Frances go ahead
to meet Charles. She needed time alone. Tears filled her eyes as
she tried to imagine her life without Jacques. How could she
write and tell Aunt Sara that her marriage had ended before the
first year?

She dawdled as long as possible, planning the evening. She
would wait until after dinner to tell Jacques she was leaving
him. She would take only her clothes, leaving the money in the
cigar box in the dresser for what he called his "operating cap-

ital." When that was gone... But that wasn't her concern
anymore.

Her hands trembled as she unlocked the door to the flat.
Jacques never arrived until dinner was almost on the table.
Where was he this minute? Was he making love to *her*?

Half an hour later there was a knock at the door. He never
bothered to use his key. Slowly, her heart pounding, she walked
to the door to let him in.

"Hello, my love." He kissed her cheek. "I'm starving. It
must be the cold air."

"I suppose." She stood in the kitchen as he walked into the
sitting room. How could he come back pretending nothing had
happened?

She was silent throughout dinner. Her eyes avoiding his, she
made a pretense of eating the wine-poached imported floun-
der that had been outrageously expensive. He ate with gusto.

"You're strangely quiet tonight," he said as she left the table to bring out the sachertorte, Aunt Sara's prized recipe. "I
hope you're not coming down with something."

Lilli stood immobile at the icebox for a moment, plate in
hand. She turned around and walked slowly to the table. Tonight Jacques's New Orleans-bred solicitude was more than she
could bear.

"No," she said. "I'm not coming down with something.
Frances and I decided to treat ourselves to lunch because this
was her last day at the shop." Her eyes met his. "We went to the
Adams Café."

Jacques dropped his gaze. "And you didn't come in because you saw me there with Mrs. Bolton," he said quietly. "Is
that why you're so quiet tonight? Because you thought I was
seeing another woman?"

"She clearly wasn't a man." Lilli lifted her head in defiance. How could Jacques make *her* feel guilty?

"Lilli, my love." He reached across the table for her hand.
She stiffened. "That's the wife of the man who's coming from
London. I've been in correspondence with him. He told me his
wife was lonesome and asked me to have lunch with her once

in a while. I was protecting our business interests. And my little wife was jealous?''

"You were holding her hand." She wanted to believe him, but instinct warned her.

"She was telling me how much she misses Lester," Jacques said. "Her husband. I was comforting her, my darling. Could a future business associate of her husband's do less?''

She wanted so much to believe him. Perhaps it was true. What kind of wife was she not to believe her husband?

"There's some whipped cream in the icebox," she said, feeling ashamed of her suspicions. "Would you like some with your coffee?''

JACQUES WAS JUBILANT when Lester Bolton arrived in town. He waited impatiently for his meeting with the railroad tycoon, convincing Lilli that this was the "important contact" who would set him up in business. She, too, was excited, but she couldn't face the thought of leaving Sydney for some outpost suitable for raising sheep.

Within two weeks of his arrival in Sydney, Lilli guessed that Jacques's potential partner was not interested. At the end of the third week, Jacques came charging into the shop to announce that Lester Bolton had offered him a job as a train conductor.

"He led me on!" Jacques was indignant. "I was sure he was ready to invest. And all he offers is a stupid job that'll lead me nowhere!''

Lilli comforted him, disappointed that Jacques had once again encountered failure, yet secretly relieved that they would be staying in Sydney. She placed a second ad in the *Morning Herald*, which brought in more orders. A woman journalist from another Sydney newspaper—out to persuade Lilli to advertise in her newspaper, Jacques suggested—interviewed Lilli. The article was extremely flattering and Lilli knew it would attract more customers.

One morning late in November, Lilli found Charles waiting outside the shop.

"Frances gave birth at four o'clock this morning! A little girl! Elizabeth Cohen. She weighs seven pounds, and she's beautiful!"

"How's Frances?" Lilli asked. "Why didn't she send for me?"

"It all happened so fast," Charles said. "She felt the first pains around eleven o'clock. By the time the doctor arrived, she was already in hard labor."

"Did she have a bad time?" Dorothy could handle the shop for the morning. She had to see Frances.

Charles laughed. "I was a wreck, I must admit. But Frances is already talking about the next baby. Lilli, I held my daughter in my arms this morning." His face was reverent. "I can't believe she's finally here."

EVERY TUESDAY night, Lilli went to Darlinghurst to visit Frances, Charles, and the baby. To her dismay, Jacques rarely accompanied her, often using the excuse of a "business meeting." Try as she might, she could not forget or excuse his condescension toward the Cohens because they were Jewish.

At dinner at the Cohens' house late in January, Lilli confided her concerns about the business—most important, her exasperation at not being able to change the formula of her creams and expand the business. It pleased her that she could talk seriously with Charles about the creams; Jacques was annoyed whenever she raised the subject.

"I see now that what I'm selling is fine for the skins of many women, but there are several *kinds* of skins. Each type requires something different. I should be offering four different creams. Can you imagine how many more women would become my customers if I could offer various products?"

"Charles," Frances said, "maybe you could help Lilli."

Charles looked uncomfortable. "Frances, I'm not a chemist."

"But you've told me yourself how much you learned about chemistry from your friend at Trinity College." Lilli knew that Charles had studied at Trinity College, Cambridge, although he had not received a degree; before receiving a degree, a student must declare allegiance to the Church of England. "You love fiddling around in your little laboratory in the attic."

"I play at it, that's true," he said, "using whatever I picked up from Robert during our four years at Trinity."

"Charles," Lilli said, "I must know how to change the formula to make a cream suitable for a woman with especially dry skin—and for very oily skin. And sometimes a woman comes into the shop and I see that her nose and forehead, perhaps, are oily while the rest of her face is dry. I have to know how to adjust the formula!"

Charles looked from one to the other and sighed. "All right, I'll try. Now, I can't guarantee that I can come up with the right formulas," he warned, "but I'll run some samples. Tell me what you're using now and the proportions."

Within two weeks Charles brought in a sample jar of cream. Lilli tested a bit on one hand. "It's just right for women with terribly dry skin!" she said triumphantly. "Charles, you're a genius!"

"Hold on there, Lilli—we have another formula to go. *Then* you may call me a genius." But he was clearly pleased.

On Purim, Lilli was invited to be Frances's guest at a party at the Great Synagogue across from Hyde Park while Charles stayed home with tiny Elizabeth. Lilli was awed by the occasion, remembering how she and Aunt Sara had observed Purim when she was a little girl. Aunt Sara would read to her the story of Queen Esther, who saved the Jews from the wicked Haman. Every time Aunt Sara mentioned Haman's name, Lilli brought out the ritual noisemaker, as did the children today, when the rabbi, reading from the Torah, mentioned Haman's name.

Lilli knew this was the moment to tell Frances that she, too, was Jewish. But she could not bring herself to say it until she told Jacques.

They left the synagogue in high spirits, with Lilli impressed by the size and enthusiasm of the congregation. Tonight she had learned that there were over 5,000 Jews in Sydney. Here—

at a time when Jews around the world were horrified by the accounts of pogroms in eastern Europe—no one made a secret of his Jewish heritage. How that would please Aunt Sara! And Frances had proudly pointed out that three years ago, when the Commonwealth of Australia was inaugurated, the governor-general had decreed that the chief minister of the Great Synagogue was to be given the same recognition as heads of other churches in the commonwealth. Frances said that Jews rose to important posts in the Australian government.

Lilli and Frances exchanged warm goodnights and hurried off to their respective homes. Lilli was startled to see the windows of her flat dark. Where was Jacques? Her heart began to pound. He wasn't off to some gambling table? Or to some woman?

She felt her face grow warm as she opened the door and let herself in. She had told herself that she believed what Jacques told her about Mrs. Bolton, yet her doubts lingered. Tense and troubled, she went into the bedroom and prepared for the night.

She had been lying awake for about two hours when she heard the sound of Jacques's key in the lock.

"Lilli?" He knew she was home because she had left a lamp on in the sitting room. "Lilli?"

She turned on her side and faced the wall, pretending to be asleep but acutely conscious of his every movement. She felt the sag of the bed beneath his weight. His body moved closer to hers. A hand crept about her waist and fondled a breast.

"Honey?" he murmured. "I'm sorry, I didn't realize it was so late. I was watching a pair of wonderful domino players over at the Union Club."

"Hmm?" she couldn't help feeling aroused. Had he been at the club, or with some woman?

"Lilli, I love you." He pressed himself against her.

For a few moments he caressed her, and then he turned her on her back and pushed her nightgown above her hips. In sudden shock, she was aware of a pungent fragrance. The scent of a woman's perfume. *So he had not been at the Union Club.* He was angry that she had gone off for the evening with Frances.

He had gone to some woman to punish her. Was it that Mrs. Bolton again? *How could she ask herself that and feel this way?*

Her hands caught at his shoulders as he lifted himself above her, thrusting teasingly between her thighs while his mouth filled hers. Their lovemaking took on a strange, startling frenzy.

Afterward, with Jacques breathing evenly in her ear, Lilli fell into a restless, uneasy sleep.

WITHIN THREE WEEKS Lilli knew she was pregnant. She lived each day in joyous anticipation. God had taken a hand. No more thoughts of leaving Jacques would torment her. The baby would bring him back to her forever. When she was a month late, she would tell him.

She knew, too, that the time had come to tell her husband of her Jewish heritage. If she carried Jacques's son, then he must be circumcised on his eighth day, as decreed by Jewish law. The child of a Jewish mother was born a Jew.

Jacques was enchanted by the news of her pregnancy. She waited for him to say that he would accept a position other than that of a sheep rancher. She waited, to tell him of her Jewish faith. *Soon.*

She was evasive when Frances questioned her about the future of the business, concerned for Lilli's health and knowing Jacques and Lilli had no other means of support. In the early months of her pregnancy, Lilli battled against sleepiness and exhaustion.

"I couldn't bear to be away from the shop when everything is doing so well," she said with a show of cheerfulness. "I can continue here until the last two months. I'm training Dorothy to handle everything while I have to be away. I'll hire another girl, too."

"If I know you," Frances said bluntly, "you'll be mixing creams when you go into labor. Lilli, you must stop pushing yourself this way."

"I'm fine," Lilli insisted. "You've said yourself, it's only in the first three months that you're so sleepy and tired."

Lilli wrote Aunt Sara about her pregnancy, wishing she could tell her in person. She could imagine Aunt Sara's joy—right away she would start sewing for her first grandniece or grandnephew.

Lilli was taken aback by Jacques's hostility when she asked if he had written his parents.

"I want nothing to do with my family. But when the baby is born, I will tell my mother."

At the end of Lilli's fourth month, Jacques—of his own volition—came into the shop to help. Lilli was pleased; he charmed their women customers and sold as well as she. He brought a comfortable stool into the laboratory so that she could sit while mixing the creams.

Charles created two additional formulas. Now the Miss Lilli line included four different creams in three fragrances, each distinguished by the appropriate label. To announce her expanded line, Lilli placed a large ad in the *Morning Herald*, at a cost that infuriated Jacques. But afterward local sales and mail orders soared. Lilli hired a girl—Mary—to help with the packaging.

Impressed by the volume of sales, Jacques went out in search of larger quarters. After a few days he found a shop with a flat above it—the shop almost double in size and the flat with a second bedroom—and supervised their moving in.

Except for missing Aunt Sara, Lilli had never been so happy. Jacques was here at her side for most of each day. She went to sleep each night in his arms. And as her pregnancy advanced, she was proud that she was still desirable to him.

One night, over dinner, she found the courage to tell Jacques she was Jewish.

"Half Jewish," he corrected after a moment of startled silence. "Your father was not Jewish."

"A child of a Jewish mother is Jewish," she said quietly. "Our baby will be Jewish." Though she spoke calmly, she trembled inside.

He paused, his face tense. "Well, call him what you like," he said at last. "It's enough that he's our child."

"I would like to join the Great Synagogue." Surprised by her own boldness, she had difficulty keeping her voice even. "I don't expect you to attend services with me," she said quickly. "I'd just like to go sometimes with Frances to the Friday evening or Saturday morning services. And it would be good to be a member, because if I'm a member, then the baby can go to the Sunday School classes there when it's old enough." She paused and took a deep breath. "And if the baby should be a boy, then he will be circumcised." She prepared herself for an explosion.

Jacques's face flushed. He avoided her eyes. "Lilli, we'll be silent about your Jewish mother until I'm established in Sydney. I don't need to labor under that handicap."

"But, Jacques, in Sydney people don't have to hide their religious faith." How could he believe that? "It's not like in Russia or Poland." Nor Bohemia, she added silently.

"I won't hear any more about this!" He rose to his feet, his chair crashing behind him. "It would not be to my advantage in business to be labeled as having a Jewish wife."

EARLY IN NOVEMBER, while preparing dinner, Lilli felt her first labor pains. But knowing it would be hours before it was time to call the doctor, she didn't say anything to Jacques. This child would arrive at a sensible hour.

She stiffened before the cookstove as she fought another contraction. Perspiration dotted her forehead and neck. She tried to remember everything Frances had told her. She was prepared for the delivery; nothing had been overlooked.

The contraction passed. Lilli carried dinner to the table. Jacques was reading the evening newspaper. She made a pretense of putting food onto her plate, but her body was noticeably tense.

"Lilli?" Jacques looked up from his paper. "Are you all right?"

"I think by morning you'll be going for Dr. Jamison," she said quietly.

"You're in labor!" His expression was a mixture of elation and fear.

"Just the beginning, Jacques. With a first baby it usually takes a long time." But it hadn't with Frances, she remembered nervously.

"You get into bed," he ordered, white and grim. "I'll go for Dr. Jamison."

"Jacques, it'll be hours before you have to bring him."

Lilli let Jacques help her into a nightgown and into bed.

"Now back to the table and finish your dinner," she ordered. "I'm not going anywhere."

Jacques put a Caruso record on the phonograph while he hastily finished his dinner, then carried the dishes to the sink to soak. When he returned to their bedroom to sit beside Lilli, she told him the pains were still eleven minutes apart. "Settle in for a long wait." She smiled, reaching for his hand. "Some things can't be hurried."

At five in the morning, despite Lilli's exhortations that Jacques delay until the more respectable hour of six, Jacques went downstairs to phone for Dr. Jamison. At twenty minutes past six Lilli gave birth to a seven-pound daughter with a mass of auburn hair and features that already resembled her mother's. She was named Janine Kathe Laval.

WHILE SHE RECOVERED from her delivery, Lilli fretted about the progress of the business. But only briefly did she worry that Jacques was disappointed over not having a son. He loved being a father. He was in and out of the flat several times a day, reporting on activities in the shop. When he conceded on the fifth day that their stock was growing uncomfortably low, Lilli insisted on going downstairs to the shop—with tiny Janine—so that she could prepare two vats of cream that Mary could put into jars in the morning.

Jacques balked at the expense when she talked about hiring a nursemaid to help with the baby so she could return to the shop. Janine would share the second bedroom with the nursemaid. "Jacques, it's a business expense," she pointed out carefully. "I can't work without help with Janine."

To her surprise, he resisted hiring domestic help even though he himself had been raised in a New Orleans household where every family of even modest means employed a "colored" nursemaid.

Lilli never considered not returning to the business. She knew Jacques was becoming restless in the shop, which made it especially important that she return as soon as possible. She realized, too, that their financial well-being depended upon her.

So, with Mrs. Phipps caring for Janine, Lilli turned back to the business, this time with an eye toward expanding. She would turn it into a "house of beauty," like the Rubinstein woman in Melbourne. She would rent the empty store next door and put in a connecting arch. She would give facials like Rubinstein—the same "treatments" that Aunt Sara had given. Profits would soar.

Alarmed by the amount of money that disappeared each week from the cigar box in their bureau, Lilli was determined to increase their income. She knew Jacques was gambling again. The time had come to put aside money that he knew nothing about. For Janine, she needed this security. She was not being a bad wife.

JACQUES WAS INTRIGUED by Lilli's plans for expansion, envisioning an enthusiastic response from the ladies of Sydney. But he argued with Lilli about her fees.

"Make them pay higher! Women appreciate what costs them a lot of money." Lilli remembered that Aunt Sara had been of the same philosophy.

Jacques appointed himself manager of the House of Beauty and supervised the workmen. When Miss Lilli's House of Beauty was formally opened, he played the handsome and courtly young host who welcomed the eager ladies into the premises and charmed them into signing up for courses of treatment.

Lilli hired two more women and trained them to give facials. Before a facial was given, Lilli herself made a point of analyzing the skin of the client and prescribing the best treatment.

After reading about all the big new stores opening up in Newtown, a heavily populated area near the city, Lilli began talking about renting a small space in such a store and setting up a clerk to sell her creams there. Jacques was incensed that she would consider such an added expense, but Frances and Charles quietly encouraged her.

Each night, as she had done since the beginning, Lilli brought home the proceeds of the day's sales. At the end of the week, Jacques would take the money—minus what he used for himself for his "daily expenses"—and deposit it in the bank. Lilli dipped into a second account—about which Jacques knew nothing—to finance the Newtown shop.

As always, she felt guilty about keeping secrets from Jacques, but she felt she had no choice. She couldn't forget that they had been in Sydney two and a half years, and Jacques was no closer to becoming a sheep rancher than he'd been on the day they arrived.

JACQUES TOSSED ASIDE the *Sydney Bulletin* and rose to his feet. He crossed to the door of the bedroom, where Lilli sat in a slipper chair near the fireplace with Janine at her breast. Her auburn hair fell in a lush cascade about her shoulders. The glow from the roaring fire in the grate cast rosy color upon her face while Janine sucked in noisy contentment.

Jacques cleared his throat, and Lilli looked up with a smile. He knew the times she nursed Janine each day were special to her. But Janine was already eight months old. Wasn't it time she stopped nursing? The sight of Janine nuzzling at Lilli's nipple was a powerful aphrodisiac, and the fact that he had to ignore his instinct to take his wife to bed this instant irritated him.

"I'm going to the club for a while, Lilli." At times like this he felt like an outsider in his own home. And he resented the constant presence of Mrs. Phipps in the bedroom next to his own. Lilli was forever shushing him when they made love, because the walls were thin.

"Be careful, Jacques," she said now. "I hear there's been trouble again with the larrikins."

"I'll just play a few games of dominoes and come home." He was impatient to get away from this domestic scene. Lilli seemed surprised by his announcement. This was the one night in the week they could make love without worrying about the old biddy's presence in the next room. This was Mrs. Phipps's night to go to her daughter's. But Janine had a nasty habit of waking up and crying at the crucial moment. Damn it, that wasn't going to happen tonight! He was getting out of here.

He hurried downstairs and out into the sharp, cold night air. Lilli probably thought it was extravagant to keep up his membership when he was doing nothing about finding a business partner. Well, to the devil with what Lilli thought. He worked like a stupid shopkeeper every day—he deserved the club membership. Not that he was truly comfortable there, but he liked talking about "my club."

He had just passed his twenty-fifth birthday, and what did he have to show for it? He'd thought when he came down here to Australia with Lilli that he would make a fortune. He was going to set the world on fire. He was always ahead of his time—that was the trouble.

He needed some excitement in his life. How the hell had he allowed himself to be trapped this way? His eyes glistened as he remembered romantic interludes in New York, then in London and Paris. No matter how tough a spot he landed in, he'd always been able to come out on top. Then he didn't have a wife and child hanging around his neck.

All at once he was aware of painful outcries and raucous laughter. He paused, peering down a darkened alley. A handful of larrikins were beating up a young boy.

"Come on, Jerry, give it to him in the gut!" a girl who could not have been more than sixteen yelled. "Let him see who's the boss!" The others joined in.

"Let go of him!" Jacques ran toward them, aware that a pair of Sydney policemen were behind him. "Go on, the lot of you!"

"Hold on there!" one of the policemen called out. "You're under arrest!"

While the two policemen went off after the larrikins, Jacques rushed forward to help the boy to his feet. "Are you all right?" he asked. "Do you need medical attention?"

"I'm—all right," the boy stammered. "I might have been dead if you'd come five minutes later. I'll be forever grateful to you."

"Do you live near here?" The boy was young, no more than eighteen or nineteen, Jacques guessed as he prodded him out of the alley into the lighted street. Still trembling, inadequately dressed for the cold night. "I'll see you home."

"I don't have a home yet." He looked down. "I just arrived in Sydney."

"This hour of the night and you don't have a home?" Jacques stared hard at the boy's delicately featured face, the troubled blue eyes. "And you'll be needing something warmer than that jacket if you're staying in Sydney." Compassion touched him as he surveyed his slight young companion. Clearly, it had been a while since the boy had eaten. "Let's go into a café close by and have a bite of supper."

"I—I don't have money."

"My treat," Jacques said expansively. "There's a quiet little place just down the block from here. I'm Jacques Laval," he introduced himself. "And you?"

"Oliver Wickersham, sir."

Together they went to the café. Jacques ordered for them, enjoying Oliver's obvious admiration. Cautiously he began to question the soft-spoken boy. He was nineteen. He had just been thrown off the family farm by his stepfather. His family—particularly the loutish stepfather—had no patience for his love of poetry and art and music. To his five half brothers and sisters, he was a misfit, a "sissy." Ashamed that she had borne her first child out of wedlock—to a man other than her husband—his mother would not come to his defense.

"You'll come home with me tonight," Jacques said. "Tomorrow we'll look about to find you a room and a job."

Jacques already had a job in mind for Oliver Wickersham. He had wasted time enough with Lilli's business. Oliver was young, good-looking, and well mannered. The ladies who came to the House of Beauty would be quite taken with him. And he sensed that Oliver was bright; he would learn quickly how to sell courses of treatments.

Jacques was whistling as he led Oliver up the stairs to the flat. Life seemed infinitely more interesting now that he was leaving the House of Beauty.

6

LILLI DIDN'T LEARN of their overnight guest until Mrs. Phipps, on her way to the bathroom at dawn, screamed at the sight of a stranger lying wrapped in a blanket on the sofa. While Jacques calmed both Mrs. Phipps and Oliver, now awakened by her screams, Lilli ran into the other bedroom to the baby's side.

"We'll all go back to sleep for another two hours," Jacques decreed, relishing being master of the situation. "At least Janine slept through this."

Back in bed, Jacques told Lilli about Oliver's experience with the larrikins. His compassion touched Lilli.

"He's alone in the world, Lilli. His bastard of a stepfather threw him out. We could put a bed in the back of the shop for him. Until he finds a job and a room for himself."

"I feel so sorry for him," Lilli whispered. "To be treated that way by his own family." For a moment she remembered her father, and the old bitterness returned.

At last Lilli fell back to sleep, her head on Jacques's shoulder. When she awoke, she heard someone in the kitchen making breakfast. Not Jacques, who snored lightly on his back. Surely not Mrs. Phipps, who vowed never to touch a stove again after feeding a family of six for many years. It must be Oliver, preparing breakfast for them. Her heart went out to him.

Lilli set up a bed at the rear of the shop for Oliver. Tacitly he assumed the duties of cleaning up the shop each evening before going up to the flat for dinner. He was gentle, eager to be helpful; and he worshiped Jacques. In Oliver's eyes Jacques was a hero, the man who had saved his life.

Lilli listened sympathetically when Oliver confided that his mother had married his stepfather in order to give him a name. His mother had been a poor farm girl, orphaned at twelve and working as a housemaid when she succumbed to the charms of the son of a middle-class sheep raiser. When the lady of the house realized the situation, the son had been shipped off to school in England and Oliver's mother had been thrown out of the house.

"She would have helped me if she could," Oliver said, lifting his head in defiance. "The best thing I can do for mum is to stay out of her life." Unexpectedly, he chuckled. "That's all I can do. The old man said he'd kill me if I tried to hang around her. But she loves me," he whispered. "At least I have that."

Four days after Oliver's arrival, Jacques admitted to Lilli that he was grooming the boy to replace himself at the shop. "He'll do fine, Lilli," he said confidently. "Mrs. Phipps is handy with a needle—she can take in one of my old suits to fit him. He has a quiet way that the ladies will appreciate. I'll show him how to welcome each new client. I'll train him to sell courses of treatment. I tell you, he has a natural gift that will be useful."

"But, Jacques, he's so young." Lilli had grown accustomed to having Jacques in the shop. Now, a virtual stranger...

"Same age as you, Lilli." Jacques laughed. "He'll talk those ladies into signing up for all the courses of treatment you can handle. Watch and see."

Lilli tried not to ask herself where Jacques spent his daytime—and sometimes nighttime—hours once Oliver had taken his place in the business. He talked vaguely again about making "new connections" via the Union Club. Was he seeing that Mrs. Bolton again? Or some other woman? All women seemed to be attracted to Jacques.

Oliver adored Lilli and the baby. An eager playmate for Jan, he was as ecstatic as Lilli when she took her first steps at ten months. At Oliver's insistence, Lilli bought one of the expensive new cameras so Jan's progress could be recorded. Oliver made dinner for them often, and even Mrs. Phipps was impressed by his culinary talents.

Lilli was pleased with the way he handled the customers, too. The women doted on him, signing up for weekly courses of treatments at his urging, lingering to confide their most intimate problems. He was especially friendly with Mrs. Allister, the French wife of an English diplomat, and persuaded Lilli to teach him French so that he might surprise her.

"Paris sounds like such an exciting city. Wouldn't you love to see it someday?" he asked Lilli while he prepared a special fish recipe and she peeled the vegetables.

"I'd like to see London." Where her father probably kept a fine town house in addition to his country manor. "And Paris. Not that I'm likely to." She laughed. "Jacques adored Paris. He lived there for a year."

"Mrs. Allister has told me all about fascinating Montmartre in Paris—where the artists live," Oliver said. "That's where her husband found her. She was an artist's model. Isn't it romantic? A poor little artist's model marrying into a rich and important English family. Now she's a fine lady." Oliver's smile was affectionate. Sadly, Lilli remembered her mother, loving the younger son in a titled English family—the man who had never come back to claim her as his wife and recognize his child. "Of course that was thirty years ago," Oliver continued, "but Corinne goes home to Paris every other year for two months."

"Corinne?" Lilli clucked in mock reproach.

"She insists I call her that privately. Sunday she has invited me to their house for tea so that she can show me the paintings by Cézanne that Mr. Allister bought years ago in Paris. She knew him well. Corinne's husband will be there for tea." He paused. "It will be very proper, Lilli."

She smiled. "I'm sure it will be."

It wasn't until Oliver had been with them for two months that Jacques explained the truth about why his family had treated him with such contempt.

"Oliver's family and a lot more in this world are still living back in the days of Queen Victoria, when poor Oscar Wilde went to prison because he preferred handsome young men to beautiful young women."

Lilli stared at him uncomprehendingly.

"People in London and Paris and other important cities realize that Victoria is dead and Edward VII has issued in a whole new way of life," Jacques continued grandly. "There's a new freedom of thought today. But in small towns and on farms, these things are not understood."

"I've never heard of such doings." Lilli felt her cheeks grow warm. "But I can't understand Oliver's family casting him out that way. I think that everyone has a right to live as he sees fit as long as he harms no one else."

But for a few days afterward, she was self-conscious in Oliver's presence. Eventually she became accustomed to the idea, and she began to understand Oliver's profound gratitude to Jacques for saving him from the Sydney larrikins and providing him with a home. To Oliver, Jacques was a king to be worshiped and served.

"Lilli—" Oliver interrupted her thoughts, a faraway look in his eyes as he slid the fish into the oven. "I think it would be nice for our ladies if we brought a phonograph into the House of Beauty so they could be serenaded by records while the girls work on their faces. It would create such a lovely atmosphere. And of course," he pointed out, "we'll specialize in records by Nellie Melba."

"That's an interesting idea," Lilli said. "We'll try it for a week and see what they say. I'll bring our phonograph from the flat."

EARLY IN 1907—several months after his arrival in their lives— Oliver asked Lilli to let him redecorate the House of Beauty. In his usual conscientious fashion, he had prepared the plans and outlined the expenses. Lilli was enthralled as she listened to him describe each change in detail. With Oliver's artistic flair, the House of Beauty could live up to its name.

"Oliver, it would be beautiful, but it would cost so much." She knew Jacques would be enraged at such extravagance just now. Without telling her, he had gone to the bank—not Charles's—and had tried to borrow money on the business. Someone at the Union Club had offered him a parcel of rural land. He was indignant when the loan was denied, completely oblivious to her shock when he told her about his efforts. *He hadn't bothered to ask her how she felt about it.* "I'm sorry, Oliver," Lilli said. "Maybe later. With the new girl I've just hired and the advertising coming up, I just can't spend more."

"Lilli, I can do most of the work myself." His face was bright with anticipation. "Don't pay me any wages until the costs are paid off."

"Oliver, I pay you so little as it is," she said gently. Oliver continued to sleep in the back of the shop and eat his meals with them. "We'll think about it in a few months," she said, seeing his disappointment.

In truth, Lilli was concerned about the shop. Jacques's representing himself at the bank as owner of the business unnerved her, and at uneasy intervals she remembered that he had access to the main bank account. It frightened her to think that her impractical husband could control the destiny of the House of Beauty.

After being turned down at the bank, Jacques was sullen with everybody except Jan. Lilli found herself looking forward to the escape of a late dinner at the Paris House with the Cohens this evening—late because they would go to Friday night services at the synagogue first. As she put Jan to bed, she wondered if Jacques would fabricate some last-minute business meeting that would keep him away from the Paris House.

She was changing from her business frock into a becoming blue-green silk made for her by her aunt when Jacques came into their bedroom.

"I have to meet a man at the Union Club in about an hour," he said offhandedly. "I don't know how you can go gallivanting with the Cohens when you see so little of Jan."

"Jacques, she's asleep!" But he'd already left the room. *She wasn't neglecting Jan!* Did he think Jan noticed that he was sound asleep in the flat until noon each day? She spent every lunch hour with Jan; and in the afternoons Mrs. Phipps brought her down to the House of Beauty, where the various ladies delighted in cooing over her. They were together every evening and all day on Sundays. Jacques thought nothing of going out in the evening. Why should it be different for the father than for the mother? She rarely went out at night, and never before Jan was asleep.

As always, Lilli was aware of the unspoken hostility between Jacques and the Cohens when Charles came up to the flat to say that Frances was waiting for them in their new Renault, a recent wedding-anniversary gift from Charles's doting mother. The automobile seemed to be a special affront to Jacques. Only the wealthy owned such contraptions, he said. The Cohens were being pretentious.

When they had ordered and sat sipping their predinner wine, Charles seemed to abandon his air of festivity. He gazed somberly at the damask tablecloth while Lilli and Frances exchanged stories about Jan and Beth. Lilli wondered what was bothering Charles, but she knew that whatever it was, he would talk about it when he was ready.

Tonight he barely touched his favorite Vancouver salmon. Lilli's eyes moved nervously from Charles to Frances.

"Lilli, we have news," Frances began, smiling encouragingly at Charles. "We have to return to London almost immediately." Lilli stared in shock. "Charles's mother is not well. She's alone, you know. She's always been so terribly independent. She's been a suffragette, and she bicycles and plays lawn tennis. At least she did. Now the doctors say she must give all that up and live very quietly. They won't even allow her to come to Sydney to spend six months with us as we'd all planned." She exchanged a tender glance with Charles. "We've decided to go back to London to be with her."

"Oh, Frances . . ." Lilli felt a terrible sense of loss.

"I've never admitted it," Frances said, "not even to Charles or you, Lilli, but I've been homesick so often. For my family and London. They've never even seen Beth because it's such a shockingly long journey, and Papa can't get away from his business for more than a week at a time."

She would be brave. "I'm so sorry about your mother." Lilli turned to Charles. "And I can't tell you how much I'm going to miss the three of you."

"You have your family and your business," Frances said. "Soon you'll hardly know we're gone."

"I'll know," Lilli said softly, tears filling her eyes. "I can't imagine Sydney without you."

LILLI LEFT OLIVER in charge of the shop so that she might see Frances and Charles and Elizabeth off on the first leg of the long journey back to London. She stood on the dock in the steamy, early January afternoon while tears blurred the sight of the stately steamer leaving Sydney Harbor.

She had known she would desperately miss Frances. Now the phone—which rang only when Frances called her each evening—was silent. For a few weeks Janine occasionally asked wistfully for Beth, and then her tiny friend disappeared from her thoughts.

Lilli became increasingly concerned by the amount of money Jacques was taking for his "daily expenses" before making the weekly deposit. She knew she couldn't ask him if he was gambling again—he would go into a rage. And she didn't really have to ask. She knew.

Most of the time he was in a bad mood. It humiliated Lilli to know that Mrs. Phipps heard him raising his voice to her when he was particularly irritated about a contact not working out. She was sure that, like Frances and Charles, Mrs. Phipps thought Jacques ought to find himself a job. That should be easy; he charmed almost everyone.

Lilli was relieved when the hot months of January and February were past. Jacques always hated the reversal of summer and winter in Australia—he seemed to take it as a personal affront. March brought pleasantly cool days and nights when the flat was comfortable. Now Jan, bless her, slept straight through the night without waking in perspiring discomfort.

Lilli left Oliver to close up the shop each day while she went upstairs to prepare dinner and be with Jan. Tonight she was surprised at the quietness above. Perhaps Jan was taking a late nap. That meant Mrs. Phipps would be dozing in a chair close by, she guessed affectionately. She was grateful for Mrs. Phipps's presence in the flat, though she knew Jacques disapproved.

The door to the bedroom shared by Janine and Mrs. Phipps was closed, which meant they were both napping. Quietly, Lilli went into her bedroom to change into slippers. Her feet ached from the long hours of standing in the shop. As she sat on the edge of the bed to change into the soft slippers made for her by Aunt Sara, her eye caught an envelope on the bureau propped against the leather-framed photograph of Jan that had been taken on her first birthday last November. She recognized Jacques's tiny scrawl on the front.

Had he forgotten to mail a letter? He would be so annoyed with himself, she thought as she rose to her feet and crossed to the bureau. The envelope was addressed to her. If Jacques expected to be tied up at the club tonight, why hadn't he just dropped into the shop and told her? But perhaps she had been busy with that awful woman from London, who insisted that nobody but "the proprietor" could touch her face.

She would feed Jan, put out dinner for Mrs. Phipps and Oliver, and wait to have her own with Jacques, she decided while she opened the envelope and pulled out a sheet of stationery. As she began to read, a shock of disbelief, of deathlike coldness, swept over her.

My darling Lilli—

By the time you receive this I will be miles at sea. I can't bear to see you working so hard while I can do nothing to save you from such drudgery. I am going to Paris, where I will draw on my family's contacts with bankers. As soon as I am settled in a position, I will send for you and Jan. I couldn't stand to say goodbye, so *auf wiedersehen*, my love, until we meet again.

Jacques

She stood immobile. The brief letter slid from her fingers to the floor. *Jacques bound for Paris?* While she was downstairs selling creams, giving a treatment, Jacques had left the flat, gone down to the dock, and boarded a ship? She ran to the cupboard and pulled the door wide. His clothes were gone. His suitcases, which he had carried halfway around the world, were gone. *Jacques was gone.*

"No," she whispered, a harsh, ugly sound in the silent bedroom. "No!"

It was her fault. She had killed his pride. *"I can't bear to see you working so hard while I can do nothing to save you from such drudgery...."* He didn't understand that she loved working with the creams. And she hadn't understood that she made him feel less than a man because all his grand ambitions remained unfulfilled while *she* was succeeding.

But even while Lilli reproached herself for driving Jacques away, she realized he must have been plotting this for months. It had not been a painful, sudden impulse. That is what he had been doing with the extra money he had taken each week—he had put it away to buy passage to Paris.

Another fear assaulted her. She reached into the bureau for the cigar box that held their weekly receipts and the bankbook. Now the box held only a few shillings and the bankbook; last night it had been crammed with pound notes. Her fingers trembling, she reached for the bankbook and opened it. Jacques had withdrawn everything except for three pounds. And the rent on the shop and the flat was due in four days.

"I saw him leaving with his suitcases when I brought Jan up from the park." Lilli whirled around to face a grim Mrs. Phipps. "You'll manage all right on your own without the likes of him."

"He couldn't bear to say goodbye," Lilli stammered. "We've been talking for weeks about his going to Paris. He's sending for us as soon as he's settled." Color flooded her face. "His family has banking contacts there—they'll help him find a position." *What family?* In the three and a half years of their marriage, there had not been one word of exchange between Jacques and his supposedly well-placed American family. Not even when Jan was born.

"Mama?" Jan's high little voice called querulously. "Mama?"

"Yes, darling!" Lilli rushed past Mrs. Phipps and into Jan's bedroom. Her poor baby. Without a father now. How could she have allowed this to happen? "It's all right, my love." She reached down and picked up her tiny daughter. "You'll be fine," she said softly, her heart filled with fear. "Mama will take care of you."

WHILE JAN PLAYED at her feet, Lilli put dinner on the stove, her hands trembling. Jacques was somewhere at sea, but here in their flat, life must go on. She stiffened at sounds on the stairs, half expecting to hear Jacques knock at their door. It had always irritated Mrs. Phipps that he never bothered to use the key.

A door opened at the flat across the hall from their own. Subconsciously she realized their neighbor was home earlier than usual. *What was she going to say when Jan started asking about Papa?*

"Mrs. Phipps," she called out. "Would you please feed Jan tonight? I just remembered something I have to do in the shop. And would you please keep an eye on the pot roast and vegetables?"

She walked quickly down the stairs, out into the cool evening, and to the door of the shop. The shop was closed for the night. Only a small light glowed inside while Oliver swept. She knocked impatiently.

Oliver glanced up, frowned, and hurried to pull the door wide.

"Oliver, I have something to tell you…." Words eluded her. She stood before him, pale and shaken, gasping for breath.

"Lilli, what's happened?" He pulled her inside and pushed her into a chair, inspecting her anxiously. "Shall I bring you a glass of water?"

Lilli shook her head. "Oliver, he's gone. Jacques has left me."

Oliver paled. "You mean he's late for dinner. I'm sure he's just tied up at the club again. Whatever gave you such a crazy idea?"

"Oliver, he left me a letter—" Her voice broke. "He said he's on his way to Paris—he'll send for Jan and me when he's settled. He—he took all the money from our bank account except for three pounds."

Oliver dropped to his haunches beside the chair. "We'll manage. Money comes in every day at the shop. There'll be enough to pay the girls and Mrs. Phipps at the end of the week. We'll be all right, Lilli." He took her cold hand in his. "Jacques knows that."

"*You* won't leave me, Oliver, will you?"

"Never, Lilli. I'll always be here. And Jacques will send for you and Janine." He said it with conviction. "You'll see."

7

For Jan, Lilli told herself, she must take charge of her life. At least she had her secret "emergency" account; that would cover the rent for the flat and shop for this month. The daily receipts would take care of all her other expenses. She would start saving again, and soon she would have another nest egg.

Weeks sped past. Both Lilli and Oliver pretended to be confident that any day now a letter would arrive from Jacques. Each night, in the aching loneliness of her bedroom, she reread the brief letter he had left behind. Was it not the letter of a man who loved his wife? she asked herself.

She worried about how Jacques was surviving; the money he had taken from their bank account might be sufficient for the three of them to live on in Sydney for a year, but expenses in Paris were high. How much would he have left after paying for his traveling? She had heard Corinne Allister confess to spending over seventy pounds *each way* for transportation to Paris. She paid Mrs. Phipps one pound a week; the girls in the shop earned even less.

Torn between her concern for Jacques and her fears that he might take up with a rich and titled Parisienne, Lilli remembered the countess in Marienbad. She suspected this was not the first adoring lady in Jacques's life.

Occasionally, anger obliterated her fears: How could he walk out on his wife and child? But she tried to push the bitterness aside. It was too painful to think that Jacques had deserted them.

She wrote nothing to her aunt or Frances about Jacques's departure. She and Oliver decided that Jacques had probably taken the fast, expensive route to Paris; he talked often about such luxury trains as the Trans-Siberian Railroad and the Orient Express. *Where was he living in Paris?*

At Lilli's suggestion—and despite Mrs. Phipps's disapproval—Oliver now slept on a cot set up in the kitchen of the flat. Too many nights Lilli lay awake until dawn, painfully aware that she slept alone in the bed she had shared with Jacques. During the day she was grateful to be caught up in demands of running the House of Beauty.

In the dark moments when she wondered if she would ever see Jacques again, she tried to convince herself that it was enough that she had Jan and the business. But there were nights when her body longed for Jacques. Was it wanton of her to feel this way? No. What happened in bed with Jacques was beautiful and right. How could she live without him?

Dreading the sleepless night ahead, Lilli started giving Oliver French lessons after dinner. He was an avid and bright pupil, and together they read *La Vie Parisienne*, *L'Illustration*, and the daily *Figaro*, a gift from Corinne Allister. He was fascinated by Paris—the Montmartre, and the aristocratic old buildings of the Faubourg St.-Germain. Lilli couldn't help imagining Jacques cavorting in the Paris night life...

In July, Mrs. Phipps gave notice. Her daughter, living in a small town near Melbourne, had persuaded her to come live with her.

"You'll find somebody," Mrs. Phipps said, seeing that Lilli was upset. "Jan's a sweet child—hardly any trouble at all."

"We'll all miss you," Lilli said. "Jan will be so upset when she finds out—"

"Jan will be fine," Mrs. Phipps said briskly. "Her father's been gone almost four months. It's as though she never knew him now."

Lilli ignored this. "I hope you'll be happy with your daughter, Mrs. Phipps. I'll place an ad in the *Morning Herald* for a nursemaid."

Of the half-dozen possible replacements Lilli interviewed, the four younger ones objected to the sleeping-in arrangements—

they preferred to work harder for lower wages in the factories and have free evenings—and the two grandmotherly types disapproved of Oliver, an unmarried young man, living with them in the flat.

"I'll bring Jan downstairs with me in the mornings," Lilli told Oliver over dinner after interviewing the last of the applicants. No nursemaid was going to tell her to ban Oliver from the flat. This was the loneliest period in her life, and he was like a brother to her. "We'll manage somehow."

Lilli didn't hold out much hope that she would hear from Jacques, but Oliver continued to talk about "when Jacques sends for you and Jan." They both agreed that he would be too proud to write until he had met with some success.

Lilli's ads continued to bring in heavy mail-order business. After putting Jan to sleep for the night, she prepared the creams in the kitchen. Oliver shipped them to their customers. Because Lilli now spent much of her day with Jan, Oliver began taking on a large share of the responsibility of running the House of Beauty. Lilli gave treatments only to very special clients. And each week she deposited an impressive sum of money in the bank. A plan gradually took shape in her mind, but she was not quite prepared to tell anyone—not even Oliver—about it yet.

On the morning of her fourth wedding anniversary, Lilli awoke with a suffocating sense of loss. It was a gray, unseasonably cold morning, the weather mirroring her mood. Where was Jacques this morning? Was he with some woman? She couldn't let herself think that.

"My darling Lilli—" His words haunted her. *"As soon as I am settled in a position, I will send for you and Jan. I couldn't stand to say goodbye, so* auf wiedersehen, *my love, until we meet again."*

The six months since Jacques had left seemed more like six years. Six impossibly lonely years. Why didn't he at least write? He loved her. It was his wounded pride that had driven him away. Why couldn't she have seen what was in his heart? It was her fault. She had been an unfeeling, thoughtless wife. She longed to throw herself in his arms and tell him how neglectful she had been. Why couldn't she? She felt light-headed with determination. Life didn't have to remain this dreary, empty vacuum. She could change it. She had money. She and Jan would go to Jacques.

But what about the shop? It was doing so well. They had security here. Aunt Sara always talked about the importance of being secure. She remembered her terror of being without money in those first months in Sydney.

For a few moments she wavered in doubt. No! They would go to Paris. She would sell the shop and start all over again. What she had done in Sydney she would do in Paris. With Oliver.

Tonight at dinner she would talk to Oliver. She would convince him that this was the right move for them. Now she couldn't wait for the day to end.

She was beset by mixed emotions. Exhilaration at her decision. Fear that she was throwing away precious security. Hope that she would be able to convince Oliver to go up with them.

At the end of the working day, while Jan sat on the kitchen floor and listened to the little music box Oliver had bought for her last week, Lilli put dinner on the stove. On their next wedding anniversary, she and Jacques would be together. They would be a family again.

"Come to the table, *ma petite*," she called. How fortunate that French was like her native language! She scooped Jan into her arms and put her in the high chair.

After Jan was bathed and in bed, Lilli bent over to kiss her goodnight. Jan's eyelids were already closing, though moments before she had protested at being put to bed. How sad, Lilli thought, that Jan had no memory of her father. And she herself had no memory...

She closed the bedroom door and went into the kitchen. Oliver was standing over the pot of stew on the stove. "You know, Lilli, I think you're learning to season right," he teased.

Lilli hesitated, overwhelmed by her need to share her decision. "Oliver, I meant to wait until after dinner to talk about this, but I—I can't wait!'' She reached for his hand, pulled him down to a chair, and sat across from him. ''I want to go to Paris. I want to be with Jacques. I want Jan to grow up with her father. Will you go with us?''

He stared at her in shock. ''For a visit?''

''To live. We'll open up a house of beauty there. Why not?''

''Lilli, just to travel there will cost a fortune.'' But Lilli's excitement was contagious. ''Of course,'' he said slowly, ''we wouldn't have to go on the expensive trains. We could travel most of the way by ship. I've saved almost every cent you've paid me. I would have the fare.''

''And I have money in the bank!'' Lilli leaned forward in excitement. ''I'll have even more when I sell the shop. Tomorrow I'll place an ad in the *Morning Herald*. Oh, Oliver, this has made me so happy!''

''Paris is a huge city.'' Oliver looked serious. ''We may not be able to find Jacques. Or he may have moved on.''

''Jacques is in Paris.'' She would not consider any other possibility. ''It's the city he loves most in the world. We'll find him. I don't know how yet, but we will. Ask your friend Mrs. Allister about where we should look for a place to live in Paris. We're going, Oliver!''

LILLI PLACED the ad in the paper. A week later, while one of the girls in the shop stayed with Jan, Lilli and Oliver went for tea with Corinne Allister. Lilli still had difficulty believing that the beautiful and elegant Mrs. Allister had, some thirty years ago, been a low-paid artist's model in Paris.

Earlier, with infinite tact and graciousness, Corinne had offered Lilli and Oliver her own and her husband's discarded but still almost new wardrobes that would be proper for their entrance into the business world of Paris. Her dressmaker would cut down four of her exquisite frocks to fit Lilli, and her husband's tailor would make the necessary adjustments so that a pair of his Old Bond Street suits fit Oliver.

''You'll look for a flat in Montmartre on the right bank of the Seine,'' Corinne said as she poured Earl Grey tea from a silver teapot into Spode cups. "But for the shop you must choose space just off the Faubourg Saint-Honoré. The shop will be tiny, but the location is superb. It will be expensive, but if you play your cards right"—Corinne's eyes sparkled—"you'll find yourselves patronized by *tout Paris*."

Lilli listened carefully to everything Corinne Allister said. In Aunt Sara's shop in Marienbad, she had served French ladies from the aristocracy and the *grandes cocottes*, kept in dizzying luxury by princes and millionaires. Once, Liane de Pougey and Caroline Otero, the most famous of all, had visited the shop—separately, of course, because they were mortal enemies. Lilli knew that these ladies—of the *monde* and *demimonde*—could make her house of beauty in Paris a success far beyond anything she had achieved here in Sydney.

"Lilli, you must remember," Corinne cautioned, "that in Paris—as in London and Vienna and Rome—beauty creams and beauty treatments are provided only in the privacy of the boudoir or in a room behind a shop. You'll bring them out in the open and the women will flock to you. The grandest ladies in Europe parade about with their faces grotesque masks of paint because there's no one—not even in magnificent Paris—to show them the proper path to beauty."

"We can add makeup to the line of creams!" Oliver said excitedly. "Delicate rouges and color for the eyelids—"

"Yes. Oh, yes, Oliver." Lilli glowed. "Colors that will enhance." If only Charles could be in Paris to help her..."We'll work on that as soon as possible." She must find a way to soften the harsh colors used by actresses in the theater.

"I'll give you the names of several friends," Corinne said. "You must write them little notes on lovely paper and tell them I suggested that they call at your shop. The first of its kind in all of Europe! Name it Chez Lilli. Oliver, you'll make friends quickly in Montmartre. You'll find someone to help you decorate the shop without spending more than a few francs here and there." She gazed out the window. "How I wish this were my year to go to Paris! Remember, the Paris season begins right after Easter. *Tout le monde* will be there! After the Grand Prix everyone dashes off to the seashore to the north. Deauville, Cabourg, Trouville. Perhaps Biarritz. It will be helpful to establish yourselves before the end of the season.''

As she headed back to the shop, Oliver at her side, Lilli sifted through everything Corinne Allister had told them. Already she imagined the kind of makeup—totally different from that worn by actresses on the stage—that would find favor with the fashionable women of Paris. But first she had to focus on her immediate problems: selling the shop, and then making arrangements to travel to Paris.

She thought of the flight with Jacques from Marienbad to Sydney. She had been just a girl then, relying on her handsome young husband. Now she was a woman with a child. With frightening responsibilities.

"Lilli," Oliver said, "you're sure you want to go through with this?"

"Yes. Inquire about our travel arrangements, Oliver. As soon as I have a buyer for the shop, we will leave for Paris."

ON A STEAMY, early January morning, with Jan in her arms, Lilli stood beside Oliver on the deck of the ship that would take them across the Indian Ocean on the first lap of the long journey to Paris. Together they watched the skyline of Sydney disappear from view. Lilli knew that it would be at least three months before they set foot on French soil, but they were on their way to Paris, and that was all that mattered.

Together Lilli and Oliver tried to entertain little Jan, who became increasingly restless as the days passed. She had celebrated her second birthday two months before and was continually frustrated by the restrictions of life aboard ship. Since her decision, Lilli had been teaching Jan French, and now she and Oliver made a game of it to keep her entertained.

Though she tried not to dwell on it, Lilli was aware of how little money was left now that she'd paid for their transportation. In her impatience to leave Sydney, she had sold the shop for far less than she had anticipated. But she would begin again in Paris, she told herself. With Oliver, and with Corinne Allister's list of prospective clients, she was sure to find new success. She would write her little notes, and the ladies would become eager to visit Chez Lilli. She herself would give treatments, and she would train Oliver to give them. They would take turns staying with Jan until the business prospered and she could again hire a nursemaid.

They crossed the Indian Ocean, the Suez Canal, and sailed over the Mediterranean to the port of Marseilles. Lilli began to feel as though she had known Oliver all her life. Enchanted by the splendor of sunrises and sunsets over the water, sharing a fear of sudden storms, they read and discussed each of the books that Corinne Allister had given them as a farewell present. Lilli was intrigued by a collection of love stories, *Les Plaisirs et Les Jours*, by a young Frenchman named Marcel Proust. Oliver confessed his French wasn't good enough to read it himself, though he did enjoy hearing Lilli tell him about Proust's view of Paris society.

Occasionally Lilli felt guilty that in her last letter to Aunt Sara she hadn't mentioned Jacques's disappearance. She knew how happy Aunt Sara would be to have her in Paris rather than far-off Sydney. Now they could look forward to seeing each other.

Aunt Sara had always claimed to prefer the French because they were the first to accept Jews as equal citizens, late in the eighteenth century. She had been especially pleased when Captain Dreyfus was cleared two years ago. Many people—non-Jews as well as Jews—had been convinced that Captain Dreyfus had been unjustly convicted because he was Jewish.

At last their ship docked in Marseilles. After being cleared by customs, they headed for the railroad station. Lilli's pulse raced as they waited for the train that would carry them to Paris; it was hard to believe that Jacques was only a few hundred miles away....

While the train sped north, she imagined her reunion with Jacques: She would be walking down a street and he would call to her in startled joy...or she would look up from a stall in the market and there he would be, staring with happiness at the sight of her.

Everything would be different this time. She would make Jacques understand that pride should not come between them. That he was more important than the business. She would be a sympathetic, understanding wife.

She refused to dwell on her suspicions that Jacques had spent many nights in the beds of other women. Instead, she dreamed only of lying in his arms again.

AT FIRST, Jan was terrified of the steaming black monster that hurtled down the tracks, but soon she became fascinated by the passing sights. That night they slept restlessly in their hard third-class seats, cheered by the knowledge that by midmorning they would be in Paris.

At dawn, while other passengers slept, Lilli looked out her window at the brightening countryside. Old stone walls, tall hedges, and ancient trees protected the large estates, surrounded by spring-green fields. Occasionally the train slowed to a crawl as it crossed a village where chickens strutted around the small houses of their owners; Lilli thought of Aunt Sara, who must now live in a place like this.

Oliver and the other passengers began waking up. Jan continued to sleep in Oliver's arms. "We'll soon be there," Oliver whispered, his face luminous. Without having seen so much as a photograph of Paris, he was already in love with the city.

Lilli's throat tightened as she recalled her wedding night aboard the Orient Express. She remembered buying a postcard of the Eiffel Tower to send to Aunt Sara before she and Jacques boarded the train that was to take them to Le Havre.

Jacques was in Paris.

When Lilli saw the skyline of the city beyond the fields, her heart pounded. Oliver had warned her that it might be impossible to find Jacques in such a huge city. Then what would she do? But that would not happen. Somehow, she would find him.

Amid clouds of smoke and steam, the train came to a halt beneath an enormous glass roof. Clutching Jan in one arm and

a suitcase with the other, Lilli waited while Oliver struggled with
the rest of their suitcases and boxes. A porter in a blue uniform with carrying straps over his shoulders gazed inquiringly,
then shrugged, dismissing their modest luggage in favor of the
label-encrusted bags arriving from such exotic cities as Venice,
Istanbul, and St. Petersburg.

"Lilli, we're here!" Oliver looked around in wonder. "We're
in Paris!"

They moved out into the courtyard where *voitures* waited to
carry passengers to their destinations. Ever mindful of their
finances, Oliver led the way to the street. Lilli flinched at the
sight of the traffic. Carriages and drays loaded with trunks
rushed to and from the station. Motorcars rolled along, emit-
ting unpleasant aromas of petrol.

"So many motorcars!" Lilli smiled as she spied a lady *coch-
ère*. In Paris, women were licensed to drive cabs.

"Mama, what's that?" Jan asked, and Oliver frowned.

"Never mind, love." Oliver motioned to Lilli to turn Jan
away from a view of a man whose head and feet were visible
while the rest of him was in a stall. "A *pissoir*," he whispered.
"Corinne—she talks so frankly about everything—told me
about them."

Following Corinne's instructions and ignoring the annoyed
stares of other passengers, Oliver led Lilli and Jan to a horse-
drawn omnibus. Corinne had told them about the Paris *mé-
tropolitain*—the mysterious underground system of trains that
linked various parts of the city—but neither Lilli nor Oliver
dared approach this labyrinthian mode of transportation just
yet. And taxis—either horse-drawn or motorized—were too
expensive.

As fluent in French as she was in English and German, Lilli
felt instantly at home in Paris—perhaps, she thought sentimentally, because she had met many Frenchwomen in Marienbad. Oliver was frustrated that he could not match Lilli's skills
with the language.

At last they found themselves in a tiny, partially furnished
garret flat on a narrow, cobblestoned street in Montmatre. To

avoid elaborate explanations—though they knew that in Montmartre conventionalities were ignored—they identified themselves as brother and sister.

"Put Jan to bed," Oliver said gently after they were settled in. "I'll go find a shop to buy food."

Over crusty French bread and strong coffee, Lilli and Oliver began making plans. They had to open a shop quickly—they needed money desperately. Tomorrow they would buy the ingredients and Lilli would start preparing her creams. Oliver would search for a shop. Both knew that the shop must be located in an area frequented by the wealthy ladies of Paris. Montmartre was fine to live in for now because the rooms were cheap, but it was definitely not the place for a house of beauty.

The next day, with the necessary purchases made, Lilli returned to their flat with Jan. Dressed in one of Mr. Allister's fine blue serge suits and a cashmere vest, Oliver went off in search of proper quarters. On their journey from Sydney, Oliver had grown a moustache in hopes of appearing older. Today he looked quite distinguished—affluent-looking enough, he hoped, to please the most discerning of landlords.

Lilli talked animatedly to Jan, who played at her feet, while she prepared her creams. Again her thoughts strayed to Jacques. He had not written because he had not yet acquired a position that would allow him to send for his wife and child. Jacques was not like other men. He dreamed such dazzling dreams. Perhaps he would walk on a side street off the Faubourg St.-Honoré, look up, and see the sign that said Chez Lilli. He would guess that she had made her way to Paris. *He would come up to the shop to claim his family.*

Lilli was aghast when Oliver returned that evening to report the rents required for even the smallest second-floor room off the Faubourg St.-Honoré were several times what she had paid for their quarters in Sydney.

As always, however, Oliver was optimistic. "I'll look for work in the evenings, Lilli. We'll manage."

"Oliver, we can't last more than three months in Paris if we pay so much."

"But if I have work in the evenings, we'll manage. I want you to see this place. It's tiny and dirty, but we'll make it beautiful. We'll use mirrors so that it'll look much larger. The colors will be a pale gray and delicate yellow. Hereafter, Lilli, you will wear a gray coat with a yellow scarf at your throat. It'll be fine, I promise you."

Lilli looked dubious. "Is the landlord agreeable to renting to us?"

"I persuaded him that we were bringing something new to Paris. Something that would delight *tout Paris*." He laughed. "I think I put him in a trance. He's willing."

Within twenty-four hours a sign in the window proclaimed the premises to be Chez Lilli, Maison de Beauté. Lilli arranged her selection of prettily labeled jars on a counter they had made from a discarded table, now covered in gray velvet, that Oliver had found in the street. From strips of wood and a discarded canvas, Oliver had fashioned a private area where Lilli could give her "treatments."

With a tiny supply of fine stationery that Oliver had bought, Lilli carefully wrote her notes to Corinne's Paris friends. Oliver delivered them by hand to their elegant houses on the rue Jacob and luxurious apartments on the rue de Varenne.

Day after day went by without a single customer appearing at the top of the stairs. Lilli was bewildered by the lack of business; she had anticipated ladies eagerly climbing the stairs out of curiosity if nothing more. She and Oliver were bringing Paris something revolutionary. Didn't the fashionable ladies realize that?

As time passed, Lilli relied on Oliver for many things. At intervals he took Jan to one of the beautiful parks to play with other children. He spent hours each day searching for work, but his still-limited French and his slight frame robbed him of the jobs he sought in the markets.

"I'm strong," he blazed over dinner one night. "I can lift as heavy a carton as any man! Tomorrow I'll go to the schools that hire male models." He smiled. "If I can find the courage to take off my clothes before strange artists—"

"Oliver, I don't understand." Lilli put down her fork. "Where are these friends of Mrs. Allister? This is the season. They should be in Paris. I hate to see you have to work like this."

"I don't know what it is." He shrugged. "They're terribly busy. But they'll come."

"Before the Grand Prix?" The Grand Prix—which would take place at Longchamps in the Bois de Boulogne on the second Sunday after the English Derby—was the signal for Paris society to take off for the seashore. "Oliver, I haven't sold one jar of cream! I haven't given one treatment!"

8

From the small square window that looked down on the street below, Lilli watched the ladies in their huge aigrette-trimmed Merry Widow hats by Rebou, their costumes by Doucet, Redfern, La Ferriere. As always she glanced at the passing men in hopes of seeing Jacques. A few feet away Jan napped in her makeshift bed—contrived from a fruit crate by Oliver.

At the sound of light laughter outside her door, Lilli turned, her heart pounding. *Her first customers!* The two ladies who entered were young and expensively dressed. Lilli suspected they were demimondaines. Their mouths were painted a voluptuous vermilion and their eyes were outlined in harsh kohl. Lilli thought a more delicate makeup would enhance their beauty.

"What is it you sell, mademoiselle?" the taller young lady asked imperiously. "You call this a *maison de beauté,* yes?"

"Creams." Lilli smiled, reaching for a pair of jars. "They are made from a secret Viennese formula handed down to my grandmother."

The two young ladies listened entranced to Lilli's eloquent sales talk, and then bought half a dozen jars. But they collapsed into self-conscious laughter when she suggested beauty treatments.

"It's such a chore to remove the coloring from our eyes," the smaller young lady said. "Do you suppose the cream will help? The cream we use after our show at the Folies Bergère is so unpleasant."

"This cream here…" Lilli reached for another jar. "Use just a bit on a piece of soft cloth and it'll remove the coloring from the eye and lips and the face." That's what she should do: *Design a cream to cleanse the skin, nothing more.*

Lilli was breathless with pleasure when her first customers in Paris left the shop. The ladies had not blinked a kohl-blackened eyelash when she named her prices—exorbitant, she thought, but Oliver had been insistent. They would tell their friends, and soon she would persuade these ladies to try a course of treatments. She couldn't wait to tell Oliver.

When Jan awoke, Lilli brought out a loaf of bread and some fruit and cheese for lunch. Her first two customers were probably lunching at a restaurant in the Bois de Boulogne—perhaps the Pavillon d'Armenonville, which Oliver told her was favored by the very fashionable.

Oliver arrived while they were eating. Lilli could tell by his expression that he had been successful.

"Lilli, I've been working all morning!" He pulled Lilli aside. "I took off my clothes. I just took poses while the students sketched. At first I was embarrassed, but to the art students it is nothing. I'm to return tomorrow morning for another three hours. And for this they pay me. Look!" He pulled franc notes from the pocket of his jacket.

Lilli continued to wait anxiously for Corinne's friends to appear. Perhaps they were away from Paris, she told herself. Her first two customers had not yet brought their friends, and she grew bored during the long, lonely hours in the shop, hours spent staring down at the sidewalk below without one stranger opening the door.

Somewhere in Paris Jacques walked the streets. Would he never walk down this one? And she worried about their finances: With the frighteningly expensive rent, she was earning almost nothing. Oliver's earnings from modeling kept food on the table and bought an occasional treat for Jan, but what would she do at the end of the month, when the rent was due?

How was she to make the ladies of Paris understand what she had to offer? Apparently her first customers were being secretive about their discovery. Would it have been better if she had gone to London? Oliver had read in an English magazine that Helena Rubinstein had opened an elegant house of beauty in London. But London was not for her. Jacques was in Paris.

On Sunday Lilli and Oliver strolled with Jan through the Bois de Boulogne, past the lovely outdoor cafés and restaurants, surrounded by forests; later they rode through the Bois atop a three-horse public coach. Always in the Bois de Boulogne she remembered that she had first been here with Jacques, as a bride....

She dreamed of taking Jan one day for tea at a café in the Bois, as did many wealthy Parisiennes. Jan would wear a blue velvet dress trimmed at the throat with lace. She would be swathed in furs. Sometimes Lilli wondered if her father was in Paris for the season. But Corinne had told them that the Channel hardly existed for the upper classes in England.

ONE DAY Oliver came back to the shop carrying a bag of fresh fruit, obviously in high spirits.

"Lilli, I have been invited to a party tonight by Monsieur Verlain, one of the art instructors. Would you be upset if I went?"

"Of course not." Lilli kissed him. "It'll be good for you."

"I thought I might be able to talk about the business to some of the ladies there," he said. "I was told that Monsieur Verlain's parties are attended by rich Parisiennes as well as students." Lilli realized that he didn't want her to think he was being frivolous. "And I always ask of everyone I meet if they know Jacques," he added.

"Oliver, go to the party and enjoy it."

The only parties Lilli had ever attended were schoolgirl affairs. In the four years in Sydney, her only friends—other than Oliver—had been Frances and Charles. Jacques had continually shocked her with tales of the parties he'd attended in London, Paris, and New York.

"Sebastien, my new friend among the students," Oliver said, "tells me that when Monsieur Verlain gives a party for the students, they sometimes last till dawn. Sebastien lives only a block away from the school. He's invited me to spend the night at his studio so that we won't have far to go to classes tomorrow. Would you be afraid to stay here alone tonight with Jan?''

"Afraid of what, Oliver?" She was happy that Oliver had found friends of his own in Paris. If only she could, too.

OLIVER STOOD next to Sebastien, perhaps four years his senior and of a more robust build, at one side of the pleasant sitting room of M. Verlain's flat in the rue de Fleurus and listened while Sebastien identified each of the paintings hanging on the stuccoed white walls.

"That's a Cézanne there," he said, "and next to it is a Picasso—he's a young Spanish painter. And that"—he pointed to a painting across the room—"is by a man named Matisse."

"Someday you'll paint like them," Oliver said softly. He knew Sebastien was sure that these three painters would someday be famous. At the moment they were considered scandalous.

"I don't know, Oliver," Sebastien said. "I try. God knows, I try. But it doesn't come out the way I like."

Sebastien turned toward the tiny entrance hall, where a new arrival was being greeted in a flurry of excitement.

"That's the countess de Nicolet," Sebastien whispered, gazing at a grossly overweight woman who towered over most of the men present. Her bleached hair, streaked with gray, was pulled back in a knot; she wore a high-collared shirtwaist and black velvet trousers—the kind favored by Sarah Bernhardt for strolls along the boulevards—and toyed with what appeared to be yards of pearls encircling her short fat neck. While a tall young art student from the school fawned over her, the countess kept one arm around the waist of a sultry-faced girl. "She's very rich and powerful," Sebastien continued. "Her husband died many years ago—in a brothel. He left her an enormous fortune." He chuckled. "Look at that idiot Claude making such a fuss over her. Claude is looking for a rich old woman to support him until he becomes famous."

"Well, you said she's very rich," Oliver said.

Sebastien laughed. "Yes, my sweet, but the countess likes young girls. Oh, she keeps one or two presentable young men in attendance—those who prefer their own sex—as bait for the sweet young things too innocent to understand. Sometimes I'm invited to be her escort, since she knows my own preferences." His fingers touched Oliver's arm.

"I didn't realize that the countess is—is—"

"That the countess is a lesbian?" Sebastien laughed again. "Here in Paris we are free to be what we like, say what we think. It's rumored that the marquise de Helboeuf—she's the sister of the duc de Morny—has boasted that she and her brother have had all the prettiest women in Paris."

In Sydney, Oliver had occasionally encountered men who regarded him with more than passing interest. Though he had not yet succumbed to their advances, he had been tempted.

"Sebastien," he said, "are Claude and I the only ones who didn't know that the countess is a lesbian?"

"I'm sure," Sebastien said. "You see the two women standing there under the Matisse?" He nodded toward a short, dumpy woman wearing a strange brown corduroy outfit and Greek sandals and a small dark woman with sharp features. "They're lesbians. Her name's Gertrude Stein and the woman with her is Alice something or other. Alice just arrived in Paris. They are at all the art exhibitions. But they're not the countess's type. The countess prefers beautiful young girls. For a while she was keeping Liane de Pougey, the most beautiful courtesan in Europe."

Not until two hours later did Oliver come face-to-face with the countess. She stared hard at him, then nodded in approval. "Sebastien, you show good taste as always. Bring your friend with you to my 'Thursday evening.'"

Sebastien looked pleased. "I've known her for over a year," he whispered to Oliver, "but this is the first time she's invited me to one of her 'evenings.' To her luncheons, to a masquerade ball, to be her escort to the theater and the opera, but never to one of her 'evenings.' Some of the most important people in

Paris will be there!'' Sebastien looked around. "Enough of this, Oliver." His eyes were amorous. "Let's go home now. We must be at the school within five hours.''

AS WEEKS SLIPPED BY, Lilli grew increasingly anxious about the business. In Sydney she had been successful. In London, Helena Rubinstein was apparently *very* successful. What was she doing wrong here in Paris?

Oliver told her that he had seen an ad of Helena Rubinstein's in an English society magazine, which stated she charged a fee of ten guineas for a course of twelve beauty treatments. When Lilli converted it into francs, she was impressed with the sum. According to an editorial in the same magazine, Mme. Rubinstein's salon was located in a Georgian town house in London's posh Mayfair.

Lilli gazed about the tiny quarters of Chez Lilli. Perhaps this was not grand enough to attract the rich social ladies of Paris. But how could she change that? And how long could she stay even here without customers? So far Oliver's earnings from modeling were their sole means of support. She was contributing nothing.

But at least Oliver was not sorry they had come to Paris. He had Sebastien, whom he adored. She had never seen him so happy. She never censured Oliver for his private tastes—that part of his life was something that belonged to *him*. Every night, it seemed, he was off to an exciting social event, sometimes with Sebastien and other students from the school, sometimes with countess de Nicolet. He told her about certain parties where men danced with men, and women with women. Where men dressed in women's attire and sang naughty songs. Lilli knew that countess de Nicolet had even taken Oliver and Sebastien to the opera.

"*Maman*..." Jan tugged at her hand. "Where's Uncle Oliver?"

"He'll be here soon, darling." Jan was restless. This was the time when Oliver usually took her to the park for an hour or two. Just then Lilli heard his steps on the stairs. "Jan, listen! He's coming now."

The door opened and a grossly fat woman, breathing heavily from the climb, stepped inside. "Really, Oliver, you should have warned me about those stairs," she said over one shoulder.

"Uncle Oliver!" Jan ran to him, knowing he would swoop her up in his arms and into the air.

"You're Lilli," the woman said before Oliver had introduced them. "I'm Countess Angelique de Nicolet. Oliver has been telling me about this *maison de beauté* you and he have set up. *This* is the entire salon?" She looked around the tiny room.

"Yes," Lilli said, her heart pounding. Oliver had brought the countess here to help them. "We have a treatment area there behind the screen."

"Oliver"—the countess's quietly reproachful gaze rested on Lilli—"you didn't tell me she was so beautiful. She could be a *grande cocotte* with no effort. A fine house of her own, a carriage, a mink coat, jewelry, whatever money she wished."

Lilli knew this was meant as a compliment, but her face grew pink with color beneath the countess's scrutiny.

"Lilli is in Paris to search for her husband," Oliver said brusquely. "This is her little girl." Lilli caught a strange exchange between Oliver and the countess over Jan's head.

The countess shrugged. "Children bore me." She sighed and turned to Oliver. "If this is the best you can do, then it must be a jewel box." She grimaced at the screen Oliver had made. "Everything must look *expensive*. I have a coromandel screen that I've grown bored with. You may have it." Clutching at her pearls, she gazed at Lilli's silken auburn hair, worn in a becoming Psyche knot. "You're right in using gray and yellow, my dear. With that hair it's perfect." Abruptly she turned away. "But that chair, Oliver. It has to go. I have a Louis XVI chair that you can re-cover in gray damask, and a Florentine mosaic table. Tonight come to my house with Sebastien to help you. I'll give you things to make Chez Lilli look as expensive as the prices you are to charge."

"You're very kind." Lilli was grateful for the countess's help, but disconcerted by the look in her eyes.

"Lilli will see patrons only by appointment. Even if they come only to buy creams." She chuckled. "That will make her seem very important. They won't understand that it's because the place is so small. I'll send some of my friends. And tomorrow night, Oliver, you'll bring her to my 'evening.'" She treats me as though I were an inanimate object, Lilli thought. "I will arrange with my *grand couturier* for her to borrow a gown for the evening," the countess continued. "She must look not only beautiful but rich. We'll say that she has arrived in Paris after enchanting Australia with this innovation of a *maison de beauté*. The first on that continent. And now—"

"I was not the first," Lilli said. "There was—"

"Who will know?" The countess waved a hand. "Tomorrow night at the usual time, Oliver. If I survive those stairs again. See me to my car now."

LILLI WAS VERY nervous at the prospect of leaving Jan with Mme. Murat, the elderly widow from the flat below theirs. It was only for three hours, she told herself, and it wasn't as though she were leaving Jan in the care of a total stranger. Jan saw Mme. Murat every day.

"Jan will sleep," Lilli said for the third time. "She'll be no trouble."

Mme. Murat smiled and led them to the door.

Lilli and Oliver made their way down the four flights of dark stairs to the street, knowing that after tonight their lives would never be the same. Ladies would come to Chez Lilli because the countess had taken Oliver and Lilli under her wing. The countess's guests at her luncheons and masquerade balls were artists and students, because she fancied herself a patroness of the arts; but her evening guests were the rich and famous of Paris.

Lilli wished that Aunt Sara could see her now, in the marvelous lilac-gray silk she'd borrowed for the evening—almost identical, according to a couturier friend of the countess's—to one he had made for Queen Alexandra of England: the same off-the-shoulder look, with the skirt narrow in the "Directoire" fashion that was causing riots on the streets of Paris. She was wearing elbow-length white kid gloves, and she carried a small gold mesh bag that was about to be launched as the newest fashion, all at the couturier's insistence.

Though it was a balmy late-spring evening, Lilli's hands were ice-cold within the gloves. As they stood before the mansion of the countess de Nicolet and waited to be admitted, she suddenly felt awkward. She tried to appear poised and faintly aloof.

An obsequious manservant admitted them to a huge marble-floored foyer, and another servant led them to the grand salon where the countess de Nicolet held court each Thursday evening. Lilli knew instantly that each piece of furniture was a priceless antique. The floor was covered with exquisite Aubusson rugs. The tall, narrow windows were draped in burgundy velvet. Three dazzling crystal chandeliers warmed the room with light. The conversations were animated, some heated in good-humored disagreement, others light and lilting like a Debussy piano piece.

The guests—most of the ladies dressed in the heights of fashion, most of the men expensively tailored—were gathered in small clusters around the room, except for a larger group surrounding the countess. "Her claque," Oliver whispered. "We must pay our respects to the countess first. Wait . . ." He spied Sebastien across the room. "You see the woman in the red satin gown, talking with Sebastien? That's Mrs. Kate Moore, a terribly rich American who collects art and worships anyone with a title."

"Do you think she may know Jacques?" Lilli whispered.

"I've asked her," Oliver said gently. "She doesn't know him. Remember, Lilli, there are thousands of Americans living in Paris these days. She couldn't know them all." But everyone American was special to Lilli. By virtue of her marriage to Jacques, *she* was an American, and it made her proud.

Lilli and Oliver made their way across the crowded room to their hostess, who stood holding hands with a beautiful young blonde in an embroidered blue silk frock that displayed more of her bosom than was customary even in La Belle Epoque.

"Lilli, do you suppose you would have time to give a treatment to Manon tomorrow?" the countess said.

"I'm sorry"—Lilli knew she was supposed to pretend that she was inundated with appointments—"but I have no free time until Monday afternoon." In the afternoon Oliver was done with his modeling and could take Jan to the park.

"Would three o'clock be all right?" the countess asked after murmured consultation with the smoldering Manon.

"That would be perfect." Lilli ignored Manon's hostile stare. "I'll expect you at three."

"Isn't that an awful dress Mrs. Moore is wearing?" The countess laughed wickedly. "I don't care if she did pay Pacquin a fortune for it. And she has no feeling for the new artists. She's forever boasting about her latest Degas. Doesn't she know Degas is a syphilitic old man?"

"She never buys American painters," Oliver whispered.

"Oliver, my darling, you are correct!" the countess trilled. "Not even Mary Cassatt. Did you know that Mary Cassatt refused to become a chevalier de la Légion d'Honneur until three years ago because before then she was asked to give a painting for the Luxembourg? Why give up a painting, she figured, for a piece of red ribbon? I don't know why she should be honored that way. All she paints are those silly portraits of mothers and babies. And everybody knows Degas helps her paint."

Lilli and Oliver listened with a show of interest to the countess's store of gossip until the arrival of the ambassador from Italy sent her charging over to welcome him. Manon took this opportunity to slide away, and Sebastien joined them.

Fighting self-consciousness, Lilli let Sebastien parade her around the room. She had long ago learned to be an attentive listener, which obviously charmed the countess's male guests. But she could barely believe that she was meeting these prestigious people—diplomats, financiers, the playwright Henry

Bernstein, the rich Countess Anna de Castellane, who was the daughter of the internationally known Jay Gould and an American by birth. There was even a Rothschild at the countess de Nicolet's evening!

Lilli and Oliver at last prepared to leave, both exhilarated by the knowledge that in the following week Lilli had four appointments to "show her creams" and three appointments for beauty treatments. Three of the ladies, not only rich but socially important, had invited Lilli and Oliver to parties, including a masquerade ball the evening of the Grand Prix.

The countess accompanied Lilli and Oliver to the foyer, an arm about each. "Lilli, in three months you will be famous in Paris if you do as I say. You'll see. The word will spread like a bonfire." She squinted in thought. "You'll meet me for lunch next Thursday. At the Pavillon d'Armenonville in the Bois de Boulogne. It's a pity that Oliver can't be with us." His modeling hours now continued into early afternoon. "But you must be seen at luncheon in the Bois. Everyone has luncheon there in the season. We must launch you properly, my dear."

CONSCIOUS OF THE FACT that she must now appear successful, Lilli let Oliver take her to a crowded shop not far from the school, where couturier frocks—worn perhaps once or twice and discarded by their jaded owners—could be bought at greatly reduced prices. With Jan perched on his shoulders, Oliver led Lilli through the maze of crowded aisles, discarding dress after dress until he found a pale olive-green silk with cascades of delicate lace.

"A bit too large in the waist, but you can take it in," he said briskly as Lilli held the dress against her slender frame. "It's perfect for luncheon with the countess. And let *me* argue about the price."

At Oliver's insistence, Lilli wore the dress to the shop, protecting it with one of the yellow dusters she had worn in the Sydney shop. Just before a customer arrived, she would unbutton the duster to reveal the lovely green silk. And well beforehand, Oliver always whisked Jan off to the park. Seeing the respect in the eyes of her customers, Lilli was glad that Oliver had talked her into buying the new dress.

She sold not only an amazing array of creams but five courses of treatments. No one seemed taken aback by her prices, which were as high as Helena Rubinstein's. Only Manon failed to keep her appointment, which hardly surprised either Lilli or Oliver.

The ladies chattered in delight over the velvet softness, the exquisite fragrances of the creams. Those who stayed for treatments were eloquent in their praise of her efforts. Lilli congratulated herself. Aunt Sara had taught her well.

"So much money, Oliver!" she marveled after they had totaled her sales on Wednesday.

"This is nothing to what will soon come in," Oliver said. But he seemed somber. He must be tired of working at the school, she realized in sympathy.

"Oliver, once we're established you'll come into the shop. Perhaps we'll find a larger place."

But he didn't brighten much at that. "Did you talk to Madame Murat about staying with Jan while you're off to lunch?"

Lilli smiled. "Yes. She's glad for the money." She paused. "I must confess, Oliver, I'm terrified. I've never been among so many grand people."

True, in Marienbad she had seen the titled and the famous ladies who came into the shop each season. But there she was a shopkeeper's niece. She had not been a part of their social lives.

"Lilli, you will be fine," Oliver said with conviction. "You have the air of a highborn young lady. You were a great success at the countess's evening. Everyone admired you!"

At the appointed hour on Thursday, Lilli, trying to appear poised and vivacious in spite of her nervousness, made her way to the Pavillon d'Armenonville. Her outfit gave her some confidence: her gown, again a wealthy lady's castoff, had been designed by Doucet; and her hat, created by Oliver, was a masterpiece of pale green silk and masses of daisies, copied from the pages of *L'Illustration*.

Before entering, she paused at the veranda, shadowed by the summer-green leaves of the towering trees. The interior of the restaurant was the quintessence of elegant luxury. Many of the pale blue lacquered tables were already occupied, and Lilli could hear light laughter, the tinkle of glasses. The maître d' approached her. In Paris it was acceptable for two ladies to have luncheon without a male escort.

"The table, please, of the countess de Nicolet," Lilli said demurely. Not a flicker of curiosity crossed the maître d's face as he led her to the table.

Her face reddening as she felt eyes following her—did they guess she was here only because of the generosity of the countess?—Lilli followed the maître d' to the countess's table in a quiet corner of the room. A pair of chairs sat at right angles around the table.

"Lilli, my love," the countess purred, "you look beautiful." She held up her face to Lilli. Understanding that she was supposed to deposit a kiss on the countess's cheek, Lilli was also uncomfortably aware of the way the maître d' frowned and looked away. For an instant she wondered if she had misinterpreted the countess's gesture—then, to her relief, the countess reached for her hand.

"Have you been busy at Chez Lilli?"

"Thank you, yes!"

"Shall I order for us?"

"Yes, please."

The countess accepted a menu from the waiter. "Alberto, tell Gaston to bring my usual champagne," she said without looking up.

After perusing the menu with the interest of one who takes her food seriously, the countess told Alberto to bring them a liver pâté, lobster, roast chicken stuffed with foie gras, and lettuce hearts. Just as he left, the champagne arrived.

Lilli had worried earlier about what she would have to contribute to the conversation. Now she realized she needn't have. Between sips of champagne and delicate bites of their rich meal, the countess kept up a steady stream of chatter, most of it gossip. Did Lilli know that Gaby Deslys—who was once the mistress of ex-King Manuel of Portugal—was said to charge a thousand francs for fifteen minutes of her time? Or that the princess de Polignac—an American before she married the prince—was said to have Jewish blood in her veins? "Her name was Winarella Singer," the countess said with distaste. "From the family that makes those sewing machines."

The countess also hated the American Edith Wharton—"a dreadful writer and her husband is such a *parvenu*." There were very few people the countess did like. She listened with a small strained smile. Would the countess drop *her* if she knew her mother was Jewish?

"You know, darling"—the countess leaned forward—"Manon is so jealous of you because you're such a lady and she's so coarse, so unrefined."

"She didn't come for her appointment," Lilli said, startled when she felt the countess's heavy thigh pressing against her own. "But all the others came," she added quickly.

"They see your lovely skin and they believe your creams will do as much for them," the countess said. "Do as I say, my love; you'll have all of Paris at your feet."

The waiter arrived with their lunch. At last the countess moved her thigh. Relieved, Lilli remembered what Oliver had told her about the women in Paris who preferred women to men. But the countess de Nicolet couldn't be one of them. *She had been married.*

While the countess raved about the cuisine, Lilli ate quietly, not tasting her food. She was too busy observing her dinner companion, trying to understand this strange new world—Manon's hostility toward her, the waiter's averted eyes when she bent to kiss the countess, the chairs arranged at right angles. *No! She was imagining things.*

As the countess told the waiter to bring them a chocolate ice with their coffee, Lilli felt the massive thigh again pressed firmly against her. Color flooded her cheeks, but she managed to reply to the countess's questions about her life in Sydney.

"Lilli, darling, when we leave here, we'll go to Jousset's for a cup of chocolate." Her eyes were bright. "I know it's early, but they'll serve us. I'm well known there."

"I must get back to the shop," Lilli stammered. "First I have to go home to pick up my little girl." She sat motionless, unable to draw away from the insistent thigh beneath the table. *If she angered the countess, then she and Oliver were alone again in Paris.*

"Later"—the countess leaned so close that Lilli could feel her warm breath—"when Oliver is home to care for the child, I'll send the man with my Renault to bring you to my house."

This time there was no mistaking the countess's intentions.

"I'm sorry." Lilli lowered her eyes. "I won't be able to accept your invitation."

9

Oliver listened in dismay to Lilli's report of her luncheon with the countess.

"Oliver, she was furious when I refused to come to her house tonight," Lilli whispered, even though Jan—playing with the paints Oliver had brought her from the school—couldn't possibly understand. "But I couldn't! Not even for the shop."

"The old witch!" Oliver was white with rage. "I made it clear to her that you were not like Manon. She saw you with Jan. Of course, Sebastien said that a child would mean nothing to a woman like Angelique. She believes what she wishes to believe. Sebastien understands these things better than I."

Lilli shook her head. "I should have understood. I hear what people say. I read. In Paris it's fashionable to be a woman like Angelique de Nicolet."

"But for a man to love men is scandalous," Oliver said. "They must pretend to be infatuated with a woman or be the subject of ridicule. Why is it that what is right for a woman is wrong for a man?"

"Oliver, I talked to the countess about Jacques. I told her that I hoped to be reunited with him here. Did she think I was so desperate to be successful in the shop that I would accept her?"

"She hoped so." Oliver looked pained. "Lilli, I'm so sorry—"

"She won't be sending customers now. We'll never see her again."

"We'll be all right." He hesitated. "Perhaps you could write another note to those friends of Corinne's."

"How can I write them again?" A few hours ago their future had seemed so promising. Now, again, Lilli wondered how much longer they could remain in the shop. "Oliver, I can't beg them to come."

"Perhaps they're away from Paris." He bent over Jan. "Tell me, my darling, what are you painting?"

Lilli began preparing dinner, her thoughts on the shop. Why, if Helena Rubinstein was such a success in London, were she and Oliver having such difficulty? She had thought Paris women would come to Chez Lilli out of curiosity, and once they were in the shop, she would be able to sell them.

Over chicken stewed in vegetables, Oliver talked about adding the new style of makeup to their beauty creams. "I wish Charles were here to help us. Lilli, why don't you write and tell him what you'd like to do?"

"Oliver, why?" As much as she tried to be optimistic, Lilli felt sick with defeat. "How much longer will we be able to stay in the shop?"

"I saw what you did in Sydney," he said earnestly. "You'll do it in Paris, I'm sure of it."

"Oliver, it'll be June in a week. Everyone rich will be leaving for Deauville or Dinard or Biarritz."

"Something will happen." His face was determined. "We will make it happen."

LILLI TRIED to remember Oliver's words as she made herself busy about the shop while Jan played with the doll Oliver had brought her. She rearranged the assortment of creams, changed the position of a mirror, moved a small gilt chair—anything to keep busy. She started at the sound of the door opening, then smiled in gracious welcome as the door swung wide to admit the tall older woman who, on a visit earlier in the week, had not only bought half a dozen jars of creams but had arranged for a course of treatments.

"You are a fraud." The woman stared at her in contempt. "Angelique told me. She apologized for exposing me to a cheap adventuress. She warned me not to use the creams. Heaven only knows what horrible chemicals you put in them!"

"I—I am not an adventuress." Lilli struggled to sound calm. "Thousands of women in Australia have used my creams and were delighted. They've written me letters."

"You are to give me back the money I paid for these." The woman dug into her huge alligator bag and brought out four jars of cream. "You are to reimburse me for the treatments I was silly enough to agree to take. Immediately. Or I will go to the police on this matter."

Lilli knew this was not a situation in which the police would care to be involved, but she knew the powerful influence of the women who moved in Angelique de Nicolet's circle. Perhaps even the police of Paris could be bent to the will of the countess and her friends.

"With pleasure." Lilli pretended to be amused. She saw out of the corner of her eye that Jan had stopped playing with her doll and was listening. "I would not wish to have you in my shop again." Her hands shook as she reached for her purse in the small Chinese cabinet behind the display table.

"Don't bother trying to attend the masquerade ball that Martine Vendome is giving after the Grand Prix," the woman said. "You will not be admitted. Her coachman—Martine can't bear the new motorcars—will return the creams she bought. You are to give him an envelope with the money she paid."

"Good day, madame," Lilli said quietly, and reached down to pick up Jan. "You have said quite enough."

Fighting back tears, Lilli took Jan to the window. So, the countess *was* exacting her revenge. She suspected that before the day was over she would have other unpleasant visitors whose presence was instigated by Angelique de Nicolet. Every cent she had earned from the friends of the countess would have to be returned. There would be so little left.

Oliver had said, *"Something will happen."* He had not expected it to be this.

A WEEK LATER, Lilli welcomed Mme. Amelie Renoir, one of Corinne's Paris friends. The wife of a French banker, Mme. Renoir was fashionable, friendly, and rich. She told Lilli that she and Corinne had been artist's models together in Montmartre. She seemed to enjoy talking about the past.

"Times are changing. More and more of the artists and writers are leaving Montmartre for Montparnasse across the river. In five years Montmartre will be full of tourists."

Mme. Renoir candidly told Lilli that while she and her husband were not received by the aristocratic old families of the Faubourg St.-Germain, they were happy to be part of the new capitalistic society that appreciated money. "Remember, Lilli, not all the elegant women in Paris come from the Faubourg St.-Germain. In Paris it's art that counts. I refuse to waste too much time in visiting and in tiresome fittings for dresses, nor do I need the reassurance of stealthy rendezvous with lovers." She laughed. "How many Parisiennes waste the hours between five and seven in discreet adultery!"

Mme. Renoir bought several of Lilli's creams, promised to return for treatments before leaving for Biarritz after the Grand Prix, and invited Lilli and Oliver to attend her salon on the following Wednesday. "If I'm lucky," she trilled, "Pierre Loti will be there."

Lilli couldn't help but smile; authors were the social lions of the new high society that had more respect for money and personal accomplishments than family background. What a different world from Sydney this was!

ON WEDNESDAY EVENING, Mme. Murat came to the flat to watch over Jan, and Lilli and Oliver left for the Renoir house. Lilli was nervous now about how much time had passed—with most of Paris society soon en route to the summer resorts, what chance did Chez Lilli have?

Oliver tried to be encouraging. "Madame Renoir will be helpful. You'll meet important writers and artists at her salon. Sebastien knows of her, too. Madame Renoir is one of those hostesses who brings together people from many circles.

There'll be titled guests as well as artists and writers. I hear the conversation there is often brilliant.''

In spite of her nervousness, Lilli laughed. "Oliver, are you trying to frighten me to death?"

Oliver had planned it so that they arrived after many of the invited guests had already gathered in the sumptuous drawing room, furnished with treasures of nineteenth-century France. Her hand lightly on his arm, Lilli paused for a moment, as Oliver had taught her, before walking into the room. Despite her youth and meager social exposure, Lilli was acquiring a distinct presence that demanded attention. Eyes followed them as they approached their hostess. Mme. Renoir was enchanted by Oliver's delicate good looks and gentle manner. And thanks to Corinne Allister, she was determined to be helpful.

"You must meet the duchess de Carpentier," she whispered. "Lisette comes from a fine old aristocratic family, but she discarded all that to be free. She is devoted to the arts." She laughed mischievously. "Especially to young painters." Lilli saw Oliver's faint smile of anticipation and surmised that he was plotting to introduce Sebastien to the duchess.

The duchess was a pencil-thin aristocratic woman of about seventy, with an air of one who has seen much and has found most of it boring. But her eyes lingered with pleasure on Oliver. Lilli guessed that handsome young men could alleviate the duchess's boredom.

"You are an artist," she said, turning to Lilli for confirmation. Lilli explained that, yes, Oliver had many artistic talents, though he was not a painter; then she launched into a lively report on Chez Lilli.

The duchess seemed fascinated. "How delightful this all sounds. Amelie," she called to Mme. Renoir, "we must do something to help these lovely people."

As Mme. Renoir came toward them, Lilli realized that the woman standing behind her was one of the countess's "unhappy customers." Apparently she had not yet recognized Lilli.

"We've had a most unpleasant experience," Lilli whispered to the duchess. "The countess de Nicolet sent patrons to us, then she—she became disenchanted." Lilli's eyes met those of the duchess. Instinctively she guessed that the duchess would understand the situation. "The ladies came to the shop. They were nasty and accusing. One even threatened to call the police because—she claimed—my creams contained harmful ingredients. It was a lie, of course."

The duchess smiled. "Old Angelique made a misjudgment. You know, my dear, I can't abide that woman. I don't care how these women live their lives, but let them do what they like behind closed doors. Angelique flaunts herself before all Paris." Her faded blue eyes held a glint of malicious satisfaction. "Amelie, we will sponsor Lilli and Oliver."

FOR THE NEXT FEW WEEKS, Lilli and Oliver were caught up in the campaign. Lisette de Carpentier's and Amelie Renoir's. The duchess arranged for the lower floor of a Louis XVI mansion owned by her late husband—and closed up since his death six years earlier—to be opened for use as the headquarters of Princess Lilli, Maison de Beauté. The second and third floors became living quarters for Lilli, Jan, Oliver, and the nursemaid the duchess insisted on hiring to care for Jan.

Embellishing on Lilli's admission of her illegitimate birth and titled Englishman father, the duchess circulated rumors in the upper circles of Paris society that Lilli was in truth the unrecognized daughter of a reigning monarch, hence the title of "princess," though in private life she was known as Mme. Laval. And with delicate malice, the duchess hinted that Angelique de Nicolet was mad about Princess Lilli and had been rejected.

In less than three months, Princess Lilli, Maison de Beauté, was a success. Lilli and Oliver worked slavishly to build a staff to handle the business. Lilli wrote Frances and Charles and asked for Charles's help in creating a line of flattering makeups. Then competition arrived in Paris. On the rue St.-Honoré, Helena Rubinstein had opened a new salon: Helena Rubinstein, Salon de Beauté Valaze. Lilli knew she had to introduce something new to keep her customers.

Oliver had supervised the redecoration of the new head-quarters of Princess Lilli, the duchess giving him free rein. He had introduced her to Sebastien, who in turn had introduced her to all the Paris antique dealers, who—after last year's financial crisis—were anxious to sell at what the delighted duchess called "ridiculously low prices." Lilli knew it was only Oliver's work at the Maison de Beauté that distracted him from his growing suspicions that Sebastien had also become the duchess's lover.

Lilli was amused by her patrons' curiosity about the identity of her father. What monarch had lingered in Marienbad to sire this young girl with the air of regal birth? Had it been Edward VII, a notorious womanizer? Don Carlos, king of Portugal? Franz Josef I of Austria-Hungary? The duchess feigned indignation that her confidence of Lilli's parentage had been circulated among the highest circles of Paris society.

Occasionally Lilli took time off to lunch at the Pavillon d'Armenonville, Restaurant de la Cascade, or Pavillon Royal in the Bois, or at Restaurant Ledoyen or Pavillon de l'Elysée in the Champs-Elysées, always in the company of the duchess and Mme. Renoir and a variety of their fawning friends, all intrigued by the mystery with which Lisette and Amelie had cloaked Lilli and her handsome young assistant. Lilli attended art exhibitions and charity bazaars accompanied by her two sponsors. Occasionally they encountered the countess de Nicolet, who was clearly having a difficult time concealing her resentment of Lilli's success. Every such encounter served only to whet the duchess's appetite for greater efforts on behalf of "Princess Lilli."

In the evenings, Lilli and Oliver often accompanied the duchess and Sebastien to Maxim's, Voisin, or Paillard's, where the guests on one night might include Prince George of Greece, Russian grand dukes, Sarah Bernhardt, Caruso, the writer Rostand, aviation pioneer Louis Blériot, and a sprinkling of the most famous courtesans. On other evenings there were dinner parties, private dances, balls, performances of ballets, operas, and the newest plays.

Late in June, Lilli and the duchess sat in a box at Long-champs for the Grand Prix. Two days later, Lilli, Jan, and the nursemaid accompanied the duchess to Deauville. A trio of "treatment girls" from Princess Lilli came along to provide services for any Deauville client who might want beauty treatments during the summer. It had been decided that Oliver would manage Princess Lilli for the summer, when almost everyone of importance deserted Paris.

Occasionally Lilli returned to Paris, only to flee when the tourists flocking into the city from other parts of the Continent and the United States became intolerable. At Deauville she supervised the treatment girls.

The duchess was delighted with Lilli's success among the important resort hostesses. Sebastien spent the summer at the duchess's villa, too; she had arranged for him to study that fall with one of France's finest artists. Meanwhile, he was her public escort—and private bedmate. Each time Lilli returned to Paris, Oliver self-consciously asked about Sebastien, clearly hoping that Sebastien's relationship with Lisette was platonic.

At the end of August, Lilli returned to Paris. The business was flourishing, and now they had to use three floors of the house for the luxurious treatment rooms. Oliver rented a cozy apartment in the rue de Varenne for himself. Lilli moved into a large apartment close by, and with the help of Oliver and Sebastien—who had a talent for discovering magnificent antiques and bric-a-brac at bargain prices—furnished it in a charming but quiet elegance.

The duchess came into the city to shop for fall and winter wardrobes at the salons of Doucet and Reboux before embarking on the autumn season's round of country-house parties. At the duchess's insistence, Lilli bought a ball gown from Doucet and a flattering plumed hat from Reboux. She was continually astonished at the prices, which would have shocked Aunt Sara, and decided to save money by hiring a seamstress to provide her with a wardrobe designed by Sebastien.

Between country-house parties, the cream of Paris society found the time to visit Princess Lilli. Lilli often came as an in-

vited guest to villas in the French countryside and advised the
other female guests on matters of beauty. Occasionally she even
brought a treatment girl with her. Letters were traveling back
and forth between Charles and her as he and a British chemist
worked on the makeups she was eager to present to her ladies.

Lilli learned how to gently reject the advances of important
men—after all, she needed their wives' business to keep Princess Lilli flourishing. And amorous gentlemen who were bachelors or widowers were politely told that she was married and
loyal to her vows, though she and her husband were currently
apart. Her clients—when they were in Paris—included such
international beauties as Consuelo, duchess of Marlborough
(née Consuelo Vanderbilt), Crown Princess Marie of Romania, and Olga de Meyer—rumored to be the illegitimate
daughter of the former Prince of Wales and Blanche, duchess
of Cariciolla.

Lilli's income soared. Her domestic staff now included a
cook, a butler, and a maid. Once a week, with autumn a
splendid backdrop, like a landscape by Corot, Lilli took Jan for
tea at a café in the Bois. Every minute of every day was occupied; there were those moments when her pleasure in her success was overshadowed by her realization that Jacques was not
here to share it with her.

In mid-December the "little season" brought the social world
back to Paris, and once again the city vibrated with the excitement of performances at the opera and the theaters. Every
night there were dinner parties, dances, balls. Knowing it was
an essential ingredient of her success, Lilli appeared nightly at
these functions, with Oliver as her escort. But every morning,
before the arrival of any of her girls, she was at Princess Lilli
with Oliver by her side.

Enjoying every moment of Lilli's success—mostly because
it was an affront to the countess de Nicolet—the duchess
watched the progress of the Maison de Beauté Valaze on the rue
St.-Honoré. When Mme. Rubinstein—in private life, Mrs.
Edward Titus—was sketched by the famous Helleu, the duch-

ess immediately commissioned a painting of Lilli by the equally famous Boldini.

Lilli was aware that her social invitations did not come from the old families of the Faubourg St.-Germain, but this was La Belle Epoque, where new money dominated society as much as old. She mingled with famous painters, writers, actors, singers, as well as the royalty that preferred the scintillating new society to that of the old aristocracy.

With the arrival of New Year's, 1909, Lilli faced the fact that this was her second New Year without Jacques. The duchess had created and circulated a story of a tempestuous marriage temporarily interrupted. Tempestuous it was, Lilli thought, but would the interruption last forever?

IT WAS AN ICY GRAY FEBRUARY MORNING and Jacques was clearly not happy as he emerged from the overnight train from Monte Carlo. He had known he would find an amiable wealthy lady to stake him in the casino. Since Queen Victoria's visit, Monte Carlo was considered respectable despite its earlier reputation as the suicide capital of the world. The most eminent ladies in society, opera, and theater were seen in the rooms and on the terrace. He hadn't known he would leave Monte Carlo in such a desperate financial state.

For almost five weeks he had enjoyed the company—and bed—of an English lady "of a certain age," who was sympathetic when his luck at the tables ran out. But then the lady's husband had arrived—as they had a way of doing—to take her to their castle on the Thames.

Jacques pushed through the crowds in the Gare de l'Est and out onto the street, wondering where he could go with so little money. Perhaps he could find himself a room on the rue Caulaincourt in Montmartre. But he would not be there for long, he thought with his usual optimism. Here in Paris he would find the success he deserved.

His pace toward Montmartre slowed as he remembered arriving in Paris with Lilli as his bride. More often than he cared to admit, he had thought of Lilli and Jan. His wife and child.

But he couldn't have stayed on in Sydney—he would have lost his mind, the way things were going. Lilli hadn't needed him; she had the shop. *He was nothing.* Colette, the French whore he'd met aboard the Trans-Siberian Railroad, had understood. He was a man ahead of his time.

After arriving from Sydney, Jacques had stayed in Paris for only three months. He was nearly penniless when a rich American widow from Kansas invited him to be her secretary and travel with her to Rome, Venice, and Florence. That suited Jacques very well, but finally her children persuaded her to return to Kansas, and they both agreed the relationship must end—clearly with regrets on her part. As for Jacques, had he not so enjoyed the luxurious living she offered him, he would have left her much sooner. As it was, he had been relieved to see her off at the railroad station, especially after he had pocketed the consolation prize she left him—most of which was soon lost at the tables in Monte Carlo.

A few hours later, Jacques had found himself a room for only a few francs a week. It didn't have a bathtub, but he was philosophical about it: He could go to the public bathhouses until his financial situation improved and he found more comfortable accommodations. He quickly unpacked, then descended the narrow, dark stairs to the street.

Emerging into the cold, dank late morning, he deliberated about where to go. The Café du Dôme always had a sprinkling of American students at its tables, but the conversation revolved around painting. He decided on the Rotonde, and headed for the long narrow room with a terrace, knowing that even on a bleak day there would be Americans gathered about the big porcelain stoves and drinking their grog *américain*. In his less affluent periods, he felt a strange need to be among compatriots.

He spent the remainder of the day wandering around the city. Paris was not at her best in February, he decided. To cheer himself up, he would be extravagant tonight. He'd have dinner at the Café Anglais, where all the rich Americans gathered. No, at the Ritz. His luck was always better with European women.

They were more understanding of his talents. Pleased with his decision, he headed for the Ritz. Never mind that it would cost almost all the money he had left.

Two hours later, after a sumptuous dinner, he left the Ritz. He buttoned his fur-lined overcoat—a farewell gift from the Kansas widow—and stopped at a kiosk to buy a copy of *Figaro*, the bible of the social world. He folded the newspaper and put it in his overcoat pocket, whistling the popular "Merry Widow Waltz" as he headed home.

Tossing his overcoat across the foot of the bed but keeping his jacket on because the room was cold, Jacques settled against a pair of pillows and began reading the *Figaro*. As always, he turned first to the page covering social events. Skipping over the fashion section and the elaborate lists of wedding presents, he focused on the names of those seen at dances, teas, the opera, the theaters. The corner of his mouth lifted as he recognized a name here and there, though he was disappointed not to find Clarissa. He had not seen her since Marienbad. Pity. Clarissa could have been most useful.

All at once he stopped: *Mme. Lilli Laval was exquisite in black velvet and pearls.* No, he told himself. It couldn't be. Lilli was back in Sydney, operating her house of beauty. This could not be *his* Lilli. It was just a coincidence.

Shivering from the chill in the room, Jacques stripped and slid beneath the covers, beset by memories of Lilli. He couldn't sleep. If she hadn't insisted on that silly business of the shop, they would be together. Lilli and he and their beautiful little girl . . .

Finally he fell into a deep, restful sleep.

When he woke up the next morning, all he could think of was Lilli. Could it be that she *was* here in Paris? It was possible, but he couldn't imagine Lilli attending a social function where the guest list included the names of the wealthiest and most famous residents of Paris.

He had to find out. He dressed quickly, cursing himself for forgetting to buy coffee and rolls for breakfast. Downstairs, he stopped in a modest café for breakfast, and read a copy of yesterday's *Gaulois* left on the next table by another customer.

Again his eyes swept the page announcing the week's social events. Again he discovered that "Mme. Lilli Laval, beautiful in jade-green taffeta," had been a guest at a ball given by the duchess de Carpentier.

His mind racing, he finished his coffee. If Lilli was in Paris, then she must be operating a *maison de beauté*. How else would she support herself and Jan? And if she was, she must be astonishingly successful.

He left the café to search for a bookstore that would sell such magazines as *Les Modes*, favored by Clarissa and her social circle. In Sydney, he remembered, Lilli had been thrilled with the results of advertising. If she were here in Paris, he would be able to find an advertisement for her *maison de beauté*. With recent editions of two of the expensive society magazines for Parisian ladies tucked under his arm, Jacques returned to his room. He settled himself on the bed and began to thumb through the first magazine. It gave him no clue as to the identity of the Paris resident who called herself Lilli Laval, and he began to doubt his suspicions. Laval was a common name in France.

He rose from the bed and reached for his coat. He had no time to waste. He had to find some wealthy widow or spinster who would be eager to hire him as her secretary. No more married women. Husbands had a devastating habit of appearing unexpectedly.

He hesitated at the door. Why not at least look through the other magazine? If his Lilli by some miracle were here in Paris and well placed, then his troubles would be over. He reached for the second magazine and began to flip through the pages. His eyes lingered for a moment on a small, elegant ad on the left-hand page, moved on to the right—and suddenly swept back in excitement to the left.

Could Princess Lilli be Lilli Laval? Princess Lilli, Maison de Beauté. He nearly laughed out loud. It must be that ridiculous story about her father being a titled Englishman. She must have taken it one step farther and dubbed herself Princess Lilli.

He couldn't just charge in on Lilli in the midst of her business day. Their meeting must be planned. His beautiful, romantic young wife would be more easily won over in a dramatic reunion. He had to make her understand why he had not sent for her and Jan. It would not be easy; she was a strong-willed woman. But he could do it. Luck was on his side. He had come back to Paris at the right time.

10

PRINCESS LILLI had closed for the night. Lilli had personally seen the last client out, as was her custom. She prided herself on maintaining Princess Lilli's personal touch: Throughout each day, she moved about the various treatment rooms giving advice, watching over her staff. She made an effort to be charming with the most difficult ladies—even those who commuted between Princess Lilli and Helena Rubinstein. Now, alone in the mansion that housed the shop, Lilli could relax.

Oliver had dashed off to some meeting with Sebastien, whose free time was now limited because of the demands of his art studies and his role as escort to the duchess. Oliver had become disturbed by Sebastien's despondency over his painting.

Lilli enjoyed this brief time alone in the salon. After inspecting each room on the three public floors, she would go home to have her dinner and dress for the evening. Earlier she had left the salon to have supper with Jan and to tell her a story before mademoiselle put her to bed.

A glance at the Viennese gilt-metal and enamel clock on the fireplace mantel in the "reception salon" told Lilli it was time to leave. She walked quickly into her private office, where her Russian sable cape, made for her by a new tailor named Paul Poiret on the rue Auber—who Oliver was convinced would soon be as famous as Worth had been—hung in a closet.

After all the long hours in the shop, Lilli preferred walking the short distance back to the apartment. She emerged from the marble-floored entrance foyer into the night air; paused to lock the massive, ornate oak door; and, drawing the fur cape around her, descended the short flight of stairs set between two pine trees whose branches soared to the wrought-iron balcony of the second floor. Swinging left onto the sidewalk, Lilli didn't notice the tall, overcoated figure behind her.

Her mind was on plans for the evening as she strode toward the apartment. There were times when she yearned for a break from the incessant socializing, but she knew how important it was to her success.

"Lilli?" a familiar male voice called out. "Lilli?"

Trembling, Lilli turned around to face the man coming toward her. "Jacques?" Could it be? *It was.* "Oh, Jacques!" Tears of joy filled her eyes as he took her in his arms and kissed her.

At last he pulled away. "Honey, you don't know how desperate I've been. I wrote you," he whispered. "Months ago. I waited day after day for a reply. I couldn't believe you would forget me."

Lilli searched his face in the streetlight. Was he telling the truth? "I couldn't bear staying alone with Jan in Sydney. I waited ten months. Then I thought I might find you in Paris— I had no idea how difficult that would be, though Oliver warned me—"

"He's here with you?"

"I couldn't have managed without him."

"Lilli," he said gently, "I wrote you to explain that I would soon have the money to bring you to Paris." So Jacques *had* written *after* she had left Sydney. But what about those long months when she hadn't heard a word from him? "Three times I wrote you." He lifted her hands to his lips. "When I didn't hear from you, I was crushed. I quit my job at the banking house." He sighed. "Even though they warned me they'd never take me back. But how could I work when I didn't know what had happened to you and Jan?"

"I'm sorry, Jacques, I—I waited until I couldn't bear it any longer."

He shrugged. "Three months ago I went to Monte Carlo. To the casinos. I couldn't face the thought that I might never see you again. I gambled at the tables and lost the money that I had been saving to bring you and Jan to Paris. I had just enough to come back here. I arrived yesterday morning."

She wanted so much to believe him. "Jacques, everything will be all right. I'm doing so well in Paris! You won't believe it!"

She took Jacques home with her and watched with pride as he admired her apartment. Despite mademoiselle's disapproval, they kept Jan up long past her bedtime. At first Jan was shy with her father, but she quickly warmed to his charms.

At last mademoiselle insisted that Jan be put to bed. Placated with promises that Papa would be here tomorrow, Jan was taken off to the nursery. Henri, the butler, was dispatched to the duchess with a note of regret for Lilli's absence at the soirée, and with a note to Oliver, summoning him to the apartment to celebrate the reunion with Jacques.

Within the hour Oliver arrived. In their eagerness to tell Jacques all that had happened in his absence, he and Lilli spent the rest of the evening interrupting each other.

At last, reluctantly, Oliver stood up to leave, his quick glance telling Lilli he understood her impatience to be alone with her husband. He knew that since Jacques there had been no one. As for Lilli, she would not dare think about the women Jacques had known in her absence. She didn't want to know about them.

While Jacques soaked in a perfumed bath, Lilli changed into the black chiffon and lace nightdress he had chosen for her honeymoon. How many nights, in the long lonely months of separation, had she brought the nightdress from its drawer to cradle in her arms, to hold against her cheek as she remembered their wedding night? She had sworn that she would not wear it until she and Jacques were reunited.

Listening to Jacques singing one of his favorite songs from a Strauss operetta, Lilli piled fresh logs on the colorful blaze Henri had started in the grate before retiring for the night. She remembered the night aboard the Orient Express, where, in the luxurious privacy of their compartment, Jacques had taken her as his wife. Soon they would be making love again....

"I chose that for you, Lilli, in a French shop on the Old Meadow in Karlsbad." She turned around to face him as he stood in the doorway of the bathroom, his clothes in familiar disarray on the bathroom floor. "Honey, you can't imagine how much I've missed you."

"Oh, yes, I can." She rushed into his arms, closing her eyes as Jacques pulled her against him. "Love me, Jacques. Please, love me."

LILLI SPENT THE NEXT FEW WEEKS, introducing Jacques to her circle of friends. Every night they went out with the rich and famous—to parties, the opera.... She was pleased that they were as sought after as a couple as she had been alone. Occasionally she felt uneasy when she glimpsed Jacques standing in a corner with some elegant woman, but Lilli told herself she was being foolish.

Every morning she dashed off to Princess Lilli. Jacques slept late, visited with Jan for an hour, then met Lilli for lunch in the Bois. Occasionally he came to the salon to take her to an art exhibition or charity bazaar, but Lilli made it clear that during the day her presence at Princess Lilli took precedence over social diversions. She and Oliver were continually working on new developments for the business.

Though Jacques talked about resuming his so-called banking career, he seemed content for now to busy himself with their social commitments, which were rapidly becoming international affairs. Distance meant nothing to the ultrarich, who hopped between Paris, London, and Vienna, to the summer resorts and to the casinos at Monte Carlo and Cannes, or to the fashionable spas at Karlsbad, Marienbad, and Baden-Baden. Only the old aristocratic families, the royalty of the republican era, seemed to resent the new society and their new money.

Early in September, Frances and Charles came to visit for a few days. Never fond of them, Jacques immediately left for a brief trip to Aix-les-Bains as part of the duchess's entourage. Charles and Frances had left their two children—Beth, who would be five in November, and her three-year-old brother,

Robbie—back in London, in the care of Frances's mother and a nursemaid.

"But I have good news for you, Lilli," Charles said, once they had settled in her sitting room and were waiting for Henri to bring them afternoon tea. "I've made contact with a chemist who I think will come up with makeup for the eyes that will look so natural no one will suspect its presence."

"Charles, you're a genius!" Lilli clapped her hands together in glee. "Some of my more daring patrons—all of them highborn ladies—still insist on wearing that garish makeup that belongs on an actress onstage. Or else they wear that ghastly white rice powder."

Charles laughed. "I'm not the genius. But I think Edward will be quite an asset to you."

Now the conversation turned to the children. Lilli was secretly glad Jacques had gone off with the duchess, though she was disturbed by the amount of cash he had taken with him. She realized that he was gambling again, but she tried not to let it worry her; they could afford some small losses if it amused him.

That evening, Oliver and Lilli took Frances and Charles to the "evening" of one of the most illustrious hostesses in France. Lilli was confident that the Cohens would fit in almost anywhere, and she was right: Charles was quickly immersed in a discussion of banking affairs with one of the Paris Rothschilds while Frances listened. Lilli herself was swept off to meet a reclusive writer who had been persuaded to attend this evening.

"Lilli, Monsieur Proust has asked especially to meet you," her hostess said and introduced her to a small, dark-haired man with large probing eyes who, despite the warmth of the ballroom, was dressed in a fur greatcoat.

"I have been told," he said without preliminaries, "that many fashionable women in Paris go to your *maison de beauté* for advice. I wish to know the intimate details about these things. For characters in a book I am writing."

"You're Marcel Proust?" Lilli asked. "The author of *Les Plaisirs et les Jours*?"

"That is nothing." He waved a hand in irritation. "I work now on a novel that is important to me. Tell me what these women I write about wear on their face."

Proust launched into a description of the society characters he was creating for his new novel. As Lilli spoke, he made notes on a slip of paper. Later, while Lilli and the Cohens were being driven home in the new Renault Jacques had persuaded her to buy, Charles told her that M. Proust's mother had been Jewish.

"Like me!" she said spontaneously. Then, remembering that she had kept this from Frances and Charles all these years, she explained how Aunt Sara had impressed upon her all her life that to survive in their world it was necessary to hide their Jewishness. Yet she suspected they guessed that Jacques had more recently been responsible for this.

"Have you visited the Jewish neighborhood?" Charles asked. "The Pletzl—part of the third and fourth arrondissements—is, I gather, rather like our East End in London."

"I must admit, I don't know it," Lilli said. "Although I do know that many Russian Jews live in Montmartre."

Charles smiled. "Most of the Jewish immigrants here have come from Russia and Romania. I'm sure your world is nothing like the Pletzl."

"I heard someone say—I believe it was Henry Bernstein...." Lilli paused, trying to remember. "He said that in the Marais, poor Jews live in squalid tenements on streets that three hundred years ago were lined with mansions."

"I think," Frances said seriously, "the French Jews battled for many years to become Frenchmen who happened to follow the Jewish religion—when it was convenient. I've read that many of them—except for immigrants—rarely attended services in the synagogues and temples. Some were even married in civil ceremonies. Then suddenly the Dreyfus affair made them realize they were a people. A people with a precious heritage."

"I know"—Lilli brightened—"we'll go together to explore the Jewish neighborhoods. I'll arrange to be away from the shop tomorrow afternoon." For the past few months, Lilli had been sending Aunt Sara copies of the Yiddish newspapers that were popping up in Paris, along with the well-established *L'Univers Israelite*. "And while you two are here, you must buy a painting. But you should talk to Oliver and Sebastien first. Something you buy today for five hundred francs will be worth a fortune in twenty years. Most of my paintings were bought for less than five hundred francs, though Oliver did manage to persuade me to pay five thousand for a wonderful painting by an artist named Matisse."

For Lilli, the Cohens' stay in Paris went far too quickly. She promised to visit them in London and to bring along Jan, who was being spoiled so outrageously by her father that mademoiselle was threatening to leave. Still, Lilli could not bring herself to scold Jacques. Jan had been without a father for so much of her young life; Lilli couldn't bear to see her own child suffer as she had.

EARLY IN JANUARY of 1910, Lilli realized she was pregnant again. She was jubilant. Over a private late supper in their bedroom, she told Jacques.

"Lilli, my darling..." He reached across the table for her hand. "A little brother for Jan. We'll be a real family."

She laughed. "With Jan, we *are* a real family."

"Lilli, every man dreams of having a son, someone to carry on his name. It's a kind of immortality." He reached for his glass of champagne. "We'll drink to our son."

Lilli raised her glass.

"To our child."

"Jacques," she said after his toast, "isn't it time you wrote your parents about your wife and family? Your parents will be their only grandparents." For the children, if not for herself, she yearned to become part of Jacques's family.

He stiffened. "No! I want no part of my family. I mean never to see them as long as I live! And you are never to talk about this again!"

Lying sleepless beside Jacques, Lilli told herself it was useless to try to reconcile Jacques with his family. Did he think it would upset her that they were not as rich and important as he had led her to believe? That wouldn't matter. As of now, Aunt Sara was their only family.

Each time Lilli expected Aunt Sara to come for a visit, she received an apologetic letter saying that George was ill again and that they wouldn't be able to make the trip. She missed her aunt more than ever. Perhaps before her pregnancy was too far advanced she could take a few days to go see her. She would take the Orient Express from Paris to Vienna, then the resort train to Karlsbad. There she could hire a car to take her to the inn that Aunt Sara was now running almost single-handedly.

When she told Oliver about the new baby, he immediately began designing an area on the first floor as a private salon. In the late months of her pregnancy, she would recline here on a gray velvet chaise longue to receive her special patrons. He made arrangements with Paul Poiret—who was causing a stir in the fashion world with his insistence that women be freed from tight corseting—to design special frocks to conceal Lilli's pregnancy as long as possible.

The months sped past for Lilli, with no opportunity to visit her aunt in Karlsbad even for three or four days. She spent hours each week with Edward, Charles's chemist friend, spurring him on to create the line of makeup she was determined to present to her adoring clients after the birth of the baby. She had to keep up with the ever-present Helena Rubinstein on the rue St.-Honoré.

As Lilli approached her ninth month, she received a letter from her aunt. George had died. Sara wanted to sell the inn; she could not bear to remain there without him; she would return to Marienbad and open up a shop again.

Lilli immediately wrote back asking Sara to come to live with them. "I'm desperate for a housekeeper," she improvised, knowing her aunt's independence. "All you'll have to do is manage the servants. We need you, Aunt Sara. And I want so much for us to be together."

Over dinner the same night, when she told Jacques about her plan, he reproached her for not first asking permission. But how could she let Aunt Sara live alone in the world?

Jacques was cool and taciturn, and Lilli was haunted by fears that he might leave her again. Then a disturbing thought occurred to her: Was Jacques opposed to Aunt Sara's living with them because she was Jewish?

While Jacques was charming when they encountered any of the Rothschilds socially, she sensed that it was only because of their extreme wealth and titles that he hid his contempt. She knew he occasionally read that awful newspaper *Action Française*, whose main purpose seemed to be to vilify the Jews of France. He had not seemed shocked when just recently the Camelots du Roi—that disgusting young gang who sold the *Action Française* on Paris streets—demonstrated against prominent French Jews at republican ceremonies and disrupted performances of plays by Jewish playwrights.

Bored by a deserted Paris in the heat of July, Jacques accepted an invitation to spend a few days at a villa in Deauville. Lilli was shaken that he would leave her at this late stage in her pregnancy. Had she threatened him with the business?

Lilli lay awake, painfully aware of Jacques's absence, and tried to imagine how she could win him back. Then she remembered Jacques's fascination with the duchess's mansion. Now, that would change. When Jacques returned from Deauville, she would say she had talked with her bankers and that they had agreed to advance her funds to buy a house of their own. Nothing so grand as the duchess's mansion, of course, but a lovely house that Jacques would enjoy showing off to their society friends. He would forget his anger about Aunt Sara— and with a large house, he would have his privacy.

Several days later, Jacques returned. Over dinner Lilli confided her plans. "Jacques, *you* must find a house for us. I can't run around Paris like this." She patted her bulging stomach.

"I've already talked to the bank—they'll let us know how much we can spend."

He looked happier than she'd seen him in months. "We'll have a floor for ourselves. And once the baby is born, we must think about entertaining. Lisette keeps saying you should have an 'evening' each week." Early in their acquaintanceship Jacques had begun to address the duchess as "Lisette," ignoring Lilli's protestations that it seemed disrespectful. "It'll be to your professional advantage to entertain."

The very next day, Jacques began looking for their new home. Lilli wrote her aunt, asking her to accept the first offer for the inn and come live with them. Nearly a month later, on the same day that Jacques came home to announce in triumph that he had found the perfect house on the avenue Montaigne, Lilli received a letter from her aunt saying she would be in Paris in ten days.

Lilli was in a private consultation with an Italian princess when she felt her labor pains. A mother herself, the princess immediately ended the consultation—despite Lilli's insistence that they continue—and Lilli reluctantly sent for Oliver to help her home and summon the doctor. Jacques was off on some errand having to do with the new house. At home, Lilli was settled in bed by Celestine, her personal maid. Within the hour the doctor was at her side. Oliver and Jan waited outside her bedroom door.

While Celestine hovered anxiously by her side, Lilli struggled to stifle the cries that rose in her throat with each pain so as not to frighten Jan.

Several hours later, the doctor could see that Lilli had abandoned herself to the pain. Celestine pressed a silken cloth against her perspiration-drenched face and throat. "Come on, Lilli," the doctor said. "Let's bring this baby into the world. Push. Again, Lilli. I can see the head now! Dark hair, like its papa."

At last Lilli heard the baby's cry. And then the doctor: "Congratulations, Lilli, you have a son."

Oliver and Jan were the first to see the new baby. Jan frowned as she inspected the sleeping infant. "He looks funny."

Lilli laughed. "We'll keep him anyway. Frederic, this is your sister, Jan, and your uncle Oliver."

As she waited for Jacques to come home, Lilli prepared herself to tell him that Frederic Laval would be circumcised, according to Jewish law. Some weeks ago she had mentioned to him that she wanted to talk to a rabbi about the necessary rites should the child be a boy. Their son had been born of a Jewish mother. He would grow up in his faith.

Despite the recent *Action Française* and the Camelots du Roi, a Jew in Paris was free to practice his religion. At one of the duchess's evenings, she had overheard a Jewish playwright and a Jewish artist remarking upon how, in France, Jews attained high positions in every field, and were admitted as chevaliers de la Légion d'Honneur and chevaliers du Mérite Agricole.

At first Jacques was indignant, but eventually he capitulated, stipulating only that the circumcision be done privately. Lilli was thrilled—especially since Aunt Sara would be arriving in Paris the morning before the traditional ceremony. Ignoring Jacques's protestations that she had not fully recovered from her delivery, she insisted on being driven to the Gare de l'Est to meet her aunt.

Jacques wasn't interested in accompanying her. "I presume you'll wish to meet her alone. Well, then, I'll be home for dinner. You will have all day to reminisce." Lilli was surprised—and pleased—by his sensitivity.

Waiting in the August heat in the Gare de l'Est, Lilli couldn't believe it had been almost seven years since she had last seen Aunt Sara. How pleased Aunt Sara would be to breathe the air of a city that included over 60,000 Jews! In Paris she would not have to hide her observance of Hanukkah, Rosh Hashanah, and Yom Kippur.

Aunt Sara's train pulled into the station. Trembling, Lilli watched the passengers disembarking. Where was Aunt Sara? At last she spied the familiar slender figure of her aunt—wearing what Lilli was sure was a copy of a frock worn by a fashionable Karlsbad guest—stepping down from the train.

"Tante Sara!" she called out. "Tante Sara!"

Lilli paused briefly to instruct a porter to take her aunt's luggage out to the waiting Renault.

"Aunt Sara, how wonderful to see you!" Tears filled her eyes and spilled over as they held each other in a tight embrace.

"Lilli! Oh, Lilli—" Her aunt was overcome with emotion. "So long since I see you."

"Aunt Sara, I have a son!"

Sara laughed. "Even I can see you're no longer pregnant. Oh, Lilli, a boy!" She beamed with pride. "How old is he?"

"A week today. Tomorrow he'll be circumcised." Lilli saw the questions in her aunt's eyes. "You know Jacques is not Jewish, but he understands that Frederic will be raised in my faith." Suddenly she was anxious about Jacques meeting her aunt—instinct told her they wouldn't get along. But Jacques was too well raised to show any ill feelings toward Jews before Aunt Sara.... "I was praying you'd be here. I would like you to be his godmother."

Arm in arm, they made their way through the bustling hordes to the street. Lilli smiled at her aunt's look of approval at the sight of the chauffeured motorcar waiting to receive them. She had told Aunt Sara of her success. She had sent extravagant gifts, and each time Aunt Sara had expressed her gratitude but insisted that Lilli "save for the future." She guessed that only now—after she'd seen the apartment, the new house, and the salon—would she truly understand just how successful her niece was.

Mademoiselle and Jan waited for them at the apartment.

"Lilli, she's lovely," Sara said upon seeing Jan. "A tiny image of you. How old is she? Wait—I remember: She'll be five in November. George kept saying, 'Go to see them. It's not like Australia—they're in Paris.' But how could I leave him alone with the inn?"

Lilli took her aunt to the nursery to see Frederic.

"Ah, you did what your mother and my mother could never do." Sara chuckled. "You produced a son."

"I don't love Jan less for being a girl. In truth I hoped she'd be a girl. What did I know about boys?"

Sara searched her face. "Lilli, you're happy?"

"I'm happy, Aunt Sara."

"I was afraid you had run off with a man you hardly knew because you'd overheard George and me talking about marrying you off to Sigmund. All these years that thought has troubled me."

"I ran off with Jacques because I loved him." Lilli took her hand. "Aunt Sara, everything I have I owe to you. Your beauty creams, everything you taught me—it was the beginning of Princess Lilli."

"Ach—never mind." Sara waved a hand. "Tomorrow morning will be the most important day of my life. I will share in the circumcision of my grandnephew. My grandchild," she added softly. "Because you, Lilli, have always been my child."

In the shadows of the waning day, Lilli sat at a bedroom window while she nursed Frederic. Aunt Sara's presence had reminded her that she could no longer sit on a fence, being neither Jew nor non-Jew. She had to make a choice. Jan was almost five; it was time she was taught about her heritage. Tomorrow Frederic would be circumcised. Paris was not Russia or Poland or Bohemia. Here they could live as Jews without disgrace.

But she knew that Jacques would fight her on this. Every step of the way.

11

LILLI WAS NOT SURPRISED when Jacques said he would not be present at Frederic's circumcision, but she did feel ashamed before the rabbi and the *mohel* when the moment came for the father to hold the child and Aunt Sara was the one who stepped forward. Jacques's excuse was that he could not stand by and watch his infant son being subjected to such pain.

It disturbed Lilli, too, that he was absent at the usual meal after the ceremony—only Oliver, Aunt Sara, and herself, along with the rabbi and *mohel*, joined in the celebration. Jacques had insisted that Lilli not invite their friends.

Ten days after Frederic's birth, Lilli was back in her consulting salon. Oliver had set up a private area so that Lilli could nurse Frederic throughout the day. To Lilli's relief, Aunt Sara had taken charge of the household, handling everything with her usual efficiency and freeing Lilli to concentrate on the business.

Fascinated by Paris, Sara discovered there was a public library in every one of the twenty arrondissements, and circulating libraries where she was able to acquire a reader's card. One day she came home breathless with the news that the Bibliothèque Nationale on the rue de Richelieu had 3 million books. "The largest library in the world, Lilli. No wonder French Jews have become so important—always they've been fine scholars, and here so many books. I hear that one-third of the bankers here are Jewish. And I hear also that in Paris there are several lady doctors and lady lawyers."

"And lady cabdrivers." Lilli laughed. "Aunt Sara, this is a new era for women."

Jacques adored his new son, though he couldn't resist making a few nasty comments about Frederic's having been deprived of proper male equipment. When he was home, he was constantly at Frederic's side—as though Jan no longer existed. She saw the hurt in Jan's eyes when Jacques came into the apartment and headed directly for Frederic's cradle. She knew that Aunt Sara, too, was aware of Jan's need to be close to her father again. Together they tried to make up for Jacques's lack of attention.

She also became concerned about Jacques's frenetic social schedule. She wanted to believe that he was being unselfish when he insisted she rest at home in the evenings rather than dash about to the usual round of parties, but she couldn't help being suspicious. The duchess, on one of her weekly visits to Princess Lilli for her facial, bluntly told Lilli to accompany her husband on his social evenings.

"Darling, Jacques is a devastatingly charming man. Don't give him such a long rein. Not with so many predatory women eager to share their beds with him."

Lilli felt a stab of fear. Had another woman already claimed him? "I'll be at your evening on Sunday," she said. Guiltily, she thought of how little time she and Jacques had been spending together lately. But it was he who had encouraged her to remain home in the evenings.... "You're a dear friend, duchess."

"Enough of such formality, Lilli. You make me feel like an old woman. Which I suppose I am." She laughed. "But to my friends I am Lisette." She hesitated. "Has Oliver spoken to you about Sebastien?"

"Only that he's working very hard at his painting."

"The master no longer wishes to teach him."

"Oh, Sebastien must be devastated."

Lisette shrugged. "He says Sebastien has an eye for line and color but he'll never be a painter of worth. We can't all be geniuses. I tried to talk to Sebastien, but he insists he's going back to his family's small farm in Provence. I shall miss him, though I suspect the person he'll really miss is Oliver, not me."

When Oliver returned later that day from a luncheon with Sebastien, Lilli knew that Sebastien had told him of his plans. All along, Oliver had ignored the gossip about Lisette's taste for young men and had convinced himself that Sebastien was faithful to him. Until now.

"Oliver, I've been thinking," Lilli said, remembering her own desolation when Jacques left her in Sydney. "It's time we expanded. We should sell our creams throughout France. But it must be handled very carefully. You'll approach an important shop in each city to be our exclusive representative. You'll have to train the salespeople to follow our methods here in Paris. It isn't enough to sell; we must educate the ladies so that they understand the importance of a beauty regime."

"Lilli, Sebastien leaves tomorrow for his family's home," Oliver said quietly. "How will I live without him?"

"You will survive," Lilli said. "You'll be busy with the business. And how long do you think Sebastien will be content to stay on the farm after all these years in Paris? Keep in touch with him. Let him know that you'll be here. Wait a month, then ask him to come to Paris to help you redecorate my house. I'll pay him, of course. Together, you and Sebastien will make it a small palace."

Oliver leaped to his feet. "I'll ask him tonight!"

"No," Lilli scolded. "Let him spend some time away from Paris. Besides, you'll be traveling through France for the next month. Oliver, think of it! Someday you'll be selling Princess Lilli creams all over the Continent!"

OLIVER SET OFF on a sales trip, offering Princess Lilli creams and talking about the new line of makeup to be presented within a few weeks. The first stop was Paris—Oliver's idea, and Lisette had agreed, saying that it would lend special cachet to the line when titled Paris ladies—including the duchess—reacted favorably. Together, the three decided the makeup would be launched shortly after Easter, when *tout le monde* would be in town for the season.

Aunt Sara supervised the move into the new house, making sure the magnificent antiques Lilli had bought at Oliver's urging from dealers hungry for cash were handled with care, as were the paintings that hung in splendor along the walls of the ornate staircases that climbed five floors: Cézannes, Toulouse-Lautrecs, Gauguins, Renoirs, Picassos, and Matisses.

Though Lilli missed his presence in the salon, Oliver's sales trip was a huge success. He even managed to coax Sebastien into returning to Paris to help redecorate the house. Once Oliver and Sebastien had declared the lower floors suitable for viewing, Jacques pressed Lilli to follow Lisette's suggestion that she set aside an evening each week for entertaining. "Lilli, it's important to your business. And to mine." But there was something in his eyes that unnerved Lilli—the same restless look he'd had before he left Sydney. She didn't understand why he refused to become a part of Princess Lilli. At this point he could be a real asset.

"Lilli"—he took her hand—"I've been thinking about a new venture." She tensed. She'd already given him money for one investment, which had proved to be a disaster. "I've been talking with some American tourists who own orange groves in Florida. They say the groves are in terrible shape because of a bad frost in January, and they—"

"Jacques, what is Florida?" She couldn't become involved in another losing deal. Not now that she was about to launch the new line.

"Florida's a southern state in the United States," he said patiently. "Beautiful country. But the citrus growers were all wrong in setting up in central and northern Florida. The groves should be in south Florida, where there's never a real frost. That's the most important requirement in growing oranges. Millions can be made with orange groves by somebody with vision. I could go there and buy up thousands of acres of land for almost nothing now. Put in a hundred thousand seedlings and in five years we'd make a mint. Lilli, it's a surefire investment."

Lilli spoke very quietly. "Jacques, I've been in negotiation with Amelie Renoir's husband about a small building at the edge of town. We're reaching the point where we need factory space to make the creams and manufacture the new line of makeup. Monsieur Renoir is willing to sell—"

"You haven't heard a word I said about Florida!" he interrupted angrily. "I suppose if it's not your idea, then it isn't worth anything!"

"Jacques, that is not true. As Oliver says, we have to move ahead—we can't stand still. We have competition now. Madame Rubinstein on the rue Saint-Honoré is—"

"You don't need the factory. You can manage without it. Instead of spending the money on that, give it to me to buy land in Florida."

"But Princess Lilli is our security. It's not a gamble. We're building a business that one day we can pass on to the children."

"That's all you give a damn about!" He was flushed with anger. "The children and the business. There's no room in your life for a husband!"

Lilli stared after him in anguish as he left the room. How could she stand by and let him squander thousands of francs on yet another "surefire investment"? Perhaps she could persuade him to take over the management of the factory. *That* would make him feel important. She would wait for just the right moment.

TERRIFIED AT THE PROSPECT of her first "evening," Lilli relied on Aunt Sara to prepare the lavish buffet for their guests. In rare good humor, Jacques had elected to supervise the choice of champagnes. Oliver insisted that the main ingredient for a successful evening was good food, plenty of champagne, and two or three important guests. "And, of course, a beautiful hostess," he added with a wink.

Lilli had consulted the duchess about the guest list, which of course was to include Princess Lilli's most devoted clients. The duchess chose an eclectic group. Among those Lilli invited were the duc de Morny, the American author Edith Wharton, Edmond de Goncourt, and a grand duke particularly admired by the duchess. Lisette had personally invited Edmond Rostand, author of the hugely successful play that had opened the year before with Lucien Guitry in the title role of Chantecler.

Even before all the guests had arrived, Lilli knew that her evening was a success. The champagne flowed. Guests compared Aunt Sara's superb buffet to that of Maxim's and Voisin. The ladies were sumptuously costumed by the finest Paris couturiers, their jewels competing with the brilliant crystal chandeliers. Conversation was lively. A cluster of guests surrounded M. Rostand.

Lilli was surprised by how much she was enjoying herself. But as the evening progressed, she became uncomfortably aware of Jacques's attentions to an older, sharp-featured American woman. Obviously wealthy, the woman had come as the guest of a British diplomat—another of the rich American expatriates enjoying the European social scene. Lilli tried to ignore him, guessing he was only doing this to irritate her.

OVER THE NEXT FEW WEEKS, it seemed to Lilli that wherever she and Jacques appeared, the American woman was there. Her name was Mrs. Adelaide Thomas. She was the widow of a New York man who had built a fortune in railroads. To Jacques she was Addie. Addie Thomas held court daily at the Café Anglais, and Lilli knew that Jacques was frequently among her guests.

Just before leaving for Cannes—in early spring, all of fashionable Paris went to Cannes or Monte Carlo and stayed until Easter—Addie Thomas was hostess at a spectacular costume ball held at her rented eighteenth-century mansion on the avenue des Champs-Elysées. Attending the ball as the auburn-haired empress Eugénie—the original long in retirement in a villa on the Riviera—Lilli wore a white satin gown with a multiflounced crinoline skirt and a tight bodice that left her shoulders becomingly bare. About her throat she wore a double rope

of pearls borrowed from the duchess. Jacques was attired as
Napoleon III.

At the head of a grand staircase, Addie Thomas, as Mme.
Pompadour, greeted her guests while from the ballroom came
the lilting music of a Franz Lehár operetta. Lilli's smile faded
when she caught the special glance between Jacques and the
American widow as the three of them exchanged perfunctory
greetings. Had Addie become another of Jacques's "distractions"? She was grateful when, a few minutes later, Lisette
swept her off to one of the several elegantly furnished reception rooms and she left Jacques in conversation with a wealthy
German industrialist.

"How dare she play at being Madame Pompadour," the
duchess—dressed as Catherine the Great—whispered. "At
Addie Thomas's age, Pompadour was long dead."

Lilli held her tongue.

"Your gown is magnificent, darling," Lisette continued.
"Did Sebastien design it for you?"

"Yes. He has *such* a flair for designing clothes."

"He ought to do something with that talent." Lisette looked
thoughtful. "Lilli, you may not realize this, but Sebastien could
one day be as important as Poiret. Believe me—I know these
things. We must help him set up his own *maison* on the rue
Auber. You and I will be dressed by him. Why did we never
think of this before? Between us, darling, we can supply him
with more customers than he can handle. Tell Oliver to send
him to me tomorrow." She reached over and squeezed Lilli's
arm. "Lilli, there across the room—it is Madame Helena
Rubinstein, who has the salon on the rue Saint-Honoré."

"I don't want to meet her," Lilli said in embarrassment.
"Please, Lisette—"

"Lilli!" A young British lord of questionable sexual
inclinations swooped down to take her hand in his and bring it
to his lips. "As always ravishing. And Lisette." His eyes crinkled mischievously. "Darlings, if I didn't know you both so
well, I'd be suspicious of an affair of the heart between the two
of you."

"Basil, do be quiet," the duchess sniffed. "And take Lilli to the ballroom and dance with her. Now if you two will excuse me, there's Madame Bernhardt just arriving—I'm perishing to talk with her."

In the crowded ballroom, while she danced with Basil, Lilli spied Jacques across the floor with Addie Thomas in his arms. She was not alone in observing him, Lilli realized in sudden coldness. The way Jacques held Addie, the way she touched his face with one bediamonded hand—surely everyone in the room must suspect.

Mrs. Thomas was at least twenty years older than Jacques and rather plain. How did it look to her clients, many of whom were here at the ball, to see Jacques infatuated with another woman? Color edged her high cheekbones. She felt humiliated. Degraded. As the queen of a beauty empire, she could not afford to appear a woman whose husband preferred another.

Now Jacques was taking Addie Thomas by the hand and off the dance floor. They were leaving the ballroom. Lilli realized she was not alone in watching their departure. Though she made a pretense of paying rapt attention to what Basil was saying, she heard not a word. *This was an intolerable situation.*

"Basil," Lilli said crisply when the music stopped, "I have a dreadful headache. Will you please see me home?"

A BLACK VELVET ROBE covering her nightdress in the chill of the dawn, Lilli sat before the fireplace in the sitting room that she and Jacques had shared. The logs were fragile lengths of charcoal bedded in ashes, with here and there a spark of red hinting at an earlier blaze.

At the sound of footsteps outside the door, she rose to her feet, white-faced and trembling. The door opened. Jacques walked in and tossed aside the cape he had worn over his Napoléon III uniform. He looked angry.

"Lilli, why did you run off without a word to me? Basil said something about your having a headache."

"You were disgusting." She spoke with quiet intensity. "Everyone in that ballroom knew what I'd suspected for weeks. You and Addie Thomas. I was ashamed to be your wife."

"Because I danced with my hostess?" He clucked, walking toward her. "Honey, I adore you when you're jealous."

"I'm not jealous." She turned away from him. "This is the first time in our marriage that I'm seeing you for what you are. I'm not that wide-eyed little girl you hypnotized in Marienbad, Jacques. I want no part of you."

"Lilli, my little love . . ." He pulled her to him.

"Let me go!" She pushed him away. "It won't work this time, Jacques."

"You're beautiful when you're angry." He lifted her from her feet and strode into the bedroom while she fought to free herself.

"How dare you treat me like this!" she blazed while he dropped her onto the bed and lowered himself above her. "Stop it this minute or I'll—"

"You'll what?" His voice was low, menacing. "You'll scream? I'm your husband, Lilli. I'm only exercising my rights."

"You dare to come to me from her?" Tears filled her eyes. How could she scream and awaken Aunt Sara and the children and the servants?

"Addie amuses me—I'll admit that, my darling wife." With one hand he ripped her nightdress. "But it has nothing to do with us."

His breath stank of champagne when his mouth settled on hers. Fondling her breasts, he pushed her legs apart. This was rape, she told herself, lying motionless as he fumbled at the buttons of his trousers with his free hand, then thrust himself within her. *If she became pregnant tonight, she would want to kill him.*

His hands were rough as they sought to elicit a response in her. How could she welcome her husband when she knew he came to her from another's bed? In the past she had always shared his desire with an intensity that lifted her to incredible heights of satisfaction. Tonight, she felt only revulsion.

At last he groaned, and she felt the liquid warmth fill her.

"Get out of my bed," she said as he lay collapsed on top of her. "Get out of this house. Tonight. Unless you're prepared to face an awful scandal tomorrow."

"Lilli . . ." He stared at her in shock.

"I mean it, Jacques. I want you out of this house. Go back to Addie Thomas. Come here tomorrow, when I've left for the salon, and pick up your clothes."

"Lilli, I'm your husband!"

"I want you out of my life. If you try to see me again, I'll divorce you and name Addie Thomas. I mean that, Jacques."

"What about Jan and Freddie? They're my children, too."

"You may see them whenever you like. Whenever I'm away from the house. But stay out of my life, Jacques. I've had all I can take of you."

Jacques stared hard at her. She gazed back without flinching.

"You are a selfish little bitch," he spat. "All you've ever given a damn about is the business. You don't deserve the children. You don't deserve me."

He stalked out of the bedroom. A moment later she heard the door to their sitting room slam shut. Lilli lay back against the pillows, the covers drawn over her torn nightdress.

What would she tell Jan about her father? Freddie was too young to know his father was gone. She didn't need him, but it tore her apart that she was depriving the children of their father. Just as she had been deprived.

12

SEVERAL WEEKS LATER, Lilli heard that Addie Thomas and Jacques had left for Cannes. When she let it be known that she and Jacques were no longer living together, she was surprised and embarrassed by the sympathy of her patrons, many of whom were content to close their eyes to their husbands' dalliances.

She thought about Edward VII, who had died last year, and his Queen Alexandra. All society considered theirs a good marriage: Despite Edward's constant womanizing, even in his later years, he was said to be devoted to his wife. Perhaps a queen could accept infidelity; Lilli Laval could not.

Once again Oliver was her escort about Paris. The relationship served them both well: For Oliver it provided a mask of respectability so that he could continue seeing Sebastien in private; and for Lilli it was a protection against the advances of wealthy men—both married and unattached—who were eager to share her bed.

Lilli was careful about her socializing, concerned that she might encounter Jacques after his return from Cannes. She knew that certain hostesses would be diplomatic about not inviting them to the same affairs. But she knew, too, that she must continue to be seen in the best Paris circles; it was important for the business. Months passed, yet her heart pounded every time she caught sight of a man who resembled Jacques.

At painful intervals she asked herself if she had been wrong in banishing him from her life. *Had* she been a bad wife? Jacques repeatedly accused her of having time only for the business. But that simply wasn't true. She was a devoted mother and wife. She had spent every evening with Jacques. He despised the business, but he certainly had been eager enough to enjoy the life it provided them. How would they have survived if she had abandoned the business?

Eager to forget her past, Lilli threw herself into promoting the new line. Her ladies were back from Cannes and Monte Carlo for the season and it was spring in Paris. Usually she loved the lovely scents of chestnut trees and flowering lilacs, the soft lush green of the trees, but this spring she was aware only of the emptiness of her bed, of Jan's plaintive questions about papa.

The ladies among her clientele were enthralled by Princess Lilli's delicate rouges, and the creams for the eyelids. When Lilli heard that Mme. Rubinstein was also experimenting with such makeup for women who were not actresses, she worked harder and faster to come up with new products. She began reading *Vogue* and *Vanity Fair*, so popular with fashionable American women. She read the ads in *Vogue* praising the "beautifully appointed salon" of Mrs. Elizabeth Hubbard, who catered to socially prominent New Yorkers. She read about beauty consultations and treatments being offered by Miss Elizabeth Arden at a fashionable New York address. It pleased Lilli that Paris—mainly because of her own efforts and those of Helena Rubinstein—was far ahead of America in beauty care.

Before the grand exodus to the beach resorts, Lilli decided to buy a small country house at Poissy, a short drive from Paris and only minutes from Lisette's villa. The children and Aunt Sara, along with several members of the Paris household staff, were installed there for the summer. Lilli tried to be there as much as possible.

Early in August, she took off a week to stay at the country house. Frances and Charles, along with the children, came to visit. Lilli relished her private hours spent strolling about the fragrant green countryside. Only with her dearest friend could she talk about the collapse of her marriage.

"You don't need Jacques," Frances said. "Jan and Freddie don't need him either. You'd be smart to divorce him, Lilli. Divorce is not a disgrace anymore."

Lilli looked shocked. "I couldn't do that!"

"Lilli, you're twenty-four years old," Frances said gently. "Most of your life is before you. You may—"

"I'll never marry again." Divorce would be the ultimate separation. She was not ready to face that yet. Perhaps later...

"One day you'll change your mind." Frances smiled. "You'll find a man worthy of all the love and passion you have to give. You were a child when you married Jacques. You were living a fairy tale."

Lilli sighed. "I keep reminding myself how Jacques walked out on Jan and me in Sydney. I made so many excuses for him then. And again when he came back into our lives in Paris. When we made love, Frances, I forgave him everything." For a painful instant she remembered the passionate nights in Jacques's arms. Then she remembered their last night together.... "But I can't forgive him Addie Thomas. As head of Princess Lilli, I can't afford to be a wife whose husband appears to be infatuated with another woman. He isn't, you know—he's playing games. Proving to himself that he's irresistible to women."

On a crisp late-autumn day, Lilli left the salon in Oliver's hands so that she might spend the morning with her aunt visiting the Pletzl, the oldest Jewish community in Paris and now home to Yiddish-speaking immigrants from Russia, Poland, Germany, and Austria. For Sara, this was a reminder of growing up in Vienna. She loved roaming the narrow streets with their kosher butcher shops, Jewish restaurants, and stores bearing signs in Yiddish.

"Lilli, smell." Sara paused outside a bakery shop to sniff the tantalizing aromas of fresh bread and cakes, the pungent scents of pickles and herring in barrels. "I feel like fourteen again."

"Come, Aunt Sara, let's go into the restaurant across the street there."

Inside, they sat at a table against the wall. They ordered gefilte fish, potato kugel, and tea—food that Lilli had not tasted
since Marienbad.

"French Jews are more French than Jewish," Sara said dryly
after the waiter had left their table. "They think because Captain Dreyfus was cleared they can forget the troubles that fall
on Jewish heads in every generation. They think they're safe."

"You know about the Camelots du Roi," Lilli said. "You've
seen the *Action Française.* There's no way we can deny that
there are Frenchmen who hate Jews."

Sara nodded. "French Jews are strangers to the Jews around
us here. *You* are a stranger to them, Lilli."

"Aunt Sara, most native French Jews are in comfortable financial situations. Here in the Pletzl there are Jews who have
fled from persecution. They have little money and little education. They don't want to become Frenchmen."

"Because they know that above all else they must remember
they are Jews. Who knows when they will have to run again?
A time may come when many of the French take up the
thoughts of those street gangs. What you call the Camelots du
Roi."

The waiter came with their food. As Sara talked to him in her
rusty Yiddish, Lilli smiled at the obvious warmth of their
communication. Aunt Sara was marvelous with people of every
social level. She carried her slim figure with a regal bearing that
elicited instant respect.

All at once a thought occurred to her. Aunt Sara had
charmed the ladies who came to Marienbad each season—she
knew how to deal with such a clientele. Why not bring her into
the salon?

"The waiter told me," Sara said once they were alone, "that
in four of the schools in one Jewish community the rule is to
close on Saturdays instead of on Thursdays as is usual—because most of the pupils are Jewish."

On their way back to the salon, they discovered there had
been a Yiddish theater in the city for four years, that the famous Yiddish writer Shalom Aleichem had lectured in Paris,

and that next season Chaim Weizmann would lecture at the
Université Populaire Juive.

"I think I will attend these lectures," Sara said.

Lilli took a deep breath. "Aunt Sara, I'd like you to come
into the salon." Aunt Sara gazed uncomprehendingly at her.
"To work with me. Oliver must spend time on sales trips. I'm
away from the salon one day every week—when I'm at the
factory preparing my secret formula. I need you in the salon."

"You need me running the house—"

"I can hire a housekeeper." Lilli leaned forward. "You'll
bring something very special to the salon."

"But, Lilli, what do I know about a fine salon like yours? I
sold creams in a little shop in Marienbad."

"You know everything about the beauty business. I saw how
you handled the ladies in Marienbad. Everything I know I
learned from you. Without you there would be no Princess
Lilli." Were those tears in her aunt's eyes? "When Oliver and
I are away, I want you in charge, Aunt Sara. If you're there, I
won't worry."

Aunt Sara hesitated. "But the children . . ."

"Mademoiselle Martine adores them. She handles them just
right. Aunt Sara, I've made up my mind: As soon as I can hire
a housekeeper, you're to come into the salon. You'll remember some of my ladies from Marienbad. They don't remember
me, of course, but they'll remember Sara Landau."

Within a week, Sara had become part of the salon staff. And
within a month, in spite of Sara's good-humored grumblings
that it was a waste of time, Lilli began including her in some of
the Paris socializing. Still a fine-looking woman, and always
fashionably garbed, she was an impressive advertisement for
Princess Lilli.

IN THE AUTUMN, Lilli proudly took Jan to her first day of
classes at a nearby private school. Someday, Lilli dreamed, Jan
and Frederic might even study at the Sorbonne. She remembered how neighbors had scolded Aunt Sara for sending *her* to
school until she was sixteen—as though Aunt Sara were one of

the rich ladies of the town. But Aunt Sara had been determined to do the best she could for her only niece. And Lilli would do the best for *her* children.

Aunt Sara was now comfortable in Paris. She visited the Great Synagogue on the rue de la Victoire, the synagogues at rue Notre Dame de Nazareth and at rue des Tournelles, attending both the 7:00 A.M. and the sunset services. She persuaded Lilli to become a member of the Great Synagogue. Soon, she decreed, Jan would attend one of the *lycées* that provided a few hours a week of Jewish instruction for children.

Late in November, Lisette reported to Lilli that she had seen Jacques and Addie Thomas at a round of country-house parties. Rumor had it they had been taken up by the countess de Nicolet.

"Angelique has never forgiven either of us," Lisette chuckled. "You for rejecting her and me for sponsoring you in Paris. Addie is dying to get royalty to her table, and Angelique is willing to help. Meanwhile, she's spreading the word around Paris that Jacques left you because he discovered you were Jewish."

Lilli was very still for a moment. "I threw Jacques out of the house the night of Addie Thomas's costume ball," she said slowly. "You know that, of course. And, yes, I am Jewish. Jacques knew that when we were living in Sydney." And now he was trying to cause trouble for her business.

"There are some in Paris who'll be shocked, my dear," Lisette said. "The Catholic upper class supported the army in the Dreyfus affair, and are hardly friendly toward Jews even today, five years after Dreyfus was declared innocent. Such bigotry is contemptible." She laughed. "Darling, how could Angelique—or Jacques—believe that your being Jewish will keep women away from Princess Lilli? Helena Rubinstein is also Jewish. Where else can they go for what your salons offer them?"

"I'm divorcing Jacques." She realized now that until then she had secretly harbored a faint hope that someday they could be reconciled. "On grounds of adultery with Mrs. Thomas. Lisette, can you suggest an attorney?"

By February, Lilli's divorce had been granted. Though Jacques fought for a financial settlement, he wanted to avoid making headlines in the Paris scandal sheets, so the divorce went through quickly and quietly. In Parisian high society, divorce was accepted. As far back as 1906, Anna Gould had divorced the count de Castellane, and two years later had married his cousin, the duke of Talleyrand-Perigord. According to French law the divorce would not be final for 300 days, but this didn't worry Lilli. She had no intentions of ever marrying again.

What with the salon, the factory, and her precious time with Jan and Frederic, she had little time to brood; and Oliver and Lisette had made a silent pact to see that her evenings, too, were occupied with theater, opera, ballet, and parties. Though there was a covert conspiracy among Lilli's immediate circle to protect her from any surprise meetings with Jacques and Addie, certain catty ladies could not resist dropping reports on Jacques's activities. Addie had announced that Jacques was to become her business manager. They were traveling together to New York so that Addie could make the necessary arrangements for him to take charge of her holdings. They would have a suite on the *Titanic* on its maiden voyage.

When he was in town, Jacques visited the house once a week to see Jan and Freddie, respecting Lilli's stipulation that he come when she was at the salon.

Lilli was secretly relieved when Paris society took off in early spring for Monte Carlo or Cannes. As usual, at the behest of devoted clients, she was a houseguest at both resorts for a period of three days each, during which time she provided consultations while a trio of treatment girls who traveled with her provided salon services. Now almost every night she sat down to leisurely dinners with Aunt Sara after her two hours alone with Jan and Freddie. Conversation at dinner was always lively. Like many Paris intellectuals, such as Anatole France, Aunt

Sara was outraged that last winter Henry Bernstein's new play, *Après Moi*, presented by the Comédie Française, had to be withdrawn because of attacks on Bernstein by the Camelots du Roi. And a Jewish dean of the faculty of law had been forced to resign because of riots.

"I thought in Paris there would be no such ugliness," Aunt Sara said one night as they discussed the campaign of the League of Rights of Man to fight anti-Semitism in France. "But this is a republic. Captain Dreyfus was cleared. French Jews have risen to important positions. Look at you, my darling. You move in the highest circles. And that other woman"— Aunt Sara never referred to Helena Rubinstein by name—"the one with the salon on the rue Saint-Honoré—she's Jewish also."

BY THE FIRST OF APRIL, society was returning to Paris. The talk at all the parties was the maiden voyage of the new sea giant, the $10 million White Star Line's *Titanic*—the largest steamship ever launched. Sailing on the *Titanic* had become the social event of the season. The fashionable were traveling from all over the Continent to embark at Cherbourg or Southampton. First-class passage cost well over 20,000 francs—over 4,000 American dollars. Lilli had been shocked when one of her American clients pointed out that the average American family lived on less than the equivalent of 5,000 francs a year.

The day before the *Titanic* sailed, Jacques came by the house to say goodbye to Jan and Freddie.

"Jan's upset that her father is going to America," the governess confided to Lilli when she arrived home. "He doesn't know when he'll be returning."

Lilli was especially tender with Jan that evening, sensing, from her daughter's rejection of her caresses, that she blamed *her* for Jacques's departure. *What kind of lies had he been feeding Jan all these months?*

"Papa will be back in Paris soon, my darling," she said. "He just doesn't know exactly when."

"He won't be back." Jan looked at her accusingly. "He's going to stay in America forever. It's all your fault!"

Not yet two, Freddie was too young to be affected by Jacques's absence from their lives; but for Jan, Lilli realized, this was a second separation. Have I been a selfish mother, she wondered, forgetting the children's needs? Was Jacques right? I've tried to do everything that was right for them. How could I have gone on living with Jacques when I knew about Addie Thomas? When all Paris knew? How many Addies have there been that I never knew about?

The *Titanic* sailed on schedule. Three days later, fighting her feelings of guilt that soon an ocean would separate her children and their father, Lilli left the salon in Sara's capable hands so that she could take Jan and Freddie to a puppet show. Afterward, she took them for hot chocolate, heaped with whipped cream, at a café in the Bois. Tears of pride filled her eyes as she gazed with love at her two beautiful children, both dressed in blue velvet.

"I have a surprise for you," she said to Jan. "I'm having the top floor of the house turned into a big, big playroom for you and Freddie. You'll be able to ride your bicycle there and roller-skate."

Jan sipped her hot chocolate. "He's too little."

"I know that," Lilli said. "But with a big playroom, *you* can have fun there when the weather's bad. You'll invite Solange and Marie and Brigitte from school to play there with you."

On the Tuesday morning after the *Titanic* had sailed, Lilli arrived at the salon well ahead of the staff, as usual. This morning, Oliver was already there, looking pale and serious.

"Lilli, have you seen the morning papers?"

"No. I never read the newspapers until evening." The look on Oliver's face alarmed her. "Oliver, what's happened?"

"It's not as bad as it sounds," he said. "The White Star Line announced last night—New York time—that the *Titanic* hit an iceberg and sank four hours later."

"Oh, my God!" Lilli turned pale.

"The Cunard liner *Carpathia* is picking up passengers, and White Star believes that two other liners are at the scene. Nobody is in real danger. This was reported in the New York and Toronto newspapers."

"Oliver, who do we know at the White Star offices? I have to know what's happened to Jacques!"

"Amelie Renoir's sister is married to someone there. But it's too early to waken Amelie—"

"I'll call her!" Lilli charged toward her office. "She'll understand."

By noon, Paris time, the earlier optimism about the safety of the passengers aboard the *Titanic* had faded. Of the more than 2,000 passengers aboard the ship, only 655—mostly women and children—were reported safe aboard the Carpathia. Lilli was distraught.

"Lilli, all the figures coming in are unofficial," Oliver said. "Many other passengers and crew may have been picked up by the two Allan Line ships."

Conversations were subdued in the various treatment rooms. Many well-known Paris residents had boarded the *Titanic* at Cherbourg. Lilli sat at her desk waiting for news from Amelie Renoir. Occasionally Sara came into the office with a fresh cup of tea. Oliver sat with her at every opportunity.

"Oliver, how could I have divorced Jacques?" Lilli said, her head in her hands. "Why couldn't I have been like other women who close their eyes to their husband's wanderings? If Jacques is all right, I'll do whatever he asks of me."

When Oliver walked into the office in midafternoon, Lilli swung away from the window, where she had been gazing unseeingly into the street below.

"Lists of survivors will be coming through very soon," he encouraged. "Jacques's name will be one of them."

"Why are the marconigrams taking so long?"

"Probably the names of those rescued are being divided by country of origin. The Paris office expects to hear very soon."

Lilli froze as her private phone rang. "Oliver, answer it—"

He reached for the phone. "Hello?" His face brightened. "Amelie, you have news?" He nodded to Lilli, smiling. "Jacques is on the *Carpathia* bound for New York!"

"I'm going to New York," Lilli said exultantly. But why did Oliver now look so upset?

"Amelie, you're sure?" Oliver asked, and Lilli sighed in impatience. Of course she was sure. Obviously the White Star Line had the facts straight.

"Oliver, ask her if the office knows where in New York the survivors will be taken. But I suppose the New York office will have that information."

"Thank you, Amelie. I'll tell Lilli." Slowly he put down the phone.

"Oliver, he's safe!" She threw her arms around him. "Book passage for me on the next ship bound for New York."

"No, Lilli," Oliver said gently. "Amelie's brother-in-law reported that the survivors' list included the names of Mr. and Mrs. Jacques Laval." Lilli stared uncomprehendingly. "Amelie's maid is a cousin of Angelique de Nicolet's cook. Amelie's maid just told her that Jacques and Addie Thomas were married at Angelique's home the night before they sailed on the *Titanic*. Addie Thomas is now Addie Laval."

13

NEVER ONCE HAD IT occurred to Lilli that Jacques would marry Addie Thomas. True, she and Jacques were divorced. What he did with his life was none of her business. But she simply couldn't imagine him with another woman.

This meant that Addie Thomas—no, Addie *Laval*—was Jan's and Freddie's stepmother. It didn't seem possible. Should she tell Jan and Freddie that their father had married somebody else? Not yet.

Over the next few weeks, Lilli tried to lose herself in the business. The new line of makeup was launched on schedule. At first it was rejected by her more conservative patrons, but by the time of the summer exodus from Paris, the new line had become a huge success.

From the occasional picture postcard addressed to Freddie and Jan, Lilli learned that Jacques and his new wife had spent June and July at her house in Newport, August in Saratoga Springs, and September at Greenbriar. A postcard arriving shortly after the New Year had been postmarked in Palm Beach. Occasionally gifts arrived for the children, though Jacques clearly had no memory of their birthdays. On Jan's birthday in November, Lilli bought an exquisitely dressed doll and pretended that Jacques had cabled Galeries Lafayette to have it delivered.

For Lilli, the streets of Paris were haunted by images of Jacques. She told herself she was well rid of him, that she was insane to be so obsessed by any man. But logic was always overruled by her heart.

Early in the spring, searching for a distraction, Lilli decided to open a Princess Lilli salon in London. She felt confident that Aunt Sara, who was respected by the staff and accepted in social circles could supervise the Paris salon and factory. She planned the move carefully. Oliver would accompany them to London. In Paris she had met influential English ladies who would spread the word about the new London salon in the elite Mayfair section.

Exactly six weeks after she had come up with the idea, Lilli—along with Oliver, the children, Mlle. Martine, Celestine, and a dozen trunks filled with gowns by Poiret and a few daring creations by Sebastien—went to the Gare du Nord for the seven-hour journey to London. She had reassured her aunt that letters posted in London before 6:00 P.M. would be in Paris by 5:30 A.M. the following morning and delivered within three hours. And telegraph offices were open from 8:00 A.M. to 9:00 P.M. in winter and from 7:00 A.M. to 9:00 P.M. in summer in the event of an emergency.

Jan and Freddie were thrilled at the prospect of traveling, first by train and then on a ship that would take them from Calais to Dover. Frances and Charles had promised to meet them at Victoria Station. Throughout the journey, Lilli was aware that she would be living in the same city as her father. What if she met him at a party and didn't even know who he was? She would hire a private detective to try to find him. Not right away, but once the London salon was established.

As promised, Frances and Charles—looking just as they had years ago—were standing on the platform at Victoria Station. Charles herded Lilli, Oliver, and the children into his car and found a taxi to take Celestine, Mlle. Martine, and their hand luggage to the glittering Hotel Savoy, where Lilli had reserved a suite. Once there, Celestine and Mlle. Martine took charge of the children and the luggage while Frances and Charles led Lilli and Oliver into the Savoy restaurant for tea.

"I knew sooner or later we'd get you to London," Charles said after they were seated. "I hadn't realized it would take a London salon to bring you here."

"Lilli, we're so proud of you," Frances said. "I've been telling everybody at the synagogue about the salon. And about how we started out in business together back in Sydney—can you believe it was almost ten years ago?" She smiled, a little sadly. "I guess I didn't do too well."

"You've done great," Charles said firmly. "Two wonderful children."

But as they talked over their very British tea, Lilli realized, with some surprise, that Frances had her regrets about not going ahead with her own shop.

BEFORE MAKING ANY SOCIAL CALLS, Lilli and Oliver set out to find a location for the London salon, as well as a house in which to live. Within a week they found a pair of adjoining Mayfair mansions for sale, and Lilli immediately began negotiating for their purchase.

Worried that she would be recognized, Lilli persuaded Celestine to spy for her at Mme. Rubinstein's salon on Grafton Street. She had learned long ago that Helena Rubinstein went regularly to check on the Paris salon, but that London was her permanent residence. Celestine returned with vivid reports of Rubinstein's brilliantly colorful decor and elegant furnishings.

"I heard from the treatment girl who gave me a facial," Celestine said as she brought out several jars of the herbal creams that were the staples of the Rubinstein line, plus small containers of rouges and eyeshadows, "that Madame Rubinstein will continue the London salon but she's moving with her family to Paris."

"Oliver," Lilli called sharply. He appeared with an inquiring smile. "Celestine tells me that the 'woman from Melbourne' is moving to Paris. Do you think it's a good idea to start a salon here?"

"I think so," he said. "London is the capital of the world now. Edward VII may be dead, but the world he created lives on."

Oliver took time out from supervising the redecorating of Princess Lilli's new quarters to dash around the city with Lilli to help her choose furniture for her house. He would live on the top floor of the salon; and for now, he insisted, all he needed was a bed.

According to Oliver's plan, Princess Lilli, London, was to be totally unlike Mme. Rubinstein's brilliantly colored salon. It would feature the delicate grays and yellows that had become Lilli's trademark, and graceful, feminine Louis XV antiques. Comfort would be emphasized in the chairs, sofas, and chaise longues, upholstered in fine damasks. The woods would be exotic rosewood, satinwood, amaranth, and tulip.

In the meantime, Lilli was swept up in London's social scene. With the English ladies she'd met in Paris, she lunched at the Café Royal, the Savoy Grill, or Claridge's, and had tea in the charming shadowed garden of the Ritz. In the evenings, with Oliver as her escort, she attended the theater, dinner parties, and saw a performance of her beloved Ballets Russes. She knew this was the way to make the contacts that would bring wealthy patrons into her salon.

Oliver took great pains to point out differences between French and London society to Lilli. Here in London, there was no equivalent to the great French demimondaines. Such women would not be seated at the Savoy or the Ritz or Claridge's. Prominent British gentlemen would shun their presence.

There were few salons. British ladies, many of whom were politically minded, inveigled ministers, ambassadors, bankers, and members of the nobility into visiting their country houses, where they pursued their personal political objectives. A sprinkling of beautiful women was always included.

Lilli began accompanying Frances and Charles to their lofty-ceilinged, stained-glass-windowed synagogue for Friday evening services and a late dinner afterward. At a sumptuous roast-beef dinner at Simpson's on the Strand, the three talked earnestly about London's immigrant problem.

"It's just as it is in Paris," Charles said. "The French and English Jews who were born and raised like other French and

English feel threatened by the Russian and German and Polish Jews, who can't understand our way of life. Remember, Lilli, they've fled from ghettos and *shtetls*. They haven't shared in the culture of their native lands. They're not Rothschilds or Goulds or Sassoons. They're shocked to see our synagogues, to hear our rabbis referred to as reverends. To them it's as though we're forsaking our heritage. They can't understand—yet—that it is possible to be both English and Jewish, or both French and Jewish. Here in London immigrants live together in the East End, cutting themselves off from the culture of the city.''

"But the children are becoming English Jews," Frances said. "They're bright, hardworking students who shine in their classes. And some of their parents attend the evening schools after working twelve hours in a sweatshop, because they realize it's important to become part of their new country."

"In the autumn," Lilli said, "I'd like Jan to attend the children's classes at the synagogue. It's time for her to know that she is Jewish."

Already Lilli had become aware of the anti-Semitism of Britain's upper crust—despite the presence of the Rothschilds, the Sassoons, and the Cassels, who were received everywhere and honored by the British court. Unaware that Lilli was Jewish, highly placed British hosts and hostesses made disparaging remarks about these august Jewish dynasties behind their backs even though they sought them as guests at balls and dinners and house parties. There was a titled British Englishwoman who confided to Lilli that she was relieved that George V did not share his father's "ridiculous affection" for Jews.

THE RUSH OF TOURISTS into London during July and August had made it fashionable for social-minded Londoners to flee the city by late June—unless court entertainments were scheduled—and Lilli took advantage of this to go to Paris with the children for two weeks. At Sara's encouragement, she decided to spend a week or two in the Paris salon.

Back in Paris she accepted Lisette's invitation to stay for a week with the children at her villa in Deauville, where she learned the tango, the slightly naughty dance that had replaced the two-step and was being denounced by Pope Pius X. Already the rage in London drawing rooms, the tango was being danced on the Deauville boardwalk at noon.

At Deauville Lilli met the former Gaiety Girls now married to lords, dukes, and counts, or to gentlemen who were simply multimillionaires. These beautiful ladies were fascinated by Princess Lilli, and Lilli returned to London convinced her new salon would be a huge success.

WHEN OLIVER pronounced the new salon ready for its formal opening, Lilli spent hours working over advertisements to appear in the *Illustrated London News*. And at last, late in August, as Londoners were returning from German-Bath season, Lilli launched the new salon with a costume ball. Oliver had talked Sebastien into coming to London for a week to help with the preparations. The second and third floors of the house were transformed into a replica of the halls of state at Versailles during the reign of Louis XV. Ladies were told to dress in the period of either Louis XIV, XV, or XVI, but the gentlemen were to appear as they liked. A chef from Foyot's in Paris was brought to London to supervise the elaborate buffet.

Among the invited guests were two dozen of Lilli's most prestigious Paris clients. Her English friends made sure the literary world was represented by the monocled Somerset Maugham and red-bearded George Bernard Shaw, the stage by Mrs. Patrick Campbell and Ellen Terry.

It was a lovely evening for all, but at several points Lilli could not help remembering Addie Thomas's costume ball. What would her life be like if she had not thrown Jacques out of their house that night? Would Jan be a happier, less moody child? Freddie, bless him, had, even at three, a buoyant nature. More than anything else in life, she yearned to see her children happy.

The following morning Princess Lilli, London, opened to receive clients. Dressed in a yellow silk caftan bordered in gray, Lilli graciously received her clients and then circulated among the treatment rooms, offering advice.

When the house-party season began, Lilli found herself a popular guest. In November, as Jan's eighth birthday approached, Lilli took her young daughter to Hanover Square to the couture house of Lucile, who in private life was Lady Duff Gordon—sister of novelist Elinor Glyn. A blue velvet dress with a touch of ecru lace at the throat was to be made for Jan so that she could accompany her mother, "just like a grown-up lady," for dinner at the Ritz.

"Mama," Jan said thoughtfully while they were being driven home from Hanover Square, "I think Papa hasn't written to me because he doesn't know we're living in London now."

"Darling, you had a postcard from Papa right after we came to London." *Always a postcard, never a letter.* "The pretty picture of a hotel called the Homestead at White Sulphur Springs. Aunt Sara sent it on to you."

"But that was a long time ago," Jan said. "Maybe Aunt Sara forgot to send them."

"I'll write and ask her, all right?" Lilli kissed her. "Now tell me, my love, what shall we have for your birthday dinner?"

"Freddie won't be with us?"

"We'll have a birthday luncheon party with Freddie and Aunt Frances and Beth and Robbie, but tonight it's just the two of us."

"Can I have anything I like?"

"Anything except champagne," Lilli said.

"Oh, I know I'm too young for that," Jan said seriously. "But Diana told me their butler allowed her to have wine on her eighth birthday. Her mother was in Monte Carlo."

Lilli was shocked by the way the highly placed English parents raised their children. *Never* would she allow her children to be brought up by servants. Every day she spent time with the children. They knew they were loved.

LILLI WAS DISTURBED by the political discussions she heard at the house parties and at dinners in fine London town houses in these early weeks of 1914. There was much talk about a possible war, dire warnings that the Continent was a powder keg, though most Englishmen seemed unaware of the ugly rumblings on the Continent. The average Englishman seemed slightly more concerned about the troubles in Ireland. From Paris, Sara wrote that many French intellectuals were convinced that Germany was preparing to attack France. She wrote, too, about the progress of a group of Jewish intellectuals who called themselves "Amis du Judaisme." They included the eminent composer Darius Milhaud, a professor at the Sorbonne; the poet Gustave Kahn; and the Grand Rabbi Israel Levi. While anti-Semitism presented no immediate threat in France, it had brought many irreligious intellectuals back to their Jewish heritage. Sara quoted from Gustave Kahn, president of the group, that "even when anti-Semitism has ceased . . . Judaism must not therefore disappear . . . Judaism represents that which must impose itself one day on all conscience, the ideal of justice. . . ."

Lilli had promised herself that once in London she would hire private investigators to try to track down her father. Now, as spring approached, she called upon a firm that advertised in a London newspaper.

"We can make no guarantees," the pompous investigator said. "But if anyone can locate your father, we can." Lilli was aware that he was covertly inspecting her simple but expensive attire. "It will be costly, I can assure you of that."

"That's fine," she said. "I'm interested in results." She deliberately kept her voice cool. "And I'm willing to pay."

On her way back to the salon, she decided she would tell no one—not even Oliver or Aunt Sara—about her search. It was not as though she meant to approach her father. She just wanted to know who he was. Who *she* was.

As the weeks passed, she was frustrated by the meager reports from the investigators. They were sending a man to Marienbad, the head of the firm wrote her—and enclosed a huge bill for services. Two weeks later another bill arrived, indicating that their man had stayed at the Hotel Weimar in Marienbad for ten days—with no lead—and had moved on to the

Grand Hotel Pupp in Karlsbad. The writer assured her that everything possible was being done to track down her father.

It was a lovely spring, promising an equally lovely summer. Early May—officially the beginning of the London season—began the traditional rounds of balls and debutante parties. On a gentle May evening, Oliver called at the house for Lilli and after his usual visit with Jan and Freddie, they left in the chauffeured Rolls-Royce—which he had convinced her to use for important social functions. The Renault was for daily transportation. "Lilli, darling," he'd chuckled, "*taxis* are Renaults."

Lilli's Rolls arrived at the brilliantly illuminated mansion of the duke and duchess of Rochester on Grosvenor Square as the first round of top-hatted young Englishmen and beautifully gowned young debutantes departed for yet another ball. The car joined the line of other Rolls-Royces, high-topped Daimlers, and highly polished broughams with coachmen and footmen on their boxes, each depositing guests before the magnificently maintained town house.

Lilli didn't feel particularly festive. She managed a smile as she stepped out of the car, but this was one of those nights when she would have preferred a quiet evening at home. Tonight she was wearing a narrow sheath of yellow silk crepe that was slit up the sides to reveal her silk-stockinged legs. She also wore the diamond and emerald necklace and earrings that she had bought only a week ago at Cartier's—after Oliver had confided that he was quite certain she was to be chosen one of the Ten Best-Dressed Women of the Year.

Lilli and Oliver entered the white-and-black-tiled entrance hall, exchanging greetings with other arrivals. "Sir Ernest Cassel is here," Oliver whispered. He knew Lilli was an admirer of the Jewish financier who had been a special friend of the late King Edward VII. "And there's Isadora Duncan going up the stairs." He and Lilli made an effort to attend the controversial dancer's performances whenever possible.

At the head of the stairs they were welcomed by their host and hostess. Earlier, a treatment girl from Princess Lilli had been sent to give the duchess a facial and makeup treatment.

"You look lovely, Your Grace," Lilli whispered.

"Pamela is a treasure," the duchess whispered back. "Oh, you must meet Mischa later." Mischa was Prince Michael Lamsaloff. Seven months ago his eighteen-year-old bride-to-be—heiress to an American oil fortune—had committed suicide only days before their wedding. "He saw you at the opera last week and was absolutely smitten."

While the orchestra played music by Franz Lehár, Lilli and Oliver walked into the ballroom. The floor was already filled with waltzing guests. At one side of the ballroom, small clusters of bejeweled ladies gathered with their masculine companions.

"Shall we waltz?" Oliver said.

Lilli took his hand and smiled. Dear Oliver... "I'd love to."

"Who is this Mischa the duchess mentioned?" he asked.

"That Georgian prince everyone's been talking about," Lilli said.

"He must be terribly rich. All the titled Russians are."

"Oliver!" Lilli froze in his arms.

"What's the matter?" He steadied her.

"Jacques is here. Across the room, dancing with Addie. When did he arrive in London?"

"Nobody has said a word about seeing him," he said. "Would you like to leave?"

Lilli wavered, her heart pounding, her mouth dry. She hadn't seen Jacques in over three years, but the hurt and humiliation of that last night was still so fresh in her mind that she trembled at the memory.

"We'll stay." She held her head high. "I won't let him drive me away. I'm going to start giving small dinner parties, Oliver." She would arrange her social life so as not to encounter Jacques and his wife. "Not an 'evening' as in Paris, but twice a month a gay, informal dinner where everyone relaxes and the conversation is exciting. Oliver, why do you think he came to London?''

"Because he and Addie were bored in America," he said.

"Lilli," a feminine voice called, its long-legged owner striding toward them, "I have a handsome man who's dying to meet you."

"Elaine, what an exquisite dress!" Lilli said. Once a Gaiety Girl now married to a munitions millionaire, Elaine was one of Princess Lilli's faithful patrons.

"I found it at Sebastien's when I was in Paris last month," Elaine said. "But, darling, Mischa will throttle me if I don't introduce him this instant. This charming, handsome man is Prince Michael Lamsaloff. Lilli Laval of Princess Lilli. And her most talented associate, Oliver Wickersham."

Lilli smiled up at the tall, fair-haired young man with dark brooding eyes who gazed at her so intently.

"Surely the most beautiful lady in London," he murmured while Elaine spirited Oliver away. "I saw you at the opera and I demanded immediately to know who you were; but before we could meet, you had disappeared."

"Are you enjoying London?" Lilli asked, aware of Jacques and Addie dancing in a corner of the room. *Why had they come to London? How long would they stay?*

"London is very different from my country," Mischa said. "But, yes, I always enjoy London. Particularly so at this moment."

Lilli saw Jacques staring hard at her from across the ballroom. He whispered something to Addie. For a moment it seemed they might leave the ball, but it quickly became clear that Addie had no such intent.

"There is a ball at the Russian Embassy," Mischa said. "Would your associate be upset if I stole you away and took you there? It's most colorful. I think you would like it."

She couldn't bear to watch Jacques and Addie any longer. "I'd love to. I'll tell Oliver that we're leaving." *What power did Jacques still hold over her? One moment life seemed whole and endurable—and an instant later everything fell apart.*

She knew that Jacques had seen her with Mischa, but she pretended not to notice him as she crossed to where Oliver was talking to a pair of effete young Englishmen, one of whom had just asked Oliver who Jacques and Addie were.

"He's Jacques Laval," Oliver was saying self-consciously. "An American. That's his wife, who was Mrs. Thomas—the widow of the American railroad tycoon."

"A morganatic marriage, no doubt," the Englishman sniffed. "She's probably twenty-five years older than he."

"Bertie, don't be so cynical," his friend said. "Perhaps it's like Disraeli and his wife. He just adored her, you know."

"I'm not sure that Jacques would approve of the comparison," Lilli said, and laughed. Disraeli—Queen Victoria's beloved "Dizzy"—was proud of his Jewish ancestry, though in a fit of pique his father had disassociated himself from his religion and had Disraeli baptized. "I'm Lilli Laval." She held out her hand. "Jacques's first wife."

"Ah..." The taller of Oliver's companions brought her hand to his lips in admiration. "The famous Lilli Laval! All of London knows of Princess Lilli."

Lilli left the ball with Mischa. As a footman summoned her Rolls-Royce, she realized with pleasure that Jacques had seen her leave with a Russian prince. He would see that she wasn't languishing in a corner—and soon he would know about Princess Lilli, London. She was surviving very well, without Jacques Laval.

14

For the next few weeks, Mischa pursued Lilli. He was handsome, young, and charming, and it was a sweet balm for Lilli's wounded ego to be sought after by one of the most eligible bachelors on the Continent.

Gossip had it that Addie Laval had rented a mansion on Curzon Street, close to the duke of Marlborough's opulent home. With Angelique de Nicolet as their houseguest, Addie was frenziedly wooing the American ambassador to arrange for her to be presented to the queen at one of the Drawing Rooms scheduled at the end of the season.

One afternoon a composed but wary Jacques appeared at the salon and asked if he could visit Jan and Freddie regularly. Lilli agreed to let him come by the house in the afternoon once every two weeks. In the meantime, she spent almost every evening with Mischa. On those nights—at parties, at the ballet, at the theater—when she saw Jacques and Addie, they only exchanged polite nods.

In June Lilli took time out from the salon to attend Royal Ascot Week. As guests at a nearby country house, she and Mischa spent long afternoons at the races, then went for relaxing evening rides in Windsor Forest. It was a happy time for Lilli; with Mischa she felt like a romantic young girl again.

But she continued to feel Jacques's presence. On Gold Cup Day, as they sat in the crowded Royal Enclosure with the Prince and Princess of Wales, she couldn't help stealing an occasional glance at Jacques and Addie's box.

After the races, Lilli and Mischa drove to London for dinner at Simpson's on the Strand. Mischa was in high spirits. He devoted himself to Lilli, making her laugh with his stories. His eyes told her that he adored her, that would do anything for her. *She didn't need Jacques.* There were a dozen men in London eager to pursue her. One of them was a Georgian prince!

"Lilli, you're pensive," Mischa said over dessert. "What thoughts fill that pretty head of yours?"

"I'm sorry, Mischa," she said. "I'm tired. All that driving and fresh air today—"

"Then you must go home and rest." He signaled for the waiter. "But first, my darling..." He reached across the table for her hand. "First tell me that you'll marry me."

She looked at him in astonishment. "Mischa—"

"Lilli, did you think I saw you only as a pleasant diversion during the season?" he said. "I want to spend the rest of my life making you happy."

"Mischa, I'm a woman with two children. I run a business." She tried to imagine sharing her world with Prince Michael Lamsaloff. With Mischa she could forget Jacques. And she would, in truth, be Princess Lilli. But... "I could never abandon my business, Mischa."

He chuckled. "I would not expect it of you, my darling. But you could find a place in your life for me." He brought her hand to his lips. "Lilli, it could be so wonderful for us."

She couldn't make a decision now. Why not? Was it Jacques?

"Mischa, give me time. I had told myself I would never marry again."

"Lilli, you're young and beautiful. Everywhere we go, men stare at you. We will be good for each other, I'm sure of it. Until now, I had no purpose in life. And it certainly will not hurt your business to have my family crest on your products." He paused. "My family might object, but you *will* be a Lamsaloff princess—"

"Mischa," Lilli said, "I have to think about this. A few days?"

He smiled. "A few days."

Later, alone in her bed, Lilli lay sleepless until the early morning light peered through the curtains. What would her life be like as Mischa's wife? He was charming and sweet. He loved her. Everyone in their circle was fond of him. Imagining passionate nights in his arms, she was startled by a surge of arousal. She'd lain alone too many nights.

He'd said that she could continue with the business. In fact he seemed proud of her accomplishments—a refreshing change from Jacques. And during the brief time he'd spent with the children, he'd been playful and kind. *At last Jan and Freddie would have a father.*

The following evening Lilli told Mischa she would marry him. She also told him she was Jewish. Would his parents try to stop the marriage?

He laughed. "Lilli, I don't care if you worship at a church or a synagogue." But his eyes betrayed him. "We will be married here in London. In a civil ceremony."

"What about your parents?" she said.

He shrugged. "I'm the younger son. Whom I marry is not of utmost importance to them. It would matter to me if they objected, and someday I will take you to meet them. You will love my country." Lilli shuddered, trying not to think of the shattering stories Aunt Sara had told her about the Russian pogroms. "We will stay at my father's palace in St. Petersburg," he said. "We'll attend a ball at the Winter Palace. We'll drive in open sleighs along the Neva. Everyone will admire my beautiful bride."

During the following weeks, Lilli started several times to write Aunt Sara about her engagement, but she always stopped midway and tore up the letter. She knew her aunt would be upset; she loathed Russian royalty, and she would be shocked that Lilli could close her eyes to the murder of so many Jews, so many Russian peasants and workingmen, with no intervention by Czar Nicholas II. But Mischa was a warm and gentle man. He was not responsible for the horrors permitted by the czar.

Reactions to Lilli's news were mixed. Oliver pleaded with her to wait six months before marrying Mischa. Charles was polite, but Lilli sensed that he didn't approve. Only Frances seemed to see this marriage as a fairy-tale experience.

"We'll be married the middle of next month," Lilli confided over luncheon at the Savoy Grill. "Mischa went this morning to make arrangements for us to sail for New York on the *Mauretania*." For a moment Lilli remembered sailing for New York from Le Havre with Jacques. How young she had been. "I'll ask Aunt Sara to come to London to stay with the children. She can oversee the salon while Oliver goes to Paris to cover for her."

"Let Mademoiselle Martine bring the children to the country house to stay with us," Frances said. "Beth and Robbie will be so pleased."

Lilli smiled. Dear Frances. "That would be lovely."

"And in the autumn, Lilli," Frances said, "do you suppose that you could find a place for me in the salon? With the servants, there's so little for me to do at home."

"Charles won't be upset?"

Frances looked embarrassed. "It took some talking. But now he understands. Remember the shop in Sydney? I loved being there."

"The minute you say you're ready, I'll find a place for you."

"I may be absolutely useless—"

Lilli shook her head. "Nonsense. You'll be fine. Nellie Sutherland, who handles the reception desk, will be leaving in September to be married. She handles all the appointments. That would be a wonderful place for you to start. By the way, did I tell you that the Arden woman is opening a salon in Washington, D.C., which is the capital of the United States? Then there's Eleanor Adair and Lillian Russell." The Gay Nineties musical-comedy star was now in the beauty-culture business. "I'm not interested in companies like Palmolive or Pond's. They're not beauty consultants."

"Lilli, I'm just curious," Frances asked. "Why *are* you going to New York on your honeymoon?"

"To cross the Atlantic twice," Lilli laughed. "Mischa says that only on shipboard will we have real privacy on our honeymoon. During the week in New York, he is taking me to visit friends at a place called Southampton."

"Lilli"—Frances looked uncertain—"you're sure about this marriage? You're not just intrigued by the notion of becoming a real princess?"

"I am intrigued," Lilli said softly. "But that's not why I'm marrying Mischa. He's charming and sweet and solicitous. And I've been so lonely, Frances."

ON JUNE 28 the world was shocked by the assassination of Archduke Francis Ferdinand, heir to the throne of Austria-Hungary, and his wife Sophie, in Sarajevo, the capital of the Austrian province of Bosnia. The leaders of Austria-Hungary were convinced that their tiny neighbor was responsible, and in the evenings that followed, the conversation at many a dinner table in high London circles centered around the possibility of war.

Lilli, however, was caught up in the arrangements for her marriage, which was to be a private affair, including only those closest to them. She discharged the private investigators, who had come up with nothing more than exorbitant bills, telling herself that she didn't care about finding her father anymore. She had Mischa now.

Mischa went to Paris to tell his mother about the marriage. Only now did Lilli realize that there was no love lost between Mischa and his father. But his mother adored her youngest son. Secret meetings were the extent of Mischa's involvement with his family. When he returned, he gave Lilli a pearl-encrusted cameo brooch as a gift from his mother, and the simple gold band that would be her wedding ring.

On a gray mid-July morning—one of London's unexpectedly cold days—Lilli and Mischa were married at a registry office with Oliver and Frances as their witnesses. Elegant and lovely in a gray velvet suit with pearls about her throat, her mass of auburn hair tucked beneath a matching toque, Lilli tried to push aside last-minute doubts. Was it wrong of her to be away from the children for three weeks? Jan understood, but what about Freddie? Both Oliver and Aunt Sara worried that she was rushing too quickly into marriage. She had known

Mischa for only a few weeks. Had he meant it when he insisted he wouldn't object to the business?

Her face softened as she remembered Mischa's instructions that she was to travel without her maid and he without his valet. No one must intrude on their honeymoon. He talked with eloquent distaste about the servant-infested life he had endured in St. Petersburg and at the family's country estate, "even when we were at Monte Carlo for the gambling in winter, in Paris for the racing, the summers taking cures." How strange, Lilli thought, that a little girl from Marienbad should end up marrying a Russian prince.

After the wedding ceremony they hurried to the Savoy Grill for the small luncheon being given them by Eleanora, the duchess of Rochester, who had introduced them. Throughout the meal, Mischa held her hand beneath the table, his eyes telling everyone in the Grill that he adored his wife.

From the Savoy they were driven to Waterloo Station to board the train for Southampton, where the four-funneled *Mauretania* waited to transport its passengers across the Atlantic. Considered by many to be the most luxurious liner ever to cross an ocean, the *Mauretania* featured a staircase paneled in French walnut, with much of the interior decoration done in eighteenth-century French. The Verandah Café was modeled after the Old English Orangery at Hampton Court. The smoking room—the sanctuary of male passengers—was fifteenth-century Italian.

Their suite had all the accoutrements of a miniature house, with two bedrooms, a dining room, a drawing room, and two baths. The furnishings were done in the graceful Louis XV, one of Lilli's favorites.

"You're pleased?" Mischa asked once they had settled themselves.

"Mischa, it's exquisite," she said. "But shouldn't we begin to dress for dinner?"

He smiled. "You're sorry that we're traveling without your maid, aren't you, darling? But I will help you dress." He bowed. "What will you wear, madame?"

"You choose, Mischa," she laughed.

Knowing they were expected at the captain's table in forty minutes, Lilli sent Mischa to change into dinner clothes while she changed into a sea-green crepe dinner dress. Right on schedule Mischa escorted her into the Francois I dining room. Like most of the passengers, Mischa was in a festive mood this first night at sea. But Lilli was haunted by memories of her first journey across the Atlantic aboard the old French liner *La Touraine*.She remembered the walks around the deck, her arm in Jacques's, and of course the nights.

Dinner was a gourmet delight. Lilli was surprised when Mischa, who admitted to a passion for sweets, refused dessert. "A touch of *mal de mer*," he said. "Don't worry, my love."

When they returned to their suite, he seemed slightly wan and uncomfortable. "I'll have the steward bring you tea," she said.

"No darling. I just need a good night's sleep. I'm sure by morning I'll be fine."

Mischa summoned a steward to help him retire for the night. As Lilli changed into one of the beautiful lace-trimmed nightgowns and matching negligees she had bought for the honeymoon, she tried to deny her disappointment. Tonight was her wedding night! The night she should be spending with her new husband.

After she heard the steward leave the suite, Lilli went in to say goodnight to Mischa. As her lips brushed his, he pulled her toward him and for a moment Lilli thought he *would* take her into his bed.

But . . . "Darling, if I sleep late tomorrow, don't be concerned," he said, releasing her.

Even though she was exhausted from the long day, Lilli lay awake until close to dawn. It was strange to be lying alone on her wedding night. In their brief few weeks together, she and Mischa had exchanged no more than brief kisses. Of course he had sensed that she was not one of those women who hopped from bed to bed. But this she had not expected. Couldn't he guess how she yearned to spend the night in her husband's arms?

Though she didn't feel refreshed when she awoke at nine o'clock, she did feel a pleasant sense of freedom: There was no need to rush to the salon; no frenzied scheduling of social engagements that in truth were business; no phone calls.

She lingered briefly in a perfumed tub before getting dressed. The door to Mischa's bedroom was closed. Quietly, she opened it. He was still asleep. She closed the door again and left their suite. After a hearty breakfast of fried eggs, bacon, and warm biscuits, she took a brisk stroll around the deck, noting with pleasure how few passengers were up and about at this hour of the morning. When she returned to the suite, Mischa was still in bed, a breakfast tray in his lap.

"How are you this morning?" She kissed him lightly on the cheek.

"I'm afraid this is going to be one of my bad trips, Lilli," he said. "I was hoping otherwise."

"Perhaps you should go up on deck," she said. "The sea air is delicious."

Mischa shuddered. "Oh, I don't *dare* stir from the bed. That would be disastrous. But don't worry about me, my darling." He gazed approvingly at her dainty summer frock. "I want everyone to see my beautiful bride."

Though Mischa's absence disturbed her, Lilli enjoyed life aboard ship. For the first time since she had opened the shop in Sydney, she felt carefree. She actually enjoyed being away from business. And everyone on board—the captain, her shipmates—was appropriately sympathetic to their temporary "widow."

Lilli avoided the spectacular glass-enclosed deck, preferring brisk jaunts on the open deck with the wind in her face. But after the second night she realized that everyone on board knew this was her honeymoon and, self-conscious at being seen alone, she retreated to the privacy of their suite.

The occasional sight of children traveling with their parents filled her with homesickness. Was Freddie crying at night because she wasn't there to tell him a story and kiss him goodnight? Did Jan feel that mama had deserted them?

MISCHA HAD MADE reservations for them at the Plaza Hotel. Lilli was enthralled with the majestic beauty of this new hotel and was further impressed by their suite, which was filled with American Beauty roses, compliments of their hostess in Southampton, Long Island.

"You'll like Katherine," Mischa said. "She's had a suite at the Southampton house redecorated just for us. And she must have driven in to welcome us personally—I'd expected her to send a car."

That night they dined with Katherine Haverstraw in the hotel's grand downstairs dining room. Over veal in a rich cream sauce, she confided that she was staying at Southampton because her husband insisted she stop dashing off to London and Paris twice a year.

"Mischa," she said, "do you see much of Consuelo?" She turned to Lilli. "She was Consuelo Vanderbilt before she became the duchess of Marlborough. Of course, she and the Duke had been legally separated for about eight years." Without waiting for a reply from Mischa, she plunged ahead. "Do you ever see dear Edith Wharton in Paris? I just adored her book—you know, the one that came out last year, *The Customs of the Country*. Now that she's divorced that crazy husband of hers, do you suppose she'll marry Walter Berry?"

"I don't know Madame Wharton," Mischa said. "I see Consuelo at an occasional affair in London. A beautiful woman." He smiled at Lilli. "But not as beautiful as my wife."

It was clear that Katherine Haverstraw was enthralled at the prospect of entertaining royalty. Lilli listened, fascinated and surprised, as her hostess told them that tomorrow morning they would be driven to Southampton, where a series of parties had been planned in their honor. Lilli wondered when she would have time to visit the salons of Elizabeth Arden, Eleanor Adair, and Lillian Russell.

She couldn't wait for dinner to be over. But while Mischa held her hand under the table, Katherine babbled on, seemingly oblivious to her companions.

At last they finished their coffee—and Katherine her last story—and she and Mischa returned to their suite. Just inside their drawing room, he pulled her into his arms.

"I'll change quickly," she whispered. "I thought we'd never leave that dining room!"

Trembling, she stood before the mirror. Auburn hair cascaded lushly about her shoulders. A becoming touch of color edged her high cheekbones. The ecru nightgown, cut at the neckline with insets of Valenciennes lace at her breast, outlined her slim, shapely figure.

Quietly, she slipped into Mischa's bedroom and paused in the open doorway. Disappointment and surprise shook her: Mischa lay on his back snoring lightly. After a moment, she turned and walked into her bedroom.

She awoke the following morning to Mischa's voice, obviously speaking to someone on the telephone. She listened. Katherine. She left the bed, pulled on a negligee, and walked into the drawing room.

Mischa looked up, put his hand over the phone. "Lilli, Katherine will pick us up with the car after breakfast. Another car will bring our trunks." He returned to the phone. "Katherine, what time will the car be here?"

Lilli looked for signs that Mischa was upset that he had fallen asleep the night before, and found none. Perhaps he couldn't relax here, she thought. She dressed quickly while Mischa ordered breakfast brought up to their suite.

WHEN LILLI AWOKE alone in her bedroom the following morning at Southampton, she knew something was wrong with her marriage. Why had she and Mischa not yet shared a bed? Was something wrong with her?

Their brief visit to Southampton sped past in a whirl of constant parties. Prince and Princess Lamsaloff were the guests of honor, with Mischa appearing as the adoring husband. And each night he retired to his own bedroom.

On the drive back to New York, Lilli was silent, interrupting Mischa's and Katherine's lively chatter only to say that before they boarded the *Kronprinzessin Cecilie* she would like to stop off at the Arden Salon D'Oro, Elizabeth Arden's new salon at 509 Fifth Avenue.

"Of course, darling," Mischa said. "We'll wait for you in the car."

Though she was excited about their new adventure aboard the elegant *Kronprinzessin Cecilie*, which was to take them and a thousand other passengers to Plymouth, Lilli's enthusiasm was dampened by the knowledge that she and Mischa would undoubtedly continue to occupy separate bedrooms. She was more than ready to be home, especially to see the children. But despite her best efforts not to dwell on the strange development in her marriage, she couldn't stop mulling over her suspicions. *Why* had he married her? To have a wife to hide behind? She felt humiliated.

On the return voyage, Mischa made no pretense of *mal de mer*. He seemed relieved, as though he felt that he had communicated their marital status to her without an ugly scene. He spent almost all his time socializing, and Lilli took refuge in Edith Wharton's most recent novel.

On the night of July 31, with the journey halfway over, Lilli and Mischa waltzed in the grand saloon, its walls adorned with paintings depicting the exquisite gardens of several Renaissance palaces and the Vatican gardens. Suddenly the "Skater's Waltz" stopped. The captain, standing pale and grave beside the orchestra, asked a dozen of the most socially prominent men on board to join him immediately in the *Rauchzimmer*—the smoking lounge.

"Mischa, what do you suppose it is?" Lilli asked anxiously as he prepared to join the captain.

"Nothing to worry about, love," he said lightly, his eyes betraying his concern.

Lilli and several other ladies were invited to join the wife of an American senator in the drawing room of their suite, where they would sit down to Viennese coffee until the gentlemen were free to join them.

"I *know* we've reversed our course!" the agitated wife of an American executive heading abroad on a financial mission said. "Only a few mintues ago the moon was shining down on the starboard. Now look at it!"

"We'll learn what it's all about shortly." Lilli tried to sound casual. "Perhaps there's some ship in trouble nearby and we're going to its aid."

"Ever since the *Titanic* I've never been really comfortable aboard ship," the wife of a Scottish industrialist said.

"Darling, we don't have to worry about hitting an iceberg in July," another wife said. "The princess is probably right— some ship is in danger and we're rushing to her aid."

Soon the ladies were joined by their husbands. Mischa came to Lilli's side and reached for her hand.

"We're in no danger," the senator said. "But the captain has received word on the wireless that war is about to be declared between the Central and the Allied Powers." A gasp filled the room. Lilli went cold with fear. "As you know, this is a German vessel. The captian has been ordered to take the ship to the nearest safe port before it can be captured by the British navy."

"The captain has assured us we have plenty of fuel and food to bring us safely into port," the American industrialist added.

"It appears to me," said an American multimillionaire— obviously eager for his shooting party to reach Scotland for the grouse—"that we have enough funds among those of us here in this drawing room to buy the ship. Let's go to Captain Polack and ask him to switch the German flag for the American flag. As an American ship, we'll have nothing to worry about— we can proceed directly to Plymouth."

Suddenly everyone was talking at once. It was decided that they would offer to pay $5 million in cash for the ship and provide a substantial bonus for Captain Polack himself. Each of the men—except for Mischa—pledged a huge sum.

Lilli, staring at the silent Mischa in embarrassment, finally spoke up. "Take my jewels. Perhaps they could be the captain's bonus." As she reached for her diamond and emerald earrings and the matching necklace about her throat, she caught Mischa's glare of reproach.

While three of the American gentleman present rushed off to consult with other wealthy fellow countrymen, the others quietly discussed the situation. Apparently the ship carried about $11 million, all of it American money, in gold and silver bullion. Certainly a prize the British navy would appreciate, especially when carried by a German vessel—the enemy.

Lilli was upset by this turn of events for reasons beyond her own safety: She wondered when she would get home to her children and her business.

Within the hour the committee returned with the news: The captain had refused their offer and had ordered resumption of efforts to have the ship's name blacked out. Black bands were painted around the tops of her four yellow funnels in order to make the *Cecilie* look like the English *Olympic*.

The *Kronprinzessin Cecilie* sped through the fog despite pleas from all to proceed more slowly. The captain's orders were to move with all possible haste. The foghorn blared as the ship headed west, but the portholes were covered with canvas lest a glint of light reveal their exact position. The atmosphere on board ship was tense and fearful.

Three nights later the ship approached Bar Harbor, Maine. Frenchman Bay, where the ship was to anchor, was unknown territory to Captain Polack. Bar Harborite yachtsman C. Ledyard Blair stayed by the captain's side as they brought the *Cecilie* into the bay and shut off her engines. At last the ship was in safe waters—among the yachts and sailboats of Maine's summer residents.

Bar Harbor was at the height of its season, its streets were crowded with those who had awakened to discover the huge *Kronprinzessin Cecilie* riding at anchor in the bay. The captain, his officers, and crew were gaily welcomed by natives and resort people alike. As visiting royalty, Lilli and Mischa were quickly snatched up by a Bar Harbor matriarch Lilli had met in London; she insisted they stay at her villa until they could make plans to sail for England on another ship.

Lilli couldn't wait to return to London. Plagued by guilt at being away from the children and the salon for so long, she had sent cables to Sara and Oliver with word that she and Mischa were safe and back in America. But for how long?

Then a new thought occurred to her: Why not open a branch of Princess Lilli in New York City? Some of her clients at the Paris and London salons were wealthy American women. They would help launch a New York salon. Then Princess Lilli would truly be international.

Before she and Mischa left for New York to board the venerable *City of Paris*, which was a neutral ship and therefore safe from attack by either the Central or Allied Powers, Lilli had made her decision: She would bring Princess Lilli to the United States. It was a challenge she couldn't resist, especially since Jan and Freddie were American citizens. In America they would be safe from the ugly war in Europe. Austria-Hungary had declared war on Serbia; Germany had declared war on Russia and on France. While the passengers of the *Kronprinzessin Cecilie* were being entertained in Bar Harbor, Germany had invaded Belgium, and Great Britain had declared war on Germany.

She said nothing of her plans to Mischa. They left Bar Harbor for New York, lingered only overnight—again at the Plaza. They made a great show of being the devoted couple whenever they were in public. No one guessed that the honeymoon couple slept in separate rooms.

DESPITE THE American *City of Paris*'s supposed safety from attack, she sailed with her lights out each night lest enemy warships mistake her for a British or French liner.

Home at last, Lilli was touched to discover that her aunt had rushed to London to be with Jan and Freddie when the cable about their delayed return had arrived. Now Lilli was anxious about Sara returning to Paris. Travel between London and Paris was prohibited except for military reasons. It required considerable effort on the part of Lilli's influential friends to arrange this.

Back in Paris, Sara wrote that most Parisians were certain there would be an Allied victory by Christmas. The English newspapers were less optimistic: They predicted the Germans would soon be within twelve hours of Paris.

Lilli said nothing to Aunt Sara about her marriage. With Oliver she was candid.

"I was afraid of something like that," Oliver said.

Lilli stared at him in amazement. "Then why didn't you tell me? Why didn't you stop me?"

"You wouldn't have believed me, Lilli. And I wasn't sure. Mischa is most discreet. I just had a strange feeling that Mischa might marry you but he'd never be your husband."

"That young American girl who killed herself…" Lilli took a deep breath. "Do you think she did it because she found out about Mischa?"

"According to the gossip, she committed suicide—she took an overdose of opium—because her father was threatening to disinherit her if she married Mischa. But she must have suspected that Mischa would not want to marry her without all that money." His eyes met hers. A quiet challenge. "What are you going to do, Lilli?"

"I'm going to the house and tell Mischa I'm divorcing him," Lilli said softly. "I want him out of my life."

She would be a twice-divorced woman, Lilli taunted herself. How had she made such bad choices in men? Never again. There would be no more men in her life. She had the children and the business. That would be enough.

15

MISCHA SAT BACK in a Louis XV chair upholstered in smoky blue velvet, the predominant color in the private drawing room of the London house, and sipped champagne while Lilli told him in a quiet, strained voice that she planned to divorce him.

He looked mildly annoyed. "Lilli, come now—don't be hasty. We have so much to offer each other. I've made you a princess. Our marriage lends cachet to your business."

She drew herself up proudly. "My business was a success before our marriage, Mischa. I don't need your name."

"Ah, foolish girl." He smiled. "As Princess Lamsaloff you will be accepted in places closed to Lilli Laval." Lilli blushed. So Mischa knew, despite her attempts to hide it, that she resented not being accepted by the old families of the Faubourg St.-Germain, by the inner circles of the British aristocracy. "As my companion you sat in the Royal Enclosure beside the Prince and Princess of Wales. You'll visit the palace in Saint Petersburg as my wife. You'll—"

"Mischa, no," she said. "Don't you understand? I can't live a constant lie. I've never been your wife. I never will be. I'm divorcing you."

He shrugged. "I'd hoped we could have a pleasant arrangement. You're young, beautiful, charming. I enjoyed being seen with you. But if you wish a divorce, then so be it."

"I'll talk with my attorneys in the morning," she said quietly. "I'd like you to move out of the house as soon as possible."

"Please understand, Lilli," he said, as though they were discussing the weather, "that I will expect a substantial settlement. After all, you're a rich woman."

She stared at him. "Mischa, you're out of your mind."

"No," he said, "just practical. By marrying me you've become Princess Lamsaloff. I won't object to your using the title even after we're divorced. I have no funds except what my mother manages to provide. My father disinherited me when he discovered me in a haystack with a stableboy. I was seventeen. So you see, my dear Lilli, I must provide for myself."

"Not at my expense!" Lilli flared. "I'll give you nothing."

"I'm sure your attorney will agree that you can manage a settlement of, say, half a million pounds."

"Not one pence," Lilli said tersely. "And you won't fight the divorce, Mischa." She fought to keep her voice even. "Because if you do, all of Europe will know that Prince Michael Lamsaloff prefers men to his wife."

"You wouldn't dare," Mischa said. "You can't take a chance on that kind of scandal."

"I will dare. Either you agree not to contest the divorce or tomorrow's newspapers will carry a full story of our unconsummated marriage." She wasn't sure she could go through with her threat—but then neither was he.

"You are a greedy little bitch," he hissed. "We will tell our friends that you refused to abandon your business to be my wife, and so we've agreed to a divorce."

"I'll accept that explanation," Lilli said. "But I want you out of this house within a week."

Mischa met with Lilli's attorneys. The divorce would go through quietly and with no exchange of funds. Lilli returned the cameo given to her by Mischa's mother, along with Mischa's wedding band. She knew Mischa would portray the "failure" of the marriage charmingly, probably intimating that she had been a cold, unfeeling bride. She doubted that it would be long before she was replaced.

With all the arrangements in the hands of her attorneys, Lilli began to plan for the opening of a New York salon. The German government was letting one ship per week travel between England and the United States without being open to attack; she would be able to make the trip between New York and London regularly.

Despite the optimism of the French, Lilli was nervous about Sara's presence in Paris. Neither Lilli nor Sara could pretend any loyalty toward Germany.

Sara vowed she would close the salon only if the German Army marched into Paris. Like most Londoners, Lilli was aware that from August 9 through August 22 the Royal Navy was transporting a British expeditionary force of 80,000 men, 30,000 horses, 315 field guns, and 125 machine guns across the Channel to France.

Sara wrote that Americans were frantic to leave Paris, though a few American college boys were joining up to serve as ambulance drivers. Frenchmen between the ages eighteen and forty-five were being mobilized for military service. In shop windows all over Paris, there were signs saying they had been closed *pour cause de mobilisation*. The Hotel Bristol was being turned into a hospital. And business—at Princess Lilli, the salons of the couturiers, the fine jewelry shops, the furriers—had dropped to almost nothing. Sara confessed, too, that there were those who held her in contempt because she bore a German name.

In London, also, wealthy Americans were rushing to sail for home. Englishmen of fighting age were being called to military service. England was ignited by anti-German feelings. No orchestra dared play Wagner—or any German composer. Dachshunds were scorned in London parks. Lilli knew to keep silent about her Berlin-born maternal grandparents—for even those who had lived in England for three or four generations were subject to insults if they bore German names.

Lilli was upset when Oliver suggested that he might have to leave Princess Lilli for the duration of the war. At Oliver's insistence, Frances was being taught every aspect of the business so she would be ready to step in for him. Lilli, expecting the worst, prepared to abandon all thoughts of a New York salon. One evening, while being driven home from dinner with Frances and Charles, Oliver tried to convince Lilli otherwise.

"Lilli, now more than ever, is the time for you to open a salon in New York. If the Germans move any closer to Paris, Sara will have to close the salon. And who's to say what will happen in London?"

The thought terrified her. "Oliver, the Germans are not going to attack London!"

He shook his head. "We don't know that, Lilli. That's why the New York salon is so important. Besides"—he smiled— "I'll feel better when you and the children are safe in New York."

Late in December, Lilli sailed from Southampton for New York with the children, Mlle. Martine, and Celestine on an American vessel, whose flag guaranteed them safe passage. Oliver had been largely responsible for their departure; though most Londoners felt that the city was safe, he was disturbed by rumors that the zeppelins, which had been carrying passengers and mail between several German cities for four years, might be used to launch attacks on British cities. From gossip, Lilli knew that Jacques and Addie were in America. *Didn't Jacques worry about the children, knowing what was happening across the Atlantic?*

Lilli planned the opening of her New York salon with her usual meticulous attention to detail. She carried with her a list of addresses and phone numbers of American ladies who were clients of the London and Paris salons. As soon as she arrived, she would telephone Elaine Harris. Elaine, the beautiful and always exquisitely dressed mother of two sons, both now in prestigious American colleges, enjoyed being the trendsetter in their ultrawealthy social circle. Lilli knew Elaine would come to Princess Lilli, New York, and the others would follow.

Upon arrival, Lilli settled her entourage in a huge suite at the Plaza. The next morning she set out to visit fashionable Bonwit Teller at the corner of Fifth Avenue and Thirty-eighth Street in search of the Elizabeth Arden line of cosmetics. Her spies had all agreed that Elizabeth Arden would be Lilli's stiffest competitor in New York. She had studied the Arden ads in *Vogue*, and began to understand that this was an era of the New Women: women who earned money and would be willing to spend it on products that would make them beautiful.

On her second day in New York, she had lunch with Elaine Harris at the Waldorf's Palm Garden. While they sipped their green-turtle soup, Elaine pointed out the city's prominent socialites—Lilli's prospective clients.

"See the man at the table directly across the room?" Elaine whispered. "That's Condé Nast."

"The man who runs *Vogue*?"

Elaine laughed. "Lilli darling, Condé Nast *is Vogue*."

"I must meet him," Lilli said.

"You will," Elaine said. "I'll plan a dinner party. Oh, and I must tell you that Mrs. Edward Titus—that's Helena Rubinstein to the rest of the world—is expected in town early next month."

Lilli stared at Elaine in shock. *More competition?* "I hadn't heard anything about her leaving Paris, Elaine. But she has two sons, I believe. And I gather her husband is an American." As she herself had once been married to an American. Sometimes it still seemed inconceivable that Jacques was no longer a part of her life. "No doubt Madame Rubinstein decided New York would be safer for her children than Paris."

"Condé tells me she'll be opening a salon here," Elaine said.

"You know, Elaine," Lilli said with pride—and just a touch of bravado—"I plan to open salons in every major city in the nation."

But in truth, Lilli didn't feel as confident as she seemed. Here she would be competing not only with Mme. Rubinstein but with Elizabeth Arden, not to mention Eleanor Adair—also on Fifth Avenue—and Lillian Russell and Elizabeth Hubbard. And she would not have Oliver at her side.

Determined to find a comfortable town house for herself and the children and the staff, Lilli spent most of her first two weeks in New York with real-estate brokers. Jan had a tutor, but Lilli was impatient to enroll her in a proper school, and Freddie was ready for kindergarten.

After a long night of indecision, Lilli called the real-estate broker to say she would sign a lease on the five-story town house on Gramercy Park, rather than the fourteen-room apartment in the east sixties. The deciding factor was the private little park surrounded by an eight-foot iron fence nearby. They would move in on April 1. Until then, they would stay in their suite at the Plaza.

She hoped to hold an extravagant opening for Princess Lilli, New York, in early June. Her next job, therefore, was to find proper quarters for the salon. Elaine insisted on Fifth Avenue. "In Paris it's the rue Saint-Honoré, Lilli. In London it's Mayfair. In New York it's Fifth Avenue. And fashionable stores are opening uptown. Bergdorf Goodman moved last year to an elegant new store all the way up on Fifth Avenue, opposite Saint Patrick's Cathedral."

Lilli chose a site midway between Elizabeth Arden's salon and the Bergdorf Goodman establishment. But later that day she heard the shattering news that Oliver had been called to military service. How would she manage without him?

Oliver wrote that the casualty lists in the London newspapers occupied columns, that the *Illustrated London News* carried pages of photographs of young British officers who had died on the field of battle. But despite the war, American businessmen were installed at Claridge's. "At a dinner party last night I heard our hostess remark that the Americans were perfectly happy about the war because they were sure to grow even richer from it. I left the party early."

Lilli worried about his safety—and about Charles, too, who had already been called into the naval reserve. Frances wrote that she was grateful for the distractions of Princess Lilli.

Ignoring Elaine's suggestion that she hire Elsie de Wolfe as her decorator, Lilli stubbornly set out to design both salon and house just as though Oliver were at her side.

As she focused on the endless details of opening up the business, it was becoming alarmingly clear to Lilli that it would be prohibitively expensive to import the materials necessary for Princess Lilli cosmetics; setting up a small factory here in New York was the only alternative. After a few days of investigating and bargaining, Lilli leased space on Ninth Avenue to serve as factory and warehouse and began hiring contractors, carpenters, painters for both the salon and the Ninth Avenue premises. Later she would begin hiring and training a staff.

Again, Charles, home on a forty-eight-hour leave, came to her aid: He had Frances send Lilli the name of a pharmaceutical firm in New York that might be able to manufacture her products.

Lilli immediately made an appointment to talk with a Mr. Evans, of Evans, Davis & Phillips. While Mr. Evans was charming and obviously impressed by Lilli's success, he pointed out that Evans, Davis & Phillips was heavily involved in filling government contracts. The United States was preparing for the day the nation might be called upon to fight.

"I'm sorry not to be able to help," he said. "But I'd like you to talk with Alex Kahn, a very able young man in our advertising department. He may be able to advise you as to other firms less involved with government contracts than ourselves." Already he was reaching for the phone. "Alex," he said briskly, "I'm sending a young lady to you. See if you can help her locate a firm that can supply her with what she needs. I explained to her that our production is all tied up."

Lilli was escorted by Mr. Evans's secretary to an office in the firm's advertising department. Mr. Kahn—slim, dark-haired, handsome—was on the phone, apparently having difficulty getting off.

"Grandma, I'll call you tonight. I'm busy as the devil right now." He smiled at Evans's secretary and waved her on. "I'll be home for dinner Friday night. I promise. How can I go for a whole week without seeing you?''

As she sat across from Alex Kahn, Lilli found herself wishing that Jan and Freddie had been blessed with grandparents. At least they had Aunt Sara.

"I'm sorry." His smile was warm. "Mr. Evans told me about your problem. This is a booming period for the chemical industry. Ironic, isn't it, that here we are enjoying the fruits of the war—"

"I'm afraid it's bad in Europe," Lilli said. "I've just arrived from London and I plan to open a salon here. I'm Lilli Laval."

"Of Princess Lilli cosmetics?" He looked astonished.

"Why, yes."

"My mother bought your creams in London. She raved about them so much that I brought them in to Evans, Davis and Phillips to have our chemists analyze them." Now it was Lilli's turn to be astonished. "I'd hoped to persuade the firm to move into the cosmetic field. But don't worry"—he laughed—"your secrets are safe. I'm afraid Evans, Davis and Phillips are too conservative to understand your business's potential. They didn't want to hear about it." He gazed at her with a disconcerting intensity. "You're missing out on a tremendous advertising angle. Miss Laval—if I may be so bold. If I were your advertising manager, I'd insist that your portrait be painted by someone very important, and that a reproduction appear on every jar of cream, on all the packaging of your products. And every ad you place in *Vogue* and *Harper's Bazaar* should carry an oval inset of your portrait."

"Mr. Kahn . . ." Lilli hesitated, her mind racing. Alex Kahn could prove invaluable to her business. "I'm just beginning to assemble a staff for my New York salon. Is there any way I can entice you away from Evans, Davis and Phillips? I'd love to have you as the new advertising manager of Princess Lilli."

"Why don't we have dinner tonight and talk about it?" he said slowly. "May I call for you at seven o'clock?"

"Eight would be better," Lilli said. "I try to spend some time with my children every night before they go to bed." That was to let Alex Kahn know she had a family. She'd noticed his covert glance at her left hand.

"Eight o'clock. I look forward to it, Miss Laval."

PROMPTLY AT EIGHT O'CLOCK, Alex Kahn arrived at her suite at the Plaza. Lilli approved of his punctuality; promptness was one of her obsessions. She wore her favorite, a yellow velvet dinner dress by Poiret. Beside her on the drawing-room sofa lay her mink coat from Revillon in Paris.

Alex was friendly but impersonal as he escorted her from the hotel to his Daimler. She wondered briefly how a young advertising director could afford such an expensive automobile. That probably meant he would expect a more generous salary than she had planned.

"The Daimler was a thirtieth birthday gift from my grandmother," he said as he helped her into the car. How had he read her mind? "I'm afraid she spoils me dreadfully. She says it's her privilege."

"Grandmothers should be coddled," she said.

On the ride to the restaurant, Alex talked about his experiences at Evans, Davis & Phillips, where he often came into conflict with the top management. "Grandma says I'm a throwback to my grandfather. His family brought him to America from Bavaria when he was three. His parents settled in Charleston, South Carolina, where my great-grandfather became a peddler." He chuckled at her quizzical smile. "My grandfather was a Confederate spy during the Civil War."

"You're not thinking about following suit?" Lilli said.

"No, I think any war is an abomination. My older brother—he was eighteen—died in the Spanish-American War. I was thirteen then. I grew up watching my parents' grief at his loss. For a dozen years on his birthday my mother never left her room."

"I worry about my friends in England," Lilli said. "And my aunt—and friends—in France." Jacques was safe—he was an American citizen.

Lilli was surprised that Alex could afford so expensive a restaurant as Delmonico's. Not until they were halfway through dinner did Lilli realize that his father was the head of one of the nation's largest mail-order companies.

"My parents were furious when I refused to go into the family business after college," he said. "I'm the only son. They've had to draft my two brothers-in-law into the business. But I'd be bored to death working in the mail-order line."

"And you wouldn't be bored working in the cosmetic field?" Now was the time to pin him down.

"No." The conviction in his voice surprised her. "It's new and challenging. And I have a million ideas about how to sell the products."

"Will you sell them for Princess Lilli?" She deliberated for a moment. "Whatever you're paid at Evans, Davis and Phillips I'm prepared to double."

He laughed. "You're a reckless lady."

"I want you selling for us. How soon can you start?"

He looked at her for a long moment. "I'll give them a month's notice. But we can begin our association in the evenings. We can accomplish a lot over dinner every night."

"Then you'll go on salary immediately. Half-salary, that is, until you're with us full-time." She lifted her glass. "Now, who would you suggest to do my portrait?"

16

EVERY EVENING, after she had spent hours interviewing prospective staff members and checking up on construction progress at the salon site and the new factory, Lilli met with Alex in her Plaza suite, where, over dinner, they planned the advertising campaign that would be launched with a lavish two-page spread in the May issue of *Vogue*. Alex convinced her that it was crucial for them to spend money on their ads. True to her promise, Elaine Harris gave a dinner party where Lilli could meet Condé Nast. Though *Vogue*'s schedule was tight, Nast agreed to fit the Princess Lilli ad into the issue, and Alex persuaded one of the editors to promise that Lilli would be mentioned in the editorial pages.

By the end of the month, Alex was officially on staff at Princess Lilli. He astonished her with his grasp of the business. He ferreted out sources that would supply them with the necessary ingredients for manufacture and took over hiring the staff for the small factory on Ninth Avenue. Lilli threw herself into training operators for the salon.

Rumor had it that Helena Rubinstein was moving ahead with a New York salon. According to a *Vogue* staff member, an ad had already been placed for the Maison de Beauté Valaze. The news unnerved Lilli. She had been prepared to face the formidable competition of Elizabeth Arden. But could Princess Lilli stand up to Helena Rubinstein as well?

Alex learned from his *Vogue* source that Mme. Rubinstein had rented quarters on East Forty-ninth Street, just off Fifth Avenue. "Arden's heard the word, too," he told Lilli one night over dinner. "I gather she's looking for larger quarters farther

up the avenue. You've got to plan the decor very carefully,
Lilli." For the thousandth time, Lilli wished that Oliver—and
Sebastien, now with the French Army—were here to advise her.
"Rubinstein will use dramatic colors and spend a fortune on
paintings to hang on the walls, and Arden will go for white and
gold and pink—the delicately elegant look. And you, Lilli . . ."
He paused, thinking. "You'll be the beautiful young princess
transforming her salon into a replica of the family castle."

"I was a princess for a few weeks," she said dryly. "It was a
bad marriage." It constantly astonished Lilli that she was so
candid with Alex. Was he a homosexual, like Oliver? No, that
was impossible. She could be candid with Alex because he was
kind and honest and she trusted him.

"You were a princess before your marriage to Mischa Lamsaloff," he said gently. "You were born a princess in your salon on the rue Saint-Honoré." Alex's respect for her
accomplishments always touched her.

Early in April, Lilli and the children moved into the Gramercy Park house. Sunlight poured into the rooms. Already the
trees in the park were showing their tight green buds, promises
of a summer splendor. If only her private life held the same
promise. As she gazed out the rear window onto the small garden behind the house, Lilli vowed that somehow Princess Lilli
would rise above the competition. This was a wonderful city.
A wonderful country. She was awed by its physical expanse. So
many cities strewn across the nation! Each the site for a potential Princess Lilli salon. But she had to be careful: She was
spending with a lavishness that could prove disastrous if New
York women did not begin flocking to Princess Lilli, New
York. Soon.

Lilli walked through each of the town house's seventeen
rooms. Yesterday the furniture had been delivered and set in
place. At this moment Freddie was in the park with Martine;
Jan was at her select private school. The servants, except for
Celestine—hanging away clothes in the master bedroom suite—
were busy helping to set up the kitchen to Bertha's liking. Lilli
savored these rare moments alone.

She had explored every antique shop in the city for the Louis XV furniture that now surrounded her. Several pieces—feminine, graceful sofas, chairs, tables, and cabinets—had been sent over by Oliver. This time she had chosen muted earth tones instead of yellow and gray for all the rooms except the bedrooms. Her bedroom was a rich mauve; Jan's a dainty pink and white, with pale carpeting. Jan had been allowed to choose her frilly white canopied bed.

On this, their first evening in their new home, Alex had been invited to dinner. Over coffee, before Martine took the children upstairs to bed, Alex promised to take Jan and Freddie to the Central Park Zoo as soon as it opened for the season. Already he had become "Uncle Alex" to the children. And he was proving himself a superb escort for Lilli whenever she chose to socialize.

Along with most of the staff, Lilli and Alex were working fourteen hours a day in preparation for the opening of the salon. So far, their efforts were being rewarded. Even the treatment rooms—each equipped with a dressing table, above which hung a mirror with carved and gilded frame, and a Louis XV armchair, its frame carved and gilded and upholstered in Beauvais tapestry—wore an air of Old World elegance. Lilli trained the treatment girls. She spent money on last-minute additions with an abandon that brought a quiet reproach even from Alex.

"Lilli, every vase in the reception area doesn't have to be a Ming," he clucked. "Suppose it's a reproduction? Who'll know?"

"I'll know," Lilli said. "Everything must be authentic."

"For Princess Lilli?" he teased.

"For a few weeks I *was* a princess," she reminded him again, chuckling. *Who* was she? If her father had acknowledged her, would she have been Lady Lilli, Countess Lilli—or perhaps even Princess Lilli?

"We're all set for the opening," Alex said, grinning in satisfaction. "The orchestra, the flowers, the caterer. I feel as though I were about to launch a debutante. But that would have been less expensive.''

''I hope people show up,'' Lilli said with rare pessimism. All of Elaine's friends would be there, she surmised. All the women who knew her from London and Paris. But to be a success, Princess Lilli would need a thousand clients on its books.

''They'll come out of curiosity. You know how Americans feel about royal titles. Princess Lilli, the salon owner, and Princess Lilli, the former wife of Prince Michael Lamsaloff, have merged. You're a royal princess forever in their minds— and that's money in the bank.'' He smiled. ''They'll come to see how a princess furnishes her salon. How she dresses. If she's really as beautiful as people say. They'll come for the free food and champagne. They'll come because everybody knows there'll be a spread in *Vogue*—and maybe they will be included. And if it looks as though the guest list is too small,'' he said with mock seriousness, ''then I'll send an SOS to my sisters and their husbands, their children, all our cousins—and my grandmother.''

''Why didn't you invite them?'' Lilli chided.

''I'm the rebel,'' Alex reminded. ''Nobody except grandma approves of my being here.'' His eyes rested on her with that intensity she sometimes found disturbing. Alex was a cherished business associate and friend, but she knew that some of their acquaintances were convinced he was her lover.

Alex knew that she would never marry again. He understood that she meant to devote her life to Jan and Freddie and the business. She was convinced he wasn't homosexual, but it was clear he kept his life uncluttered by women. Like her, Lilli told herself, Alex was fascinated by the future of the cosmetic industry, and this dominated his every waking moment.

''Do you think *Vogue* will admire the salon?'' In more confident moments she adored the delicate grays and yellows of the three Princess Lilli salons, the graceful Louis XV antiques, the exotic woods. Alex had said the salon must be distinctly different from those of Arden and Rubinstein. It must bear her imprint.

"They'll love it," he soothed. "Lilli, you know what my grandmother would say about you? She'd say *'Sie ehrgehrt sich.'*"

Lilli stared at him, puzzled. "German is my native language," she apologized, "but I don't understand what you said. Is it some special dialect?"

"Lilli!" His eyes lit with laughter. "I was speaking Yiddish. Mangling it, grandma would say."

"Where did you learn Yiddish?" Lilli stared blankly at him.

"I must confess," he said, "I know very little. My parents never speak it. My grandmother is fluent in Yiddish—like most European Jews. But here in America, German Jews like my parents think it's disgraceful to speak Yiddish."

"Alex, you're Jewish?"

"Lilli," he said, "with a name like Kahn, did you think I was Irish?"

"I—I never thought about it." She blushed. "If I did, I suppose I thought of it as a German name."

"Does it bother you?" Alex asked quietly.

"Why should it? I'm Jewish."

Slowly her voice filled with emotion. She talked about being raised covertly as a Jew, about her grandparents, who had been born in Berlin and died in an anti-Jewish riot in Bratislava, thirty-five miles from Vienna. He knew already that she was born in Bohemia and under what conditions.

Unexpectedly Alex chuckled. "I believe Jan and Freddie are the one-quarter Jew that might be acceptable in quarters that reject a one-hundred-percent Jew."

"They're being raised Jewish," Lilli said with pride. "In America they are free to be whatever they want."

ON THE OPENING NIGHT of Princess Lilli, Lilli received her guests, with Alex at her side, in the spectacular marble foyer that sparkled with jewels and Waterford crystal chandeliers.

"Mama, why can't we stay longer?" Jan turned her most winning gaze on Alex after being told by a stern Martine that it was time to go home.

"Because mademoiselle says you must go home and go to bed." Lilli took Jan's small face between her hands, kissed her, and then turned to Freddie. "My beautiful babies—"

"I'm not a baby," Jan said. "I'll be ten in November."

"Ten is a very special birthday." Alex dropped a kiss on her forehead. "May I take you out to dinner on your tenth birthday? At the Plaza?"

Jan's face was incandescent. "Mama, may he? You can't say no to Uncle Alex!"

"He may," Lilli said solemnly. "Now scoot because mademoiselle is angry with me."

Alex had been right—nearly all of those invited showed. Lilli wished Oliver could be here with them.

After the last guests had departed, Lilli and Alex sat in her private consultation room while the caterer's staff cleaned up. Over Viennese coffee, they talked about the future of the business, both too exhilarated to feel tired.

"Lilli, it's not the salon that will bring in the most money," Alex said. "It'll be the fine department stores to whom we sell Princess Lilli products—only the elite stores. Let Pond's and Palmolive sell to the drugstores and Woolworth's."

"In Paris I shipped my creams to shops throughout France," Lilli said. "That's why I was able to open the London salon. But in England I hadn't expanded to this point when I left."

"Lilli, we'll do it in America," Alex said excitedly. "We have a tough fight ahead, but we'll be there right beside Arden and Rubinstein. As soon as we can afford it, we'll open another salon. That's important, even before we go into selling to department stores. The salons lay the groundwork for the retail trade." He looked thoughtful. "Lilli, you've spent so much on this one. Are you sure—"

"I can afford it, Alex." But the figures from that last bill danced across her mind. She *had* been spending a lot of money. Still, Alex was right, it was time to move ahead. "I've done marvelously in Paris and London. I own property in both cities that should bring in over a million American dollars. A friend in London—a friend from Sydney, Charles Cohen—

advised me well. If need be, I can sell the houses in Paris and London and the country house at Poissy."

"It'll be difficult to sell property in Paris or London just now." He looked worried. "You know how close the Germans are to Paris." Lilli flinched. Sara had been adamant about keeping the Paris salon open. "And with all the damage the zeppelin raids are doing in outlying London, the British will be wary of buying."

"We'll borrow from the banks." She refused to be intimidated. "I heard tonight from one of our ladies who enjoys bearing bad tidings that Elizabeth Arden has leased larger quarters farther up Fifth Avenue, just as you said she would. She's spending a fortune on it. It seems she's quite annoyed that we've launched Princess Lilli, New York, and she's furious that Helena Rubinstein is opening up here."

"I think we should start thinking of Philadelphia next."

"Why not Palm Beach?"

"No," he said firmly. "Leave Palm Beach for Elizabeth Arden to exploit. It'll only be profitable for three or four months a year," he predicted. "And then there's the Jewish problem."

Lilli stared at him. "What are you talking about?"

"Lilli, there are cities in America where Jews have always been accepted. There are others that are proud of their rejection of Jews. We don't need to start off with a handicap."

"I didn't think this applied to business."

"It applies to people," he said gently. "For instance, I'm told that Elizabeth Arden never hires a Jew. Like you, she caters to wealthy women. Do you think she wants to take a chance antagonizing any of her society ladies?"

"We won't even ask an employee her religion!" Lilli flared. "And I wouldn't want clients who feel that way."

He patted her hand. "We'll avoid such complications. Leave Palm Beach to Elizabeth Arden. Let's think about Philadelphia."

As THE MONTHS SPED PAST, Lilli became increasingly confident that the New York salon was a success. Still, she was caught up in the competition with Arden and Rubinstein. In the fashion magazines, Helena Rubinstein was calling herself "the greatest living beauty exponent"; Elizabeth Arden announced that she had "given her life to the study of this subject both here and abroad, in Paris, London, and Berlin." Lilli was quoted as "being gifted with a secret family beauty formula that was the foundation of all feminine beauty."

Lilli's face regularly graced editions of *Vogue* and *Harper's Bazaar*. She was photographed with Jan and Freddie for *House & Garden*. Her youth—she was twenty-eight, as opposed to the maturity of Mme. Rubinstein, who was forty-five, and Miss Arden, who was approaching thirty-eight—was their primary focus: Advertisements were designed to convince prospective patrons that they, too, could appear as young as Princess Lilli if they used her products.

As for opening new salons, the race was on. Lilli opened Princess Lilli, Philadelphia. Both Arden and Rubinstein retaliated by opening new salons—Rubinstein in San Francisco, Arden in Boston. Alex predicted this was only the beginning.

Princess Lilli products were cautiously moved into a few fine department stores across the country. Lilli herself, accompanied by a pair of treatment girls, visited each city to demonstrate how their products were to be sold and promoted. Nervous, dressed in her beautiful Paris gowns, she talked to ladies' groups, playing the young and beautiful Princess Lilli to the hilt. While she was gone, Alex moved into the house and took care of Jan and Freddie.

Sara stayed on at the Paris salon, even though the government had fled Paris for Bordeaux. She lived on one floor of the house on the avenue Montaigne; the rest of the house, with Lilli's approval, had been turned over to the government for use as a nursing home. Now Lilli turned over the country house at Poissy to the government to use as a hospital.

Sara wrote that Christmas, 1915, had been grim in Paris. Rather than attending parties, Parisians went to midnight masses. Gone, too, were the ubiquitous crusty rolls.

Sara's letters chilled Lilli; they were filled with reports of the deaths of husbands, fathers, sons of the women who had worked at the Paris salon or the factory. The mother and sister of one of her favorite treatment girls were killed in their small village by German bombs. Word filtered through of the deaths of menfolk of her numerous clients both in Paris and London. These were men she had known socially—some no more than boys.

For London, too, it had been a dark Christmas. Tens of thousands of English soldiers had died. Civilians had died in the zeppelin raids. Lilli wrote Frances repeatedly, asking her to send Beth and Robbie to live with her in New York, but Frances insisted she couldn't bear to be separated from them.

At widely spaced intervals Lilli received notes from Oliver, but they were frustratingly brief. He said he was well, and that he was eager for news of the New York salon and grateful that Jan and Freddie were an ocean away from hostilities.

Americans were involved in the war effort. In New York it was fashionable for debutantes and young matrons—as well as for women "of a certain age"—to join the motor corps of the National League for Women's Services. Dressed in their smart uniforms, they drove staff cars and ambulances around the city. Women were moving out of the kitchen into the offices, shops, and factories to meet the accelerated need for workers. In America, business was booming.

On a midafternoon early in April 1916, Lilli's secretary, the vivacious and pretty young Peggy O'Connor, dashed breathlessly into Lilli's office. "Princess Lilli, there's a gentleman here to see you." Under Alex's orders Lilli was always addressed as Princess Lilli to emphasize the firm's trade name.

Lilli smiled. "A salesman, Peggy?" Peggy had been told to direct all salesmen to Alex.

"No, ma'am." Peggy's eyes danced. "It's Mr. Laval." From the many newspaper interviews, all the staff knew of Lilli's two marriages. Peggy held out an engraved calling card.

Stunned, Lilli was silent for a moment. At intervals, she still caught herself thinking of Jacques. Lately, though, he seemed to have dropped out of sight; there hadn't been mention of the dashing M. Laval and his wife, Addie, in the society and fashion weeklies, such as *Town Topics* and the *Tatler*, for months. She had assumed Jacques knew she was in New York, but there had been no postcards for the children, as in earlier years.

"Please show him in, Peggy. And leave the door open."

Lilli arose from her chair, angry at herself for this absurd sense of panic. *Why was Jacques here?*

She pretended to be busy with a sheaf of letters when she heard his footsteps—and she hoped he would not see that her hands were trembling.

"Lilli!" He came toward her quickly, smiling. "You look lovely. As beautiful as ever."

"The children have almost forgotten they have a father," she said quietly. "It would be nice for them if you could remember to write once in a while."

He looked only slightly embarrassed. "That's why I came back to New York. I knew about the salon here. Lilli"—his eyes searched hers—"let me see the children."

"I've never denied you that, Jacques. But remember, you haven't seen them in two years. Freddie may not even recognize you."

"I'm proud of your success, Lilli." He said it firmly, but the words sounded hollow. She knew how he hated her success. "I'm sure Jan and Freddie are proud of their beautiful mother."

"I'll give you the address and the phone number." She reached for a sheet of paper. "Please check with Martine before going over."

"I've missed you, Lilli," he said softly. "There's never been anybody like you."

"You haven't changed, have you?" she said. "How's Addie?"

"Addie's divorced me." His smile was rueful. "She's gone back home, to a kind of retirement. She blames me for some of her unfortunate business investments. How could I have known the world was about to explode into this crazy war? Oh, Addie won't ever be poor, but she won't live the way she once did—"

"Lilli..." It was Alex. They both turned. "I've worked out that deal with I. Magnin's in California—" He stopped, seeing Jacques. "Excuse me, I didn't realize you were busy."

"Mr. Laval is just leaving," Lilli said. "Jacques, this is Alex Kahn, my associate. My former husband, Jacques Laval."

"I'll call Martine about seeing the children," Jacques said abruptly, obviously insulted by Lilli's dismissal. She remembered now that Martine and Jacques had never liked each other. "Nice meeting you, Mr. Kahn."

Relieved, Lilli walked to her chair. Alex closed the door and crossed to a chair beside the desk.

"Lilli," he said, "is Jacques's appearance in New York going to upset you?" She had confided in him about her marriage, and he was concerned.

"No," she replied. "Except that Jan will be difficult to handle after she's spent an afternoon with him. Jacques always manages to charm her and I become the enemy. Now, tell me about the deal with I. Magnin."

As LILLI HAD EXPECTED, Jan was ecstatic at seeing her father again. And though Freddie didn't remember Jacques, he, too, was charmed. Lilli tried not to resent their anticipation when every Wednesday and Saturday he arrived with gifts for each child. Lilli suspected that his generosity came easily; Addie had probably paid for the divorce—though of course not as extravagantly as Jacques would have liked.

During the next few weeks, Lilli approached each social engagement with trepidation, knowing that Jacques would be circulating in search of a third wife and they moved in the same circles. There had to be a woman in his life. A woman with money.

Every time she didn't find Jacques among the guests at a dinner, ball, or house party, she was at once relieved and disappointed.

As time went on, she began looking forward to the children's accounts of their father's visits. Lately he had begun taking them for little trips about the city—with her permission, of course. She was surprised by his sensitivity to the children's need to see him, and began to wonder if perhaps he had changed.

With the approach of summer, Lilli settled Jan and Freddie—along with Martine and part of the domestic staff—in the house she had rented for the summer at Southampton, which was close enough to the city for her to visit on weekends. Martine informed Jacques that the children would be at Southampton for the summer months.

During July and August, the New York and Philadelphia salons would close on Saturdays. Alex began his campaign to have Lilli take a week or two off in August. "Lilli, you can't spend the rest of your life working fourteen hours a day," he said on a humid night in early June while they pored over designs for packaging of a new face cream. "Take two weeks and go out to Southampton and lie in the sun."

"The sun does terrible things to the skin, Alex," she said. That was what she told her clients.

"Then stay under an umbrella." He leaned forward. "You can't afford to look tired. You're supposed to be the epitome of youthful beauty."

"Do I look tired?" she asked anxiously.

"You look beautiful." There was an intensity to his words that made her blush. Immediately, he lightened the mood. "And a little tired."

"I'll go out to Southampton for a week in early August, Alex. I promise. And I'll be going out tomorrow night for the long weekend."

17

L<small>YING IN BED</small> in one of the guest rooms—decorated by Elsie de Wolfe—at Donna and Bob Allen's Southampton beachfront estate, Jacques cursed under his breath and he reached to shut off the alarm clock. Dimly conscious of the cool, sea-scented morning air spiced with the perfume of roses growing on a trellis past a bedroom wall. Damn, six in the morning was an ungodly hour to arise! None of Donna's other guests—a Russian grand duke and a Hungarian count on the prowl for rich American wives—would be stirring for at least three hours. But Jessie, the luscious little maid Lilli had hired for the summer, had told him Lilli was on the beach every morning no later than seven during these three-day weekends.

Jessie thought it was terribly romantic that Lilli's ex-husband was trying to win her back. It didn't seem to matter a bit that she and Jacques had only recently dallied in the back seat of Donna's Pierce-Arrow.

He hadn't been smart about Addie, that much he knew. He shouldn't have been so stupid as to let her catch him with that overheated little laundress.

Lilli was the only woman he'd ever loved. Why did she treat him as though he were her profligate son rather than her husband? No man should have to beg from his wife. And who was this Alex Kahn? He must be her replacement for Oliver. Women like Lilli usually had some homosexual in tow.

In a burst of energy Jacques leapt from the bed and stalked to his bathroom to prepare for a rendezvous Lilli would not be expecting. He was whistling by the time he emerged from the shower. Why had Lilli divorced Mischa? Rumor had it the marriage had lasted less than a month. Had Mischa been a washout in bed? Lilli was a passionate woman—and he was the man who knew how to make her happy.

Lilli and he belonged together. Jan and Freddie needed a father. He felt a surge of paternal pride—he had given Lilli two beautiful kids. And he'd helped her in the business when she needed it most. He would never have played around with Addie if Lilli hadn't pushed him into it. If she had listened to him, he'd have an international business in operation by now. That was the trouble with Lilli—she never listened to anybody.

He held his razor under running water and planned his approach. At heart, Lilli was a prude. A thousand to one she hadn't hopped into bed with anybody until she married the Russian prince. The only way to reach Lilli was to throw her flat on her back.

Unexpectedly Jacques was aroused. If Lilli had been the type, she could have been the richest demimondaine in Paris. He'd seen the way men looked at her. Why wasn't she here right this minute? He'd make her understand they belonged together forever. She was young, beautiful—and rich. A passionate woman like Lilli needed a man in her bed.

In white flannel slacks, navy jacket, and rubber-soled Keds, Jacques went downstairs. He paused for coffee at a table on the expansive open veranda that faced the ocean. The sky was a magnificent, cloudless blue. The early-morning sun cast gold glints upon the breaking waves. He glanced at his Tiffany watch—a gift from Addie. Time to hit the beach. Lilli had taken the Albemarle house—the equivalent of about one city block down the beach. He felt exhilarated by the challenge that lay ahead.

Taking off his Keds and socks, he rolled up his trouser legs and, with sock-stuffed shoes swinging by the laces, headed toward the water. A swift glance to the right showed him an empty stretch of beach. He saw a pair of fishing vessels far out to sea. Gulls hovered over the waves or sauntered over the sand, leaving footprints in the sand. Jacques walked slowly, enjoying the shock of the cold water on his bare feet.

He stiffened at the sight of a woman approaching the water's edge. By her quick, graceful step, he could tell it was Lilli. He quickened his pace. He wasn't going to take any chances this time. His whole future depended on it.

She wore a blue and green striped taffeta bathing suit with three ruffles forming the skirt. Except for her elegance, he thought, she looked like a little dancer at a Paris music hall. Lilli had traveled far in the almost thirteen years since he had married her in Karlsbad.

"Lilli!" he called out. "Lilli, how wonderful to run into you this way!"

She looked stunned. For an instant he was afraid she would turn and flee. But then she seemed to regain her composure. "I would never expect to see you awake at this hour." She paused. "Or haven't you been to bed yet?"

He ignored the implication. "I woke up early to walk on the beach. Great for clearing the head. I'm staying at the Allen's house for the weekend. Donna and Bob Allen. He's the stockbroker."

"I'm right down the beach." Her eyes were veiled.

"Lillie..."—he paused long enough to give her a wistful look—"as long as I'm out here, will it be all right if I drop by to see Jan and Freddie?"

"The children are always glad to see you." She was tense, Jacques noted. A good sign.

"I must confess I was hoping to run into you out here. It was the first thought that came to my mind when the Allens invited me. So I could see Jan and Freddie," he added quickly. "I dreaded the thought of not seeing them all summer. It took me a long time to grow up, Lilli. Now I realize what I've lost by my stupidity." Their eyes met, only for a moment. "I've a great job," he continued enthusiastically. "I'm working for Bob Allen. My being here is actually part of the job. Bob figured I might make some important business contacts out here." That would impress her.

"There's plenty of money out here," she said quietly.

"Let's walk along the beach for a while, Lilli. Please."

"All right." She began to walk, and he fell into step beside her. "Oliver's in the British army. I'm sure he hates it, but he seems determined to do his duty."

"Who's in charge of the London salon?"

"Frances Cohen. She's a real jewel."

"God, Lilli, this brings me back to Sydney," he said, "to walk along the water this way. Remember the night I made love to you in a carriage driving along the quay?"

Her face was suddenly warm with color. *She remembered.* "I should get back to the house. I make a point of having breakfast with the children when I'm out here. Why don't you drop by later?"

Jacques could tell that she was flustered. Good. She probably wished they were back together in that crummy flat in Sydney.

LILLI LAY BACK in a chaise on the loggia of the Albemarle house, the new book of poems by Carl Sandburg beside her, while Jan helped Freddie build a sand castle on the beach. It would have been a sublimely peaceful moment had she not met Jacques this morning. Since then, she had thought about little else.

Jacques seemed to have found a place for himself at last. He was selling stocks and bonds. He ought to be good at that, she acknowledged. He had the persuasive charm of the perfect salesman. She assumed that Bob Allen expected Jacques to bring in prospective clients and then would step in himself to close each deal.

Never in all their years together had she ever seen Jacques awake at seven in the morning, unless he had not yet gone to bed for the night. How old was he? She was twenty-nine; he must be thirty-six. In four years he would be forty. Next year she would be thirty. God, the years were hurtling past.

"Papa! Papa!" Jan ran toward Jacques, with Freddie right behind her. "Come see the sand castle we're building!"

Jacques tossed Jan into the air as though she were three rather than ten, then picked up Freddie. Tears stung Lilli's eyes as she watched father, daughter, and son.

Jacques stayed with the children until Martine came out to call them to their early dinner.

"Papa, you'll be back tomorrow?" Jan demanded.

"I'll be back tomorrow," he said after a quiet glance at Lilli. "Scoot." He playfully swatted her on the rump.

Lilli rose to her feet. Alex was driving down from his family's house in Amagansett to take her to a charity dinner in Southampton. "The children enjoyed their afternoon with you," she said politely. "I'll tell Martine you'll be here again tomorrow." But tomorrow afternoon she would not be here watching the children. Martine would be with them.

"Thanks, Lilli," Jacques said.

"I have to go upstairs to dress for a charity dinner." She avoided his eyes. *She mustn't care that he looked at her as though he were holding her in his arms.* "Goodbye, Jacques."

THROUGHOUT THE EVENING, Lilli tried to dismiss Jacques from her thoughts. There was no room in her life for him. She knew him too well. Addie had thrown him over, and now he needed another woman in his life. Perhaps he was doing well with the Wall Street firm, but she doubted that his salary could meet his taste for the high life.

"You've been quiet tonight," Alex said after he brought her home. "Would you like to talk about it?"

"I'm sorry, Alex," she said. "I'm still tired. Don't worry— I'm sure I'll unwind by the time we go back into town Monday morning."

"This confirms it, Lilli," he said. "You're taking time off in August. You'll come back bursting with fresh ideas. And while you're out here, I'll come out and work with you for a long weekend on the packaging for the new cream." He knew that she wanted their packaging to be as eye-catching as Elizabeth Arden's.

"Alex... Stay here at the house instead of going out to Amagansett. It will save you all that driving." But the truth was she wanted him around—as a buffer between her and Jacques.

LILLI WAS RELIEVED when at last the summer ended and she no longer had to worry about running into Jacques at every party. Whenever they met, she was unable to sleep that night, and she sensed that Alex was wary of him. Jacques, on the other hand, seemed to regard Alex with playful indulgence, as if—unlike many of their acquaintances—he knew that Alex was not her lover.

In mid-September, when Alex was on a trip to Boston to explore sites for a new salon, Lilli received a letter from Oliver saying he had been wounded in the leg and was in a hospital in France. "At least, now I'm out of this rotten war. The doctors won't say yet if I'll be able to walk without crutches; but even if I can't, I can still return to the salon...."

Lilli read the letter over and over. Her first instinct was to try to get to France to see him. Merchant ships—carrying a handful of passengers—were still crossing the Atlantic, but most people felt it was too dangerous these days. She couldn't risk her life when she had children to raise.

What if it was worse than he said? Oliver was always trying to make things easier for her. What if he was dying alone somewhere in a military hospital?

She'd write Aunt Sara in Paris—maybe she would be able to go see him.

"Princess Lilli..." The door was flung open and Peggy came into the room. "Arline is having an awful time with Mrs. Fitch. Could you—"

"No," Lilli said brusquely. "Tell Arline to handle it. I have to leave the salon." She saw Peggy's astonishment. "Peggy, I'm going home." She held up the letter. "A very dear friend has been wounded in France."

"Oh, Lilli..." Peggy hurried forward, the more formal "Princess Lilli" forgotten. "But he'll be all right," she said. "If he's able to write you, then he must be all right."

Lilli didn't bother to call for the car; she flagged down a taxi. She glanced into Gramercy Park before going into the house: Martine and the children were not there. Perhaps they had gone home.

As she entered the foyer she heard the sound of the children's laughter. Jacques was with them—she heard his voice. Despite his work schedule, he saw them every Wednesday and Saturday afternoon.

Lilli hurried to the entrance of the small sitting room. Jacques was in the corner; Jan and Freddie were at his feet, entranced by whatever he was saying.

"Jacques," she said urgently. "Jacques, I'd like to talk to you."

He looked up. "Jan, Freddie, go up to the playroom now. Your mother and I have to talk." He smiled, but his eyes were serious.

"Papa, not yet," Jan said, but Freddie was tugging at her hand.

"Jan, come on," he said. "Mama wants to talk to Papa."

Lilli closed the door behind them. "I've just heard from Oliver." Her voice broke. "Jacques, he's been wounded."

"How bad is it?" He pulled Lilli down to a sofa.

"Here's the letter." She didn't trust herself to tell him.

Jacques carefully read the brief letter.

"So he'll have a game leg." He shrugged. "Like Oliver says, at least he's out of the war."

Jacques rang for a maid and ordered tea, remembering how a cup of hot tea had always soothed Lilli in moments of stress. In the quiet of the sitting room they sat and talked about Oliver, remembering the past. Jacques insisted they tell the children about their "hero uncle," making light of his injury.

When Martine knocked and told them it was time for the children's dinner, Lilli explained that tonight she must be excused. She felt a pang of guilt at Martine's look of surprise: She had never missed this hour with the children.

"Martine," Jacques said gently, "we've had some unhappy news about Oliver."

"Mon Dieu!" Martine said, white and trembling.

"He's going to be all right," Jacques said. "But he was wounded. He's in a hospital in France."

"I'll light a candle for him," Martine whispered. "Such a fine young man."

"Martine, would you please phone Mrs. Harris for me and tell her I can't be there for dinner tonight. Explain to her what has happened." Elaine Harris knew Oliver from the London salon. She would understand.

After dinner, Jan insisted on rushing in to kiss her father goodnight. Lilli was wistful. A perfuntory peck was all she ever received from Jan.

"Oh, Papa, I wish you lived with us again," Jan said, her small face wistful.

He smiled. "Sleep well, my darling."

Jan remembered only the good times with Jacques, Lilli thought. How could she have forgotten his earlier favoritism toward Freddie? Had Jacques changed?

He seemed reluctant to leave. Feeling in need of company herself, she invited him to stay for dinner. Jacques knew, more than anyone else, how much Oliver meant to her, that he was the brother she had never had. She rang for Celestine and asked her to tell Henri to serve dinner for two in the garden.

It was dusk by the time dinner was served in the tiny garden, where a faint breeze stirred the green lace of a young willow. Light peered through the rear door of the house, and a pair of candles cast flickering shadows on the damask-covered round wicker table.

"All we need is an orchestra playing Strauss waltzes, and I'd feel as though we were dining at the Bellevue Café in Marienbad," Jacques said, sipping his wine.

Lilli smiled, a bit nervously. "Aunt Sara worries about her old friends in Marienbad. There's so much trouble there now."

"Isn't there trouble enough for her in Paris?" For a moment the old Jacques surfaced. "Only a stubborn old woman like Sara would insist on staying there."

Lilli didn't taste a bite of the gourmet meal Bertha had prepared. Their talk was filled with memories—Oliver sharing her panic when they learned of the sinking of the *Titanic*, happy times in Paris and London.

"You're chilly out here." Jacques put his hand gently on her arm. Not a star shone in the heavens. Dark clouds passed over the moon. "Let's have coffee in the house."

By the time they finished their coffee and generous slices of Bertha's superb Black Forest Cake, it had started to rain. Lilli offered to send Jacques to his small apartment in the east sixties in the car.

"Oliver is fine," he said as they waited in the foyer for the car. "You'll see. There'll be another letter soon." He kissed her on the cheek as Henri opened the door and stood by with umbrella in hand. She blinked once as a raindrop hit her, and then he was gone.

TEN DAYS LATER, Lilli received another letter from Oliver, in which he said he was about to leave the hospital for a nursing home—and that he would walk for the rest of his life with a slight limp: "Nothing that will cause me any problems. Meanwhile I'll be living in a beautiful château in the south of France for three or four months, being spoiled deliciously."

Immensely relieved, Lilli felt she was now free to leave New York for a tour of several department stores that were to feature Princess Lilli cosmetics. On these out-of-town trips, Alex had insisted that Peggy travel with her to oversee all train and hotel arrangements, to handle the hiring of a limousine in each city, and to see that a maid was available to care for Lilli's wardrobe.

After hearing of Lilli's trip from the children, Jacques called and offered to stay with them at the house in her absence. She hesitated. Usually Alex stayed with them when she was away.

"Lilli, it will be a gift to me to spend more time with them," he said. "Jan and Freddie are all I have to show for my life."

Lilli knew that if she rejected his offer—and she was convinced Jan and Freddie already knew about it—Jan would hold it against her forever. Anyway, Alex would probably be relieved not to be tied down with the children. "All right, Jacques."

EVERY NIGHT, when Lilli phoned home and talked to the children, they chattered gaily about their evenings with their father. Apparently Jacques was with them every possible moment.

"Papa's teaching me to play bridge!" Jan said. "And tomorrow he's taking us to the zoo!"

The trip was going well. At the end of the first week, Lilli phoned Alex at his apartment late at night.

"Lilli, try to relax on these trips," he said. "The New York salon and the factory will survive without you for two weeks."

She laughed. "I know, Alex. *Nobody's* indispensable."

"You are. Still, I think we can survive for two weeks." He hesitated. "Everything all right with the kids?"

"They're fine." He must feel he had been replaced. "Busy with school now."

"Shall I meet your train when you come in? It is next Tuesday, isn't it?"

"Yes, but it'll be awfully late, and you get up so early. I'll have Martine send Henri with the car. Don't work too hard, Alex."

"Hey, that's supposed to be my line," he said. "Grandma says we're both obsessed by the business."

"She's probably right. But never mind that. What's happening with the new packaging?"

A WEEK LATER—close to midnight—Lilli's train pulled into Grand Central Station. Peggy directed a pair of porters to transport their luggage to the waiting car, and the two women walked out into the cavernous, sparsely populated central area of the station.

"Your train was right on schedule!" a cheerful voice greeted them.

"Jacques!" There he was, beaming, coming toward her, his arms outstretched.

"It seemed positively rude to let you return after two weeks away with nobody to greet you," he said. "I had the devil of a time convincing Jan and Freddie that they couldn't stay up until you were home." He eyed Peggy.

"Jacques, you've met my secretary," she said. "Peggy O'Connor.

The two exchanged smiles; quickly he turned back to her. "How was the trip?"

"Great. With so many women going into business and industry because of the war boom, sales are soaring."

"I suppose cosmetics build morale," Jacques mused, placing himself between Lilli and Peggy. "Think of it, Lilli! You're performing a patriotic service."

In the car, as Jacques prattled on about the children, Lilli found herself noticing his warm body, the scent of his shaving lotion. How many years had it been since he had shared her bed? Henri dropped Peggy off at her apartment, and then drove on to the house. Lilli's heart began to pound. Jacques was planning to spend the night.

As soon as they arrived, Lilli went to her bedroom, leaving Jacques to find his way to one of the two guest rooms on the second floor. She knew it was late, but she needed to relax before she could sleep. She drew a bath and soaked in the tub for nearly half an hour before reaching for a lushly thick lilac towel. Why did she still feel like a romantic schoolgirl sitting beside Jacques? And why had he not gone to his own apartment tonight?

Jacques was fighting for a place in her life again. But that would never happen. She had everything she needed. The children. The business. Aunt Sara and Oliver and Alex. *She could survive in this world without Jacques.*

She reached into a drawer for one of the rose satin nightgowns she had bought at B. Altman. Over the years, exquisite nightwear had become one of her passions. She pulled the nightgown over her auburn hair, down around her curvaceous, slim body. For a moment she inspected her reflection in the full-length cheval mirror. She looked like a woman preparing for a night of lovemaking.

The light knock at her door startled her. She reached into the armoire for a matching negligee and walked in bare feet toward the door. One of the children must have woken up from a nightmare.

"Just a minute..." She tied the negligee around her waist, then pulled the door wide. It was Jacques, in pajamas and bathrobe.

"I saw the light under the door, so I knew you were still awake." He held out a sheaf of papers. "I thought you'd like to see these drawings Freddie did while you were away. He made them especially for you." His eyes lingered on the rise of her breasts beneath the rose satin.

"Thank you, Jacques." She refused to look into his eyes.

"Lilli," he said, "I've never stopped loving you."

She froze, managed a smile. "I find that hard to believe Jacques."

"I've made some awful mistakes, honey...." Suddenly, he was inside, closing the door behind him. "The only real thing in my life was you. You and the kids." He pulled her close. "The only thing that ever stood between us was the business. I couldn't compete, Lilli."

"I think you'd better go to your room." Her voice was uneven.

"Lilli, please don't send me away."

She closed her eyes. His mouth came down on hers. His arms drew her closer. Thirteen years fell away: She was a sixteen-year-old bride, wildly in love with her husband.

He carried her to the turned-down bed.

"Jacques, this is ridiculous...." But she knew she was powerless. He took off his robe and pajamas, revealing a body that was still slim and muscular, deeply tanned from the Southampton weekends.

"Lilli, remember, you're a woman." He slid one hand beneath the neckline of the satin gown.

"A divorced woman, Jacques." *She wasn't his wife anymore.* His hand moved lower.

"Lilli, you're not a little girl now. You're a beautiful, fascinating woman, and we'll both go out of our minds if we stop now."

She wasn't Princess Lilli now. She was Jacques's bride.

18

FROM HABIT, Lilli woke early. She would meet Alex at the salon before the others arrived and bring him up to date on the department-store tour. Today would be busy: two private consultations in the morning; a trip across town to the factory to work with the chemist on the right tones for the new rouges; lunch in her office with Alex to go over the new advertising layout; tea at Sherry's with three ladies from the Women's War Relief Committee.

But she couldn't concentrate on all of that now. Jacques was asleep in her bed. She had to make him understand that last night was just a casual incident.

She started at the light knock on her door: Celestine, with her breakfast tray. On most mornings she had breakfast by her bedroom bay window, which looked out over Gramercy Park. She cherished these few minutes of solitude.

"Celestine," she called, "I'm running late this morning. I'll have breakfast at the salon."

"*Oui*, madame."

Reaching for the jacket of her burgundy velvet Poiret suit—just right for tea at Sherry's—Lilli debated about waking Jacques. She mustn't let him back into her life simply because he made her so passionate that she forgot all reason.

"Jacques...Jacques, wake up."

He mumbled, frowned, opened his eyes. "Honey..." He smiled, reached for her hand.

She stepped out of reach. "I have to leave for the salon. Henri will be driving Jan and Freddie to school in about twenty minutes. I think it would be best if you were back in your apartment before they return. I wouldn't want them to think that—"

"That Papa's moved back home?" He sat up. "Lilli—"

She stood by stiffly, not moving a muscle. "There's no point in confusing the children. Last night was a mistake, Jacques. It won't happen again."

She pulled on her jacket, grabbed her burgundy leather purse, and left the room. Why did Jacques have this hold on her? Why did she allow Jacques to upset her this way? She had wanted nothing more than to lie in that bed again with Jacques. He gloried in being a stud, she told herself in distaste. For women who could afford him. She had taken him back into her life once. She was not so obsessed that she would do that again.

OVER THE NEXT FEW WEEKS, Jacques continued to appear at the house every Wednesday and Saturday afternoon, often staying with the children until Lilli arrived home. Each time, Jan—who was now "grown-up" enough to dine with her mother—asked him to stay for dinner. On these nights, Lilli always left the table immediately after dessert on the pretense of a business meeting.

Jacques was becoming a presence on the social scene—most often at a charity ball or dinner as the escort of an older, married woman. At a dinner party early in January, she found herself seated beside him.

"What do you hear from Oliver?" he asked.

"He's having a long convalescence," she said. Alex, on her right, was being monopolized by a committeewoman eager to enlist his help in persuading his father to contribute to yet another war charity. "But he hopes to be back in the salon in another few weeks."

"Has the salon been damaged?"

"There's been some damage, but, thank God, none of the staff was hurt. Frances has sent her children to their country house with her mother. It's hard to believe that while we sit here at dinner, people in England and France don't know if they'll be alive tomorrow. I've begged Aunt Sara to close the salon and try to get passage to New York. But she refuses to leave Paris."

"For all Wilson's talk about keeping us out of the war, a lot of people are sure we'll be dragged in—and soon."

"What a terrible thought!" Lilli said.

"If the Germans are not stopped, they could show up right here on our shores. Even Wilson must realize that."

"America has always seemed so sheltered," she said. Was it selfish of her to pray that the United States stayed out of the war? She knew that the French and the British were furious that American soldiers were not fighting beside them.

"I know men who're taking bets that we'll be actively fighting within six months," Jacques said. "I've thought about enlisting, while I can still choose a branch of service. If we have a draft, nobody knows where he'll end up."

Shocked, Lilli stared at Jacques. The thought of him in uniform, fighting in war-torn Europe was unnerving.

"Jacques, you'll be thirty-seven. If there's a draft, they'll be calling up men under thirty."

"In England and France, *every* able-bodied man is fighting." He was annoyed at her mentioning his age. "I'm unmarried—a natural choice."

The lady whom Jacques had escorted to dinner now claimed his attention. Lilli stared at her plate, pretending to eat. If there should be a draft here, would Jacques be called up? *But he was a father: Men with children would not be taken first.* She had to believe that.

OVER THE NEXT FEW WEEKS, Lilli was preoccupied with the possibility of Jacques's being drafted—or enlisting. In February, fresh tensions erupted in the United States when, before Wilson's second inauguration, the Germans resumed unrestricted submarine warfare against all merchant ships—including American vessels. While mass meetings for peace were being held in New York and other major cities, Wilson cut diplomatic relations with Germany. Later in the month, American newspapers carried a story—uncovered by British

Intelligence—of a German plot to back a war between Mexico and the United States. In March, German submarines sank five American merchant ships. Now Americans were demanding war.

Early in March, the Russian workers revolted. In Petrograd, regiment after regiment of cossacks mutinied to join the rebelling mobs that were attacking police stations and looting shops. On March 15, Czar Nicholas II abdicated. A provisional government took over.

One gray early evening in March, as Henri drove Lilli home from the salon, she noticed the flags hanging before private houses, apartment buildings, shops, even churches. Everybody knew it was a matter of days before President Wilson would announce that America was entering the war.

As she let herself into the house, Lilli heard Jacques talking to Jan. Freddie must have already eaten his dinner.

"Papa, my teacher says we're going to have to fight the Germans," she was saying as Lilli walked into the sitting room. A cozy blaze glowed in the fireplace.

"I'm afraid that's likely, my love." Jacques glanced up at Lilli with a wry smile. "I'll probably enlist in the navy."

"No!" Suddenly Jan began sobbing. "I don't want you to fight in the war! You'll be killed!"

"Jan, Papa isn't going off to fight in the war." Lilli swept Jan's small, trembling body into her arms, her own heart pounding. Jacques could be so unpredictable. Did he imagine himself a war hero? "Darling, stop crying," she said. "If you don't, Papa might not stay for dinner." Jacques never refused an invitation to dinner.

Over dinner, Lilli was glad Jacques kept up a stream of amusing stories, with Jan hanging on his every word. Later, after Jan had been put to bed, they shared a bottle of wine in the sitting room.

"Jan's awfully upset about the war," Lilli said. "She remembers that Oliver was wounded—"

"But Lilli, we can't close our eyes to what's happening." He refilled her glass. "If I have to fight, Jan will have to accept it—just like other little girls have."

Lilli winced. If anything happened to Jacques, Jan would blame her forever. She would blame herself.

"Even if there's a draft," she said, "you won't be called up right away. You're over thirty." She diplomatically refrained this time from reminding him how much over thirty. "And you're a father."

Jacques chuckled. "Whose former wife is raising his children, my darling. Remember, I'm not exactly solely responsible for their support. I doubt I could afford even their fancy private school."

"Jacques, please, you mustn't think of enlisting." She tried to keep her voice even. "There's nothing romantic about war."

"What do I have to keep me here?" She heard the challenge in his voice.

"Jan and Freddie."

"They don't need me. They have their mother."

"Jacques, I don't want you to enlist!"

"Lilli, give me a reason for living." He reached for her glass of wine and put it beside his own. "Honey, we never should have split up. We belong together forever."

No.

"It didn't work before. It won't work now." She was trembling as he reached to pull her into his arms.

"We'll make it work." His mouth merged with hers and her arms closed in about his shoulders.

Where was her will?

FOUR AFTERNOONS LATER, in the drawing room of the Gramercy Park house and with only the children and the household staff in attendance, Lilli and Jacques were married by a judge whose wife was a devoted client of Princess Lilli. Alex had been out of town on business for a week. Lilli had decided she would tell him about the marriage after he returned.

The decision was a carefully considered one: She knew he would disapprove; he wouldn't understand why she had revived a marriage that had failed twice. But her marriage to Jacques would not change *their* relationship. She would have to make Alex understand that.

Jan, of course, was ecstatic that Papa would be living with them again. They didn't bother with a honeymoon; Jacques simply took up residence in the house and continued at his job on Wall Street. Lilli allowed him to persuade her to invest a sizable sum in stocks he was handling, though secretly she checked these out with Alex before agreeing.

Almost imperceptibly, Jacques's attitude toward Alex began to change. He became increasingly condescending, dropping disparaging remarks about Alex's contribution to the business, all of which Lilli made a point of ignoring. He regarded Alex as competition, and Lilli could see why: She saw more of Alex than of Jacques. Usually they had lunch together every day. Throughout the day, they were in and out of each other's offices. Alex was like an extension of herself.

On April 6, Congress declared war against Germany, and Lilli found private—but guilty—solace in the knowledge that as a married man with two children, Jacques would not be called up for service. She had not yet heard from Aunt Sara in reply to her news that she and Jacques were married again. Like Alex, Aunt Sara would disapprove—and would say nothing.

Lilli was upset when Alex came to her early in May to say he was offering his services to his country. "How can I do less, Lilli? You'll manage without me." Alex was thirty-two. Only men between twenty-one and thirty were subject to the draft.

"It won't be easy, Alex."

"You'll manage." His eyes were tender. "Lilli, this country has been very good to my family. I have to do whatever I can."

From the moment Alex left, it seemed, her life was in turmoil. She had known she would miss him in the daily running of the business, but she had not realized how much she would miss his cheerful presence at her side, his caring, thoughtful nature. She was relieved when she got word that he had been stationed in a federal office in Washington, D.C., safe from German bullets and bombs. And thanks to Alexander Graham Bell, they were able to talk on the phone at least twice a week. Despite what she knew had to be a frenetic schedule, he somehow found time to work on advertising for Princess Lilli, and to pursue starting yet another salon. The war seemed only to accelerate the success of the field.

Then—with over 9 million men registering for the draft—Jacques came home that same June day and announced he had joined the Red Cross. He was pulling strings to be stationed in Paris. Within thirty days he would be in France. *Why?* Lilli asked herself. But she knew the answer. Jacques's ego was at stake: He would rather risk his life than admit he was "over-age" for the draft.

Jacques convinced Jan that he wouldn't be in any danger. Lilli wanted to believe he would be safe behind the lines, but she couldn't help worrying.

With shattering swiftness, the day of Jacques's departure arrived. He was to leave at midnight on a supply ship bound for France. Both Jan and Freddie sat at the dinner table with their parents on their last night together. Jacques knew only that he would be stationed first in Paris.

"I'll see Sara, Lilli," he said. "Perhaps I can persuade her to come to New York now."

"Papa, will you shoot people?" Freddie asked.

"No, Freddie. I'll be with the Red Cross. We'll help those who are hurt." Jacques smiled encouragingly, and tears filled Lilli's eyes. Jacques could be so tender with the children—when it suited him.

At last, protesting as always, Jan and Freddie went to bed. A few minutes later Jacques took Lilli by the hand and walked with her up to their bedroom. Tonight their lovemaking held a special urgency. Before midnight Jacques would leave the house to board the blacked-out supply ship. Lilli tried to block out of her mind the terrifying realization that the ship would have to make its way through a maze of German submarines. And no one could foretell when the war would end. Jacques and she could not know when they would see each other again.

"I'll go with you to the ship," Lilli said later, as Jacques dressed again.

"No," he said, reaching for the jacket of his uniform. "I want to go away with my last sight of you here in our bed." He seemed almost gay at the prospect of going off to war, Lilli thought.

"Jacques, be careful." She kissed him. "Darling, *be careful.*"

MAIL FROM EUROPE was excruciatingly slow in arriving, so Lilli knew it would be weeks before she heard from Jacques. Still, she phoned home every morning to check with Martine. She had written Aunt Sara that Jacques would be stationed with the Red Cross in Paris. How comforting it would be to have word about Aunt Sara after all these months!

One hot late-August morning, Lilli took the train to Washington to spend some time with Alex over their new fall campaign. He had managed to find her a room in a quiet hotel in this overcrowded city.

As she stood in the huge Union Station, swarming with people—many of them men in uniform—Lilli was afraid she would never find Alex. Then she spied him, pushing his way toward her. Her eyes filled with tears when she saw he was in his army lieutenant's uniform. It was the first time she had seen him out of civilian clothes. Every man in uniform seemed so vulnerable.

"Lilli!" He pulled her into his arms and kissed her lightly. "Oh, it's good to see you!" He held her away and scrutinized her face. "You look wonderful."

"I miss you, Alex."

"I've arranged to take off the rest of the day." He reached for her valise. "Let's get you settled in the hotel and then have lunch."

Over lunch at the Hotel Willard, Alex suggested they go back to his small apartment. "People are not concerned about proprieties in wartime. Don't worry, Lilli," he chuckled, "your reputation won't be sullied."

"Of course we'll go to your apartment. I can't very well spread the layouts I've brought along across a tea table."

At Alex's small, charmingly furnished apartment, they planned Princess Lilli's winter promotion. As always, the conversation turned to the prospect of opening a new salon.

"Rubinstein and Arden are moving out like crazy," he said. "We can't let them get ahead. I know we're facing bad inflation, but the profits will make up for every cent you spend."

Insisting that going out for dinner was a waste of their precious time, Alex began cooking for them. "My repertoire is limited, but how wrong can I go with steaks, baked potatoes, and salad? Anyhow, there's a hospital just five blocks away." Lilli laughed. She missed Alex's light humor. "I have a special meeting at ten this evening," he said. "I was able to get off the hook for everything except that."

"It sounds like our schedule at the salon. What exactly do you do?"

"Dull office work." He shrugged. "Keeping records, checking on supplies, arranging shipments."

"You will be staying here in Washington, won't you Alex?" What would she do if he were shipped overseas?

He took her hand. "I'll be here for the duration, Lilli. At least that's what my colonel tells me."

At 9:40 P.M., Alex left Lilli standing in front of her room at the hotel. She'd already told him she planned to return to New York on an early-morning train.

"I'll pick you up at the hotel and take you to Union Station," he said.

"Alex, you don't have to do that. I know how busy you are."

"I want to," he said. "Damn the war. I'll pick you up at six-thirty. We'll have time for coffee and toast before I put you on your train. There's only one dining car—you might find yourself without breakfast until you're five minutes out of Pennsylvania Station."

Before going to sleep, Lilli phoned New York and checked with Martine. The children were fine, asleep. Feeling oddly peaceful, she lay back in bed. But tonight she couldn't sleep. She was too stimulated by the hours she'd spent with Alex. He always brought out fresh ideas in her.

Sometimes she felt guilty that she was obsessed with the business in the midst of the war. But Alex always insisted she was performing a patriotic duty by lifting the morale of women, not only in America but in England and France. And the checks she sent to various war charities did slightly assuage her guilt....

THE NEXT MORNING Lilli waited in the hotel lobby until Alex's car, with an army corporal at the wheel, picked her up and took her to Union Station. In the car, Lilli listened while Alex discussed some last-minute ideas for their winter advertising budget. When they pulled up before the station, Alex led her to a coffee shop, where they had toast and coffee. A few minutes before the train was to depart, they pushed their way to the gate where the New York-bound train waited.

"Take care of yourself, Lilli." Alex bent to kiss her goodbye. The kiss deepened...and then they separated, both shaken.

"It was good to see you, Alex," she said. "I'll talk to you soon."

FRESH FROM A BATH in his newly acquired suite at the Ritz, Jacques sat at a sun-washed sidewalk café on the Champs-Elysées and sipped Pernod. His uniform was clean and crisply pressed—for the first time since his arrival. He knew, from the covert glances of passing young mademoiselles, that he could have taken any one of them back to the suite at the Ritz. But not today—he had other plans. What luck to have run into Sheila Wainwright his first week in Paris! When he'd first met her—back in London, when he was still married to Addie—gossip about her escapades had been endless.

Still, Jacques couldn't help eyeing the swishing posterior of a particularly seductive Parisienne until she was out of sight.

On sunny days like today, he found it impossible to believe that the city was so close to the front lines. The only sign of trouble was the lack of tourists lingering at the cafés or strolling along the avenue with their cameras.

Some other Americans had chosen to remain in Paris despite the war. Edith Wharton stayed on, working with the French Red Cross and French-American Relief. Harry Lehr remained with his rich wife. Elsie de Wolfe was involved in caring for the wounded.

Four weeks of driving an ambulance back and forth between Paris and the front lines, driving until he was ready to collapse from exhaustion, had certainly killed Jacques's taste for war. God, he was tired and tense and sick of the sight of death and physical pain! Would he ever clear his mind of the visions of those soldiers they carted from the trenches to hospital beds? Missing arms, legs, eyes. Screaming in their agony. They were so goddamn young! They made him feel old. But of course he wasn't. He'd certainly proved that to Sheila in an empty ambulance last week. At least for those few moments, he had been able to forget the horror, dirt, and blood of war. He had been shocked by his fear. But, hell, you'd have to be stupid not to be scared with shots flying and bombs falling all around you.

Then he saw her. There was no mistaking that tall, slim figure; she even looked good in her Red Cross uniform. But who the hell was that with her? Oh, yes—Amy something or other. He'd met her somewhere. Attractive, and with an incredible pair of breasts. She was from a British working-class family, if he remembered correctly. Sheila, on the other hand, came from one of Britain's wealthiest families. In fact, the only reason she and Amy had joined the American Red Cross was because one of her parents' connections had seen to it they would be assigned to Paris. "London's so depressing, with all the bombings."

"Waiting long?" Sheila asked, dropping into a chair and reaching under the table for his knee.

"Five minutes or so." He waited for an explanation.

She ignored it. "Amy has a twenty-four hour pass, too," she said.

"Are we expecting someone else?" he asked.

"Darling," she purred, her hand caressing his thigh, "haven't you learned there are times when *trois* is *très* exciting?"

"I wasn't sure you'd agree." He signaled a waiter. "I have a suite at the Ritz that would be most honored by your presence. *Both* of you."

Sheila giggled. "I figured you'd be there. We just happen to have a suite there ourselves."

"Do you realize it took a war for me to stay at the Ritz?" Amy said. "Before the war, I lived in two rooms with my mother, father, and sister."

"Where did you two meet?" Jacques asked after the waiter had taken their orders.

"We were both working at the same hospital," Sheila said. "And we were going crazy with boredom. The parties were *so* dull." Suddenly her face was serious. "So many boys we both knew were not coming back from the war. It's very hard to face that when you're twenty-two. So we decided to find some excitement for ourselves. Why else go on living?"

Jacques laughed. "Sheila, chuck the melodrama." But he understood. In America they'd sat out the war for two and a half years. *Reading* about the fighting, the bombings, the casualties was one thing; being part of it was an ugly reality.

"You know, before the war I swore I wouldn't give up my virginity until I was married," Sheila said.

Amy winked. "That didn't stop you from enjoying yourself, darling. You told me so. You did everything but."

"I brought us a little treat. Maybe it was a bit unfair, but I helped myself to the hospital supplies. Have you ever tried morphia, Jacques?" She patted the small case that lay on the empty chair beside her.

"On occasion." He felt oddly defensive. Did this little slut think he was too old to try anything new? He knew about chloroform *and* morphia—after all, they were available from almost any chemist in London. "Though I can live without heroin."

"Wonderful!" Sheila clapped her hands. "Later we'll drug ourselves into glorious oblivion. Think you're man enough for the two of us, Jacques old boy?"

They ate quickly and returned to the Ritz. First Jacques went up to his suite alone. A few minutes later, Sheila and Amy knocked at his door. "Come in," he yelled from the bedroom. "The door's open."

Naked and passionate, Jacques crossed to a table and poured champagne into three glasses.

"Darling, don't waste that." Sheila reached for him.

"I wouldn't dream of it." He ran his hands down her back. "But aren't you a bit overdressed?"

"Not for long, Jack," Amy said, and laughed.

Jacques grimaced. She could at least pronounce his name right. But now she was taking off her clothes, and she had a glorious body.

He realized immediately that the girls wanted to be in charge, and he was perfectly content to follow their lead.

Time raced by. Their bodies became sleek with perspiration. At alarmed moments Jacques worried that he might fail to perform, but the two girls were incredibly canny. Who the hell had taught them to drive a man to such frenzy?

At last, they lay back, exhausted, entangled.

"Why don't we go downstairs for dinner?" Jacques said. "And then come back up here for sweet dessert. You *do* have the morphia?"

"Oh, darling, yes," Sheila murmured. "*My* treat."

LILLI TRIED TO READ between the lines of Sara's latest letter. From Jacques she had received only a postcard, which appeared to be a jaunty effort at optimism. Aunt Sara wrote that she had met Lisette de Carpentier for luncheon at the Ritz—where the duchess had been living since turning her house over to the French government—and looked across the room to see Jacques dining with a pair of young women. "Jacques told me he has been in Paris for over a month. He's driving an ambulance for the American Red Cross. So many young English girls here, Lilli. I suspect they're attracted by all the men in uniform."

Jacques had not bothered to look up Aunt Sara. It was difficult to forgive him for that. Was Aunt Sara trying to tell her that Jacques was forgetting his marriage vows with American Red Cross girls? He must be driving an ambulance between Paris and the front. The Germans were rarely less than sixty-five miles from the city. "We live with the constant sounds of cannon fire," Aunt Sara had written. "But that is reassuring. It means our guns are between us and the Germans."

Lilli put the letter aside when Peggy came in to report that a difficult client was insisting on talking to her. "I don't know what she wants to complain about. She insists she won't talk to anybody but you." Peggy sighed. "She may be the wife of some important Belgian official, but she's an obnoxious woman. Do you want me to tell her you're too busy to see her?"

"I'll talk to her," Lilli said.

Peggy ushered in a tall blonde, in her late forties, and introduced her as Mme. Memling. With a smile, she accepted Lilli's offer of a seat across from her Louis XV writing table; but she waited for Peggy to close the door before speaking.

"You come originally from Marienbad, yes, Mrs. Laval?" The question—and the accent, which hinted of German rather than Belgian background—took Lilli by surprise.

"Yes."

"Your native language was German?"

Lilli stiffened. "I am an American citizen, madame." Occasionally the anti-German hysteria in America had reached out to include her. "My husband was born here. Our two children acquired their father's citizenship. What is it you wish, madame?"

"I'm here on behalf of the German government," Mme. Memling said, smiling faintly at Lilli's obvious shock. "You were born in Marienbad. Your grandparents were born in Germany—"

"I've told you, I'm an American." Lilli tried to keep her voice from shaking. "I'm a loyal American citizen."

"Good." Mme Memling smiled. "It is necessary to keep this attitude. I was born in Berlin, but I work for Belgian relief here in New York and in Washington."

"Madame Memling, please. What is it you wish of me?"

"You own one of the most elegant beauty salons in Paris," she said, "and another in London. You own property in both countries. If you choose to be helpful to the German government now, then the German government will be helpful to you later, once it occupies London and Paris. As it will."

The conviction in her voice sent a chill through Lilli. "Madame, I've told you. I'm an American citizen. My husband is in Europe with the American Red Cross. I have two children, both American citizens." Then a daring thought occurred to her: Maybe she could be useful to her adopted country by playing along with this woman. "I—I can't think how I could be useful to the German government." She made a pretense of appearing ambivalent.

Mme. Memling smiled. She had caught the scent of victory. "You have much to lose if you turn us down. Everything you own in the conquered countries. All we ask of you is a little of your time."

Lilli sat silently, assessing her position. "What would you require of me?" she asked finally.

"Your presence in Paris for a few days to—"

"Paris is out-of-bounds to everyone except high-ranking military personnel and the Red Cross," Lilli interrupted. But she felt a surge of excitement at the prospect of being there. Seeing Sara. *Seeing Jacques.* "Not even soldiers on leave are allowed in Paris."

"Come now, Mrs. Laval. You have friends in high places. You've lent your house to the French government. Now don't worry, we understand that this was a good business move—like your contributions to French and British relief. We will show you how to arrange to visit Paris. It is logical for you to want to go to Paris, yes? You have your salon there, your house, your factory. You worry about them. You worry about your aunt.'' Lilli started. They had done their homework. ''You speak fluent French and English. You are the right person for this assignment.''

''How long would I have to stay there?'' Traveling across the Atlantic in wartime was slow—she'd be away from the children for weeks.

''No more than four days in Paris, Mrs. Laval. There is a special meeting scheduled there among French, English, and American officials. We know they will decide on the date for a tremendous drive against us. We must be prepared. They will be staying at the Crillon, where you will stay. You will contrive to socialize with them. Not difficult for a beautiful young woman with an international reputation.''

''But—I wouldn't know how to go about getting such information from them.''

''You will be told how to elicit—in a seemingly innocent fashion, of course—the facts we need. You are a sophisticated woman, Lilli. You understand men. Under the right circumstances they talk freely.'' So, Mme. Memling meant for her to sleep with one of these high-ranking officials. ''In these ugly times they'll be grateful for your company. You'll sail for Liverpool, go down to London for two days.'' *She would see Oliver and Frances and Charles.* ''It's natural that you are concerned for your London salon. From the train you will go directly to Claridge's. You'll be contacted about the Channel crossing.''

She would see Jacques.

''When do I leave?''

''In six days.'' Mme. Memling nodded in approval. ''You are to meet with our group here in New York tomorrow evening. We'll discuss—''

''It will have to be postponed until the following evening,'' Lilli said. *She had to talk to Alex.* ''I leave for Washington, D.C., in the morning. We're planning to open a new salon there. It would seem odd if I didn't show up for important appointments.''

"If anyone asks, you explain that because of your generosity to the war effort, you received special permission from the French government to visit your salon. You'll admit that you're eager to go there because your husband is stationed with the Red Cross in the city." Mme. Memling rose to her feet. "I'll phone to set up our meeting. You understand it would be inadvisable to confide your mission in Paris to anyone? Even to your husband?"

"I understand."

LILLI WAITED UNTIL she was sure Mme. Memling had left the salon before reaching for the telephone. She had to talk to Alex. He would help her find the proper parties to consult. He would help her become a German agent, reporting to the U.S. government. It was unreal and frightening—but something she must do.

19

In a crowded restaurant, colorful military uniforms of many nations on display, Lilli and Alex sat at a small damask-covered table in the corner.

"It seems absurd that they would approach *me*, Alex."

"Not at all." He looked grim. "They figure a German victory in France and London would be a serious financial threat to you."

"I thought it was important for me to pretend to agree to work with them. I was sure you'd know whom I should contact."

"These people know you're in Washington today?" he asked.

"Yes, but they think it's for business. I said we were considering opening a salon here, and that I had appointments today that had to be kept."

"The Memling woman accepted this?"

"Absolutely."

"Madame Memling has been under suspicion for months, but this is the first actual link we've had to—"

"*We?*" Lilli stared at him. "Alex, are you with Army Intelligence?"

He nodded. "I'm sorry, Lilli, but obviously I couldn't tell you about this until now. Anyway, after lunch we'll go to my apartment. We'll meet with my colonel there. It wouldn't be wise for you to go to Army Intelligence headquarters. At worst—if they've followed you down here—they'll think we're having a wartime affair in addition to discussing business for the salon." He chuckled. "That's a hell of a lot safer than thinking you're playing double agent." Though he seemed casual, Lilli knew he was nervous about her being involved this way. "Lilli, you don't have to go through with this. You can tell Memling you've had second thoughts. Damn it, you're not trained in espionage! This is insane."

"Alex, I have to go through with it," she said quietly. "It could be very important. Nothing will happen to me." She reached across the table and covered his hand with hers. "Just tell me what to do."

At 3:00 A.M. on a Tuesday morning of the following week, in a dense fog, Lilli boarded the small, camouflaged ship that was to take her to Liverpool. She would share a cabin with one of the nurses—a grim, middle-aged woman whose only concern seemed to be that someone other than nurses or doctors had the audacity to take up passenger space on the ship.

From the nurse, Lilli learned that the crossing would take anywhere from ten days to two weeks and that they were leaving New York Harbor without a convoy to protect them in the dangerous Atlantic. Except for a pair of high-ranking nurses—including Lilli's cabinmate—the nurses slept on deck wearing their life belts. Lilli had been provided with a rubber life suit that contained packets of emergency rations in the event the ship was sunk.

For nine days, over a choppy sea, the ship traveled without an escort, though it was armed with half a dozen eight-inch guns. Lilli spent her waking hours going over in her mind every small detail drilled into her head by both German and American Intelligence, refusing to dwell on the obvious dangers that lay ahead: She would come out of this alive.

She worried about the children. Jan had been intrigued that she would be seeing Jacques in Paris, but Freddie had clung to her when she'd kissed him goodbye, as though he knew that this was not the festive trip to Paris—"to see Papa and Aunt Sara and the salon"—that she pretended. Only now did Lilli realize how exhausted she had been. She spent hours each day dozing on the deck. She couldn't wait to see Aunt Sara again. They had never expected another long separation.

Wouldn't Jacques be amazed to see her in Paris! Somehow they would have to find a way to spend a few hours together. Aunt Sara was living in the apartment above the salon. She would have to check with the Red Cross to see where Jacques was billeted.

She had been disturbed by the tone of Sara's references to Jacques in her most recent letter, but she told herself she mustn't jump to any conclusions; Jacques had changed this last year.

In the late afternoon of the ninth day of their crossing, the ship was joined by two British destroyers. This meant they were in the danger zone. Countless pairs of eyes scanned the water for a periscope. That night Lilli slept fully dressed, her life suit within reach. She could feel the constant zigzagging of their course as the engines pounded in the night.

The next day the ship docked at Liverpool. Lilli could barely contain her excitement. In a few hours she would be in London. She would see Oliver and Frances and Charles. And London—though letters from Oliver and Frances had warned her that wartime London was not the London she had known.

Emerging from the train in Victoria Station, she was struck by the sight of groups of soldiers saying farewells, clearly on their way to the battlefields of France. And then she saw the amputees, painfully making their way through the crowds.

She was trembling when she climbed into a waiting taxi and asked to be taken to Claridge's.

Sandbags were everywhere. She remembered Oliver writing that the roof of Buckingham Palace was covered with sandbags to protect the royal family. Streetlamp shades were painted black or green. Searchlights and antiaircraft guns were silent reminders of German planes dropping death and destruction upon the city. Soldiers were everywhere, drilling wherever there was an open square. There was a mournful quality to those who walked the streets.

When she arrived at the hotel, Lilli was told that Countess Irma de Nemur would call on her at nine the following morning. This must be her "contact," who would accompany her to Paris. Now she could phone Oliver.

He was at the salon.

"Lilli, I can't believe you're here!"

"Can you meet me for dinner?" she said. "I leave for Paris the day after tomorrow."

"Of course," he said. "We'll have dinner at the Savoy." The Savoy had become their "celebrating place."

"Is Frances there?"

"No. She just left for the day. She'll be so excited when she finds out you're in London!"

"Shall I phone and ask Charles and her to join us for dinner?"

"Of course."

"Are the children all right, Oliver?"

"Still in the country with Frances's mother. Frances and Charles visit every weekend."

"And Sebastien?" Lilli realized it had been months since Oliver had mentioned Sebastien, off fighting with the French Army.

"Lilli—" His voice cracked. "I'm sorry. I haven't been able to tell you. Sebastien—Sebastien gave his life for France."

"Oh, Oliver, I'm so sorry. He was a sweet, talented man."

"Word came through eight months ago," he said. "I just couldn't talk about it."

"Oliver, I'm going to call Frances now. Come up to the suite as soon as you can. We'll have a chance to talk before dinner."

In less than forty minutes, Oliver was sitting beside Lilli while she poured tea for him. Even in these first few moments together, Lilli noticed a change in Oliver: His boyish airs seemed to have disappeared. The slight limp he dismissed with a shrug.

Oliver accepted without question her explanation that she was here on government business. "You were always a pretty courageous lady, Lilli," he said with a smile.

"I may not be able to see you after tonight, Oliver," she said. "Do you understand?"

He nodded. "Be careful, Lilli. We love you."

"Of course I will." She took his hands. "And when this insanity is over, you'll come to New York. You won't believe the way the children are growing!"

Oliver told her that the air raids were now occurring even in daylight. The basement of the salon had become a neighborhood shelter when German planes flew overhead. He told her, too, of the losses suffered by members of the salon staff.

After an hour or so, Frances and Charles arrived, and they all left the hotel for the Savoy. Though the streets were filled with people going to the theater or the opera or their favorite restaurants, Charles had to drive without headlights—another concession to the war. Over dinner, Lilli listened in shock as her friends talked of close brushes with death.

"But there'll be no bombings while you're in town, Lilli," Oliver said. "The Germans wouldn't dare."

AT NINE O'CLOCK SHARP the following morning, Countess Irma de Nemur arrived at Lilli's suite. A tall blonde in her forties, like Mme. Memling, she was exquisitely dressed and had an English accent that sounded to Lilli as though it had been acquired. Also like Mme. Memling, her cover was that of a Belgian refugee.

"We will cross the Channel early tomorrow morning," the Countess said crisply. "I'm accompanying you to buy gowns by Monsieur Poiret. The salons seem to be doing some business despite the war." She shrugged. "The Paris officials know you are bringing a friend. The story is that we know each other from your days in Paris. We spent country weekends together and holidays at Deauville. We'll share a suite at the Crillon."

"Will I have time to visit my salon this afternoon?" Lilli asked.

"No." She looked irritated. "We have much work to do. We can afford no mistakes."

For the rest of the day, Irma de Nemur and Lilli practiced their story. Over dinner in the suite, Irma announced they would go to bed early. They were leaving early in the morning.

TWICE, THE BOAT that was to take them across the Channel turned back because of mines. On the third try, they made it across. But it was close to midnight before their train pulled into the Gare du Nord. Upon leaving the train, they learned that earlier in the evening there had been another air raid on the city. On the train into Paris, Lilli had been sure she heard the sound of gunfire in the distance.

They took a taxi to the Hotel Crillon, driving through streets lighted only by the moon. Here, too, life seemed to go on undisturbed by the war: People went out to the theater, the opera, and the ballet; they dined in the best restaurants and entertained in their homes.

Lilli received an enthusiastic welcome at the Crillon. Irma and she were escorted to a choice balconied two-bedroom Louis XV suite with a view of the Place de la Concorde. The elegant sitting room had a high curving ceiling and an exquisite crystal chandelier. A pair of cloisonné vases and an antique clock sat atop the fireplace mantel.

"Draw a bath for each of us," Irma ordered the maid standing at the door. "We're absolutely exhausted. Then you may unpack."

EXCITED TO BE BACK IN PARIS, Lilli hadn't expected to sleep that first night. But she did—a deep, dreamless sleep. When she awoke, Irma was standing in the doorway of her bedroom.

"I've ordered breakfast sent up," she said. "It should be here any moment."

"Thank you." Lilli tossed aside the coverlet. "I think I'll call my aunt first."

"Later," Irma said. "After breakfast, we'll go to the salon."

"I should contact the Red Cross," Lilli said, "to find out where my husband is billeted."

"I'm sorry, Lilli," Irma said. "He has been transferred to hospital duty in the south of France. I didn't want to disappoint you until it was absolutely necessary."

Who had done this? The Germans? And why? To keep her from telling Jacques why she was here? They didn't trust anyone. But she had made her commitment.

She shrugged. "I *am* disappointed, Irma. But there's nothing I can do, is there?"

The morning was gray and cool. Lilli picked at the hearty breakfast Irma had ordered. She couldn't wait to get to the salon. At last, they left the hotel and flagged a taxi.

Lilli was trembling as the taxi dropped them in front of the salon. In one hand she held the B. Altman shopping bag that contained the coffee she had brought across the Atlantic and the Channel for her aunt. Her heart pounded as she gazed at the charming old mansion that stood proudly before her, slightly damaged now from German bombings.

"We'll stay here perhaps an hour or two," Irma said. "Then we'll have lunch at the Ritz. It must appear that we're here to enjoy ourselves, Lilli. Remember that."

As soon as she stepped into the salon Lilli was surrounded by her treatment girls, most of whom had been with Princess Lilli since its first days. With tears in her eyes, she hugged them all.

"Lilli! Oh, my God, it is you!"

She turned. There was Sara, arms outstretched, coming toward her. "However did you manage to get here? How could you take such chances?"

Lilli laughed. "I pulled strings. I'm here for only two days—to see you, the salon, and to buy some dresses from Monsieur Poiret. I hear the salons are 'half open.'"

Sara eyed Irma. "For old customers like you, of course."

"Aunt Sara, this is Countess Irma de Nemur," Lilli said. "Do you remember hearing about my old friend Irma, whom I met years ago at a house party in Deauville? Well, she was stranded in New York—her husband is a Belgian who was in

America on business—and we ran into each other on the street!
Irma, this is my aunt, Madame Fielding. She's been my mother
since I was seven." Fighting tears, she hugged Sara again. *Why
wouldn't Aunt Sara listen to reason and come to New York?*

Sara took her two visitors on a tour of the salon and then
suggested they both have facials. "Gigi is marvelous," Sara told
Irma. "You will be delighted with her." She deposited Irma in
a treatment room and pulled Lilli into another room. "Lilli,
what is this?" she whispered. "That woman is not Belgian. Her
French is far from perfect, and German is clearly her first language."

"Aunt Sara, I learned German as my first language—"

"Lilli," Sara said, "tell me the truth. Why are you here with
her?"

"Because of the American government," Lilli said softly.
"Please, you must not ask questions. I may not be able to see
you again before I leave. Do you understand?"

Slowly, Sara nodded, her eyes filled with fear. "Yes."

"Irma told me that Jacques has been transferred to the south
of France," Lilli said. "Do you know anything about that?"

"I've seen Jacques once since he arrived, Lilli," Sara said
briskly. "I know nothing of his whereabouts. I heard, though,
that several of the American Red Cross workers had been
transferred. Some have a tendency to live too high."

"I doubt that I will see him," Lilli said quietly. Had some
scandal erupted that sent Jacques and the others away from
Paris? "Aunt Sara, can't I persuade you to come to New
York?"

Sara almost visibly recoiled. "And leave the salon? No, I will
stay here, where I belong."

At last, with reluctance, Lilli stood up to leave. She kissed
Sara goodbye, and together she and Irma left the salon. In the
taxi on the way to the Ritz, Irma congratulated Lilli on the
quality of the salon services. "No wonder you look so young,
my dear. When this stupid war is over, you *must* open a salon
in Berlin."

They lunched lengthily at Maxim's—where the grand paneling, the elegant mirrors, the traditional lush display of roses, even in wartime, reminded Lilli of the halcyon days when Oliver, Jacques, and she had been the toast of Paris. How long ago it all seemed!

"Tomorrow we will shop for clothes," Irma said. "After all, that is supposed to be my reason for coming to Paris with you." She smiled in satisfaction. "I will buy at least two day dresses and an evening gown."

Irma was pleased when two elderly gentlemen whom Lilli had known since her first year in Paris stopped by the table to greet her. Again Lilli stuck to her story explaining her presence in Paris.

From Maxim's, they returned to the Crillon. Irma insisted on spending the remainder of the afternoon coaching Lilli for her evening activities. She had been delighted to discover that Lilli knew Richard Lindsay, President Wilson's representative at the secret conference in Paris.

"Lilli, why didn't you tell me you knew him?"

"Because you hadn't told me who would be conferring in Paris." Lilli had met Richard Lindsay in the privacy of Alex's apartment in Washington so that she would be able to recognize him in the dining room at the Crillon.

"There will be General Aumont—no doubt traveling with his usual military escort," Irma said. "And Lester Williams, who is here to speak for the British government. They'll confer all day, then relax over dinner. When you've been seated in the dining room, you'll be able to see Richard Lindsay. Send over a magnum of champagne. You'll be invited to join them."

Wearing a black velvet gown and pearls, Lilli left the suite and headed for the dining room. Tonight, Irma would have dinner alone in their suite. As she stood in the luxurious Crillon elevator, Lilli went over her instructions. Of the three representatives of the Allied Powers, only Mr. Lindsay knew why she was here. She had been briefed on exactly what to report to Irma: any information American Intelligence wanted to have delivered into German hands, or any false information about military plans for the American troops being rushed through training.

There was only a small crowd in the dining room tonight. With the windows draped against the night, the atmosphere was warm and festive, filled with the tinkling of glasses, the occasional pop of a champagne cork, and the mingling of voices. During the war, it wasn't unusual to see a lady hotel guest dining alone. Women were making such progress: they held jobs that once had been closed to them; they fought—even in a war—for the right to vote, and at this moment a woman-suffrage amendment was being considered in the U.S. House of Representatives.

As planned, Lilli pretended to suddenly notice Richard Lindsay, and ordered a magnum of champagne sent over to his table. The gentleman with him had to be Lester Williams. But where was General Aumont?

Just then a tall man in military uniform—a general's uniform—walked into the dining room. Six soldiers stood at the entrance. Lindsay and Williams stood up, and from the exchange of handshakes, Lilli guessed that this was their first meeting of the day. The general must have just arrived from the front.

As soon as the waiter approached the gentlemen's table with the champagne, Lilli and Richard went through the charade of discovering each other. Lindsay crossed the room to invite her to join them for dinner. Smiling, Lilli stood and followed him to their table.

It was just a pleasant dinner party, though Lilli was unnerved by the realization that General Aumont was fresh from the battlefield. The general and Williams seemed delighted by the gaiety Lilli introduced into the atmosphere. Teasing Lindsay about his limited French, the general decided they would speak in English. Lilli tried to ignore the heavy cigarette smoke, which she loathed, and to focus on the superb blanquette de veau.

All at once a shattering wail penetrated the room. Lilli froze.

"Ah, yes, the *sirène*," the general said. "Another raid." Then he picked up his fork and continued to eat.

"Should we remain here?" Lester Williams asked politely.

"Oh, the planes won't arrive for at least twenty minutes after the first alert," the general said. "It is always this way. Let us finish this superb meal."

20

Lilli and her companions continued with their dinner as though nothing had happened while the other guests were accepting the waiters' entreaties to go down to the *cave*. The lights had been turned off and candles were being passed around.

"I have not had a meal like this in months," General Aumont said, "and I'll be damned if I'll be stopped by a raid." He paused. "Forgive my language, madame."

Lester Williams looked around nervously. "Perhaps Madame Laval should go down to—"

"No," Lilli said. She had no choice but to stay with her companions as instructed. "This will be something to tell my children."

When an illustrious French general spoke, his words were honored. Though the dining room was deserted, one waiter stayed to serve them. To Lilli, the meal seemed interminable. The waiter cleared the table and returned with their chocolate soufflés.

They ate their soufflés and tried to talk over the sounds of guns. The general talked nostalgically about a prewar dinner party. Lilli was aware that the gunfire was coming closer. Then all at once there was the deafening sound of planes overhead.

"Madame Laval, come with me to the windows," the general said, extending his hand. "Something, as you said, to tell your children."

As she stood at the window, she noticed an odd light patter outside. She looked questioningly at the general.

"Shrapnel," he said.

Close by, a bomb hit a building. Lilli shuddered. How many died at that impact?

"General, I think we should retire to the *cave*," Lindsay said firmly. "This could continue for an hour."

At last the *breloque*—the all-clear—was sounded. Lilli and the three men returned to the dining room to be served their coffee. She wondered where Irma had gone during the raid. The Countess had not been in the *cave*.

Accompanied by his military guard, General Aumont went up to his suite. Lindsay and Williams escorted Lilli to her suite before going to their own. Lilli unlocked the door, walked into the small entrance foyer, and stared in astonishment. A short, pudgy man in his fifties sat beside Irma on the sofa.

"Well?" Irma demanded. "What happened with them?"

"We had dinner together," Lilli said uncomfortably.

"This is Ernst," Irma said. "He and his partner were in the dining room tonight—sitting separately, of course. They will be there each night that Aumont, Williams, and Lindsay meet there. They will see that all information you bring us goes directly to Berlin along with their own findings." Ernst nodded, expressionless, as he pulled a notebook from his jacket pocket.

"I'm having dinner with the three of them again tomorrow evening—" Lilli began.

"When do they plan to leave Paris?" Irma leaned forward. "It's important we know that. There will be no major American drive until then."

"Not for another four days at least."

Irma glanced at Ernst. "Why are they staying here so long?"

"I couldn't find out." Lilli tried to look apologetic. She had been warned not to supply too much information from this first encounter. "I suspect they're waiting for some military personnel to join them here." True, but of no use to Irma and her friend. "Possibly General Pershing himself." Not true.

"His men are being used as replacements?" Irma said. "Is that what Pershing will discuss? Lilli, we need facts!"

"Pershing won't allow the American forces to be used as replacements, Irma." Alex's colonel had stressed the importance of conveying this to the Germans. "The general means for American soldiers to fight independently."

"Not all Allied generals agree with him," Ernst said, taking notes.

"But Pershing will hold out," Lilli said. "Both Lindsay and Williams are sure of that. Our French general is irritated at Pershing. He's anxious for replacements."

"Were you able to learn the number of American troops that will be coming over?" Irma asked.

"Irma, they would hardly be so open with me," Lilli said. But she added specific facts, as instructed by Alex's colonel.

Irma looked pleased. "You must cultivate this Mr. Lindsay in a more personal way, Lilli. I don't have to tell *you* how to make a man more responsive...."

"Are you saying I should sleep with him?" Lilli pretended to be amused. "That should not be difficult to arrange." She and Lindsay could make a pretense of a romantic interlude.

Irma turned to Ernst. "This attitude of Pershing's about the American soldiers must be known in Berlin. Make sure the news goes out tonight."

Before dismissing Ernst, Irma questioned Lilli over and over, until at last she seemed satisfied with the information. Then the two women went to their separate bedrooms. Tomorrow Lilli and Irma were to shop for clothes at the salon of M. Poiret. In the evening Lilli would dine with the three men again. By that time the information Lilli had planted would be in the hands of the Germans.

LILLI WAS ASTONISHED by the abandon with which Irma spent money—until she realized the shopping spree was financed by the German government. How strange to be shopping at Maison Poiret while the guns from the front could be heard in the dressing rooms!

Lilli tried to inveigle Irma back to Princess Lilli for another beauty treatment, but Irma insisted they return to the hotel and plan for the evening. "Lilli, tonight I will be dining with you," she said.

"But they're expecting me alone." How would she be able to tell Richard Lindsay that they must be careful what they said in front of Irma?

"You'll explain that I'm an old friend who's traveling with you. You said nothing to them about me last night?"

"No, I thought that would only complicate the situation."

"Then you'll tell them when we go downstairs," Irma said. She smiled slyly. "I doubt that they'll object to yet another feminine companion at dinner."

At six o'clock sharp, Lilli and Irma left their suite and headed for the Crillon dining room. The night was unseasonably cool. Lilli wore the new dinner dress she had bought that afternoon. Normally a quietly elegant dresser, tonight she wore a gown with a gold brocade bodice and flame chiffon skirt. The brocade jacket was lined in flame silk—Lilli's gesture of personal defiance against the war.

Irma wore body-hugging black satin, the neckline daringly low. In the soft lighting of the dining room, she looked lovely. As the two women walked into the dining room, Lilli spied Ernst at an inconspicuous table that hugged the wall.

Lilli struggled to hide her unease as she introduced Irma to the three men. She saw a glint of surprise in Richard Lindsay's eyes and sensed his approval. *He thought she had brought Irma along for cover.*

Irma talked about her work with Belgian relief, and to Lilli's dismay, General Aumont seemed to believe her. She prayed he would be wise enough—despite the prodigious amount of champagne he was consuming—not to say anything that shouldn't be said.

"I know it was frivolous of me to rush over to Paris with Lilli this way just to shop," Irma said, "but we all live under such tension."

"This insanity will soon be over," Lindsay said with an optimism that gave Irma an opening.

"You mean because the Americans are coming over to fight in the war? Are they really sending over a whole army to fight beside our French and English troops?"

"Pershing arrived in June with his first troops," General Aumont said: a well-known fact, Lilli realized with relief. "There will be many more." Information that American Intelligence wanted Berlin to know.

As Irma talked to the general and Lester Williams without learning anything concrete, Lilli caught a hint of suspicion in Richard Lindsay's eyes. At their Washington meeting, nothing had been said about her traveling with a Belgian countess.

Lilli tried to channel the conversation into a discussion of the Paris theater, knowing that changing to a lighter topic would infuriate Irma.

"What the devil?" The general, staring at the dining-room entrance, stood halfway up, then sat down again. "Paul!" he gestured impatiently. "My nephew," he explained.

A young French officer in a crumpled uniform arrived at their table and bowed politely to each of the others as the general introduced him. "I'm sorry for my appearance," he said, sitting down in the chair the maître d' had supplied. "I'm afraid I'm rather disheveled. But Paris maître d's understand."

Paul was clearly delighted to be seated between the two ladies. In a burst of exuberance, he ordered another bottle of champagne. Irma immediately engaged him in private conversation while the others reminisced about prewar Paris. Lilli noticed Richard's uneasy glances in Paul's direction throughout the evening, but Paul seemed more enthralled with Irma's cleavage than her conversation.

Later, Paul entertained them with amusing anecdotes about life in the French Army. "The word came through that you were in Paris on some hush-hush mission," he said to the general, "so I decided it was the perfect time to come into the city for dinner and a hot bath. May I use your bathtub?"

"How did you know I'd be at the Crillon?" The general pretended to be gruff, but Lilli suspected this was a favorite nephew.

Paul laughed, his eyes still on Irma. "Uncle Raoul, you always stay at the Crillon."

"Would one of you gentlemen have a cigarette?" Irma asked.

Instantly, the general brought out his silver cigarette case and offered it to her.

"Thank you." She smiled, took a cigarette, and waited while the general lit it for her. "When Lilli and I were shopping today, I picked up a pair of cuff links for my husband. Now I'm not sure he will like them." She turned to Paul. "Would you look at them and tell me if you think they're attractive? If not, I'll return them tomorrow."

Paul rose to his feet. "Why don't you show them to me now?" he said, turning to the others. "If you will excuse us?"

"Of course," the general said. "But don't keep the Countess waiting."

Lilli was upset. Paul had been drinking. God only knew what he might unwittingly reveal under Irma's trained questioning. Yet she had been instructed not to divulge her role to anyone other than Richard Lindsay, who already knew.

"I think I must tell you gentlemen," she began, her voice so low they had to lean forward to hear, "the Countess is a German agent. I'm sure she's taking Paul to our suite to pry information from him about the Allied plans."

The general and Williams stared at her in disbelief.

"It is true," Lindsay said. "Madame Laval is here on behalf of American Intelligence. The Germans believe she is working with them."

Slowly the general rose to his feet. "I will deal with this situation. Please excuse me."

"There's another German agent sitting at a small table against the wall," Lilli said. Surely Ernst was watching. "The small man in a dark business suit. Sitting alone."

"There's no one sitting alone, Lilli," Lindsay said.

Lilli pretended to drop her purse. Bending to retrieve it, she made a swift survey of the dining room. Lindsay was right—there was no sign of Ernst.

"He must have seen General Aumont leave directly behind Irma and Paul," she said quickly. "The general had left his cigarette case on the table—obviously he had not planned his departure.''

"The general could have gone to the men's room. The agent couldn't know—" Lester Williams paused. "Could he?"

Lindsay's gaze settle on the entrance. "The general's guards went with him. He knows." Lindsay was grim. "And we don't know where he has gone."

"He works with a partner," Lilli said, "who's somewhere in the dining room. He knows he's safe—I wouldn't recognize him." The two agents must have guessed that *she* had sent the general and his guards off in pursuit of Irma and Paul. That was why Ernst took off.

"We'll have to wait for the general's return before we make a move." Williams looked in the direction of the maître d'. "Let's order dessert, shall we?" They pretended to be unaware of the unidentified German agent watching their every move.

A waiter came forward and they ordered dessert. Williams ordered dessert brought for General Aumont, too.

"Can't have the general missing out on his sweet," he said, chuckling. "I doubt that this is included in field rations."

The trio at the table were in a silent conspiracy to appear to be enjoying the evening. Williams launched on a humorous story about a country-house party hosted by the Prince of Wales just before the war. His voice was slightly louder than normal because, Lilli surmised, he meant to convey to Ernst's partner that nothing ominous was happening at their table. "The general's had her picked up," Williams said softly, realizing Lilli could not observe this from her place at the table. He looked at Lilli. "She's being taken out under military guard. His nephew is accompanying the party." Lilli was aware that other diners were caught up in the drama being enacted beyond the dining room entrance. "I say, you're in a difficult spot, Lilli," Williams said nervously. "Those two agents must have guessed what happened."

"Here comes the general," Lindsay whispered.

"I've had the Countess taken in for questioning," he said as he sat down. "Paul's sobered up. He's gone along to help." He turned to Lilli. "We should have a deposition from you—"

"We have a more pressing problem," Lindsay said. Then, as briefly as possible, he explained the situation.

The general listened carefully while he ate his dessert. "She must be spirited out of Paris immediately," he said. "Out of France."

"Lilli," Lindsay said, "take off your jacket and let me drape it across the back of your chair. Let's all please try to appear relaxed. In a few moments, Lilli—leaving your jacket—go out of the dining room as though you're heading for the ladies' lounge. *Get out of the hotel.*"

"I can go to my salon if I can find a taxi," Lilli said, trying to keep her voice even. "My aunt lives in the apartment on the top floor."

The general shook his head. "They'll look there first. Tell Maurice at the desk that I wish you to be taken out through the kitchen and to wait for me in my car. He'll understand."

When their waiter approached the table with their coffee, they changed the subject and began talking animatedly about the current production at the opera.

"Now," the general ordered as soon as the waiter had left their table. "I'll wait another two minutes and join you in my car."

Lilli reached into her gold brocade purse and pretended to inspect her reflection in her compact mirror. Then she rose to her feet, smiled as though excusing herself, and walked toward the dining-room entrance.

Which one of the men—or women—sitting at the other tables was Ernst's partner? Whoever it was planned to kill her.

21

LILLI FOUND Maurice and delivered the general's message.

"This way, madame." Maurice realized the urgency of the situation, as the general had said.

Maurice led her outside to the general's car. The soldier at the wheel was polite and unquestioning when Maurice explained the general's orders.

Moments later, General Aumont sat next to Lilli in the rear seat and gave his chauffeur instructions.

"We're driving to my field headquarters," he said as the car moved down the blacked-out Paris street. "At field headquarters you'll be transferred into a Red Cross ambulance. By dawn you'll be in Calais. Passage will be arranged for you on an Allied ship crossing the Atlantic or on a boat sailing across the Channel. I promise you, we'll have you out of France by morning."

After they had left Paris behind, they drove through devastated villages and abandoned trenches. They passed a convoy of ambulances carrying casualties to a Paris hospital. Anguished cries of the wounded and dying filled the air. On the outskirts of yet another deserted village, Lilli saw an overturned baby carriage in the ruins of a house where only a mantelpiece stood above the rubble. She shivered. Thank God Jan and Freddie were safe in the United States!

In America people were horrified by the *idea* of war. Women lived in fear for the lives of husbands, boyfriends, and sons—but they had not come face-to-face with the reality of war: the agony of the wounded and dying, the villages devastated by the destruction.

Approaching the front, they saw stretches of farmland and orchards scored by shellfire; soldiers on night patrol; more ambulances, filled with wounded. At field headquarters General Aumont escorted Lilli to his improvised office to wait until an ambulance arrived to carry her to Calais. Here she signed the deposition dictated by the general to a corporal who was serving as his secretary.

"Thanks to you, Lilli," the general said, "we have the Countess de Nemur in our custody. And in Berlin, because of your efforts, they are poring over false information that will be most useful to the Allied cause. When this war is over, France will show its gratitude."

Within an hour, Lilli was in a Red Cross ambulance, a French Army jacket draped over the arm of her gold brocade and flame chiffon gown. As dawn crept over Calais, she was helped aboard the destroyer that was to take her to Liverpool. Alone, surrounded by early-morning mist, she stood on deck and watched the shoreline of France disappear. When would this horror end?

An hour later a young officer asked her to come to the wireless room.

"You will be met at Liverpool by a British army escort who will see you to your ship," the British officer in charge of the warship said, pacing the length of his office. For a moment the respect in his eyes gave way to a twinkle. "There will be an army nurse there, and a valise of clothes that, we hope, will be the proper size."

At that, they both laughed.

"Thank you, captain," Lilli said. "It would be most uncomfortable to cross the Atlantic dressed this way!"

The trip across the Channel was slow because of mines, but uneventful. Pacing the dock in Liverpool was Lilli's escort, who took her to the American troopship, its hull painted black and funnels gray, its decks packed with bags of sand and "protection" coal. Guns with impressive firing ranges were set up at strategic points to defend against German submarines.

A British nurse handed over the suitcase containing her homegoing wardrobe. "A wireless from Paris gave us your approximate size," she said apologetically, "but I suspect the shoes are too large."

"I'm very grateful for *anything*," Lilli said, smiling. "Thank you."

In her tiny stateroom, the original woodwork had been stripped from the walls, the portholes covered; the lavish linens from the ship's days as a luxury cruiser had been replaced by army issue.

Now that she was at last on her way home, Lilli worried about Jan and Freddie. She wondered, too, if she had been foolhardy in taking on so risky a mission. What if she had been killed? Who would take care of her children? Aunt Sara was wonderful, but she was getting on in years. Jacques wasn't reliable. Frances and Charles would be responsible, but they lived in England. Jan and Freddie were American citizens by birth; they must be raised as Americans.

Lilli spent most of the trip dissecting her marriage. She had deluded herself into believing Jacques had changed. But he hadn't joined the American Red Cross out of bravery—he had wanted some excitement, he had loved dashing about Paris in uniform. Leave it to Jacques to find a trail of welcome beds. No doubt he had been involved in the scandal that sent a coterie of Red Cross workers out of Paris.

When this awful war was over and Jacques came home again, she would be his wife, but she would not be blind to his shortcomings. The children would have their father. They would be a family. That she owed Jan and Freddie.

EXCEPT FOR ONE ENCOUNTER with a ship that was slow in hoisting its flag, the trip across the Atlantic was uneventful. At last they pulled into port in Maine. Lilli remembered arriving at Bar Harbor on the *Kronprinzessin Cecilie*. Could it have been only three years ago? It seemed like a lifetime.

Dressed in the uniform of a British nurse, Lilli traveled by train to New York. She arrived at the house tired, but relieved to be home. Martine greeted her.

"The children are still at school, Madame Lilli. They've missed you so."

"Never again," Lilli said, "will I leave them for so long."

Martine eyed Lilli's uniform. "I see there was trouble."

"Yes, there was." Lilli smiled. "But I'm all right now, Martine."

"Mr. Kahn has called every evening for the past four days," Martine said, taking Lilli's bag. "And he's been here twice to visit with Jan and Freddie. He said he's in New York on business. Such a fine man." Martine adored Alex.

"I'll call him right away." She couldn't wait to talk to him. Perhaps she could persuade him to come over for dinner.

"Madame!" Henri came into the foyer, Celestine at his heels. "We're so glad you're safely home!"

"I'm sorry I couldn't try to find your families," Lilli said. Martine, Celestine, and Henri had families in villages close to Paris. "After the war, I'll send you all home for a vacation. And I promsie you, that day will be soon."

"I'll go down to the kitchen to tell Bertha you'll be home for dinner," Martine said happily. "You know, Madame Lilli, I lit a candle every day that you were away."

Upstairs in her bedroom, Lilli kicked off her shoes, reached for the phone, and dialed Alex's number. She let it ring six times, until the operator came on to say her party did not answer.

Not until two hours later—after a long talk with Peggy at the salon—was she able to reach Alex. His voice sounded crisp and businesslike over the phone.

"Alex, I'm home," she said softly.

"Thank God!" She heard the relief in his voice.

"When can you come over to the house?"

"For dinner?"

"Wonderful." She was impatient at the delay, but she understood. After all, Alex was not in New York on vacation.

Shortly before three, Henri drove to the school to pick up Jan and Freddie. Lilli waited at the window, barely able to contain her excitement. When she had sailed for England, Gramercy Park had been summer-green. Now the trees were gold and red. The nursemaids and their charges were bundled up against the crisp autumn air.

She watched Henri pull up before the house, step out and open the car door. Jan and Freddie spilled out onto the sidewalk, laughing and talking as they scurried up the steps to the front door. Lilli rushed to open it.

"Mama!" Freddie threw himself into her arms. "You were gone so long!"

"Mama, Freddie's been just awful," Jan said. "Miss Martine lets him get away with anything!"

Lilli and the children settled in the family sitting room. Both Jan and Freddie were disappointed that she had not seen Jacques.

"You could have stayed longer and found out where Papa was," Jan said accusingly.

Lilli felt a stab of anger, but held it in. "No, darling, I couldn't. When this war is over, then I can tell you why."

Late that afternoon the doorbell rang. Lilli guessed it was Alex, though he was not expected for another hour and a half. "Henri, I'll get it," she called, hurrying to the entrance foyer. Her heart pounding, she pulled the door wide.

"Lilli!" Alex swept her into his arms. "God, I've worried about you!"

"It's marvelous to be back." She had always loved it when he held her. His arms were so strong, comforting—like an older brother's. But this time was different. "It was crazy in Paris, Alex—"

"I knew only that you were en route to the States." He released her. "And that because of your help some German spies had been apprehended."

"It's all over now." *Why was she trembling this way?* "Let's have a glass of wine to celebrate. We have a lot of catching up to do."

First Alex insisted on hearing a detailed report of her trip. In his daily communications with the Washington office, he had learned only the basic facts. He told her that Mme. Memling had been taken into custody in New York.

"I'm sorry, Lilli, but the colonel wants to see you in Washington for one final meeting. We could take the train down together tomorrow. My work here is finished."

"Tomorrow would be fine," she said. "Then I can settle down to business again."

EARLY IN NOVEMBER the world was shaken by the news of the Bolshevik Revolution. On December 3 the new Russian government began armistice talks with the Central Powers. Russia withdrew from the war, giving Germany 1.3 million square miles of Russian territory, which included 62 million Russians, and three quarters of her iron and coal resources, thereby depriving the Allies of Russian support.

Only days later Lilli returned to the salon to find a gaunt, shaken Mischa. The American debutante he had married after Lilli divorced him had gone down with the *Lusitania*. Her wealth had been in trust, so he was now virtually penniless. He had discovered that he could buy his family's safety back if he took quick action, but none of his society friends were interested in providing the funds. Lilli was their only chance for survival. Reluctantly, she agreed to arrange for the necessary transfer of funds through a Swiss bank.

"Lilli," he said, lifting her hand to his mouth, "you are a true princess."

By the end of 1917, the Allied forces had overcome the U-boat peril. Over a period of four months, thirty-one German submarines had been destroyed.

In the spring and summer, when the Germans made a desperate offensive against the Allies, they seemed closer to a breakthrough than at any time since the first year of the war. In a drive along the Aisne River, five German divisions drove through Allied troops and charged toward Paris. Many residents fled the city. But soon headlines revealed that in the second battle of the Marne, American divisions at Château-Thierry, Belleau Wood, and Cantigny had moved into battle to stop the German tide.

Over the past months Lilli had received a few letters from Jacques. They were brief, colorful, and melodramatic. While Lilli knew enough to discredit most of his stories, she let Jan share in his bragging. In addition to duty as a driver for a military hospital in the south of France, he did admit to a social life that included several prestigious French ladies and gentlemen—including Count Robert de Montesquieu.

As usual, Lilli poured herself into work, but she was distracted by these new feelings for Alex. She wondered: Did he share these feelings? It didn't seem possible. He acted as though he cared only about his work. Princess Lilli was as much his creation as hers. Lilli remembered the girls who pursued him—like that lovely young girl fresh out of Radcliffe who came to the salon just before he left for Washington—to solicit funds from him for some Jewish charity drive. *So young.* And yet Alex brushed all those pretty, available young girls aside. For now. But the day might very well come when he'd give in to his family's wishes and start a family of his own.

Once every six or seven weeks, she went to Washington for a conference with Alex. She justified the trip by telling herself that they accomplished far more in one evening together than in dozens of phone calls and letters. Alex was involved in his military activities twelve to fourteen hours each day, but he somehow found time to work with her on Princess Lilli. The long hours took their toll: Every time she saw him, he looked paler, more tired. But he was convinced the war would be over—and it would be a victory for the Allies—before the end of the year.

Now there were Princess Lilli salons in New York, San Francisco, and Philadelphia. Alex had plans for salons in Washington, D.C., and Boston, but he agreed with Lilli that this must wait until the country was no longer at war. Together they concocted new products for the Princess Lilli line.

The battle between Helena Rubinstein, Elizabeth Arden, and Princess Lilli continued unabated.

For Jan's thirteenth birthday, on the first Saturday in November, Lilli had a luncheon at the Ritz that included a dozen of Jan's classmates. Tears of pleasure welled in Lilli's eyes as she sat at one end of the table listening to the girls' squeals of delight at their expensive party favors.

How lovely Jan was! Tall, just beginning to show the graceful curves of womanhood, she had long, lush auburn hair that she was continually begging Lilli to let her cut into the new Irene Castle bob.

The high point of the luncheon was the two-tiered birthday cake, brought to the table to the accompaniment of a string quartet. Jan looked so grave and proud as she cut the first slice. This was an occasion she would remember, Lilli told herself. How often had she felt she'd failed her daughter?

ON NOVEMBER 7, 1918, word that the most terrible war in history had finally come to an end ricocheted around the world. New York erupted into jubilant celebration. Ship and tugboat whistles blew. People poured into the streets—singing, blowing tin horns, snake-dancing. Fifth Avenue and Broadway were so clogged with people they had to be closed. From office buildings workers tossed a blizzard of ticker tape and shredded paper. But by evening the joy had died. The newspapers said the report was false.

Four days later Lilli heard the sounds of "extras" on the street. In robe and slippers, she raced down the stairs. Henri had already run out to buy the "extra."

"This time it's real!" he said, coming back in, his eyes shining with tears.

Domestic staff and family sat together at breakfast this morning. It was a day no one would ever forget.

"Mama, when will Papa be home?" Jan said. "Next week?"

"Darling, it'll take a little while," Lilli said. "There are not enough ships to bring everybody home immediately. But Papa will be home soon. I promise."

Lilli had tried a half-dozen times to get a call through to Alex in Washington, but lines throughout the country were jammed. She was worried about him. No matter how many times he insisted that his work involved no personal danger, she knew there had to be times when his life was in peril. But now he would be home. They would see each other every day.

She was happy that Jacques was coming home, too—but only for the children's sake. She was not looking forward to having him in her bed again—the shadow of all those other women between them. Right this moment he was probably celebrating the end of the war with some little Red Cross worker, or a nurse, or a French girl.

She would maintain the pretense of their marriage for the sake of the children, but she knew that at last she was free of her obsession for him. Still, the victory was a hollow one.

22

A FEW DAYS BEFORE CHRISTMAS, Lilli was interrupted in the midst of a private consultation to take a phone call.

"Doris, is it important?" Lilli was impatient with her secretary, well trained by Peggy in salon practices.

"Yes, ma'am!" Doris glowed. "It'll only take a minute."

"Mama!" Jan's voice was electric with excitement when it came to Lilli over the phone. "Papa's home! He came home just as Henri brought us from school!"

"Darling, that's wonderful," she said. "Ask Bertha to make a Black Forest cake for dessert tonight."

There was a long pause. "Aren't you coming home right now? Papa's having a bath, but he said he'd be out in ten minutes."

"I'm in the middle of a consultation." *Why was she always so defensive with Jan?* "I'll be home as soon as I've seen my afternoon appointments. Goodbye, Jan."

"Lilli, what do I do about this awful dry skin?" The imperious Broadway actress brought her back to the business at hand. "I can't bear it!"

"My new cream," Lilli said automatically, reaching into a hand-painted enameled box on her desk. "It's not yet scheduled for distribution. Alex will kill me for letting it out of the salon just yet, but it'll do marvelous things for your dry skin. You'll be the first to enjoy it."

At six, as usual, Doris came into the office to tell her Henri was waiting to drive her home.

"Thank you, Doris. Tell him I'll be there in a few minutes." She reached for her Russian sable cape, which Freddie kept insisting made her look like a movie star. Jacques would understand that she simply couldn't walk out on her appointments at the salon just because he had come home, she reasoned. What she wasn't ready to admit was that she was deliberately delaying seeing him.

"Alex, I'm going home." She paused at the door of his office. Alex glanced up from the spring ad campaign spread out on his desk. They had spent the past three evenings working with an artist on the packaging. Everyone talked about Arden's packaging. They had to match it. "Jan called earlier." She tried to sound enthusiastic. "Jacques arrived this afternoon."

"Ah," he smiled, "there'll be celebration in the Laval household. Jan must be terribly excited."

"She was furious that I didn't leave the minute she called."

"You know, you could take a few days off—"

"We're much too busy." She didn't want to be home with Jacques. "See you in the morning, Alex." She smiled, moved on down the hall and out into the street. Henri was waiting beside the car in the cool, crisp early evening. He opened the door for her.

When she arrived at the house, she heard Jacques's and the children's voices. She walked slowly down the hall to the family sitting room. Jacques sat on the sofa with Jan leaning against one shoulder and Freddie at his other side.

"Lilli!" He sprang to his feet and rushed toward her. He was still in Red Cross uniform. "Honey, it's wonderful to be home!"

He kissed her, and she felt nothing.

"You're looking marvelous." He held her at arm's length and inspected her. "Lilli, you are amazing—you never age."

"Not true." She laughed. "But it's a pleasure to hear it, anyway."

Jan's face was disapproving. "Mama, you took an awful long time to come home."

"I had to finish up my appointments. Did you ask Bertha to make a Black Forest cake for dinner?"

"Mama, Papa almost got killed three times!" Freddie said. "Papa, tell her!"

Little was required of Lilli for the rest of the evening. As Jacques and the children kept up a lively stream of chatter, she observed her husband. The year and a half had not been kind to him. High living and too much drinking had thickened his waistline, and his face was slightly bloated.

But in spite of Lilli's silence, the atmosphere was festive. Bertha had outdone herself with the meal, and Jacques was clearly out to be his most charming. Lilli realized that wives across the nation were celebrating the return of their men in uniform. Why did she feel that Jacques's presence was an intrusion?

Tonight it was Jacques who ordered the children off to bed at a respectable hour. From his gaze, Lilli knew he was anticipating a passionate reunion.

"I'll bring a bottle of champagne up to the bedroom," he said as soon as the children were gone. "God, Lilli, it's been so long—"

"I'll go on upstairs."

She could feel Jacques's eyes following her as she left the room. She remembered their last night together. She had been so afraid for his safety. He had not let her see him off on the ship. *"I want to go away with my last sight of you here in our bed."* In how many other beds with how many other women had he lain since then?

Tonight she ignored the lacy black nightgowns that Jacques liked, choosing instead one of the ecru satin gowns with delicate lace inserts at the neckline. She didn't want Jacques to make love to her.

She settled herself in bed with the current issue of *Vogue*. Why was he taking so long to come upstairs? Then she heard him, whistling a Strauss waltz as he came down the hall. He opened the door and came into the bedroom with a tray bearing a bottle of champagne, two glasses, and a plate with a serving of the Black Forest cake.

"You hardly touched dessert," he scolded, placing the plate on the night table at her side of the bed. "Enjoy, while I change for bed."

He put the tray on the tulipwood commode and disappeared into the dressing room. Lilli reached for the plate, dug a fork into the dark, rich cake.

As he emerged from the dressing room in one of his Chinese robes, Lilli caught the scent of his shaving lotion. He poured two glasses of champagne and brought them to the bed.

"I haven't tasted cake like that since I left for the war, Lillie."

"Not even at those lovely parties in the south of France?" she said.

He looked surprised—and annoyed. "They didn't happen often. Everything was in short supply in France. We were at war, Lilli."

"I was in Paris last year," she said softly.

He looked startled. "The devil you were!"

"I was, Jacques. I couldn't talk about it until the war was over." Slowly, she gave him an edited version of her activities on behalf of the American government.

"That bastard Alex let you go into something like that?"

"He was just the connecting link. Actually, American Intelligence requested I take on the assignment. I'd hoped to see you in Paris, but then I learned you'd been shipped to the south of France. Something about a scandal..." *Why was she doing this?*

He gulped his champagne. "Oh, that. That was ridiculous. Drugs disappeared from a hospital cabinet. Because half a dozen Red Cross workers had access to it, we were *all* transferred." He looked at her playfully. "You thought I was mixed up with some woman, didn't you? You were jealous again." He untied the sash to his robe.

"Jacques," she said. "I was disappointed at not seeing you." *But that was before she had regained her sanity.*

"How could you bring yourself to leave the children?" he said softly. "How could you have put yourself in such danger?" He pulled off the robe and let it drop to the floor.

"In treacherous times we do what must be done." She couldn't help noticing that his shoulders were still broad and muscular—but he had the beginning of a paunch.

"Drink your champagne, my darling Lilli." He walked toward the lamp on the commode.

"I've had enough." Lilli set the glass on the night table.

"How do you stay so absurdly young?" he clucked, dropping to the edge of the bed. "At this moment—with your hair down like that—you look about seventeen, not thirty-three."

"Thirty-one," she said.

He leaned forward to kiss her, one hand reaching for a breast. She felt herself responding. No one had made love to her for so long.

"Turn off the lamp," she whispered.

He switched off the lamp and stretched out beside her. With one hand he prodded the nightgown from her shoulders until her breasts were free. The other hand slid beneath the ecru satin up the length of one thigh, fondled until a low sound of excitement escaped her.

"Jacques..." She gripped his shoulders as he held a taut nipple between his lips.

Slowly he lifted himself above her, content for a moment to burrow between her heated thighs. She thrust one slim hand between them, found him. Allowed her fingers to dart in the light movements he always enjoyed.

"Oh, Lilli," he whispered. "That feels good."

"Now, Jacques." She couldn't wait any longer. "Please, now."

She cried out softly as he entered her. Together they moved until, at once, they exploded in passion. They lay together quietly, their bodies limp. After a few moments, he kissed one earlobe. "For a little while," he said, "when I first came home, I thought you'd forgotten how it could be with us."

Long after Jacques had fallen asleep, Lilli lay wide awake. What kind of woman was she to make love to a man she loathed? But what had happened between them tonight was only a physical need; it wasn't love.

Jacques slept with his back to her. Once they would have slept entangled together, her head on his chest. She left the bed, reached for the robe that lay across the chair, and pulled it about her in the coolness of the night.

She sat on the cushioned bay window seat, pushed aside the drapes, and gazed out into the night. A light snow was falling, forming a white coverlet over the park. Usually the snow made her feel peaceful; not tonight. She was determined that her life would not change because Jacques was home. Certainly, for Jan and Freddie that was not the case. But *why* did the small attentions that Jacques provided—*when he was in the mood*—enrich their lives so much? What would her life have been like with a father?

LILLI'S WISH CAME TRUE: Jacques's return to the house on Gramercy Park brought little change to her routine. As always, she was awake at 7:00 and at the salon no later than 8:30. Jacques, she gathered, slept till noon. He made no pretense of returning to his job with Bob Allen's firm.

Unless they had a dinner party to attend, she and Jacques had dinner each night with Jan and Freddie. Their acquaintances knew she allowed herself three nights a week for socializing; the other nights were reserved for conferences with Alex, their staff artist, their chemist consultant, the factory manager—whatever was required at the moment. Jacques enjoyed being "the extra man" at social events on those nights when Lilli did not accompany him.

As in Sydney, Lilli kept cash for Jacques in an enameled box in a dresser drawer in their bedroom. He had charge accounts at Brooks Brothers and Tiffany's, and Lilly bought him a Stutz to drive around the city.

One unseasonably warm March morning, Alex charged into her office with an effervescent smile. "I've just told Doris to see that all your appointments for the day are switched. Get your coat. I'm driving you out to Southampton."

Startled, she looked up from her work. "Alex, this is my day to be at the factory—"

"Tomorrow you'll go to the factory." He crossed to the closet and pulled her coat from the hanger. "This morning you're looking at a house that's just going on the market. I have the keys. If you like it, you can tie it up before prospective buyers line up for it. It's right on the water, Lilli. You'll love it."

In twenty minutes they were in Alex's Daimler on their way to Southampton. The air was caressingly warm, the sky a brilliant blue, and Alex's enthusiasm for the house was infectious. To Lilli, this unexpected day away from the salon was a precious adventure. She rarely got the opportunity to cast aside all responsibilities and be just "Lilli."

"We'll stop for lunch in Southampton," Alex said. "Is that all right with you?"

Lilli laughed. "If you're sure you can wait to show me this fabulous house."

"I'll control myself." For an instant his eyes left the road to rest on her. "It's ridiculous to keep renting out here. And there's always the possibility you won't find a rental. And anyway, I'm selfish." He turned back to the road—but not before Lilli saw the hunger in his eyes. "I want to be sure you're close to Amagansett so I'll have a short run on summer weekends. We know we can't escape from business just because the calendar tells us it's July or August."

Lilli launched nervously into a discussion about the next site for a new salon. Arden was in Southampton and Atlantic City, but Alex advised against these two areas: Southampton was too limited, and the more elegant hotels in Atlantic City—such as the Ritz-Carlton—were said to be "restricted."

With little traffic on the roads, they reached Southampton in record time, lunched, and drove to the oceanfront house that was up for sale. It was a large, rambling, unpretentious house with a magnificent view of the sea. Alex was right: Lilli knew instantly that she would buy it.

"Of course, you mustn't expect to be invited to join the Meadow Club or the Beach Club," he said. "Jews are not accepted for membership."

"Alex, I won't come out to Southampton to socialize," she said, "except with the sea and sun."

"I knew you would love it." He was pleased. "You'll use a local lawyer. We'll stop by and make arrangements today."

Lilli was reluctant to leave the house. How different her life would have been, she thought wistfully, if it had been Alex she'd met in Marienbad almost sixteeen years ago. But she thanked God every night that he had come into her life at all.

LILLI FOUND IT increasingly difficult to avoid Jacques's persistent efforts to discover the status of her finances. He tried regularly to prod her into buying stocks through Bob Allen's brokerage office. She surmised that although he was no longer officially associated with the office, he would receive a commission if her account was substantial. As they dressed for a performance at the opera tonight, she tried again to talk him out of it.

"All liquid cash goes into opening the new salons, Jacques. And into introducing new products. We can't afford to stand still in the cosmetic field—the competition is tremendous."

"You know, it *could* backfire," he said ominously. "You could wind up with nothing."

"That's not true. We have the houses in New York, Southampton, London, Paris, and Poissy. Property is always security." He had no comprehension of the value of her art collection, new additions acquired for her regularly by Oliver.

"You think small, Lilli," he said with distaste. "Mentally, you're still a small shopkeeper."

As the weeks sped past, Lilli tired of hearing Jacques's constant highly colored tales about the dangers and hardships he'd endured in France, though Jan and Freddie seemed endlessly fascinated by every detail. And again she became increasingly concerned with Jacques's blatant favoritism toward his son.

She was delighted when Alex invited Jan and Freddie to go with him to his grandmother's house for the family seder the first night of Passover. She still remembered Aunt Sara's efforts to provide her with a semblance of a seder in their tiny flat in Marienbad.

A few days after the seder, Freddie came down with chicken pox, and Jacques acted as if his son were dying. As she watched him hover about nervously, Lilli realized that Jacques simply hadn't been around during all the other childhood illnesses.

"Shouldn't he have a trained nurse?" he asked from the doorway to Freddie's room. Earlier he had warned that if Freddie threw up, he would immediately leave the house. How, Lilli wondered, had Jacques managed to drive an ambulance in France?

"He has Martine and me—that's quite sufficient. It's a very mild case."

"Suppose you catch it? Don't those things leave scars?"

"If they're not properly cared for," she said, "but grown-ups rarely catch it."

Freddie was fretful. "Mama, it itches."

"It won't in a minute, darling." Lilli noticed that Jacques was still standing in the doorway. "Oh, for God's sake, Jacques, you're not going to catch it. I'll sleep here in Freddie's room until he's well." Martine would take care of him during the day and she would take over at night.

Exactly two weeks later, Jan came down with a severe case. Her temperature was high and the rash looked painful. Jacques went off to a house party at Tuxedo. Brushing aside all suggestions that she hire a trained nurse, Lilli had Doris cancel all of her appointments for the next week and she moved into Jan's room.

"Mama, I'm too old to have chicken pox," Jan said one afternoon while Lilli slathered her back with lotion. "It's all Freddie's fault. *He* gave it to me."

"Darling, two other girls in your class came down with it. Before you." Thank God, Jan's fever had broken.

"Mama, will I have awful scars?"

"Of course you won't. That's why I'm always here putting on the lotion. So you won't have scars."

"Mama," Jan whispered, "I love you so much."

"And I love you," Lilli said, tears filling her eyes. Nothing within memory had brought such pleasure.

WITH SCHOOL OVER until autumn, Lilli prepared for the summer. Except for Celestine, who would remain in the city with her, the staff would go with Jacques and the children to the Southampton house, now redecorated and ready to receive them. As in previous summers, Lilli would spend long weekends there.

In August, Oliver came to New York for four weeks on a combined business and pleasure trip. Midweek he stayed with Lilli at the New York house; immersed himself in Princess Lilli, New York; and lunched with Condé Nast and several Broadway leading ladies whom he knew from the London salon. He made a point of visiting the Fifth Avenue department stores to familiarize himself with the latest Rubinstein and Arden products.

To Lilli's delight, Alex and Oliver established an instant rapport. Every night that Oliver was in the city, the three of them gathered at Alex's apartment or at the Gramercy Park house for dinner and long, involved conversations about the future of Princess Lilli. For long weekends Lilli and Oliver drove out to Southampton, both grateful for the release from the stultifying Manhattan heat.

This year Alex avoided the Southampton house except for Oliver's first weekend there, when Lilli gave a dinner in Oliver's honor. Southampton summer residents included several women who knew Oliver from the London salon. Alex claimed that the new fall promotion required his presence in the city. He planned on no more than four brief weekends at the Amagansett house, where his family was spending the summer.

Lilli was surprised and dismayed by Jacques's reserve toward Oliver. The children, however, more than made up for it:

They insisted vehemently that they remembered their uncle Oliver.

It wasn't until after the dinner in Oliver's honor that Lilli understood Jacques's strange reserve. With his battle-acquired limp, Oliver was an authentic war hero. He had outdone Jacques. And Jacques was not a man who enjoyed being outdone.

On Freddie's ninth birthday late in August, Lilli arrived from New York minutes before the birthday dinner was to be served to find Jan sitting alone on the sprawling veranda staring gloomily out to sea. Haltingly, she explained that Jacques had rented a yacht for the day and had taken Freddie and his playmates out for a daylong cruise.

"Papa didn't invite me to go along," Jan said softly. "They're all out there on the yacht, but Papa didn't take me."

Lilli's heart went out to her. How *could* he?

"Jan, he probably thought you'd be bored with all those little boys," she said. "Are you hungry, darling?"

"Yes."

"Then you and I are driving into town to have our own dinner." God only knew when Jacques and Freddie would return. "When Papa and Freddie come home, we'll have birthday cake with them."

As Henri drove them to the restaurant, Lilli did her best to lift Jan's spirits. She searched her mind for warm memories. The time she took Jan for her eighth birthday luncheon at the Ritz in London. How beautiful she had looked in that blue velvet dress!

"Just you and me, darling," she said. "We didn't take Freddie."

Jan stared out the window. "He was too young."

"And remember when Uncle Alex took you out to dinner on your tenth birthday? To the Plaza? Without Freddie or me. And then there was your last birthday party, at the Ritz—"

"Freddie was there," Jan pounced. "You brought him along."

Lilli sighed in defeat. How could Jacques be so unthinking? How could he go back and forth in his warmth toward Jan? But this time she knew why. Jacques saw Jan, now moving into adolescence, as a reminder that he was no longer a young man.

On the drive back to the house, Lilli talked vivaciously about taking Jan into town with her so that they might shop for a school wardrobe. But Jan—who shared her mother's love for beautiful clothes—didn't even seem to hear her.

"Mama, Papa doesn't love me because I'm ugly," she blurted out in the darkness of the car.

Lilli was shocked. "Jan, you're beautiful! Darling, look in the mirror!"

"I'm ugly," she said. "Nobody will ever love me."

"I love you," Lilli said softly. "Uncle Alex loves you. Uncle Oliver, Aunt Sara. Charles and Frances. Martine and Celestine and Henri. Jan, so many people love you."

But Lilli cried inside, because she knew her daughter didn't believe her.

23

LILLI WAS FURIOUS when Jacques left for a house party in White Sulphur Springs a day before Jan's fourteenth birthday. He was charmingly contrite, but refused to change his plans. Again, Alex came to the rescue and took his adopted niece out for a festive birthday dinner and to the theater. Lilli sensed a deepening hostility in Jan toward her father.

When Jacques returned, several days before Thanksgiving, he was attentive to Jan and Freddie, and he tried to be amorous in bed with Lilli. He was even friendly toward Alex when he paid a visit to the salon. But on Thanksgiving eve, after the children had gone up to their bedrooms and he and Lilli were alone, Jacques revealed what he had on his mind.

"Lilli, I have too much time on my hands." He dropped an arm about her shoulders. "I should settle down to some business activity. I think I should be your business manager." He sounded deceptively casual. "You have too much on your hands to worry about investments."

"Jacques, I don't need a business manager." She was polite, wary, and firm.

"You can't let money sit in the bank drawing a paltry three percent interest!" he exploded. "I could invest it properly, multiply it a thousand times! I—"

"Jacques, I don't have money lying around in savings banks," she said. Not that she was going to tell him where it *was* invested. Her advisers were Oliver in art, and Alex in real estate. "It's all tied up in the business. I don't need a business manager." She hesitated. "If you're serious about wanting something to do, you'd probably be a great success as a liaison with our retail outlets—"

"I'm not going to be a traveling salesman!" he snapped. "Don't try to make me your errand boy." He glared at her, then stalked from the room.

Lilli went down to the kitchen and made herself a cup of tea. Now that it was over, she was trembling from the encounter. Under no circumstances would she let him handle her finances. He had no understanding of money, and if he realized the extent of her fortune, he would try to live like the Aga Khan.

When she went upstairs to their bedroom, she discovered that Jacques had stormed off to sleep in one of the guest rooms. Tonight she welcomed his absence from her bed.

THE FOLLOWING EVENING, Lilli came home for dinner with Jacques and the children, then returned to the salon for a conference with Alex and the French-born woman who was about to leave for Paris as a sales representative to stores throughout France. This was one of the more exciting aspects of the business that had gone into eclipse.

Sara had written that Rubinstein was becoming more active outside Paris than Princess Lilli. Even the Arden woman's products were being stocked by a few pharmacies in Paris and on the Riviera. Sara was ~~determined that Princess~~ Lilli would again be the world leader in cosmetics.

After Lilli sent their new French representative home with Henri in the Rolls, she and Alex settled down to continue a conference that had been cut short that morning when Lilli had been summoned to advise a temperamental Broadway star about the proper choice of eyeshadows for a photographic session.

"Candice Rollins give you a bad time this morning?" Alex asked.

"Not really," Lilli said. "She needed some coddling. She's looking in the mirror and seeing the years creep up. But let's get back to what you were saying this morning." She leaned forward. "How can we throw away all the business that's coming in from the drugstores and specialty shops? That represents a substantial profit."

"Lilli, it's time to reorganize." Lilli saw the glint in his eyes and prepared for battle. Fighting with Alex over business details was stimulating—and ultimately rewarding. "We can't afford to allow Princess Lilli to expand into a mass-market line that's sold everywhere. We must always remember that there's something very special about our products—it's the prestige line that women are eager to pay more for because that makes *them* special. In New York, henceforth, we'll sell only to stores located on Fifth Avenue."

"What about Stern's?" Lilli said. "That was one of our first accounts."

"If they want to sell Princess Lilli," Alex said, "then they'll have to move to Fifth Avenue. We'll fill orders on hand, but in the future the sales force will be selective."

"But, Alex, you said no more specialty shops. How can we *not* sell to I. Magnin?"

"We'll sell to only the most exclusive specialty shops—like I. Magnin," Alex said. "This country is about to see an unprecedented boom. Women will be delighted to buy the most expensive line of cosmetics in the field. We'll have higher earnings than ever," He chuckled. "And we're going to spend like hell on advertising."

When Henri returned with the car, Lilli instructed him to drop Alex at his apartment before taking her home. Sitting beside Alex in the car on the way, Lilli was conscious of a nagging regret that the evening was over. Lately she had dreaded returning alone to the silent house.

"It was a good evening," Alex said. "We've accomplished a lot."

She nodded. "You're right about our prestige policy. It'll pay off."

While Henri pulled away from the curb, Lilli's eyes followed Alex across the sidewalk and into the elegant apartment building. In some odd fashion, being with Alex—fighting

good-humoredly but intensely over the course of Princess
Lilli—was a bit like making love.

She leaned back against the lush gray upholstery and remembered the rare moments when she and Alex had fleetingly
exchanged emotions that went beyond that of close friends. She
kept telling herself that Alex filled the same place in her life as
Oliver, but she knew that was a lie.

Alex was happy with their relationship, wasn't he? He didn't
seem to want the complications of a woman in his life. And she
was a married woman. A *twice-divorced* married woman. That,
at least, was over. No matter how Jacques infuriated her, he
would remain her husband—in name.

When Henri pulled up before the house, she was surprised to
see her bedroom lighted. Jacques had gone to some charity affair tonight, and she hadn't expected him home until dawn. He
liked to sit around a table at the Ritz with his companions,
ranging from society acquaintances to Broadway celebrities and
best-selling authors. Before the war, society women and actresses never shared a table. All that was changed now. And
Jacques enjoyed being mentioned in the new gossip column of
Cholly Knickerbocker. What had brought him home so early?
she wondered as she climbed the stairs, the wall adorned by a
selection of vibrant Van Goghs bought by Oliver. Had he decided to make up for his absence from their bed last night?

Despite her cynical view of Jacques, Lilli admitted to arousal
tonight. She would never sleep with Alex, she taunted herself.
She would have to make do with what was available. Her husband. It would be an exercise in passion—devoid of love. Sec-
ond-best, but nonetheless desirable.

Approaching their bedroom door, she heard the strains of a
Strauss waltz. Jacques must have brought a Victrola into their
room. Perhaps he planned to evoke memories of those romantic nights at the Bellevue Café in Marienbad. Well, he needn't
have bothered.

Lilli opened the door. Jacques was sprawled across the bed
in one of his Chinese robes. "You look tired, honey," he said.

"When are you going to stop this crazy rat race with the business?"

"It's necessary." She walked into the dressing room. He could never understand what the business meant to her. It wasn't the money, though that certainly brought its rewards. And it wasn't only the security for the children. Princess Lilli, Inc., was *hers*—*her* creation, *her* success story.

Tonight she chose one of the sheer black nightgowns that Jacques always said excited him. She was tense and tired. Making love would relax her. She would try not to think about the man who would be her partner.

"You look absolutely wanton," he murmured when she walked back into the bedroom. "Like a delicious French *co-cotte*. Come to bed and show me how great you are."

WHEN LILLI HAD showered and changed into another gown, she was surprised to find Jacques awake, sitting up against a pair of pillows.

"It's chilly," she said, crossing to the radiator.

He yawned, stretched. "Lilli, take off next month and go down to Palm Beach with me."

"You know I can't." She paused. "Well, maybe for four or five days. Jan and Freddie would probably enjoy some sun in winter."

"I meant just the two of us." He reached for her hand. "And don't you think we ought to consider boarding school for Jan? She's old enough. They might teach her some manners."

She stared at him. "I'll never send the children away to boarding school." She tried to keep her voice even. "When Jan finishes high school, she'll go to college. That's soon enough for her to be away from home."

"Damn it, Lilli, she's my kid, too!" He dropped her hand.

"Jacques, you can say what you like—Jan's not going to boarding school." She slid under the coverlet and reached to switch off the bedside lamp.

"I'm going down to Palm Beach in two weeks," he said coldly.

"Before the season opens?"

"I thought I'd look around to see what properties are available down there. If we don't build a house now, we'll pay ten times as much in two years. Addison Mizner and Paris Singer are making it into the top winter resort in the country. Mizner has just built a marvelous house—really a castle—for the Stotesburys. The grounds go from Lake Worth right to the Atlantic. The house has thirty-seven rooms, a forty-car garage, half a dozen patios, a swimming pool and—"

"Jacques, we're not the Stotesburys." She had heard about the Stotesburys' "El Mirasol," built at a cost of a million dollars and still not completed. "We're not building a house in Palm Beach."

"But, Lilli, it's a sensational investment! Everybody's building in Palm Beach. The Munns, the Phippses, Harold Vanderbilt, Rodman Wanamaker—"

"I'm opening a new salon in New Orleans." Jacques grimaced, and Lilli remembered that he had no affection for his hometown. It disturbed her that Jan and Freddie had no contact with grandparents, aunts, uncles, or cousins—all because of Jacques's rejection of his family. "I assure you, Jacques, another salon is a better investment than a house in Palm Beach." She suspected that one of the major attractions for him was Palm Beach's new Everglades Club, where socialites gathered nightly, in season, to gamble.

"I'm leaving in the middle of the month." He turned his back to her. "I'm sick to death of the beastly cold up here."

Jacques was asleep when Lilli arose in the morning. When she returned from the salon and went to their bedroom to change for dinner, she found every sign of his presence had been removed. He had settled himself permanently in one of the guest rooms: her punishment for refusing to buy a house in Palm Beach. It was a punishment she welcomed.

LILLI WAS PLEASED when Alex took Jan and Freddie to a Hanukkah party his sister Esther was giving for her children. In a rush of guilt, she asked Peggy to choose a menorah for her at

Tiffany's so that she and the children could light the Hanukkah candles.

The party reminded Lilli of how she had neglected the children's religious education. She joined a neighborhood synagogue, rejecting the illustrious Temple Emanu-El, to which Alex's family belonged. She understood his need to keep his professional and family lives apart. It was all right for him to take the children to a seder or a Hanukkah party; to introduce her into his family life would be inappropriate.

She arranged for Hebrew instruction for Freddie. Jan refused, and Lilli backed off; lately she avoided any conflict with Jan. But Freddie had to learn Hebrew. In less than four years, they would celebrate his bar mitzvah.

This year she arranged for the children to receive both Hanukkah and Christmas gifts. At Passover, she promised herself, they would somehow manage to have a seder at home. *She* was Jewish. Therefore her son and daughter were Jewish.

At midnight, January 31, 1919, Lilli, Alex, and the children welcomed 1920 with champagne while the usual New Year's Eve sounds filled the streets. Earlier, Alex had taken them to the theater to see Fred and Adele Astaire in *Apple Blossoms*, the romantic operetta by Fritz Kreisler and Viktor Jacobi. Jan and Freddie had been impressed when their mother and Uncle Alex took them backstage to meet the stars. Now almost nine and a half, Freddie was considering a career as a dancer.

"What about medical school?" Lilli teased Freddie tenderly. For the past year—ever since his closest friend had been saved from death by the skills of a surgeon—Freddie had talked about becoming a doctor.

He shrugged. "I can do both."

"Freddie, you are so silly," Jan said. "Mama, don't you think it's far past his bedtime?"

"Absolutely," Lilli agreed. "And yours, too, young lady."

"Oh, Mama." Jan sighed, submitting to a goodnight kiss.

"Happy New Year, darlings." Lilli hugged each child.

"Thanks for the champagne, Uncle Alex," Jan said sweetly.

"Our last chance," he chuckled. "In a couple of weeks the Eighteenth Amendment should go into effect. Then drinking will be illegal."

Alex stayed with Lilli to discuss their plans for the New Orleans salon. Lilli was relieved that Jacques was away celebrating New Year's at the Breakers in Palm Beach with his high-living multimillionaire socialites.

Shortly past one, Alex rose to leave. Lilli walked with him to the front door. With the familiar mixture of sadness and regret, she watched him leave, turned, and went upstairs to her bedroom.

EARLY IN JANUARY the bank informed Lilli that Jacques's checking account was heavily overdrawn. She made the necessary deposit. When she received yet another note from the bank three weeks later, she again came up with the necessary funds—but not without being angry. She couldn't understand how he could spend so much money. Then the canceled checks arrived and she saw he was gambling again.

She wrote Jacques a strong letter, insisting that he stop appearing at the Everglades Club's gambling tables, or return immediately to New York. It was sinful to throw away all that money. Yet his absence from her life was welcome.

Jacques returned to New York early in March with a becoming suntan, made fashionable by Gabrielle Chanel, also known as "Coco." But on close scrutiny, his suntan did little to disguise his puffy face, the jowls that showed the first sign of sagging. Despite his expensive tailoring, his spreading waistline was painfully obvious. Approaching forty, he looked his age—and more.

On this first evening home—after Lilli apologized for a business conference requiring her presence—Jacques remembered a party being thrown by one of his Palm Beach playmates, also just returned to New York. Lilli was relieved when she returned from the salon and Jacques was still out. She guessed he would not be home until dawn. They had not made love since the night he tried to persuade her to send Jan to boarding school. The same night he had meant to persuade her to buy a house in Palm Beach. She would never again make love with Jacques without wondering what was behind his amorous mood.

Over dinner his second night home, Lilli informed him she was making arrangements to spend the month of July in Paris. Sara was eager to see the children, and she herself would visit their prime accounts in France. They would spend weekends at the country house at Poissy.

"Mama, can we sail on the *Mauretania*?" Jan asked. "Everybody says it's the only way to go to Europe."

"Lilli, you can't be serious about going to Paris in *July*," Jacques said.

"Why not? The children are out of school, and it's a slow period in the salon."

"I wouldn't mind going in April," he said. "But don't count on me to spend a summer month in Paris. The heat and the tourists, Lilli! How can you expect to enjoy it?"

"You aren't going with us, Papa?" Freddie said. Jan stared ahead. "You said Paris was your most favorite city in all the world!"

"In the right seasons, yes." He looked nervous. "No, I'll hold the fort out at Southampton."

After dinner the children went to their rooms to do homework. Jacques insisted that he and Lilli go to a speakeasy. "Everybody in Palm Beach was talking about the 'speaks,'" he said. "They hadn't started up yet when I went down for the season. I guess I'm behind the times."

"You mean people wintering in Palm Beach stopped drinking because of Prohibition?" Lilli's smile was skeptical.

Jacques laughed. "You'd have to be naïve to believe that. We would leave the beach sightly past noon to go to a prelunch cocktail party. The drinking is always at somebody's house. After dinner there is a round of parties with plenty to drink. I would usually check them all out, then settle on the most amusing. After all, who wants to be bored?

"We're going to Jack Kriendler and Charlie Bern's 'Twenty-one,'" he said. "It's over on West Forty-ninth Street."

At "21," Lilli settled for white wine. Jacques was drinking far more than Lilli ever recalled. He was in high spirits, pleased at discovering a number of Palm Beach friends present. He was only fleetingly irritated when Lilli insisted, slightly past midnight, that he take her to their waiting Rolls-Royce.

"That's right, my darling Lilli," he said. "You have to be at your Temple of Beauty tomorrow morning."

Henri hurried from behind the wheel of the car to open the door. With a flourish, Jacques instructed him to "take Madame Lilli home," dismissing his offer to return to pick him up later. It was as though she had spent the evening with a stranger, Lilli thought as Henri drove her home. She was uncomfortable in the speakeasy scene. The brazen flouting of the law—absurd as the law was—disturbed her. In fact, the whole postwar atmosphere—the almost hysterical gaiety, the frenzied determination to enjoy every minute of every hour—disturbed her. In this new decade, it seemed a sin to be bored.

Lilli knew that Jacques would not be home till dawn. She would be asleep if he came into her bedroom. Even if she were not, she would pretend to be. Lying awake in the darkness, she remembered how she had once adored Jacques. It didn't seem possible.

24

IN THE FOLLOWING WEEKS, Lilli went to dinner parties, to the theater, to the opera, with Alex as her escort. It was a wonderful theater season and together they saw *Beyond the Horizon* by Eugene O'Neill, whose *Emperor Jones* was scheduled to open in November; *Sally*, the hit musical by Jerome Kern, Guy Bolton, Clifford Grey, and Joseph Urban; and *The Jest*, with John and Lionel Barrymore.

As usual, Jacques slept till noon, then lunched at the Ritz, the Plaza, or the Waldorf. He dropped in at the stockbrokerage firm each afternoon—on the pretense of working with Bob Allen again—before heading for the Lorraine or the St. Regis for tea. He spent every evening at a different speakeasy. He made no effort to include Lilli in his social life, for which she was grateful.

In June the Republican party nominated Warren G. Harding for president and Calvin Coolidge for vice president. Just before Lilli was scheduled to sail for Europe, the Democrats nominated James M. Cox for president and Franklin D. Roosevelt for vice president. A woman-suffrage amendment had passed both houses of Congress and was being ratified by an increasing number of states. This nineteenth amendment to the Constitution was expected to become law in time to permit American women to vote in a national election for the first time in history.

In July, Lilli and the children—along with Martine and Celestine—sailed for Europe on the *Mauretania*. Each morning, Lilli settled herself in a deck chair to read Sinclair Lewis's *Main Street*, which was creating a sensation across America.

The month in Paris, with weekends at the country house at Poissy, was a time of joy for Lilli. Twice, Oliver visited them in Paris, and Frances and Charles came down with their children for a long weekend at the country house. As always, Lilli cherished her private time with Frances. On long, peaceful walks around the countryside, she talked about the problems in her marriage. She wished Frances lived in New York. There were moments, she thought, when two women could be closer than husband and wife.

It was a period of infinite relaxation, and Lilli relished every minute of it, even though she felt in Paris the same forced gaiety that permeated the atmosphere in New York. She loathed the defiant declarations of the young—on both continents—that their parents had made a mess of the past and that the future offered nothing.

When Lilli returned to New York and went out to settle the children in the Southampton house until school opened, Jacques—staying in the guest room—announced that he would be leaving in a few days for Newport, where he would be a houseguest of the Allens. "Donna and Bob bought this marvelous 'cottage' there. It's so much more chic than Southampton"—*chic* had become Jacques's favorite adjective—"and Bob feels we can make good business connections there."

"Next Wednesday is Freddie's birthday," she said quietly.

"Don't worry, I'll be here." He looked annoyed. "But I'm leaving the next day. I really don't want to miss the boat races."

Lilli suppressed a sigh. Apparently, Jacques's enchantment with his son had evaporated. As soon as Freddie could no longer be referred to as "an adorable little beggar," Jacques seemed to have lost interest. At ten, Freddie was already as tall as Lilli.

The postwar era—a time when every woman wore lipstick and mascara and eye shadow; when corsets had given way to girdles and, for some, nothing at all; when women smoked in public and thought nothing of applying lipstick at a restaurant table—offered a wealth of new freedoms. Prosperity, Americans were told, would soar. Lilli threw herself into a fresh wave of expansion for Princess Lilli.

She began to experiment with a variety of lipstick shades. Alex suggested creating a new line of eye shadows, each shade to bear the name of a feminine stage or movie beauty: the Gloria Swanson, the Marilyn Miller, the Clara Kimball Young, the Katharine Cornell, and the Alma Rubens.

In addition to Elizabeth Arden bringing out new lipsticks, bath products, and skin lotions, and Helen Rubenstein developing breakthroughs in the scientific aspects of her products, Lilli now had to cope with the newer firms springing up around the country: Dorothy Gray, who had once been with Elizabeth Arden; Richard Hudnut; and Primrose House.

Princess Lilli began advertising with a lavishness that startled its competitors. Alex used his contacts to get Lilli mentioned frequently in the editorial pages of *Harper's Bazaar* and *Vogue*, in the much-read columns of Cholly Knickerbocker and Louella Parsons, and in the pages of *Photoplay* and a half-dozen other fan magazines. Lilli dutifully appeared at the requisite parties with Alex as her escort—except for those rare evenings when Jacques was in New York.

Late in the spring of 1921, Alex came into the office at the end of the business day to tell Lilli that half of the New York salon staff was quitting and going to one of the lesser competitors. She was shocked.

"Alex, why?" she said. "We pay the highest salaries in the business."

He nodded. "And you're courteous and kind to every girl in the salon. People say Rubinstein and Arden are absolute tyrants."

"Then why would they leave us? When Betsy's mother was in the hospital, I advanced the money to pay the entire bill. I loaned Celia the money for her sister's funeral. They all know that in an emergency I'll see them through."

"Doris has done some detective work," Alex said, settling himself on Lilli's green velvet sofa. "The girls who've left were given contracts guaranteeing them each a mink coat at the end of their first year of employment. I guess that's irresistible bait."

Lilli deliberated a moment. "Then I'll start a new policy. An all-expense paid two-week vacation each summer—you work out the details, Alex. And at the end of five years, passage to London or Paris and all expenses paid for two weeks."

"With each girl spending part of those two weeks in our salon in the chosen city," he added. "That'll add a dash of class to the staff. And we need a new twist in the salons—some kind of tie-in with the European spas. After all, everybody knows you're from Marienbad."

"We have our exercise classes and the steam baths—"

"We should play up the Old World angle." He leaned forward, squinting in concentration. "Arden and Rubinstein are offering eternal youth. Princess Lilli must offer eternal youth with a hint of mystery. Lilli, I want you to go to Europe and hire a dozen girls from Marienbad to work in the New York salon. Eventually each will become a manager of a salon—"

"But what about immigration laws?"

He smiled. "With our wartime records, I think we'll be able to make arrangements."

"I could go in June," Lilli said. "You know, Freddie wants to go to camp this summer with two friends. And I've promised Jan she could go to Paris with a school group—an advance 'sweet sixteen' present."

Alex shook his head in bewilderment. "She told me she's never really *seen* Paris because she went before with her mother."

"Alex, she lived there as a child!"

"Suddenly Paris is the wonderful, wicked city every young American has to see," he said. "But don't worry, with a school group she'll be chaperoned to death."

"I'll talk Aunt Sara into going with me to Marienbad," Lilli said. "And, Alex, I'll make arrangements for bottled water from the springs of Marienbad to be sent to the New York salon. We'll use the water in the treatments! If this is well received, then we'll use Marienbad springwater in all the salons. Perhaps even in some of the lotions."

"Lilli," he said, "is there really something special about Marienbad springwater?"

"Perhaps. But you know what Aunt Sara has always said: 'The secret ingredient of my cream is hope.' That's the biggest secret ingredient in all beauty products."

Lilli planned to leave for Europe in June. Since she would not be back before Jan left with her school group, she took Jan to lunch at the Sert Room at the Waldorf. Still presided over by Oscar, this restaurant was one of the few that had survived Prohibition.

Lilli listened to Jan chatter on about Paris and worried. At the salon she'd listened to anxious mothers' stories about "petting parties," boys who wouldn't dance with girls who wore corsets, and the public smoking and private drinking of teenagers. Jan wouldn't be sixteen until November. Why did they all try to grow up so fast?

Two days after that lunch, Lilli sailed for Southampton aboard the *Mauretania*. At Southampton, she took the boat train to London. Oliver went with Lilli to Paris, to take over the Paris salon while Sara accompanied Lilli to Marienbad. She could hardly believe it had been eighteen years since she had run away with Jacques. Eighteen years . . . and now she was returning a wealthy woman with an international reputation. Marienbad, too, had changed. A republic since the end of the war, it was now part of Czechoslovakia.

As the train pulled into the small railroad station, Lilli could see that little had changed from the day she had left.

"I never thought I'd see this town again," Sara said. "How many of those we knew are still here? How many have died?"

On the way to the Hotel Weimar, they passed Aunt Sara's shop. "Lilli, it hasn't changed a bit!" Sara surveyed the facade of the small shop. "*We've* changed. Would George have ever believed that you and I would be staying at the hotel where he was a waiter?"

Lilli laughed. "In the royal apartments, yet!"

"By the way, how did you ever manage that in the height of the season?"

"Alex took care of it. He has a way of bringing off these things. He thought I should interview the girls in a setting that will tell them we offer them brilliant careers."

"Wait till our neighbors and the girls who went to school with you realize that Lilli Laval is Lilli Landau," Sara said with pride.

"And Sara Landau is head of Princess Lilli, Inc., Paris," Lilli said. "Remember Mrs. Brunner, who lived next door? Always telling you to get married so you wouldn't be left alone in your old age!"

"I brought a present from Paris for Mrs. Brunner." Sara winked. "Expensive enough to make her understand I don't worry about my old age."

At the hotel, the management gave them an effusive welcome. The manager told them that the guests presently at the hotel included a few ex-kings, a maharaja, and a dozen rich American tourists.

The management was aware that Mme. Laval was both wealthy and famous. In the days ahead, Lilli was grateful to be tied up with the business. For her, it was a bittersweet homecoming. Sara seemed to enjoy visiting old acquaintances, but Lilli was haunted by the memory of her mother's tragic death, and she began wondering again about her father. She *did* remember happy times, too: her innocent infatuation with Jacques, and those wondrous nights at the Bellevue Café. The flood of memories was too much for her. She was glad when she and her aunt were on the train back to Paris.

On her return to New York, Lilli and Alex decided the "European Spa Treatments" would be offered first in the New York salon and then in the others. Lilli herself undertook the training of the dozen girls, and Alex made arrangements for their housing, providing a chaperon to escort them about the city. Soon, several of them would be transferred to salons in other cities.

Elizabeth Arden was introducing exercise classes and Helena Rubinstein was touting the value of diathermy. Princess Lilli European Spa Treatments were advertised in *Vogue* and *Harper's Bazaar* and *Town & Country*. The three firms were engaged in another aggressive campaign for a most lucrative market.

JACQUES TRAVELED the super-rich social circuit, and Lilli was appalled at his extravagance as each new flock of bills arrived. She tried to be philosophical: This was the price of maintaining a semblance of a marriage, and she had made that choice. Still, she could complain to him about his continual absence from the children's lives.

Late in February, when the Palm Beach season was ending, Lilli received a phone call from Jacques. Indignant, scared, and defensive, he told her that he was in jail in Miami, accused of rum-running. "All I did was to rent this yacht for a four-day cruise through the Caribbean for myself and three guests. How was I to know the crew was smuggling rum into Miami! The stupid police are claiming I'm mixed up in it. Get me the best damn lawyer in this country and get him fast. And tell him to bail me out of this hellhole!"

She was shaken by the image of Jacques in jail. And what if her clients heard about this? She couldn't risk a blemish like that on her business—nor, for that matter, for Jan and Freddie's sake.

"I'll make some calls, Jacques. You'll need an attorney who can go right into the courts and post bail." *Was Jacques involved?*

"Lilli, this is the only call the bastards will let me make," he said. "Contact that lawyer right away!"

Lilli left her office to look for Alex. She found him in conference with one of the copywriters from the advertising department.

"Alex, I have to talk to you."

He looked up, instantly aware that she was upset. "We'll talk later," he said to the copywriter, and rose to his feet. "Let's go back to your office, Lilli."

It wasn't until they had settled themselves on her sofa that Lilli explained the situation.

"Jacques claims he had nothing to do with the rum-running. The truth is, Alex, I don't know whether to believe him." She took a deep breath. "But I'm willing to do anything to clear him. It would be awful if the children found out he was in jail."

"My father has a close friend who's a judge in Miami," Alex said. "I'll call him right away. We'll do everything we can."

"I don't care what it costs," Lilli said. "Just help me get Jacques out of this mess. For the children's sake, Alex."

He laughed. "You know, a lot of everyday, normal people are involved in bootlegging. Grandma was telling me about some respectable neighbors of ours up in Amagansett—year-round residents—who're bootlegging. It's become a major industry in Nassau and Suffolk Counties because it's comparatively easy to operate just off the beaches—"

"And it's being dominated by gangsters!" Lilli flared. "Please, Alex, don't try to whitewash Jacques."

"What I'm trying to tell you is that you mustn't feel personally disgraced because Jacques has been arrested. Prohibition is a law that is being flouted even by our lawmakers. I know two congressmen who have stills in their Washington town-house basements."

"I can't help it, Alex—I'm ashamed of him," Lilli said softly. "I feel tainted."

Within twelve hours, Jacques was out on bail, but he was under orders to remain in Florida. Now Lilli waited for the team of lawyers and the judge who was a friend of Alex's father to go into action. Alex explained that members of the crew were to be paid off to testify that Jacques was not part of the operation, though it was devastatingly clear he had financed their setup.

"I'm warning you," Alex said, "it'll cost a lot."

"I don't care. I'll pay whatever it takes."

In mid-May, Lilli returned to the salon from a charity fashion show at the Ritz-Carlton to find Alex waiting for her in her office.

"Lilli . . ." He drew her inside and closed the door. "It's all right. Jacques has been cleared."

"Oh, thank God!" She hugged him. "And thank *you*, Alex. How did I ever survive before you came into my life?"

He smiled. "Somehow, you did rather well. From a tiny little shop in Sydney to Princess Lilli, with salons already in Paris and London when I met you."

For a moment the atmosphere was tense with emotions both fought to keep hidden.

"I have to do something to keep Jacques out of further trouble," she said. "And not just because of the children. I can't afford to be part of some sordid scandal, Alex. You know how it would hurt business—"

"Why don't you set him up in a new salon? Not with any power," he added, seeing her expression, "but as a figurehead. Just keep him too busy to go looking for trouble."

She shook her head. "He won't do it."

"He will if you insist. Tell him that unless he does, you'll cut off his funds." He squinted in thought for a moment. "What about a salon in Hollywood? That would be a great area for us. Remember when Gloria Swanson was in the salon? She talked about our opening up out there. The salon will cater to Hollywood stars. It'll be marvelous publicity. Every woman in southern California will want to go where the movie stars go."

"Jacques might be intrigued by that." In this new decade, celebrities in the entertainment world were far more fascinating to the American public than socialites. Fan magazines were everywhere. From coast to coast, millions of newspaper readers devoured Louella Parsons's latest tidbits of gossip about Hollywood stars.

"Lilli, don't just ask Jacques," Alex said. "*Tell* him. He'll cave in fast once he understands you mean it."

"All right, Alex." It was worth a try. "We'll open a salon in Hollywood." It was a few months earlier than they had planned to begin groundwork for a new salon, but why not? "I'll buy a house out there. You've talked about how people are pouring into the Los Angeles area. Real estate is sure to boom. I suppose you're right, Alex. If I'm firm, he'll go along."

Lilli saw Jacques for what he was. A forty-two-year-old man whose handsome face and magnificent body had given way to time beyond his actual years. Profligate living had taken a devastating toll. Now Jacques was the darling of the dowagers rather than the debutantes. And those dowagers with an eye for younger men brushed Jacques aside.

BACK IN NEW YORK, Jacques was at first outraged by Lilli's plan. But then, realizing he had no recourse, he became intrigued at the prospect of being part of the Hollywood scene. By early June, when he visited the Southampton house, his spirits had lifted.

Alex left for the West Coast aboard the Twentieth Century. He phoned Lilli from his suite at Hollywood's Alexandria every night to brief her on his activities. Within four days of his arrival, he had found the perfect site for Princess Lilli, Hollywood, and was already negotiating with the real-estate broker.

"Lilli, aside from the salon, the property is a fine investment," he reported. "At least a hundred thousand people a year are pouring into this area, all of them hoping to buy homes."

After a week of haggling, Alex bought the property, and hired a contractor to make some minor structural changes. He and Lilli planned to consult a New York-based decorator, already chosen, to make sure the Hollywood salon featured the trademark gray and yellow motif. In two weeks Peggy, who would be the *real* head of the salon, was to come out to hire and begin training staff. Once the hiring was completed, Alex would return to New York.

In August, as usual, Jacques left Southampton for Newport to visit the Allens at their forty-room French Renaissance "cottage." Lilli reminded him that he was expected in Hollywood in late September for the opening of the salon.

"Darling," he drawled, "of course I'll be there. Nobody stays at Newport past August. It simply isn't done. But I am planning to take off the month of January to run down to Palm Beach. Don't give me that look—even your treatment girls take a vacation." Lilli held back the reminder that the treatment girls did not take a month off, and certainly not after less than four months on the job.

A few days after Jacques took off for Newport—and with Freddie spending the month of August at a camp in Switzerland and Jan in Italy with a school group—Lilli prepared to leave for California.

"Why don't you stop off in New Orleans on your way back?" Alex said. "I know it'll be hot as hell there in the summer, but—"

"I was thinking about that," Lilli said.

Nobody, not even Alex or Aunt Sara, knew about her dealings with private detectives. Two weeks ago, assuming she would stop off at New Orleans if she was already in California, she had hired a prestigious private investigator to locate Jacques's family. She'd told him that her mother-in-law, in poor health, was nostalgic about a distant younger cousin with whom she had quarreled bitterly many years ago. His name was Jacques Laval, and he had left New Orleans around 1900. If the detective couldn't locate Jacques, then she would like information regarding his parents' present whereabouts.

She didn't want to *meet* Jacques's family, she told herself. It was more that, for Jan and Freddie, she needed to know *who* they were.

"You haven't been at the New Orleans salon except for the opening," Alex said, drawing her back. "This is the perfect opportunity."

Lilli laughed. "I suppose I can bear the heat for two or three days."

"Good," he said. "I'll arrange everything. We'll have a reception at the salon. All the newspapers will send photographers. You'll speak at Maison Blanche. It'll be great for business."

Again Lilli was caught up in traveling; but instead of Peggy, it was Doris and Celestine who traveled with her. One day, Lilli promised herself, Jan would travel with her. It was Lilli's greatest hope that the business would one day be Freddie's and Jan's.

Upon arriving in Los Angeles, Lilli's party of three was met by Peggy in a chauffeured gray Rolls-Royce and driven to the new Ambassador Hotel on Wilshire Boulevard.

Lilli's instinct told her that the Hollywood salon would be a success. She charmed the new staff, who were clearly delighted that Princess Lilli herself had come out to inspect the new salon. Her guest appearance at I. Magnin brought a record crowd of women who were eager to listen to Princess Lilli's words of wisdom about beauty, curious to see if she was as beautiful as her photographs.

Though she stayed in California only four days, Lilli took time out to find a house for Jacques. The first day she found one on Crescent Drive in Beverly Hills: with its parklike lawn, swimming pool, and elegant, spacious rooms, it was sure to impress him. And its value was certain to increase in this escalating building boom. She was not, she told herself, being ridiculously extravagant. After all, it was important to keep Jacques happy in his new position.

ON FRIDAY MORNING, Lilli stepped off the train in New Orleans's Terminal Station. She knew Jacques would be furious if he knew she would soon have a full report on his family. Yesterday morning, from Hollywood, she had talked with the New Orleans detective she had hired. Her luck with detectives was improving. This one had come up with nothing on Jacques, but he had located Jacques's mother.

Lilli inspected her diamond wristwatch. It was 9:30. Mr. Swift, the detective, would be at his office awaiting her arrival. Within an hour she would know about Jan and Freddie's grandmother. She felt absurdly elated. She doubted that Jacques's mother was even aware that he had two children.

"Please follow us to our car outside," Doris told a pair of porters. "It's a gray Rolls-Royce. I insisted on a Rolls," she said to Lilli. As part of the Princess Lilli legend, Alex had long ago decided that Lilli always be driven in a gray Rolls-Royce. "But the chauffeurs for their rental all wear black uniforms."

Celestine dabbed at her forehead with a linen handkerchief. "No one will notice. Who can think in this heat?"

"I can't wait to soak in a cool tub," Lilli said. "Oh, but that will have to wait, Celestine. The chauffeur will drop you two off at the hotel and then drive me on." She tried to sound casual when she saw the surprise on their faces. "I promised to stop by to spend an hour or two with an old friend who's staying here for a few weeks."

"She's staying in New Orleans in summer?" Celestine asked.

"Some family crisis," Lilli lied. "I explained I'd be totally tied up at the salon and at Maison Blanche the rest of our time in town. This seemed the best time to see her."

"As soon as we're settled in our suite, I'll go over to Maison Blanche to check on the arrangements for your appearance tomorrow," Doris said. "I hope not all of New Orleans is off to the lake or in the country in this hot weather."

"I'm sure there'll be a substantial crowd," Lilli said. "And the newspapers will carry a full report. Doris, make sure we have the new photographs for the press."

As they walked through the thirty-foot-high arch at the terminal's entrance, Lilli spied the waiting Rolls-Royce.

"Celestine and I will take the luggage in a pair of taxis," Doris said. "Then you can go directly ahead."

"Thank you, Doris." Lilli was glad to avoid the detour to the hotel.

Within fifteen minutes, Lilli was sitting in a comfortable chair across from Roger Smith, while a ceiling fan valiantly worked against the dense morning humidity.

"Miss Landau," he said in a musical southern accent, "we located Jacques Laval's mother here in the city."

"You're sure this is the Jacques Laval to whom my mother-in-law refers?"

"It's not an uncommon name in New Orleans," the investigator said with a faint smile, "but you gave us the exact date of birth. There is only one Jacques Laval born on that date. His father deserted the boy and his mother when he was no more than four or five." *So Jacques was an only child. And he talked about a "houseful of brothers and sisters."* "His father was a charming but irresponsible gambler. He left his wife, Daisy Laval, in very bad circumstances, and never showed up again. She took in sewing to raise herself and her son. The son, Jacques Laval, left New Orleans when he was eighteen to join a theater company." His smile was wry. "I gather that even at that age he was quite a ladies' man. His mother's wealthy customers remember him well."

"Did his mother hear from him after he left New Orleans?" Lilli imagined the young Jacques, fascinating to his mother's customers. In how many of their beds had he lain, envious, no doubt, of the luxurious surroundings in which they lived?

"She received occasional postcards from him in the early years. From a variety of cities. There was never a return address. Her last communication with him was a brief note along with a string of beads she received over twenty years ago. The postmark was Paris, France." *So Jacques had been in Paris before he came to Marienbad.*

"Would his mother be willing to see me?" she asked.

Swift shook his head. "I don't think that would be advisable."

"She's angry with Jacques, isn't she?" Lilli said. "She has reason to be."

"It's not quite that." The investigator seemed to be searching for words. "She's failing mentally as well as physically. Sometimes she's normal, and then she drifts off into some vague—perhaps happier—past. Some of her old customers still hire her for simple sewing, but she is barely able to care for herself financially. I'm afraid it's only a matter of time before she'll be placed in some charitable institution."

"I won't let that happen," Lilli said sharply. "Mr. Swift, I'd like to arrange a trust that will care for her comfortably as long as she lives. Would you know of a New Orleans attorney who can handle this for me?''

WITHIN HALF AN HOUR Lilli was sitting in the tastefully furnished private office of Charles Adams, attorney-at-law.

As briefly as possible, she explained that she wanted a trust set up for Mrs. Daisy Laval, to provide for a comfortable small house and all living expenses, plus a housekeeper/companion. She knew that Adams would not question her about the arrangements.

''I've been thinking about how to explain this to her,'' Lilli said. ''I'll go over personally to tell her that one of her ladies from many years ago wishes to arrange for her care. I'll explain that this lady has retained you to represent her.''

''Would you like me to go with you?'' Adams asked.

''I think I'd like to see her alone,'' Lilli said quickly. ''I'll explain that you'll come to see her. Please let Mrs. Laval choose her house, and make sure her companion is carefully screened. My New York attorneys will be in touch with you about the financial arrangements.''

Adams walked her to the waiting Rolls-Royce, and Lilli told the driver to take her to the address the investigator had provided. She leaned back in her seat, tense and fighting tears. How could Jacques have treated his mother so badly? How could he have deprived Jan and Freddie of a grandmother?

As they drove through the city to the edge of town, the neighborhood grew progressively worse. At last the driver pulled up before a ramshackle cottage, its paint cracked and peeling, its small veranda sagging, its half-dozen steps a hazard to anyone who attempted to climb them. Yet Lilli noticed the vibrant color and rich fragrance of the flowers nestling beside the cottage. Clearly, the garden had flourished under someone's affectionate care.

Noting the chauffeur's look of concern, Lilli assured him she would only be a few minutes. Then, slowly, she made her way up the decaying steps and to the veranda. She was about to come face-to-face with Jacques's mother. Deserted by her husband and then by her son. How like Jacques to walk out on responsibility! And like her own father...

She knocked on the screen door, patched in spots to keep out the mosquitoes that had once been the scourge of New Orleans.

"I'm coming, dear," a small, high voice called from somewhere beyond the tiny sitting room. Through the screen door Lilli saw the faded sofa, the torn rug, the bric-a-brac on the paint-chipped mantelpiece.

"Good morning, Mrs. Laval." Standing before Lilli was a thin woman dressed in a frayed but clean cotton frock, a string of colorful beads about her throat. Her hair was graying and flyaway, and her eyes were vague as she stared uncertainly at her caller. Once she must have been quite pretty, Lilli thought. But Jacques must resemble his father; she saw none of his features in this pale, lined face. "May I come in?"

"Oh, my, yes." Daisy Laval managed a smile as she pushed the screen open. "Now let me see...are you the lady who wanted the baby sacs? Sometimes I just don't remember too well."

"No, I'm a friend of one of the ladies you sewed for a long time ago." She hesitated. "Mrs. Edwards? You remember—she moved up to New York months ago."

Lilli's gaze settled on the clutter of faded snapshots on the console table behind the sofa: a mother's collections of photographs of her only child. Each photograph was identified in small, neat script: "Jackie, eighteen months"; "Jackie on his second birthday"; "Jackie, five years old." The most recent was of a strikingly handsome young man, looking older than the years claimed by the inscription: "Jack, fourteen."

Lilli's eyes moved back to Daisy. The cheap beads about her mother-in-law's throat had to be those sent by Jacques from Paris over twenty years ago.

"I seem to recall a Mrs. Edwards." Daisy Laval's voice trailed off. "They lived in that big white house on Saint Charles Street at..." She shook her head as though to clear her mind. "I guess I don't rightly remember."

"Mrs. Edwards is getting on in years, but she remembers you with much affection." Lilli knew she was talking too fast. "Why don't we sit down," she said, "and I'll tell you how she'd like to help you...."

DRIVING BACK TO THE HOTEL, impatient to soak in a cool tub and change, Lilli tried to piece together Jacques's growing-up years. Already handsome—and no doubt charming—at fourteen, he must have been spoiled by his mother's rich lady clients. He must have looked at their way of life and vowed to have it for himself. This explained his fascination for high living, his near-reverence for the socially well-placed. She understood, yes; but she could not forgive.

25

As Alex had predicted the Hollywood salon became an instant success. Peggy wrote that Jacques spent two or three hours each afternoon there. He was charming, flattering to their patrons, and delighted when he was summoned by a rising young movie actress to give his approval on a hairstyle or a new shade of lipstick or eye shadow.

Occasionally Jacques dropped brief letters to Jan and Freddie, both of whom were wide-eyed that he was on first-name terms with such Hollywood stars as Bebe Daniels and Norma Talmadge and Marion Davies. They bubbled with excitement when he sent a photograph from an issue of *Photoplay* showing him at a Hollywood gathering. At least, Lilli told herself, Jacques was no longer involved in bootlegging.

Now that Jan was a high-school senior, much of the talk at dinner concerned her choice of a college. Her grades were excellent and at last she decided to apply to Vassar. Not all of her classmates had elected to go to college; several would be making their debuts the following winter.

Freddie was studying for his bar mitzvah in August. Though Jacques made no comment about it, Lilli and Freddie both sensed his disapproval. He wrote Freddie that he had joined the Episcopal church in Beverly Hills.

"Papa says he joined the Episcopal church because it's 'chic,'" Freddie said over dinner. "What's he talking about?"

Lilli tried to appear amused. "Papa's decided it's fashionable to be Episcopalian." In the movie center of the world—known to be dominated by Jewish producers—Jacques became an Episcopalian because he thought it was chic.

"Papa told me once that I was only one-quarter Jewish," Jan said. Lilli stared in shock. She had never suspected that Jacques ever discussed their Jewishness with the children. "He said you were half Jewish and he was Christian, so that made Freddie and me only a quarter Jewish."

"Jan, I am Jewish, and that means my children are Jewish. If your father decides he wishes to be an Episcopalian, that's his privilege. But I doubt he'll ever appear at church services. Only at 'chic Episcopalian weddings.'"

Lilli was looking forward with pride to Jan's graduation. Her daughter's going to college was a fulfillment of her own dreams. She was disappointed, however, when Jan refused to come to work in the salon for the summer. It seemed like the right time for Jan to start familiarizing herself with the business, but...

"Mama, I'm going to Vassar in the fall—I'll need the summer to shop for clothes," she said. "Besides, nobody in my class is going to work."

"It's not disgraceful to work, you know." Was she spoiling Jan? *She* had come into Aunt Sara's shop in Marienbad when she was twelve. "Women today go out into the business world, Jan."

"Nobody in my class," Jan said coolly. "Some of them are going to Europe for the summer. That might be fun. I could shop in Paris."

"May I remind you that you went to Paris with Freddie and me three summers ago?" Lilli said. "And the summer before last you went to Paris with that group from school. This summer you'll stay home."

Three evenings later, Lilli came home from the salon to be told by a worried Martine that Jan had come home from school, announced that she would not be down to dinner, and locked herself in her room.

"I'll talk to her," Lilli said. Somebody at school had probably said something disparaging about the new way Jan was wearing her hair; that was all she needed to be convinced she was ugly.

But it wasn't until Lilli warned that she would have Henri break the door down that Jan finally let her in. Lilli's throat tightened at the sight of Jan's tearstained face.

"Darling, what happened at school to upset you this way?"

"I don't want to talk about it." Jan sat on the edge of her exquisite canopied bed and stared at the delicate pink carpeting.

"Jan, whatever is bothering you we can talk about."

"You can't do anything about this!" Jan snapped. "I'm not going back to school. Not ever. I hate those awful girls."

"Someone said something to you," Lilli began. "Darling, you can't take everything literally."

"Erica Hampton said I was going off to college because I knew I'd never be invited to make my debut next winter. Because I'm Jewish. She said no Jewish girl *ever* becomes a debutante." Jan stared accusingly at her mother.

Lilli didn't know what to say. Even here in America it was not always comfortable to be a Jew. That was a fact of life. Jan would have to live with this absurdity.

"Did Erica ever consider that Jewish girls might not want to be part of that silly social whirl?" Lilli said.

"The girls at school say being a debutante is wonderful."

"Jan, darling, it's much more exciting to go away to college than to spend all your time running around to balls and dinners and fashion shows. You always say you hate big parties. I can't tell you how proud I am that I'll have a daughter in college!"

Jan looked at her coldly. "I won't go back to school."

"Of course you'll go back. You're graduating next month. You need your diploma for college. And for your graduation you'll have a party that will outshine any debut of the year."

For a moment, Jan considered it.

"Nobody will come," she whispered.

"*Everybody* will come. It'll be photographed for an issue of *Vogue*. It'll be written up in the *New York Times*. Jan, every girl in your school will be envious."

Lilli threw Jan's graduation party in the huge Crystal Room of the Ritz. She personally made sure that everything would be perfect: the menu; the music, to be supplied by Howard Lanin's orchestra; the extravagant floral decorations by the fashionable Fifth Avenue florist Max Schling; the fine champagnes—because this would be expected despite Prohibition.

Jan was alternately ecstatic and terrified as the big day approached. "It'll be awful," she moaned. "Everybody will laugh. Not one boy will want to dance with me. I'll spend the whole evening in the Ritz ladies' room!"

"Jan, you'll be the prettiest girl at the party," Lilli said. "Every boy there will be cutting in—you'll see."

At last the evening of the party arrived. Breathtakingly lovely in a sea-green bouffant tulle by Callot, Jan was convinced she looked plain and gauche. Every one of the 200 people invited attended the party, Lilli noted with satisfaction, and the atmosphere was elegant and festive. No debut could possibly be better conceived or executed.

A photograph of Jan by the famous Baron de Meyer was to appear in *Vogue*. Photographers from all the newspapers were present. After the party, Jan, triumphant in its success, told Lilli that even Erica Hampton had been impressed. It was like a preseason debut, Erica had said. Jan was ecstatic.

In September, Jan took off for Vassar, and Lilli began worrying: about the young men Jan would be meeting at college, "petting parties" in the back seats of cars, the drinking parties, the alarming way dresses were moving upward to knee-length . . .

In November, at Lilli's insistence, Jan came down from Vassar for Freddie's bar mitzvah and the elaborate reception to be held afterward at the Ritz. Aunt Sara, at her own instigation, came from Paris. As they took their places in the synagogue, Lilli was concerned by Jan's obvious discomfort. For the last three years Jan had found excuses to avoid the Hanukkah parties and the seders to which Alex routinely invited her. Obviously she was uncomfortable at being a Jew.

In her own mind her children were Jewish. A child followed the religion of its mother. Somehow she had failed to instill this in Jan. It was not enough to be a Jew in her heart. To attend services only for the High Holidays. She should have set an example for the children.

The services were about to commence. From his place on the *bimah*, Freddie's eyes sought hers. She smiled and lifted a hand. Sara, always so reserved, was dabbing at her eyes with a handkerchief. Like herself, Lilli knew, Aunt Sara was remembering the years in Marienbad when they hid their Jewishness from their neighbors, when no Jew was allowed to be a member of the Municipal Council.

"Lilli, I'm proud of you," Sara said after the ceremony. "You've brought your son up to be a Jew. I'm glad I lived to see this day."

When Sara, insisting she had to get back to the business, sailed for France one week later, she took back plans worked out with Lilli and Alex for the opening of a salon in Cannes. After talking at length about Elizabeth Arden's successful salon in Nice, a Princess Lilli salon in Cannes seemed the next logical step. Oliver would help Sara set up the new salon. Next would be Monte Carlo. And Alex and Oliver agreed that a factory must be established in London to eliminate dependence on the Paris factory, which was now working at capacity.

Lilli was disturbed by the extravagant claims of the various cosmetic firms. While a New York State act calling for the licensing of cosmeticians had been put through, no restraint was put on the manufacturer's claims. The result was that every cosmetic firm proclaimed miracles for those who bought their products. Alex suspected that in time the government would intervene.

For the cosmetic industry, this was a golden era. Beauty-culture courses were being offered in major cities across the nation. Beauty operators were lured with stories of high salaries and heavy tips. Women flocking to the field were soon joined by men, eager to share in the earnings available to knowledgeable operators.

In the spring of 1924, Alex persuaded Lilli to buy her own building on Fifth Avenue. It would be called the Princess Lilli Building. After reading about it in the paper, Jacques phoned Lilli from Hollywood and demanded that his name be on the deed as co-owner.

"The building will belong to Jan and Freddie," Lillie said. "The company will pay rent. It's some kind of tax arrangement the attorneys worked out." She wondered if he would believe her.

"Damn it, Lilli, what am I getting out of this? I'm working my ass off out here—and for what?"

"For a salary that's ten times what you deserve." He wasn't working more than three or four hours a day. "And a fully staffed residence that costs you nothing." All she wanted was for him to stay in Hollywood and out of her life. Only twice a year now did he appear at the New York house: early in August, when he was en route to Newport; and early in January, when he was en route to Palm Beach.

"I need a new car," he said defiantly. "Jacques Laval of Princess Lilli shouldn't be seen driving a broken-down Stutz. I should have a Rolls—people out here expect it of me. And a chauffeur."

Lilli paused. She had to do whatever was necessary to keep Jacques happy in Hollywood. "I'll make arrangements for a new car," she said. "It will belong to the Hollywood office, for tax purposes. Peggy will handle the details out there."

"Give my love to the kids," he said brusquely.

"Of course. Goodbye, Jacques." Jacques had no love to give anyone, she thought bitterly. He was too wrapped up in himself.

Lilli began working every evening at the house, in a room set up as her home office. Alex would come over for dinner, and afterward they would settle down to plot future campaigns. Every night she and Freddie and Alex sat down together at the dinner table. It was almost as though they were a family, she thought one night—except that sometime between eleven and midnight Alex would leave for his own apartment, and she would go upstairs to her lonely bed.

Occasionally Jan swept down from Vassar to spend a few days at home. When summer vacation approached, she announced she wanted to go with three classmates to Venice and Rome. Lilli acquiesced. Freddie asked to have a school friend as his guest for the summer at the Southampton house. The classmate's parents were divorced, each going his separate way. "Jimmy would be sent to camp again, Mama," Freddie said. "Can he stay with me at Southampton for the summer?"

"Of course, darling." Lilli was grateful for this warm, sweet son. "I'll be out for long weekends through July and August." Martine would take care of the two boys.

As always, Lilli was consumed by the business. It was her way of escaping from the reality of her life: the fact that she was married to a man for whom she had only contempt, that she was in love with a man she could never have. Alex understood that close friendship was all they could ever share—but without him, Lilli knew she could not survive.

LILLI BEGAN LOOKING forward to Jan's graduation from college, hopeful that some magical change in her daughter's thinking would bring her into the salon. When Freddie graduated from high school, he would go on to college and then to medical school.

After the summer in Venice and Rome—with a brief stopover at the family house in London—Jan came to the Southampton house before returning to Vassar. Jacques appeared for a weekend, en route to Hollywood after his usual month in Newport. Bronzed, thicker than ever around the middle, he was condescending toward everyone and fought constantly with Jan. Lilli was relieved when he left.

In April the following year, Lilli went to Europe to check on the London, Paris, Cannes, and Monte Carlo salons—and to visit Oliver, Frances, and Charles in London and Aunt Sara in Paris. Then on to a long-delayed visit with Lisette at her country estate outside Paris. The duchess, now eighty-seven and frail, was eager to see her protégée.

"Lilli, you are a young and beautiful woman still," she said. "There should be a delightful man in your life."

"Lisette, I have no room in my life for a man."

"I know you, Lilli." Lisette's eyes were wise. "You have a great capacity for love."

Lilli was silent for a moment. "I love a man," she said. "I'm with him constantly at the salon. We see much of each other in the evenings, though not as lovers. I'm grateful for what we have."

"It's a gift to be able to love," Lisette said. "I thank God that I, too, am blessed with this."

The few days with Lisette were happy and sad for Lilli. Happy, of course, because she was with her dear friend. Sad because she knew this might be the last time she saw her. More than ever, she was aware of the passing years.

Lilli stayed in Paris for another two days before taking the boat train to Cherbourg. She would have loved to persuade Aunt Sara to move to New York, but she knew her aunt had established a world for herself in Paris. She must not deprive her of that.

On the return to New York aboard the beautiful *Aquitania*, Lilli couldn't wait to get back to Alex and the children. Jan was to spend much of the summer with a college group touring the Southwest. Before returning to New York, Jan wanted to stay at the Hollywood house with her roommate, Vanessa Grey, for a week. Vanessa had ambitions—unknown to her parents—to become a movie star.

Though it was three years away, Freddie was already talking about college. How empty the house on Gramercy Park would be when he, too, was off at college. But when Freddie started college, Jan would have been out of Vassar for a year. Lilli cheered herself. She would still have one at home. Until Jan married. Already, three of Jan's former classmates were married. *Dear God, she felt so old.*

ACUTELY AWARE of the *Aquitania*'s quarantine off Staten Island, Alex feigned interest in the lively conversation around the beautifully laid dinner table in the Murray Hill house where he had been born and raised. It was still known as "grandma's house," though his parents had lived here since their marriage and his mother had long managed the household. In earlier years, before the tragic deaths of two of her young daughters in childbirth, Grandma Kahn had divided her time between the Murray Hill house and those of her daughters, who had both married Charleston men and returned to live there.

Out of deference to Grandma Kahn, the house had barely been changed since her arrival there with her husband and three children in 1868. They had fled the problems of reconstruction in Charleston, South Carolina. Grandma was fond of pointing out that other southern Jews—including the Strauses of Georgia, the Lehmans of Alabama, and the Baruchs of South Carolina—had left the South to improve family fortunes. They had been able to buy the fine brownstone house with the money Grandpa Kahn had earned—trading on his own account—as a Confederate spy in Europe during what Grandma Kahn still referred to as the War Between the States.

The dining-room walls of the Kahn house remained covered in red damask. The furniture was the mid-Victorian that had been so fashionable right after the Civil War. Sometimes Alex's mother wistfully talked about the bright chintz rooms favored by Elsie de Wolfe, but everyone knew that redecorating was not an option as long as Dora Kahn was alive.

It was a tacit rule that business was never discussed over dinner. Instead, conversation usually revolved around current events or the latest philanthropies favored by "the family." Tonight Alex's younger sister, Esther—an avowed feminist— was outraged by the news that John T. Scopes in Dayton, Tennessee, had been arrested for violation of a state law forbidding the teaching of the theory of evolution.

"I may go down there for the trial," she said. "I've never heard such nonsense!"

"Alex, we're having a small dinner party Saturday night," his mother said quietly. "Won't you arrange to be here?"

"I'll probably be tied up at the office." It was Alex's automatic response. Without a doubt, this would be yet another opportunity for his mother to parade before him some well-placed young lady interested in marriage.

"That business has become an obsession with you." His mother, who made a point of never losing her temper, also made a point of getting her message across. "You're forty years old, Alex. How long before you marry and raise a family?"

"It's true, son," his father said. "You're the only one to carry on the family name. It's bad enough that you won't have anything to do with the business."

Alex sighed. They'd been through this a million times. "Papa," he said, "you have Adam and Jesse in the business. You keep telling me what a great job they do."

"But sons-in-law are not sons," said his older sister, Frieda, who occasionally let her resentment of this show.

"No offense to Adam and Jesse," Henry Kahn said with a bow to his two sons-in-law—ignoring Frieda—"but I still would like to see my son take over when I retire. And that day is fast approaching."

"Grandma," Alex said, "I've brought one of our new creams. Would you try it out and give me your opinion?"

"Alex," she laughed, "I'm eighty-three years old. A beauty cream is going to make me look sixteen?" But she was obviously pleased that he was consulting her.

As soon as he could respectably do so, Alex left the house and headed back to his own apartment. These weeks without Lilli had been trying. Whenever she was away, or he was off on a business trip, he felt an emptiness in his life. If the family suspected where his affections lay, they never said so.

In his charming apartment, Alex sat before a fire in his living room until well past midnight. He couldn't possibly sleep, knowing that soon Lilli would be back here, with him. He knew his place in her life. But he refused to accept it.

UPON HER RETURN, Lilli was almost immediately swept up in Alex's campaign to bring out new products in time for Christmas. Aware of America's love affair with Hollywood, Alex began featuring the Hollywood salon and its movie-star clients in many of the ads.

Unfortunately, all was not going smoothly at the Hollywood salon. Peggy was having problems with Jacques. He was constantly overstepping his bounds, giving orders where he had no business interfering. He threw a New Year's party at the Hollywood house that far exceeded their annual entertainment budget. Louella Parsons reported in her column that he planned to move into film production.

A few days after Lilli had written a blistering letter to Jacques about his extravagances, Jan arrived home from Vassar on a late Friday evening train. Freddie had gone up to his room to study. Alex and Lilli were in the house office working on the summer advertising schedule when Jan appeared in the doorway.

"Darling, how wonderful to see you!" Lilli hurried to her side.

"I came home for the weekend." Jan was clearly agitated. "Mother, I must talk to you."

"We've done enough work for this evening." Alex rose to his feet. "Welcome home, Jan." He crossed the room and leaned over to kiss her on the cheek. "You're looking beautiful, as always."

"Thank you, Uncle Alex."

Lilli saw Alex to the door, then returned to Jan, who was sitting on the edge of a chair.

"What's happened?" Lilli asked. "Did something go wrong at school?"

"It wasn't school." Jan was digging into the depths of her Mark Cross purse. "It's Daddy!" She pulled forth three scraps of paper and thrust them toward her mother. "He ought to be ashamed of himself!"

Lilli looked at the items Jan had circled in ink. According to Louella Parsons, *Photoplay*, and *Movie Play*, Jacques was having a "torrid affair" with a blond starlet who had appeared thus far in two small but flamboyant roles. She gave her age as twenty-two. Lilli's face tightened when she saw the photograph of Jacques with his arm around the short-skirted starlet—and the caption identifying him as the "on-and-off husband of Princess Lilli, the cosmetics queen." Undoubtedly this young actress expected Jacques—who talked now about becoming a film producer—to catapult her to stardom.

"We can't believe everything these columnists say," Lilli said, handing back the clippings.

"When Vanessa and I went out to Hollywood and Daddy took us to the Patent Leather Room at the Ambassador, he told us to pretend we were his girlfriends! He wouldn't let us go to the salon because he was afraid Peggy would tell everybody I was his daughter. It's degrading to have your father chasing after somebody practically your own age. All the girls at school read Louella Parsons!"

"Jan," Lilli said, "nobody has ever been able to tell your father how to behave. I divorced him once because of that."

"Are you going to divorce him again?"

Lilli hesitated. "Yes," she said quietly. "It was a mistake to have remarried him. I did it because I thought it was right to bring your father into your and Freddie's lives."

"I don't want him in my life. I can't wait until you divorce him. I never want to see him again."

THE NEXT MORNING Lilli wrote Jacques that she was suing him for divorce; that it would not be a "quickie" Reno divorce—she didn't have the time to take up residence out of New York City; and that her attorney would contact him about a financial settlement, since it was inadvisable for him to continue at the salon.

Her private phone rang at eight the following morning. "What the hell's bugging you?" he yelled. "I've been playing your cute little game! What more do you want?"

"Jan has been very upset about your affair with that young actress," said Lilli. "And I find it most distasteful. We've had no marriage for years, Jacques. Let's put an end to it."

"You can't get away with this, Lilli. Not again!"

"Jacques, shut up. My lawyer will be in touch with you. He'll work out a—"

"I'll fight you in court if you try to go ahead with this." His voice shook. "I'll—"

"You'll agree," Lilli said, "because you wouldn't want it known to your friends that Jacques Laval deserted his mother and let her become a charity case."

"What are you talking about?" His voice was a mixture of rage and bravado and alarm.

"I was in New Orleans. I saw your mother." She remembered his fictional childhood: the Louisiana plantation and the fine mansion in New Orleans, his rebellion at going to law school and joining his father's law firm. "Several older ladies for whom she used to sew had been keeping her solvent, but the time came when—"

"You sneaked behind my back. How dare you, you conniving little bitch! How many people have you told already?"

"Nobody, Jacques. And I'll tell no one, provided you give me no trouble with the divorce. Otherwise, it'll be in all the columns."

There was a long silence. "All right," he said at last. "But I keep the Rolls and the house. And a settlement of a million in cash."

"You'll work it out with the lawyers," Lilli said. She didn't care what it cost.

After she hung up, Lilli crossed the room, sat at her dressing table, and stared hard into the mirror. She was trembling. Couldn't he understand that it was humiliating—not only to Jan but to herself—that he was pursuing a girl almost half her age? She inspected her reflection. *In a few days she would be thirty-nine years old. One birthday from forty.* She had wasted her life on a man who had given her nothing in return. No—he had given her Jan and Freddie. But what about the years ahead?

The symbol of youth and beauty to the richest women in the world was terrified of growing old.

26

DURING THE DIVORCE proceedings Lilli was uncharacteristically tense and irritable at home and in the salon. She was even hostile to Alex. But nobody understood: In the midst of her beauty empire—her magnificent town house, her circle of famous and important friends—she felt frighteningly alone.

By late February the settlement had at last been arranged and the divorce papers filed. The grounds were adultery, acceptable in New York courts. And there was certainly no doubt about their truth. Now Jacques was urging her to go to Reno for a quick divorce—impatient, she assumed, to buy himself a new young wife. How long before he squandered the fortune he was receiving as a settlement?

There had always been men in pursuit of Lilli Laval. Now she no longer laughingly brushed them aside. She no longer spent her evenings working with Alex; she no longer relied on Alex as her escort. She appeared instead on the arm of one prominent bachelor, widower, or divorcé after another. All of it was dutifully reported by Cholly Knickerbocker—who of course had no way of knowing that Lilli rejected the advances of each one.

Every night she stared into her mirror and thought about these men. Were they interested in her because she was rich and successful? Certainly it was not that they were fascinated by Lilli Laval. How could they be? *She'd be forty on her next birthday.*

One gray October morning, tired from a late evening at "21," Lilli arrived in her office to find Alex sitting in a chair beside her desk.

"Problems?" She remembered guiltily that she had been short with him last night when he had suggested a working dinner.

"Lilli, I have to tell you something. When we finish the current campaign, I'm leaving the firm."

Slowly she pulled off her coat, tossed it on the sofa, and sat down at her desk. *This couldn't be happening.*

"I never thought *you* would succumb to the competition." How would she survive without Alex? "Is it Rubinstein or Arden? What did they offer you that was so irresistible?"

"I'm not leaving to go to somebody else, Lilli," he said. "I could never do that."

"Alex, please, you can't walk out on me." Alex was the one constant in her life. The one person she could depend on in any emergency. "I know I've been a bitch these last weeks—but I've been upset. Alex, you're my dearest friend—I need you."

"You need no one." He smiled. "You're Princess Lilli. A legend in your own time."

"Oh, Alex, don't give me that! I'm a woman facing forty. Those jars and bottles with my portrait—that's Lilli fifteen years ago! She's gone."

"Lilli, that's not true—"

She shook her head. "I look in the mirror, and I see. Maybe I can hide for a while behind my own beauty preparations, but the good years are gone."

"You're a beautiful woman," he said sternly. "Your life is just beginning. What is all this nonsense? Is it because Jacques is chasing after young girls? Do you think you have to compete with those silly little flappers? Lilli, you are a magnificent woman. Haven't you noticed the men who are dying to be your lovers?" She couldn't help but notice the bitterness in his voice.

"Well, for your information, none of them ever has. And anyway, it isn't me they're fascinated by. It's the image of the rich, important Princess Lilli."

"So you're frightened of turning forty." He smiled. "Ah, Lilli, life—like a good wine—should improve with the years. Twenty to thirty is tough—especially for this generation, which seems to feel cheated by our generation. Thirty to forty improves. And what we make of the years that follow depends upon how we handle them.''

"Alex, I don't think I know how to handle them," Lilli whispered. "What's the matter with me? Three marriages and three divorces. Why do I make these awful mistakes?"

He chuckled tenderly. "Nothing is wrong with you. It's just that you save your best thinking for the business. In some crucial personal situations, you've acted on impulse. You were little more than a child when you married Jacques, and still very young—and vulnerable—when you married Mischa. And now," he teased, "you're reacting like the warm, sweet, emotional woman you are."

"When I was sixteen," she said, "I thought the high point of my life would be when I discovered who my father was. Then I gave up on that and—" She paused at Alex's look of puzzlement. She hadn't told him about her father. "My dear, dear friend, let me tell you a story about the girl who was Lilli Landau."

She told him what she knew about the father she had never seen, about her efforts with the private detectives.

"When I remarried Jacques, my only thought was to give Jan and Freddie a father again. Something I never had."

Alex stood up. "That does it. We're leaving the salon in the competent hands of the staff, Lilli, and we're driving out to Amagansett for the weekend."

"But there's so much work to do..."

He waved a hand. "The work will keep. And Freddie is a big boy now. I think he'll let you have a weekend off. I'll drive you to your house so you can pack a few warm things and then we'll head for the beach."

"Alex, this is ridiculous. How can we—"

"Shhh—I hear Doris down the hall." He put a finger to her lips. "We'll explain we're heading off for a private conference and we won't be back in town until Sunday night. Doris will reschedule any appointments you have today or tomorrow." He smiled. "That's an order."

BY THE TIME they were out of the city—in Alex's new red Stutz with its top down—the gray in the sky had given way to a glorious blue. Alex had not bothered to stop at his apartment to pack; he kept a closet full of clothes out at the Amagansett house.

"Nobody else goes out there after the end of September," he said, "but I like to run out at odd times throughout the fall. Before we left I phoned the handyman, who keeps an eye on the wood for the Franklin stove and the fireplaces. With the fireplace and the stove in the kitchen, it's warm enough. I consider it my runaway place." He laughed. "Where I go to lick my wounds. Did I ever tell you how we came to buy it?"

"No."

"Thirty years ago, one of Grandma's New York friends—a retired admiral's wife—told her about a fine summer boardinghouse out there. Grandma was tired of going to Long Branch—what she called the 'Jewish Newport'—so she decided to give Amagansett a try. When the rest of the family shied away, I was drafted. I still remember taking the train to Sag Harbor, from there going by Jerry Baker's stagecoach. In those days, that was pretty much the only way to go."

"It's hard to remember a time without cars. Speaking of which, how much farther before we get there?"

"Sit back and relax. It's another two hours." He smiled. "Grandma loved that summer at Mrs. Hand's boardinghouse. There were several in town, along that incredibly wide Main Street with its arch of trees. Beautiful old elms. It's more like a colonial New England village than a little town way out on Long Island."

Gradually, Lilli found herself relaxing as she listened to Alex talk about the summer at Mrs. Hand's boardinghouse and the subsequent building of their own beach house three years later. Though she hadn't met any of them, she had come to feel that she knew Alex's family. All the women in Alex's family patronized the Rubinstein Salon—originally to show their disapproval of his deserting the business, and later simply out of habit.

Halfway there, Lilli drifted off to sleep. When Alex woke her, they were in the driveway of the beach house.

"It's big but unpretentious." He gazed at the rambling clapboard house sitting on a faint rise at the edge of the beach. "Come on, let me show it to you."

Lilli understood immediately why Alex loved the house. It was warm and comfortable and tranquil, the only intrusion the distant sound of the waves and the occasional caws of the sea gulls.

"Let's go get some groceries," he said excitedly. "We'll have lunch at a little place in town, and tonight *I'm* cooking dinner."

They ate a hearty lunch, shopped at the grocery, put what they had bought in the icebox and went for a walk on the beach, deserted except for a cluster of sea gulls and a lone Irish setter. When Lilli tried to talk about Alex's proposed trip to Europe—mainly to reassure herself that he had abandoned any thought of leaving Princess Lilli—he held up his hand. "I said *no* talk about business this weekend. Let's turn around, shall we? I'll show you where rumrunners are supposed to be doing business on dark nights."

When they tired of walking, they sat on the dunes and rested a while, then walked again. Now, while they sat watching the huge orange sun drop majestically toward the horizon, Alex talked about early Jews on Long Island. The son of Asser Levy—one of twenty-three Jews who had fought beside the Dutch and arrived in 1654 in what was then called New Amsterdam—had settled in East Hampton in 1730. A Jewish pioneer merchant named Aaron Isaacs, who had set up business in Sag Harbor, married and converted to Christianity.

"Aaron Isaacs was the grandfather of John Howard Payne, who wrote 'Home Sweet Home,'" he said.

"People convert to make their lives easier," Lilli said, staring out to sea. "I could never do that. Even though it might make life easier for the children. I just couldn't."

"Your one-quarter-Jewish children," he teased.

"Their grandmother was Jewish. Their mother is Jewish. *They* are Jewish," she said stubbornly.

"Lilli, look at that sun." He pointed to the red-gold ball, now settled on the horizon. The sky was bathed with color. "This is one of the reasons I love Amagansett."

When they returned to the house, they discovered Josiah, the handyman, standing over a blaze in the living-room fireplace.

"It's gonna be cold tonight, Mr. Alex," he said, his eyes resting on Lilli for a surprised instant. "I got a fire goin' in the kitchen stove, too."

"Thank you, Josiah. How's the family?"

For a few minutes Alex and Josiah exchanged family news. Then Josiah took off with a promise to leave fresh fish on the kitchen steps early in the morning.

Lilli laughed. "He thinks we're out here for a high time."

"I've never brought anybody out to the house," Alex said. His eyes met hers with sudden intensity. "I've thought about you often when I've been out here. I knew you'd love it."

She reached out a hand to him. "Alex, don't ever leave me. No matter what you say, I could never survive without you."

"I couldn't bear seeing you with those other men." He took her hand.

"Nothing ever happened," she whispered. "I was running away."

"Lilli, I love you. I've loved you since the day you walked into my office at Evans, Davis and Phillips."

"I think I've always loved you, Alex. I was just too stupid to realize it."

His arms closed in about her. They held each other as the birch logs in the grate crackled.

"Lilli . . ." His eyes sought hers. Passionate yet questioning.

"Oh, yes, Alex." She lifted her mouth to his again, abandoning herself to emotions too long submerged.

He released her gently and began removing pillows from the wicker sofa, placing them on the floor before the fireplace. He held out his arms. "I've waited so long for you, Lilli."

THEY WERE NO LONGER a part of the rest of the world, Lilli told herself as they sat on the porch and watched the sun rise over the ocean. Not until the rosy circlet moved above the horizon and merged into a dazzling gold did they go into the kitchen to prepare breakfast. As Josiah had promised, they found fresh fish—cleaned and ready for the skillet—waiting on the kitchen steps.

They ate and made love and talked. As she told him of her pain and anguish at never knowing her father, he held her in the curve of his arms and soothed her as though she were still that hurt little girl in Marienbad.

Lilli was shaken by the depth of her feelings. Jacques had been part of a childhood fantasy: the romantic knight on a white charger who had rescued her from a dreaded marriage. He had become a habit. A responsibility. A third child.

Was there a place in her life for this kind of love? She was almost forty. She had a daughter who would soon be twenty-two. A son who was seventeen. Love was for the young.

SUNDAY CAME too quickly. Lilli and Alex drove back to Manhattan in the afternoon. Only now did they discuss his plans to spend two weeks in Europe to explore sites for new salons. He wanted to leave almost immediately. She realized he sensed she needed time—a separation—and she was grateful.

"Lilli, come to the house to meet Grandma tonight," he said as they drove across the Queensboro Bridge. "Mama and Papa are away at their house in the Berkshires for a week, but Grandma will be there; she insisted she didn't want to go." He chuckled. "She said it was time Mama and Papa had some time alone together."

"Alex, it isn't right just to barge in," she said. She was not ready for the commitment Alex had in mind. And yet she knew she loved him. "Another time—"

"Tonight, when Grandma's all alone." His eyes were warm and tender. "I'd like Grandma to be the first of the family to meet you."

LILLI WAS NERVOUS when she and Alex were ushered into the mid-Victorian drawing room of the Kahn house, but at the first sight of Dora Kahn, her nervousness vanished in the warmth she felt from the kindly old woman. Mrs. Kahn was small and round with perfectly coiffed white hair and penetrating brown eyes. Lilli guessed she had once been a beautiful woman. It surprised Lilli that after so many years in New York, she still spoke with the musical accent of her native South Carolina.

"Alex, you never told me she was so young and beautiful," Mrs. Kahn scolded, holding Lilli's hand.

Lilli laughed. "Not that young. I have two grown children. At least, Freddie insists that at seventeen he's grown."

Mrs. Kahn seemed to know that tonight was a special occasion, and she was clearly pleased that Alex had finally opened an avenue between his business and his family. Between his family and *her*.

Over dinner, conversation was lively. Mrs. Kahn was fascinated by the details of the business, which until now Alex had discussed only superficially. At the end of the evening, Mrs. Kahn walked them to the door and kissed Alex, then Lilli. "You're a great lady," she said to Lilli. "A real *mensch*." Lilli laughed, remembering how Alex had said his parents shied away from speaking Yiddish. But Dora Kahn would do as she liked in this world, and for that alone Lilli respected her.

Four evenings later—dreading what would be a five-week separation—Lilli saw Alex off as he boarded the *Mauretania*, on which he had been able to book a first-class cabin because of a last-minute cancellation. The atmosphere was very convivial, very youthful. The *Mauretania* was the favorite of the younger set, as the ship's advertising gaily reported. Lilli gazed with tender amusement at a host of young people milling about the decks. Here and there she saw a familiar face. Young girls who looked as though they had just walked off pages from *Vogue* or *Harper's Bazaar*.

"I'll miss you, Alex," she said quietly when he had kissed her goodbye. "Take care of yourself. You're very precious to me."

On the way back to the house, Lilli remembered her loneliness at their earlier separations. She had told herself it was loneliness for a very dear friend. Now it would be more painful loneliness. What did the future hold for them? Was she being impulsive again? If nothing else, life had taught her not to trust her heart alone.

ALEX DISEMBARKED from the *Mauretania* at Cherbourg and took the boat train to Paris. He planned to spend a few days selecting new sites for future salons, but his primary reason for being here was personal: Lilli would never be a totally free woman until she had tracked down the man who was her father.

When he returned to New York, he would bring with him the name of the titled Englishman—living or dead—who had given Lilli's mother a child, and then callously married another.

27

In Paris, Alex and Sara sat before a cozy fire in the sitting room of Sara's apartment. She toyed nervously with the heavy gold band on her left hand.

"Alex, I understand what you're saying. Perhaps long ago I should have made an effort to learn the identity of Lilli's father, but I was sure he would never acknowledge her. Like many men who came to Marienbad in the season, he found a young girl to his liking and had his pleasure with her—it meant nothing more." She shrugged. "How are we to know what is right for another?"

"Lilli hired detectives, who sent huge bills and no information," Alex said. "There must be a way to track this man down."

"You're the one who has tracked down spies," she said. "After the war, Lilli told me all about it."

"Lilli's mother never gave you any hint?" he asked.

She shook her head. "Nothing."

"I know from the reports the detectives gave Lilli that they talked to personnel at the Hotel Weimar. They say they came up with nothing. What about someone close to Lilli's mother? A girlfriend?"

"Kathe had one special girlfriend," Sara said. "Elspeth. As I recall, she moved with her mother and sisters to Karlsbad shortly before Lilli was born."

"What was her last name?"

Sara frowned. "Let's see...it was such a long time ago. Wait a minute...Mayer! That's it: Elspeth Mayer."

"She moved from Marienbad to Karlsbad," Alex said.

Sara nodded. "She may have married. Her sisters may have married. I don't know if the mother is still alive."

"Thank you, Sara." Alex took her hand. "Somehow I'll find this Elspeth Mayer. She may be the link to Lilli's father."

"Lilli blames me for not finding her father," Sara said unhappily. "When she was very young, we had such fights about it."

"Lilli loves you very much," Alex said. "Perhaps as a young girl she was angry, but no more, I promise you. With age comes understanding."

"I have some old photographs," Sara said. "One is of Kathe and Elspeth, taken when they were fifteen. Perhaps it will be helpful." She rose to her feet. "It's in a box in my bedroom."

The following day, Alex was aboard the Orient Express en route to Vienna. At Vienna, he took the train to Karlsbad. He had no difficulty getting a room at the Grand Hotel Pupp, now that the season was over. He began his search for Elspeth Mayer.

People in the resort town were friendly, but they didn't seem to know anything about Elspeth Mayer. Fighting despair, he stopped in a small café for coffee and to rest his tired feet. When the one waitress in the café came to serve him, he asked in his shaky German about Elspeth Mayer, showing the faded photograph of Kathe and Elspeth.

"I'm sorry," he said. "The picture was taken a long time ago."

The pretty young waitress stared at the photograph in astonishment. "Grandma!" she called excitedly to the buxom older woman sitting behind the cash register. "There's a man here asking for you."

A few minutes later, Alex was having a cup of fragrant strong coffee with the woman who had been Elspeth Mayer before her marriage thirty-seven years ago. Elspeth plied him with questions about Sara and Lilli, and was thrilled when he told her about Princess Lilli. It was only when he asked about Lilli's father that Elspeth was wary.

"I moved away from Marienbad when Kathe was still pregnant," she said. "After three or four years, we lost touch. Then I heard how she died. Poor Kathe. She was so pretty. So sweet."

"Lilli has tried all these years to learn the identity of her father," Alex said. "She doesn't want to approach him, she just wants to know who he is. Please. It's terribly important to her."

"Kathe said no one was ever to know." Elspeth toyed with the tablecloth. "Ah, he told her such things—that he was coming back to Marienbad in a few months, that they would marry and go together to live in Paris. She never heard from him again."

"She would want to put Lilli's mind at rest," Alex said. "Please tell me his name."

"I don't know," Elspeth said. "Kathe called him Edward. But I can give you a picture of him and his mother, taken at a party in London. He gave it to Kathe that summer in Marienbad. It's from a London newspaper. The *Morning Star*. When Kathe realized she was carrying his baby, she gave me the picture to keep for her. She was afraid her sister would find it. Will that help?"

"It'll be an enormous help," Alex said.

ALEX SPED THROUGH the business that had ostensibly brought him to Europe, then hurried to London. With Oliver's assistance he was able to track down Lilli's father within twenty-four hours. The man in the photograph—the man who had left Kathe Landau carrying his child—was Viscount Edward Linley.

"Oliver, how can I meet him?" Only to size the man up, Alex told himself. So that he could prepare Lilli, if he decided to arrange a meeting.

"I'm afraid I'll have to do some reconnoitering first," Oliver said. "I know one daughter slightly—she's a client of the salon. The older daughter is married to a diplomat stationed in Bermuda."

That same evening, Oliver reported to Alex that Viscount Linley was spending December and January at his daughter's home in Hamilton, Bermuda. The youngest daughter was to join her father and sister shortly.

"What will you do, Alex?" Oliver asked.

"I'll find a way to take Lilli down to Bermuda," Alex said. "I'll bring her face-to-face with her father. What she does then is her decision."

Alex had written nothing to Lilli about any of this. He prayed it wouldn't turn out to be a mistake. According to Oliver, the viscount's two daughters were spoiled, arrogant women. As for the viscount himself, all they knew was that he had been a widower for twelve years and was part of the international set.

LILLI PACED the length of her office. Alex's ship had docked this morning. Any moment now he would walk in the door, with news of Aunt Sara and Oliver, and Frances and Charles. She had missed him more than she thought possible.

Her face lighted at sounds of voices from the reception area. The girls were greeting him. She ran out into the hall.

"Lilli!" He freed himself from the circle of girls and came toward her. "I missed you so much!"

"You were gone so long!" She pulled him into her office and closed the door behind them. Tonight, she promised herself, they would celebrate properly.

He kissed her, swaying with her in his arms. "I always forget you're so little," he said. "My fragile Dresden doll."

She laughed. "Now get out of that hot coat and tell me what's been happening. You've said so little in your letters. The plans for Cannes sound exciting. Did Aunt Sara go with you?"

"Lilli, sit down," he said quietly, tossing aside his coat and hat. "I have something to tell you."

Holding her hands, Alex told her about his secret trip to Karlsbad and his further explorations in London. She didn't say a word until he had finished.

"You did that for me?"

"Don't you want to know who he is?" he said.

"Yes," she whispered. And yet, after all these years, she wasn't so sure . . .

"He is Viscount Linley," Alex said. *She would have been Lady Lilli Linley.* "I didn't meet him, though I'd hoped to—he's visiting his married daughter in Bermuda."

"My half sister," Lilli said.

"There are two half sisters. Lilli, we're going to vacation in Bermuda for a few days," Alex said. "You'll have a chance, I hope, to meet him."

"How can we do that?"

"I'll find a way. Lilli, I want you to meet your father."

"I'm scared," she said. "Oh, Alex, I've never been so scared of anything in my life. After all this time . . ."

"Now don't rush into this," he said. "It's very likely he'll pretend he never knew your mother."

"I don't care about that. I just want to see him."

"Good. I've made some inquiries. The Furness line doesn't begin sailing to Bermuda until January first, but we can take the Royal Mail Stream Packet from New York. It leaves every Saturday year-round at eleven in the morning. You'll love Bermuda. It's beautiful and peaceful—no cars are allowed. About twenty years ago there were a few automobiles, but they frightened the horses and there was an accident, so the vile city machines were banned!" He chuckled. "I think Bermuda must be the quietest place in all the world."

"I understand the Princess is a beautiful hotel." Now Lilli remembered clients talking about winter months in Bermuda. "Very much Old World elegance. But if you'd rather stay at the Bermudian or the Inverurie . . ."

Alex was frowning. "My family keeps a house down there," he said. "There's a resident staff. It's comfortable and on the water. Ten years ago, when Bermuda was becoming popular with Americans, Papa did some checking on the Princess. Their ads read as they still do, 'Restricted Clientele.' At that point Papa took a long lease on a house because Grandma was enthralled with Bermuda. He didn't know the policy of the other hotels. He didn't want to expose the family to any ugliness."

"Oh, Alex," Lilli said. "It's everywhere, isn't it? Even in so beautiful a place as Bermuda."

"But there's much to enjoy there," he said.

"You know," Lilli said, "it *is* a bad time to be going away. There's the Christmas rush at the salon and last-minute shipments from the factory—"

He held up a hand. "We'll be gone just nine days. And we'll work on board ship. Away from the phones and all the other interruptions, we'll get a lot done. And don't worry about Freddie—he's working so hard at school he'll hardly notice you're gone."

Three days later, on a blustery Saturday morning, Henri drove Lilli and Alex to Pier 42 North River, where they boarded the *Araguaya*, bound for Bermuda.

"We're running away from snow and sleet and icy winds," Alex said as they watched a gray Manhattan disappear from view. "We're moving into eternal spring."

The brief voyage was deliciously restful. Lilli realized Alex was making an effort to distract her from the purpose of the trip. At intervals they discussed, argued, and made decisions about the Cannes salon and the projected one in Rome. Alex was an extension of herself, Lilli thought with pleasure. But she must be sure before she made another commitment. She had already divorced two men.

She woke early on Monday morning, instantly aware that within a few hours they would be in Bermuda.

"Cold?" Alex asked, pulling her into his arms.

"Just nervous," she said. "No meeting in my life has been so important."

"We'll dress in a little while and go to breakfast."

"We should pack—"

"Later." He pulled her close. "Right now I have something else in mind."

Alex always knew what was best for her, she thought as her arms closed around his shoulders. With him, she could forget everything else in the world.

After breakfast—with their trunks and hand luggage packed—Lilli and Alex went on deck. "The North Rocks are just ahead," he said. "But we're not likely to see them, be-

cause the ships try to keep a distance—the reefs are dangerous. The first land we'll see is Saint George's Island. Bermuda
is a collection of islands."

"When were you here last?" Lilli asked.

"About seven years ago. I popped over for a couple of days
when I was looking into Miami as a possible salon site. But
Grandma and Mama and my sisters spend at least a couple of
months down here each year."

They watched while the ship moved over the brilliant blue
water. Alex pointed out the octagonal tower of St. David's
Lighthouse. The ship continued its course through the Nar-
rows—the only passage adequate for large steamers—and
through the outer reefs, toward Hamilton Harbor. After passing through the channels among the islands—some wide ex-
panses of beach, others dotted with white cottages set in groves
of cedar—the ship rounded a point and the colorful, crowded
port St. George, with its white and yellow limestone houses, its
tropical broad-leaved trees, lay before them.

The vessel skirted St. George's, and paused at Grassy Bay,
where the mail was taken off.

"That's Gibb's Hill Lighthouse," Alex said. "We'll go there
one morning and climb to the top for the best view of Bermuda. You'll love it."

Now they were drawing close to Hamilton Harbor, the ship's
course marked by large numbered black-and-white checkered
buoys. "See those clock towers?" Alex said. "They're at the
cathedral and the Sessions Houses. There's the Hamilton Hotel. And just beyond it, the Bermudian."

They went through the customs formalities with astonishing
ease. A discreet tip to the room steward, Alex whispered, would
rush their trunks ashore. A ship's steward had already taken
their hand luggage to the dock. Smiling native porters carried
their luggage to one of a lineup of waiting carriages. A cable
had been sent to the house to announce their arrival, but Alex
had instructed the houseman, Simon, not to bother to meet
them; they would take a public carriage.

"Alex, I can't believe the color of this sea." Lilli gazed in awe at the crystal-clear blue water.

"We'll take one of those tours in a glass-bottomed boat," he said, prodding her toward the carriage. "Then you can see the coral and the weeds and strange animal life at the bottom of the sea."

"I must find time to go to Trimingham's," Lilli said. "Jan and Freddie would love some cashmere sweaters." How strange to be talking like a tourist when her purpose here was so desperately serious!

The carriage drove them away from the wharf at the foot of Queen Street and out into a residential area. Lilli was fascinated by the charm of the scenery as they drove over narrow, dazzling white, winding roads lined with cedars and orange trees. Hedges of red hibiscus and pink oleanders everywhere, with blue morning glories entwining themselves in the hedges. The sea sparkling in the sun, the beach a pristine white and pink. The waves becoming swaths of frothy pink chiffon.

"Did you notice the terraced roofs of the houses?" Alex asked. "They're constructed that way to catch the rain. That's Bermuda's only water supply. Our house is just ahead. It's right on the water. A pleasant, unpretentious house. There are no mansions here like the ones you've seen in New York or London or Paris. Here the homes of even the richest residents are like what you'd expect to find in an affluent American suburb."

The carriage pulled into the driveway of a two-story white limestone house surrounded by spacious verandas. The garden was in glorious bloom. Another native came forward to help them with their luggage. Behind him a small, round, black woman waited on the veranda.

"Welcome to Bermuda, Mr. Alex." Lilli knew this was Simon. His teeth were a dazzling white against his dark skin. "It's been too long, sir."

"Simon, my mother never stops bragging about how wonderful you are with the garden. Lilli, you've heard much about Simon and Rosita."

"Mr. Alex!" Rosita came toward him. "It's so good to see you here again."

"Simon, Rosita"—Alex turned to Lilli —"this is Mrs. Laval, who'll be my guest here."

Rosita swept Lilli off to a private suite—usually Grandma Kahn's rooms—with windows and veranda overlooking the sea. If she closed her eyes, she thought once Rosita had left, she could almost pretend this was her and Alex's honeymoon.

Why didn't she trust herself to make such a commitment? But perhaps she was being silly; after all, Alex hadn't even asked her to marry him. Still, she knew all he needed was a sign from her.

Immediately after lunch, Alex went off to phone his mother's friends, who lived on the island year-round. Lilli waited for him on a veranda overlooking the ocean.

"We're invited to tea at the Witherspoons' later this afternoon," Alex said, coming out onto the veranda. "They're both British by birth and they socialize with the British colony. They're sure to ask us to be their guests at some social functions while we're here."

"Did you ask them if they knew Viscount Linley?"

"Lilli, that's not the way to do it." He reached for her hand. "Maybe we won't meet him our first evening in Bermuda; but I promise you, before we leave, we will."

"But that's leaving so much to chance—"

"Don't you trust me?"

She smiled. "You know I do."

"Then let's have Simon drive us to Front Street and I'll show you some of Hamilton until it's time to go to the Witherspoons'."

"Should I dress for tea?"

"Tea is casual in Bermuda." He inspected her simple gray jersey Chanel suit. "You might add your pearls."

Simon drove them to Front Street and left them when Alex said they would take a carriage to the Witherspoons' at teatime. Meanwhile, they strolled along Front Street, which followed the water for half a mile. They paused to gaze at the

windows of a succession of shops, lingered at Trimingham's.... But not for a moment did Lilli forget that somewhere on this island her father was about to have his afternoon
tea.

"Have you ever seen such a charming business district?"
Alex asked, obviously trying to distract her from anxious
thoughts. "People call it the finest commercial street anywhere in the world."

At the appointed time Alex and Lilli took a carriage to the
Witherspoons'. At their destination, the driver turned off the
road into a circular driveway through tall wrought-iron gates
and pulled to a stop before a modest white colonial.

Mr. and Mrs. Witherspoon, an older retired couple who had
been New Yorkers for thirty years, were delighted with their
new guests. Mrs. Witherspoon informed them they were invited to a dinner party the following evening and to a military
ball the next night. Alex went to elaborate lengths to explain
that Lilli was here with him on business. During the daytime
hours, he told them, he and Lilli would be involved in conferences with a local perfume manufacturer. But Lilli knew these
meetings would be brief. Alex also talked about Simon and
Rosita to reassure the Witherspoons that he and Lilli were
properly chaperoned. Darling Alex, Lilli thought in tender
amusement. He was concerned about her reputation, although in 1926 the Witherspoons would hardly have been
shocked that she and Alex were sharing a bed.

"Tell me, Lilli, is what we hear about the speakeasies in New
York all true?" Mrs. Witherspoon asked. "As you can imagine, Bermuda is doing well with all the rum-running."

"I must confess," Lilli said, "I rarely have time to visit the
speakeasies."

"I can assure you," said Alex, "you're not missing a thing.
Occasionally I go to Jack and Charlie's or 'Twenty-one' or
Leon and Eddie's with out-of-town buyers who're eager to see
the New York 'speaks,' but I wish the government would do
away with Prohibition before more people are blinded or killed
from bad bootleg whiskey."

AFTER A FULL DAY of playing tourist in Hamilton—shopping for sweaters at Trimingham's, an eighteenth-century chest at Wm. Bluck & Company, a tartan handbag at H. A. & E. Smith Ltd., an exquisite pin at Astwood Dickenson—Lilli was both happy and apprehensive. She changed dresses three times before Alex insisted the green velvet Poiret was perfect for their dinner engagement.

The Witherspoons called for them in their carriage. Mrs. Witherspoon made no effort to hide her pleasure at escorting the internationally known Princess Lilli. Within minutes of arriving, Lilli knew that neither her father nor her sisters would be present, but she hid her disappointment well. Two of the British ladies present patronized the London salon and were enthralled to have Princess Lilli herself at dinner.

LONG AFTER Alex had fallen asleep, Lilli lay awake beside him. Had she and Alex been naïve to think they would meet Viscount Linley and his daughters here?

"Lilli?" Alex murmured.

"Did I wake you?"

"Darling, don't be disappointed that your father wasn't there tonight." He pulled her close. "We have several days ahead of us."

"Alex, why can't I just phone his daughter's house?" *Her half sister's house.* "Why can't I just ask to see him?"

"Because it would be wrong for *you*." His hand moved beneath the light blanket and caressed her breast. "Meet him socially first. Then you'll know if you wish to identify yourself to him."

"Alex," she said, "you're so good to me."

"Shall I show you how much I love you?" he whispered.

"Oh, yes," she said, "please do."

28

FOLLOWING BREAKFAST, Lilli and Alex set off for a day of sightseeing. She was looking forward to the military ball this same evening. It was the social event of the month, and chances were Viscount Linley would attend.

It was a wonderful day. They hired a carriage and rode out to visit Gibb's Hill Lighthouse in Southampton, climbing the stairs to the highest point in Bermuda for a breathtaking view of the islands, the Sound, and the Atlantic. They were driven to the quaint and lovely Tom Moore's Tavern—built in 1652, with huge fireplaces and windows of cedar paneling—where the Irish poet lived and wrote about Bermuda over a century before. In the afternoon they went out in a glass-bottomed boat. They watched a rose-and-gold sunset over the water, and then Alex insisted Lilli rest before leaving for the ball. The day had been pleasantly warm, the sunlight brilliant; but now a cool breeze swept the island.

In a hot, perfumed tub, Lilli tried to relax. *What was her father like?* He must have been handsome to win over her young, impressionable mother. Just as she had been won over by Jacques. Why was it so important for her to meet the man who had so neglected her mother? Her oldest sister, who had never married, was Lady Alicia Linley. The other sister was now Lady Augusta Reynolds. According to Alex, Oliver didn't like either of them: Whenever they came to the salon, they were demanding and patronizing.

Lilli stepped out of the tub and began to dress. Earlier, Rosita had laid her evening gown across the bed. Celestine had been astonished that Lilli was traveling without her maid. In truth, except for her weekends on Long Island, this was the first time since opening her first salon that Lilli had taken a trip totally unrelated to business.

While she adjusted the clasp of the magnificent pearls she had bought for herself at Cartier's on her thirty-fifth birthday, Alex knocked and came in.

"You're wearing my favorite dress," he said, his eyes trailing over the chic, graceful, black georgette Poiret frock, cut to display her creamy-white shoulders and long, slim legs.

Lilli smiled, and twirled before him. "I'll always be loyal to Poiret. He made my first designer gown. I was entranced."

"It's cool tonight," he said. "What are you wearing as a wrap?"

"My chinchilla cape. I'll get it." She felt more nervous tonight than she had at her first "evening" in Paris.

Alex reached for the cape when she returned and draped it about her shoulders. "I'm very proud to be escorting such a beautiful lady," he murmured. "Every man at that ball will be envious of me."

"A woman of my age?" Lilli lifted an eyebrow. "Only the French appreciate a woman of 'a certain age.' "

Lilli and Alex went downstairs to await the arrival of the Witherspoon carriage. On the way to the ball, they chatted about the day. Alighting from the carriage, they could hear the sounds of the orchestra playing Vivian Ellis's "Spread a Little Happiness"—the English hit song Lilli and Alex had heard last night and that Alex had thought was a new Gershwin song, so similar was the work of the two composers. Let it be an omen for her future, Lilli thought.

As they entered the elaborately decorated ballroom, Lilli surveyed the dance floor, sprinkled with women in chic Paris frocks and men in formal attire or dashing military or naval uniform. Her smile was warm as Mr. Witherspoon introduced her to the receiving line.

When the orchestra switched to an American import, "Lady Be Good," Alex led Lilli onto the dance floor. "Relax," he whispered. "The evening's just beginning. No more than half the guests have arrived."

Lilli focused on a couple standing in the entrance. "There's Kathy and Richard Conway." She knew their next move. "I met them two or three times in London at dinner parties at my friend Eleanora's house—you know, the duchess of Rochester. They'll probably know the viscount and his daughters. Let's go over and greet them. But let *me* make the inquiries. I have a perfect opening."

For a few moments the Conways and Lilli talked about the duchess of Rochester and London while Alex listened with a show of interest. Then, casually, he intervened.

"Would you know Alicia Linley and her sister, Lady Augusta Reynolds?"

"Oh, yes." From Kathy's slight frown, Lilli guessed the two ladies were not favorites of the Conways'. "In fact, I'm sure they'll be here tonight. As well as their father, Viscount Linley."

"The viscount never misses a chance to mingle with young and pretty women," Richard Conway added dryly.

"I was at our London salon just recently," Alex said. "Oliver asked me to give his regards to the two ladies. They're clients of the salon."

"There's Alicia now," Kathy said. "The blonde in the pink crepe with all the beads. Shall I introduce you?"

Lilli managed a fixed smile as they were introduced to Lady Alicia Linley and her elderly escort. *She had not been fantasizing as a little girl. She had a family. This was her sister. Jan and Freddie's aunt.* She was startled by Alicia's resemblance to Jan. To *herself.*

"How sweet of Oliver to send his regards," Alicia said with affected sweetness. "He's such a love. He always helps when I'm having a problem with a difficult operator." She turned to Lilli, faintly condescending. "And Frances is a darling, too. No one would ever guess she was Jewish."

"No," Alex said, "we don't walk around with identifying tags."

Alicia's mouth dropped open. "Would you excuse me, please?" she said, cold as an Arctic wind. "I think my father's just arrived. I must speak with him."

"Well," Lilli said, "it looks like the London salon has lost one client. No loss, I'm sure, as far as Oliver and Frances are concerned."

Lilli's eyes followed Alicia. The man she was approaching—a rather tall, corpulent man who once must have been handsome but was now coarse and dissipated—was Viscount Edward Linley. *Her father.* Watching his gaze move about the ballroom, settling lasciviously on a particularly attractive young woman, Lilli flinched.

"Are you all right?" Alex said.

"Fine." But she felt cold and sick. Her father reminded her of an older Jacques. She and her mother, both so careless with their love...

"The resemblance between you and Alicia is startling," Alex said. "Except for that petulance of hers."

Lilli was relieved that the Witherspoons joined them to introduce other friends. But even while they chatted gaily, she was distracted by Alicia and the viscount. When she saw a taller redhead join them, Lilli knew instantly that it was Augusta. Her features were less fine than Alicia's but the resemblance, again, was so striking that Lilli's heart pounded.

Dancing with Mr. Witherspoon, Lilli looked above his shoulder directly into the eyes of Viscount Linley, who appeared to be mesmerized by her. For an instant she feared he had noticed her stare. The music stopped. He came forward and slapped Mr. Witherspoon on the shoulder. "Witherspoon," he said, "who is this marvelous young woman you're monopolizing?" Lilli heard Richard Conway's voice: *"The viscount never misses a chance to mingle with young and pretty women."*

Unfailingly polite, Mr. Witherspoon introduced them. A summons from his wife across the ballroom left Lilli alone with the viscount.

"My daughter tells me you're the talented lady who heads up the Princess Lilli cosmetic firm," he said, holding her hand. "How sad for London that you went off to the States. Will you be here long?"

"Just a few days." She pulled her hand away.

His eyes lingered on the curve of her breasts. "Aren't you divorced from that fellow Laval? I thought I read something about it in the *Tatler*."

"Yes." Lilli looked around the ballroom for Alex. He was being introduced by Mrs. Witherspoon to the commanding officer of the Bermuda garrison.

"I say," he said, "why don't we meet for a pleasant little dinner tomorrow night?" His eyes brazen now. She was a divorced woman, therefore fair game.

"I think not," she said coldly.

He flushed. "You women in trade are strange. What kind of family do you come from?"

Lilli lifted her head, her eyes meeting the viscount's with cool disdain. "My mother was a wonderful lady. Unfortunately— though it matters little to me because he was never part of my life—my father was an utterly worthless bounder."

LILLI AND ALEX cut short their stay in Bermuda and left for New York the following day. For Lilli, the loveliness of Bermuda had been spoiled by her encounter with her father. She told herself—and Alex—that she was finally at peace, that she was free of the obsession that had haunted her most of her life. She had seen her father and her half sisters and she now knew she wanted no part of any of them. Yet she couldn't deny that it hurt to know that her father was a pompous lecher and her sisters shallow, arrogant women.

After dinner on the first of their two-night return voyage, Lilli and Alex went on deck to watch the moonlight cast its glittering silver glow over the dark water. They stood at the railing, for a moment the only passengers on deck.

"It's beautiful," Lilli said softly. "I wish the trip was longer than two nights."

"Lilli, I've waited a long time to ask you." He made no effort to touch her, but the urgency in his voice startled her. "I want most desperately to marry you. I hate the nights when I have to leave you to go back to my empty apartment."

"You know I love you," she said. "More than I thought I could love any man. What I felt for Jacques—even in the best moments—was infatuation. And I don't have to tell you about Mischa. But because I love you, Alex, I must be sure that marriage is right for both of us. I don't want to marry you only because I'm afraid of growing old alone."

"Darling," Alex said, "what *is* this insane fear you have about your fortieth birthday? You come from hearty stock. Look at Sara—sixty-five and looking forward to another twenty years in the Paris salon! Lilli, half your life lies ahead of you. Let me share it with you."

"Alex, please." She kissed him lightly. "Just give me a little time. I couldn't bear to hurt you."

BACK IN NEW YORK, Lilli and Alex were caught up in the rush of Christmas business. When Jan came home for the holidays, she was withdrawn and secretive. Realizing she had probably been pressing Jan too hard to join Princess Lilli after graduation, Lilli refrained from reminding her that this was her senior year at Vassar and she had no plans for her life beyond college.

During the Christmas vacation, Jan spent little time at home, disappearing almost every evening for a social engagement with Vanessa. Lilli worried about the young men she and Vanessa were meeting. Why hadn't Jan brought her young men to the house? *Was she ashamed of her mother?*

Somewhere in her bright young head, Lilli guessed, Jan blamed her for Jacques. She had chosen a husband who was a rotten father. Freddie seemed to survive this with less trauma—but Freddie was five years younger than Jan. Jan remembered when she had been her father's spoiled little darling—before Freddie took her place, and she was eventually discarded altogether.

Determined as ever to go to medical school, Freddie would be entering his senior year of high school in September. At frustrated moments Lilli wondered what would happen to her cosmetic empire with no heir apparent.

Shortly after New Year's, Jan returned to college, with a new wardrobe. Lilli often wondered at how her daughter spent money, thinking perhaps it had something to do with the fact that Jan had not yet accepted her Jewishness.

The night after seeing Jan off, Lilli, feeling lonely, went into her daughter's bedroom. The room was a shambles from Jan's last-minute packing. Lilli sat on the edge of the bed. A crumpled mauve nightgown lay across the foot of the bed. Lilli reached for it and brought the satin softness to her cheek. She could smell Jan's delicate floral perfume on it.

Noticing a copy of *Photoplay* lying facedown on the floor beneath Jan's night table, she reached down and picked it up. Circled in red pencil was a photograph of Jacques with a young starlet who wore an evening dress indecorously low. Below, underlined in red, was a gossip item to the effect that Jacques Laval was "playing house" with the actress.

Lilli ripped the page from the magazine and tore it to shreds. She should have banished Jacques from their lives when he married Addie Thomas. She should not have let him come back and hurt Jan this way. Clearly, Jan blamed her for Jacques's behavior. How could she ever change that?

WITH THE CHRISTMAS RUSH OVER, Alex focused on further expansions for the business. He was training a team of women to travel around the world and set up Princess Lilli departments in stores on every continent. He was determined to make Princess Lilli household words around the world.

In the face of Alex's seemingly endless energy, Lilli was especially concerned about her own recent fatigue. Lately she had been waking up every morning tired. She also had no appetite; she turned away even the breakfast tray that Celestine brought to her bedroom at 6:30 every morning.

After two weeks of this, she began to worry in earnest. Fearful thoughts of cancer taunted her throughout the day. She couldn't afford to die. Jan and Freddie needed her. After a week of sleepless nights and exhausted days, she phoned Dr. Bernstein, Alex's family doctor, who eight years ago had become her own physician. Telling no one of this appointment—not even Alex, who would be terribly worried—Lilli left the salon on the pretext of a luncheon appointment.

The day was cold and blustery. Determined to keep the appointment secret, she hadn't even called for Henri. Instead, she hovered at a curb on Fifth Avenue until she hailed a taxi.

By the time she stepped out of the taxi, huge flakes of snow had begun to fall. She hurried across the sidewalk to Dr. Bernstein's building. Perhaps she was just being melodramatic, she thought as she opened the door to Dr. Bernstein's wood-paneled reception room.

Dr. Bernstein's secretary greeted her with a warm smile. "He'll be with you in just a few minutes."

"Thank you."

She sat at one corner of the brown leather sofa and reached for the current issue of *Literary Digest*. She flipped the pages nervously, thinking how grateful she was that Dr. Bernstein had managed to schedule an appointment for her so soon after a call. He knew she was not a hypochondriac.

She looked around the empty room. At least she didn't have to worry about small talk with any other patients. But each passing minute seemed painfully long. Then a door opened and Dr. Bernstein's nurse, folder in hand, summoned her inside.

"You're looking well," he greeted her jovially, but his eyes were serious. "Alex been overworking you?"

"I just feel rotten," she said.

"We can't have that, can we?" He reached for her file.

For the next few minutes, she answered his questions.

"Let's see . . ." he said, "you're a few weeks from forty—"

"That's right." All at once her heart was pounding again.

"All right, let's have a look at you." He buzzed for his nurse. "Go along with Elise. I'll be right inside."

Despite the almost excessive warmth of the suite of offices, Lilli was cold as she dressed again in the small examining room later. Dr. Bernstein's eyes had been opaque, his face impassive when he told her they'd talk in his office in a few minutes. She was conscious of an odd, inquiring look on his face.

Now she sat again in the chair across from Dr. Bernstein's desk and tried to prepare herself for whatever he had to say. He cleared his throat.

"Lilli, you've had two children."

"Yes." Her throat was dry. What did that have to do with anything?

"All indications are that you're going to have a third."

Lilli stared in shock. *She was pregnant. She was carrying Alex's child.*

"I was sure it was cancer or an ulcer." Her laughter was shaky. "I should have recognized the signs!"

"I realize this is quite a shock"—he knew she was divorced from Jacques—"but the pregnancy can be handled discreetly. I can arrange for you to go—"

"Dr. Bernstein, I'm thrilled to be pregnant again! I've been secretly married for three months."

"Alex?" Dr. Bernstein asked, and it was Lilli's turn to be astonished. She hadn't realized that their affair had been so obvious.

"Yes—but please, don't say anything to anyone until he can tell his family."

"You're in excellent health, Lilli. There's no reason in this world why you won't have a fine baby. Congratulate Alex for me."

Lilli walked out into a world that seemed new and wonderful. She felt young again, and blessed. This new child would unite Alex and her forever. She stood indecisively for a moment before a telephone booth. She called Alex's private line.

"Alex, meet me for a late lunch at the Salle Cathay at the Saint Regis."

"When?" He seemed startled, but asked no questions.

"I'll be there in ten minutes."

Lilli was seated at a choice table in the elegant Salle Cathay when Alex arrived, struggling to hide his anxiety.

"I've ordered for us," Lilli said tenderly. "Everything you like."

"Is this a special occasion?"

"Darling, yes." She reached across the table for his hand. "I think you're going to have to marry me, Alex. How else can we tell Grandma Kahn we're presenting her with a great-grandchild?"

29

LILLI INSPECTED HER REFLECTION in her bedroom mirror as Celestine moved a button on the skirt of the olive-green velvet suit Alex himself had chosen for her to wear at their wedding this afternoon—to take place in the drawing room of the Kahn house. Thank God, the jacket concealed her already expanding waistline!

She and Alex had told everyone they had been married in a civil ceremony in Bermuda. Nevertheless, Alex would not take up residence at the Gramercy Park house until they had been married in a religious ceremony. Both brushed aside his mother's suggestion of a June wedding at Temple Emanu-El with a dinner after at the Płaza, saying they preferred to be married quietly and immediately.

"Madame Lilli, you look just beautiful." Celestine beamed. Lilli suspected Celestine was aware of her pregnancy and approved.

"We'll have to be leaving soon," Lilli said.

Her domestic staff—along with the Kahn servants—would be present when the rabbi married them. Alex's immediate family and Freddie would be there. But Jan would not come down from Vassar for the wedding. Now a senior, she claimed that because of an upcoming exam she would not be able to be there.

Lilli started at the brisk knock at her door.

"Mother?" Freddie called anxiously. "It's almost time to leave."

"Come in, darling," she called.

He opened the door and walked into the room, looking proud and handsome. Lilli had hoped to have Jan as her maid of honor, and she had been hurt when Jan refused. Though Alex's mother was too polite to say as much, Lilli suspected she didn't want to have the children in the wedding ceremony.

"You look beautiful," Freddie said.

"Thank you, Freddie." How lovely to be told by your child that you looked beautiful!

"I'll bring an umbrella to protect your clothes." Celestine was gazing out the window at the snow that was beginning to fall. "Why couldn't it have waited until tomorrow to snow?"

"Celestine, the snow is delightful," Lilli said. Today was very special to Lilli. Three times she had gone through a civil ceremony. They didn't count. Today, when she and Alex took their vows before a rabbi, she would have her first real wedding. Her only regret was that Aunt Sara, Oliver, and Frances and Charles could not be here to share her joy. "And we don't have to worry about traveling tonight. We're staying at the Plaza and going down to the Homestead tomorrow."

"Mother, you can't be late for your wedding," Freddie said, pretending to be stern. "I hope you'll be so happy. You deserve it."

Lilli left the house with Freddie on one side and Celestine, holding an umbrella over her, on the other. This was a fairy tale come true, she thought: This was the marriage for which she was born.

The Kahn house was a bower of red and white roses. A red velvet canopy had been set up at one end of the drawing room. Chairs had been arranged in rows for the guests. The servants were gathered in the rear. Lilli went through the wedding ceremony in a joyous haze, aware every moment of Alex's happiness, Freddie's approval. Grandma Kahn beamed.

After dinner, which was held in one of the private rooms at the Plaza, Lilli and Alex went up to their suite. In the morning they would board a train that would take them to the Homestead in Hot Springs, Virginia. Within a week they would return to New York and the business.

On their return, they planned to tell the family of Lilli's pregnancy.

JAN STOOD at the window of her darkened dormitory room and stared out at the falling snow. It was all over now. Uncle Alex was her stepfather. How could her mother have been so stupid as to ask her to be maid of honor?

She blinked as the lights went on. "Why were you standing here in the dark?" Vanessa asked.

"Because I *like* looking out at the snow without the lights on inside."

"Oh, come on, Jan," Vanessa said, "are you still fuming because your mother got married?"

"It's her fourth wedding ceremony," Jan snapped. "That's almost obscene."

"You can't blame her for divorcing your father," Vanessa said, "even if she had to do it twice. And everybody knows now that Prince Lamsaloff is a homosexual."

"She's forty years old."

"So what? Women don't dry up and die when they turn forty. Charlie Adams told me that the most passionate women he ever knew were over forty." Vanessa giggled and threw herself into a chair, her short skirt rising high on her thighs. "He says they're much more fun than girls our age. And so appreciative. That woman he's spent every weekend with bought him that new Essex."

"I don't think I'll ever marry." Jan settled herself across the foot of her bed. "I mean, with all these divorces, why bother?"

Vanessa laughed. "Don't be ridiculous. It's much more exciting to be a divorcée than an old maid. Remember what Freud says about obeying your libido."

"You've never read Freud," Jan said.

"No, but he did say you should obey your libido. I don't know. If I did, I'd never get to class!"

"Anyhow, most of the boys we know are disgusting," Jan said. Not one of them would ever ask *her* to marry him. She wasn't gorgeous like Vanessa, or "fast" like Dottie. She never knew what to say to them—except "No" when they tried to drag her into the back seat of their "struggle buggies."

"If we want to go down to New York next weekend," Vanessa said with a little smile, "Cole says he and his roommate will take us to Harlem to the Cotton Club. With *mucho* hooch."

"I hate gin," Jan sniffed. She hated any alcoholic beverage, but you couldn't tell that to the boys. Vanessa pretended to like everything. "Everybody knows gin is what they serve in Harlem. And I don't know his roommate. Blind dates can be such flat tires."

"You know, you are practically living in a convent," Vanessa said. "This is our last year at school—we're supposed to be having one big party. You are the prettiest girl on campus." *Why did Vanessa keep saying that? It wasn't true.* "You could have any boy you wanted if you'd stop being so standoffish."

"Can't you talk about something besides boys?" Jan started thinking about her mother and Uncle Alex again. The wedding and the dinner party were over. Mother had said they would spend their wedding night at the Plaza. She closed her eyes, trying not to think about them in bed together.

"We can talk about after college," Vanessa said offhandedly. "Have you said anything to your mother yet about going to Paris with me in the fall?" Vanessa had abandoned aspirations to become a movie star when she learned how early in the morning movie actresses had to be at their studios. Now she had persuaded her parents to allow her to study painting in Paris.

"It's too early to talk about Paris," Jan said. "Not until closer to graduation."

IT WASN'T UNTIL after their honeymoon, at the end of a Friday evening dinner at the Kahn house, that Lilli and Alex broke the news of her pregnancy. Tears of joy filled Grandma Kahn's eyes as she swept her granddaughter-in-law into her arms. Alex's parents seemed pleased, too, but they were more reserved. She knew that his marriage—so long awaited—to a three-times-divorced woman was not their first choice.

Freddie was the first one Lilli told when they arrived home. His first reaction was astonishment, then concern.

"Freddie, I'll be fine," she told him. "I'm not the first woman to have a child at forty, you know."

"You look about twenty," he said with pride. "I never told you, but Jimmy has an awful crush on you."

"Never mind Jimmy. Did I ever tell you that I love you very much?"

"A few million times." He grinned. "I love you, too."

While Freddie and Alex settled themselves in the library to listen to the news, Lilli went up to her bedroom to phone Jan. She was worried about Jan's reaction to her pregnancy. Jan had always loved Alex, yet she had refused to attend the wedding. So, Lilli reasoned, despite her hostility toward Jacques, she must still love her father.

At first, Lilli talked about the week in Virginia. Then she told Jan about the baby. Her heart pounded at the long silence on Jan's end of the line.

"So that's why you rushed to marry him."

"Jan, Alex and I were married in Bermuda." Her hands were shaking. "We both wanted a religious ceremony. This was not a 'have to' wedding."

"Well," Jan said coolly, "I hope you'll have more time for this baby. You don't *have* to work now."

"Jan, you were never neglected." Lilli was shocked. All these years Jan had resented her involvement in the business?

"Goodbye, Mother."

Lilli heard the click of the phone. Anger and frustration hit her. *She had been a good mother. She had not neglected her children for the business.*

Lilli said nothing to Alex about the confrontation with Jan. She was grateful for the comfort of his nearness as she lay awake far into the night. Her daughter didn't realize how much she was loved. Where had she gone wrong?

As THE WEEKS PASSED, Lilli worried about Alex's parents' continuing reserve toward her. She knew that he, too, was unhappy about it. For Alex's sake—and the baby's—she was determined to break down the barrier between them.

One day, when Lilli knew that Alex's parents were at the Bermuda house, she invited Grandma Kahn to lunch at Ratner's on Delancey Street. Alex had told her that this was one of his grandmother's favorites.

While Henri drove them downtown, Grandma Kahn reminisced. "Back around 1906 or 1907, my husband—may he rest in peace—came home one day to tell me about this wonderful restaurant he had just discovered on Pitt Street. Until he died in 1912, we used to go down regularly every Sunday evening for dinner."

"I should have taken Aunt Sara down there when she was here for Freddie's bar mitzvah," Lilli said. "She loved the Jewish restaurants we found in Paris."

Settled at a comfortable table in the large Ratner's, opened on Delancey Street in 1918, Grandma Kahn pointed out celebrities at nearby tables, dining between their shows at the nearby Loew's Delancey.

Over gefilte fish, Lilli confided her anxiety about Alex's parents' attitude toward their marriage. "I thought when I told them about the baby, they would be overjoyed," she said. "Like you."

"They worry," Grandma Kahn said gently. "Unlike some of the Jewish families in their circle, my son and daughter-in-law don't fight to be assimilated. We wish to be thoroughly American, yes—but not to give up our Jewish heritage. It's possible for Jewish Americans to serve their country well without sacrificing their five thousand years as a people."

"Grandma, Alex's child will be raised Jewish. As Freddie and Jan have been. If that is all that concerns them, assure them that Alex's child will know he's Jewish."

"Alex is the family's only chance of carrying on the Kahn name," Grandma Kahn said. "I had one son. And my son lost his older boy in the Spanish-American War. They're praying for a Kahn grandson—one that won't forsake his Jewish culture."

"I promise you, Grandma," Lilli said, "that will never happen." But if their baby should be a daughter, they would love her as much as a son.

LILLI WAS DISTRAUGHT when Jan not only told her not to come to Poughkeepsie for graduation, but also confided that she planned to feign sickness and skip the ceremony altogether.

"It's so silly, Mother. All that fuss over picking up a college degree. What will I do with it, anyway?"

Lilli had seen the major events of this year as Jan's graduation and the birth of the baby. Sara had been torn between coming to New York for Jan's graduation or for Lilli's delivery. Now there was no conflict. Sara would arrive at the end of July. Lilli expected to give birth sometime around the middle of August.

On graduation day Vanessa tried to persuade Jan, who was settled in bed with a copy of *The Great Gatsby*, the novel by F. Scott Fitzgerald, to get up and join the commencement exercises. But Jan refused.

"My mother was so excited about meeting your mother," Vanessa said. "Did you know that she left Elizabeth Arden for Princess Lilli when we were freshmen, mainly because we were roommates?"

Jan shrugged. "Mother gives occasional private consultations. Tell your mother to make an appointment." It was irritating the way everybody made such a fuss over Mother, as though she were royalty.

"Sure, she gives private consultations," Vanessa said. "For Gloria Swanson or Ina Claire or Gertrude Lawrence—or maybe Queen Mary of England."

"You'd think they would have met socially by now." But Vanessa's mother was *Social Register*, Jan remembered. Mother had friends who were highly placed socially, but there were affairs to which Princess Lilli, in "trade" and Jewish, was not invited. Intellectuals, artists, and entertainment-world celebrities formed Princess Lilli's court.

"I have to go now. I wish you'd stop being so stubborn."

"Go fly a kite, Vanessa."

Jan turned back to her book, but she couldn't concentrate. The festive sounds of the commencement exercises filtered into her room. It would have been silly to let Mother come up and make a big fuss over her graduating. Everybody would have crowded around Mother—the fabulous Princess Lilli—as though she were a scientist who had made some earthshaking contribution! At *her* age Mother had already been famous all over Europe. She'd been considered one of the most beautiful women on the Continent. How did graduating from Vassar compare with that?

Jan decided to spend the summer out at Southampton. Vanessa would stay with her, since Vanessa's mother would be in the south of France. They'd swim and play tennis, and in the fall she'd go to Paris with Vanessa. She could handle her mother.

FROM COLLEGE, Jan and Vanessa went to New York, staying only long enough to pack a proper wardrobe for a Southampton summer. The Gramercy Park house seemed strange to her now. It wasn't *their* home anymore. It was mother's and Uncle Alex's home.

Jan was relieved that her mother would not be out at the beach house at all this summer. Uncle Alex—so proud that he would soon be a father—insisted they stay close to the obstetrician and hospital. Didn't Mother realize how awful she looked, parading around at the salon with her stomach out to there? She looked ridiculous, even if her maternity clothes had been designed for her by Captain Molyneux.

At Southampton Jan and Vanessa attended an endless stream of parties. Lilli didn't belong to either the Meadow Club or the Beach Club—they didn't accept Jews—but Jan and Vanessa were invited regularly as guests. Vanessa's family was *Social Register*, so Vanessa was accepted everywhere. At least nobody at the Meadow Club or the Beach Club would ever say anything to *her*. Jan was only one-quarter Jewish, but she was never really comfortable at either club.

Early in August, Jan and Vanessa prepared to go into New York for a few days to shop for their wardrobes. They'd be sailing next month, Vanessa reminded. They needed fall clothes. Summer clothes would be out.

"Jan, talk to your mother," Vanessa said. "We have to book passage when we're in the city."

"Okay." Jan paused. "Aunt Sara arrived yesterday. Mother will be in a good mood. And Aunt Sara would *love* to have me in Paris." But let neither of them get the idea that she would work at the Paris salon. Paris was for fun.

LILLI WAS ECSTATIC that Aunt Sara was in New York and would be with her when her child was born. "I feel so fortunate," she said over dinner with Alex and Sara. "As though I'm beginning a whole new life."

"As I began a new one, when you brought me to Paris," Aunt Sara said softly. "I'd thought my life was over when I lost George."

Henri appeared in the doorway. "Madame Lilli, a phone call for you."

"Is it Freddie?" Lilli asked. Jan rarely called.

"Yes."

Ten minutes later, Lilli returned to report that Freddie and Jimmy, his closest friend, would be back the following day from their camping trip at Lake George.

"I can't wait to see him," Aunt Sara said, and paused at Lilli's gasp. "Lilli?"

"I think so," Lilli said quietly. "Now, Alex, relax," she laughed, because his face was suddenly drained of color. "This isn't my first child."

"I'll call the doctor." He was already on his feet.

"Aunt Sara, hold his hand," Lilli said, laughing. "He'll be a nervous wreck if this child is slow in coming." She hesitated, startled at the swift arrival of the second contraction.

"I'll call the doctor and have Henri bring the car around," Alex said. "I want you in the hospital as soon as possible."

Though Alex never said anything about it, Lilli knew he worried about her going through delivery at her age.

"I'm going to be all right," she told him. "By morning you'll be a father."

JAN STIRRED, aware of a persistent noise close by. She'd been dreaming. Something strange. Vanessa would say, "Aha, you have a complex about sex!"

Realizing the irritating noise was the buzz of the telephone on her night table, Jan swung across the bed and reached for the receiver. "Hello?" In the darkness of her bedroom, it was impossible to see the face of the clock.

"Jan, it's Uncle Alex. You have a new sister. Victoria Kathe Kahn. She's exactly"—he paused for an instant—"one hour and three minutes old. She weighed in at seven pounds seven ounces."

"That's wonderful, Uncle Alex." She tried to sound enthusiastic. God, what time was it? It had to be close to dawn; the sky was lightening. "How's Mother?"

"Fine," he said. "She said you're due in town tomorrow."

"Right." She lay back against the pillows. Couldn't Uncle Alex have waited till morning to call? "I'll go straight to the hospital."

Alex talked for another few moments, then they hung up and Jan tried to go back to sleep. With no luck. She felt alienated from her whole family. Her mother was beginning a new life. What room would there be for her and Freddie?

30

ON THIS HOT and humid mid-August morning, Jan sat at her dressing table staring in distaste at her reflection—not seeing the luminous sea-green eyes, the lovely arrangement of delicate features, the becoming halo of auburn hair. She listened to the morning sounds in the Gramercy Park house. After looking in on the baby, Uncle Alex had left for the salon. Home from the hospital for a week now, Mother was in the nursery with Vicky. She wasn't nursing this child but insisted on giving each bottle, except the 2:00 A.M. feeding, herself. In another few minutes Mother and Aunt Sara would have breakfast together in the alcove off the kitchen. Then, Jan thought, she would go downstairs.

Vanessa had left yesterday to spend a week with her father in Saratoga. She had left with strict orders to Jan to talk to her mother about spending a year in Paris. This was a good time to ask—while she was all dewy-eyed about the new baby and Aunt Sara's being here.

Impatiently, she began brushing her hair. It was goofy the way Uncle Alex and Freddie hung over the baby's crib all the time. To listen to those two, anybody would think this was the only baby in the world. But Mother was scheduled to go back to the salon in another week. Not even a new baby would keep Princess Lilli away from her kingdom.

Jan heard the nursery door open and close. Mother was leaving the baby with the new nurse to go downstairs. Aunt Sara was already down there having her first cup of coffee of the morning. Jan rose to her feet. *Go down and have this out with Mother.*

When she arrived at the cozy breakfast alcove, Jan forced a cheerful good-morning. *She couldn't wait to get out of this house. She didn't belong here anymore.* Not until Bertha had served their breakfast did she announce her desire to go to Paris with Vanessa next month.

"What is this madness," Lilli said, "going chasing off to Paris?"

"Vanessa's going," Jan said. "To study painting. I thought I might study fashion design."

"You've been away from home for four years of college," Lilli said flatly. "That's enough for now."

"Vanessa's my best friend." Color touched Jan's high cheekbones. "She expects me to go with her."

"I don't like what I hear about young Americans in Paris these days." Jan noticed that Lilli was folding over an edge of the tablecloth, which she always did when she was upset. Now she turned to Sara. "What do they expect to find in Paris they can't find at home?"

"Jan, perhaps your mother might feel differently about Paris if you came into the salon," Sara began. "After all, one day you'll—"

"I don't want to come into the salon." To be monitored every minute by Aunt Sara! "I would hate it."

"Jan, please—stay home for a year," Lilli said. "If you're still in the mood to study fashion in Paris, we'll talk about it then."

"Mother! You act as though I were twelve years old!"

"Sometimes you act like it." Lilli turned away. "I don't want to hear another word about it."

WITH REBELLION IN HER HEART, Jan saw Vanessa off on the glorious new *Ile de France*. It was outrageous that she wasn't sailing with Vanessa! Mother was just being mean and petty. Heaven knew, she could afford it! Every few months some magazine wrote about her being one of the richest women in America.

After Vanessa's departure, Jan slept till noon each day, then went shopping at Saks, Bonwit's, and Altman's with her usual abandon. Occasionally—when she knew no one would notice—she wandered into the nursery to visit with Vicky. It was hard to believe that this warm, sweet-scented tiny person was her sister. And it surprised her that in spite of her anger toward Lilli, she felt warm toward this pretty, happy baby.

Out of boredom, Jan let herself be talked into serving on various charity committees, though she carefully avoided those favored by Alex's mother and sisters, just as she avoided their efforts to include her in their social lives, which revolved around a closely knit circle of German-Jewish families. Even though they did their best to make her feel at home, she always felt like an outsider.

She was escorted by various young men-about-town, none of whom pursued her past the third or fourth date, because she rejected all efforts at "petting"; and if this didn't discourage the pursuer, she made it clear she intended never to marry. She wrote Vanessa regularly about how dull her life in New York was: "All the boys who trail after me look at me and see my mother's bank account. Or else they're betting on how soon they'll get me in bed."

Vanessa was ecstatic about Paris, which was apparently full of Americans. "And darling, the dollar goes so far!" Vanessa took classes, spent her afternoons hanging around the Café du Dôme and La Rotonde drinking *marc-cassis*. There were parties every night. After every letter, Jan was consumed with jealousy.

For a while Jan was fascinated with jazz. Then it was the movies. For a few weeks she wished passionately she looked like Clara Bow, who drove men wild. A Yale football player had even tried to commit suicide when Clara Bow broke up with him. But now all the movie magazines were talking about a new actress named Joan Crawford. Jan had long since lost interest in her father's romantic dalliances. She didn't even look for his name in the movie magazines anymore. She told herself that he was gone from her life forever.

At a Valentine's ball Jan met Scott Jamison, a soft-spoken young man who seemed mesmerized by her. When she told him she hated liquor and thought the Charleston was ugly, he didn't seem shocked in the least. One night he timidly invited her to come up to his apartment on Park Avenue; he seemed almost relieved when she turned him down. He had graduated from Harvard three years ago and worked with his father, who carried on the family's investment-banking firm. He seemed uncomplicated and undemanding. For Jan, he was the ideal escort about town.

In the spring her mother shocked her with the news that she was pregnant again. Vicky was only eight months old.

"Alex would be so happy if we had a son to carry on the family name," Lilli said.

Jan was appalled. "Doesn't he care about you? At your age, to go through this again?"

"I want his baby," Lilli said gently. "My children are my riches. I want to have another while I can."

"It's awful for your figure to be carrying a baby in your forties," Jan said.

"I'll survive that." Lilli's smile was tender.

"I have to dress." Jan rose to her feet. "Scott is taking me to the *Follies* tonight."

"You're seeing quite a bit of him these days, aren't you?"

"He's convenient." Jan shrugged. "And at least I don't have to spend the evening fighting him off." After the first try, he'd never again tried any silly ploys to get her up to his apartment.

In May, Lilli was approached by a Wall Street investment firm with an offer of $12 million for the business. Wrapped up in marriage and motherhood—and convinced that neither Jan nor Freddie would ever become part of Princess Lilli, Inc.—Lilli discussed the offer endlessly with Alex. They agreed that perhaps this was the time to sell.

"But not the Paris or London salons," Lilli said.

"Never," Alex said. "Those will remain in the hands of Sara in Paris, and Oliver and Frances in London." He hesitated, troubled. "Lilli, are you sure you want to do this?"

"Twelve million dollars is a great temptation." She smiled. In truth, she had not been able to forget Jan's accusation that the business had made her an inadequate mother: *"I hope you have more time for this baby."* She didn't want Vicky and the child she carried to feel that way. "But what about you, Alex? Won't you miss the business?"

"We've brought it to the heights," Alex said. "Our creation, Lilli. Perhaps this is the time to let go."

"Will you go in with your father now? You've always said you hated the mail-order business."

"I'm needed there. Papa would like to come in only two or three days a week. He can't do that when Frieda's husband is so ill." It was unlikely, Lilli knew, that her older brother-in-law would ever return to the firm. "Yes, I'd like to move into the family firm," he said. "I think I can bring something to it now."

"Then we'll agree to the sale." Lilli leaned forward and kissed her husband. "You'll have a full-time wife. The children will have a full-time mother."

"Lilli, don't ever feel guilty that you were involved in the business all these years. You were—and are—a fine mother."

Lilli smiled. If only Jan felt that way.

ON AN EARLY EVENING, Scott drove Jan out to Great Neck to a party at his family's estate. Only now did Jan realize the extent of the Jamisons' wealth. Approaching through a long driveway past magnificent gardens, Roman statuary, and a huge swimming pool, the house was an Italian Renaissance showplace, furnished with impeccably chosen antiques. In addition to a *Social Register* guest list, those at the party included such celebrities as George S. Kaufman, Gertrude Lawrence, and Oscar Hammerstein II.

Aware of Mr. and Mrs. Jamison's covert scrutiny, Jan also sensed their disapproval of her, and she realized with a shock that she was probably the first girl Scott had brought home. It was common knowledge, too, that Lilli Laval—now Lilli Kahn—was Jewish.

"Scott, do we have to stay?" Jan asked after an uncomfortable exchange with Scott's two sisters, both married into "upper-crust" New York families, both clearly sharing their parents' hostility toward her.

"No." Scott seemed angry; he, too, had felt his family's hostility. "But before we leave I'd like you to meet my great-grandmother."

"Is she at the party?"

"She lives in a cottage at the rear of the estate." He led her to French doors that faced out on the garden. "There's a shortcut through here. Then we'll drive back to New York."

Hand in hand, Jan and Scott walked through what seemed like acres of gardens. "It's just ahead," Scott said. Moments later, Jan saw the lights in a modest little house that appeared to be part of the servants' quarters. As they approached the door, they heard the strains of Al Jolson singing "Kol Nidre," the haunting song that had brought the audience to tears the night Jan and Scott had seen *The Jazz Singer*.

"Great-grandma is ninety-one," Scott said as he knocked at the door. "But she's still sharp as a whip."

The door was opened by an elderly black woman in a brightly flowered cotton dress. "Miss Rachael said you'd be comin' to see her tonight, Mist' Scott," she said fondly as she held the door wide for them to enter.

"Scott?" a warm, thickly accented voice called. "Come into the parlor. Mattie'll bring us cake and coffee."

Scott led Jan into a tiny parlor decorated in the early Victorian fashion and comfortably cluttered with family portraits of four generations. In a mahogany rocker sat a small, round woman wearing what Jan guessed was a wig. Her face was remarkably unlined for her years, her eyes faded but lively and inquisitive.

"Scott, you've brought a young lady to meet me!"

"This is my second favorite girl," he said, turning to Jan. "Great-grandma is number one."

She chuckled. "The family keeps me hidden away here in the back. I think they're afraid I might embarrass them before their *goyishe* friends." Jan's eyes widened in astonishment. *Scott's family was Jewish?* "My grandson and my son might call themselves Jamison," she said, noting Jan's surprise, "but a look back in the family history would tell the world they were born Jacobowitz." Now she turned to Mattie, who was staring, seemingly enthralled by Jan. "Mattie, bring us wine tonight. And the *rugelach* I baked this morning."

Jan understood the special relationship between the old lady and Scott. Anyone Scott brought to her would be "on their side." Mrs. Jacobowitz reminisced about her arrival at Castle Garden over seventy years earlier—"Ellis Island didn't open for immigrants until 1892"—and spoke with pride about how she and her husband had brought their infant son to this new land.

"But my children got fancy ideas," she sighed. "The mama with the accent from the old country and the kosher kitchen embarrassed them. But enough of me. Tell me about your family, Jan." Great-grandma Jacobowitz exuded a warmth that brought tears to Jan's eyes.

As Jan told them about her mother and stepfather, it became clear that Mrs. Jacobowitz knew about Princess Lilli. And she nodded in admiration at the mention of the Kahns. "You see, Scott?" Mrs. Jacobowitz beamed. "It's like I always say. You don't have to forget you're a Jew to become a *mensch* in America."

When they were ready to leave, Mrs. Jacobowitz held her face up to Jan to be kissed. "I knew when a girl caught Scott's eyes, it would be somebody special," she whispered. "He is the only Jamison I respect."

On the way back to Manhattan, Scott told Jan about his family's determination to bury their Jewish background.

"Great-grandma is the only holdout," he said. "My grandfather was determined that nothing would block his progress in the business world—and he was convinced that being a Jew would do that. So they became Jamisons. They joined the Episcopal church. They were delighted when their son and three daughters all married gentiles." *Then Scott was half Jewish.* "Our parents raised my sisters and me to marry Christians. We knew we were Jewish because of Great-grandma, but the children were not allowed to discuss it. The family avoided schools and resorts and country clubs that had even a sprinkling of Jews." Scott chuckled. "I never would have made a 'final club' at Harvard if they'd known I was Jewish."

"I was never conscious that being Jewish was different until a girl at school taunted me about not being invited to make my debut," Jan said. "Occasionally Mother tried to remind us that we were Jewish—lighting Hanukkah candles and observing the High Holidays. I think those are the only days Mother ever stayed away from the salon."

"I'm not marrying by religion," Scott said. "Will you be my wife, Jan? I don't care where you worship. All I want is to make you happy."

Jan's mouth dropped open in astonishment. For the past few weeks, she had been avoiding the thought that one day Scott might propose. She hadn't expected it to be tonight. But married to Scott she would be somebody new. Janine Jamison. She and Scott would have a house of their own. A life of their own.

"Is happiness so important?" she said quietly.

"Yours is to me."

She was touched. People usually called her "shy." How did Scott know she was unhappy?

"What makes you think I'm not happy now?"

"I see it in your eyes," he said. "I know, we're supposed to be the Lost Generation. We don't know what to do with the messed-up world our parents handed us. But yours is a different kind of unhappiness."

She laughed. "Don't tell me. You've been studying Freud."

"You don't have to answer right away—" He leaned forward eagerly.

"But I will." She gave him a dazzling smile. "Yes, Scott, I'll marry you."

He pulled her into his arms and kissed her—a bit more chastely than she would have liked, pulling away quickly.

"When?"

"In October. Autumn is a lovely time for a wedding." She hesitated. "I wouldn't want a big church wedding. I hate that sort of thing."

"It would make Great-grandma very happy if we were married in her cottage. By a rabbi." He paused, waiting for her reaction.

"Fine—by whomever you like." She could afford to be generous. Scott was sweet and mad about her. They'd have a beautiful apartment of their own and probably a country house as well. *Mother couldn't tell her what to do anymore.*

AS JAN AND SCOTT HAD ANTICIPATED, his parents were upset about his engagement. More upset when they realized Jan would not be married in the Christian faith.

"If there's to be no church wedding," Scott's mother said while they sat in the Jamison library, "then you must quietly elope and be married by a justice of the peace. After a suitable engagement period, of course."

Scott and Jan exchanged a quick glance; that meant October was out.

"We'll be married by a rabbi first—in Great-grandma's cottage," Scott said. "Jan and I both want it that way."

"I suppose that can be kept private." Mrs. Jamison was clearly exasperated. "It's important to your father, and it's good for business for him to be a member of the best clubs. I don't have to tell you how many major transactions are consummated within the walls of the University Club or the Union Club. It would be deplorable if your father had to resign."

"He won't have to resign, Mother." Scott's smile was bitter. "Jan and I will be married by a rabbi in Great-grandma's cottage—with no one there other than Great-grandma and Jan's family. We'll elope the next day and have a civil ceremony. The public one."

Only now did Jan tell her mother of the impending marriage. Lilli was delighted. She listened with a sentimental smile to their plans for the secret wedding to be held in the cottage at the rear of the Jamison estate. She agreed gracefully to Scott's self-conscious request—relayed by Jan—that she be silent about his grandparents' and his father's conversion.

"Scott is a fine young man," Lilli said, hugging Jan. "I know you'll be happy together."

"There's no need to write Daddy about the wedding," Jan said. "It's not as though this is going to be a big affair or anything."

"I never write to him," Lilli said quietly. "I don't even know if he's still in California."

"Freddie hears from him once in a while." Jan saw her mother's look of surprise. "Just postcards, which he answers. I don't get them anymore, since I never write."

"Your father will probably see the announcement in the *Times*." Lilli's smile was cynical. "I'm sure he still reads the society pages."

As the mother of the prospective bride, Lilli gave the newspapers the announcement of Jan and Scott's engagement. Scott's mother insisted on a splashy engagement party at the family estate in Great Neck. Jan knew her prospective in-laws were relieved that her mother and stepfather would not attend the party—using Lilli's advanced pregnancy as an excuse. Scott gave her an outrageously expensive diamond and topaz ring from Cartier's. Topaz—signifying fidelity—was Jan's birthstone.

The wedding was tentatively scheduled for the following June. Scott's mother talked effusively about a wedding at St. James Episcopal Church, where several converted families, including the current generation of Strauses, had been married.

At polite intervals, Scott's parents invited Jan and Scott to dinner. Jan dreaded these occasions. His parents, so nervous that she and Scott might give them away, would ask politely about her mother's health—avoiding any mention of Alex—

and then about her father—her *Episcopalian* father. Beyond that, conversation was excruciatingly sparse.

More often, Scott came to the Gramercy Park house for dinner. He had enormous respect for Lilli and Alex. Scott and Uncle Alex always got into serious conversations about the stock market. Both were concerned about the wild speculating that seemed to infect everybody, from bootblack to billionaire. Lilli admitted to no interest in stocks; long ago she'd decided to invest only in real estate and art. At times Jan suspected her mother regretted selling Princess Lilli, Inc.— whenever anybody talked about it, she had such a pained look in her eyes. She said she was afraid the people who'd bought the company would run it into the ground. Why should Mother care? They'd paid her $12 million for it.

On late-summer Sundays, Jan and Scott drove out to the Great Neck estate to see Scott's great-grandmother, who was thrilled about the coming marriage.

Late in October, Jan and Scott returned from the theater to be told by an agitated Martine that Lilli had gone into labor and was in the hospital.

"We'll go right over," Scott said instantly. "What hospital?"

"Scott, nothing might happen for hours." After all, it *was* mother's fourth child—nothing would go wrong.

"We'll keep Alex company," he said. "Maybe he'll do the same for me one day."

Jan felt color flood her face. She had managed to blot out of her mind all thoughts of what married life would bring. So far, all she and Scott had exchanged were a few kisses. He was old-fashioned—he respected his future wife. What would it be like to be in bed with him? She and Vanessa talked a lot about sex, but they really knew so little.

"Let me get a coat," Jan said.

"Call me the minute you have word," Martine said. "We'll all be in the kitchen having tea."

JAN AND SCOTT sat on a sofa in the hospital's maternity-floor waiting room while Alex, who rarely smoked, lit endless cigarettes, each snuffed out after a puff or two.

"Alex, she'll be fine," Scott said.

"It seems so long." He was pale and his hands shook. "I wish to hell they'd let me be with her."

"Have you chosen a name?" Scott asked.

"Louis Emanuel Kahn," Alex said with pride. "For my grandfather and for my brother who died in the Spanish-American War."

Scott smiled. "And if it dares to be a girl?"

Alex shook his head. "It's a boy. My grandmother had a dream last week."

A few minutes later the obstetrician came into the waiting room to confirm the dream. Lilli had presented Alex with a seven-pound son. Jan sighed in relief. Thank God, it was over. Alex was ecstatic. He kissed Jan, hugged Scott, and rushed off to see his wife and son.

Jan and Scott waited at the hospital until they could see Louis Emanuel Kahn. Lilli was sleeping, Alex told them, while the three of them got a glimpse of the small red face, topped by a tuft of dark hair, that emerged from a blanket in a nurse's arms.

"Looks just like his mother," Alex boasted. "I can see it already. I'd better call the house. The whole staff's waiting up."

JAN FELT MORE AN INTRUDER than ever when Lilli came home with little Lou. Uncle Alex, Mother, and the two babies were a family. When Freddie—now in his first year at Harvard—came home over the weekend to see the baby, she thought he would feel the same way.

"Jan, you're crazy," he said. "I think it's great."

She was startled when Lilli, over dinner two days before Jan's birthday, while Alex grinned in approval, told them she wanted them to start looking at houses in Great Neck, or wherever on the Island they would like to live. Their wedding present would be a house.

"Not Great Neck," Jan said quickly. It was too near Scott's family.

"Darling," Lilli said with a smile, "wherever you like."

Mother couldn't wait to have her married and off her hands, Jan told herself as she toyed with her duck à l'orange. All Mother could think about were Vicky and Lou. She'd given up the business for them.

"We'll start talking to brokers," Scott said, his expressive face showing his gratitude. "It's wonderful of you to be so generous."

All at once Jan felt the pressure of her wedding. She and Scott were supposed to start looking for a house; her mother kept coaxing her to start shopping for her trousseau; Scott's mother and father had already planned a trip to Palm Beach early in February for three weeks to be away from the city at the time of the elopement.

"Mother, do you mind if we don't hang around for dessert and coffee?" Jan ignored Scott's look of reproach. He had a passion for sweets, especially Bertha's desserts. "I hate getting to the theater at the last minute."

"Jan," Scott said, "we have plenty of time."

"No, we don't." She stood up. "I'll run upstairs for my coat."

As Jan sat in the darkened theater beside Scott, she tried, without much success, to concentrate on the play. Everybody said *Holiday* was deliciously amusing, but tonight all she could think about was the fact that she didn't want to get married. *She wanted to go to Paris.* Vanessa was staying in Paris even though her year was up. The Greys didn't know Vanessa was having an affair with an American art student from Pittsburgh.

Jan sat through the Philip Barry play with clenched teeth. The prospect of a house on Long Island which *she* would have to run, seemed like a prison sentence. What would she do out there after Scott dashed into the city every day to the office? And he would want to have a family right away. She saw the way he looked at Vicky and Lou. The day after tomorrow she would be twenty-three years old, and she had done nothing with her life, except go to school. She wasn't ready to settle into the trap of being a wife and mother. There had to be more to life.

With the audience still applauding and calling for another curtain call, Jan was pushing her way past knees and into the aisle. It would be awful, but she had to tell Scott the engagement was over.

"Scott, let's go to a 'speak,'" she said with a show of enthusiasm when they were out in the crisp November cold.

He stared at her in astonishment. "You hate 'speaks.'"

"Not tonight," she said flippantly. "Let's go over to the Park Avenue—it's decorated by Raymond Anthony Court in red and black and gold. Somebody said it looks like a *Follies* set."

"You barely touched dinner. Why don't we drive down to Chinatown first for chow mein?"

"All right. But then we'll go to the Park Avenue."

OVER THE NEXT WEEK, Jan dragged Scott to a series of speakeasies, up to Harlem to the Cotton Club and to Connie's Inn, while he protested—puzzled by this new side of his bride-to-be—that he had to be at his office at a respectable hour each morning. When he talked about driving out to Long Island to look at houses a broker had discussed with him, Jan airily brushed this aside.

She knew she had to tell him the engagement was off. She took the cowardly route—she called him on the telephone.

"Scott, I know this sounds crazy—I should have realized it long ago. I don't want to get married—not to anybody." Her words tumbled over each other. "I'm sorry. I'm just not ready to be tied down that way."

"Jan, we'll postpone the wedding," he said after a moment of stunned silence. "We'll wait until next fall."

"No." Her voice was involuntarily brusque. "And I won't be seeing you again. I'm sorry. I'm truly sorry. I'll have Henri bring my ring to you at the office."

"I want you to keep it, Jan." His voice cracked. "Please, do that for me. Wear it sometimes—and remember that I love you."

"But, Scott, it's terribly expensive—"

"I'll never give it to anyone else. I'd like you to have it forever."

"I'm sorry, Scott. I didn't mean to hurt you this way." With a shaking hand, she put down the phone.

It was over. She wasn't engaged any longer.

31

CHURNING WITH IMPATIENCE, Lilli waited for Alex's secretary to put her through to him. She was still trembling from hearing Jan's news. She had been so happy when Jan became engaged to Scott. She was sure they would have a fine, substantial marriage. She and Jan were so much alike, it worried her. She feared Jan would make the same mistakes she had.

"Good morning, darling." Alex sounded warm and reassuring, but she sensed his anxiety. She never called him during business hours.

"Could you meet me for lunch, or are you all tied up?"

"Lilli, I'd untie a gordian knot to have lunch with you. How about the Ritz? It's a great day for vichyssoise."

"The Ritz it is." She tried to keep her voice even. "One o'clock?"

"One o'clock." He hesitated. "The kids all right?"

"They're fine. At least Vicky and Lou are, Alex." She had to tell him. "Jan's broken her engagement. But we'll talk about it later. I'll see you at one."

Wearing one of her cherished Chanel suits, she waited at a corner table in the Ritz dining room. Life never seemed to settle into a calm pattern. She worried about Jan, and she fretted over what was happening with Princess Lilli, Inc., in the hands of the new owners. They had no real feeling for the cosmetic industry. According to reports around town, they were talking about going mass market. How wrong for Princess Lilli!

Lilli's face lighted as she spied Alex coming toward her. She relished his strength. His sense of responsibility. Despite his protestations to the contrary, she knew he was not enjoying his hours at the office—it was a family responsibility, which Alex would never shirk. Like her, he missed the day-to-day creativeness of keeping one step ahead of the competition.

"Darling, that suit will still be superb twenty years from now." He smiled and kissed her.

Not until they had ordered did Lilli talk about Jan.

"Did she say why she broke the engagement?" Alex asked.

"Only that she wasn't ready for marriage. That it would be unfair to both of them to go ahead with it." Lilli sighed. "I never really know what's going on in Jan's head. Freddie talks to me. She bottles everything up inside."

"So many young people are rushing into marriage these days, then rushing into the divorce courts. Don't push her, Lilli. Let her feel her way through this." He reached into his jacket pocket and pulled out an article neatly cut from the *Wall Street Journal*. "There's another article about the new direction of Princess Lilli." His face tightened in distaste. "I'm not sure I did right in encouraging you to sell."

"You miss the business, too," Lilli said. "Oh, Alex, we were out of our minds to sell."

JAN SPRAWLED ACROSS THE BED, a copy of *The Bridge of San Louis Rey* open but facedown on the bedspread. She let her private phone ring unanswered. Scott was still trying to get through to her. Couldn't he understand it was over? As soon as he had started calling, she'd sent his engagement ring back.

She was glad her birthday was over. Right now she hated any kind of celebration. There was Thanksgiving to go through. Freddie would be home from college—that would make it easier because Mother would be all involved in having him here. She was so tired of sitting down to dinner every night under Mother's reproachful gaze. And Uncle Alex looking so damned sympathetic.

The phone stopped ringing. She'd told Martine and the others to tell Scott she was "out of town for an indefinite stay" whenever he rang on the downstairs phone.

She had not left the house for two weeks, except to take a few brisk turns around the park each day. She was turning down all invitations. She was withdrawing from all the silly committees. How long before Mother gave in and let her go to Paris? A secretive smile lifted the corners of her full mouth. Mother would get all upset and frustrated and talk to Uncle Alex. And Uncle Alex would say, "Poor little kid, let her go stay with Vanessa just for a few weeks."

She left the bed to cross to her desk. She'd written Vanessa about breaking off the engagement. She'd hinted she might be coming to Paris soon. Wouldn't it be the cat's meow to celebrate New Year's in Paris? Maybe she could, with a little luck.

Jan sat up as an envelope was slid beneath her bedroom door. Henri always brought up her mail as soon as it arrived. When she saw the square mauve envelope, she knew it was from Vanessa. Vanessa's mother had the envelopes made up specially twice a year.

Avidly she read the tight purple-ink scrawl. Vanessa applauded her act of rebellion; all parents cared about was marrying off their kids and seeing them make the same mistakes they'd made. She and Chuck had thought about getting married but had decided to live together for six months first: "We stayed one week in Chuck's apartment and one week in mine. We have to keep both places so our folks don't find out—you can bet that would be the end of the checks every month."

Suddenly it occurred to Jan how to get to Paris. Mother was not in the salon, so it wasn't likely she'd run into Mrs. Grey on the rare occasions Vanessa's mother was in New York. She'd have Vanessa write that she was being married in Paris. In late January. And of course Jan *had* to come over to be her maid of honor.

In Paris she would be *somebody else*. She'd be gay and charming and sort of mysterious. Maybe she'd have an affair, too. It was screwy not to have slept with *somebody* before you got married.

EARLY IN JANUARY, Jan sailed at midnight for Paris on the *Mauretania*. Her mother and Alex insisted on seeing her off, remaining until the final warning—"Last call for all those going ashore"—echoed through the ship. She was leaving on the assumption that she would return in four weeks. When Vanessa left for her supposed honeymoon, Jan was to go to Aunt Sara's Paris house. Jan had no such intent.

As she watched the Manhattan skyline disappear from view, Jan promised herself she would be like all those other gay young Americans who were making the *Mauretania* the vessel of the "younger set": She would enjoy every minute aboard ship.

As she had expected, there were fewer passengers in January than in the warmer months, but that didn't stop the crew from making every aspect of the sailing a gala event. The bar was set to open at the twelve-mile limit, and already a crowd of women in backless evening gowns and men in white-tie evening garb were lining up to sample Dutch Schultz champagne. Brushing off an interested young man, Jan went to her stateroom—and discovered a dozen red roses on her dressing table, with a note from her mother and Alex. Roses were her mother's favorite flower. She preferred gardenias.

Despite her earlier intention to play the carefree flapper aboard ship, Jan spent much of her time in her stateroom, flipping through pages of *Town & Country*, *Spur*, and *Vogue*. She took brisk, solitary walks around the deck early in the morning and watched the early sunsets before having dinner alone in her stateroom. But she wasn't lonely. She kept herself entertained with romantic fantasies about being on her own, in Paris. Away from her family, she told herself, she would at last feel like an adult.

After docking at Cherbourg, Jan boarded the boat train for Paris. Vanessa was waiting for her at the Gare St.-Lazare. In a rush of kisses and laughter, the two girls followed a porter to the street, where Jan's hand luggage was packed into a taxi. Her trunk would be delivered later.

"Darling, I knew you'd make it!" Vanessa said, inspecting Jan with approval. "You know, I like your hair that way, but there is this fabulous man in Montmartre who does marvelous things with hair."

"Then I'll try him," Jan said. Vanessa looked surprised: Jan had always been wary of hairdressers; usually she would simply wait until the spirit moved her to snip her bobbed hair herself.

"Jan," Vanessa said breathlessly, "you're not going to believe this. The same night you left on the *Mauretania*, Chuck decided we really ought to get married."

"Vanessa, you're sure?"

"Darling, I was sure three months ago—I was just waiting for Chuck to see the light. We'll be married in Paris, but the family won't know that." She giggled. "Neither Chuck's nor mine. Neither family will consider us married unless we have one of those huge New York weddings that take up a quarter of a page in the *New York Times* and is reported in *Vogue* and *Harper's Bazaar*. I wrote Daddy—after all, the father of the bride pays the bills. I have to catch up with Mother. I'm not sure if she's in Palm Beach or Nice."

"I'll be your maid of honor here in Paris," Jan said. "I can't bear going back to New York soon. But you'll be coming back to Paris."

Vanessa was silent for a moment. "Chuck says we'll have to live in Pittsburgh. At least for a while. He'll go into the steel mill with his father." Jan's mouth opened in astonishment. "But he won't stop painting. He'll paint on weekends and evenings and on vacations. He doesn't want to become one of those mad painters like Vincent van Gogh."

"When will you be leaving?" It hadn't occurred to her that Vanessa might leave her alone in Paris. But no matter what, she would *not* stay with Aunt Sara or work at the salon. She was in Paris to have a marvelous time. On her own.

"Chuck's arranging our bookings now," Vanessa said. "It will probably be in about three weeks."

The taxi pulled to a stop. Vanessa lived in a Montparnasse flat that was expensive by neighborhood standards but extremely modest by hers. They transferred Jan's luggage from the taxi to Vanessa's flat with the help of the driver and the concierge. She was in Paris, she thought happily. There was *nobody* here to tell her what to do. She was Jan Laval, liberated!

JAN HAD LIVED IN PARIS as a child. She had visited in later years. But she was seeing a new Paris now: the Paris of postwar, expatriate Americans—painters, writers, musicians, students. Vanessa and Chuck's turf included Harry's New York Bar, the Café du Dôme, Jimmy's Falstaff Bar, and the Deux Magots—where Picasso could be seen daily. Occasionally Chuck holed up at his studio to paint, but never for longer than a few hours. The rest of the time they were an inseparable trio, spending their nights first in Vanessa's flat and then in Chuck's, Jan taking the bedroom at the couple's insistence, while they slept in each other's arms on the wide sofa in Vanessa's tiny sitting room or on the daybed that served as a sofa in Chuck's. Jan buried her face in her pillow to muffle the sounds of their lovemaking.

They slept till noon each day, awoke to croissants, black coffee, and fruit, and sometimes exotic omelets Chuck claimed he'd learned to make in the kitchen at Elsa Lee's, where he had worked during one lean period when a check from home was late in arriving.

In the afternoons Vanessa and Chuck took Jan to Sylvia Beach's bookstore, Shakespeare & Company, where they browsed through the books, occasionally pausing by the fireside to read one, and inspecting the endless photographs of famous writers—both living and dead—lining the walls. Other afternoons they went to art exhibitions or to see an American film at the Paramount or the Grand Guignol.

Every afternoon they stopped at an expensive café for lunch, where they would meet other Americans. Jan was shocked when, at lunch one day, Chuck pointed out a wreck of a woman with a baby stare and identified her as Pearl White.

"The movie star? The *Perils of Pauline* Pearl White?" Jan couldn't get over the transformation.

"She hasn't made a movie in four years," Chuck said, "and that one was filmed here in Paris. She belongs to another era."

In the evenings they made the rounds of student parties, where they talked avidly about Dada, Gertrude Stein, Michael Arlen, and Eugene O'Neill. From the parties, they roamed to the bars. Chuck preferred Harry's Bar, whose wood-paneled walls were festooned with college pennants from all over the United States. He always grew sentimental around midnight, when somebody sat down at the piano to play. He talked about how Hemingway had always hung out at Harry's before he'd left Paris, two years ago. They'd all read *The Sun Also Rises* and Hemingway's short stories.

On the night after Chuck had picked up his most recent check at the American Express office, he took the two girls to see Josephine Baker, who was appearing at La Plantation. The following afternoon, Chuck decided they would go to the Ritz for five o'clock tea. Abandoning their casual Montparnasse wardrobe, Jan and Vanessa donned Chanel dresses and brought out their fur coats. Chuck shopped hastily at Old England on the boulevard des Capucines for an appropriate suit.

Feeling as though they were making a brief return to the world they had sought to leave behind, the three young Americans were escorted to a table at the Ritz.

"There's Scott Fitzgerald!" Vanessa said. "The blonde beside him must be Zelda. Who's the other couple?"

"Cole Porter and his wife," Chuck said. "Porter wrote the music for the revue at Des Ambassadeurs last year. The Porters throw great parties."

Jan couldn't stop staring. "He's written some gorgeous songs."

"There are two American colonies in Paris," Chuck said. "Cole Porter and Scott Fitzgerald and Elsa Maxwell and Elsie de Wolfe—the whole so-called international set, who go to

Sherry's or to the Tienda Oyster Bar for lunch, the Ritz or the Pavillon Colombe for tea, dinner at Ciro's, a midnight supper at Le Perroquet. And those like us, living in Montparnasse. Of course, *everybody* goes to Harry's Bar and to Jimmy's."

"What about the serious American writers and artists?" Jan asked. "When do they find time to work?" She thought of her mother, who had spent endless hours six days a week at the salon and *still* talked shop with Alex at home.

Chuck's smile was wry. "They're all dull, uninteresting people, Jan darling. Who cares about them?"

Jan and Vanessa did visit Aunt Sara, who loved hearing every detail about Vanessa's imminent marriage. Nothing was said about Jan's broken engagement. Jan suspected her mother must have warned Aunt Sara to stay away from the subject.

When Chuck was at his studio, Vanessa and Jan went to the little galleries on the rue Bonaparte, and shopped at the Galeries Lafayette. Vanessa took Jan with her to the salon of Jeanne Lanvin to order a gown for the New York wedding.

Then suddenly the day arrived—lit with the pale winter sunlight of Paris—and Jan stood with Vanessa and Chuck while they were married in a village just outside the city. Afterward they drove back to Paris and went to the Ritz for dinner. In the morning Vanessa and Chuck would take the boat train to Cherbourg and board the *Ile de France*. And then Jan would be alone in Paris.

FOR THE FIRST FEW DAYS, Jan luxuriated in having the tiny apartment to herself. She felt totally free as she wandered around the city. Friends of Vanessa's and Chuck's phoned to invite her to parties. Tim Watkins, an art-student buddy of Chuck's, pursued her feverishly. But gradually, with Vanessa and Chuck gone, Jan began to tire of Paris.

She was not alone. Many Americans had come over expecting to find life in Paris one big party. Many of them talked vaguely about writing the Great American Novel or painting a masterpiece or composing an opera that would set the music world on its ear. But Jan suspected that most of them, like

Chuck, eventually went back home after rebellion against the "routine" lives they thought they had left behind forever.

Two weeks after Vanessa and Chuck departed, Jan went with Tim to see Bricktop, the red-haired, freckle-faced Negro singer who was the current rage in Paris. "Bricktop brought the Charleston to Paris," Tim whispered to her while the audience applauded wildly at the end of a song. "She taught the Prince of Wales the black bottom."

Jan was aware of the blatant stares of a man at an adjacent table. He was ignoring his three companions—a heavyset middle-aged man and a pair of young blondes who looked like high-class whores. Even before she heard his atrocious French as he ordered a drink, she knew he was an American. But he was not like the Americans she had met in Paris. He was still young—not much over thirty, she surmised—and strikingly handsome in a rough-hewn, almost vulgar way. A man sure of himself. Vanessa would have said, "Oooh, he's loaded with sex appeal!"

Shortly after Tim decided they'd go to Jimmy's for Pernod, Jan noted that her admirer was leaving. She felt disappointed—ridiculous, of course; she hadn't spoken a word to him. She pretended to be amused by Tim's storehouse of Paris gossip while they made their way to Jimmy's, but all she could think about was the tall, broad-shouldered, dark-haired man who had been watching her.

When they arrived, Jimmy's was crowded, noisy, and filled with smoke. Tim made it clear that he was in the mood for serious drinking, and Jan had no intention of keeping up with him. But he wouldn't notice—he was too busy trying to convince himself he was the next Great Talent to light up Paris.

Just when she was growing restless—and alarmed at Tim's consumption of Pernod—she noticed her dark-haired friend from Bricktop's standing in the doorway. He smiled at her. Quickly, she lowered her eyes. Vanessa would have smiled back.

"Hey, you know, I feel lousy—" Even in the muted lighting of the bar, Tim looked white. He staggered to his feet. "I think I'd better go to the little boys' room—"

"I'll get home alone," she said quickly, praying he'd make it before he was sick.

The dark-haired man had been watching, and seemed to understand the situation. He dropped a sheaf of bills on his table and approached Jan as she rose to her feet. "I'll see you home," he said quietly.

He didn't take her directly home. Instead, they went for coffee at a cozy bistro and talked till dawn. She had never known anyone quite like Tony Gambarelli. He had been born in a small town seventy miles from Chicago but had lived in Chicago since he finished high school. Occasionally he went home to see his mother and father, as well as a half-dozen married sisters and brothers, and their husbands and wives and children.

"Every two or three years I come over to Italy. My grandmother still lives there. But this time I had a hankering to see Paris. Right now she's here with me. She came to take care of me." He smiled. "She cooks and cleans and yells at me for being a bad boy who keeps terrible hours. I'm hoping to persuade her to go back to Chicago with me when I leave."

"Paris is like a zoo," Jan said. "I mean, the Americans' Paris. It's like being on a perpetual roller coaster."

"You hit the nail on the head," he said, nodding in approval. "But Americans don't know the real Paris. All we know is the circus. Why do we hang out at Jimmy's Bar or Harry's or wherever other Americans hang out? You know what we have to do, Jan?" His smile, perfect white teeth against a Florida tan, was dazzling. "We have to go out there and discover the real Paris." His eyes narrowed. "You speak the lingo well."

"I lived in Paris when I was very young," she said. "Then we lived in London until I was nine."

"I mean to see a lot of you, Jan Laval," he said softly. "Starting tomorrow. How about lunch? On the Champs-Elyseés, at noon?"

NOT UNTIL she had known Tony almost a week did he kiss her goodnight. It was, she suspected, a calculatedly casual kiss that left her yearning for more. He seemed pretty damned smart about women.

Only Vanessa knew that no man had ever made her feel passionate before. All she had ever known—and she was twenty-three years old—were the greedy, sloppy kisses of a gin-soaked male mouth. Except for Scott. Scott had kissed her as though he were afraid she would fall apart. In the Roaring Twenties, Scott *respected* her!

It wasn't long before Tony was monopolizing Jan's days. He loved being a tourist, and she knew the sights well. Together they visited the Tuileries Gardens, the Palais Royal, built by Cardinal Richelieu in the seventeenth century, and the Louvre. On the Left Bank they paused at the Pont de la Tournelle to admire the view of the great Cathedral of Notre Dame, lingered in the Luxembourg Gardens, and stopped for coffee at the Café de Flore.

She admired Tony's honesty about his past. He told her about being poor as a little boy. He wasn't poor now—that much she knew by his clothes, and by the way he spent money. But he never mentioned what he did for a living. Whatever it was, he had to be good at it: How else could he afford to take off an undetermined amount of time like this?

One spring day, after a long luncheon at the Ritz, Tony suggested a drive in the country. "I know this great little inn where we can have an early dinner," he said. "The man who runs it told me it was built in the early eighteenth century." He chuckled. "Yeah, I know—to Americans that sounds ancient, but to Parisians it's almost modern. When I was driving to Paris from Rome with my grandmother, the car broke down right in front of the inn. My grandmother and I had dinner and stayed for the night." He laughed. "All she could think about was how expensive it was going to be. I couldn't make her understand that it was all right."

"It's a beautiful day for a drive in the country," Jan said, her heart pounding. His grandmother and he had stayed the night there. Was that a gentle hint that he meant for them to do the same? If so, she'd already decided that she wouldn't say no.

With Tony at the wheel of his Mercedes, they left Paris in mid-afternoon. The sky was a cloudless blue, the air spring-sweet. Tony cursed in colorful Italian each time he took a wrong turn. Finally, at dusk, they arrived.

"They'll look at us and think, These crazy Americans," Jan said as he helped her out of the car. "Expecting to be served dinner at such an hour."

As they were welcomed and ushered into a tiny dining room, deserted at the moment, Jan realized that Tony must have phoned ahead. And from the way the waiter inspected her, she knew he expected them to stay the night. Had Tony been here with other women? Besides his grandmother? But she wouldn't think about that now. At last she'd met a man who excited her. Somebody who wasn't just another boy. Tony was waging a slow and careful campaign. That meant she was special.

They dined beside an open window that offered a breath-taking view of the moon hiding behind clumps of dark clouds. The temperature had dropped and the air felt cool. Tony gestured for the waiter to close the window against the night chill.

The dinner was superb. Tony ate with relish. Jan hardly tasted the food. All she could think about was *later*, when Tony would take her upstairs to the room they would share for the night.

Someone came to start a blaze in the fireplace grate, and their waiter arrived with dessert. Jan made a great fuss over their gâteau St.-Honoré and the rich, aromatic coffee made from freshly ground beans.

While they lingered over coffee, rain began to pelt the earth. Lightning flashed across the sky. "It would be crazy to try to drive back to Paris in this," Tony said softly.

She nodded. "Yes, it would."

They were escorted to a large, square, corner bedroom furnished with a French Empire sleigh bed and wall-hung canopy, an armoire, and a pair of walnut bergère chairs drawn up before the fireplace, where logs crackled in welcoming warmth.

Before leaving, the maid showed off the adjoining private bathroom, which in earlier centuries had been a child's room.

"Listen to that thunder," Tony said, reaching for her.

Jan felt like Joan Crawford in *Our Dancing Daughters*. She remembered when Dolly Conrad had brought those books about sex to a pajama party when they were fourteen. At the time, Jan couldn't believe that people really did *that*. Dolly and some of the other girls squealed and said it must be exciting, if you were really crazy about the boy.

"Does thunder make you passionate?" He held her so tightly she was having trouble breathing. "It does me."

"Wild," she said huskily. She'd die if he guessed she was a virgin. But Vanessa said you could fool almost any man if you handled yourself right. "When are you going to kiss me?" she said, lifting her parted mouth to his.

Suddenly his mouth was on hers, his tongue pushing between her teeth. One hand moved within the low neckline of her dress to fondle a breast. Her arms closed around his shoulders. Her heart pounded while his hips moved against hers.

She laughed shakily when their mouths parted. "We didn't even bring our toothbrushes."

"I think we'll survive," he said dryly. "Take off your clothes."

She stared for a startled instant. She had expected some preliminaries. But Tony was turning off the lamp on the commode. Now he reached to unbutton his trousers.

She tried stalling. "It's cool."

"Then go over by the fireplace." He stepped out of his trousers and draped them across a chair, reaching now to strip away his shorts.

"Mmm, lovely." She stood before the blaze; then, trying to appear nonchalant, pulled her dress over her head and kicked off her shoes. Standing before him in teddy and stockings, she still felt like a character in *Dancing Daughters*. She restrained an impulse to throw her clothes back on and run off.

"You are sensational," he said, his eyes taking in the full length of her.

"You must have gotten that tan on one of those nudie beaches," she said, feeling madly sophisticated.

"I didn't miss an inch," he grinned, and stepping forward he reached over and slid down the straps of her teddy. Provocatively slow in removing the teddy—pausing to kiss velvet skin, prodding the stockings down her long, slim legs. As he lifted her in his arms and carried her to the bed, she hoped he had brought along some "protection." Had he expected her to be one of those girls who carried condoms in her vanity? She knew about the girls who came to the frat dances at Yale and Harvard and Columbia with enough "protection" for a harem.

"I'll be back in a moment to warm you up," he said, and disappeared into the bathroom.

Trying not to shiver in the coolness away from the fire, she stretched out in what she hoped was a provocative pose. After tonight, she would be a woman. She was glad Vanessa had been so frank in discussing sex. Tony would never guess that she was a virgin.

"Cold?" He came out of the bathroom. Protected.

"Warm me up," she said, trembling.

He lifted himself above her and burrowed his mouth between her breasts while his hands separated and fondled her thighs. She felt the first experimental thrusts, and her hands closed in about his shoulders. They moved together in growing frenzy.

"Honey," he said gently, "let me in."

"Oh, yes, Tony!" She tried to relax.

With one tearing wrench, he was inside her. She cried out. And then, to her surprise, she was moving with him, savoring every feeling. She wished it would never end.

They lay together without moving for a few moments. She felt so relaxed—yet exhilarated. She had never imagined that it would be like this.

Tony stood up and disappeared again into the bathroom. Jan pushed aside the covers and slid between the sheets. She lay there quietly, listening to the sound of the rain hitting the windows.

Tony came back into the room, a grin on his face. "You never did it before, did you?"

She blushed. "I'm sorry, Tony. I know it's ridiculous—I'm twenty-three years old."

"I think it's wonderful," he said, sliding into bed beside her. "I think *you're* wonderful."

DRIVING BACK TO PARIS in the morning under a blue sky, Tony told Jan about growing up in the small midwestern town, the youngest of seven children.

"If you live in New York," he said, "you don't know how the rest of the country lives. There are millions of people in the States who've never touched alcohol, never been inside a 'speak.' Their idea of a big Saturday night is to go to a movie. They furnish their houses on the installment plan, one piece at a time. Five dollars down, ten dollars a month." His face tightened. "I'd die if I had to live like that. Actually, I did—until I left high school and went out to earn a buck."

"People like that don't come to Paris," Jan said. How *did* Tony make his money?

"All most Americans know about Paris is what they hear on the radio or see in the movies," he said. "Hey—why don't we run down to Antibes tomorrow? Just for a few days. I could do with some sun."

She would have said yes if he'd suggested the Arctic Circle.

"Sure. What time shall we leave?"

JAN AND TONY became inseparable. Ten days after they returned from Antibes, he took her to Rome—where he disappeared for long hours each morning to attend to "business." Jan lolled in bed in their flat—borrowed from a friend of Tony's—that overlooked the Spanish Steps, and decided that her life was unbelievably exciting. For Easter, Tony decided they would fly to Portugal for a few days. Terrified of flying, she pretended wild enthusiasm for this next grand adventure.

Often, when they were in Paris, Tony slept over at her flat, or they drove out to the inn for a night. Jan understood that since his grandmother was there, it was impossible for him to take her to his apartment on the rue de Varenne. Jan refused to let herself think about him returning to Chicago. All that mattered was *now*.

Tony was in love with her. He hated it when other people intruded in their lives. He resented her monthly luncheons with Aunt Sara at a café on the Champs-Elysées; he resented it when acquaintances—people she had met with Vanessa and Chuck—came over to their table at restaurants. Even though he knew she was mad about him, he was jealous of other men. Like Vanessa with Chuck, she would wait until Tony decided it was time to ask her to marry him.

A softness touched her face as she remembered Vanessa's last letter. Vanessa was three months pregnant. She and Chuck were ecstatic. Jan tried to imagine being pregnant by Tony. *When would he ask her to marry him?*

32

LILLI SAT AT HER DESK in what used to be her office at home and frowned as she reread Jan's letter for the third time. How could she make Jan understand that it was time to return to New York? Alex was probably right—she should stop sending the monthly checks. But she couldn't face the possibility of Jan's being in financial need. She was so headstrong; there was no guessing what she might do.

"Another letter from Jan?" Alex's voice startled her. She had not heard him come into the house. He made a habit of leaving the office at five sharp so they could spend two hours with the children before sitting down to dinner.

Sighing, Lilli nodded. "She's been in Paris for over five months." *Alone*—the traitorous reminder intruded on Lilli's thoughts. She and Alex had been invited to Vanessa's elaborate wedding and reception in New York. About the same time, Vanessa had phoned—no doubt at Jan's prompting—to confide that she had been married earlier in Paris, with Jan as her maid of honor, but that no one else was to know. "Aunt Sara sees her occasionally but can't pin her down. She still talks vaguely about 'studying fashion.' What is Jan *doing* in Paris?"

"Rebelling," Alex said gently. "Give her time, Lilli."

"Why can't she rebel at home?"

"Lilli, you can't spend the rest of your life trying to protect her. She's a woman now."

"I worry about her."

"Remember, my love, we can't go through this world without traumas. You can't take her hard knocks—she has to do that for herself."

"Let's go up to the nursery," Lilli said. This was her favorite time of the day. "But remember, we're having dinner early. We're taking Grandma downtown to see Molly Picon." She reveled in the knowledge that Vicky and Lou not only had warm and attentive grandparents but had a great-grandmother who made a point of seeing the children every day. Alex's family included Jan and Freddie in their affection, but Jan had never accepted this.

"I ran into Scott this morning," Alex said on their way upstairs. "He's a nice young man."

"He's still in love with Jan," Lilli said. "They could have had a good marriage."

Alex squeezed her hand. "Not unless Jan was ready for it. So how was *your* day?"

"Oh, Alex, I feel so restless. I had two committee meetings with your mother." Since selling Princess Lilli, she had been active in several philanthropies close to the heart of Alex's family. "I spent time with Vicky and Lou. I made calls to Southampton about opening up the house next week. That should be enough—"

"You miss the business, don't you?" His face was serious. "I read an article in the *Wall Street Journal* this morning that'll disturb you. As it did me."

Lilli stopped dead. "About the business?"

"They're serious about going mass market. All the way— including sales to Woolworth and the other five-and-dime chains."

"Alex, they'll ruin everything I worked so hard for." Tears filled her eyes. "What can we do?"

"We can start buying stock."

"We can't buy up enough to be major stockholders. There won't be that much on the market. We can't control the company's direction." Then all at once excitement gripped her. "Alex, get me a list of all the women stockholders. There *is* something we can do. Maybe not to control the company, but to give the board of directors second thoughts."

He grinned. "You're going to write all the women stock-holders, warning them the new owners are headed on a course that'll ruin the business."

"I'm writing personal letters. I'll write every woman stock-holder, even those with only a handful of shares. I'll tell them that only a woman understands the cosmetic industry, and that the way the company's going, the value of their stock is sure to drop—"

"And we'll put out word that we're ready to buy every share that comes on the market." Alex seemed excited now, too. "But remember, the stock has gone up insanely since you sold." There had been a few sudden downturns in the stock market, but these had been brief. Stocks were booming. "I don't know if we'll be able to buy a controlling interest—even if the shares come on the market—without divesting ourselves of every-thing else."

"Alex, I want my company back," Lilli said quietly. "Even if it means selling everything."

"There's no guarantee that even your letter-writing cam-paign will bring enough shares into the market, Lilli."

"We'll wait and watch. And I'll collect proxies from those who don't sell. They'll trust me to act in their best interests be-cause they know I want the company to be successful. Some-day Vicky and Lou will run Princess Lilli. That will be our legacy for them." She pulled him close. "Help me, Alex."

EARLY IN OCTOBER—when Paris was mercifully free of the hordes of summer tourists—Tony decided that he and Jan should spend a few days in London. They settled in a luxuri-ous suite at the Savoy. This was a business trip, Tony told her, which meant he would be tied up during daytime hours; but in the evenings they would go out to dinner and on to the theater and nightclubs.

"We'll go to the 'Midnight Follies' at the Hotel Metro-pole," he said, seeing Jan frown at the prospect of being alone all day. "We'll dance at the Princess Restaurant and the Florida and the Embassy. I hear the Prince of Wales shows up every Thursday.''

She pouted. ''But what'll I do during the day?''

''You lived here as a little girl,'' he clucked. ''You must have a dozen places you'd like to see.''

''I guess so.'' She shrugged. ''I'll visit Oliver and Frances at Mother's salon. And shop.''

''Good girl.'' He kissed her. ''Tonight, let's have dinner at the Ritz. You said that was where your mother used to take you for birthday dinners when you lived here, right?'' He grinned. ''What a pity we can't borrow your mother's London house for this visit.'' Tony seemed to love borrowing houses, villas, apartments. It made him feel important.

''Oliver lives in an apartment in the house,'' Jan said. ''He plays host to whomever Mother invites to stay there during the course of the year.''

''But we're not invited.''

''I don't think Mother or Oliver would approve.'' Jan laughed. *If she and Tony were engaged, they could stay at the house.*

As they walked into the restaurant at the Ritz, Jan was conscious of approving stares. She wore an expensively simple turquoise chemise that showed off the high thrust of her breasts, her narrow hips, the beautiful slim legs that she dismissed as ''ridiculously skinny.'' She was aware of an uneasiness in Tony, a certain swagger that in anybody else she would have considered vulgar. He was totally at home in Paris, Rome, Antibes—wherever they traveled. Why was he uncomfortable here in London?

Midway through dinner, Jan saw Oliver, still slender and handsome, sitting across the room at a table for four. He seemed uncertain that it was truly she. She hesitated for an instant, then lifted a hand in greeting. Smiling brilliantly, Oliver excused himself to his companions and hurried to her table.

''Jan darling, I had no idea you were coming to London.'' He leaned forward to kiss her. ''Why aren't you at the house?''

"I'm here with two friends from school," she said nervously. "We arrived today and we'll be leaving in four days. They thought it would be fun to stay at the Savoy." Her face grew hot when she saw a glint of disapproval in Oliver's eyes as they rested on Tony. "This is Tony Gambarelli from the States," she said cheerfully. "Tony, this is Oliver Wickersham—my adopted uncle and Mother's longtime business associate. They started Princess Lilli together."

The two men exchanged wary greetings. Did Oliver believe the story about the two friends from school?

"I'll come to the salon in the morning," she said, before Oliver had a chance to suggest phoning her at the Savoy. "Will you take me to lunch?"

He bowed. "Wherever you like."

OLIVER WAS IN A MEETING with the art department when Jan arrived at the salon the next morning, but Frances was there to greet her.

"Jan, I can't believe you're a grown-up young lady! The image of your mother. Come, let me show you around the salon."

After Jan had been fussed over by the London staff, several of whom remembered her as a little girl, Frances took her back to her own office.

"Are you having lunch with Oliver and me?" Jan asked, uneasy at the prospect of dining alone with him.

"No. I have a consultation I can't break," she said. "With a member of the royal family. What about our having lunch tomorrow?"

"Fine," Jan said. "You can tell me all about Beth and Robbie."

Oliver came into Frances's office and swooped Jan off to lunch. When she professed a preference for French food, he took her to a small restaurant in Soho, where they were given a quiet corner table. After they had ordered, Oliver leaned forward, suddenly serious.

"Jan, what the devil possessed you to have dinner with Tony Gambarelli?"

"I told you," Jan stammered. "He's from the States. Chicago. He's a friend of a friend."

He stared at her in disbelief. "Don't you know who he is?"

"What do you mean?"

"Tony Gambarelli is a notorious American gangster! A bigtime bootlegger. His name pops up regularly in those American newspapers your mother sends me. I just read last week that he's in Europe to sit out a gang war!"

"That's another Tony Gambarelli." Jan was trembling. "It's a common enough Italian name."

"Jan, his face has been plastered across the New York tabloids," Oliver said grimly. "I recognized him right off. You didn't know?"

"No." Jan's voice was barely audible. So much she had not understood before was clear now. Tony was in Europe because he was hiding out—he would be killed back in the States.

She was disgusted by the image of him involved in a gangland war. Tony as another Al Capone. *But maybe Oliver was wrong.* She had to give Tony a chance to clear himself, didn't she?

"I won't see him again, Oliver," she said sweetly. "I promise."

ON THEIR RETURN trip to Paris, Jan tried to bring herself to question Tony about his life in Chicago. Each time, she couldn't quite say the words. Then, as they drove in a taxi from the Gare du Nord to her flat, Tony mentioned casually that his business in Europe was finished and that he should be returning shortly to Chicago.

"What about you?" he asked. "Ready to say goodbye to Paris?"

"I think I *have* had enough." She hesitated. When would he say *"Why don't we get married?"*

"I have to make a quick trip to Rome to dispose of Grandma's little house," he said. "She's going to Chicago to live with my folks."

"Oh, she finally agreed?" If he'd known before they went to London that he was leaving for Chicago, then why hadn't he mentioned it?

"I'll make arrangements for a stateroom for us and another for Grandma on the *Mauretania* or the *Berengaria*." He leaned forward and gave the driver directions to his apartment. "We'll let Grandma make dinner for us tonight. She makes the best tortellini alla bolognese in all Europe."

Jan glowed. Tony was taking her to meet his grandmother! He wouldn't do that if he didn't mean to ask her to marry him. What would it be like to live in Chicago? Would Tony's family like her? Would they be upset because she wasn't Catholic? Tony laughed sometimes about the way his mother ran to early mass every morning. They'd have to have a civil wedding—she wouldn't convert.

But what about Tony's business? For a moment, doubts again tugged at her. No, Oliver was wrong. People in London thought every American was a gangster.

Tony's Paris apartment was furnished so ornately that it was almost vulgar. He had explained there were no servants except for a man who came in to do the heavy cleaning; his grandmother insisted on doing everything else herself.

"Tony!" His grandmother, a short, stout, white-haired woman in her seventies, kissed him. "You look skinny. Four days away from my kitchen," she clucked. "Eating in cafés all those days."

"Grandma, this is Jan. I've been bragging to her about your tortellini alla bolognese."

"You're hungry. I'll go right away into the kitchen and cook for you." She inspected Jan with admiration. "Such a pretty girl, Tony!"

His grandmother bustled off to the kitchen. Tony pulled Jan to the window to point out the view. She was startled at the sight of the photographs scattered around the living room.

Most of them of a little boy and girl. The boy appeared to be about six or seven; the girl a couple of years younger. Tony's nephew and niece, she guessed.

"We'll go back to your flat later," he whispered. "Grandma might guess, but she doesn't have to know."

"Tony," his grandmother said later over espresso, "when you go to Rome, buy toys for me to take with me to Angela and Victor." She leaned toward Jan. "Let Tony's children have toys from where their great-grandmother lived."

Stunned, Jan turned to Tony. For an instant he seemed guarded. Then he smiled. "They're great kids, Jan. Smart as a whip, both of them."

"I didn't know you had children," she said softly.

"A man like my Tony should reach thirty without children?" His grandmother chuckled. "What's the matter you give Marie only two? She's young and strong—she could have five or six. Thank God, they stopped that crazy business in Chicago. You can go home again."

"Tony, I'm awfully tired from all the traveling today. I'd like to go to my apartment now." Jan understood. This was their way of letting her know about his family.

She thanked her hostess for dinner, wished her well in her new home in America. She was cool and silent as Tony took her downstairs.

"Don't drive me home, Tony. Just find me a taxi."

"Honey, don't be upset." He tried to pull her to him, ignoring passing pedestrians. "Nothing has to change for us."

"Everything's changed, Tony." She wrenched herself free. He was married, a father, and a gangster. "I never want to see you again."

"Jan, I'll be in New York more than in Chicago. It'll be like in Paris—we'll be together most of the time."

"You lied to me!" she said through clenched teeth. "You let me believe you were free. Oliver told me who you were—I didn't believe him!"

His face darkened. "So I'm a bootlegger. It's big business. I'm not any different from any other successful big businessman. We fight every way we know how to climb to the top. Whether it's selling liquor or steel or grain." Except that Tony eliminated his competition with bullets.

"I must have been out of my mind," she said bitterly. "Go back to your family."

Sitting alone in a taxi on her way back to the flat in Montparnasse, Jan thought about Tony's grandmother. To her it was all right that Tony played with a young American girl. It was expected of him. It was the Old World way of life. How different from Scott's great-grandmother.

Suddenly she couldn't wait to go home.

THREE DAYS LATER, Jan was on the boat train for Cherbourg. She didn't care that a check would be arriving from her mother momentarily. She had enough money for a tourist third-class cabin on the *Berengaria*, sailing from Cherbourg tonight. Anyhow, she told herself, it was smart today to travel "poor." Everybody—that is, everybody her own age—said it was more amusing.

The summer rush of ocean travelers was past, and once again Jan was glad not to be swept up in the frivolities of shipboard life. She needed to be alone. Throughout the trip, she berated herself for being so naïve about Tony. She still couldn't believe that she had run out on Scott—so sweet and considerate—into the arms of a married American gangster!

Her first two mornings aboard the *Berengaria*, Jan felt faintly nauseated. The sea was pleasantly calm. Why should she feel seasick? It seemed to pass after lunchtime—and alarm zigzagged through her. She was two weeks late. *She'd never been late.* Again, she was aware of a touch of queasiness. She could be pregnant. She and Tony hadn't always been careful.

She was revolted by the thought that she might be carrying Tony's child. Maybe she was wrong. Maybe it was just nerves. It had been an awful shock to learn the truth about Tony. This whole thing could just be part of her reaction to what had happened at Tony's apartment.

Now, each hour aboard ship seemed endless. Each night was plagued by insomnia, despite a constant sleepiness. If she *was* pregnant, she decided, she would ask her mother to find an abortionist. Mother knew all kinds of people. She'd find a doctor who would take the baby.

By the time she arrived at the Gramercy Park house, Jan was convinced she was pregnant. Now she was almost three weeks late.

Henri's face lighted up when he opened the door. "Your mother will be so pleased, Miss Jan. You must phone her right away. She's with Mrs. Kahn."

"I will, Henri. Where's Alex?"

"Mr. Alex is down in Washington for two days," Henri said. "And Mr. Freddie is up at his dormitory." Freddie was now a sophomore at Columbia. "Of course, he's home for dinner often."

"Jan!" Martine's voice echoed down the hall. "Oh, how good to have our little girl home again!" *What would Martine say if she knew her "little girl" was pregnant?*

After she had been welcomed by the staff, had fussed over Vicky and Lou before they left for the park, and was settled in her room, Jan phoned her mother.

"Darling, how wonderful to have you home!" Jan heard the relief in her mother's voice. "I can't wait to see you!"

"I have to talk to you, Mother."

Lilli hesitated. "I'll be there in twenty minutes."

In slightly less than that, Jan faced her mother in the privacy of her bedroom.

"Mother, try not to be too upset," she said, her throat dry. "But you have to help me. I'm pregnant." She saw the color drain from her mother's face.

"I gather you don't want to marry the baby's father."

"He's married. I discovered that just before I sailed for home. And even if he weren't, I wouldn't marry him. I must have been out of my mind." She felt humiliated—not because she'd had an affair, but because she was pregnant by a man who revolted her. "You know so many people. Find me a doctor. Somebody who'll arrange an abortion."

"Jan, no," Lilli said gently. "You're carrying a precious little life."

"I don't want this baby." Now her voice was shrill. "Mother, please help me!"

"Jan, if your grandmother had undergone an abortion, neither you nor I would be here today."

"I don't want this baby!"

"Darling, you're not some poor little girl whose life will be ruined," her mother began. "We can—"

"Don't you remember your own bitterness at being illegitimate?" Jan flung at her. "About never knowing your father?"

"Jan, an abortion is dangerous. And there's no need. We can—"

"It's not dangerous in the hands of a competent doctor." Yet, there *had* been moments when she'd already felt an unexpected tenderness for the baby growing within her.

"Jan, marry Scott," Lillie said. "He's still in love with you. Whenever we meet, he asks about you. He was terribly hurt that you broke off the engagement."

"Hurt enough to father another man's child?" Jan said. In truth, marriage to Scott hadn't occurred to her. With Scott and the baby, she would have a family. But how could she expect Scott to want to marry her now?

"Let's work on this," Lilli said.

"Mother, there's no time to play games!"

"I'll have a small welcome-home dinner party for you on Friday. I'll invite Scott. He'll come, Jan. He still adores you."

ON FRIDAY EVENING, in the charming dining room of the Gramercy Park house, Jan sat beside Scott at a dinner party that included her mother and Alex, Freddie and a current girlfriend from Barnard, and Alex's niece and recent bridegroom. Scott was obviously delighted at being invited to a family dinner. If he was upset about the shocking drop in prices on the stock market during the past three days—which was ominous news for the nation—he managed to hide it. While joined politely in the conversation at the table, his eyes lingered at every possible moment on Jan, as though he could not believe she was really back.

Despite her mother's exhortation that they not talk businesss at the table, conversation inevitably turned to the stock market. Even the best stocks were taking a beating. For the past seventy-two hours, the radio had blared out bulletins. All over America, investors—large and small—were unable to meet margin calls. Still, this morning's newspapers assured their readers that the market would adjust itself.

"I don't like what's happening in Germany," Alex was saying in response to a question from his nephew-in-law. "Hitler and his Nazi party are becoming stronger. They're behind the desecration of Jewish cemeteries in Germany. They fomented agitation against that medical congress in Wiesbaden because it included Jewish doctors. If Hitler isn't checked, God knows what he and his Nazis will be doing in ten years."

"He's right," Scott said. "Look what's happening in Palestine. The British ignore their promises about helping to provide a homeland for the Jews while the Jews are being massacred—mutilated—by the Arabs."

Scott was still drawn to his Jewish roots, Jan thought, listening to the crackling conversation about the table. He was a good man, as different from Tony as day from night. But if he asked her to marry him again—and it would have to be soon—he'd have to know about the baby.

"How's your great-grandmother?" Jan asked Scott while the others resumed anxious conversation about the state of the stock market.

He smiled. "Vowing to live to be a hundred. You made quite a hit with her."

"She's a wonderful old lady."

"Would you like to drive out to see her tomorrow afternoon? The leaves are turning. We'll have a beautiful view all the way out." He was leaning forward eagerly now. "We could have dinner at a great fish place not far from the house. It's right on the water.''

"I'd like that," Jan said.

All through dinner the next night, Jan could tell that Scott was deliberately holding himself in check, fearful of pushing her too fast. When he took her home, he lingered with her in the family sitting room over a glass of wine, obviously reluctant to leave. Jan knew her mother had made a point of being upstairs in the master bedroom with Alex.

"Would you like to see the new Cole Porter show?" he asked as he was about to say goodnight. "It's supposed to be terrific."

"It sounds like fun," she said softly. Even though she was drawn to Scott's tenderness, she felt so guilty. "Goodnight, Scott." Impulsively she reached up and kissed him lightly on the mouth.

"I'll pick up tickets for Tuesday night. We can go out for an early dinner before the performance."

Walking up to her bedroom, Jan decided to tell Scott on Tuesday that she was pregnant. She couldn't go on with this charade.

LILLI SAT AT HER DESK and paused for her midmorning cup of tea, a collection of the morning newspapers at hand. While a drizzle cast a shadow over the city, she scanned the headlines. Stalin proclaimed communism was sweeping the world. Mussolini made the same claim for fascism. Hitler, according to news from Berlin, was recruiting many thousands of middle-class Germans who were terrified of communism. Except for the *Times*, New York papers predicted banking support would rescue the stock market from its alarming slump.

At the sound of Vicky and Lou laughing in the hall, Lilli stood, intending to join them for a few moments before they were taken across the street into the park. But the ring of her private phone stopped her. She reached to pick up the receiver. Only a handful of people used this line—all of them close to her.

"Hello?"

"Lilli, have you heard?" It was Alex, sounding serious. "All hell has broken loose on the stock exchange. It's far worse than Black Thursday last week." Lilli knew that Alex and she were all right. He always insisted they buy nothing on margin. "Are you ready to go all the way on buying up whatever shares of Princess Lilli come on the market?"

"You know I am!"

"I'll pass the word along," he said. "God, Lilli, it's a rotten situation on the exchange. A lot of people are being wiped out. What's happening today will affect the world for the next fifty years. But by the end of today, you may have enough stock to control Princess Lilli again."

"Alex," Lilli said slowly, her mind racing, "what's happening with Scott's firm? His father's firm, that is."

"I don't know," he said after a moment. "Some investment bankers will survive. Others will be in bad shape." He hesitated. "Lilli, has Scott talked to Jan yet about marriage?"

"Not yet, at least as far as I know. They were supposed to go to the theater tonight. I'd hoped he'd say something then—"

"You're concerned that he may be too distraught about business to bring it up. God knows what his financial state will be after today."

"I'm going to have a talk with Scott," Lilli said. "He's in love with Jan. If he wants her, now's the time."

Lilli told Henri to bring the car to the front of the house. While she waited for him to arrive, she turned on the radio, switching impatiently from one station to another for the most up-to-date news on Wall Street. Even the announcers, reading off bulletins, seemed shaken by the reports of the worst financial disaster in history.

Dressed in one of her favorite Chanel suits and a cloche, Lilli settled herself in the gray Rolls and gave Henri directions to the offices of Scott's firm. As they cruised into the Wall Street area, Lilli was astonished at the number of policemen visible. The streets were clogged with people hurrying from banks to brokerage houses in a desperate effort to save themselves from being wiped out. Clusters of people, ignoring traffic in their panic, made driving a painfully slow process. A crowd was gathering in front of the stock exchange, and as they passed Trinity Church, Lilli saw hordes of people pouring inside for the noon service.

"Miss Lilli, I'm not sure it's safe for you here," Henri said as he parked.

"I'll be all right, Henri. I won't be too long."

Lilli pushed her way across the crowded sidewalk and into the building. In the crowded elevator, a man stood in the corner, weeping. "I'm ruined!" he wailed. "It's gone! Everything's gone!"

Shaken, Lilli stepped off the elevator at Scott's floor and headed for the offices of his firm. From behind the door to the reception room she could hear the babble of voices. She reached for the doorknob, turned it, walked into the crowded room.

At one side of the area, a harried switchboard operator was trying to answer a flood of calls while several strident conversations were being carried on around the room. The receptionist was losing patience with someone on the other end of her phone.

"I told you, sir, he can't talk to you now! He's not taking any calls!"

The air was fraught with panic. In the corridor, Scott's father, ashen and grim, was trying to soothe a client.

"I'd like to see Mr. Scott Jamison," Lilli told the receptionist.

"I don't know if he can see you—"

"He'll see me." Lilli's was the only serene voice within hearing range. "Tell him Lilli Laval is here."

Within moments Scott came out. "I'm so sorry, Mrs. Kahn; everything's crazy today." He paused, his eyes questioning.

"May we go to your office?"

"Of course." He took her arm and led her down the corridor to a corner office. He closed the door behind them while Lilli sat in a chair facing the desk.

"Mrs. Kahn, is Jan all right?"

"Jan is..." Lilli searched for the proper word. "Jan's upset. She has something she must tell you—she planned to do this tonight after the theater." Lilli hesitated. "*If* you and Jan will be going to the theater tonight, after what's happened today..."

"We're going," Scott said quietly. "I think we can use a few hours of sanity in this insane world, don't you?"

"Jan is going to tell you about those long months she spent in Paris." Lilli took a deep breath, and paused. *Was this the right thing to do?* What choice did she have? "She went through a bad love affair."

Scott flinched. Then his face softened. "Poor kid."

"She realized on the ship coming home that she was pregnant," Lilli said. Scott stared in shock. "She knows now that running off to Paris that way was just an act of youthful rebellion, that breaking off with you was a ghastly mistake." She leaned forward. "I don't expect an immediate answer, Scott— but if you're willing to marry Jan under the circumstances, I'm prepared to invest one million dollars in a new firm to be headed by you."

"Mrs. Kahn, I don't even need time to think," Scott said softly. "I love Jan. I'll marry her as soon as it can be arranged." He smiled. "I'd marry her without the million dollars. But it'll be nice to know I'll be able to support her in a comfortable fashion."

Lilli leaned back in her chair, realizing now how tense she had been. "You mustn't tell Jan that I was here," she said. "Tonight after the theater she'll confide in you. Then ask her to marry you. She must never know that I was part of this."

"I understand. But please remember, I would marry Jan without the money."

"It's ironic," Lilli said, rising to her feet, "that in the midst of such chaos in the world, I feel very happy today."

33

WHILE ALEX HELD HER HAND, Lilli watched with tears of pleasure in her eyes as the rabbi married Jan and Scott in the living room of his great-grandmother's house. The proud old lady walked with the groom to the altar. Lilli and Alex had given away the bride. Nearly destroyed by the stock-market crash, Scott's parents had gone off to visit one of their daughters who lived in Charleston. Scott and Jan hadn't even considered inviting them to the wedding. The only other invited guests were the staff of the Gramercy Park house.

Lilli had convinced herself that Jan was happy—that at last this difficult, moody child of hers was settled in a good marriage. Jan loved Scott. And he would be a fine father to her child. No one would ever know that it was not his own. No one would ever know that she had intervened to bring this marriage into being.

At Lilli's other side, Freddie, struggling to appear serious, focused on the ceremony. Lilli cherished her older son's zest for living. She was blessed, she thought sentimentally. Four fine children, Alex—and soon a grandchild!

She had written a brief note to Jacques about Jan's marriage. The note would be forwarded by her attorney together with Jacques's next monthly check. She assumed he was still in California. In keeping with Jan's original request, he hadn't been invited to the wedding. Jan wanted no part of her father.

Lilli was exhilarated, though sorry for the unhappy circumstances that made it possible, that through the shares she and Alex had bought up on the falling market, plus proxies she was already obtaining, she would once again be the head of Princess Lilli, Inc.

After the ceremony, limousines drove the wedding party back into New York for a dinner party at the Ritz-Carlton. Jan and Scott were going on to the Greenbriar in White Sulphur Springs, West Virginia, for a one-week honeymoon. Then they would return so that Scott could speedily launch his new firm. They would live in a duplex at the elegant Dakota Apartments on Central Park West, an area shunned by his parents because it was "too Jewish."

At Scott's suggestion, Lilli had announced her financial backing a day after Jan told her that she and Scott were being married. He preferred this, he said, to lying to Jan about "private backers." Lilli described the venture as a wedding present from Alex and herself. At first, for a terrifying instant, Lilli had feared that Jan suspected. But her suspicions had evaporated once Jan was swept up in the wedding plans.

The day after the wedding, Lilli and Alex went to work at putting Lilli back in charge of Princess Lilli, Inc. In the shattering aftermath of the stock crash, they encountered few obstacles. While Alex continued with his own business, he also continued advising her. Once again, the office in the house was the scene of nightly consultations.

Every Friday evening, Jan and Scott came to the house for dinner. The one sad event during Jan's pregnancy was the loss of Scott's great-grandmother, who died peacefully in her sleep. Scott and Jan had hoped she would live to see this great-grandchild. But there was happy news, too: In February, Jan was thrilled to hear of the birth of Vanessa's daughter, Tracy. Their firstborns would be only months apart.

Lilli was pleased to see how much both Jan and Scott looked forward to the baby's arrival. She wished, though, that Jan and Scott were closer to *his* parents. She suspected that the elder Jamisons were embarrassed that Scott's Jewish mother-in-law had saved the family from financial ruin. Scott had brought his father into the new firm.

As Jan's due date came close, Lilli grew increasingly tense. Alex teased her about not being able to go through labor for her daughter. Early in May, just as she and Alex were sitting down to dinner, Scott phoned to say he was taking Jan to the hospital.

"We'll be right there," Lilli told him.

"Have your dinner first," Scott insisted. "A first baby won't come *that* quickly."

"We'll be there in an hour, Scott," Lilli said.

When they arrived at the hospital, Lilli and Alex found Scott anxiously pacing the waiting room. "Why won't they let me be with her?" he said. "Why does she have to go through this alone?"

Lilli hugged him. "She's not alone, you know. She's going to be just fine."

"Looks like this is going to be a long night," Alex said. "I'll go get us coffee."

The hours crept by. Occasionally Jan's doctor emerged with brief reports. "She's carrying a large baby—we must be patient." *A large baby when, publicly, Jan wasn't due until July.*

"She's having poor contractions."

At last the doctor came to tell them that Jan's contractions were strong now. "Still ten minutes apart," he said briskly, "but we're in business."

The three-in-waiting drank endless cups of coffee. Alex at determined intervals offered his cheerful conviction that any minute the doctor would tell them the baby had arrived.

Finally, with pink streaking the sky, the doctor came from the labor room to announce that Jan was in hard labor. Alex reached for Lilli's hand as she sat white and still. Everyone said that a mother forgot the pain of labor after delivery. *She* remembered.

"I hope you're giving her an anesthetic," Scott said.

"I'm afraid we have a problem right now," the doctor said. "She's in hard labor but not much is happening. I've advised a cesarean section, but Jan's against it." He frowned. "She insists on going through with a normal delivery."

Lilli saw Scott clench his hands so tightly the knuckles went white.

"May I talk to her?" she asked. "Or may Scott try to change her mind?"

"She anticipated such a request." The doctor's smile was wry. "She doesn't want to see anyone." He paused in thought. "We'll give her one more hour. That's about all she can take."

Fifty minutes later the doctor came toward them with a broad smile. "Congratulations, Scott!" He extended a hand. "You have a son."

Scott's face lighted. "Jan's all right?"

"She's exhausted, but she'll be fine."

"Thank God, it's over." Lilli clung to Alex.

"When can I see them?" Scott asked.

"In a little while." All at once the obstetrician's face was guarded. Lilli's heart began to pound. "That was a big boy. Eight pounds, seven ounces. And she's not built for that." He cleared his throat. "It was a rough delivery. The baby's arm was broken. But an infant's bones heal quickly. I just want you to think about that when you see that tiny arm in a cast."

JAN LAY BACK, exhausted, against the pillows. Early-morning sunlight streamed into her suite as Scott walked slowly into the room.

"Did you see him?" Her voice was barely above a whisper. "His arm is broken."

"I saw him. That arm will heal fast." Scott bent to kiss her. "He's a handsome little guy. Looks like his mother."

"With that mop of dark hair?" She laughed. She had not thought of Tony once in the last few months of her pregnancy. And then she saw the baby. She thanked God she had Scott, and now Gregory Randolph Jamison—named for her great-grandfather and Scott's great-grandmother. Her private little world was complete—*without* Tony.

"Great-grandma would be so proud," Scott said quietly. "She'd be proud to know he'll be raised Jewish."

But in the weeks to come, it became clear that Gregory suffered from more than a broken arm. The pediatrician first called in an orthopedic specialist, then a team of specialists. Scott and Lilli and Alex pretended it was just a matter of time before Gregory's left arm was normal, but Jan was terrified.

The specialists reported nerve damage. At one year, Gregory would undergo surgery. Despite the presence of a full-time nurse, Jan fussed over him constantly. If he was fretful, she couldn't think about anything else. If he sneezed, she worried he was coming down with flu or pneumonia.

In early December, Vanessa—two months pregnant—arrived with tiny Tracy and Tracy's nurse for a ten-day visit. Though reluctant to leave Gregory during the day, Jan accompanied Vanessa on her Christmas-shopping spree through Saks and Bergdorf's and Altman's. Vanessa admitted that Chuck thought it bad taste to be extravagant when so many people were hurting financially.

"Chuck's family came out of the stock crash smelling like a rose," she confided over luncheon at the Plaza, "but Chuck feels so guilty that we're living well while more and more people are joining the breadlines. He says that with wheat down from one thirty-five a bushel to seventy-six cents now, the farmers are having a terrible time. Some of them are losing their farms to the banks. And he keeps talking about how in the first nine months of this year, anywhere from sixty to eighty banks a month have closed. He says last month it jumped to two hundred thirty-six. Chuck's mother and I spend most of our afternoons on charity committees." She grimaced. "Boring."

"I stopped reading the newspapers. It all sounds so depressing. But not everybody's hurting from the Crash. My mother and Alex are doing fine. You said Chuck's family is all right."

Vanessa chuckled. "Oh, his father complains that steel production is down forty percent, but you can be sure Chuck's parents will go down to Palm Beach next month in their private railroad car. And have you heard all the stories about Barbara Hutton's debut later in the month? It's a three-parter: Tea for five hundred guests at her parents' Fifth Avenue house, with Meyer Davis providing the music; dinner and dancing for five hundred at the Central Park Casino; and on the twenty-first a formal ball at the Ritz-Carlton for one thousand. It's going to be the splashiest debut in ages. Chuck says it *has* to cost sixty thousand dollars."

"Scott and I aren't doing much socializing these days," Jan said, suddenly serious. "Vanessa, I can't help feeling that what happened to Greg's arm is all my fault."

Vanessa stopped eating. "Jan, that's crazy. Anyway, you said the doctors will operate in May. He'll be fine then."

"They don't know. They're guessing." She closed her eyes for a moment. "And it is my fault. I should have let them do the cesarean."

"Jan, you don't know that. I thought Scott said the damage must have happened in the early months—that it had nothing to do with the delivery."

Jan shook her head. "If I'd agreed to a cesarean, Greg's arm would be all right."

"It's *not* your fault," Vanessa insisted. "In a few years Greg and my kids will be playing baseball together. Chuck says if it's a girl, he's stuffing her right back."

LILLI WAS AT THE HOSPITAL on the May morning when Gregory was taken into surgery. While Alex went out for coffee, she sat beside Jan and Scott and talked cheerfully about Freddie's graduation from Columbia a year hence, and his hopes of being accepted at medical school.

"Freddie will make it," Scott said. "He's bright and he's hard-working." He managed a chuckle. "I can't imagine who he inherited those traits from."

Within three days the doctors conceded that the surgery had been futile. They talked about another procedure in a year or two. Worried by Jan's depression, Lilli summoned specialists from all the country for consultations about Gregory's arm. At present, all agreed, nothing could be done. "But next year or the year after or perhaps five years from now, someone may come up with a treatment that will be helpful," a specialist from Texas told Jan and Lilli after a particularly arduous examination. "We'll keep in touch."

THE NATION WAS IN the depths of depression that was worse than any experienced in America. Almost 10 million were unemployed. Stores and factories closed. Thousands of families lost their homes when they were unable to keep up mortgage payments. Breadlines and soup kitchens appeared everywhere.

Yet millions of Americans were only slightly affected—or affected not at all. Government workers—whether federal, state, or city—and workers in the few industries that seemed to be weathering the rough times continued their daily lives as though nothing had happened.

It quickly became clear to Lilli that the cosmetic industry would survive—and survive brilliantly. Princess Lilli would continue to expand. The wholesale business and the salons would be untouched by the terrible slump—there were more than enough women eager and able to buy Princess Lilli products and to patronize the salons.

Lilli was happy to be back at the helm of her company. She was no longer sole owner, but she was in command. Unfortunately, more often than ever, her concern for her grandson—and her daughter's obsession—overshadowed her happiness.

Six months after the first operation, Gregory was in surgery again. Jan had been told about a "miracle doctor" in Chicago who had achieved great success with infants suffering from nerve damage. It was innovative surgery, regarded with skepticism by the doctors Lilli had covertly consulted, but Jan insisted on giving it a try.

Lilli waited with Jan and Scott until at last the doctor emerged from surgery. Instantly, the three were on their feet.

"He came through the surgery in fine shape," the doctor said. "You can go in to see him in a little while." He paused. "But I'm afraid there was nothing we could do to restore that arm."

As always, Alex tried to distract Lilli with the business. "Lilli, I've been thinking about a new promotion," he said as they sat alone over coffee in the family sitting room after a small dinner party Lilli had planned to lift Jan's spirits. "You must hire a press agent. Someone who'll keep Princess Lilli constantly in the public eye."

"Alex, we already advertise heavily. Why do we have to hire someone for that?"

"This is a new era," he said. "Every day millions of people read the gossip columns. It's not enough anymore to be mentioned in *Vogue* and *Town & Country* and Cholly Knickerbocker's column. We need Winchell, Mark Hellinger, Louis Sobel. We'll go out once or twice a week to places like El Morocco and 'Twenty-one' and the press agent will plant items about Princess Lilli."

"Do you have someone in mind?" She knew full well that he did. He never brought anything up without having explored all the options.

As they discussed this new approach to publicizing the firm, Lilli recognized the validity of what Alex said. The competition between Rubinstein, Arden, and herself was fierce. Mme. Rubinstein had recently bought back her company from Lehman Brothers, who'd acquired it little more than a year ago. She was sure to launch some dramatic new product. Dorothy Gray, with her own building on Fifth Avenue, was not to be ignored either.

"There's a 'nail man' calling on the beauty salons who bears watching," Alex said. At intervals, Alex made personal calls on the neighborhood beauty salons as a "researcher" for the cosmetic industry. "His name is Charles Revson. He's selling 'nail enamel,'" Alex said humorously, "and he's pushing shades that are not those harsh reds we see everywhere. He's sharp."

"Alex, what about our developing some new shades of eye shadow?" Lilli asked. "Oliver talked about this in his last letter. He and Frances are enthusiastic about it."

"Sounds great." Alex nodded. "Have you talked to Dick about it?" Dick Weisberg was their head chemist.

"I thought we'd meet with him together." Lilli frowned. "Alex, what am I going to do about Jan? She's so depressed about Greg."

"Lilli, you can't fix everything. But God gave us *two* of our most important body parts—two arms, two legs, two eyes, two lungs, two kidneys. Gregory will be able to do almost everything except play golf, hold a baseball bat, drive a car. If Jan doesn't smother him with her anxiety, he will be just fine."

UNEMPLOYMENT WAS growing worse. Wages had dropped by sixty percent from 1929 standards. "Brother, Can You Spare a Dime?" was one of the most popular new songs. President Hoover reduced his own salary by twenty percent and persuaded the vice president and nine members of his cabinet to do the same.

In late May—when Lilli and Alex attended Freddie's graduation from Columbia—a "bonus army" of about 1,000 exservicemen arrived in Washington; by June that figure had risen to 17,000, all of whom camped out in Washington to demand the cashing in full of soldiers' bonus certificates. A bill was passed by the House but was killed by the Senate. The government provided the veterans with return transportation, but 2,000 refused to accept. In July, federal troops, under General Douglas MacArthur, dispersed them.

Lilli and Alex—and subsequently Scott, to his family's indignation—became active in the presidential campaign of Governor Franklin Roosevelt, a Democrat selected by his party that June. Freddie, too, spent the summer—before beginning his studies at Harvard Medical School—working on the campaign.

In November, Roosevelt won by a landslide. The following March 4 he was inaugurated. Lilli, Alex, Jan, and Scott gathered around the radio to listen to his inaugural address. All four were impressed by the new president's stirring statement that "the only thing we have to fear is fear itself." The following day, a Sunday, the president called a special session of Congress and proclaimed a national bank holiday. The following

Sunday he held a "fireside chat" over the radio to discuss re-opening the banks.

Lilli and Alex were optimistic about Roosevelt's "New Deal." Banks across the country were beginning to reopen; by the end of March, more than seventy-five percent were in operation again. Scott was working hard at keeping his business out of the red. When Jan told Lilli that he missed dinner about three nights out of every week, she suspected that Scott was upset by Jan's obsessive concern with Greg and sought refuge in work.

Shortly after Greg's third birthday, Lilli brought a Viennese specialist to New York to look at her grandson. She had deliberated painfully before making the decision, knowing that another disappointment might push Jan even deeper into her depression. As she feared, the kindly specialist told them that nothing could be done. He advised that Greg be raised to ignore his handicap as much as possible. "He's a bright, healthy child. He has a loving family. He'll never want financially. Be grateful, Mrs. Jamison."

Lilli was disturbed when only a few months later Jan began to talk about another "miracle doctor" she had read about in some tabloid. She understood Jan's desperation, but it would be unconscionable to subject Greg to more surgery. It was time Jan had another child, she told herself. Knowing she ran the risk of being a meddling mother-in-law, she decided nonetheless to discuss this with Scott.

She met him for lunch at a quiet restaurant near his office. He assured her that he was against further surgery. "We can't put Greg through any more of this. Jan's got to accept him as he is. She's spoiling him rotten." He sighed. "She still blames herself for that arm, but she's not helping by letting him think he can get whatever he wants by crying."

"Scott, perhaps if Jan had another child . . ."

"I've thought of that, too." His eyes were pained. "Jan and I talked about that almost two years ago. I persuaded her that we should try. When nothing happened, we consulted a doctor. I'm sterile. That's why Greg is so important to us. But I won't let Jan put him through more surgery. Not unless there is some real hope for improvement.''

WHILE MANY SALONS struggled to survive over the next few years, Princess Lilli prospered. After much deliberation, Lilli and Alex decided to open a new salon in Rome, where Arden was already established, and another in Monte Carlo. They traveled to both cities with an entourage that included Vicky and Lou, the children's nurse, Lilli's current secretary, and Celestine.

Both Lilli and Alex recoiled from operating in Berlin, though Arden was running a successful salon there despite the Nazi party's edict that female members refrain from wearing make-up at official meetings. "Apparently that doesn't apply to male army officers," Alex said when he heard about the ruling. "American tourists talk about their wearing rouge and powder on Berlin streets."

Lilli and Alex were aware, too, that as Jews they would not be welcome in Berlin. Like many American Jews, they were disturbed by the stories they'd heard about the Hitler regime. All Jews were barred from the professions; they had been dismissed from university posts and government service. Nazis smashed the windows of Jewish-owned department stores. Bands of Nazi youths painted swastikas on the walls of buildings. Jewish children were excluded from public education. Some Jews in a position to do so were fleeing Germany, though strict quotas set up by other countries had limited this.

In open defiance of the Treaty of Versailles, Hitler had begun conscription to create a "peacetime" army of thirty-five divisions. He focused on creating an air force, started to build submarines. The other powers protested loudly, but they took no action. Of all the foreign leaders, only Churchill seemed aware of the dangers Hitler and the Nazi party presented to the rest of the world.

When their business in Rome and Monte Carlo was completed, Lilli, Alex, and their entourage moved on to Paris to spend a week with Sara. While in Paris, Lilli arranged to transfer ownership of the European salons to Sara because of the new tax structure in the United States. The English business, for the same reason, would be turned over to Oliver and Frances.

Sara, too, was frightened by what was happening in Germany. "Over in America you forget how close Berlin is to Paris. In Europe we have nightmares about Hitler. I remember how it was in Bratislava—thirty-five miles from Vienna," she added for Alex's benefit. "My mother and father went to visit a cousin. They died there in a riot against the Jews. Hitler is singing a familiar song."

From Paris, they went on to London for a week with Oliver, Frances, and her family. Frances and Charles were upset about the anti-Semitism being promoted in London by Sir Oswald Mosley and his British Union of Fascists. As always, Oliver was wrapped up in the business; he dismissed Mosley as a road-company Hitler.

"They hold rallies right in the heart of the East End," Frances said indignantly. "Chanting 'The Yids, the Yids, let's get rid of the Yids!'"

"There's an anti-Semitism in England unlike anything we've ever seen, Lilli," Charles said somberly. "God knows where it will end."

LILLI AND ALEX returned to New York to find the cosmetic industry in an uproar. What had been only a rumor from Washington had become a reality: Roosevelt's New Deal had brought a bill before Congress to place a ten-percent luxury tax on cosmetics.

Manufacturers and consumers across America were outraged. Women in cities across the nation paraded around federal buildings with placards demanding that the bill not be passed: "We need lipstick as much as toothpaste!" "Makeup No Luxury, a Necessity!" But the Senate and House were composed largely of men—women, such as longtime Congresswoman Jeannette Rankin of Montana and Congresswoman Florence P. Kahn of California, were a minority—and these men saw makeup as a luxury. The bill was passed.

For the first time in the history of the cosmetic industry, representatives of companies, large and small, convened to find a solution. Though the industry was clearly doing well, they voted to pass the tax on to the public. The consensus was: "A woman will pay whatever it takes to try to make herself beautiful."

Lilli was one of the first dissenters. A few weeks later, Dorothy Gray advertised that her company was absorbing the tax. Arden countered with an ad stressing that her patrons were receiving full value, even with the tax. Industry leaders gathered again and came up with a fresh resolution: The tax on cosmetics—lipstick, rouge, powder, mascara—would be passed on to buyers; the tax on treatment lines—creams, tonics, lotions—would be included in their prices.

"We'll survive this," Lilli told Alex as they discussed the new regulations over after-dinner coffee at the house. "It won't cut down sales either at the salons or at the stores handling our products. All it means, actually, is a headache for the book-keepers."

34

LILLI LEFT THE SALON in midafternoon to meet Freddie, who was coming home from medical school for the winter intersession, at Pennsylvania Station. As Henri waited in the Rolls, she crossed the sidewalk outside the salon with her usual brisk pace, drew the collar of her Russian sable coat closely about her throat, and stepped into the car. Leaning back in the seat, she closed her eyes for a few minutes. She had taught herself to use such brief—and rare—periods alone for what Alex called "recharging her batteries." It wasn't until the car pulled up before the station that she opened her eyes.

On her way inside, she dropped a bill into the collection kettle of the Santa Claus standing outside the large building. She and Alex contributed faithfully to many charities. Despite their personal wealth, both were conscious of the destitution that still pervaded the country, even as 1936 approached.

After several confused minutes, she found the arrival track of Freddie's train. As usual, she was early. She waited with a gathering crowd, boisterous with holiday spirit.

It had pleased Lilli that since Greg's arrival, Freddie and Jan had grown closer. Freddie showed a tenderness toward little Greg that seemed to dissipate all of Jan's earlier hostilities. Jan now seemed as proud as Lilli that Freddie was at a top medical school.

At last the train pulled in. Lilli waited impatiently for Freddie to appear among the crowds spilling out onto the platform.

"Mother!" She turned, saw a hand waving at her. "Be right there!"

She watched with pride as he pushed his way toward her. "Darling, you look wonderful." She threw her arms around him. "It's so good to have you home!"

Arm in arm, they made their way through the station and out to Thirty-second Street and the waiting car. Henri stood on the sidewalk, smiling in welcome. Leaning back in the car, with Freddie beside her, Lilli thought how precious moments like these were.

"Did you know, my love," she said, "that you're home for the last night of Hanukkah?"

He laughed. "Does that mean there's a present for me?" In the past, Lilli had always arranged for a small gift for each night of the holiday.

"For you and for Vicky and Lou." She nodded. "And for Jan and Scott and Gregory. They'll be over for dinner tonight."

"Oh, Mom, I almost forgot—you won't mind if I leave right after dinner? I'm going to see *Porgy and Bess* with Phyllis Winthrop." He grinned self-consciously. "She's this girl I met at a dance at Harvard."

Lilli was surprised. Freddie had always insisted he had no time for a social life, that the demands of medical school took precedence over everything. "Is that the Roger Winthrop family?" *Social Register*, ultraconservative, Lilli recalled. If she remembered correctly, Roger Winthrop was credited with fervid anti-Roosevelt remarks.

"Yeah." Freddie cleared his throat. "But Phyllis isn't like her family. She's a real liberal. She never misses a play by Clifford Odets."

"We'll move dinner up half an hour so you won't have to rush," Lilli said.

"Great. Oh, I almost forgot a news bulletin. It looks like you'll have me home after graduation. I'll be interning at Bellevue."

"Freddie, how marvelous!" Lilli glowed. "My son, Dr. Frederic Laval."

Over dinner, conversation focused on conditions in the world. The invasion of Ethiopia by Italian troops in October. The escalating agony of Jews in Germany. The assassination of Louisiana's powerful demagogue Huey Long.

"Most Americans think of Hitler as a ranting idiot," Alex said in frustration. "They don't realize he's a menace to the whole world."

Lilli remembered Aunt Sara's anxiety about the Nazis. About the closeness of Berlin to Paris. With the vast expanse of this country, most Americans forgot how close the Nazi menace was to all of Europe. She would try again, though she knew it was futile, to persuade Aunt Sara to leave the Paris salon and come to New York.

LILLI WAS PLEASED to see that the cosmetic industry was not suffering from the luxury tax. Before the end of 1935, she and Alex, along with other wealthy families, such as the Strauses and the Rockefellers, set up trust funds for their four children in order to avoid the new tax schedule going into effect on January 1, 1936. Jan and Freddie would receive the income from their trusts immediately, Vicky and Lou at the age of twenty-five. All four children would gain control of the trusts at thirty-five.

In early 1936 most Americans focused their concern on the economy. Though there were those who optimistically insisted that the country was emerging from the depression, there was no denying that millions were still hurting. Two million were barely able to provide a meager subsistence for their families through newly set up WPA jobs. Former president Hoover told a Republican meeting—in a speech broadcast on national radio—that the freedom of Americans was in peril. He warned that in this election year the country was moving toward crushing taxes and a dictatorship.

In March, Hitler defied the Treaty of Versailles a second time by sending German troops into the Rhineland. Almost at the same moment Premier Mussolini, in Rome, told the Italian Cabinet Council that he would accept "in principle" the

League of Nations' invitation to negotiate peace in Ethiopia. Hitler and Mussolini were causing a great deal of anxiety throughout the world.

In April the *Palestine Post* reported on Arab attacks that left nine Jews dead and scores hurt. Lilli and Alex spent tense evenings talking about the future of the Jews in Germany, in Palestine, and in Poland. Chaim Weizmann declared that the Jews in Poland were doomed.

IT GREW APPARENT from Freddie's letters that Phyllis was becoming important to him. Lilli tried to tell herself it didn't matter that she was not Jewish; after all, Freddie himself was only one-quarter Jewish; just let him choose a sweet, bright girl who would make him a good wife. But the night before Freddie was scheduled to come home for the spring intersession, she couldn't sleep.

"What's wrong?" Alex asked.

"I woke you. I'm sorry."

"No, I was awake. I couldn't stop thinking about that Jew-baiting fascist Father Coughlin. What's bothering you, Lilli?" He reached for her hand.

"I think Freddie's serious about Phyllis Winthrop."

"Now, Lilli, we haven't even met her. Don't make a snap judgment. If Freddie's in love with her, then I suspect she's a fine girl." He hesitated. "You're unhappy that she's not Jewish, aren't you?"

"That's part of it," she said. "And I tell myself that it's wrong, that people are people—where they worship, where they come from, shouldn't count. But I don't think the world has reached the stage yet where we can view life like that. What's happening in Germany makes me especially aware of what it means to be Jewish."

"Lilli, if Freddie is happy with Phyllis Winthrop, then you'll be happy. I must admit, I've never particularly admired Roger Winthrop either. I've only met him a few times, but he sure is a stuffed shirt. If a family didn't hop right off the *Mayflower*, he dismisses them as riffraff."

"I've met Cynthia Winthrop." Lilli frowned. "She doesn't come to the salon. She's devoted to Elizabeth Arden and that spa of Arden's up in Maine. What does she call it? Maine Chance?"

"Well, what about Cynthia Winthrop?"

"She's cold, arrogant, and empty-headed." Laughter lit her eyes. "If Freddie married Phyllis, she'd have a fit. Phyllis may be thrown out of the *Social Register*."

"Don't you think you're jumping the gun just a bit, my darling? I mean, Freddie may not even be serious about Phyllis. Remember, he has years of internship ahead of him."

Lilli sighed. "Alex, when does life become uncomplicated?"

He laughed. "When we're dead. Did I ever tell you that you're a fascinating woman even at one in the morning? And without Princess Lilli cosmetics?"

"I'm forty-nine years old," she marveled. "Where have the years gone?"

"Shut up and let me make love to my wife."

She might be forty-nine, Lillie thought with satisfaction, but with Alex she felt like nineteen.

THE APRIL NIGHT was unseasonably warm when Freddie and Phyllis emerged from the blue and white striped Colony bar after a dinner that included the Colony's famous crepes suzette. The Colony held a special place in Freddie's affections; he remembered those festive afternoons when his mother had interrupted her hectic schedule to bring Jan and him here for ice cream.

"When do you go back to school?" Phyllis asked. She was annoyed that he kept dodging her hints about marriage.

"I told you, day after tomorrow."

"I'm not sure when I'll be able to run up to Cambridge again." She glanced up at him from beneath her perfectly mascaraed lashes, one hand unconsciously smoothing the silken sweep of shoulder-length blond hair. Since the Christmas break she had been to visit Freddie half a dozen times. They had never

been to bed together, though they'd done "everything but."
"Mother's trying to persuade me to go to Paris at the end of
this month."

"Are you going?" He would have to work his tail off these
next weeks, but he looked forward to the weekends when
Phyllis popped up on campus. Her younger sister was in a so-
rority house at Radcliffe, so she camped out there for a night
or two.

"I haven't decided. Why don't you come up to the house
with me and make up my mind?" She traced a finger along his
chin. "Mother and Dad won't be back from the Caribbean
until tomorrow afternoon, and the servants are all off for the
evening."

Freddie had known for weeks that Phyllis was ready to go all
the way with him, but something held him back. Maybe because he knew if he did, he'd end up marrying her. The years
of internship and residency were rough enough without the
added responsibility of a wife.

"Let's go, baby." Every guy at school drooled when he
looked at Phyllis. But she came up to Cambridge to see *him*.

They hopped into Freddie's Packard—a twenty-fifth-
birthday present—and drove to the Winthrop town house.
Phyllis leaned against him as they walked arm in arm to the
door. Inside the black-and-white-marble-floored foyer, Freddie pulled Phyllis into his arms. "Let's go up to my room," she
whispered. "And don't worry—the servants won't be back for
hours."

They hurried up the stairs. Inside the large, square bedroom, the walls, draperies, rug and upholstered chairs were
pristine white, the furniture stripped and bleached. Phyllis
closed the door, locked it, and turned to Freddie with a provocative smile. "I'll bet I can undress faster than you."

In the heated silence of the bedroom, their eyes fastened on
each other, they stripped to skin. By the time Phyllis had peeled
away her lacy brassiere and satin panties, Freddie thought he
would explode. His mouth was dry with excitement when they

moved into each other's arms, bodies touching. Her smooth, cool skin seemed to intensify the warmth of his own.

"You're cold," he said in surprise.

"Not inside," she whispered.

With a groan he swept her off her feet and carried her to the bed, without bothering to turn down the white lace and satin bedspread. His mouth groped for one dark nipple while his hands fondled between her thighs.

"Freddie, put it in." Her voice was thick. "Hurry!"

He plunged into her, and together they moved to a swift climax, her nails ripping into his shoulders. He lay on top of her, perspiring, knowing that in a few minutes they would make love again. He realized now that Phyllis had "gone all the way" before. When Bob had said she wasn't a virgin, he'd almost knocked his teeth in.

But it didn't matter. Phyllis was sensational. He wondered if he'd got her pregnant. But that didn't matter either. He knew he was going to ask her to marry him.

PHYLLIS SAT at her large, modern, triple-mirrored dressing table and concentrated on her makeup while her mother paced the bedroom.

"Your father will be furious when he finds out about this. How can you *think* of marrying the Laval boy? Everybody knows his mother is Jewish—*and* his stepfather."

"Mother, his father is Episcopalian. His mother is half Jewish. You can tolerate one-quarter Jewish, can't you? Especially when it comes with all that money." Everybody knew about the children's $10-million trust funds.

Mrs. Winthrop sighed and lowered herself into the white velvet armchair that flanked the dressing table. "Then I'll announce the engagement in the Sunday *Times*. You'll be married at Saint Bartholomew's—"

"I'm working on that," Phyllis said. "Freddie's so damned devoted to his mother and stepfather."

"Phyllis, you're twenty-three years old. You've been 'out' five years. Couldn't you have done better than this?"

"I'll be safe, Mother. You won't have to worry about me anymore."

Three times she had been sure she was pregnant. Twice she had just been late. But on the third occasion, her mother had been a nervous wreck until Dr. Raleigh arranged for her to go into his private sanatorium for a quiet little D&C.

"Has he told his mother?"

Phyllis giggled. "He woke them up at two this morning to tell them. I'm going over tonight to meet the family. Right now I'm trying to convince him to forget about interning at Bellevue. It's so unchic. I'm sure Daddy could get him into a more suitable hospital."

ON A SWELTERING JUNE AFTERNOON, Lilli stood beside Alex with a tight little smile while a judge married Freddie and Phyllis in the library of the Winthrop home. Under normal circumstances, she would have admired the late-seventeenth-century interior, executed ten years earlier at great expense by Elsie de Wolfe. She tried to tell herself that Phyllis was a lovely charming girl, that Freddie had chosen well. Yet both she and Alex sensed an arrogant coolness beneath the beautiful exterior.

Freddie had been candid about his battle with his bride over the wedding ceremony: Phyllis had almost broken off the engagement when he refused to marry her in an Episcopalian ceremony, so they had finally compromised on a civil ceremony. Cynthia Winthrop was telling everyone that the young couple had eloped and that upon their return from a honeymoon in Biarritz she and her husband would have a reception for the newlyweds.

Lilli was relieved when the ceremony was over and the couple had been toasted with champagne. Phyllis disappeared with Freddie to supervise the gathering of her thirty pieces of honeymoon luggage. Despite the supposed elopement, Phyllis had assembled an extravagant trousseau, grudgingly provided by her father. She and Freddie were to sail at midnight aboard the *Ile de France*.

The atmosphere in the Winthrop library was one of forced conviviality. Cynthia Winthrop had shocked Alex and Lilli with her description of the lavish Ritz-Carlton reception planned for Freddie and Phyllis. To Lilli, especially, it seemed obscene to spend a fortune on one evening's entertainment when the country was in the depths of a depression.

"Obnoxious people, Freddie's in-laws," Alex said once they were at last within the privacy of the Rolls. "But then, Freddie's married to Phyllis, not her parents."

"Alex, why did he marry her?" Lilli asked. This cold, petulant girl was the last person she would have expected.

"Because, my love, she probably got him into bed, and he mistook excitement for love."

"Can you believe the reception Cynthia Winthrop is planning?" Lilli winced. "When people are standing in line at soup kitchens and breadlines, how can she spend fifteen or twenty thousand on a party?"

"The Winthrops were barely grazed by the Crash," Alex said. "And I suppose they feel they have to show the world— their world—that they're still very rich." He reached for Lilli's hand. "What's happening with the battle of the school?" Jan was resisting sending Greg to school in September. She insisted he should be privately tutored first.

"It's useless for me to talk to her. Ever since that little girl in the park made some remark about Greg's arm, she's terrified his feelings will be hurt in school."

"He'll be hurt worse if Jan doesn't let him move out of that satin cocoon." Alex frowned. "He needs to play with somebody besides Vicky and Lou. Damn it, he's going to have to live with people! He'll adjust if she'll let him."

"I was on the phone with Scott this morning," Lilli said. "I told him to have it out with Jan. For Greg's sake."

Lilli worried about Jan's marriage. Scott was a fine young man, but if she didn't change her ways, Jan could lose him.

JAN SMILED at the newly hired nursemaid—their eighth; all her predecessors had been fired; the seventh had been asked to leave after Greg reported the woman had slapped him.

"Mrs. Ruggles, I'd like you to start tomorrow if that's all right," she told the motherly Englishwoman. "Your room is all ready for you."

"What time will I be taking Gregory to school tomorrow morning?" Mrs. Ruggles asked. "I can go back later for my things."

"Greg doesn't go to school." Last night in one of their infrequent long-distance telephone conversations, Vanessa had referred to Greg as "His Royal Highness." Jan knew Vanessa thought Greg was dreadfully spoiled. But Vanessa left her children in a nurse's care almost all the time. "We plan to have Greg tutored at home," she said evenly. "I'm in the process of making arrangements now."

Mrs. Ruggles's expression was opaque. "Yes, ma'am. What time would you like me to arrive tomorrow?"

After Mrs. Ruggles had left, Jan went upstairs to look in on Greg. As always the door to his room was slightly ajar: He hated having the door shut. A night-light glowed in the darkness. He was asleep. Jan stood by his bed for a few moments, fighting the urge to pull him into her arms.

She heard sounds in the downstairs foyer as Frank welcomed Scott home from the office. Scott had promised he'd be home for dinner tonight. She tiptoed from the bedroom and moved out into the hall. Scott was coming up the stairs. She held a finger to her lips to indicate Greg was asleep. "Dinner will be ready in about half an hour," she whispered.

He leaned forward for the routine nightly kiss. "Come keep me company while I wash up for dinner." He kept his voice low. "Greg behave himself today?"

"I took him to the park in the morning." Greg rarely joined in the play with the other children. "In the afternoon he played with Vicky and Lou." Henri drove the children and their nurse to the apartment three or four afternoons a week to play with Greg. "I think he'll like the new nurse."

Scott looked surprised. "I didn't know Marie had left."

"I fired her yesterday. Scott, I was furious. Marie slapped him!"

"Did she tell you that?" he asked with the calm that often irritated her.

"Greg told me. He said she slapped his hand when he pulled a lamp plug from the wall. He was so upset."

Scott dropped his jacket across the back of a chair. "Jan, maybe that slap on the hand would make him understand he'd just done something dangerous."

"You talk to a child. You don't hit. That poor little baby—"

"I spoke with the principal at Vicky and Lou's school," Scott began, "and even though school started last week, they're willing to accept Greg in their first grade if he comes in right away."

"Scott, I told you. I'd rather have him tutored for a year or two. He's so little to be pushed out into the world."

"School will be good for him. Jan, you can't protect him from life forever. He needs to be around children his own age."

"He plays with Vicky and Lou all the time." Her throat tightened. "You've been listening to Mother again, haven't you?"

"No. I've been listening to a little voice inside me." His face softened. "It's time for him to go to school. I made an appointment for you for tomorrow."

"I just want everything to be right for him." Her voice broke. She knew he was right, but she was terrified by what the children would say to him. "I just don't want him to be hurt. He's too young. Why did I let it happen to him?" She closed her eyes. "Why didn't I listen to the doctor?"

"Jan, honey, it's not your fault." He pulled her close. How many times during the last six years had he said this? "Greg will be fine. Just give him room to breathe." He took her face between his hands and kissed her.

"Scott, don't be angry with me. I couldn't bear it. I know it must sometimes seem like you have a mother for your child but no wife—I worry so about Greg's future."

"Greg will never lack for anything," Scott reminded her. His arms pulled her close. "Bless your mother for setting up the trust funds. Even if the business fell apart—and I don't expect that to happen despite these rotten times—we know we're financially safe."

"I worry about Greg." Her eyes pleaded for understanding.

"I know." She was aware of passion welling in him. She knew that too often she avoided making love because she was anxious about some incident during the day that had upset Greg.

"Tell Clara to hold dinner."

"All right," she whispered, startled by her own arousal. Maybe afterward she could persuade Scott to agree to keep Greg out of school for another year.

35

BECAUSE VICKY HAD BEEN DOWN with chicken pox and had missed the glittering reception that introduced the new line of Princess Lilli perfume and dusting powder, Lilli took her to lunch at the Colony.

Unlike Jan and Freddie, Vicky and Lou took a great interest in Princess Lilli. Every few weeks Lilli brought them—and sometimes Greg—to the salon and the offices and even the factory. They were fussed over and admired by the personnel, and told about the various aspects of the business. Lilli now had a crown prince and crown princess—and Greg, third in line of succession—to inherit the Princess Lilli, Inc., dynasty.

Noticing the stares at her younger daughter, Lilli felt a surge of pride as they walked into the Colony. Vicky's hair, dark like her father's, was worn in the new pageboy style and framed a face that was a replica of her mother's. Unlike the reserved, aloof Jan, Vicky was effervescent and outgoing.

"Can I order anything I like?" Vicky asked, her eyes skimming the surrounding tables.

Lilli laughed. "Anything except champagne."

"I'm too young for that," Vicky conceded, and suddenly leaned forward in a glow of excitement. "Mother, is that Claudette Colbert?"

Lilli turned. "Why, yes it is. Would you like to meet her?"

"Oh, no!" Vicky said. "I just want to look at her. Wait till I tell the kids in my class that I had lunch across the room from Claudette Colbert!" Now Vicky inspected her deliberately quaint green velvet dress that emphasized her sea-green eyes. "Is my dress pretty?"

Lilli hugged her. "It's lovely." She remembered the traumatic scene three weeks ago when she had bought Vicky the tiny squirrel coat for Hanukkah. At first Vicky had been ecstatic. She tried it on, deciding it was even prettier than the coat being worn to parties by her "best friend." She stroked the soft gray fur. And then, suddenly, tears welled in her eyes. "It was a squirrel, like the ones in the park," she sobbed. "Like a whole bunch of squirrels. And now they're dead because of me."

A waiter arrived and they turned to their menus.

"Mother, isn't that Phyllis over there?" Vicky frowned. She had little affection for her sister-in-law.

"Yes, it is." Lilli forced a smile.

"I hope she doesn't see us," Vicky whispered. "I don't want her to come over here."

"Phyllis is having lunch with a friend. She wouldn't want to join us." Lillie tried to sound casual. "If she's still here when we leave, we'll stop by and say hello."

Phyllis had come to dinner at the house only three times since the wedding, and she had never invited her in-laws to their apartment on Fifth Avenue, overlooking Central Park. Freddie was too loyal to say that Phyllis was giving him a rough time, but Lilli knew it was true. Phyllis didn't want him to be close to his family. His *Jewish* family. Poor darling, he always looked so exhausted when he popped in at the salon or the house to visit briefly whenever he had a free hour. He spent grueling hours at the hospital. But he loved medicine—working at something you loved didn't bring on that aura of frustration and unhappiness she sensed in Freddie at unwary moments.

Lilli turned her thoughts back to her ebullient young daughter. Vicky had dismissed Phyllis from her mind. *Claudette Colbert was here!* Lilli wished she could do something to make life happier for Freddie. How much easier it had been to make things "right" when they were younger. Phyllis didn't realize how lucky she was to have a husband with Freddie's warmth and loyalty and sense of responsibility.

When finally Lilli and Vicky finished their lunch and stood up to leave, Lilli noticed that Phyllis was deep in conversation with another young woman. She doubted that Phyllis had noticed them. "Come on, Vicky." Lilli tugged at her arm. "We really should stop by for a minute to say hello to Phyllis."

"How nice to see you two." Phyllis smiled, but not before Lilli saw a flicker of annoyance in her eyes. "Vicky, what a lovely dress!"

Phyllis went through the motions of introducing her friend, another recently married postdebutante. They talked briefly, and then Lilli and Vicky went out to the waiting Rolls.

"Lou says Phyllis is beautiful." Vicky crinkled her nose. "Boys are so silly."

PHYLLIS SAT BACK in her chair in the breakfast nook—which Freddie called the "most friendly" of their eleven rooms—with a bored smile. Why the hell had she rushed straight home from the performance of *On Your Toes* instead of going on with the others to El Morocco? Freddie, a fellow intern he had brought home from Bellevue, and the pretty little nurse who was the intern's fiancée drank black coffee and spent the entire evening talking with irritating intensity about the Spanish Civil War. She wished Freddie wouldn't show up with these people at strange hours. All they ever talked about was the hospital or the trouble in Spain.

"The International Brigade is already taking shape," Freddie said. "Men are coming into Spain from all over the world. They're being trained in a small town called Albacete."

"They're going to need doctors like crazy," Bernie, the other intern, said somberly. "I understand a group called the American Friends of Spanish Democracy is working to set up a hospital."

"My father says that if the Loyalists defeat the Conservatives in Spain," Phyllis said with deceptive innocence, "then all of Europe will turn Communist. It'll be awful for America."

"Phyllis, it's democracy against fascism!" Freddie said. "The Loyalist cause is the cause of justice and decency and morality!"

"We know what's happening in Mussolini's Italy," Bernie said. "We know about Hitler and his Nazis in Germany. We've got to stop fascism in Spain before it takes over the world."

"Bernie, we ought to be leaving," his fiancée interrupted, and turned to Phyllis with an apologetic smile. "We both have early shifts tomorrow."

"Yeah." After fleeting eye contact with her, Bernie leaped to his feet. "Thanks for having us over, Phyllis."

Phyllis played the charming hostess as she walked with the others to the door. God, she'd thought they'd never leave! She didn't care how brilliant Bernie was supposed to be—he was a bore. And his fiancée, from some little midwestern town, dressed like someone who worked in a five-and-ten.

"I'm going to sleep around the clock on Friday," Freddie said as he walked down the hall to their bedroom.

"Now remember, we have theater tickets for Friday night," Phyllis said. "Don't you dare let yourself be dragged into the hospital on some emergency." She had thought it would be exciting to be married to a handsome young doctor, but five or six times a month she had to show up at a party alone because Freddie was tied up at the hospital.

"Phyl, I'm sorry my hours are so crazy." He smiled. "But you knew you were marrying an intern."

"I don't think you give a damn when you're called in on your days off," she said. "All you care about is the hospital."

"I'm learning every time I walk through that hospital entrance," he said quietly, almost reverently. "This is the most important time of my medical career. It'll be different once I'm in practice." He dropped an arm about her waist.

"Freddie, I don't want to have to call some girlfriend to go with me to see *You Can't Take It with You* on Friday night," she said. "This Friday let them draft somebody else. It's a marvelous comedy. Everybody's predicting it'll win the Pulitzer Prize."

"You know what I'd like to see?" His face lit up. "If it's still on, that is: The WPA *Living Newspaper* thing on Ethiopia."

"I'd loath it." Phyllis kicked off her high heels and began to undress. "Who wants to spend an evening watching some sordid play about Ethiopia?"

"A lot of people, judging from the ticket sales." He crossed to one of a pair of art-deco chests and reached into a drawer for pajamas. "Phyl, we have to care about what goes on in the world."

"Why?" She dropped her dress across the back of a chair. "I'm so sick of hearing you and Bernie and that stupid girlfriend of his cry about how the Spanish peasants and workers are hungry and downtrodden."

"Without compassion we're uncivilized. We can't shut our eyes to what's happening in the world. We have to take a stand." He hesitated. "Bernie's talking to the administration about taking time off to go to Spain. The Loyalists are shockingly short of doctors."

"Bernie's the kind of idiot that would do a thing like that." Stripped down to lace bra and panties, Phyllis reached into the closet to pull down a robe. She'd soak in a bubble bath for a while then settle down in their small sitting room to read *Gone with the Wind*. Freddie got up at six. She slept till noon.

"Phyl, I'm considering going with him." Freddie's face was turned away from her.

She looked up. "Are you out of your mind?" To go dashing off to fight in that stupid civil war with a bunch of illiterate Commies fighting against the landlords and the bankers and the church? What would people think? "How can you go and leave your wife?"

"It wouldn't happen for another two or three months," Freddie said, his eyes focused on tying the strings of his pajama trousers. "And you'd be well provided for while I'm gone. Phyl"—he turned to face her—"it's something I must do."

Phyllis stared at him in shock and rage. "What will people say when you walk out on a wife of seven months?"

"They'll think you have a husband with a social conscience. That is, if they're real people. The other kind I don't care about."

"But all my friends will laugh at me," she shrieked.

"Don't dawdle too long in the bathroom," he said. "I could try to stay awake." When he reached for her breast, she pulled away.

"Don't bother." She stalked into the bathroom. She'd be damned if she'd sleep with him *tonight*.

Slamming the door behind her, Phyllis dropped her red velvet robe on the zebra bathroom rug and inspected herself in the mirrored wall of the bathroom. She unhooked her bra and let it fall to the floor. Her hands moved over her breasts. She *did* have a nice body.

She couldn't believe what Freddie had said about going to Spain. He meant it, too. Freddie could be such a jughead when he thought he was right. Most of the time she could twist him around her little finger, but not when he got that look in his eyes.

She leaned over the marble tub to run a warm bath, then crossed to the dressing table for the bottle of Elizabeth Arden's Eight Hour Cream. She would wash her face and let the cream soak in while she was in the tub. Her eyes glinted with amusement as they rested on the elaborate lineup of Princess Lilli creams and cosmetics that stood on one side of her wide dressing table. She knew it made Freddie furious—though he'd never said a word—that she ignored the bottles and boxes of Princess Lilli that his mother had sent to the apartment while they were on their honeymoon.

Relaxing in the tub, positioned so that she had a perfect view of herself in the mirrored wall, Phyllis suddenly realized who would be her ally in keeping Freddie from running off to Spain: Lilli.

That was it. She settled back into the tub. She would call her mother-in-law tomorrow.

SEATED IN HER OFFICE—looking beautiful and elegant in a black wool Mainbocher frock—Lilli listened while Phyllis told her about Freddie's determination to join the International Brigade in Spain. Intellectually, she could understand her son's desire. Americans from all walks of life—students, writers, bricklayers, engineers, artists, dock workers—were caught up in the frenzy to stop the march of fascism. But emotionally, as his mother, all she thought about was the danger he would face. She felt sick at the prospect of his being under fire, only minutes from death.

"You know how stubborn Freddie can be," Phyllis said. "But he adores you, Lilli. If you talk to him, he'll understand how ridiculous this is. To take off in the middle of his internship!"

Lilli toyed with her emerald and ruby wedding band. She knew Phyllis was not concerned about Freddie's interrupting his internship; it was that his going off so soon after their marriage reflected badly on *her*.

"I know the one way you can keep Freddie home," Lilli said after a moment. "Get yourself pregnant, Phyllis. Freddie will never leave your side for a night."

Phyllis's eyes widened in shock. Her mouth dropped open. Involuntarily one red-nailed hand touched her flat stomach. "But so soon?" she objected. "We haven't even been married a year."

"If you want to keep Freddie here, you'll get pregnant," Lilli said softly. "I guarantee he won't give Spain another thought." He might think about it, she admitted to herself, but he would decide to stay home with his wife.

Phyllis stood up and reached for her mink coat, lying across the back of her chair. "Thank you." Her voice was cool. "I'll have to think about it." She hesitated. "Please don't tell Freddie we talked about this."

"I won't. But, Phyllis, please—*don't delay*."

Late in the afternoon, Lilli came out of a staff conference to find Freddie waiting in her office. She knew instantly that he had come to talk about the International Brigade. She listened without showing a flicker of emotion. Everything Freddie said, she, too, believed in—but she was not prepared to sacrifice her son to her ideals.

"Freddie, how can you leave in the first year of your internship?" she said. "You can make a contribution to humanity as a doctor. You—"

"Mama," he said gently, "I have to do this. Just as you had to go to Paris in 1917. It'll be at least three months before Bernie and I can leave, but we're already in touch with the proper people."

She waited until he had left the salon, then she telephoned Phyllis. "Freddie was just here," she said. "I talked to him. I couldn't change his mind. It's up to you now, Phyllis."

PHYLLIS STEPPED out of a perfumed bath and reached for a towel. Freddie should be home any minute. He laughed at the way she was in and out of the tub two or three times a day—but he always got so passionate when she came into their bed with her skin soft and sweet-scented.

She dropped the towel to inspect herself in the mirror, grimacing as she imagined her firm, flat belly swollen with pregnancy. But Lilli was smart. Having a baby would tie Freddie to her forever. He was the kind that worshipped family.

She would hate being pregnant; but once the baby was born, there'd be a nurse to take care of it. She smiled, imagining herself as the beautiful young mother. Freddie would commission a portrait of her, holding the baby; it would appear in *Vogue* and *Town & Country*. He wouldn't dare run off to join that idiotic fighting in Spain.

She heard him in the foyer. She had told Mary to schedule dinner for an hour later than usual. She paused at the mirror to smooth violet eye shadow on her lids and run a brush over the silken length of pale hair that fell to her shoulders. Then she opened the bathroom door slightly, allowing the steamy fragrance to filter into the bedroom.

"Freddie?"

"Yeah."

She pushed the door wide, poised there with the towel draped carelessly about her. "Darling, I can't bear it when you're angry with me."

"I'm not angry." His eyes trailed over her.

"I told Mary to hold dinner an hour." She dropped the towel, moved slowly toward him.

"Oh, baby. . ." He pulled her to him.

"Take off your clothes," she whispered. "I want to touch you everywhere. I want to feel you everywhere."

As WEEKS RACED BY with no word that Phyllis was pregnant, Lilli worried that Freddie would run off to Spain. On this cold April night, with unseasonably late snow falling over the city, she sat in the library at the house and tried to listen to Alex, who was talking about the rumors that the Federal Trade Commission was about to bring malpractice suits against some top cosmetic firms on grounds that their advertising made false claims.

"We'll come out all right," he said, "though I gather that Rubinstein, Richard Hudnut, and Yardley are in trouble." He paused. "You're thinking about Freddie, aren't you?"

She smiled. Again he'd read her mind. "Every time I read another article about the Spanish Civil War, I shiver."

"I'll go down to the kitchen and make us some tea." He rose to his feet. "You always feel better after a cup of strong tea."

"Let's have it in our room," she said. "It's almost eleven—we've talked enough business for the night. Henri put wood in the grate before he called it a night. I'll start the fire." They loved lying in bed on cold nights, gazing into the fire.

In their bedroom, Lilli lit the newspaper that laced the chunks of wood and watched the flames dance around the bits of kindling. She started at the sound of the phone—the private line, used only by family members. She walked over to the night table, sat at the edge of the bed, and picked up the receiver. "Hello?"

"Did I wake you?" It was Freddie.

"No, darling. How are you?"

"Wonderful news, Mama! Phyllis is pregnant!"

"Oh, Freddie, I'm so happy!"

"Of course, I'll have to give up this business of going to Spain with Bernie. But I think Phyllis will be much happier with a baby. She told me to wait until the morning to call, but I couldn't." He laughed.

"I'm so glad you called tonight. I'll adore having another grandchild."

They talked for a few minutes, and when Alex arrived Lilli put him on the phone.

Had she been wrong in persuading Phyllis to become pregnant? Was she a meddling mother-in-law? What mother would have done less if she could? And maybe with a child, Phyllis and Freddie would have a real marriage.

36

LILLI'S REVIVED HOPE for Freddie's marriage soon faded. As she watched his moods seesaw between a baffled depression and exhilaration, she knew they reflected Phyllis's moods. Once, when Freddie admitted to impatience with his wife's extravagances, Lilli tried to convince him that once the baby was born Phyllis would settle down.

In early July, Lilli and Alex, along with Vicky and Lou and the usual entourage, sailed for Europe. They planned to stay first at the London house, visit the salons at Rome, Cannes, and Monte Carlo briefly, then divide their time in France between the Paris house and the small country house at Poissy.

They arrived in London only weeks after the coronation of George VI, which, except for the June wedding of the Duke of Windsor and Mrs. Simpson, seemed to be the favorite topic of conversation in the city. Lilly enjoyed spending time with Oliver—still slim, handsome, and distinguished at fifty-one—and with Frances and Charles and their children, both of whom were now married and pursuing their careers.

During dinner at the handsome Cohen house, they heard over the wireless that the Japanese had invaded China again and were fighting at Peking.

"It seems there's no corner of the earth that's immune to war," Alex said.

Charles nodded. "I know. And it's heartbreaking to watch a man like Winston Churchill, who's done so much for Great Britain, being treated now as a man past his time. He seems to be the only one who sees what's happening in Germany and

Italy. All Chamberlain thinks about is keeping Hitler and Mussolini happy."

"Most of the British prefer to close their eyes to what's happening," Frances said. "They prefer to think peace will go on forever."

Lilli and Alex sent the children to Paris, along with the rest of their party, and then set off for Rome, Cannes, and Monte Carlo. Though Rome appeared to be enjoying a great economic recovery, Lilli and Alex were ever conscious of the shadow of Mussolini and his Blackshirt followers. Conservative newspapers in many countries praised Mussolini for saving Italy from communism, but Lilli and Alex could not ignore his gangster methods.

"Mussolini?" The head of the Rome salon shrugged with an enigmatic smile. It was dangerous to express an opinion in fascist Italy. "All I know is that he has made the trains run on time."

Lilli and Alex spent only a day each in Cannes and Monte Carlo before heading for Paris. There, Lilli spent most of her time with Aunt Sara, who was enthralled with Vicky and Lou. Before their departure, Lilli again pleaded with her aunt to retire and come to live with them in New York—to no avail.

"Lilli, darling, Paris is my home. My second life. I'd be happy except for that monster Hitler and his Nazi party."

When it came time to leave, Lilli felt a special poignancy in saying goodbye to Aunt Sara. On the trip back to New York aboard the *Normandie*, she and Alex spent hours dissecting the state of the world. Ominous rumors filtered throughout Europe. With Hitler and Mussolini supplying General Franco with arms and troops while Russia was sending the Loyalists planes, pilots, and tanks, Lilli thanked God every night that Freddie was not fighting in Spain. Though Roosevelt preached against isolationism, most Americans felt protected by the oceans that separated them from Europe and Asia. But many Europeans felt war breathing down their necks.

BACK IN NEW YORK in early September, Lilli was caught up in business. Like all major cosmetic companies, Princess Lilli was constantly under pressure to develop new products. And the field was becoming increasingly crowded. Now in addition to Arden and Rubinstein, there was Coty, Dorothy Gray, Chanel, Hudnut, Yardley, and that new man Revson. Unlike Coty, which used a lot of full-page, full-color ads, Revson favored smaller ones. But Alex insisted he was a man to watch.

The only time Lilli escaped business was with the children. It became a ritual now for Jan, Scott, Freddie, and Phyllis to come for dinner on Friday evenings. Usually Jan and Scott left Greg and a playmate at home with Mrs. Ruggles. Whenever Greg, Vicky and Lou were together, all they did was fight. Lilli suspected that Phyllis came only because Freddie insisted on it. But on the first Friday in November, he arrived alone and early.

"Phyllis says she won't leave the house until the baby is here," he said. "She says she hates the way she looks."

"She's due late this month, darling. Try to be patient with her."

"There's more." His face was apprehensive.

"Let's go into my office."

In Lilli's office they sat on the sofa facing the fireplace.

"Phyllis is insisting on a cesarean section," Freddie said.

"What does the obstetrician say?"

"He says it's unnecessary. There's no reason why she can't have a normal delivery."

"Why does she want to go through surgery?" But Lilli knew immediately: Phyllis wouldn't tolerate any suffering.

"She says it's ridiculous for women to go through the pain of labor," Freddie said. "She says all her friends are having their children by sections. 'Barbara Hutton had *her* baby by cesarean section,'" he mimicked. "Phyllis can't seem to understand that any kind of surgery entails danger. I can't change her mind, Mama."

"Jan's doctor wanted her to have a section," Lilli said slowly. "The doctors agreed she shouldn't have to go through that much pain. She fought for a normal delivery."

"Does Jan still have that crazy notion that she's responsible for Greg's arm?"

Lilli nodded.

"Then it won't help to ask Jan to talk to Phyllis," he said.

"I doubt that anybody, except her obstetrician, can change her mind, Freddie."

"He's even given up. He says that maybe it *would* be best for her—emotionally, at least. But I worry. I worry like hell."

One week later—insisting that the doctor not delay lest she go into early labor—Phyllis entered the hospital. The following morning a section was performed. The child was a boy. Freddie was ecstatic. But Phyllis was furious to discover that the surgery, too, was painful. She refused all visitors for a week. Lilli dropped by the hospital every day to see her second grandchild, David Evan Laval; and at Freddie's request, Lilli instructed her attorney to inform Jacques, when his monthly check was sent, that he had a second grandchild. Neither Freddie nor Jan had heard from their father in years. According to Lilli's lawyer, he had been living in Miami for over a year.

Without consulting Phyllis, who was not nursing the baby and considered herself too fragile even to hold him to give him his bottle, Freddie arranged for circumcision on the eighth day, as decreed by Jewish law, though the procedure was performed by a physician rather than a *mohel*. It soon became clear to Lilli that Phyllis regarded her son as a novelty, fit only for showing off to her friends. "She acts like she's the Madonna in those paintings by Raphael that we saw in the Metropolitan," Vicky said.

To Lilli's astonishment, Jan and Phyllis began seeing each other. She watched with apprehension as Phyllis swept Jan into her café-society world of El Morocco, the Stork, "21," and the Colony. Freddie was too busy at the hospital and with David to have time left over for much else. Lilli suspected that he closed his eyes to Phyllis's socializing.

When Jan complained that Scott spent endless evenings at his office, he acknowledged to Lilli that he was avoiding being caught up in Jan's new social whirl. "I hate sitting around in a nightclub until all hours," he said. "I *can't* do it and handle business the next day. I don't know why Jan can't understand this."

"It's her way of escaping reality. You know how she worries about Greg."

"She's talking again about another operation." He sighed. "I won't let Greg be put through another, Lilli. According to Freddie, what this new man is doing is still in experimental stages. When he can show some success, I'll consider it." Scott looked tired and tense, Lilli noted. Why couldn't Jan understand that she ought to consider Scott's feelings, too? "Did she tell you," he said, "I suggested we adopt a child?"

"No." Lilli was taken aback. Jan confided in her less and less.

"She won't hear of it. It would be good for Greg. Jan spoils him badly. With another child in the house that might change."

"I'll talk to Jan about letting Greg spend the summer with Vicky and Lou at the Southampton house," Lilli said. They wouldn't be happy about it, she thought uneasily, and Martine would have her hands full. "It'll be good for him to be with other children for a while."

In March 1938, Grandma Kahn died in her sleep. She was buried beside her husband. Lilli and Alex grieved but were grateful for the years they had shared her life. That same month, after Hitler had secretly supported a Nazi movement in Austria and Nazi conspirators had assassinated that country's chancellor, Dollfuss, Nazi troops marched across the Austrian border in a quick, bloodless conquest. Though she respected Austria's efforts to establish itself as a democracy after the world war, Lilli harbored little love for the country of her grandparents. They had been murdered in an anti-Jewish riot at Bratislava.

Surrounded now on three sides by Germans, the Czechs were justifiably frightened for their future. Like her aunt, Lilli was especially concerned about what was happening in Czechoslovakia. Marienbad was Czech territory now. It was hard to believe that the girls she had grown up with in Marienbad now stood in the path of Hitler's troops.

Letters from Oliver and from Frances and Charles warned that war was imminent. Sara agreed, and worried that France was unprepared to fight.

"If there's going to be a war, we'll lose the foreign markets," Alex said on a Sunday afternoon in July while he sat with Lilli on the veranda in Southampton. "I think it's time we expanded into the South American market." Arden was already operating successfully there.

"We should start stockpiling raw material," she said. It was terrifying to think of the world once again on the brink of war. "Oh, Alex, it seems so awful to sit and talk like this about another war!"

"I pray we're wrong. But we have two madmen on the loose. If Hitler and Mussolini have their way, they'll rule the world."

"Mother!" Vicky came running up from the beach and into Alex's arms. One of the great joys of Lilli's life was the warmth Vicky and Lou shared with Alex and her. "Daddy," Vicky said, "make Greg go home! Lou and I spent hours on our sand castle, and he just kicked it in!"

IN LATE SEPTEMBER, Hitler demanded that the 3.5 million Sudeten Germans in Czechoslovakia be placed under his rule, claiming the Sudetenland would be "the last territorial claim I have to make in Europe." The Czechs were prepared to fight, but at the Munich Conference on September 30, Chamberlain of Great Britain and Daladier of France bowed before the demands of Hitler and Mussolini. Chamberlain returned to London to declare that the Munich agreement meant "peace for our time."

Lilli and Alex sat by the library radio and waited for the evening news reports on the Munich Conference. Now a surgical resident, Freddie had dropped by after being on call for twelve hours, and was eating with relish the plate of cold chicken and salad Bertha had brought him.

"David is asleep by now," he said. His face took on a soft glow that mention of his son always evoked. "Phyllis is at some charity affair." The glow disappeared. "With Jan, I think."

Lilli knew he wasn't happy with Phyllis. He was making the best of the marriage because of David. "Those two are thick as thieves," he said.

"I'd never have guessed it. They're so different," Lilli said.

"Jan's going through a rough stage right now," Alex said gently. "Greg can't seem to adjust to school. He's transferred to a new one this term."

"Did you know Phyllis keeps yapping at Jan to go to her psychiatrist?"

"No." Lilli was startled.

"Try to persuade her not to," Freddie said. "God knows, he hasn't done anything for Phyllis."

Lilli frowned. "I didn't know Phyllis was seeing a psychiatrist."

"Only because several of her friends are. It's *the* thing to do. That's all Phyllis talks about these days. On those rare occasions when we talk, that is."

"How's my second grandson?" Lilli asked, determined to shift Freddie into a brighter mood. "I haven't seen him for three days."

"David's fine. Phyllis is annoyed because he isn't walking yet. I keep telling her he'll walk when he's ready. The pediatrician said the same thing when she called him."

"It's time for the news." Alex reached over and turned on the radio.

Would there be war in Europe? Lilli wondered as they listened to the newscast. Would Freddie feel it was his duty to go to fight? Thank God, he had not gone off to Spain. Just last month they'd heard that his friend Bernie had died there.

No, Lilli told herself with shaky conviction. Freddie was a married man with a child. He belonged here. He was *needed* here.

IN ANTICIPATION of losing foreign markets, Lilli and Alex made two trips to South America in the ensuing months to set up retail operations in Rio de Janeiro, Caracas, and Buenos Aires. Reluctantly, the elder Mr. Kahn now conceded that Alex had brought about admirable efficiency in their mail-order business and agreed that Alex turn over the reins to his son-in-law. So Alex was free again to give all his time to Lilli's cosmetic empire.

Despite the constant pressure of the business, both Lilli and Alex were concerned about the state of Jan's and Freddie's marriages. "I thought I'd work hard and become successful, and I'd be able to do everything for the children," Lilli said one hot late-August night as she and Alex sat alone after dinner. Both Freddie and Scott had come for dinner. Jan and Phyllis, along with the children, were out at the Southampton house. "I don't want Jan to lose Scott. He's a fine man."

"I don't know how much more Freddie will take of Phyllis," Alex said. "Would it upset you if they divorced?"

"Freddie's like me—he's stubborn. He won't break up his marriage until he's hit over the head." And what then of little David? "David barely knows his mother. That's why I can't understand this friendship between Jan and Phyllis. Jan's devoted to Greg—just the opposite of Phyllis."

"It might be better if she was less devoted," Alex said. "He's a spoiled brat." Alex rose to his feet. "Why don't we have a cup of tea while we listen to the late news?"

They knew the news would be depressing. France and England, aware of their peril in the face of Hitler and Mussolini aggressions, were committed to defend Poland should Germany attack. They were trying to enlist Russia in an alliance, but Stalin was refusing.

Lilli and Alex settled themselves before the radio. Henri knocked and came in with a tea tray.

"The world was stunned today to learn that Russia and Germany have signed a nonaggression treaty..." the newscaster began.

"Good Lord!" Alex was white with shock. "They're supposed to be the bitterest of enemies!"

"Alex, what does it mean?" Lilli, too, was shaken.

"It means," he said grimly, "that the days of peace in Europe are numbered."

Seven days later—on September 1—the world learned that the German Army had crossed the Polish borders. On September 3, Britain and France declared war on Germany. Lilli sent frantic cables to Sara and Oliver, pleading with them to come to New York. Knowing it was useless, she wrote Frances and Charles and urged them, too, to join her in the New York offices of Princess Lilli.

Both Sara and Oliver insisted they would remain at their posts. "I'm an old woman, my darling," Sara wrote. "France is my adopted country. I sat out one war. I'll sit out another."

Oliver still bore a souvenir of the First World War, though he had never allowed his limp to change his way of life—a fact that Lilli constantly pointed out to Jan. He was determined to be involved as best he could—though clearly it would be as a civilian—in this war. Frances and Charles, too, were determined to stay in London.

In less than three weeks, Poland was crushed. Russian troops joined the Germans in partitioning Poland. On November 30, Russian troops invaded Finland. The French took their positions behind their supposedly impregnable Maginot Line while the Germans settled behind their Siegfried Line. Each side engaged in minor raids, dropping propaganda leaflets. To the newspapers this was "the phony war."

"Barrage balloons hang over the Thames," Oliver wrote. "Antiaircraft emplacements have been built along the docks and in Victoria Park. At night, the city is blacked out. Many of London's children have been evacuated to rural areas. All we do is wait for an attack that doesn't come."

Frances wrote that at least 25,000 refugees from Germany and Austria were said to have entered England—some illegally—since 1933. British newspapers welcomed these refugees, who were usually highly trained or with sufficient funds to be an asset to England, though there were complaints by some professionals—and by the rabid Right—that they were taking over business that belonged to British citizens.

From Paris, Sara wrote that workers were leaving their jobs, as they had in 1914, to join the fighting. It was almost impossible to buy heating fuel. Because of the shortage of servants and heat, many of the wealthy were closing up their houses and huge apartments to settle in at the Ritz and the Crillon. Rumor had it that the French Army was unprepared for war and that Paris would fall at the will of the Germans. But life went on. Business at the salon and to the retail outlets continued as usual.

Then in April 1940 Nazi troops took Norway and Denmark, smashing the courageous resistance of Norway's fighting men and of the British troops that had been sent to help. A month later, Winston Churchill took over for Chamberlain, and at the same time the Germans launched a massive attack, sweeping through Holland, Belgium, and Luxembourg.

Along with everyone else around the world, Lilli and Alex stayed by the radio as bombs fell on these countries, paratroopers jumped, and a wedge of tanks and troops rushed the French line and pushed toward the English Channel. Belgium surrendered. In and around Dunkirk, 400,000 British and French troops seemed abandoned. But within a week British destroyers, along with a flotilla of small crafts—any vessel large enough to stay afloat, including motorboats and fishing vessels—rescued 340,000 British and French soldiers from the beach in an effort that stunned the world.

Life in Paris continued to be normal until word seeped through at the end of May that Nazi troops were heading for the city. Suddenly everyone was fleeing, jamming the roads to the south. In a matter of days—or perhaps weeks, at most—the Germans would enter the city, and Paris was helpless to defend itself.

One sunny morning, Sara sat at her eighteenth-century desk and tried to decide what to do. She was Jewish. She had no doubt that French Jews would be rounded up and sent to camps. But she had lived in Paris for thirty years. This was her home.

The door to her office burst open. It was Emilie, her long-time second-in-command. "Sara, you must leave Paris." She was white and trembling. "They say the Nazis will be here in two weeks at the most. You *know* what they will do to the Jews."

"Emilie, your son-in-law is still an undertaker?" Sara asked quietly.

"Yes."

"Then I know what we must do. Call Monsieur Gaspard, the attorney. Ask him to come as quickly as he can. Tell him this is an emergency. And have your son-in-law at the house this evening."

"Sara, what will you do?"

"Tonight I will suffer a fatal heart attack. Your son-in-law will arrange for a quick funeral, as the Jewish faith requires. Make sure he pretends to bury me in a Jewish cemetery," Sara said with bitter humor. "The salon will revert on my death to Lilli, an American citizen. Germany is not at war with America—the salon will remain open, with you in charge."

"But you, Sara? What will you do?"

"Monsieur Gaspard, for a price, will find me new identification papers. I'll become another woman, the housekeeper at Lilli's house in Poissy. And whatever I can do to help France, I will do."

"Sara, I'm so afraid."

"You're a Frenchwoman, Emilie. You will not be afraid. The day will come when France will be free. Remember that."

"I don't dare write Lilli what is happening," Emilie said. "Suppose the letters are censored?"

Sara thought for a moment. "Try to get Lady Mendl on the phone, if she's still in Paris. She's American—she'll be returning to the States, and she'll tell Lilli what has happened."

ON JUNE 14, word came through that the Germans had entered Paris. Lilli paced the library as she and Alex listened to the news. It was shattering to imagine Paris in the hands of the Germans. She remembered now how it had been in 1917, when the Germans had been at the edge of the city when she had been there. But they had never entered the city.

There was a knock at the door. Lilli turned. It was Freddie, pale and obviously shaken. "It's too late now to get Aunt Sara out," he said.

"Oh, God." Lilli turned to Alex. "Not only is she French, she's a Jew. Alex, what will they do to her?"

"Lilli, she's a seventy-eight-year-old woman. They'll do nothing to her. But because she's Jewish they'll close the salon and the factory. French Jews with money must be fleeing like mad. But, of course, we all know your stubborn Aunt Sara won't run."

"They'll round up the Paris Jews and send them to camps." Lilli's voice was shrill. "Why didn't I insist she leave last year?"

"Lilli, you tried. She wouldn't listen." Alex sighed. "The French were totally unprepared to defend Paris."

"I'm sure Congress will take some action about raising a larger army," Freddie said slowly.

Lilli stared at her son in shock. Freddie would be thirty in August—he had a child of his own. Surely he wouldn't be drafted.

"We can't stay out of this much longer," he said.

OVER THE NEXT FEW WEEKS, Lilli thought of little else but her aunt's safety. She took comfort in the fact that since America was not at war, mail service would continue to and from Paris, and also to London. Every day she hoped for mail from Paris.

In early July, Lilli received a phone call from Lady Mendl, who had just arrived from Europe via Pan Am's *Yankee Clipper*. She told Lilli that Sara was taking refuge at the Poissy house under false identification papers. Emilie would write that Sara had suffered a fatal heart attack. Emilie would continue to operate the Paris salon as long as the Nazis permitted it.

At the same time, the cosmetic industry had recently been stunned by the passage of the Food, Drug and Cosmetic Act.

Now each package offered for sale had to indicate the amount it contained, along with a listing of its ingredients and an explanation of its purpose. For Princess Lilli and Arden, this was not a serious problem, but for other manufacturers it was. Offending ingredients had to be replaced, new formulas developed. And for every manufacturer it meant repackaging.

At the same time there was a scramble for new markets. Both Rubinstein and Arden were moving into pharmacies and chain drugstores. Lilli fought with Alex about following them into these markets. She worried that it would tarnish Princess Lilli's prestigious image. Alex felt they had no choice. "We've lost most of our European market, Lilli. The entire American cosmetic industry is hurting."

"Not Arden," she said. "According to Emilie, her salon in Paris is doing well, and so are retail sales."

"Forget about Arden. Forget about the European market. We need more outlets here in America."

She sighed. "All right then, let's offer a special line for the chain drugstores and pharmacies. Instead of Princess Lilli, let's introduce Mademoiselle Lilli."

He jumped up, began pacing. "Lilli, that's it! We'll launch it within four months. With a big promotion. Basically the same products, but with a different fragrance and different packaging. It'll be a smash!"

ON THE FIRST SUNDAY in December, Phyllis entertained a group of young women socialites at a fund-raising tea for British children. After the guests had left, Phyllis and Jan kicked off their shoes and collapsed on a sofa in the library.

"We sure collected a lot of loot, didn't we?" Phyllis giggled. "They knew if they didn't kick in, they wouldn't be invited to my New Year's Eve ball."

"I've got to go, Phyl," Jan said. "Greg will be home soon. Scott took him ice skating in Central Park."

"Relax, baby." Phyllis yawned. "They'll survive without you."

"Where's Freddie?"

"You know your brother. Always at the hospital. Some patient's taking a long time to die." She gazed at Jan. "You talk to Scott yet about running down to Palm Beach with me next month?"

"Phyl, I don't see how I can." They went through this every year. She couldn't take Greg out of school simply because she wanted to spend a month in Palm Beach. "Let's listen to some music."

"I'll see what's on." Phyllis rose to her feet and crossed to switch on the radio.

"—attacked Pearl Harbor in Hawaii with devastating results!" A newscaster's agitated voice came on. "Four American battleships are known to have been sunk . . ."

"Freddie isn't here—we don't have to listen to the news." Phyllis switched to another station.

"Phyllis, wait!" Jan was pale with shock.

But no station was playing music on this crucial afternoon of December 7, 1941. Jan and Phyllis listened to a replay of what had been reported earlier plus additional news just arriving.

"Phyllis, that means the country is at war." Alex and Mother and Freddie and Scott kept saying the United States would be dragged into the war. "I can't believe it!"

"Freddie will enlist for sure," Phyllis said. "Remember how badly he wanted to go to fight in Spain?"

"Phyllis, no—"

"What about Scott? How old is he?"

"Thirty-eight. Two years past the draft age." But Jan's heart was suddenly pounding. Scott had such a strong sense of responsibility. He might consider it his duty to enlist.

"Freddie's thirty-one," Phyllis said. "He'll go in as a doctor, of course. He'll look terribly handsome in an officer's uniform."

"Phyllis, don't talk like that!" Jan stood up. "I have to go home. I don't want Scott fighting. He has to remember he has a wife and child to think about!"

She loved Scott. Until now, she hadn't realized how much.

37

THE CRYSTAL CHANDELIER that hung above the beautifully laid dining table lent a soft glow to the room on this late-March evening. Lilli tried to pretend this was a festive occasion. She was surrounded by her husband, her four children, a grandson, and her son-in-law and daughter-in-law. Only little David, too young to be awake at this hour, was missing.

She smiled as she saw the way Scott and Jan looked at each other across the table. The only good thing to come out of this war was their reconciliation. Fear gripped her as her gaze moved to Freddie—so handsome in his army air force uniform. Even Alex was finding it difficult to appear cheerful tonight.

The night of the attack on Pearl Harbor, Freddie had come over to tell her that he was enlisting. She had tried to prepare herself for this, had told herself that sooner or later he would have been drafted, but shock and fear had overwhelmed her. And she knew this war would not be over quickly. She would do anything to keep him in this country, pull whatever strings she and Alex could think of, if it would keep him out of the fighting. It was unpatriotic, she knew, but her heart ruled, and all that mattered was that her child was in danger.

Though Freddie was only their stepgrandson, Alex's parents, too, were concerned about his going into the service. All over the country mothers must be experiencing the same emotions. Lilli ached for the mothers and fathers of those who had lost sons or daughters at Pearl Harbor.

"When do you have to return to camp?" Jan asked Freddie, and Lilli was brought back to the dinner-table conversation.

"I'm taking a late train tonight," he said. "I was lucky to get this weekend pass."

"I went down to Kentucky to see him last weekend," Phyllis said, pouting. "But I spent most of the time alone in the most awful hotel room."

"We were lucky to get a room at all," Freddie said. "This is wartime, Phyllis. I'm being transferred to Wright Field out in Ohio." He turned to Lilli with a grin. "Maybe you'll open a salon out there and come visit me."

"I had tickets to see Gertrude Lawrence in *Lady in the Dark* last night—you know how hard they are to get." Phyllis looked to Jan for support. "And Freddie refused to go."

"I preferred to spend the time with David and you," Freddie said gently.

"With David and me and the radio newscaster, you mean."

"It was grim to see General MacArthur pull out of Bataan," Alex said. "Even though it took a presidential order to remove him."

"We still have soldiers and nurses there," Scott pointed out.

"True," Freddie said. "But from what we know, they're greatly outnumbered. They're in a rough position."

Lilli frowned. When would this talk of war end? Thank God, Lou and Greg were too young to be involved. Her face softened as she gazed at her two youngest children. They both adored Freddie, and they were so proud of their brother in the army air force.

Right after dessert, Freddie asked if anyone would mind his leaving. "I want another look at David before I go." He smiled. "I'm probably the proudest father in my battalion."

"I'll come out to visit you in Ohio," Lilli said, and Alex nodded. "Keep me posted."

After the others had gone, Lilli, Alex, Vicky, and Lou settled in the library to listen to the news. "At least we have radio," Alex said in an effort to lighten the mood. "Remember the last war? We had to wait for newspaper extras."

"Do you think the war will last till I'm old enough to enlist?" Lou asked.

Lilli turned on him. "Don't even think such a thing! Worry about your bar mitzvah."

"Vicky," Alex said calmly, "why don't you go out to the kitchen and bring us some ice cream?"

"Why can't Lou do it?"

"Because girls do stuff like that," Lou said. "Boys bring in wood for the fireplace and shovel snow."

"That's so silly!" Sighing with an air of martyrdom, Vicky left the room.

Lilli followed her, mostly to escape the depressing news on the radio.

"I can't stand Phyllis," Vicky said as she dug into the container of ice cream. "All she talks about is dancing with servicemen at the Stage Door Canteen. She thinks she's so patriotic. She's just uniform-crazy."

"Vicky, you know I don't like it when you talk this way. Watch it—you're making that serving way too big."

Vicky scowled. "I mean it, Mom. Phyllis thinks because she's so pretty she can get away with anything. Well, Jan's prettier. Only she doesn't know it."

"Both my daughters are beautiful," Lilli said with pride. "Okay, honey, that's enough. Now let's take this inside before Lou comes tearing out here."

IN APRIL the nation learned with anguish of American and Philippine prisoners taken at Bataan and forced to march eighty-five miles in six days on a ration of one meal of rice. By the end of this "death march," 5,200 Americans and even more Filipinos had died. On April 18, Americans were cheered by the news that a bomber group led by Major General Doolittle had hit Tokyo. Early in May American forces inflicted heavy losses on the Japanese fleet in the Coral Sea, but at the same time General Wainwright was forced to surrender Corregidor.

Unknown to Freddie, Lilli and Alex pulled all the strings they could to keep him in the United States. When he telephoned to say he was on a twenty-four-hour pass—too brief to fly to New York—Lilli flew to Ohio by charter plane to spend just three hours with him. She and Alex had given enough of themselves in the First World War, Lilli told herself. Let Freddie be safe in this one.

In late June, Doris interrupted Lilli and Alex's conference with their new ad agency to tell them that Freddie was calling from La Guardia Airport. "I'm in town for only a few hours," he said. "I'm going to the apartment to see David and Phyllis, then I'll come over to the house. It may be late—"

"Darling, any time." She knew this was a special visit. "We'll wait up for you."

"He's on alert," Alex said quietly when Lilli, pale and shaken, put down the phone.

"I'm sure of it. Alex, what happened? We were assured he'd be kept here at home!"

"Doctors are needed desperately overseas." He reached for her hand. "But perhaps we're both jumping to conclusions. Maybe he's just on a twenty-four-hour pass."

STANDING BEFORE HIS APARTMENT, all Freddie could think was that it might be years before he stood here again. It might even be the last time. But knowing the heavy casualties in American troops, he'd had no choice but to volunteer for overseas duty. How could he remain in his safe little niche when so many were dying?

"Mr. Laval, welcome home!" Eunice, the current maid, smiled broadly. "Mrs. Laval just got here a few minutes ago."

"Thank you, Eunice. Is David home?"

"He's at a birthday party. I expect he'll be home in about an hour."

"Thank you, Eunice."

Freddie swept past her and down the hall to the master bedroom suite. Phyllis was seated at her dressing table in a black lace bra and black satin panties. She swung around, looking irritated. "Freddie! Why didn't you call and tell me you were coming?" She rose leisurely and walked toward him.

"There was no time." His mouth went dry at the sight of her. It had been months since they'd made love. "I'm on alert, Phyl. I'm shipping out."

"Oh, Freddie!" Her eyes widened. Not with shock, he realized—now she could boast about her husband fighting overseas. "Would you like a quick shower?" she asked. "I'll take you with me to the fund-raising party over at the Plaza—"

"I have no time to go to a party. I'm flying back to Ohio tonight." He pulled her close.

"Darling, they'll hate me if I show up late." But he saw the passion in her eyes.

"It won't be all that late." He unhooked her bra. "You can say you had a rendezvous with your husband."

This wasn't the way an overseas-bound husband should feel, he told himself while his hands roamed about her sleek, narrow frame. It was more like being with a high-priced prostitute.

"Freddie," she whispered, "lock the door."

When he went back into the bedroom, Phyllis was spraying the pillows with Blue Grass, a popular Elizabeth Arden scent. She lay down on the bed. Instantly, he was beside her. He took her in his arms, content for a moment just to hold her close, to feel her warm body against his.

"Freddie, kiss me everywhere," she whispered. "Make me go crazy."

SHOWERED AND DRESSED, Freddie lay back on the bed against a mound of pillows and watched while Phyllis put on her makeup. She took such pains with it that there was no point in trying to converse. He listened for the front door; Phyllis had told him that David would be home shortly from a party. For what he had just shared with Phyllis, he thought, he might as well have gone to one of the houses favored by army brass. It was David—and his family in the Gramercy Park house—that had brought him rushing to New York for what might be his last time.

He heard footsteps in the hallway and jumped up. "There's David!"

"Darling, you *will* be careful?" Phyllis paused for a moment, smiling prettily.

"Of course I will." He ran out into the hall. "David!"

"Daddy!" David flew into his arms. "Daddy, are you going to stay home now?"

Playing with David in his room, Freddie realized that Phyllis had left without saying goodbye. He stayed with David until Mrs. Ames came to take him out to the kitchen for his dinner. Then he left, hailed a taxi, and drove downtown to the much-loved house on Gramercy Park.

As he was welcomed by Henri, he heard his mother's voice, then Alex's, in the library. They knew, he thought tenderly, that he was shipping out. They knew, too, what war was all about. Growing up, he had been enthralled by his mother's stories about her brief career as an agent for American Intelligence, and had coaxed Alex to confide his own adventures. But never once had either failed to make him understand the horrors of war, the price to be paid. He wasn't going off to Phyllis's glamorous war but to mother and Alex's very real, very ugly war.

THROUGHOUT DINNER Lilli found it impossible to take her eyes off Freddie. Though she and Alex had guessed that he was on alert, hearing the words had been more of a shock than she expected. Vicky and Lou looked so somber, almost in awe of their brother. Jan and Scott, hastily summoned for this last dinner before Freddie was shipped out, had arrived with false cheer and a bottle of champagne.

After dinner Lilli stood by while Jan and Scott said their farewells. Scott was defensive about not being in uniform. He had registered for the draft, but as a husband and father he was thus far exempt. Lilli knew that Jan was terrified he might follow Freddie's lead and decide to enlist.

Freddie said goodbye to Vicky and Lou and sent them off to bed. "Tomorrow's a school day," he said. "Can't have you two messing up because you stayed up too late with me."

Now it was just the three of them—Alex, Freddie, and herself—standing in the foyer. No one dared say anything. Lilli's eyes moved to the clock. Henri was standing by to drive Freddie back to the airport.

"Take care of Mother, Uncle Alex." Freddie embraced his stepfather.

"You know I will."

Freddie turned to his mother. "Take care of yourself, Freddie. You're very special to us." The words sounded hopelessly inadequate, she thought as they held each other.

Lilli stood at the door and waved goodbye as Freddie was settled into the car. She refused to cry. Let Freddie's last image of her be with a smile on her face.

They had no way of knowing whether he was headed for North Africa or England or the Pacific. And they wouldn't know until the card arrived giving them an APO number.

She was another mother who would spend sleepless nights worrying about a child in uniform. Praying that he would come home to her again.

AFTER SIX INTERMINABLE WEEKS, the postcard with Freddie's APO number arrived: He was somewhere in the Pacific. Lilli hung on every mention of the Pacific in the news. In August, U.S. marines landed on Guadalcanal in the Solomon Islands. And in August Phyllis told Jan, who then told Lilli, that she was pregnant again.

"She figures she's due in March. I don't think she's terribly happy about it," Jan said to Lilli over lunch at the St. Regis. Lately, it seemed to Lilli, Jan had been growing disenchanted with her sister-in-law. "She's complaining she won't be able to be a hostess at the Stage Door Canteen after another month or so."

"I'm sure the canteen will survive without Phyllis." Lilli couldn't keep the sharpness out of her voice. But she couldn't help being thrilled that another grandchild was on the way. "What does she hear from Freddie?"

"I think you hear from him more often than she does," Jan said. "Phyllis hates writing letters."

"I write every night," Lilli said softly. "Of course, I don't know how many of them he gets." Several times a week she stopped by to visit with little David.

"Mother..." Jan hesitated. "How long do you think this war will last?"

"Darling, who can say? You're worrying about Scott, aren't you?"

Jan nodded. "He feels so guilty, with Freddie out there. He practically flinches at the sight of every man in uniform."

Lilli paused. "Jan, there's something I haven't told you . . . Alex is going back into uniform." Jan stared at her in shock. "He's been talking about it for several weeks. He'll be stationed here in New York. At a desk job." Even at fifty-seven, Alex refused to sit out the war.

"Oh, God," Jan said. "Now Scott will really be upset."

"I'll ask Alex to talk with him," Lilli said. "If the business can survive under his father's guidance, then I'm sure Scott could make a contribution here at home."

Within two weeks Alex was back in uniform—and Scott began arrangements to turn over the business to his father for the duration of the war in order to accept a position with the government. He would remain in New York, for which Lilli was grateful. More than ever, she wanted her family to stay in close touch.

She continued to worry about Oliver, Frances, Charles, and their children and grandchildren in London. She worried about the staffs of the London and Paris salons and the branches in the south of France. The London house had been damaged in an air raid and the salon had narrowly missed being destroyed. She knew nothing about the Paris salon or her house. No word had come through about Aunt Sara's whereabouts since the visit from Lady Mendl, over two years ago. Lilli assumed that, under her new identity, Sara had not dared to write before the

United States entered the war. And now, of course, contact was impossible. Lilli continued to blame herself for not insisting that her aunt join her in New York.

SARA WATCHED while the four German officers billeted in the small house a few kilometers outside Poissy climbed into cars to head for a night in Paris, as they had every Friday night since arriving. The couple Lilli had hired long ago as caretakers had fled when the Germans marched into France, so Sara lived here alone, surviving on the cash and jewelry she had brought with her from Paris. She trusted few these days. Her only friend was the village priest. Nobody in Poissy knew that she and Father Michel were part of the French underground, helping Allied airmen who had been shot down over France to escape.

Father Michel was presently hiding a British flier in the village church, but now the airman would have to take refuge in the secret cubicle off her bedroom because Father Michel feared the church would be searched; someone had told the Gestapo that a British parachute had been discovered in a nearby field. Father Michel knew her Nazi houseguests went into Paris on Friday evenings. The open drapes in her bedroom window were a signal that they had left.

Sara stood at the front door in the early twilight while the car disappeared in a cloud of late-summer dust. She was worried; night fell so late this time of year, and Father Michel had said that he would have to wait until dark to bring the flier to the house. Later, when they thought it was safe, he would be moved to the south.

A damp chill had fallen on the house with the fading of the afternoon sun. She went inside for a sweater. Pulling it about her shoulders, she paused, listening to the light clop of the horse that pulled Father Michel's cart. She hurried outside. The cart was headed for the barn. Ostensibly, Father Michel was bringing her firewood—a simple act of charity for an elderly parishioner.

"I couldn't wait any later," Father Michel told her as he began removing the wood from the cart. A young man in uniform lay beneath a small pile of kindling in the corner. "The Gestapo is searching the whole town."

"Come inside." Sara nodded to the young British officer. "With four Nazis billeted in the house, it isn't likely they'll search here."

Over coffee, they plotted the next destination of the British flier, briefing him on his contacts. Sara was pleased that he spoke French—she'd never been totally comfortable in English. She told him about Lilli's salon in London and about her efforts on behalf of American Intelligence in the First World War.

"We must take no chances," Father Michel said as Sara carefully removed the third cup and saucer, and the young Englishman nodded in agreement.

Sara led the way up to her bedroom and to the secret cubicle, concealed by a pine dresser, which she and Father Michel quickly moved. Inside, there was barely enough room for a narrow cot. A small, circular window, like a ship's porthole, provided the only light and ventilation.

"Remember," Sara said as the flier settled himself in, "four Nazi officers are living here in the house. You must *not* come out—not even once. I'll bring you food and coffee when they're gone."

"We'll send you on to your next stop as soon as possible, and then—" Father Michel stopped short at the sound of a car.

In an instant, they had moved the dresser back into place and returned to the kitchen. They pretended to be sitting at the table over coffee as they heard the tramp of boots down the long hall.

A Gestapo officer, accompanied by four soldiers, walked into the kitchen. "You are both under arrest for conspiracy against the Fatherland." He gestured to the soldiers to take over.

While they were being marched to a waiting car, Sara caught a glimpse of a face peering from behind the now-shut window—but only for an instant. The soldiers hadn't seen him, she told herself. And the underground would know that she and

Father Michel had been arrested. They would take over the rescue mission.

LILLI RETURNED to the salon from a fund-raising committee meeting for Jewish war refugees to find Alex waiting in her office. She knew immediately he had bad news.

"Alex, what is it?"

"I just received a letter from Oliver. It's Sara, Lilli. A British flier she hid in the house at Poissy came to the salon to tell him. She was taken into custody by the Gestapo—"

"Alex, no!"

"I'm afraid so. Oliver investigated further. She's interned at Ravensbrück in northern Germany."

"The concentration camp?" *Aunt Sara in a concentration camp?* "It's my fault, Alex—" Her voice broke. "I should have insisted she come here to us. It's my fault!"

Alex held her in his arms while she sobbed. Aunt Sara was in that awful place, and there was nothing she could do to help her. All the money, all the connections, meant nothing.

38

EARLY IN MARCH, Phyllis's mother—with whom Lilli had no contact except for occasional social encounters—phoned to tell Lilli that Phyllis had given birth early.

"It's a girl. She weighs just four pounds. She'll be baptized Carol Elena—when her physical condition permits."

"Will she be all right?" Lilli was worried. To come into the world so tiny! "And Phyllis—how is she?"

"The baby is in an incubator. How do you think Phyllis feels? Another cesarean section. I think your son might have shown more restraint. To put Phyllis through this in the middle of a war—"

"Mrs. Winthrop, women have babies even during wars." What did Phyllis or her mother know about what was happening to fighting men overseas? Their lives were little changed. Phyllis had been furious because she had to bribe her maid and cook to get extra ration coupons for shoes.

Lilli ran around the salon looking for Alex. Breathlessly, she told him about the baby's birth. "I'm going over to the hospital, Alex. Right now."

"Don't bother asking to see Phyllis," he said. "I'm sure she won't want to see you."

"I know that." Tears filled her eyes. "I'm going to see Freddie's daughter. Alex, she's so little."

Together, Lilli and Alex went to the hospital and stood before the glassed-in area that housed the incubators.

"She's got a strong voice for such a tiny girl," Alex chuckled, holding Lilli's hand. "And stop looking so worried. You've talked to the doctor—he says she's doing fine."

But Lilli didn't stop worrying until Carol passed the five-pound mark. Phyllis insisted that Carol remain at the hospital until she weighed seven pounds. According to Jan, Phyllis was already making the rounds of the nightclubs again.

Letters from Freddie were increasingly rare now, but Lilli knew he would be happy to learn about his new daughter, so she continued to write every night. Vicky and Lou, too, wrote Freddie at least once a week. Lilli also made a point of seeing David and Carol regularly, though she saw little of their mother. Even Jan rarely saw Phyllis these days—she told Lilli she suspected that Phyllis was having a string of brief affairs. "It's not because she's worried about Freddie and is looking for comfort in the arms of other men, Mom. I don't think Phyllis is capable of worrying about anyone other than herself."

Jan and Scott came to the house regularly for Friday-evening dinners. The talk always revolved around the war. Freddie could say little in his letters, and even with the care he took, cut-out segments showed the censor's hand.

The fighting in the Pacific was bitter, with malaria and other jungle diseases taking a terrible toll. Allied troops had to face Japanese soldiers who were required by the fanatic code of *bushido* to fight to their deaths. On November 1, 1943, American troops landed on Bougainville. Twenty days later, U.S. marines landed on Tarawa and army troops on Makin, in the Gilbert Islands. In December, U.S. troops landed on New Britain. Casualties were heavy in these operations.

In March 1944, Vicky arranged a small first-birthday party for Carol at the Gramercy Park house. The party was attended by David and a collection of his small friends, an assortment of nurses, and Lilli. Lilli took snapshots of Carol and David to send on to Freddie. She doubted that Phyllis would bother.

Lilli treasured Freddie's letters. He wrote that he was optimistic about the outcome of the war, and was convinced he would make it home. "If I haven't been wiped out by now, you can be sure I'll come through safely. And I'm learning more here, on the move, than I'd ever dreamed possible. I know I'll be a better doctor for having served over here."

Many Americans grew optimistic as the year progressed. The Allied forces were on the offensive both in Europe and the Pacific. Many people were predicting victory before the year was over, but responsible leaders warned that there was much fighting ahead. American and British troops were fighting in Italy. For the first time, Allied troops were moving through prewar Japanese territory.

Within five weeks of each other, Alex's mother and father died. Lilli was especially sad for Vicky and Lou: They had lost their much-loved grandparents, and Sara, who was their other grandmother, was in a German internment camp. Lilli's first thought was that Vicky and Lou were too young to come to grips with such tragic losses, but then she remembered she had been only five when she had walked into the modest little flat in Marienbad to find her very young mother dead.

In April, American troops invaded New Guinea. On June 4, the Germans were driven out of Rome by Allied tank units. On June 6, the Allies established beachheads in Normandy. The D-Day invasion involved more than 4,000 ships, 3,000 planes, and troops that eventually approached over 4 million. The next month Saipan was taken by Americans after twenty-five days of brutal fighting. Lilli slept little these nights, knowing Freddie was somewhere in the Pacific.

In late July and August, Lilli, Alex, and Vicky and Lou spent every night by the radio listening to reports of the bloody fighting at Guam. After twenty days, Guam fell to the Americans. As she listened to the reports, Lilli reminded herself that Freddie was a doctor, not a combat officer. But knowing Freddie, she was sure he would be where he could be most helpful—where the fighting was heaviest.

"Lilli, we didn't have a 'sweet sixteen' party for Vicky," Alex said, grinning at his daughter. Like many Americans in wartime, Lilli and Alex kept festive occasions to a minimum. "Why don't we do something special for her seventeenth birthday?"

"Daddy, take us out to dinner and to see *I Remember Mama*," Vicky said. "Everybody says it's terrific."

"Okay. I'll see if we can get tickets." Alex gave Lilli a questioning look. "What's your second choice? *Oklahoma*?"

"Mother and I saw it when you were down in Washington," Vicky said. "Second choice would be *Voice of the Turtle*."

"Not at your age, young lady." Lilli turned to Alex. "If you can't get tickets for *I Remember Mama*, ask for *The Skin of Our Teeth*, or *Jacobowsky and the Colonel*."

THE EVENING of Vicky's birthday, Lilli heard Celestine calling her: "Miss Phyllis on the phone—"

"Thank you, Celestine. I'll take it in the library."

"Lilli, something awful has happened!" Phyllis's voice was shrill. "I just received a telegram from the War Department. Freddie's listed as 'missing in action.'"

Lilli took a deep breath, fought for control. "Now, Phyllis, let's not panic. He's just missing. You know what the fighting's been like in the Pacific. I'm sure we'll hear from him soon." She felt cold and frightened. More frightened than she ever had in her life.

"I suppose I ought to call all our friends," Phyllis said.

"I suppose you should. Goodbye, Phyllis."

Lilli sat absolutely still by the phone. She could not—would not—believe that Freddie had been killed in action. He was missing—hiding somewhere from the Japanese. Her mind moved back through the years, remembering all the precious moments with her older son. Always such a happy child. Warm, bright, compassionate. He couldn't be gone.

"Mother?" Lou stood in the doorway of the library. "Is Daddy home yet? Martine says Bertha's ready to serve dinner."

"Tell Bertha to hold dinner." *She would not cry.* "For about an hour. Daddy will be home then. And go find Vicky and come back here with her. There's something I have to tell you."

Vicky was the first to speak after Lilli told them.

"Sure, Freddie's all right," she said in shaky defiance.

"I'm going to keep writing anyway," Lou said. "So he'll have letters when he's found."

They sat together in the library and talked about Freddie. Then Alex arrived. He was determinedly calm. "You know Freddie—bright and resourceful. The fighting out there has been horrendous—he's probably hidden away in the jungle there, a few steps ahead of the Japanese. He'll probably stay there till the Americans come in and make it safe to emerge." He held Lilli's hand in his. "Did you call Jan?"

"Not yet. I was waiting for you to come home."

"Call her," Alex said gently. "And then we must tell Martine and the others."

IN THE MORNING, at Jan's insistence, Lilli called her attorney for Jacques's phone number. Someone—a family member—had to tell him about Freddie.

Her hands trembled as she waited for someone to pick up.

"Hello?" At last, a woman answered. Now she remembered that Jacques had remarried three years ago.

"May I speak to Jacques, please?"

There was a long pause. "Who is this?"

"Lilli Kahn. I was Jacques's first wife. I have news for him about our son, Freddie."

"He's not here. I'm Mrs. Laval now."

"When may I talk to him?"

"You can't. He's been dead seven months."

"I—I'm sorry, I didn't know."

"He told me when I married him he was a wealthy retiree. He left me nothing except a bunch of bills! So *that's* where the checks that came each month have been going. To pay the bills he left—" Jacques's latest wife sounded scared. She had been endorsing Jacques's checks these seven months and cashing them.

"My lawyer will be in touch with you," Lilli said softly. "A small trust set up for Jacques will be turned over to you." She hesitated. "Where is he buried?" For all the ugliness between them, she felt an unexpected sense of loss.

"He was cremated. He said he didn't want people staring at him in a coffin; I was to sprinkle his ashes in the ocean. I did it like he asked. We had a wake for him in his favorite bar down here.''

ON AUGUST 25, with Allied troops pushing the Germans from French soil, the underground rose up to liberate Paris. Shortly after the world knew that Paris was free again, Lilli received a long letter from Emilie, long Sara's second-in-command in the Paris salon. The salon, like most of Paris, had been undamaged during its years in the hands of the Germans.

"We had to close, like Molyneux and Chanel, but most of the fashion and beauty firms stayed open during the occupation. We look forward to your arrival in Paris when the war is finally over. We know you will reopen Princess Lilli, Paris.''

Emilie had no word of Sara. She urged Lilli to write and tell her what she knew of her dear friend's whereabouts. During the German occupation she had not dared go to Poissy, but immediately after the liberation she had gone there. The house had been destroyed. No one in the village seemed to know where Sara had gone.

Lilli was relieved that Paris was free again. She had been worried about her staff in the Paris salon and the workers in the factory. She worried, too, about the havoc the new V-1 rockets were causing in London; though Oliver belittled the new Nazi weapons, she was aware of the death and destruction they were causing.

Lilli's conviction that Freddie was alive was what kept her from falling apart. Her worst moments in the passing months were when letters began to be returned with the notification "Missing in Action" stamped in red. All indications pointed to a speedy end of the war. But on the same day that the world was stunned by the sudden death of Franklin Roosevelt—April 12, 1945—Lilli learned from Phyllis that Freddie's status had been changed from "missing in action" to "killed in action." According to the War Department, he had been shot down off the coast of Guam while on a medical evacuation mission. The plane, with all on board, had sunk.

"I don't believe it," Lilli said tightly as Alex gazed at her in anguish. "Alex, something inside me tells me Freddie is alive. I don't care what that telegram says. Freddie is coming home."

On May 7, Germany surrendered to the Allies. The surrender was signed in General Eisenhower's headquarters in Rheims. Lilli waited anxiously for some word of Aunt Sara. After days of searching, Oliver came up with sad news: Only weeks after her incarceration, Sara had died of a heart attack. She was to be honored posthumously by the French government. The medal would be forwarded to Lilli, to rest beside the one given to her for her services in World War I.

American leaders were convinced that the war in the Pacific would be over in a matter of weeks. On August 14—eight days after the atom bomb had been dropped on Hiroshima—President Truman announced the unconditional surrender of Japan. At last, the world was at peace.

On Freddie's thirty-fifth birthday—in mid-August—Lilli didn't go to the salon. Alex stayed home with her. He understood that today she could not face a world that accepted Freddie's death. Only Vicky was as convinced as her mother that Freddie would come home to them now that the war was over.

Lilli was grateful that Vicky had chosen to attend Barnard College right in New York, though she dismissed her daughter's passion for the Broadway theater, just as she dismissed Vicky's declaration that one day she would be an actress. She was determined that Vicky and Lou would come into the business.

Lilli was stunned and furious when she learned that Phyllis had hired a battery of lawyers to try to wrest away control of Freddie's trust—due to be turned over to him on his thirty-fifth birthday—from the bank.

"Can she do this, Alex?" she asked.

"We'll talk to the lawyers tomorrow. I don't think so." But he looked concerned. "As I recall, the terms of the trust call for the money to be held in trust by the bank for Carol and David until they're twenty-five."

"Then we'll fight her! She'll squander every penny, Alex."
Ten million dollars.

"Don't worry, Lilli. We'll be there tomorrow afternoon when
our lawyers meet with hers."

Suddenly Lilli realized how tired Alex looked. The long
hours, the seven-day weeks he had put in during the war, were
catching up with him. She should take him away for a rest. But
she couldn't bring herself to leave New York when each day the
tabloids carried some story about a soldier or sailor, believed
missing in action, who had surfaced very much alive.

The next day Lilli and Alex sat in on a heated meeting with
the attorneys. Phyllis was claiming—untruthfully—that she
couldn't raise her children in the manner to which they were
accustomed without access to Freddie's trust fund. The first
meeting ended with Phyllis's attorneys insisting they would go
to court.

The following day Alex called their attorneys to arrange another meeting to discuss a compromise. The meeting was
scheduled for early the following week, though their attorneys
were convinced that Phyllis wanted to take the case to court.
Much as Lilli recoiled from a public battle, she was determined that the trust be handled properly.

"Lilli, are you sure you want to go to this meeting?" Alex
asked. "Let me go alone. Phyllis upsets you so."

She managed a smile. "I have to be there, Alex."

Lilli and Alex were the first to arrive at the attorneys' offices. They sat with the two men around a conference table and
discussed various aspects of the case. Again, Lilli realized how
pale and tired Alex looked. How dare Phyllis put them through
this!

At last Phyllis's team of attorneys was ushered into the room.
They waited another twenty-five minutes for Phyllis to appear, offering no apology for the delay. She looked beautiful
and detached, but there was a glint of triumph in her eyes. She
sat back in her chair, her long, nylon-clad legs crossed at the
ankle. She pulled a cigarette from a silver case and waited for

one of the men to light it for her. After an awkward pause, the younger of her attorneys leaned forward with his lighter.

Alex's hand reached for Lilli's while the attorney began to negotiate. Almost immediately the arguing became heated. Phyllis interrupted to accuse Lilli of trying to prevent her from having what was rightfully hers because it would mean acknowledging that her son was dead.

"You are being absurd, Lilli. Freddie is dead. You'll have to accept that." She flicked ashes across the top of the fine oak table while an attorney reached belatedly for an ashtray.

"I suggest we allow the attorneys to handle these negotiations," Alex said brusquely. "We have—"

Suddenly Alex stiffened, grasped at his chest, and fell forward across the table.

"Alex!" Lilli screamed and stumbled to her feet. "Alex—"

"I'll call an ambulance!" One of their two attorneys charged toward the door.

"No!" Alex gasped, massaging his chest. "It's just indigestion. I'll call Bill Bernstein when we get home and—"

"I'll call him now." Lilli ran out of the room.

It seemed to take years for the receptionist to summon Dr. Bernstein to the phone.

"Yes, Lilli?"

Briefly, she explained the situation.

"I'll send a private ambulance immediately." His voice was calm but firm. "I want Alex in the hospital."

Lilli stood by while Alex, chalk-white and obviously in pain, tried to assure the others that he was all right. She was only dimly aware that Phyllis had left. Let her have her money, she thought in disgust. Who had time for such ugliness?

The ambulance arrived in record time, and Lilli went with Alex to the hospital. When they arrived, Dr. Bernstein was there to greet them. Lilli was told to wait in a private suite. She phoned the house to ask Martine to track down Vicky and Lou and send them to the hospital. Jan and Scott were out of town for a few days.

Lou arrived first, pale and breathless. Vicky appeared a few minutes later. Perhaps she shouldn't have scared the children this way, Lilli thought as she held them in her arms, but she'd been selfish; she needed their support.

At last, Alex was wheeled into the bedroom of the suite. "Didn't mean to be so dramatic," he murmured as he went by.

"Don't talk, Alex." Lilli looked at Dr. Bernstein. The look in his eyes turned her to ice.

"A private nurse will arrive shortly," Bernstein said. "I'll go make the arrangements now."

Signaling to Lou and Vicky to keep Alex busy, Lilli walked with Dr. Bernstein into the sitting room of the suite and to a window looking down on the busy Manhattan street.

"How is he, Bill?"

"I wish I could be hopeful. I'm afraid we can only wait and see."

"Can't you do something? Bill, he's—"

"Everything that can be done has been done." She felt the weight of his hand on her shoulder. "I'll be back in a few minutes."

She returned to Alex's bedside. Vicky was leaning over him, holding one hand. Both of them had tears in their eyes.

"Hold my hand, my darling..." With great effort, Alex lifted his hand. She took it, felt the warm, familiar pressure. "You've been so good for me, Lilli."

His hand went limp.

"Alex?" No. *No, she wouldn't believe it*. "Alex?" She took a deep breath. "Lou, go find Dr. Bernstein." She must not fall apart. "Tell him to come instantly."

FOR WEEKS Lilli wondered what was left in her world. First she had lost Sara, now Alex—and Freddie was still missing. More than ever, she wouldn't believe that Freddie might be dead. Even Jacques's death had been a shock. Alex had been only sixty. She had imagined another twenty or more years with him at her side. Now, at fifty-eight, she was alone.

The loneliness was unbearable. She thanked God for Jan and Scott, Vicky and Lou. Those first few weeks they never left her alone in the house she had shared with Alex for eighteen years.

Again she threw herself into the salon, to see her through the long days and longer nights. At times, running the vast Princess Lilli empire without Alex at her side seemed inconceivable. But she knew she must. She still dreamed of the days when Vicky and Lou would join the business. Lou was enrolled at Columbia. He planned to become an accountant. In time, he would head Princess Lilli's accounting department.

Once it was possible again for civilians to go to Europe, Lilli left for London. The joy of reconciliation with friends and staff was dimmed by what she saw of the ravages of war. Charles and Frances's son, Robbie, had lost a leg in battle, and several workers in the London salon had been killed.

Oliver went with her to Paris to reestablish the salon there. Again there was the joy of reconciliation—but for Lilli, Paris was a stranger without Sara. She and Oliver went out to see the house at Poissy, now a shambles. Standing before the remains of the small country house, Lilli felt as though she were watching the years parade before her. And remembering, she felt her life coming together again. Suddenly, she couldn't wait to return home to her children and grandchildren. How selfish of her to abandon herself to grief, to run off leaving her children to grieve alone!

TEARS OF PLEASURE filled Lilli's eyes when she saw her welcoming committee—Jan, Scott, Vicky, Lou, and Greg—standing on the pier and waving. They swept her off to an early lunch at Jan and Scott's apartment.

"Why didn't you take a ship that landed on a weekday?" Vicky teased. "Then I could have cut classes."

Lilli asked about David and Carol, her face softening as she thought how much they were like Freddie when he was a child. Though Jan and Phyllis had drifted out of their earlier close friendship, Jan had dropped by regularly in Lilli's absence to see them.

"They're fine, Mother," Jan said, a little too brightly.

"Something's wrong." Lilli looked at each of them. "What's happened to David and Carol?"

"Nothing, Mother." Vicky patted her hand. "They're wonderful. I saw them in the park yesterday afternoon. They asked when you'd be back."

"Jan," Scott said quietly, "we have to tell her." He turned to Lilli. "The children are well. But Phyllis has decided she doesn't want them seeing any of us. She had her attorney advise us that none of Freddie's family would be welcome at her home. I gather she'd prefer that they never realize their father was part Jewish."

"How dare she!" Lilli exploded. "After I allowed her to take over the trust fund!" She sat silent for a moment, her mind racing. "Phyllis will not stop me from seeing my grandchildren. I don't care what it takes."

LILLI CHECKED HER WATCH as a particularly long-winded copywriter discussed a segment of the new summer advertising campaign. "I'm sorry," she interrupted crisply. "I have an important appointment. We'll continue with this tomorrow morning."

Henri was waiting at the curb with the Rolls. Right after the war, Lilli had offered him a generous pension plus a small house outside of Paris, but he had chosen to remain on the job. Like herself, she guessed, he would die in retirement.

"It's so nice out," she said as Henri pulled the car door open for her. "The children will be in the park."

Four afternoons a week Lilli left the salon to spend an hour with David and Carol. She had quickly discovered that Phyllis was away from the city more than she was there—off to Palm Beach or Newport or Paris or the Riviera, wherever wealthy socialites were appearing in the postwar world. It proved easy to arrange these little "visits" with the maid and housekeeper. The nursemaid was reluctant, however, to let Lilli bring the children into her own house. She longed to bring her children and grandchildren together, as she had been able to do when

Alex was alive. She remembered how pleased Alex had been when Freddie had solemnly shared in the observance of all the Jewish holidays.

Early in 1947, Lilli learned from a patron of the salon that Phyllis was engaged to be married. "Darling, didn't you know?" the chic socialite asked. "*Everyone's* been talking about it."

"No, I seldom see Phyllis. Who is she marrying?"

"Carter Logan the Third. The shipping-company Logans, though I gather *he's* in real estate."

"I hope Phyllis will be very happy." Quickly she changed the subject to a benefit ball both women would be attending the following week, then excused herself and hurried back to her office.

She was trembling as she sat at her desk and thought about David and Carol sharing their lives with a stepfather. At nine, David barely remembered his real father. Carol had never even seen him! Why did it have to happen this way?

She reached for the phone and dialed her attorney's office. She would ask for a complete report on Carter Logan III. She had to know more about this man who was to take Freddie's place in her grandchildren's lives.

39

LILLI READ the report on Carter Logan III over for the third time. He was in his forties, divorced, no children. He was considered an aggressive and shrewd real-estate operator. Wealthy from his inheritance, he was nonetheless dedicated to multiplying his fortune. Too busy, Lilli interpreted, to take an active part in raising two young stepchildren.

In June, Phyllis and Carter were married quietly in a judge's chambers. After a lavish reception at the Plaza, they left for a three-week honeymoon at the Grand Hotel on Mackinac Island in Michigan. Instinct told Lilli that somewhere in Logan's business enterprises there was an angle that could help her spend more time with her grandchildren. She began to check into his real-estate activities.

Not long after the newlyweds returned to New York, Lilli learned that Carter's real-estate syndicate was buying up property that would allow him to build an impressive office structure on Madison Avenue. Surveying the area, she found a five-story brownstone sitting on a prime piece of land. She immediately went to her real-estate broker.

"Sorry, Mrs. Kahn." The broker leaned back in his chair. "The elderly couple who own that property refuse to sell. Carter Logan has been doing his damnedest for six months to change their minds."

"Mr. Hollis," Lilli said quietly, "I want that house. Tell them I'm prepared to offer them one million dollars."

The broker stared at her. "It's not worth anywhere near that!"

"To me it is." She smiled. "Please make the offer."

As Lilli anticipated, the owners accepted her bid, and the closing was arranged. She knew that soon she would be hearing from Carter. By now he had bought or contracted for every foot of property in the area for his office building, designed to be one of the tallest and most modern anywhere in Manhattan.

A week after the closing, Carter phoned Lilli and asked if they could meet. She told him she was happy to oblige. When he arrived for a conference in her office at the salon, she suspected—from his nervousness—that Phyllis had provided him with a distorted image of her former mother-in-law. She inquired politely after Phyllis's health, wished them every happiness, and, with the amenities out of the way, waited for his approach.

"I'm quite certain the figure the former owners quoted me has been much escalated," he said, "but I know also that you are an admirable businesswoman. You're aware that I need that piece of property before we can start to build. I'm willing to pay one million for it."

"The figure I paid, Mr. Logan, *was* one million." Lilli looked him straight in the eye. "That is all I ask for it, plus one personal stipulation: I want a written agreement from Phyllis that David and Carol—my grandchildren—will be allowed to spend one day out of each week with me."

He looked startled, then paused, thinking. "I'm sure Phyllis will be amenable to that."

"Good." She stood up. "Bring a notarized affidavit to that effect to the closing. The property will be yours."

OVER FRIDAY-NIGHT DINNER, on the eve of the closing for the brownstone, Lilli told her family about the negotiations with Carter.

"Lilli," Scott chuckled. "I would never want to cross *you* in any action."

"When do we get to start seeing David and Carol?" Vicky asked. "I mean, outside of your clandestine meetings?"

"We'll see them every Sunday," Lilli said. "Beginning this week."

"I bet Phyllis won't even know they're here," Jan said. "She's too busy with her social life to notice *anything*. Once she and Carter have been married for a while, I'm sure she'll be running out of the city most of the time."

"I'm happy that David and Carol will become part of the family again." Lilli gazed about the table. "I'm happiest when I'm with my family."

She only wished that Alex could be here to see how she'd brought David and Carol back into the fold. He would have been proud of her. Would she ever stop missing him?

Since there was no way she could keep track of how Phyllis handled Freddie's trust fund, Lilli established—privately—trust funds for David and Carol. It made her happy to know she was providing them with a lifetime of financial security. But recent events had given her a new perspective: Money had not kept Freddie from dying in Guam; money had not helped Alex survive his heart attack. In the end, money wasn't really worth a damn.

LILLI TOLD HERSELF that life was made up of a series of compromises. Gradually, she was learning to accept her losses. As always, she was grateful for the distractions of the business. She was determined to make Princess Lilli even more prominent in its field, and she was keenly aware of new competition, particularly Charles Revson. His innovation for "Revlon" of matching nail polish and lipsticks was causing a sensation. She became obsessed with creating a new perfume. When she was at last satisfied that this had been developed, she launched an electrifying advertising campaign. It was almost as though Alex were beside her.

Of course, she had her worries: She wished Vicky would abandon her ambition to become a Broadway actress and begin showing an interest in the business. It would be satisfying to know that Vicky and Lou would be there when the time came for her to step down. Not that she planned on it anytime soon.

In the fall of 1947, Lilli returned to the salon from a business luncheon to be told by her secretary that an army officer had called twice on what he reported was "urgent personal business." She was to phone him as soon as possible.

"Thank you, Annette." Lilli settled herself at her desk. "Anything else?"

Annette briefed her on other messages and left the office. Lilli frowned. Why on earth was an army officer calling her? Was it something to do with a posthumous award for Alex? She hesitated, then reached for her private line and dialed the number. A local number, she noticed.

Within a few moments she was connected to Colonel Waters. "This is Lilli Kahn," she said. "You phoned me?"

"Oh, yes..." There was an uncomfortable silence. "Please understand, we have not been able to confirm officially what I'm about to tell you. But the U.S. naval headquarters in Guam has informed us that a man identifying himself as a flight surgeon in the U.S. Army Air Force has surfaced in Guam. He has asked that you be notified—"

"Freddie?" *It was happening. Just like she had kept telling herself it would.* "My son, Major Frederic Laval?"

"That's the name he has given us." Colonel Waters was guarded. "He has no dog tags. We're in the process of confirming identification. He's currently undergoing tests in the navy hospital in Guam."

"Is he all right?"

"He's fine. This is just a routine medical checkup. He was held prisoner, along with a flight nurse, since 1944. By Japs—hidden away in the caves in Guam—who were unaware that the war was over."

"I'll go to him. I'll fly—"

"We can send you out by army plane," the colonel said. "The government is aware of your own record in World War One and your husband's in both world wars. Tell us how soon you can be ready to leave."

Within hours, Lilli was on a U.S. Army plane, wishing that Alex could be beside her. Before leaving, she had asked Jan to tell Phyllis what was happening. There was no doubt in her mind that the man was truly Freddie. Would he be upset to discover that Phyllis had remarried? Probably not. It would be another embarrassing situation, to be corrected with a divorce. Phyllis had given Freddie two children, but she had never really been his wife. He hadn't even asked that she be notified. He had asked that his mother be told, Lilli thought. He knew how she had mourned him.

IN HER SHEEREST black chiffon negligee, Phyllis paced about her bedroom like a caged tigress—chain-smoking, constantly pausing to check the time. What the hell was taking Carter so long? She'd told his secretary it was urgent, that he was to come home immediately.

She froze as she heard Carter's voice in the hall; he was talking with Raymond. She rushed to the door of their bedroom and out into the hall, forgetting Carter's demand that she not display herself before Raymond in her negligee. Carter didn't have to know that Raymond saw her in much less.

"Carter!" she called imperiously. "It certainly took you long enough to get here!"

"I was in a board meeting." He sounded testy as he hurried up the stairs. "What is it? Did something happen to the children?"

"To their father! Carter, Freddie's alive! His mother is flying to Guam right now to be with him."

He turned pale. "I'll call the lawyers immediately."

She threw herself into his arms. "How could Freddie do this to me? How will I ever face our friends again?"

"We're not the first couple to find ourselves in this kind of situation." Carter quickly regained his poise. "You'll go out to Reno for a divorce from Freddie. We'll be remarried the moment the divorce is final."

"Suppose Freddie refuses to let me divorce him? Suppose he wants to come back to me? He's such a nut about the kids."

"Let him have custody."

"No." She pulled away. "I won't give Freddie and his bitch of a mother that kind of satisfaction. They can see the children once a week. That's it. I'll never forget how Lilli manipulated us for visitation rights."

"Phyllis, you want the divorce, don't you?" *Why was Carter looking at her that way? Did he think he would get out of their marriage this way?*

"Darling, Freddie will agree to the divorce." All at once she felt secure. "He wouldn't want a scandal that would embarrass his precious children. Have your attorneys handle it. They'll know what to do." But she would keep the children, she thought with vindictive satisfaction.

THE FLIGHT TO GUAM—with several brief stopovers—seemed endless. All Lilli thought about was seeing Freddie again, holding him in her arms. This wasn't a dream that would disappear with the morning.

At last she caught sight of the sun-washed Guam beach from her window. During the turbulent landing, she closed her eyes and prayed until she felt the wheels hit the runway. A military jeep stood by to take her to the hospital. She trembled as she was escorted through a series of corridors, her voice uneven as she tried to make small talk with her guide.

"Mother?" There he was, standing in the narrow corridor, looking just as he had in June 1942—except that he was thinner and tanned. "Oh, Mother!" His voice cracked.

"Freddie!" They embraced. "My baby." It was real. He was alive. "I prayed it would happen this way. I always knew you'd come home to us."

Freddie took her inside his room and explained how Debbie Lawrence, the flight nurse who had gone down on the plane with him, had pulled him into a life raft she managed to get into the water. They were the only two who had survived the crash.

"You'll meet Debbie later," he said. "I know you'll like her." From the look on his face, Lilli suspected that he was in love with her. "It was only because I was a doctor and she a nurse that the Japs kept us alive," he said. "We took care of three badly wounded among them in the caves."

"I'll be personally indebted to her forever," Lilli said.

He brightened. "Why don't I bring her here?" Within a few moments, Freddie returned hand in hand with a small, pretty young woman, also in pajamas and robe. "Mother, this is Debbie."

Lilli drew the dark-haired nurse into her arms. "Thank you. Thank you for saving my son."

Debbie laughed. "I needed someone to help me row." But her eyes were serious. "I doubt if I could have endured these years without Freddie."

"Your family must be as excited as we are."

"I grew up in foster homes," Debbie said, "none of them especially happy. I worked my way through nursing school and joined the army air force early in the war. I have a few friends scattered about, but no family." She smiled shyly.

"Mother, do you have pictures of the children?" Freddie's face glowed in anticipation.

"What kind of a grandmother would I be not to have pictures?" Lilli reached into her purse, remembering now that Freddie had never seen his daughter—only the snapshots she had sent with her letters.

Freddie gazed long at the pictures, tears of joy and pride in his eyes. "David's almost ten," he told Debbie, handing her some of the snapshots. He seemed reluctant to let go of them. "Carol must be almost four. I've never seen her."

"David remembers his daddy." Lilli knew instinctively that it was a question on Freddie's mind. "And Carol knows about her father, who was a hero in the army air force."

"What about Phyllis?" All at once Freddie was uneasy.

"She married again," Lilli said gently. "Of course, it's not legal."

His face showed no emotion. "Our marriage was dead before I enlisted. She can file for divorce and remarry her current husband." He hesitated. "As soon as Phyllis divorces me, Debbie and I will be married." He paused. "There's something else, Mama. I won't ever be a surgeon again. I injured my right hand in the crash.'' He held up his hand: two fingers wouldn't bend. ''But I can still practice medicine—among the poor. And Debbie and I will fight for peace in the world. What happened in this decade must never happen again.''

''It can't.'' Lilli nodded. ''You know now about the United Nations. It's dedicated to international peace.''

''But Debbie and I have read about the 'cold war,' '' Freddie said softly, ''and we worry. We were told about the atomic-bomb tests at Bikini Atoll in the Pacific last year, and—''

''Please, let's have no such thoughts today.'' Lilli hugged them both. ''Freddie, this is the most wonderful day in my life. You're safe and well.''

LILLI, FREDDIE, AND DEBBIE arrived at the Gramercy Park house at dusk. The family, as well as Martine and the other staff members, had assembled in the library, waiting to welcome him home.

After a brief shy period—which Lilli attributed to Debbie's presence—Vicky was her normal effervescent self, hanging on her older brother's every word. Lou was, as usual, reserved but warm. He kept staring at Freddie as though to reassure himself that his brother was really alive.

''Where are David and Carol?'' Freddie asked finally, disappointed that the children were not there.

''The governess is bringing them over,'' Jan said. ''They should be here soon.'' All at once her face was serious. ''Phyllis asked if you would call her lawyer to confirm that you're willing to go along with a Reno divorce.''

''Of course.'' Freddie exchanged a relieved glance with Debbie. ''What's his number, Jan?''

''Scott has it.'' Jan frowned. ''To listen to Phyllis, you'd think your return was an affront to her reputation. I don't think anything has shaken up her family so much since the election of FDR.''

Freddie reached for the slip of paper Scott extended. "She can leave for Reno tonight, provided we agree to certain conditions."

They were all silent while Freddie talked with Phyllis's lawyer. Lilli listened anxiously as they discussed joint custody. Freddie didn't seem happy. Lilli guessed Phyllis meant to retain custody. At a signal from her, he brought up the question of the trust fund. Even Phyllis realized that now this must be turned over to Freddie.

Within a few minutes he was off the phone. "Phyllis's lawyer pointed out that no court would give me custody of the children—it always goes to the mother. But the children can come to me once a week and I can have them for four weeks during the summer. Phyllis is leaving for Reno right away. The trust fund—minus what Phyllis has gone through—reverts to me. We've agreed to an amount for child support."

Freddie reached for Debbie's hand. In six weeks he would be free to marry her. He turned to his younger sister and brother and his nephew. "I can't get over how you kids have all grown up."

"I'm a sophomore at Barnard," Vicky said, "and Lou's a freshman at Columbia."

"And you, Greg . . ." Freddie punched him playfully. "You were the runt of the litter. Now you're taller than I am."

Greg was looking at Freddie's hand. "What happened?"

"It was hurt in the crash. The bones didn't knit properly." Lilli watched Jan's tense observation of this exchange, knowing that Freddie was deliberately making little of his injury in light of Greg's handicap. "So I won't be a surgeon." He shrugged. "I can still practice medicine. I can still work for peace. I can do a lot of things."

At Henri's appearance, Lilli ordered everyone into the dining room. Then the doorbell rang and Freddie charged down the hall to the door, pulling it open. Lilli was right behind him.

The governess stood at the door, flanked by David and Carol, both impeccably dressed. For a moment Freddie was speechless.

David was the first to speak. "Daddy?"

"David . . ," Freddie paused before he leaned forward to embrace his son. "You grew an awful lot while I was away." Now Freddie turned to Carol. Her sea-green eyes were wide and uncertain. "And this is Carol," he said softly, dropping to his haunches before her.

"Are you my daddy?" she whispered.

"I'm your daddy." He lifted her in his arms and kissed her.

"Carol looks just like you," Lilli said with pride. "Just like David."

Carol turned to her. "Grandma, can we have ice cream?"

Lilli laughed. "If you eat your dinner. Come, let's all go into the dining room."

Lilli gazed about the table. This was one of the beautiful times in her life—when she was surrounded by her children and grandchildren. Now that Freddie was home, David and Carol would see much of their father. She and Freddie would make sure of that.

40

LILLI WOULD HAVE BEEN HAPPY in the ensuing months, except that she sensed Freddie's frustration at not being able to see David and Carol when he pleased. As Jan had predicted, Phyllis was often away from the city; but the servants were afraid to allow the children to visit with their father or grandmother at any other than the specifically allotted times.

In July, when Freddie and Debbie came out to spend a month at the Southampton house, they were able, per the agreement, to bring David and Carol with them. Lilli, too, took off a week at the beginning of July and another at the end of the month to spend with Freddie, Debbie, and the children.

Vicky came out for the weekends. To Lilli's irritation, she was taking summer courses at a drama school, and seemed to love them.

In September, Vicky and Lou returned to school, but both came down from their respective campuses most weekends, which delighted Lilli. Vicky said her campus was practically deserted from Friday afternoon until Monday morning because so many Barnard students commuted. Lou said he came home to catch up on sleep.

When Phyllis announced that she had rented a house in Palm Beach shortly before New Year's with the intention of remaining there until late March, Vicky was angry that Freddie didn't go into court to demand custody of his children.

"Mother, Phyllis is *never* in the city." Phyllis, it seemed, dashed off in one direction and Carter in another—though Carter's trips were largely for business. "If she didn't scare the servants to death, David and Carol could move in with Freddie and Debbie or with you for most of the year. If we didn't sneak around to see them, they'd die of loneliness!"

"Vicky, be patient. When you're as old as I am, you'll understand that it's important to sit back and wait for the right moment to act in situations like this."

AFTER EACH OF HER WHIRLWIND TRIPS to the salons and retail outlets about the country, Lilli made a practice of spending time in the New York salon to chat with longtime patrons and offer a pleasant word to newcomers. In late February, back from a West Coast trip, she knocked lightly and invaded the treatment room where a gossipy society matron—a patron of the Princess Lilli salons in various locales—was being pummeled by a Swedish masseuse.

"Lilli, have you heard the latest about your ex-daughter-in-law?" the lady asked archly.

"No." Lilli prepared herself. "Why don't you tell me, Rita?"

"Well, Carter is demanding a divorce. He caught her in bed with the chauffeur. Of course, he was only confirming what everybody else had long known. I hear her parents are so furious they won't even talk to her."

Lilli smiled. "Carter will make sure she ends up without a cent of alimony." *And Phyllis without funds would be open to a deal.*

Lilli hired a private investigator to learn the details. Earlier than planned, Phyllis had returned to New York to fight the divorce. Carter had moved out of their apartment and into a suite at the Plaza. He refused to talk to her except through his attorneys. Rather than go through an ugly New York divorce—sure to be splashed across the tabloids—he agreed to send her to Reno for a six-week divorce. When she returned, she would have six months to vacate their duplex. She would receive an allowance for that period only. After six months, Phyllis would be out on her own—with her family cold and unreceptive.

Lilli phoned Phyllis to set up a meeting.

"Why do you want to see me, Lilli?"

"To discuss a business arrangement that could provide you with a million dollars. Tomorrow morning at ten, Phyllis, in my office at the salon."

Lilli gave orders to Annette that no one was to disturb her while she was with Phyllis. At fifteen minutes past ten, Annette ushered Phyllis into Lilli's office and left the two alone.

"Phyllis, I won't beat about the bush," Lilli said after the door had closed. "I know your financial situation. I'm willing to pay you one million dollars if you'll sign over full custody of David and Carol to their father. Arrangements will be made for you to see them, but legally Freddie will make all decisions concerning their care." Her heart pounded as she watched Phyllis's expression. Phyllis was quiet for barely a minute before she nodded.

"Okay, it's a deal. By *certified* check. And I'll want my attorney to clear the papers."

David and Carol moved into the charming house in Irvington that Freddie and Debbie had recently bought. Someday—but not now, Freddie told Lilli—the children would be told about their grandmother's "deal."

Vicky was appalled. "Phyllis is so rotten! Imagine, taking money for her own children!"

"Vicky, I'm grateful that she did," Lilli said. "Of course, Freddie and Debbie are ecstatic."

"But it's wrong that she should come out so comfortably."

"Darling, Phyllis creates her own hell," Lilli said softly. "Don't be vindictive. Be happy that the children are away from her."

HER SPIRITS SOARING, Vicky emerged from the subway at Twenty-third Street and Fourth Avenue and headed toward Gramercy Park. This morning she had received notice that she had been accepted as an apprentice at a summer-stock company in upstate New York. It was the first major decision she had ever made for herself in her whole life. She had cut her first class to dash over to the coffee shop at 112th and Amsterdam where Lou always had breakfast to tell him her news.

"You're *paying* to be an apprentice," he'd teased. "Fat chance they'd turn you down!"

She'd have to tell Mother tonight. For two years she had talked about breaking into theater after Barnard, and graduation was only weeks away. Mother still had that obsession about Lou and her going into Princess Lilli. Jan said it had been the same way when she and Freddie were young. Why didn't Lou come right out and say he wanted to be a writer?

College had been more than an education for her, Vicky thought as she walked toward the house. It had taught her how the rest of the world lived. Before college she had never set foot in a subway. She'd known nothing about running down to Klein's Annex—only a five-minute walk from the house, but it might as well have been in another country—to shop for bargains. Budgeting had been a foreign word to her. She would be twenty-two years old in August, and as long as she could remember, people had been saying, "Oh, you're Princess Lilli's daughter!" She couldn't spend all her life being the daughter of a living legend.

Of course, it was great not to have to worry about money. She wouldn't start receiving the income from her trust until she was twenty-five, but Mother kept her checking account healthy. Sometimes she'd felt uncomfortable that Linda, her roommate, had to work so many hours each week to be able to stay in school.

Back at the house, Vicky went straight up to her room to study until dinnertime. Tomorrow evening she was meeting Linda to go to a playhouse down in the Village to see an Ibsen revival. Afterward, they'd meet a couple of boys from Columbia at that new coffee shop on East Fifth Street. Why was she feeling so guilty about not going to the salon?

Around 6:30 Vicky heard the first sounds downstairs that told her the family was beginning to arrive for the Friday-night dinner. Sometimes she was annoyed that they had to be home for this weekly ritual, but she always enjoyed the get-togethers. With the children, they were ten at the table—when Greg showed up. He had a way of weaseling out at the last minute.

Sometimes, even now, she missed seeing Daddy sitting there at the head of the table. Daddy had been the family arbitrator. She wished he were here to make Mother understand that she and Lou had a right to run their own lives.

"Vicky?" It was Lou, knocking on the door.

"Yeah?"

"You tell Mother yet?"

"No. I'll tell her tomorrow. I don't want to spoil her Friday night." But she'd told Mother for years that she didn't want to be part of the business. Mother just didn't want to hear her.

Freddie and Debbie were in the library with David and Carol. Jan had just arrived. "Scott's coming straight from the office," Jan said as Vicky and Lou walked in. "He had a late conference. And Greg should be here any minute." But by the way Jan said it, Vicky knew she wasn't sure. "All excited about graduation?"

Vicky shrugged. "Not really." She'd be excited about landing a part in a Broadway play—even a three-line part.

Within a few minutes the entire family—except for Greg— was settled in the library, awaiting word from Henri that Bertha was ready to serve dinner. Freddie announced that David planned to follow in his father's footsteps and go to medical school.

Freddie wasn't seriously disturbed that his war injury prevented him from performing surgery, Vicky thought. He and two other war-veteran doctors were running a storefront clinic on the Lower East Side, and he and Debbie were all involved in a group concerned about the future use of the atom bomb.

Henri arrived to announce dinner.

"We won't wait for Greg," Lilli said. "He's probably tied up with something at school." Mother always worried about upsetting Jan, Vicky thought. Jan had a chip on her shoulder because Mother had had two more children after *she* was already grown. But Vicky knew that Jan loved her half brother and sister.

Jan brightened. "That must be Greg at the door now."

Greg was a pain. He could be *so* charming when he was in the mood, and so nasty when he wasn't. He was always sweet to strangers. He was actually quite good-looking, though Lou said he ignored all the girls they knew. Was he waiting for Princess Elizabeth to come over from London to go out with him? He seemed to think that because of his arm, everybody ought to bow down and cater to him.

"All right," Lilli said after Greg had deposited a swift kiss on her cheek, "let's all go in to dinner."

THE NEXT MORNING, Vicky went downstairs earlier and with a good deal more apprehension than usual. She knew her mother would be in the breakfast room having coffee and reading the *Times*. Right after their usual morning kiss, Vicky told Lilli about the apprenticeship at the summer-stock company. She waited, her throat tight, watching her mother's expression.

"You're quite sure about this, Vicky?"

"Quite sure."

"And when you come back from summer stock?" Vicky saw the pain in her eyes.

"I'll take classes and make Broadway rounds." And in the fall, she would tell her mother that she planned to get her own apartment.

"I suppose it would be sticky-sentimental to suggest I give a graduation party for you?" There was a touch of hostility in Lilli's voice.

"Nobody does it these days, Mama."

"Well, I'm going to adore sitting there at commencement," Lilli said softly. "Jan refused to attend the exercises, but I was there for Freddie's graduation and I'll be there for yours and for Lou's, God willing."

"Mother, you're still young!" Mother might be sixty-two, but she looked twenty years younger. She certainly *acted* twenty years younger.

"Never mind." Lilli waved a hand. "Will you be leaving soon after graduation?"

"Two days later. Mother, it's going to be so exciting!" She wished her mother could share her excitement.

"I'm sure it will be, darling. But remember, there's always a place for you in the business. Someday, it'll belong to my four children."

VICKY WAS ECSTATIC to be part of the summer-stock company, though the work was grueling. She painted scenery, helped out in the box office, set up props, distributed handbills. In the last play of the season, *Carousel*, she had a walk-on, along with Marcia Finch—with whom she shared a small attic room in the house where the company lived for the summer. She dreaded going back to New York. But at least she wouldn't be going back to the old life. She and Marcia would get an apartment together. For the time being Marcia would go back to her room at the Rehearsal Club.

"The apartment will be cheap," Marcia said on the ride back to Manhattan one early September morning. "My budget is tight." After two years at a small Georgia college, Marcia had come to New York and worked as a typist for almost a year. She'd managed to save enough to pay for her apprenticeship and provide a tiny nest egg.

"Paula says we can work part-time through one of the office temporaries," Vicky said. "We'll make rounds the rest of the time."

"We have to try to get a part in one of those companies operating non-Equity," Marcia said. "It's a showcase. Agents come down."

"My mother is going to be shocked when I tell her I'm not coming back home." Vicky dreaded the confrontation.

"Don't worry about it—she'll get used to the idea." Marcia smiled. "But my mother would be, too, if my family lived in New York." Marcia's family—her father, mother, and four younger sisters—lived just a step above poverty in a small Georgia town.

"Johnny said to try his old building over on East Seventh Street," Vicky said. Johnny was currently being kept in style by an older woman. "His landlord loves having show-biz people in the house—he's a frustrated playwright."

Before returning to the Gramercy Park house, Vicky went apartment hunting with Marcia. Johnny's former landlord showed them a tiny apartment consisting of two cell-like bedrooms, a minute living room, and a fair-size kitchen. The rent was forty-six dollars a month. The two girls grabbed it.

As Vicky had anticipated, her mother was shaken that she was not returning to the family house, and that she and Marcia had gone ahead on their own and rented an apartment. "But what's wrong with the house?" she said. "I thought you loved it here."

"Mother, I do. But I'm twenty-two years old. It's time I was out on my own. At my age you were married, a mother, running Princess Lilli in Paris!"

For an instant Vicky thought her mother was going to lose her temper. But she knew Lilli prided herself on understanding the mood of the times. And this *was* a time when girls her age were striking out for independence.

"Darling, do what makes you happy." She leaned forward and kissed Vicky tenderly. "But please—let me see you every once in a while, okay?"

VICKY AND MARCIA threw themselves into the fast-growing Off Broadway scene. They haunted the Off Broadway theater groups that were sprouting up and around town, grateful for small parts even in bad plays that ran for only two or three nights. Following the advice in a copy of *Show Business*, they went to a photographer and had "composites" made up. They made the rounds of agents submitting talent for the TV programs filmed in New York. Marcia was ecstatic when an agent prepared to send her for a walk-on in a mystery series, until it became clear that the agent expected her to spend a night or two with him as well.

"Vicky, I don't know how to handle those creeps."

"They're not all like that," Vicky said cheerfully. "You'll find other parts. Better ones."

Late in the spring, surprised by Lou's curiosity about the Off Broadway world, Vicky invited him up to the apartment for dinner on a nonrehearsal night. She and Marcia were in rehearsal for a Chekhov revival four nights a week, and were thrilled that for the first time they had substantial roles. From nine to five, three days a week, they worked at clerical jobs they had gotten through a temporary-employment agency. The other two days, they made rounds. Vicky was determined to survive on her own. Though her mother protested she didn't need to work, Vicky was aware of the respect this decision had earned her.

Watching the clock while she changed from office dress to warmer clothes—their landlord was stingy about providing heat—Vicky worried about Lou's finding the apartment. Would he remember she'd changed her name to Victoria Wright? Vicky Kahn was not a name for show business. They doorbell read "Wright-Finch." She'd felt a bit guilty about changing her name, but Mother seemed to understand.

Lou arrived ten minutes early, with a bottle of champagne tucked under his arm. He was breathless from rushing up the four flights. "No cracks about the apartment," Vicky whispered as she led him past the kitchen into the living room. Marcia had gone downstairs for lettuce for their salad after declaring that what was on hand was not fit for hungry actors.

"Hey, I think it's great," he said. "I mean, it's your own place!"

"You can do the same, you know." Sometimes she felt like smacking Lou, the way he mooned around Mother, always so anxious to please her. "You'll be out of Columbia in five weeks."

"I'm headed for Harvard Business School."

"Come on, Lou, you know you don't really want to go. What about your writing?"

"I don't know enough yet to write," he said softly. "There's time ahead for that."

"Mother's pushing you into Harvard Business School as part of her strategy to drag you into the business. You swore you'd never do it."

"I'm going on to graduate school because that'll keep me out of the army. Mother and Freddie are both convinced there'll be war in Korea. Those border clashes between North and South Korea are more than just guerrilla attacks."

"You're doing it to make Mother happy."

"She's been through two wars. You know how she suffered all those years Freddie was away. I couldn't put her through that again."

"Lou, I love Mother as much as you do. I have terrific respect for what she's accomplished. But we have a right to do what we want with our own lives."

"She's hurt that you never ask her up here."

"I can't. Not until it looks better." She paused at a rap on the kitchen door. "That's Marcia. She must have forgotten her key."

Marcia came in and was introduced to Lou.

"I went over to Ratner's to pick up onion rolls," she said as Vicky reached for the lettuce to prepare the salad. "I ate one on the way home." She laughed. "We sure don't have onion rolls like Ratner's in Columbus, Georgia."

"Did you teach Vicky to cook?" Lou said. "Otherwise I may be taking my life in my hands."

Lou liked Marcia, Vicky decided. She was pleased. She had avoided taking Marcia home with her because she felt uncomfortable about her family's wealth. Maybe she would now.

Maybe she'd have the nerve to invite Lou and Roger Knight up for dinner. Roger was almost thirty, but what was seven years' difference at their age? And she wouldn't be inviting him up just because she hoped he'd cast her in his next play, which he expected to be Equity. He was fascinating: tall, dark, and handsome—and bristling with energy. Everybody thought he was terrific. Once, when Roger was particularly pleased with the way she handled a scene, he'd grabbed her and kissed her. It certainly wasn't like the goodnight kisses from the Columbia students who used to be her social life. This was a whole new world.

Before Lou left, he promised to attend the opening performance of the play in which both Marcia and she would be appearing.

"We don't get paid," Marcia said. "But there's always the chance that some agent will come down and see it."

VICKY WAS DELIGHTED when Lou came down for their Off Broadway opening, and was thrilled when he expressed what seemed to be genuine admiration for her performance. Still, she didn't let anyone else in the family come down to see her—she was still too insecure. In the fall, she promised Lilli and Jan, they would be invited to see her. If she got a decent part.

Roger was already talking about having her read for a part in the Equity play he hoped to produce and direct. The script was an original, and Roger was convinced it would be a hit. She was excited, too, about being a member of the summer-stock company Roger was to direct in Rockland County this season. An Equity company—definitely a step up the ladder. Marcia would be playing the Borscht Belt hotel circuit with a non-Equity company; but at least she was being paid, she told herself—that made her a professional.

Marcia worried that Vicky was seeing so much of Roger. She'd carelessly mentioned that she guessed Roger was sleeping with their leading lady, Denise Cantrell. Marcia was like an old-maid aunt, Vicky thought affectionately—scared to death she was going to jump into bed with Roger. Marcia didn't know she was just waiting for the invitation. *She* didn't care whom he was sleeping with!

Ten days before they were to leave for the Rockland County playhouse, Roger threw a party for the company in his studio apartment on East Fifth—one of the few modern buildings in the area. She had never been to Roger's apartment before. So far they'd shared only passionate kisses in the playhouse after the others had gone, or in the dark hallway of the apartment she shared with Marcia.

She liked the casual way Roger had furnished the studio—not with things picked off the sidewalk at night, like so many apartments of would-be actors and actresses. He had chosen each piece with care. While the others became involved in a hectic game of charades, she had delegated herself to set up the buffet, composed of last-minute shopping at the delicatessen and at Ratner's. It was a tacit admission that she was "Roger's girl."

When the others began to leave—including Denise—Roger invited Vicky to stay and help him wash dishes and pick up. She kicked off her high heels and went into the kitchenette.

"I didn't tell the others my great news," he said, pulling her away from the sink. "I signed the contracts for the new play. We'll go into rehearsal in early October. An Equity company—and a great part for you." He ran one hand across her breasts. "You're good, Vicky. I knew that the first time you read for me. With any luck at all, this play can take us both to Broadway."

"Roger, how wonderful!"

"You're pretty wonderful yourself."

Tonight when he kissed her, she knew she would not be going back to her own apartment. She'd call Marcia. Later.

"It's so damn hot in here," he said. "Let's make ourselves more comfortable." He swung her about and unzipped the back of the tiny-waisted, full-skirted turquoise and white print. Vicky had bought the dress at Bergdorf's but pretended to have picked it up at Klein's Annex. None of her new friends knew she was Vicky Kahn, daughter of beauty empress Lilli Laval.

In moments her dress lay at her feet. She closed her eyes while Roger took off her bra and brought his mouth to her breast. Her hands caressed his unruly dark hair. She didn't care if he had been sleeping with Denise. It was over. Denise had gone home, and he'd asked her to stay. Was she imagining it? Somewhere she heard the lyrics of the song on the radio—"My Foolish Heart."

Roger lifted his mouth to hers for a brief touch, then took her by the hand and led her to the Hollywood bed that served by

day as a second sofa. She felt deliciously decadent wearing only
nylons, garter belt, and mauve silk lace panties. She sat at the
edge of the bed while Roger moved about the room, switching
off all lamps but one.

At last he came and stood beside her. Slowly, he unsnapped
her nylons and peeled first one and then the other down her
long, slim legs. She remembered Paula analyzing men one night
when the girls of the summer-stock company gathered in her
room for prebedtime talk. "Men are damned unromantic. They
make this great pitch, they get you in this terrific mood, then
they drag you into the bedroom and say, 'Take off your
clothes.' "

She waited while he unhooked the garter belt and guided the
mauve silk panties to the floor. "Beautiful baby." He swept her
legs onto the bed, and without taking his eyes from her, he
stripped to the skin. "I see a great future for us, Vicky—in
many ways."

LATER, in the curve of Roger's arm, his body warm and hard
against hers, Vicky remembered Marcia.

"I'd better call Marcia."

"She'll understand." Roger threw his leg across hers.

"I've never stayed away overnight before." She saw his look
of astonishment. "Marcia's a worrier. Don't move. I'll be right
back."

41

VICKY WAITED through the summer for Roger to talk about their getting married. She tried to convince herself that he was waiting until the play opened and their futures seemed assured. Occasionally she wondered if it would bother him that she was Jewish. Not likely. People in the theater never seemed concerned about ethnic backgrounds. Nor was there any reason to bring it up—though eventually she knew she'd have to. If she married Roger, it would have to be by a rabbi or a judge.

She was astonished when, toward the end of the summer, Lou drove up with their mother, who was just back from another European business tour. Nobody here knew that Lilli Laval was her mother. Not even Roger. She was grateful that Lou came backstage alone first to ask her to join them for a late supper. She hastily explained to Roger that she was dashing out—without even bothering to remove her makeup—for a quick supper with her mother and brother.

Beautiful and elegant in a casual summer silk, with a mohair stole draped across her shoulders in deference to the country night chill, Lilli waited in the back seat of Lou's new Dodge hardtop. Mother was the greatest advertisement for her products, Vicky thought with pride. Some catty columnists insisted she'd had several face-lifts.

"Vicky, you were excellent!" Her mother leaned forward and kissed her. "I was truly proud of you."

On the way to the restaurant, Vicky told her mother and Lou that she was scheduled to start rehearsals for an Off Broadway production in the fall. Though she knew that her mother was trying to show enthusiasm, Vicky sensed her disappointment that she hadn't changed her mind about coming into the salon.

Over dinner they talked mostly about family. Greg would start his senior year at Columbia in September. Freddie and Debbie were putting all their energy into a group lobbying against the hydrogen bomb. Lilli suspected that Jan felt less remorse about Greg's arm these days, since it would keep him out of the Korean War after graduation.

"Freddie says the only way we'll ever have peace in the world," Lilli said, "is to eliminate poverty and illiteracy."

"And it'll help if we can learn to control world population," Lou said. "Can you imagine what that'll be by the year 2000 if some action isn't taken?"

Vicky stirred uneasily. She hoped she wasn't about to increase the population. If she was two days late these days, she got nervous. Neither of them wanted her to get pregnant. Not at this stage in their careers.

"How're David and Carol?" Vicky asked.

"They're fine," Lilli said. "I brought Carol into the salon one day last week. She had a marvelous time."

Vicky laughed. "Into all the makeup, I bet!" Clearly, Mother was already planning how one day Carol would come into the salon. She and Lou had grown up hearing all the details of the business over the dinner table. Every new shade of eye shadow, powder, rouge, lipstick that was introduced, every new cream that was developed, every new advertising campaign that was plotted.

"Darling, do you need anything?" her mother asked.

"Not a thing." Vicky laughed. "I'm doing what I've always wanted to do. I'm an actress!"

NEW YORK LOOKS GORGEOUS, Vicky thought as the station wagon bringing the company back into the city rolled down Broadway early in the morning, before the city came fully alive. Marcia had been back from her hotel circuit for two days now, but there would be nothing happening around town for at least two weeks. It would be good just to do nothing for a little while.

Marcia knew that Vicky and Roger had lived together all summer. But Vicky had made Roger understand that once they were back in the city, she would return to her own apartment. He still hadn't said a word about marriage.

He rented a tiny office on Second Avenue and hired Vicky as his assistant, though she received no salary. She was startled to discover that his coproducer—a sole investor—was a woman. Immediately, Vicky was aware of Lola Randall's hostility toward her. A flamboyantly attractive woman somewhere in her late forties, Lola had just divorced a wealthy garment manufacturer and had emerged with a huge settlement because she'd tracked him down in forty-eight counts of adultery with a series of models. He'd admitted later that she'd missed a few.

At the end of her third week as Roger's assistant, Vicky told him she didn't think that Lola liked her.

"Honey, don't worry about Lola. But she's Lady Moneybags—we have to handle her with care. Oh, about dinner tonight." Vicky had invited him to her place for dinner. "I can't make it. Lola wants to talk about our trying to line up some Hollywood name for the male lead."

"Do you think you can do it?"

"With enough money for bait—and some luck."

"Is that why you've been holding up on a casting call?"

"I'm persuading her to up the budget. I talked about bringing somebody east for a six-week run. With a Hollywood name, we might even be able to move the play uptown."

"What about me? Do I stay in the young lead?" She didn't trust Lola.

"Vicky, you're perfect for it." He gave her his most dazzling smile. "Lola knows that. Remember, I'm coproducer and director. You're in this production." With a hasty glance around, he pulled Vicky into his arms for a passionate kiss that washed away her anxieties.

On her way home, Vicky thought over what Roger had said. "He'd have no trouble bringing some Hollywood name—

somebody eager to make a splash in New York theater—into the company. It was a terrific play. A great part for a young male star. Vicky sighed. She wished there were something— even a walk-on—for Marcia.

Was Roger sleeping with Lola Randall? He'd do *anything* to direct an Equity company in town. He wasn't in love with Lola. Was he in love with *her?* He kept saying he was mad about her. Why wasn't he mad enough about her to marry her?

IMPATIENTLY, Lilli thrust a sheaf of papers dealing with the latest market research on the cosmetic industry into her brief-case. Everybody in the country was concerned about infla-tion, but Princess Lilli couldn't stand still. Lilli was convinced that her decision to set up salons in Milan and Madrid and ex-pand the factory in London was a good one.

The salon was empty now except for the cleaning crew. It was time to go home to dinner. With Vicky in her own apartment and Lou away at school, she had dinner served on a tray table in the library on the nights when she was not at some special function. She read the *Times* or watched "Burns and Allen," "Mama," or "Our Miss Brooks" while she ate. After dinner, she would go into the house office she had set up long ago so that Alex and she would have a comfortable place to work in the evenings. Here, she always felt a special closeness to Alex.

After arriving home, Lilli went up to the master bedroom suite and changed into gray velvet slacks and a yellow silk blouse. While she was changing, Jan called.

"What do you hear from Vicky, Mother?"

"I've seen her once since she came back from stock. She calls once or twice a week, though she's rather vague about what's happening. God bless Alexander Graham Bell."

"I had lunch with Debbie. Freddie went down to Washing-ton to talk with some lobbyists. Debbie says he's terribly upset that Truman's pushing ahead work on the hydrogen bomb."

"Isn't the atom bomb bad enough?" Lilli sighed. And now there was the war in Korea. "Did you hear on the news last night that the Red Chinese threatened to intervene if U.N. forces cross the thirty-eighth parallel?''

"I don't understand all this war talk," Jan said, "though Scott certainly is concerned. I don't know if the fighting in Korea or that business about *Red Channels* disturbs him most. Every time his father and mother come over for dinner, they have a fight over which way the country's going. His father is convinced Joe McCarthy is the savior of the nation, and Scott hates McCarthy, of course. I like it better when he's glued to the TV watching baseball, but not even Ralph Kiner can keep him away from the news now."

"How's Greg?"

"Working hard at school. He'll graduate cum laude. He's disappointed that it isn't magna cum laude. Scott and I can't make him understand that we're damn proud of the cum laude." Jan hesitated. "He feels rotten when his classmates talk about being drafted. He knows he won't be."

"He should be glad about that. What does he plan to do after college?"

"He doesn't know. He made it clear that he won't come into the firm with Scott. He's been talking vaguely about working in a museum. He does have an eye for art."

Of all Lilli's children and grandchildren, it was Greg who was impressed by her art collection—carefully selected by Oliver, and worth millions. Someday they would hang in a museum, but she meant to enjoy them in her home and in the New York salon during her lifetime.

"It seems to me that a student should emerge from college with a profession of some sort, even if he doesn't go on to graduate school. But I suppose a college education would be an asset working in a museum."

"We promised Greg a summer in Europe." Jan laughed. "I don't know why we all think we have to have a summer in Europe after college."

"Make sure he lands in some kind of job after the summer. He can't spend the rest of his life drifting around the world."

"Oh, he'll find himself." Jan paused. "I have to go dress now. Scott and I are seeing *Member of the Wedding* tonight."

This evening Lilli ate a hasty dinner and then settled herself in the office to study the market research she had brought home. Revson continued to be her most threatening competition. While Elizabeth Arden was still a competitor to be watched, she was so wrapped up in her horses now that she had ceased to be the main threat. Rubinstein, still a cosmetic tycoon at what was whispered to be eighty years old, had captured a substantial chunk of the market, but like Arden was not a serious concern. It was Revson who kept Lilli on her toes.

After finishing her reading, she prepared for the interview tomorrow with the woman from *Fortune*. Princess Lilli, Inc., was celebrating its thirty-fifth anniversary in the United States, and the promotion department was playing this to the hilt. They'd scheduled her for interviews on Jack Paar's show and on a few new series.

Lilli stopped writing, leaned back, rubbed her eyes. She was one of the ten wealthiest women in the United States. Her name was one recognized around the world. So why did she feel like a failure? She knew why: She had created a dynasty that was shunned by her daughters. At least she had Lou. He'd promised to come into the business. Princess Lilli would have an heir.

AT SECOND AVENUE and Seventh Street, Vicky stopped to buy a small bunch of chrysanthemums. They'd be pretty on the dinner table. She'd planned to bring Roger home for dinner to help cheer up Marcia. After checking her bank balance on her return from the tour, Marcia had gone back to temporary work. She was depressed that she had found nothing in the handful of non-Equity plays being cast so far.

Climbing the stairs to their apartment, Vicky thought of Marcia and Roger's fight last night. Marcia was right. Roger should have put her on salary. He didn't *know* she didn't really have to worry about money. Working for him kept her from drawing a check each week from the temporary agency that had been sending her out before the summer.

It would be great if Lola would put up enough money to pay a Hollywood name to play the male lead. The playwright, a professor at a college in New England, could be in town for weekends only. Roger said he was out of his mind with excitement at having his play produced.

As she approached the door of the apartment, Vicky smelled the rich aroma of herbs and spices coming from inside. Marcia really liked cooking. She'd promised to put on a pot roast as soon as she arrived home.

"Hi." Marcia pulled the door wide. "Oh, mums! How nice."

"Roger can't make it tonight, Marcia. He's tied up with business. Did you go over at lunch to see about that children's play deal?"

"They're setting up a road tour," Marcia said. "With what they're paying, we'd all be on a starvation diet." She frowned apologetically. "Vicky, I hope you won't be mad. I invited somebody over for dinner. I thought we'd need a fourth."

"Why should I be mad? Who's coming?" Vicky reached for a vase.

"Howard Grossman. You know, the law student I told you about who's working part-time in this office where I've been for the last nine days. He works awfully hard, pushing his way through Columbia, and he seemed kind of lonely today. I don't think he has time for much of a social life between studying and working. Don't get that look, Vicky. He's not a prospective boyfriend. He's just a friend."

Vicky grinned. "I'll make the salad. My major contribution to our kitchen duty. When's Howard coming?"

"He'll be here in about half an hour. Sure you don't mind?"

"Marcia, no. Without help we'll be eating that pot roast all week."

Howard Grossman arrived just as Marcia had decided the pot roast was done.

"I could smell that all the way down the stairs," he said. "Reminded me of home."

Howard was about Vicky's height in heels. He towered above petite Marcia. As Marcia introduced them, Vicky decided she liked his scrubbed good looks, his casual manner. He wasn't spectacular like Roger, but he had an appealing charm. Marcia could do much worse than Howard Grossman, even if she did say he was just a friend.

The couple of times Marcia and Lou were together she'd thought they might have something going. But, of course, Lou was all tied up with school and then she and Marcia had both gone off for the summer. And now Lou was up at Cambridge.

Howard relaxed over dinner, keeping them laughing with stories about law school. He came from a small town north of Phoenix, Arizona. His father ran a retail store there that had been founded by his grandfather. Early in high school Howard had known he wanted to come to New York. "I figured two generations in Arizona was enough. I came to New York as soon as I could swing it. I went to school in Arizona, worked summers to save up money for law school. My family helps, but living in New York is expensive."

"Why did you choose law?" Vicky asked.

"I wanted to make money." He shrugged. "I figure a sharp corporate lawyer can make more than a schoolteacher. That's what my mother does. And I sure didn't see myself selling men's suits for the next fifty years."

"When do you graduate, Howie?" Marcia asked.

"The end of next semester." He bowed his head in prayer. "Then I worry about the bar exams."

Vicky enjoyed this dinner far more than she had expected. Everybody she knew these days was involved in the theater. It was a pleasant change to be with somebody who was interested in other things. Daddy would have liked Howie, Vicky thought as she listened to him speak with contempt about *Red Channels*, which had blacklisted such talents as Irwin Shaw, Lillian Hellman, Paul Draper and Dorothy Parker.

"They list people as being part of some so-called suspect organizations that haven't existed since the late Thirties," he said. "They're ruining careers. Ruining lives."

"You should get together with my brother Freddie," Vicky said. "He's always running down to Washington to lobby against the hydrogen bomb. But they can't say anything about Freddie—he was a hero in World War Two."

At the end of the evening, Vicky suspected that Marcia liked Howie more than as a friend. She decided to do her best to promote this. Howie *was* special.

"You like Howie, don't you?" Marcia said after they'd finished up the dishes and had collapsed in the tiny living room before going to bed. Marcia smothered a yawn. "I'm tired. But I'd be wide awake if somebody called to say I had a part in something. Maybe I should have gone out with that children's group."

"You wouldn't have gained a thing. Besides, the season's just starting."

"Joel Zabriskie is casting a lot of TV bits. I know I'd get some of them if I could bring myself to play his game. Maybe I'm just not ambitious enough. I won't sleep with him for a job."

"Marcia, Zabriskie is just one agent. Plenty of them don't audition on their couches."

"What's with Roger? You said he's rented a theater. When will he start reading people?"

"I found out just today. He's trying to sign up a Hollywood name. If that goes through, he'll set the rehearsal schedule right away."

"It's a great part for you."

Vicky had known right off that she and Marcia would be friends forever. Of all the people she'd met Off Broadway, Marcia was the one who wouldn't be bursting with envy if she made it big in the theater. Marcia was like a sister—more even than Jan, who was twenty-two years older.

"Let's go to sleep." Vicky pulled herself to her feet. "We both have dates with desks in the morning."

But Vicky couldn't sleep. She couldn't stop thinking about what Roger had told her earlier. If he was able to sign up a Hollywood name, the play would take on far more importance career-wise for all of them. It meant major advertising. Major newspaper reviews. Every agent in town would come down. *It could be a springboard to Broadway.*

VICKY HUNG OVER Roger's shoulder while he carried on a tense telephone conversation with Tim Dalton's agent in Hollywood. Dalton was a hot young star, but before that he had been—briefly—a shining light in the Broadway theater.

"Of course we'll work out the rehearsal schedule to fit in with Tim's plans. I just have to be sure he'll sign to play six weeks—otherwise my backers won't come through with the money." He was listening to the agent now. He smacked Vicky on the rump and grinned. "Absolutely. I'll have the contracts out to you in forty-eight hours." Roger put down the receiver. "Baby, we're in business!"

"Tim Dalton is signing?"

"He's signing!" He pulled Vicky across his knees. "We start rehearsing in three weeks, which means casting like crazy. Tim's got just enough time between pictures to handle this, and he's mad about the script."

The tiny office became chaotic. Vicky was entrusted with preliminary screenings. Possible candidates were asked to leave résumés and photos. Roger chose the ones Vicky was to call to come in for readings. Vicky was alone in the office much of the day. Roger and Lola auditioned from 10:00 A.M. to 10:00 P.M. at the playhouse. An early-December opening date had been established.

Once all the casting, except for one difficult character role, had been set, the office settled down into a less hectic scene. Now Roger spent the mornings at the office, then met Lola for lunch at Sardi's or the Colony. Vicky saw him only two or three evenings a week.

Three days before they were scheduled to begin rehearsals, Vicky walked into the office to discover Roger in a heated telephone conversation with Lola.

"Lola, cool it," he was saying. "We can't throw out the script and start all over! We've got Tim Dalton arriving in town tomorrow. The cast, except for the old man, is signed to contracts. We—'' He sighed and nodded. ''All right, Lola, I'll come right over.''

''What's happening?'' Vicky stared in bewilderment. ''Lola said she loved the play.''

''She's been doing business with one of those firms that investigate people at so much a name. You know, looking for Commies. It seems our professor playwright fought in Spain on the side of the Loyalists. He—''

''A whole brigade of Americans fought in the Spanish Civil War! On the side of the Loyalists. Are they calling the whole Abraham Lincoln Brigade Commies?''

''I don't give a shit. All I care about at this moment is convincing Lola she can't throw away a whole production—and all the money invested—because this professor is a Commie.''

''*You're* calling him a Commie? Because he fought with the Abraham Lincoln Brigade?''

He sighed. ''There's more. Back in the Thirties, when he was a student at City College, he was a member of the Communist party. Just for a few months, but that's enough—''

''Tell him to change his name. He has to know what's going on in this country. He'll understand.''

Roger squinted in thought. ''You know, he's *dying* for production. He'll probably agree. But first let me go over and talk to Lola.'' He reached for his jacket. ''I have to make her understand we won't have a picket line outside the playhouse because we're doing this guy's play.''

Roger didn't return to the office until late that afternoon. He'd called Vicky earlier to get the playwright's phone number in New England. She'd been churning with anxiety ever since.

''What happened?'' She was on her feet the instant he walked through the door.

''The professor's changing his name. Lola's willing to go along with that.''

''I think it's awful he has to do that. But you have saved the production.''

Roger obviously wasn't happy about the name change. He seemed awfully tense. "There's more, Vicky." He dropped his jacket across a chair and settled himself behind his desk. "Lola's checked out every member of the company with those people." He looked reproachful. "Why in hell didn't you tell me your name is really Kahn?"

She hesitated. "I—I guess I didn't see any reason. Everybody in show business changes his name. Does it bother you that I'm Jewish?"

"It bothers me that you're Fred Laval's sister!" He stood up. "Half sister, but that's enough to cause trouble."

"What kind of trouble? He can't be listed in *Red Channels*. He's not in radio or TV."

"One of the organizations that does these investigations for business firms has a dossier on him. He worked with a group that sent aid to the Loyalists in Spain during the civil war there. He's signed petitions for suspect groups. Now he's lobbying down in Washington against the hydrogen bomb."

"He was a major in the army air force during World War Two," Vicky said, furious at this attack on her brother. "He was decorated by the government for heroism!"

"Vicky, we can't use you in the play." He looked at her coolly. "We can't take the chance of somebody finding out that he's your brother."

She stared at him in disbelief. "Roger, my name on the program will be Victoria Wright."

"The playwright can get away with it. Not an actress. There'll be interviews and all kinds of publicity. *Somebody* will find out, Vicky." He took a deep breath. "Lola says you have to go. You'll be paid for rehearsals and two weeks of performances—"

"I don't want the money! Because some idiots have decided Freddie's a Communist, you're throwing me out of the play?"

"Honey, it has nothing to do with us personally." He reached for her hand. She backed away from him.

"It has everything to do with us!" Tears of rage filled her eyes. "I never want to see you again!"

42

VICKY AND MARCIA sat at the kitchen table while the lighted oven, its door open, provided some relief from the dank early-November chill. The predinner cups of coffee with which Vicky had fortified them were forgotten after an initial swig. Their faces were serious as Vicky told Marcia about what happened earlier in Roger's offices.

"I don't think other Off Broadway producers are going out witch-hunting." She mustered a defiant smile. "Most of them don't have money in their budgets for that."

"Nobody makes a living working Off Broadway." Marcia sighed, crossing her legs. "You need Broadway or TV to pay the rent and eat." But they both remembered the stink that arose when Ed Sullivan invited the dancer Paul Draper to appear on "Toast of the Town." And now Jean Muir, slated to play the mother in the upcoming TV version of the "Aldrich Family," was under attack by Red-baiters. "Vicky, this is crazy."

"What's really hairy is that these creeps can paste a label on somebody like Freddie. How can they make anybody believe that a flight surgeon who served heroically in the Pacific is dangerous to the country? Marcia, you know what this means. You're my roommate—you'll be suspect, too. If you want me to move out, I'll understand."

"Nobody is splitting us up." Marcia's cheeks flushed in anger. "Remember when we talked about the blacklisting when Howie was here for dinner? I thought it was disgusting, but I couldn't imagine that it would ever touch us. Anyhow, I'm glad you broke off with Roger. I never liked him. I didn't like what I heard about him."

"Do you suppose Freddie knows he's considered a Commie?"

"Probably. But I think you ought to tell him what's happened."

"I'll call him tomorrow." Freddie and Debbie hadn't yet moved from Irvington into the Manhattan town house they'd bought on East Nineteenth Street. "It's not like I'm blaming him. It's not his fault that some people in this country have gone nuts. So now"—she smiled bravely—"it looks like I'm back to reading the casting calls in *Show Business*."

Vicky's old insecurities came surging forward again. She had so little background, nothing substantial to give her the kind of confidence she needed when she walked into a producer's office. She wondered if there really was any point in making TV and Broadway rounds.

At a quarter to eight the next morning, hoping to catch him before he boarded a commuter train into town, Vicky phoned Freddie.

"Honey, he leaves the house before seven," Debbie said. "They're seeing patients in the clinic by eight, which is one of the reasons I insisted we move back into the city. He won't be a slave to a train schedule. And children do grow up in Manhattan."

Vicky laughed. "Freddie did. All of us did. Think of all the advantages."

"Vicky, is something wrong?"

"Not really." She wanted to tell Freddie first. "But I have to talk to Freddie."

"Call him at the clinic. He may keep you on hold for a while, but eventually he'll come to the phone."

Vicky was casual when she talked to Freddie, but she knew he understood that she wasn't dragging him off to lunch on a whim. "I'll meet you at Reuben's at two," he said. "I have to be in the neighborhood, and I'm in the mood for my favorite—Nova Scotia, cream cheese, and fried onion sandwich. Plus cheesecake, of course.''

Once they were seated and had ordered, Vicky explained what had happened. He was genuinely upset. "Oh, God, Vicky, I know how important that part was to you!''

"I thought you ought to know," she said. "I mean, that they're trying to label you a Commie.''

"I knew. But I didn't expect it to affect *you*. We've got all those vigilantes out there—the American Legion, the Catholic War Veterans, the DAR, too many to name. This craziness won't last. It can't. We can sit it out.''

"Sure we can.''

"You're coming up for David's bar mitzvah next Saturday, aren't you?''

"Of course, Freddie. We're *all* coming.''

VICKY AND MARCIA decided to eliminate their TV and Broadway roundmaking after Broadway gossip told them that blacklisted performers were receiving the same treatment in theaters as on the television scene. So far neither Actors Equity, Screen Actors Guild, nor AFTRA had gone to bat for their members.

They focused instead on the sprinkling of Off Broadway groups in rehearsal or preparing to go into production. It was always a hassle to keep non-Equity people in a cast, because they could—and often did—walk out without a moment's notice when something better came along.

Vicky knew that Roger's company was in rehearsal. With a Hollywood star in the cast, the play was the hottest prospect Off Broadway. The newspaper gossip columns carried items about Tim Dalton and the girl who had replaced Vicky. The press agent was dropping hints about a romance. Vicky fumed in silent frustration as the opening date of Roger's production came close. Losing the part that could have taken her to Broadway was what hurt most—not losing Roger. The Roger Knight she had been in love with did not exist.

A few days before Thanksgiving, Vicky invited Marcia to the Gramercy Park house for the holiday meal. When Marcia mentioned that Howie would be alone that day, Vicky invited him also. Mother was always pleased when she and Lou brought friends home.

Vicky and Freddie had agreed not to tell Lilli why she had lost the part. When Lilli asked, Vicky shrugged it off with the explanation that the producer had simply decided he didn't want her in the company. Vicky suspected that if the business with Freddie had not come up, Lola would have dreamed up another reason to get rid of her. Obviously, Lola meant to have a clear field with Roger.

Vicky and Marcia were dressed and waiting when Howie arrived to pick them up for the midafternoon Thanksgiving dinner. "You're sure your mother won't mind your bringing me?" he asked.

"Are you kidding?" Vicky laughed. "She's thrilled when there are a lot of people around the dinner table." She had not told her mother that Howie was Marcia's boyfriend, but she had hinted as much, lest she jump to the wrong conclusion. "Especially on holidays."

Howie grinned. "Sounds like my mother."

Howie knew her real name was Kahn. He knew Freddie was her half brother. She doubted, though, that he had put facts together to realize that her mother was Lilli Laval of Princess Lilli. She was sure of this when they arrived at the entrance to the town house on Gramercy Park.

"You moved from this to East Seventh Street?" he said as Henri appeared at the door to admit them.

Vicky smiled. "It *was* a change."

The three of them went to the library, where Lilli and Lou waited to welcome them. Lou seemed delighted to see Marcia. When he was introduced to Howie, he became quiet. Vicky assumed that he thought Howie was Marcia's boyfriend. The couple of times she had seen Lou and Marcia together, Vicky had felt an electricity between them. But then Lou had gone off to school. Was he sorry that Marcia appeared involved with

Howie? *She* wasn't. She and Marcia and Howie were close friends.

In minutes, Jan and Scott arrived, and right behind them came Freddie and Debbie and the children. Now the atmosphere in the library crackled with holiday spirit. Carol looked darling in a green velvet dress and matching tights, her lush, honey-colored hair tumbling about her shoulders. All the women in this family—even tiny Carol—had the same green eyes.

As always, Greg was late, but Vicky saw the furtive admiration in his eyes when he looked at Marcia. Greg would graduate from Columbia in June. He'd wheedled Jan and Scott into giving him a summer in Europe. What would he do after that? He said he'd never go into business with his father. But who else would put up with his arrogance?

"Every year on Mother's Day," Howie was saying to Lilli, "I send my mother a gift of Princess Lilli perfume. It's always been her favorite."

"Give me her full name and address later," Lilli said, "and I'll see that one of our gift collections goes out to her—because she has such a charming son."

Her mother was really taken with Howie, Vicky decided. She was glad. But moments later, as they settled themselves about the dining table, she was disconcerted when Freddie inadvertently gave away the real reason for her being dropped from the play.

"Darling, you didn't tell me." Her mother looked pained.

"I'll survive." Vicky shrugged. Would she, the way this craziness was escalating? "Freddie and I didn't want to worry you—"

"And with my big mouth, I came out with it." Freddie smiled apologetically. "I'm sorry. It's just that Debbie and I live with this situation almost every hour of the day. What's happening in this country is incredible."

"A couple we know in the city had invited us to a post-Thanksgiving cocktail party on Sunday," Debbie said. "People Freddie's known since college. Yesterday the wife phoned to ask us not to come. She said our political activities made it too embarrassing for them."

The conversation turned to blacklisting, and then moved to a sober assessment of the fighting in Korea, which Freddie called an American anti-Communist crusade. Vicky noticed Greg's sullen anger at this turn in the conversation. Jan said he was upset because he was not subject to the draft. Would Howie be pulled into service after graduation? Vicky shuddered. She hadn't even considered it.

It wasn't until eight o'clock that Vicky, Marcia, and Howie left the house. It had been a good day, Vicky thought as they walked down Second Avenue toward the apartment; but tomorrow the rat race began again.

She couldn't stop thinking about Freddie's after-dinner quotation of an Einstein statement: *Radioactive poisoning of the atmosphere and hence annihilation of any life on earth has been brought within the range of technical possibilities . . .* She began to understand Freddie's and Debbie's obsession with the fight against new atomic weapons. She felt guilty at being so emotionally involved in something as "frivolous" as breaking into theater when the world was in such an awful state.

"It's strange." Howie's voice brought her back. "During World War Two, everybody was so conscious that we were fighting a war. Already, thousands of American soldiers are casualties in Korea, but here at home it doesn't seem as though we're at war. Except," he added quietly, "for those families who've lost somebody in Korea."

VICKY AND MARCIA made the rounds on the days they weren't working at temporary office jobs. In the months ahead, each won two small parts in non-Equity productions, but none of the plays went beyond the third rehearsal. Two companies gave up because of the heavy turnover in cast and a lack of money for advertising. The other two were unable to acquire licenses for their hastily set up playhouses—capacity, sixty or seventy— because of the need for new exits, new wiring, separate "johns" for boys and girls, or other items too costly for their budgets.

Late in the spring, Vicky snared a role—tiny but showy—in an Equity Off Broadway company. The production was rumored to be bankrolled by the playwright, who was prone to temperamental outbursts. Vicky went through the rehearsal period in constant fear that she would be dismissed. She took a deep breath of relief when they prepared to open for a week of previews. She was still in the cast, though she suspected the run would be brief.

Her family was scheduled to come to the opening, but she had asked her mother not to bring a theater party of friends. It would be humiliating to have them see her in such an awful play. She had even told Lou not to come down from Cambridge. Only Marcia and Howie would be at the first preview. Still, it was an Equity company. Some critics would show up.

Early in the afternoon of their first preview, Vicky received a phone call from the director. In a cool voice he told her that she was not to appear at the playhouse that evening—or ever. She was being replaced by the general understudy at the playwright's orders. "You'll be paid, Vicky. We're going by the Equity rules—"

"Why am I not playing?" *Please not the same story again.*

He paused. "Because of your Communist connections."

"Equity won't let you get away with this!"

"They'll complain, but you are being paid, so they can't do anything. I'm sorry, Vicky." He didn't sound sorry. "I'm just carrying out instructions."

When Marcia came home, Vicky told her she was out of the play.

"You know what I'll do with my check, Marcia? I'm donating it to Freddie's protest group."

VICKY WAS ASTONISHED when Marcia turned down a part in another summer hotel package. "Once on that circuit was enough, Vicky. It won't lead to anything else. The hotels give us great dinners. We pay most of our salary back to the producers for room and board. I'm better off working for the temporaries." She paused, thinking. "Maybe I've lost my wild ambitions to make it big in the theater. I'm going back to school at night to earn a degree. I don't know what I'll do with it, but it seems more important to me than a rerun of last summer.''

Vicky told herself this was a time for learning. She signed up for acting classes three times a week during the approaching summer. Off Broadway would be dead until mid-September. In March she had been furious when the board of directors of SAG—the Screen Actors Guild—stated it did not believe that the House Committee on Un-American Activities was "in the witch-hunting business." In June she was equally enraged when the council of Actors Equity, after condemning the blacklist, issued a similar statement.

She sensed her mother's frustration that two of her children were being falsely labeled and she was unable to clear them. Mother was not accustomed to situations she couldn't handle.

With the arrival of hot, humid weather, Vicky succumbed to her mother's pleas that she go to the Southampton house on weekends with Marcia and Howie. Lou was staying at the beach house for the summer—secretly writing a play. Occasionally Jan and Scott would come out, as would Freddie and Debbie and the children. Greg was off somewhere in Europe. Lilli herself was dashing about the country on business in the company's new plane.

On the Friday afternoon before their second weekend in the Hamptons, Vicky hurried over to the salon for a poodle cut. Afterward she would pick up Marcia and Howie in midtown. In her quiet little way, Marcia had made it clear to Lou that she was not romantically interested in Howie—and that his sister *was*.

Sitting under the dryer, Vicky sorted through her feelings for Howie. She really flipped for him, but it wasn't what she had felt for Roger. She'd been infatuated with Roger—he was the Great Young Director with a dazzled young clique at his feet, and he'd professed to be mad about her. It had been fun—at the time, anyway. With Howie it was different. She could easily see herself spending the rest of her life with him. At unexpected moments when they were together, she'd look up and find Howie's eyes on her. She knew he was in love with her, but why was he so damned reluctant to come out and say so? Instinctively she knew that he was having trouble coping with the fact that her mother was one of the richest women in the country. What would he feel if he knew about her own trust fund? What difference did the money make in how they felt about each other? Marcia said she should show Howie she was in love with him, that most of the time women had to make the first move.

"You're dry." Felicia interrupted her thoughts as she touched the rollers. "Let me comb you out."

Vicky took a taxi from the salon to the garage to pick up her car, a Citröen. Both Marcia and Howie had arranged to leave their offices early on Fridays during the summer so they could avoid the frantic Friday-afternoon exodus from the city. Vicky drove from the garage up Madison to the corner of Forty-third, where Marcia and Howie were waiting.

"You had your hair cut!" Howie said as he slid onto the front seat beside her and Marcia settled in the rear with their luggage. "You look like Elizabeth Taylor in *A Place in the Sun*."

"It's sensational on you," Marcia said. "On most girls it looks like a dust mop."

Vicky smiled. Mother would be delighted if she married Howie. Would it upset her to know that Marcia and Lou were in love? Debbie wasn't Jewish, but mother loved her, and Freddie and Debbie were raising David and Carol as Jews. What would happen if Marcia and Lou decided to marry? Of course, Lou had another year at Harvard ahead of him . . .

They arrived at the Southampton house to discover that only Lou—in addition to the staff—would be out this weekend. This was the weekend she'd make Howie open up about his feelings for her, she told herself. She finished her unpacking in minutes, changed into a swimsuit, and ran across the hall to Marcia's room.

"Why don't you take Lou to a drive-in after dinner?" she said as she came in.

Marcia looked at her in mock horror. "Take your darling brother to a passion pit?"

"He won't need a second invitation."

"Vicky, Lou's so sweet." All at once Marcia was somber. "But your mother won't like it when she finds out we're serious. I mean—she'll expect Lou to marry in his own faith."

"Worry about that later. Lou and I can twist Mother around our little fingers." *Could* they, she wondered, in a situation like this?

"When it comes to a showdown, I'm not sure," Marcia said. "You know how he feels about your mother."

"I know how he feels about you. I don't think it's Mother's decision to make. Come on. Change into your bathing suit and let's test the water."

WITH A GREAT SHOW of being casual, Marcia and Lou went off to the drive-in to see Judy Holliday in *Born Yesterday*. A beige cashmere sweater draped about her shoulders, Vicky reached for Howie's hand and led him from the house and onto the beach.

"You didn't want to go to the drive-in, did you?" Her heart hammered as they gazed up at the star-splashed sky.

"Not when I could be alone with you."

"Howie," she said softly, "I think I'm in love with you."

He smiled. "I know I'm in love with you."

"Then why keep it a secret?"

"Because I'm in no position to be serious about us. I don't even know yet if I'll pass the bar exams—"

"Oh, Howie, stop talking so much." She turned and kissed him.

They'd never shared more than a casual goodnight kiss. Tonight they held each other with startling hunger, their bodies pressing heatedly against each other.

"Oh, wow!" Vicky said after they pulled away. "Why did we waste all those months?"

"We'll waste more," he said, "if you're thinking what I think you are." But he held her close, swaying with her in the cool night air. Her sweater lay on the sand at her feet now, but she wasn't cold.

"Howie, I think I should tell you about my 'dark past.'" She laughed shakily. "I thought I was in love with Roger. I was just starstruck."

"I don't want to hear about it." He kissed her on the forehead, then on the eyelids. "From now on there's only Vicky and Howie—nobody else. But we're not sleeping together until we're married."

"Let's elope," she said, and he laughed.

"We can't tell anybody about us until I'm set up in a law practice. Vicky, I wouldn't let your mother support us."

"Oh, Howie, you are so noble. In another fourteen months I draw the income from my trust fund." She felt him stiffen. "Darling, it's not a disgrace to have money. In fact," she giggled, "I've been chased by men who had nothing else in their minds."

"All right, then. But nobody is to know except Marcia and Lou, until I'm earning a living. Of course, don't expect to be supported in the style your mother taught you to enjoy."

EARLY IN THE FALL, a flurry of press releases announced Princess Lilli's new television series, "The Princess Lilli TV Theater," starring Donna Devan. The ad agency had convinced Lilli it was time to expand from radio into TV. Predictions were that within a year there would be more TV sets than radio sets drawing audiences between 9:00 P.M. and midnight.

Within ten days after the announcement of "The Princess Lilli TV Theater," 1,103 letters and telegrams had poured into the cosmetic firm's offices, demanding the company fire Donna Devan because she was "pro-Communist in her sympathies." The advertising agency was bombarded for its part in packaging the show. Unnerved, the agency president called for a conference with Lilli.

On a lovely autumn afternoon, Lilli sat at the head of the fifteen-foot-long, hand-tooled, leather-topped table in the salon's newly redecorated conference room and smiled tightly while top officers of the ad agency—with millions riding on the Princess Lilli account—told her why the star of "The Princess Lilli TV Theater" must be bought off.

"We have to pay off Donna's contract and replace her," her account executive said. "Her appearance on the show will devastate sales." Lilli knew he was worried that the agency might lose one of its most lucrative accounts. "Princess Lilli can't afford to be involved with her."

"I've yet to see what Donna Devan has done to merit this kind of treatment," Lilli said coolly. "She's one of the finest actresses in theater and films. If you recall, it was a coup when you were able to sign her for the show."

"Lilli, we've shown you the reports, the listing in *Red Channels*, the articles on her in the *American Legion* magazine and in *Counterattack*." The account executive was trying to hide his exasperation. "You can't afford the association on national TV. There are five million TV sets in this country today."

"Be more specific, please." Lilli might have been pouring tea at a charity affair. Only her eyes told the cluster of men and women gathered around the table that she was furious.

The account executive read from a report: " 'Donna belonged at one time to the American Committee for the Protection of the Foreign Born. She sent a congratulatory telegram to the Moscow Art Theater. She was a member of the American Labor party. She supported Henry Wallace'!"

"These associations mean nothing," Lilli said. "Donna stays on the program." She gazed around the table at the shocked faces. "I won't be part of this smear campaign."

Long after the others had left, Lilli sat alone in the conference room. For her, this confrontation highlighted the fact that Princess Lilli, Inc., was no longer a family-owned corporation. At the moment, she owned thirty-seven percent of the stock. While she sought constantly to buy additional shares when they came on the market, she was in control now on the strength of the proxies she managed to hold. She knew that because of her decision today, a fight could arise at the stockholders' meeting three weeks from now.

Thoroughly absorbed in her thoughts, Lilli left the conference room and returned to her office. She remembered the radio and television assumption that a thousand letters represented the view of an audience of 1 million. Could there possibly be a million Americans—even with Joseph McCarthy on the loose—who believed the security of the nation was in jeopardy because Donna Devan was to appear in a TV series?

Where did those letters come from? Could it be an organized campaign? She would *not* be intimidated by *Red Channels, Counterattack,* right-wing gossip columnists, or Joseph McCarthy's underground network of paranoid vigilantes. She needed some answers, and she needed them *now.* Howard Grossman was the man to ask: He'd welcome a side assignment, and he shared her contempt for Joseph McCarthy. She reached for the phone and dialed Vicky's number. No answer. She'd keep trying. Now was the time to take action. Freddie and Debbie were down in Washington for three days with the children while Freddie spoke before some committee. She would talk to him when they returned. Lilli Laval—Lilli Kahn—was not without influence.

Not everybody bowed down before the name-callers. Edward R. Murrow, Walter Lippmann, the Alsop brothers, Drew Pearson, Elmer Davis, the Luce magazines—all remained sane amid this craziness. McCarthy had labeled the *Washington Post* "the Washington edition of the *Daily Worker,*" and referred to the *New York Times* as the Communist daily's uptown edition.

It wasn't until she was about to leave the salon for the day that Lilli caught up with Vicky. She explained she had a freelance assignment for Howie. "Bring him over for dinner, Vicky. Afterward, we can talk."

Lilli sat at her desk immersed in thought. Was Vicky serious about Howie? He was bright and hardworking. The few times she'd seen him, she'd admired his manners, his sense of decency. She knew Vicky saw him often—he was helping her through this insanity in the theater. Vicky was twenty-four. It seemed unlikely she'd ever come into the business. It would be good to see her happily married. Of course, she could be married and still come into the business.

Leaving the salon, Lilli remembered Alex's favorite saying: that life never ran smoothly until death. At moments like this, he seemed very close to her. Other women marveled that she brushed aside the men who clamored to pay her attentions. For her, there was no choice. She had her business and the family—and her precious memories. She was sixty-four years old. She would never be able to believe that a man who looked at her did so with anything other than an appraisal of her fortune on his mind.

She always felt a kind of sadness at the parade of women in her age group who signed up for endless courses of treatment at the salon in a frantic effort to appear young and beautiful for their young—and well-paid—lovers. The business was her lover. No one could come after Alex.

LILLI HAD PROMISED herself she would not discuss the business at hand until after dinner, but Howie introduced the subject when he brought up a recent suicide that had been blamed on Joseph McCarthy. Immediately, Lilli launched into a report on the angry letters regarding Donna Devan that had come into Princess Lilli and its advertising agency.

"I'd like you to be a part of a team I'm forming to fight this insanity, Howie. You'll be paid on an hourly basis." She shook her head as he prepared to dismiss the idea of payment. "Princess Lilli can afford it," she chuckled. "And you'll earn it."

Clearly enthusiastic about this venture, Howie began asking questions. He was shrewd. He had legal training. Lilli knew he would see aspects of the case that she was too angry to see.

"I'd like to have a look at those letters," he said. "There may be some pattern."

Lilli couldn't wait to get started. "Certainly. I'll have Henri bring the car around when we've finished dinner. We'll go right over to the salon."

Within an hour, the three of them were sitting around the conference table with the mailbags emptied along its length. Howie was on his feet, skimming through the letters.

"Look at these!" He held a cluster of letters. "They're exact copies. And they're not coming from all over the country. They were all mailed from Manhattan, Bronx, Brooklyn, and Queens. It was a campaign set up right here in the city. Phony mailing addresses with signatures, sure—but the postmarks tell the story!"

"That's just what I suspected." Lilli nodded in satisfaction. "A handful of rabble-rousers pretending to be the voice of the country."

"What are you going to do, Mother?" Vicky asked.

"The series goes on with Donna Devan. I don't care if we receive a million letters."

"It could affect sales," Howie said.

Lilli stared in disdain at the pileup of letters and telegrams. "Princess Lilli can afford to lose sales. I will not be intimidated by these people. I know they won't stop with smearing Donna Devan. I'll be next. After all, they've already labeled my son and my daughter Communists. Why should I escape? But they won't be expecting a fight—and that's what they're going to get."

Yet Lilli was mindful of the imminent stockholders' meeting. Only the proxies she held gave her control. Would they be swayed by the fear that sales would plummet and dividends would shrink? At a time when General Foods and Pepsi-Cola were knuckling under to the name-callers, could Princess Lilli hold out?

43

THE FAMILY RALLIED AROUND Lilli in her battle to defy the name-callers. Shaken but defiant, Donna Devan gratefully put herself in the hands of the team of high-powered and expensive press agents Lilli had hired. Lilli herself issued a series of statements refuting Devan's Communist affiliations. She announced a press conference to be held at the New York salon, and in a whimsical moment decided to have it catered by the Russian Tea Room.

The reporters were greeted by Lilli, Donna Devan, Freddie, a retired American general, and a popular congressman in the grand drawing room of the salon, opened only on state occasions. While the ladies and gentlemen of the press enjoyed blini, Beluga, and icy Slavic vodkas, Lilli and her crew made eloquent statements designed to soothe the most paranoid. Lilli's career as a double agent during World War I was colorfully exploited by the congressman, a former intelligence officer. Freddie's experiences as a flight surgeon in the Pacific and his dramatic return from the dead were outlined by the general. Alex's service during two world wars were lauded. Donna Devan's overseas USO activities during World War Two were demonstrated by film clips and photographs, and highlighted in the dramatic recall—previously plotted—of an army sergeant, now a newspaper reporter, who had taken refuge along with Donna's USO troupe during a bombing raid in the South Pacific.

The following day, newspaper headlines quoted the congressman and the general. There were columnists who countered with snide comments, but Lilli was optimistic. "We may lose some sales, but we can sit this out."

As she had feared—but refused to voice—some of the minority shareholders at the annual meeting rebelled, and she won by a painfully narrow margin. She reinforced her orders to the brokers to buy whenever Princess Lilli stock came on the market. And to buy *at any price*.

As always when under stress, Lilli pushed herself to develop new ideas for Princess Lilli. "The two older ladies"—Arden and Rubinstein—and Revlon seemed to spend extravagantly on advertising. She made a series of trips around the country to a dozen Princess Lilli salons and to oversee the training of new demonstrators in the department stores that sold the Princess Lilli line. She was astonished when Greg shyly asked if he could have a job at the New York salon. "Just for a little while," he said. "Until I figure out what I want to do with my life." Lilli knew that Scott was insisting he not fall into the young-playboy role.

On impulse, Lilli began taking Greg along on her trips: Maybe this grandchild would surprise her with talent for the business. Greg's major task on these trips was to be charming to their new demonstrators and to encourage them to remain with Princess Lilli. Lilli was irritated by the constant turnover. Demonstrators played musical chairs, flitting from one top cosmetic house to another as enticing offers came their way. She remembered that Jan always said Greg had an eye for beauty.

In June, Lou would graduate from Harvard Business School. He would become part of Princess Lilli, Inc. Like his father, David would eventually become a physician, but Lilli hoped that Carol—always fascinated by visits to the salon—would join her one day in the business. For her children and grandchildren, it was important that she retain absolute control over the Princess Lilli empire.

AS THE TRAIN pulled into Penn Station, Lou put aside the notebook in which he had been writing and brought his valise down from the luggage rack. He hadn't called home to tell his mother he'd be home this weekend. She wasn't expecting to see him until she came to Cambridge in three weeks for graduation. He'd phoned Marcia on impulse last night and told her he'd be arriving early this afternoon. She was sure she could take time off from the office to meet him at the train. Marcia knew this was not an ordinary visit home. He was coming down to talk about their future.

The train slowed to a crawl and stopped. Carrying his weekender, Lou pushed toward the door. He was both excited and afraid about what he had to say to Marcia. She might be angry, he warned himself. She might walk right out of his life. He shuddered at the possibility.

"Lou!" Marcia waved to him over the shoulders of others waiting at the gate. "Over here!"

He pulled her into his arms.

"Are you hungry?" she asked, after they had kissed.

He laughed. That was always his mother's first question when he came home. "Starving," he said, "for you."

"Howie and Vicky found this great little restaurant down on MacDougal Street. Shall we?"

They hurried out of the station and hailed a taxi. While the driver swore at the sluggish traffic, Lou pulled Marcia into his arms and kissed her again. "I missed you," he murmured. "I always miss you. What have you been doing while I've been up in Cambridge breaking my back?"

"Working at the stupid office. Going to classes in the evening. Vicky dragged Howie and me over to dinner at your mother's house several times."

"Still satisfied to forget about the theater?"

"I love the theater." She spoke softly. "But I don't have the drive to make it big. It's not a compulsion with me, the way writing is for you. I've been through my big rebellion. My place in the theater is in the audience."

"What about Vicky? Is she back making rounds?"

"No. She's taking classes. She has real talent, Lou, but I suspect she's more interested in helping Howie make it as a lawyer than in building a career for herself. She's working in his office as his receptionist." Marcia giggled. "She's even learning to type so she'll be able to do his briefs."

As Marcia had promised, the softly lighted, rustic restaurant was sparsely occupied. They were led to a corner table and given huge handwritten menus. With their waitress gone, Lou was suddenly impatient.

"I meant to set the stage for this better," he said softly, "but I can't wait. In three weeks I'll be out of school. I want nothing in this world so much as to marry you." He paused. "But we *do* have some problems."

"I know." Her voice was tender and solemn.

"Would you be willing to be married by a rabbi? For my mother's sake."

"Lou, I'd marry you in a Moslem ceremony if I had to," she whispered. "The words don't count. It's what we feel for each other."

"One problem down, one to go." He took a deep breath. It wasn't right to ask this of Marcia, but he had to. "Would you be willing to raise our kids in the Jewish faith?"

"Lou, I have three sisters. I'm sure they'll all be married in the church. Their children will be baptized. Let the rabbi have our children."

"When?" Lou reached for her hand across the table. "When can we be married?"

LILLI WAS THRILLED when Lou and Marcia told her that in late September, when the Georgia heat had subsided, she and Lou would be quietly married by a rabbi in her hometown. Marcia's parents, a hardworking, family-oriented couple, had at first been reluctant, but then had realized Marcia and Lou were deeply in love. They were impressed by Lou, and Lilli suspected they were pleased that their daughter would be financially secure forever.

Two days before the wedding, the family flew down en masse in the company plane. A whole floor of the city's poshest hotel had been reserved for them. Marcia had flown home two weeks earlier to prepare for the wedding. Vicky was to be maid of honor. Carol was ecstatic at being a junior bridesmaid, along with Marcia's youngest sister. Marcia's family was instantly charmed by Lilli, enthralled that she was giving Lou and Marcia a town house quite near her own as a wedding present. For Lilli, the only sorrow of the day was that Alex could not be there with them.

On the flight back to New York, Vicky persuaded Howie that there was no need for them to wait until he was established as a lawyer for them to marry. "You'd be cheating me of years," she said. "Darling, please, let's get married on Thanksgiving."

"You're a conniving woman," he whispered. "Taking advantage of me like this, when my defenses are down."

"I'll tell Mother," Vicky said. "And don't you think I'm sleeping alone tonight!"

VICKY AND HOWIE were to be married on Thanksgiving Day in the spacious living room of the Gramercy Park house, by the same rabbi who had married Jan and Scott twenty-three years earlier, with only immediate family present. Howie's parents and younger sister were to fly in from Arizona and stay at the house.

At the last moment Vicky decided to wear a traditional wedding gown. Lilli used all her connections to have a designer gown made. She was amazed at her own sentimental reaction to this wedding. Despite another of the endless crises in the business—a competitor had just raided the coddled staff of the San Francisco salon—she took on all the details of planning the wedding herself.

Promptly at two in the afternoon on Thanksgiving Day, the pianist began the music that brought the guests to the rows of small gilt chairs set up for the occasion. White lilacs, lilies, and white chrysanthemums filled the room. Her face radiant, Lilli—exquisite in a yellow chiffon princess-line gown by Dior—watched from the upper-floor landing while Carol, looking serious and sweet and pretty in her yellow bridesmaid's gown, began her careful walk down the staircase. Marcia, the matron of honor, followed, wearing a green gown by Givenchy.

"Darling, don't dawdle," Lilli called to Vicky, who was fussing with her rose-point lace veil. She wore a high-waisted white satin gown with a bouffant skirt and carried a bouquet of tiny white orchids. "It'll be time for us to go down in a moment."

With Lou as his best man, Howie waited before the red velvet *huppah* while Lilli escorted her younger daughter down the stairs and to the canopy, which represented the wedding couple's future home.

While the rabbi conducted the ceremony, Lilli gazed about the room, her eyes pausing to rest for a moment on each family member. Scott sat with one arm around Jan, as though reliving his own wedding. Freddie and Debbie held hands. David seemed uncharacteristically solemn. Only Greg seemed disinterested. No, Lilli corrected herself—self-conscious.

She knew Jan worried that Greg would consider himself an unlikely candidate for marriage because of his physical handicap. None of them had ever been able to convince Greg that he was a normal human being. He repeatedly refused any psychiatric help, and took refuge in being supercilious and aloof. But she would not let her concern for Greg spoil her day, she told herself. Her four children were happily married. She had fulfilled her obligations as a mother.

For a moment, her eyes met Howie's mother's in warm communication. Howie's parents were happy that he had married a girl in his own faith. In small towns, Mrs. Grossman had confided, this was often a problem. They respected the money that would come with Vicky, without being awed by it. And Evelyn Grossman confessed that she looked forward eagerly to the day when Howie and Vicky would make her a grandmother. Lilli couldn't have agreed more.

LILLI CELEBRATED New Year's Eve, 1952, with a family party. Except for Alex's absence, her life was full. She was surrounded by children and grandchildren, two sons-in-law and two daughters-in-law whom she loved. And she had Lou and Greg in the business.

Earlier in the evening—midnight London time—she had phoned to wish Oliver and Frances and Charles a Happy New Year. She knew they would be together this evening, as had been their practice for many years. She had been momentarily disconcerted when Frances hinted that perhaps the coming year would be her last in the business. Frances was five years older than she. Seventy. Aunt Sara had been going strong at seventy-eight when the Germans invaded Paris. Only a war had driven Aunt Sara from the business.

She'd persuaded Frances that it was ridiculous to give up her place in the salon when she still enjoyed being there. She herself refused to imagine the day when she would step down as head of Princess Lilli.

It astonished Lilli that Greg stayed on at the salon, though she suspected that Vicky was correct in her blunt assessment that he was there because he enjoyed looking at beautiful women. Vicky and Lou were both happy in their marriages, Lilli told herself with satisfaction. Even Jan—always tense and restless—seemed to be relaxing now that Greg was occupied, though she thought Scott probably doubted that Greg would remain at Princess Lilli.

At eleven, they sat down in the Louis XV dining room, softly illuminated by the Waterford crystal chandelier, for the final supper of the year. She had planned the festive menu with Martine: coriander prosciutto with pineapple, onion soup with port, a roast rack of lamb, Belgian endive and grapefruit, an artichoke soufflé and brussels sprouts. For dessert, Freddie's favorite chocolate mousse. At the end of the meal they would welcome the New Year with Dom Perignon.

They were dawdling over their mousses, caught up in reminiscences of the past year, when the sounds of whistles and horns outdoors told them 1953 had arrived. Henri appeared with the chilled champagne. Lilli insisted he remain to toast the New Year with the family. In a little while she would go out to the kitchen to wish the others on the staff a Happy New Year.

She was proud that her domestic staffs—except in Paris during World War Two—and her salon and factory employees showed such loyalty. In the trade, Arden and Revlon were considered revolving doors.

Champagne glasses in hand, the family left the dining room for the library. Henri had laid a fire in the grate. Freddie dropped to his haunches before the tall marble fireplace. He enjoyed the small routine of coaxing the fire into a hearty blaze while Scott offered good-humored advice. Carol yawned repeatedly, but seemed determined to remain awake.

Lilli's face softened as her eyes lingered on her youngest grandchild. Carol had been only two when Alex died, but to Alex she had already been a replica of "Grandma Lilli." Would Carol someday come into Princess Lilli?

"Darling, come sit over here with me." Lilli patted a place beside her on the smoky blue velvet love seat that flanked the fireplace.

"I'll take her upstairs in a few minutes," Freddie mouthed silently over Carol's head. Freddie, Debbie, and the children were to sleep over tonight, in what Lilli suspected was a yearly pact not to leave her alone on New Year's Eve.

When Carol was asleep in the curve of Lilli's arm, Freddie came to take her in his own arms and off to bed. Lilli excused herself to go out to the kitchen to wish the staff a happy holiday. When she returned to the library, she found the family divided into companionable clusters. David and Greg sat playing chess by the window. The four women—Jan, Debbie, Vicky, and Marcia—were somberly discussing the imminent inauguration of Eisenhower, the first Republican president elected in twenty-four years. This was a family that had campaigned vigorously for Adlai Stevenson. Even David and Carol had been involved.

Clustered before the fireplace, Freddie, Lou, and Howie discussed the president-elect. Lilli was drawn by Howie's earnest analysis of why Eisenhower had won the Republican nomination when so many Republicans had been sure Taft had it sewed up.

"Television won the nomination for Eisenhower." Howie reiterated the beliefs of many. "We all saw what happened at the convention in Chicago. When there was all that clashing about seating the delegates from Georgia, Texas, and Louisiana, the Eisenhower team jumped in to massacre the Taft supporters. Right there in front of the television cameras, they carried on about the 'smoke-filled rooms' and the 'Taft steamroller.' It was the beginning of a whole new era of electioneering."

"Howie, have you ever thought about going into politics?" Lilli asked. "You seem to have a feel for it."

He looked embarrassed. "It's not my style. I like digging in behind the scenes, not being out there making speeches. I'm not even crazy about having to make court appearances."

"Then why did you go into law?" Freddie asked.

"To make a decent living. A law degree seemed like a trust fund. Remember, I'm a depression child." Howie smiled wryly. "Corporate law is not exactly the most exciting job in the world."

"You liked pinning down the source of the crank letters that came in against Donna Devan," Lilli said.

"But that wasn't a legal situation. That was research."

Lilli shook her head. "You have a sharp, analytical mind. How would you go about doing market research for a cosmetic line?"

Lou laughed. "What brought that up?"

"Mr. Charles Revson. Every time Revlon brings out a new product, he spends a fortune on market research, my spies tell me. And it pays off, even though he steals ideas from all of us. Tell me, Howie, how would you research a new moisture lotion?"

Across the room Vicky listened in disbelief to the lively conversation between her mother and her husband. Clearly stimulated, Howie was shooting a barrage of questions at her mother. Did Mother think she could pull Howie into the cosmetic business? He'd spent three years in law school!

"What did you think about *The Old Man and the Sea*?" Jan's voice intruded and Vicky realized the others had expressed an opinion.

"I loved it," Vicky said quickly. "I think it's the best thing Hemingway's ever done."

While Vicky tried to appear absorbed in the discussion about Hemingway and Steinbeck—whose *East of Eden* Marcia had just read—she was drawn into the electric exchange between her mother and Howie. Howie was bright. Of course he was coming up with ideas Mother thought were great. But that didn't mean he should jump into a job in market research for Princess Lilli. He was a lawyer.

Vicky suggested she and Howie call it an early night. She didn't want Howie to be sucked into Princess Lilli. It would be like moving back home again. Living in her mother's shadow again.

She said nothing about her anxieties as she and Howie drove home. They left the car in the garage and walked the half-block to the house, Vicky clutching the collar of her Jacques Fath cloth coat about her throat. She refused to wear furs.

"It was a great party," Howie said while he unlocked the heavy oak front door. "Your mother's an amazing woman."

"Was Mother trying to appoint you to her unofficial board of directors tonight?" she asked, trying to sound flippant, as they climbed the stairs to their bedroom. "She has a wonderful talent for using people close to her." She frowned. That sounded hostile. She hadn't meant it to be.

"She asked me to consider coming to work for her." All at once Howie was serious.

Vicky stared at him. "You're a lawyer. Is Mother setting up a legal department?" She tried to sound amused.

"She's talking market research." Howie crossed to the fireplace where logs had been laid in the grate in readiness for their return. Their domestic staff was limited to a couple who came in daily. Vicky had guessed that Howie would prefer sleep-out help. "I have to admit I'm intrigued."

"What do you know about market research?" Vicky threw her coat across a chair and kicked off her shoes.

"I could learn." He focused on coaxing the paper-laced quartered log into a blaze. "I think I've taken well to luxury living. A wife who thinks nothing is more romantic than a woodburning fireplace, though I shudder to think of the cost of logs bought in a city market." He laid aside the brass-handled poker and reached to pull her close. "I'd feel less like a kept husband if I were earning some real money. And your mother talks high figures."

"Don't decide right away, Howie. Please. Think it out."

"I will." He kissed her throat tenderly. "Right at this moment I have other things on my mind. We've never made love before a roaring fire."

"This one isn't roaring yet."

He smiled. "It will be."

Watching him poke at the fire, she wondered if Howie had already decided to go to work for her mother. She loved Mother, but she didn't want to be pulled into the Princess Lilli empire. She had grown up hearing the beauty business at the dinner table every night. If Howie worked for Princess Lilli, it would be the same all over again.

He reached for a pair of loose pillows on the sofa near the fireplace and dropped them to the floor. "Madame, will you share my lair?"

44

LILLI WAS DELIGHTED WHEN, shortly after the New Year's Eve party, Howie appeared at the salon to say he would like to become part of Princess Lilli's research department. She loved the way he threw himself into the various aspects of the business; he was determined to learn everything about the cosmetic industry. She recognized, too, that Howie, with his youthful enthusiasm, was creating hostility among others in his department.

"He's as brash as hell!" Ernie Schuman, the department head for fourteen years, said. "He drives me nuts with all his questions. What did law school teach him about the business?"

Lilli tried to soothe him. "He's learning from you."

But she was irritated in coming weeks by Ernie's subtle hints that he'd be happier if she fired Howie. That would not happen, even if Ernie issued an ultimatum. She was always fair to her employees, but she would not allow them to run her company. Perhaps, she surmised, Ernie resented someone twenty years his junior questioning long-standing tactics.

Late on a June afternoon, when most of the staff was gone for the day, Howie appeared at her office door looking troubled.

"I've been suspicious about Ernie for weeks, Lilli." He sighed as he dropped into a chair beside her desk. "He's selling your ideas to the competition." Lilli stared at him in shock. "You know the new hair-care line?" Lilli was about to introduce this as part of her "total beauty" campaign. "I followed Ernie last night. He had a meeting with Ransome, the head of

Evalina Cosmetics, at a restaurant on West Eighth Street." He chuckled. "Thank God Ernie's so nearsighted and too vain to wear his glasses outside the office. He couldn't see me. He gave Ransome a large manila envelope."

Lilli was shaken. "How do you know it was our hair-care campaign?"

"I've been talking to this artist who left Arden to go to Evalina. You always say you admire Arden's packaging. Anyhow, I told him I'd put in a good word for him if he approached you about a job at Princess Lilli." He grinned. "It's not a raid. I heard via the grapevine that he isn't happy there." Many employees found Elizabeth Arden difficult. "I met him for coffee this afternoon. He told me Evalina's all steamed up about a new hair-care line that was just brought to them. Out of nowhere, he says, they've decided to move into hair care."

"I'll fire Ernie first thing tomorrow morning." Lilli was grim. Did this damn thievery never stop? "From today on, Howie, you're head of the market-research department."

He was hesitant. "I don't have the experience."

"You have the instinct, imagination, and integrity. You'll gain experience."

"Thank you, boss." He smiled. "I'll try not to step on any more toes."

Lilli was proud to see Howie moving up in the Princess Lilli hierarchy. Eventually Lou would become head of the accounting department. Even for her son she would not oust a competent employee. Greg appeared happy with his casual, low-responsibility duties. She would have preferred to see him display more ambition, but she'd resigned herself to his weaknesses.

Sometimes she wasn't sure that Lou enjoyed his work. He was thoroughly competent, mixed well with the others in his department. He was liked and respected—and it had nothing to do with his being the boss's son. Yet there were moments when she looked into his eyes and saw a kind of frustration.

When Vicky announced late in the autumn that she was pregnant, and seven weeks later Marcia came forward with the same news, Lilli was rapturous. More than ever now she was determined to bring more shares of Princess Lilli stock under family control. New generations of family would come into the business. Carol had taken over as the crown princess, the role relinquished by her two aunts.

ON NEW YEAR'S EVE, 1953, Lilli again gave a family party. Earlier in the day there had been the usual lavish affair for staff and patrons at the salon. Now the family gathered in the library to wait for Henri to announce that the festive supper was ready to be served. This year Greg was missing. He had begged off to attend a party with friends. When Scott made an effort to apologize, Lilli brushed it aside. "Scott, the young seek out their own. It's natural." She caught the wistful glance David shot his father. "And if David has a party, then let him go to it."

David's face lit up. "You won't be angry, Grandma?"

"Not if you give me a New Year's Eve kiss before you take off."

"It's hard to believe David will be going to Columbia in September," Debbie said softly.

"I know." Lilli smiled. "It seems just a short time ago that Freddie was waiting impatiently for his freshman year at college."

"The way things are going around this town," Vicky said, "we're about ready to put this one on the list for a good nursery school." She patted her slightly protruding stomach while Howie dropped an arm about her shoulders. Carol glowed. She was fascinated by the prospect of two new babies in the family. For almost eleven years she had been the baby in the family.

In moments, Henri appeared and summoned them to the dining room. Freddie extended one arm to his mother and the other to Debbie. "Ten years ago today Debbie and I were Japanese prisoners. Times sure have changed, haven't they?"

Over Bertha's superb supper, they spoke with relief about the end of the war in Korea, and about the way more and more people were becoming disenchanted with Joe McCarthy.

"I love what Eisenhower is supposed to have said about him when his advisers told him to cut down McCarthy," Scott recalled: "'I just will not. I refuse to get into the gutter with that guy.'"

Inevitably, the conversation turned to Princess Lilli.

"Elizabeth Arden always manages to come out with the most exquisite Christmas packaging," Lilli said, her annual complaint. "I often wish Oliver were here in New York to work with the packaging department. In the early days he was so wonderful at designing our packages."

"Are you still unhappy about the theme of the summer campaign?" Howie asked.

"We need something fresh." Lilli sighed. "I know we have Mademoiselle Lilli for the mass-market trade, but instinct tells me we should pick up a share of that market with Princess Lilli products as well, even though they are expensive. Somehow the approach keeps eluding us."

"Remember what you dreamed up at lunch yesterday, Lou?" Howie turned to his brother-in-law.

"What did Lou dream up?" Lou was being his usual reserved self, and Howie was trying to make him talk.

"It was just some silly little idea that crossed my mind." He looked embarrassed.

Lilli exchanged a brief glance with Howie. "Tell me about it."

"Well . . ."—Lou looked uneasily around the table—"I figure a lot of women may think Princess Lilli is for the rich. They may be scared away by its prestige. I mean, it's only sold in the finest department stores and specialty shops—"

"Over two thousand of them," Howie interrupted. Lilli gestured for Lou to continue.

"I was thinking of something like, 'You don't have to wait to win a sweepstakes to buy Princess Lilli products. Treat yourself well—you're a princess.'"

"I like it," Lilli nodded. "It's rough, but it just might be the hook we need. Let's sit down with the advertising department. I want you to help us develop the new campaign, Lou. You're coming to it with something new!"

"You could play up the princess bit with the model you hire for the campaign. A girl who's not only beautiful but regal."

"Wearing a diamond tiara from Van Cleef and Arpels," Lilli added. "A copy of the one Arpels designed for Napoleon to give to Josephine."

"That sounds wonderful!" Marcia beamed at her husband. "Lou has such a creative mind. He should be able to use it for more than routine business problems."

So Lou *wasn't* happy in the accounting department. Why hadn't he come and told her? If Lou preferred to create their advertising campaign, then let him move in that direction. Whatever he wanted was his.

"Lou, I'd like to sit down and talk with you about our brochures," she said casually. "We need a fresh approach there, too. Start thinking about it."

TOUCHED AND PLEASED by this side of her younger son, to which she had been blind, Lilli put Lou to work. He was full of enthusiasm, bursting with ideas that Lilli embellished and acted on. At last a child of hers shared her joy in Princess Lilli.

In early May, Vicky gave birth to her first child, a baby girl whom they named Betsy, after Howie's late-grandmother. Five weeks later, Marcia gave birth to a son, to be named for Alex. A son to carry on the Kahn name, Lillie thought tenderly. She curtailed her usual traveling for months in order to be close to her new grandchildren: Betsy and Alex, who might one day be at the helm of Princess Lilli, along with their fathers and Carol.

Lilli continued to worry that she had not yet acquired enough stock to give her guaranteed control of the company. Her shares had crept up to forty-three percent; still, only the proxies she held assured her total control. So far they were all loyal to her, but how could she be sure this loyalty would continue? The cosmetic field was constantly changing. Chances had to be taken. Stockholders might one day disagree with her.

In early October, Lilli flew to London on a DC-4—a tedious fourteen-hour flight—for her annual conference with Oliver and Frances. From there she flew to Paris and on to their other salons across Europe. It still astonished her that wealthy and important men pursued her. She didn't realize that at sixty-seven she was still lovely and vibrant.

Back at the New York salon, Lilli discovered that a new receptionist had been hired in her absence. She suspected it was Greg's doing—and that he was enamored of the attractive young blonde. Though Constance Harris seemed charming and efficient, Lilli couldn't bring herself to like this new receptionist. Greg didn't seem to realize he was quite a "catch." Jan would be destroyed if Greg was roped in by some girl who only wanted his money.

HANDSOME IN HIS Brooks Brothers suit and London-tailored shirt, Greg strolled about the lounge area and chatted with each of several ladies waiting to be summoned to their treatment cubicles. It was his duty to keep tempers unruffled, egos smoothed, ladies flattered by his attentions. He knew it irritated his grandmother that he seemed satisfied with what she regarded as a menial position at Princess Lilli. She didn't know how he enjoyed circulating among the salon patrons, many of them young and beautiful. The operators, too, were often young and attractive. When he'd been in his early teens, he had waited eagerly for those occasions when his grandmother paraded him—along with Vicky and Lou—around the salon.

Today he was waiting for the reception desk to be clear for a moment so he could talk to Connie without anyone overhearing. His mouth went dry when he just looked at her. God, she was built! And it wasn't just the body. She had that gorgeous face. He had been dying to ask her out since her first day on the job. He was twenty-four years old and he'd never had a real date with a girl. No girl in his life, except those whores he picked up when he was desperate. Always scared to death afterward about what they might have given him, though everybody said it wasn't so terrible these days because of penicillin and the sulfa drugs.

He thought he was dreaming it that first week Connie was working at the salon, but the message was coming through loud and clear. Constance Harris looked at him and got hot pants. He saw it in the way she gazed at him with those sexy blue eyes, her mouth half parted and moist.

Now. Connie was alone at the desk. He wasn't so hot, he mused, that he didn't notice how chic she looked in that navy striped flannel in the new H-line dreamed up by Dior and already ripped off on Seventh Avenue. He liked women to dress smartly.

With an unconscious tug at his Countess Mara tie, Greg crossed the room. "Hi, gorgeous," he murmured in his best Tony Curtis imitation.

"Hi, Greg." A little-girl whisper that didn't match the rest of her.

"Busy tonight?" he asked casually. Maybe she had never even noticed his left arm. *Maybe she didn't care.*

"Not very." She leaned forward slightly so that he caught the scent of her perfume. It was a salon rule that every female on staff wear the latest Princess Lilli perfume. On Connie it seemed to take on special qualities.

"How about picking you up about eight? We could have dinner at 'Twenty-one.'" He saw her eyes widen. "Afterward, we'll drop by El Morocco for a drink." He would have preferred the Blue Angel, but he guessed she'd be more impressed by Elmo.

"Eight o'clock is fine." She used her best, faintly breathless Marilyn Monroe voice.

"Where do I pick you up?"

"I live on West Seventy-third," she said, and scribbled down the number. "Just ring the bell and I'll come down. I'm in a fourth-floor walk-up."

"Now, remember," he said, "eight sharp. Be ready because I may be double-parked." He knew she would be impressed by his Porsche Spyder—it was the same model James Dean drove.

After dinner they'd go to his apartment. It had taken him a year, but Mother finally bought him a one-bedroom co-op on East Sixty-seventh. She was relieved that he'd given up running with that swinging young jet-set crowd he'd been messing around with that summer in Europe after graduating from college. Their favorite pastimes were racing cars, orgies, and daisy chains. He wasn't ready for that. He'd never be ready for racing cars—he was glad he was able to drive at all.

CONNIE STEPPED out of the shower and wrapped herself in a deep-pile lilac towel. In the bedroom, Ron was singing along with an Eddie Fisher record on some disc-jockey show while he read the *Wall Street Journal*.

"Hey, baby," he called through the half-open bathroom door. "You don't want to keep the boyfriend waiting. Not a boyfriend who drives a Porsche Spyder."

"How do you know what he drives?" She walked into the bedroom in bare feet. If this deal went through, she'd be walking on carpeting three inches thick.

"I made it my business to know everything about Greg Jamison." His eyes trailed over Connie as she dropped the towel to the floor and hovered before an open dresser drawer. "I told you when you married me, Connie. I mean to make a million, and that calls for shrewd planning."

"I hate playing with this kid," she pouted. Ron was thirty-one. She was twenty-seven. They'd been married two years, but she still could make him hot as a pistol.

"You'll play with me later," he said. "We *need* Greg. If I come up with the right deal, we're set up in business. Rogan's group has a lot of money to invest, and I'm his boy if I can deliver."

"Now, remember, don't hang around tonight." She giggled. "Go see Brigitte Bardot's new movie. I'll take care of you later."

"My guess is he won't come here. He'll take you to his place—a co-op his parents bought for him. Not that he needed them to buy it. Lilli Laval set up a million-dollar trust fund for him."

She wiggled into a pair of black lace panties. "You read that in the *Wall Street Journal*?"

"From my private source." He slapped her on the rump. "Now get going, baby."

GREG WAS FEELING smug when he and Connie left "21" and headed for the Porsche. She had flashed him a sexy smile when he suggested going up to his apartment to listen to his "rock 'n' roll" records. "How did you guess I'm just mad about rock 'n' roll?" She clung to his arm—his *good* arm. He felt a pang of insecurity.

"You remember last year when Alan Freed had that rock jamboree in Cleveland? I flew out for it. So many people showed up at the stadium, the show had to be canceled."

"My radio stays on WINS," she said as he helped her into the car. "Just waiting for Alan Freed."

Greg was aware of Connie's approval as they walked through his plush lobby to the bank of elevators. She knew Lilli Laval was his grandmother—had she expected him to live in a hovel?

Alone in the elevator, he pulled her to him, sliding his right arm beneath her cloth coat. Tonight, he knew, he would not be rejected. Tonight the humiliation of his "passion-pit" encounter his last year in high school, when a supposedly overheated girl had gotten the giggles because he had to pull his arm away from her to unzip his fly, would finally be a thing of the past. *It wouldn't matter to Connie.*

"Wow!" Connie stared in delight as he led her past the foyer of his apartment into the starkly modern black, white, and red living room.

"My mother brought some decorator over from Paris to do the apartment." He crossed to the bar.

"No more drinking for me, Greg." She paused, smiled coyly. "I have to be at the salon at nine-thirty tomorrow morning."

"Okay," he pointed to a wall unit holding a colorful display of records, a television set, and a record player. "Choose some records and put them on the player. I'm going to change into something more comfortable."

In the bedroom he stripped, tossed his clothes onto a chair and pulled on a tiger-print silk robe he'd bought on a trip to Tangiers the previous autumn. For a moment he paused beside the bed, imagining Connie's creamy naked body sprawled across the black fake-fur spread.

From the living room he heard the explosive sounds of the Ravens' "Rock Me All Night." He hurried in and stopped dead. Connie was on her feet, writhing with the music. Stripped down to the black lace panties, black bra, black garter belt, sheer black nylons.

"What took you so long?" Her Marilyn Monroe bosom had all but spilled from her bra.

"Just building up the suspense." He untied his robe.

"It'll be our secret," she said softly, moving in close against him. "Nobody at the salon has to know."

"Nobody." He would have agreed to anything as he fumbled with one hand for the hooks on her bra. At last the strip of lace fell to the floor.

Suddenly she pulled away. "Catch me!" She ran toward the bedroom, her creamy white breasts bouncing. He was right behind her, his heart pounding.

"Honey, you're young and healthy." She gave him a look of reproach as he pushed her across the bed. "There's no rush."

"Anything you say." He let her pull him onto the bed and on his back beside her.

She slid out of her panties and tossed them to the floor. Still in garter belt and black nylons, she crouched beside him and with one vermilion-nailed hand fondled him while she dropped feather-light kisses on his thighs. He followed her lead, maneuvering her into position above him. He nearly laughed out loud when he realized that her inner thighs had been dabbed with *Arpege*.

At last they separated. He lay back, breathing heavily. The pungent taste of her in his mouth. Waiting for her next move.

"Now," she purred, straddling him. "Okay, Greggie boy. Let's ride to paradise!"

GREG WAS OBSESSED with Connie. He didn't understand why she wouldn't see him every night. Ten days after their first date—over dinner at a small French restaurant—he pleaded with her to move into his apartment.

"Sweetie, my brother would kill me. He doesn't understand girls like me. To Ron, I'm his sweet little baby sister. All he's interested in is his business."

"What does he do?" He realized now that he had never given a thought to Connie's family. He was surprised to learn she shared an apartment with her brother.

"Ron's a promoter, really. Right now he's setting up a cosmetic company. Nothing terrific like Princess Lilli, just a small operation. But they're probably not offering high enough salaries. Could you find out for me what people like Princess Lilli's product manager and Nadine, the fashion coordinator, and that woman who's head of the demonstrators are paid? All the key people, Greg. Then Ron'll know if they're offering too little."

He looked at her, startled. "I don't know about those things, Connie."

"But you can find out, Greg. A list of salaries of the top people." Her knee nudged his under the table. "Then maybe Ron won't be upset because I keep refusing to go out with his partner."

"I'll try to get the figures for you." The thought of sharing Connie with another man was intolerable.

"I'll cook dinner for you tomorrow night at your place. Bring the figures with you."

Greg glanced at his watch. He hated wasting time in a restaurant when Connie made such a point of being home by eleven.

"Why don't we have coffee at my place?"

"Tonight I'm going straight home—I have to wash my hair and do laundry. But tomorrow's Friday. And I'm off this Saturday. I just might tell Ron I'm sleeping over at a girlfriend's apartment."

Greg brightened. "Sensational."

THE NEXT DAY, Greg left the salon with the rest of the staff, as usual. He'd given his apartment key to Connie so she could go ahead and start dinner. It was understood that he'd be slipping back into the salon. He strolled around the block, pausing at the corner of Fifth Avenue until he saw Lilli, always the last to leave, emerge and walk to the waiting Rolls.

Once Henri had driven out of sight, Greg let himself into the salon again. He headed upstairs to the accounting department. Check the files. He ought to be able to find the figures fast and get right out of here. Connie would be thrilled when he brought her the salary list. They'd have dinner and then make love.

In minutes he found what he wanted. His hands trembling, he scrawled names and figures on a sheet of paper. What harm could this do Grandma? A small company trying to start up a business needed all the help it could get. Dad was always saying how hard it was to be a small company in this generation of biggies. And Connie sure would show her appreciation. He broke out in a sweat just thinking about it.

OVER THE NEXT THREE WEEKS, Greg was shocked by the mass exodus of Princess Lilli employees. They couldn't be going to Ron's company, could they? And what if they were? Cosmetic companies were always raiding somebody else's staff or stealing a hot new idea. He'd grown up hearing tales about how Elizabeth Arden had once hired away Helena Rubinstein's whole sales staff, how Mme. Rubinstein had hired Miss Arden's ex-husband as her sales manager, how Charles Revson stole from everybody.

Grandma wouldn't stew for long, Greg told himself. Everyone in the company was all excited about the new lipstick package they were launching for the summer trade. It was very hush-hush; but Connie said that from the way everybody talked, this new lipstick case was expected to sell 5 million.

"I'm dying to see it," Connie said one night in bed. "All the operators at the salon have seen it. I guess I'm not important enough."

"I have to go to the factory tomorrow. One of those damn tours again." Occasionally people from the out-of-town or out-of-country salons were brought to New York to see the New York salon and the factory. It was his duty to show them around. "I'll filch one of the samples and bring it to you."

A week later Connie told Greg that she wanted him to meet Ron that evening. "He has an absolutely sensational idea, sweetie. About bringing *us* into his business."

Greg was startled. "He knows about me?"

"Not about us personally," she giggled. "Only that you were so sweet about getting those names for him. Ron says the business is going to make everybody in the field sit up and take notice. They're just starting off, and the orders are pouring in."

"What could I do?" He was flattered that Connie was trying to bring him together with her brother.

"Ron will explain everything tonight. Let's have dinner at that little French place."

Throughout the day, all Greg thought about was being in business with Connie's brother. Becoming an important business executive on his own, without Her Royal Highness, Princess Lilli! The prospect was tantalizing.

By why had Ron asked *him* to come into business? Quickly he dismissed the thought that his money had anything to do with it. Ron probably figured he'd bring in a lot of know-how; he'd been exposed to the cosmetic business all his life. But what the hell did he really know? Now doubts infiltrated his mind. He could run a salon. He'd learned that much. Of course they'd want to open up a salon. Connie and he would run it.

Connie and he might even get married. The family couldn't stop him; he wasn't a minor.

At the end of the day, he and Connie left the salon separately, though only minutes apart. Nobody at the salon guessed about them, he thought triumphantly. They'd handled it well.

Ron was waiting for them when they arrived at the restaurant, and Greg was immediately impressed by him. Ron Harris was sharp. He knew all the angles. And tonight Greg saw another side of Connie: She had learned a lot about cosmetics.

"The company is ready to expand way beyond what Ron planned in the beginning. They've got great new ideas," she said enthusiastically. "The salesmen are all steamed up."

Ron suddenly looked serious. "Only one problem is holding us back. The backers are insisting I bring in a token amount of the investment before they put up more money to expand the factory so we can make shipments. And you know we have to ship fast, before somebody else steals our ideas and comes out on the market with them. They expect me to bring in half a million. I've raised a quarter of a million. That's as far as I can go." He looked expectantly at Greg.

"I can't put my hands on any cash until my twenty-fifth birthday next May." They thought he would be Ron's partner! "And then I only get the income from my trust—I can't touch the principal until I'm thirty-five." Maybe he could talk to Mother and Dad. Invest in Princess Lilli's competition? No matter how small the company, they'd consider it treason.

"Oh, Greg." Connie trailed a finger down his back. "Can't you borrow it? It would be awful if we lost out on this when Ron's come so far with it."

He paused. He couldn't stand it if Connie walked out on him.

"Let me try to think of something. Maybe I can persuade my mother to let me hock some of her jewelry." He turned to Ron. "I wouldn't know how to do it. If I brought you some jewelry, would you know how to raise cash on it?"

Ron's eyes narrowed. "That could be arranged. We won't get market value, but it could put us over."

"Then I'll try." Greg stood up.

"We have to move fast," Ron said. "My people won't hang around indefinitely."

Greg couldn't get to sleep that night. He knew if he failed to come up with money—or jewelry—he would lose Connie. He couldn't let that happen. At dawn, fortifying himself with scotch on the rocks, Greg lay on the living-room sofa and planned his next move.

45

AT CLOSE to 1:00 P.M., Greg collected his attaché case and left the salon. Ostensibly he was going out to lunch and on to some salon errand. He knew Lilli would be tied up for at least two hours in another of her many business luncheons. Last year a private dining room and kitchen had been installed on the top floor of the Princess Lilli building. A chef was brought over from Paris because Lilli had a passion for gourmet French food.

Out in the brisk November cold, Greg flagged down a taxi and gave the driver his grandmother's address on Gramercy Park. His heart was pounding as he contemplated the course ahead of him. Grandma was leaving late today on the company plane for a conference at the factory in Rio. Her luggage had already been dispatched to the plane. As usual, she would be accompanied by her private secretary and maid. She would be gone ten days. On her business trips, Lilli took very little jewelry: only her rope of Harry Winston pearls and the single strand of black pearls reputed to have belonged to Marie Antoinette, plus earrings that had been designed to wear with each. She'd worn the black pearls today with her new black Chanel suit and white silk blouse, which was her tribute to the comeback this year of the legendary Coco Chanel. A faint smile touched Greg's mouth as he remembered his father's reproach to his grandmother only last month. "Lilli, you shouldn't keep your jewelry in the house. Even in that Oriental cabinet, it isn't safe."

But his grandmother—normally so realistic—refused to keep her jewelry in a bank vault, because it meant a trip to the bank each time she chose to wear something from her magnificent collection. Everything was in the secret drawer of the cabinet she had bought years ago on a trip to the Far East.

Despite the cold, Greg's hands were perspiring as he paid the driver. Nobody would suffer except the insurance people, he told himself. Nobody would ever know who had taken the jewelry. They couldn't arrest the whole household staff.

He rang the bell and waited. He'd explain to Ron that his mother was letting him have her jewelry but that nobody was to know because his father would be furious.

Tonight, Connie would cook dinner for him at the apartment. She would sleep over. And tomorrow morning they would turn the jewelry over to Ron. They wouldn't leave the salon just yet. They'd wait a few weeks.

"Good afternoon, Mr. Greg." Henri seemed surprised to see him. "Madame isn't home."

"I know. I've just come from her office. She sent me over to pick up some papers she left in her sitting room. She's in the middle of a conference right now and needs them."

Greg hurried up the stairs to the master bedroom suite. Carefully, he closed the door behind him and crossed to the eighteenth-century Oriental lacquered cabinet that sat between a pair of tall, narrow windows in the sitting room. He deposited the attaché case on the top, pulled out the drawer that concealed yet another drawer. His grandmother's jewelry collection, reputed by appraisers to be worth millions, lay before him.

He scooped up a handful of glittering necklaces and bracelets, and a square-cut emerald ring. Enough, he told himself, to satisfy the demands of Ron's associates. He dropped the jewelry into the attaché case, slammed it shut, and whistled as he strode from the room.

LILLI RETURNED from Rio three days before Thanksgiving. She made a point of always being at the Gramercy Park house for Thanksgiving, New Year's, and the eve of the first seder of

Passover. These were times of family gatherings that were precious to her.

By eleven on Thanksgiving morning, savory aromas drifted through the house from the basement kitchen. Lilli had slept late and had breakfast served in her sitting room. After breakfast she had gone over the sketches for the new packaging, which she had brought home with her last night. Now she prepared to dress for dinner.

She chose a softly bloused gray alpaca from Dior's autumn collection. She would wear her emerald necklace, she decided—Alex's favorite. She changed into the gray alpaca frock, slid her feet into gray suede pumps, and crossed to the cabinet that was her jewelry depository.

Her face drained of color as she stared into the secret drawer. What had happened to some of her best pieces? None of the staff would have stolen from her. She would stake her life on that. As for outsiders, there was always someone in the house, and long ago Alex had arranged for the installation of a security system. *Who could have taken her jewelry?*

Lilli hurried into the hall and called downstairs to Martine. Had there been a plumber, an electrician, some repairman? The jewelry was insured, of course, but money wasn't the issue. She'd loved some of those pieces.

"Martine, some of my jewelry has been stolen," she said as Martine appeared at the head of the stairs. "I just can't believe it!"

"Oh, madame!" Martine was aghast. "You're sure of this? You didn't take it with you to Rio?"

"Martine, you know me. I take only my pearls when I travel. Has there been a repairman in the house while I was away? I know that none of the staff would do this."

Martine paused, thinking. "I don't recall any repair people," she said. "But perhaps we ought to ask Henri."

Henri was summoned.

"There's been no stranger in the house, madame. No breach in the security that I know of. Shall I phone for the police?"

"Please, Henri," Lilli said, and then stopped him. "Wait. Let's make sure we've overlooked no strangers coming into the house. Let's go back to my last day in the city. Let's think very carefully. Was there a grocery delivery?"

"Yes," Henri said, "but the man didn't come into the house." He squinted in thought. "No. I brought the boxes into the kitchen for Bertha myself. There was the grocery delivery and the postman and Mr. Greg—"

"Greg?" Lilli froze.

"He came to pick up those papers you needed for your conference."

"Yes, of course." Lilli managed a faint smile. *She hadn't sent Greg to the house.*

"Shall I call the police now?" Henri asked.

"I think it's best that I talk with the insurance people first." She needed time to think. "And please don't say anything to the others. I wouldn't want to spoil their Thanksgiving."

Lilli waited until she was sure that both Henri and Martine were downstairs before she reached for the telephone. Greg was not expected for dinner—he'd come up with some story about going to Connecticut to spend the long weekend with a friend from college.

"Jan, I want you and Scott to come over right now. And bring Greg with you."

"Mother, I just spoke to Greg on the phone. He's about to leave to drive up to Connecticut." Jan sounded anxious.

"Connecticut will have to wait. Bring Greg with you."

GREG STOOD white and shaking before his parents and his grandmother. He'd been so stupid to think that Henri would forget his visit that day.

"I want to know why you took my jewelry, and who has it now," Lilli said. "Is Constance Harris involved in this in some way?"

"I feel sick," he whispered. "I think I'm going to throw up."

"No, you're not. I want to know everything that's happened between Constance Harris and you. And I want to know *now*."

Haltingly, Greg confessed the whole story—his infatuation with Connie, the list of employees and their salaries that he had filched for her, the sample lipstick case he had given her...

"Greg, how could you?" Scott stared at him in shock. "Steal from your own grandmother!"

"Jan, sit down," Lilli said gently. She knew that Jan was remembering the man who was Greg's natural father.

"I'm going to be sick," Greg gasped, a hand to his mouth.

Lilli turned to Scott. "Take him into my bathroom."

"Mother, it's all my fault," Jan whispered while Scott hustled Greg into the bathroom.

"It's *not* your fault. It has *never* been your fault. Stop blaming yourself, Jan. Greg has needed psychiatric help for a long time. Now he's going to get it. I'll tell him frankly: Either he signs himself into a sanatorium immediately—and remains there until the doctors assure us he's a responsible human being—or he goes to prison. I don't have to tell you what he'll decide."

"Oh, Mama..." Jan hadn't called her that since she was twelve. "But what about the jewelry? It's worth a fortune!"

"Your happiness means more to me than a fortune in jewels," Lilli said quietly. "I won't report this to either the police or the insurance company. It's a family matter. We'll salvage what we can, but what's important is that Greg learn to become the decent human being he was meant to be."

"You'll do this for your grandson?"

"I'm not doing this for Greg. I'm enraged and affronted by what he's done. I'm doing it for you. Because your happiness is at stake."

As Lillie held Jan in her arms, she realized that the final vestiges of hostility between them had disappeared. At last, her daughter had come home to her.

FOR THE FIRST FOUR WEEKS, no one was allowed to visit Greg at the sanatorium. After that, Jan and Scott drove up to visit him every Sunday. They reported that he was remorseful, often depressed, sometimes rebellious, always blaming fate for what had happened. The doctors recommended a lengthy stay.

Connie Harris had been fired, and Lilli's attorneys threatened Ron Harris with arrest for receiving stolen goods. But Ron knew this would involve Greg and guessed Lilli would do nothing that would bring her grandson up on criminal charges. Harris Cosmetics scooped Princess Lilli on their new lipstick package, with sales that established them in the industry.

Frustrated by this little coup, Lilli launched a new line for men: Prince Alex. It was conceived in secrecy, the campaign developed by Howie and Lou and the advertising and marketing staffs. Lilli was astonished at the sparkling copy Lou created, especially the press releases, each of which, she always maintained, had more impact than a dozen ads. She had no inkling of Lou's frustration at having to abandon the novel he had been secretly working on at night and on weekends.

Late the following summer, Prince Alex and a men's boutique of the same name were launched with ads in *Esquire*, *Vogue*, *Town & Country*, and *Harper's Bazaar*. A spectacular press party was given at El Morocco; another party, for society and entertainment personalities, took place aboard a rented yacht that sailed around Manhattan.

Lilli was proud of Lou's success in creating attention-grabbing copy and press releases not only for Prince Alex but for Princess Lilli and Mlle. Lilli. She was equally proud when Lou and Marcia confided in October that in seven months she would be a grandmother again.

Lilli relished the knowledge that her four children were all happy in their marriages. It was as though Freddie had never been married to Phyllis; Debbie was such a fine mother to his children and a wonderful wife. David—now a student at Columbia—and Carol saw Phyllis once a year when she visited New York. She lived in Paris.

As time passed, Jan grew optimistic about Greg's treatment at the sanatorium. Even Scott, always cautious, expressed his conviction that Greg—in his grandmother's words—would become a *mensch*.

LIKE OTHER cosmetic-field leaders, Lilli watched the continually astonishing progress of Charles Revson, who had bought a new TV show, "The $64,000 Question," for Revlon. Howie was urging Lilli to move into TV on a larger scale.

Lilli became increasingly aware, too, of the small but enterprising Estée Lauder line. Howie had enormous respect for the Lauder gimmick of giving away free samples. Now Lauder was introducing "gift-with-purchase," which other houses were ridiculing as poor business policy. Lilli called a conference to discuss this new approach to selling.

Shortly after New Year's, a dozen key executives gathered with Lilli, and on her instructions Howie outlined the Estée Lauder ploy to increase sales volume: Customers who purchased a specific amount of Estée Lauder products at a designated department store would receive a gift of sample items selected from cosmetics or creams or lotions they were promoting at that time. The gimmick could be repeated at different stores during the course of the year.

"It won't work." Lilli's controller was adamant. "It's far too expensive. And once it's started, it'll be hell to stop—both the department stores and the customers will expect it. You won't see Revson jumping on this bandwagon."

"You're absolutely right," Howie said, and Lillie turned to him in surprise. Last night he had been enthusiastic about their going into gift-with-purchase. "Revson's dealing with mass market, like we are with Mademoiselle Lilli." Lilli suppressed a smile. Aware of his youthfulness and brief tenure with Princess Lilli, Howie was being diplomatic. "But for our major line—our prestigious Princess Lilli—it's a natural. I suspect Arden and Rubinstein and Gray are already considering it, despite all the unfavorable talk about town."

"I think we should hold off"—the fashion coordinator always backed up the controller—"until we see how gift-with-purchase is accepted."

"I can give you an idea of how it's being accepted," Howie said. "At stores like Saks and Altman's, velvet ropes are being used to keep the would-be buyers in a line. I spoke to my wife about her reaction to the gift-with-purchase. She thinks it's intriguing. I talked to my sister-in-law, and to my mother and sister out in Arizona. Every woman I've talked to likes the idea."

"Then we'll do it." Lilli stood up, her decision made. She was secretly pleased that Howie had consulted Vicky.

IN MAY, Marcia gave birth to a second son, to be named Stephen—for his great-great aunt Sara. They followed the Jewish tradition in choosing a name beginning with the same letter of the alphabet as that of the person being remembered. Three weeks earlier, Vicky and Howie had exuberantly announced that *she* was pregnant again. Lilli rejoiced at hearing of each new grandchild. Carol, at thirteen, was especially close to her grandmother. Whenever Carol's school schedule permitted, Lilli took her along on trips to the salons and department stores.

In June, Greg was released from the sanatorium. He planned to take a position in his father's business. Profits at Princess Lilli were soaring to the point where Lilli, on her attorney's advice, decided to establish the Alex Kahn Foundation. Lilli was delighted when Jan expressed a wish to work with the foundation.

In August, Freddie and Debbie were in Chicago, along with David, for the Democratic National Convention. Everyone in the family was behind Adlai Stevenson. Each night of the convention Lilli and Carol—staying with her grandmother at the Southampton house while her father and stepmother were in Chicago—sat in front of the television set to watch the nomination of the man who had become almost a family idol.

Late in August the family gathered for a long weekend in Southampton. Though this was ostensibly a holiday, Lilli summoned Howie and Lou after dinner on the first night to what had become the Southampton house office for a discussion about the international market. Princess Lilli was now sold in seventy countries throughout the world, but Lilli was ever in search of expansion. Ever determined to keep the stockholders on her side.

"Let's go for a walk on the beach," Marcia said to Vicky as they finished a game of Monopoly at the cozy breakfast-room table. "If you feel up to it, that is." Vicky was now in her sixth month.

Vicky stood up. "Of course I'm up to it."

The little ones—Betsy, Alex, and Stephen—were asleep in the new nursery wing. Freddie, Debbie, and Carol were in the library watching Jackie Gleason on TV while David alternated between watching TV and reading—usually during commercials—MacKinlay Kantor's Pulitzer Prize-winning novel, *Andersonville*.

"I'll run upstairs for sweaters," Marcia said. "I'll only be a minute."

Marcia suspected that Lou would be upset if he knew what she was about to confide to Vicky, but she loved him too much not to try to help him. Lou had to make his mother understand he had a right to live his own life.

Marcia paused briefly to look in on the children, though both nurses were close by, then hurried downstairs with the two cashmere cardigans. In comfortable silence, she and Vicky left the house to walk the fifty feet to the beach. The moon lent a silver sheen to the waves that rolled with mesmerizing music onto the shore.

"You're upset about something, aren't you?" Vicky said.

"Sort of. I'm upset about Lou. He shouldn't be tied down writing advertising copy and press releases."

"I thought Lou enjoyed that."

"He did at first. It took him out of the accounting department. But now it's draining him. You know how many evenings he and Howie spend with your mother, working on one campaign or another.''

"I know." Vicky smiled. "There are so many nights when Howie calls up at the last minute to say he won't be home for dinner. But to him it's exciting and stimulating."

"For the last year, Lou's been working on a novel. He wouldn't let me tell anybody—not even you. But lately he's had no time at all for it, and I can see it's eating him up inside. It's absurd for Lou to keep working for the company when he wants to write. We don't need the money. We can live well— luxuriously—on the income from his trust. And he's not indispensable at Princess Lilli. He's awfully good, but he can be replaced."

Vicky nodded in understanding. "He can't bring himself to hurt Mother, can he?"

"Vicky, help me convince him he has a right to pull out. It's time for Lou to cut free of his mother and do what he feels is right for himself."

"It won't be easy," Vicky said. "Lou's always felt compelled to do whatever pleases Mother. Even when he was a little boy."

"But he's a man now. He's got to cut the tie!"

THE FOLLOWING EVENING Marcia and Vicky together confronted Lou. At first angry that Marcia had revealed their secret, he gradually relaxed enough to discuss the novel with Vicky.

"How do I know I'm any good?"

"I know you're good," Marcia said. "You owe it to yourself to give yourself a chance to prove it. You can't put in the long hours writing copy for Princess Lilli and write a novel, too. And it isn't necessary. Thank God, you don't have to worry about supporting yourself and a family. Do you know how many writers would sacrifice ten years of their lives for that assurance? You owe it to yourself—and to the children and me." Only for Lou and the children could Marcia be so impassioned.

"It would be wonderful," he mused, "to know that I could spend as much time as I liked at the typewriter."

Marcia leaned forward urgently. "Do it, Lou. Tell your mother. She'll survive, I promise you." She wouldn't think now about how upset Lilli would be.

"Marcia's right," Vicky said. "Mother's a tough lady. And she can't have it her way all the time. She's got Howie. It's time to let you off the hook."

Lou laughed. "Okay, you win. I'll tell her I'll stay another three months. That should be long enough, shouldn't it?"

LILLI SAT at her desk and listened with a tightening of her throat as Lou opened his heart to her. All this time, while she had gloried in Lou's coming into the company, he had been cherishing other ambitions. She had spent her lifetime building a dynasty for her children, and all of them had shunned it—except for Vicky's husband.

"I've not been the mother I hoped to be," Lilli said quietly when he had stammered his confession. "I want you to do what's right for you, darling. You have no obligation to stay with the business." She hoped he didn't sense her hurt, her sense of desolation at losing him.

"You've been the best of all mothers. *I* wasn't entirely honest."

"If you change your mind and decide you'd like to come back, you know there's always a place for you." Marcia had pushed Lou into making this decision, she thought with anger. Why couldn't Marcia have let him be? He had a flair for the business. In time, he would have come to love it, as Alex did. *He was so much like Alex.* "After all, one day the business will belong to you children. I'll be seventy my next birthday. How long can I expect to remain at the head of Princess Lilli?"

"Mother, you don't look fifty. You'll be the head of Princess Lilli thirty-five years from now." For what? she thought. For a business that might go into the hands of strangers? She had poured her whole life into her business. *Why did Marcia do this to her?* "Look at Helena Rubinstein," Lou said. "People in the industry say she has to be over eighty, and she's still going strong. Elizabeth Arden isn't far behind her. In the cosmetic field, you're still a young woman.''

''When will you be leaving, Lou?''

He'd told Vicky and Marcia three months, but... ''I'll stay another six months. You should be able to ease me out comfortably by then.''

Long after Lou left her office, Lilli sat at her desk and tried to sort out her feelings. She would never be able to feel quite the same toward Marcia again. Damn it, why couldn't Marcia have given Lou time to come to love the business the way his father had?

46

LILLI TRIED TO PRETEND that her feelings toward Marcia were unchanged, but she knew Marcia sensed her hostility. This son was replaceable in the business—but not in her dreams for Princess Lilli. *Alex's son belonged at the helm of Princess Lilli.*

In November, Vicky gave birth to a second daughter, named Kathy for her great-grandmother. November would be an eventful month for the family, Lilli remarked as she hovered with Howie before the hospital nursery to inspect this newest edition. Jan and David also celebrated birthdays in November.

At the annual Christmas party at the salon, Jan confided that Greg was in love.

"Who is she?" Lilli was pleased. Marriage might be the best thing that could happen to him.

"She was a nurse at the sanatorium. It was her first job. When Greg left, he continued to see her."

Lilli hesitated. "Is she Jewish?"

Jan laughed. "I was waiting for you to ask. Yes, she is. Her name is Anne Levine. Her parents died in a car crash when she was seven. She was an only child and raised by her grandmother, who died seven years ago. She worked her way through nursing school. Greg says they're very much in love." Jan hesitated. "He says she doesn't care at all about his arm, and that she refuses to let him be depressed about it."

Lilli smiled. "I like the sound of this Anne Levine."

"I was amazed when Greg insisted he wants a traditional wedding. Small—just family—but with Anne in a white wedding gown with a veil and all the trimmings."

"Jan, let me give them the wedding." Suddenly Lilli realized that in this way she could bridge the gap between Greg and herself.

Lilli was happy to be caught up in wedding plans again. Happy that at last Jan was finding such pleasure in Greg. On the night of the wedding rehearsal—with Carol enchanted at being a bridesmaid again—Greg confessed to his grandmother that he was bored with investment banking. "It's dull. I don't know how Dad stands it year after year. At the salon everything was so different. Beautiful. There was a special feeling there." His smile was eloquent. Lilli saw something of herself in him. Greg felt as she did about the salon. He understood that women came to the salon with eagerness and hope, knowing that when they left they would be more attractive. For all the special ingredients the chemists strove to put into their products, the most important, as Aunt Sara had always said, was hope.

"Greg, do you think you could run a salon?"

He looked at her for a long time. "I can't think of anything more exciting. Yes. I could run a salon."

"I'm opening in Phoenix. I know it's strong Arden territory, but there's room for us. Would you and Anne be willing to live in Phoenix?"

"Anne will do anything that'll make me happy."

"Then it's settled," Lilli said briskly. "You'll be in charge of Princess Lilli, Phoenix."

LILLI ALLOWED GREG increasing leeway as she recognized his ability to make the Phoenix salon another jewel in the Princess Lilli chain. Anne worked with him in the salon. She was obviously thrilled by the new life-style her marriage had brought to her. She and Greg were building a large, sprawling Spanish hacienda with a swimming pool on several acres at the edge of Phoenix. In the meantime, they lived in a rented house belonging to a retired industrialist on a yearlong trip around the world.

Secretly, it disturbed Lilli that Lou was out of the salon. Though he and Marcia never missed a Friday-evening family dinner, she felt there was a rift between her and the two of them. From Vicky, she learned that Lou was hard at work on his novel. Lilli found it impossible to understand how he could prefer writing a novel to taking over a world-renowned cosmetic dynasty.

She was certain Greg would do well with the Phoenix salon, but she also knew that his talents would not expand to taking over for her one day. Her hopes focused now on Carol. Freddie and Debbie teased her about spoiling Carol on those frequent occasions when she stayed with her grandmother. Freddie and Debbie were deeply involved not only in the peace movement but in civil rights. Their activities took them across the nation.

Carol's presence in the Gramercy Park house was especially precious to Lilli when word came that Charles had died of a stroke, and when five weeks later Frances followed him in death. She was reminded, too, of her own mortality—and of the fact that until she owned fifty-one percent of Princess Lilli stock, she could not consider her life's work completed.

In late September, Carol and Lilli, along with most of America, watched the activities at Central High School in Little Rock, Arkansas. President Eisenhower had sent almost a thousand paratroopers to quell the violence that erupted when nine black students tried to enroll in the newly integrated school.

"Grandma, how can they treat those kids like that?" Carol was outraged.

"Times will change, darling," Lilli said. "Be proud that your father is one of those fighting for the change." But let this child not follow in her father's footsteps. Let Carol come with her into the business.

In the increasingly hectic jungle of the cosmetic industry, Lilli was introducing new products by the dozen, almost all of which proved successful. She battled with the new advertising agency to come up with a TV show to match Revlon's "$64,000 Question." Revlon had become her most formidable competitor.

In addition to heavy advertising, Lilli fought for editorial space in magazines and newspapers. Photographs of her on her seventieth birthday proclaimed to the world that Princess Lilli products kept the founder of the company beautiful and young far beyond her years. Rubinstein appeared far younger than she was, but she was no longer a beautiful woman. Arden, several years younger than Rubinstein, also looked younger than she was, but she had never been beautiful either.

Early in the summer Lilli announced that she had bought extensive property adjoining the house at Southampton. By the following summer there would be a family compound, with separate houses for Lou and Marcia, Vicky and Howie, Jan and Scott, and Freddie and Debbie. She waited impatiently for Oliver's arrival in New York. Knowing he was devastated, as she was, by the deaths of Frances and Charles, she hoped that six weeks in New York would refresh his outlook.

During Oliver's visit, Lilli tried to be with him as much as possible. Of those early days in Sydney, only she and Oliver remained. It was hard to believe they were both seventy years old; they didn't act or feel like seventy. But they had reached the age where funerals were more frequent in their lives than weddings. She would not let herself become maudlin. She had lost dear ones, but her life had expanded to include seven grandchildren. And those who were gone lived in her memory. Not a day passed that Alex was not with her.

When she saw Oliver off at the airport, she reminded him she would be in London the following spring. "God bless the airlines," she laughed. "We're never really far apart."

During the autumn and winter, Lilli drove to Southampton to check the progress on the houses under construction. When she returned in the spring from a week in London—and quick visits to the European salons with Oliver—she ordered the beach house opened so that she might run out for a day or two when her schedule permitted. The prospect of a compound, where she would be surrounded by children and grandchildren, delighted her.

In May, Lou and Marcia came to the family Friday-night dinner and announced excitedly that Lou had sold his novel. "The advance is very low," he said, "but I'll be published!"

"Lou, I'm proud of you," Lilli kissed him, then turned and kissed Marcia. "I'm proud of both of you," she said softly. "When will the book come out? We'll have a magnificent party."

"Not for a year," Lou laughed. "And there's more news. Marcia's pregnant again."

Lilli was radiant. "Another family jewel."

In the fall of '58, Lilli emerged from a conference with the packaging department to learn from her secretary that Vicky was waiting for her in her downstairs office. Though Lilli maintained a lavishly appointed office on the floor that housed her top-level executives, she spent part of each day in her street-level salon office, with its charming private garden. Here, she confided to family, was the heart of Princess Lilli.

Now she was worried. Had something happened to one of the children? She couldn't remember Vicky ever coming to the office this way. *What had happened?*

"Hi, Mother." Vicky turned around in her chair with a bright smile. "I thought it was time we had a special talk—and it seemed right to have it here in your office."

"The children are all right? And you?"

Vicky laughed. "Oh, I'm fine. I don't know whether this is my own idea or Howie's—you know how he charges home every night oozing with shoptalk. But I think I'd like to come into the business. I'm restless. I adore Betsy and Kathy, but I need more in my life than the children and the house. And I'd see more of Howie if I were working with him. I'd like to be involved in marketing. Howie says I come up with some good ideas." She paused, looking a little shy.

"Vicky, that's wonderful news!" Lilli glowed. "When would you like to start?" Her dream was coming true. Vicky was bright and imaginative—she would learn fast.

"I don't care—tomorrow, anytime. I won't be depriving the kids. I'll spend hours with them every day."

Lilli heard the guilt in her voice. "Darling, don't feel guilty. Women are having families and careers today without depriving their families. I raised my children and worked." Suddenly she remembered Jan's reaction to her working. But Jan's frustrations didn't really have anything to do with her mother's working. Lilli had at last arrived at peace with herself on that score. "I can't tell you how happy this makes me. You and Howie together in the business. Like your father and me." Her face was luminescent. In time she would step down, and Vicky and Howie would head Princess Lilli.

But when Vicky left the office to go upstairs and tell Howie of her decision, Lilli again grappled with the realization that her hold on Princess Lilli depended on her control of proxies. Again she berated herself for selling out all those years ago. Revson had gone public in 1955, but he controlled his company. Rubinstein controlled hers. Elizabeth Arden owned her company. She would not rest until she had a majority of the shares in Princess Lilli—but the precious few percent she needed remained elusive.

In MID-NOVEMBER, Lilli went to spend a week with Greg and Anne in Phoenix. The salon was doing well, and her appearance caused quite a stir socially. Greg arranged for a reception at the Arizona Biltmore. There was newspaper and TV coverage. Anne insisted on taking a day away from the salon to drive Lilli north along the tedious route through Wickensburg, Prescott, and Camp Verde into the midst of awesome "red rock country."

While driving with Anne, Lilli suddenly understood what Vicky had been trying to tell her about presenting a new line of youthful cosmetics. Though "red rock country" had been formed millions of years ago, there was an exultant spirit of renewal here. The colors, the incredible formation of the rocks, were at once ageless and young.

She would send Vicky and Howie out here. They could go to Cottonwood to visit his parents for a couple of days. And they would return to create a "Red Rock Country" line that would appeal to the eighteen-to-thirty-four age group. The illusion of the campaign would be that the new line was created in this marvelous country. Clean, pure, bursting with health. It would be Vicky and Howie's baby, *their own line*. And it would tie Vicky forever to Princess Lilli.

ON THE NIGHT FOLLOWING Carol's sweet sixteen party at the Four Seasons, Lilli gave a postbirthday family dinner at the house. The first to arrive on the blustery March evening was David, in his senior year at Columbia, and looking forward to his first term at medical school in September. He brought a box of red roses for his grandmother and white roses for his sister.

"I've rearranged my travel schedule," Lilli said as Henri took the flowers to put them in water, "so I'll be in town for your graduation."

Within ten minutes the library was filled with the sounds of lively conversation. Her face reflecting her love, Lilli gazed at Carol, who reflected the sweetness and compassion of Freddie. She was grateful for Carol's presence in the house whenever Freddie and Debbie were off on either peace or civil-rights missions. And she was proud of her son's efforts: Freddie and Debbie were the conscience of the family.

Lou and Marcia arrived last, Lou carrying a package. "A present for you." He held it out to her.

"Lou, how sweet of you."

Slowly, Lilli unwrapped the package. She smiled as she inspected the book jacket. Lou's novel. Now that she held the product of his labor in her hands, it was exciting that her son was a novelist.

"It's the first copy," Marcia said. "Open it and look inside."

Lilli opened the book, turned past the title page, and read the dedication. Tears welled in her eyes. *To Mama, with love and gratitude.*

"Everybody, come and see Lou's novel!" she called out. "This is the very first copy. We must have a party, Lou. We'll hire a top publicist. I want the whole world to know my son has written a marvelous novel."

Lou laughed. "Mother, you haven't even read it."

"If you wrote it," she said, "it's marvelous."

Late that evening, when everyone except the staff had left the house, Lilli settled herself in bed to read Lou's novel. She had never felt so close to her son. How wrong she had been to try to keep him in the business. And how proud Alex would be that his son had made a place for himself in the world! Alex's father had tried to hold him in the family business. Alex had rebelled—as Marcia had helped Lou to do. Thank God for Marcia. Lilli had no doubt in her mind that Lou would be successful with his writing. After all, he was Alex Kahn's son.

Her children might move into other fields, Lilli told herself as she put Lou's book down, but Howie had brought Vicky home to her. In July and August, when the shows would be held all around the country to introduce the new Christmas items, Princess Lilli would stress its new Red Rock Country line for the younger purchasers.

Lilli knew there was some consternation among stockholders about the enormous investment she was making in Red Rock Country. She also knew that it might take two or three years—or even longer—for the line to move into the black. Why was it that one stupid move in her lifetime could forever haunt her?

She could have been at peace in her world—except for that four percent of Princess Lilli stock.

47

A COOL NIGHT BREEZE drifted into the library of the Southampton house, a pleasant contrast to the blistering heat of the day. The three in the library—Lilli, Vicky, and Carol—were unaware of the weather. The drama in the Los Angeles Sports Arena—the scene of the July 1960 Democratic Convention—held them captive.

Tonight, the supporters of John F. Kennedy battled those of Lyndon B. Johnson for the Democratic nomination for the presidency. Earlier primaries had demonstrated that Adlai Stevenson, Hubert Humphrey, and other candidates were out of the running. At this moment an impassioned Eleanor Roosevelt was making a last-ditch plea from the visitors' gallery for Adlai Stevenson, long the idol of many liberals. His appearance on the convention floor earlier had brought such affectionate applause that, fleetingly, hope had welled in the Stevenson-worshippers.

"What chance did Stevenson have?" Vicky said bitterly when Mrs. Roosevelt was seated again after thunderous applause. "Who could fight the Kennedy millions? John Kennedy has had every weapon at his disposal—TV, newspaper ads, direct mail, even his own Convair to fly him around the country."

"I can't bear the intellectuals who've shifted to Kennedy," Lilli said with contempt. Carol knew her grandmother was forcing herself to become involved in the convention. She was still shaken by Henri's sudden death from a heart attack five weeks ago.

"They admit that Stevenson is the best man, but they're sure Kennedy will win for them. Best doesn't count."

"I think it might be exciting to have John Kennedy as our president," Carol said softly. Lilli and Vicky frowned. "I think this is an exciting time to be alive."

They turned back to the television, but Carol's thoughts went back in time. In February, in Greensboro, North Carolina, four young black men had walked into the F.W. Woolworth store on South Elm Street and sat down at the lunch counter. It was the beginning of a movement that swept across the country—to other Woolworth stores, to Kress, Liggett, and Walgreen. Civil-rights demonstrators from Harvard, Yale, MIT, and Brandeis joined the movement. Through this past spring and summer, the protest expanded—and slowly the protesters made progress. Carol was proud that her father and stepmother had been among them, though she couldn't really understand the depression that settled over her grandmother and Vicky with the nomination of John Kennedy.

Like some of her classmates at school, Carol was intrigued by the charismatic young man with the Bostonian accent who would fight against the Republican candidate to be nominated later this month. When she returned to the city, she would become a volunteer for him. That would be almost as exciting as being a freshman at Barnard in September. Maybe next summer Dad and Debbie would let her join in their work, the way David had been doing for several years now.

On the night of November 8, the girls at Carol's floor of the dorm gathered in their lounge to watch election returns on TV. As the hours passed, the atmosphere grew increasingly tense. It was predicted that this would be one of the closest elections in U.S. history.

Slowly the cluster of girls thinned. Carol disappeared briefly to change into pajamas and robe, returned to rejoin the dwindling gathering. A shout of triumph echoed through the lounge when at dawn, with Michigan narrowly going to Kennedy, newsmen were indicating Kennedy had won.

"There could be a reversal!" a Nixon follower said. "We won't know for sure until morning."

But Carol went to sleep convinced that John Fitzgerald Kennedy was the president of the United States.

By the end of her freshman year, Carol knew she would go into social work. She knew, also, how this would disappoint her grandmother. But there was no need to tell anyone yet.

For Lilli's seventy-fifth birthday in April 1962 the family planned a surprise birthday party at Le Pavillon. Carol was delegated the task of bringing Lilli to her favorite of French restaurants. The evening before the party Carol called with a preplotted story. Her grandmother must have dinner with her, her friend Suzanne, and Suzanne's father to discuss Suzanne's possible talents for a career in cosmetics.

"Let's dress for dinner, Grandma, even though it's only with Suzanne and her father," Carol coaxed ingratiatingly.

"For dinner at Le Pavillon I always dress," Lilli assured her. She saw through the subterfuge.

All through the following day Lilli went along with the pretense that her birthday had been forgotten, though whispered consultations she intercepted between Howie and Vicky were blatant hints. Somewhat earlier than usual she left the salon and went into the waiting car. Even Ralph, the new chauffeur, was in on it, she noted.

At the Gramercy Park house she ordered a bath to be drawn, though normally she preferred a brisk shower. Tonight she would soak in a perfumed bath and contemplate her future, she told herself indulgently when she was alone. Her maid was dismissed for the evening.

She had harbored thoughts these past months about stepping down as head of Princess Lilli on her seventy-fifth birthday and remaining only in an advisory capacity. But tonight, as she inspected her reflection in a full-length mirror, she felt ambivalent about this move. Neither Rubinstein nor Arden was stepping down.

The woman that stared back at her from the mirror appeared in her early fifties. Her hair was only slightly lighter than when she was fifty years younger—by virtue of the bottle, of course, because lighter was more becoming with the passage of time. Her face—as Aunt Sara's had been—was remarkably unlined. No, she was good for another five years—at least.

For tonight she chose a slim, elegant black velvet from St. Laurent's first collection at his own couture house. It was a perfect background for her emeralds and would be dramatic in the setting of Le Pavillon's cerise damask upholstery and arrangements of roses.

Right on time, Carol appeared at the house. Ralph drove them to Le Pavillon. On the way, Carol talked enthusiastically about school and the newly formed Peace Corps.

"It seems so silly to be going to college when I could be working with the Peace Corps," she said casually.

"It's not silly at all." Lilli tried to hide her concern. "Education is important. You can make a more valuable contribution to society with a college degree."

"That's what Dad said." Carol made a face. "But I'm old enough to join the Peace Corps. You only have to be eighteen."

"Why don't you think about it after college," Lilli said. But perhaps, like Vicky, Carol needed to have a taste of the world first. Still, she wanted to see Carol in the business while she was alive.

Lilli walked into the restaurant with Carol at her side. Freddie and Lou came forward and escorted her to the table.

"Happy birthday, Mother!"

She looked around the table, and tears came to her eyes. Greg and Anne had flown in from Phoenix. David had come down from medical school. Everyone was here, except for the babies of the family.

"Did you think we had forgotten you?" Lou asked after she had been warmly kissed.

"Not *all* of you." Lilli chuckled. "But I love it, anyway."

It was an evening rich with reminiscences. Vicky and Lou were always fascinated by Jan and Freddie's recollections of the years in London—and Jan insisted that she remembered being a tiny girl in Paris. Lilli's eyes rested on Anne, who looked radiant tonight. She was the best thing that ever happened to Greg.

The conversation took a somber turn when someone raised the question of President Kennedy's insistence that U.S. troops in Vietnam were "not combat troops in the generally understood sense of the word"—though they had been instructed to "fire to protect themselves if fired upon." While they waited for the table to be cleared and dessert served, Lilli excused herself and went to the powder room. She gestured to Anne to accompany her.

"Anne, I couldn't bear waiting another minute to ask you." Lilli linked an arm through hers. "Are you pregnant?"

Anne looked startled, then pleased. "Yes. We were going to tell you later. Nobody else knows yet. How did you guess?"

"You have that I'm-pregnant-and-thrilled-about-it glow about you." Lilli kissed her. "You've given me the most beautiful birthday present in the world."

When Lilli and Anne returned to the table, the men were still in a deep discussion about the situation in Vietnam: They all feared escalation. The women—except for Carol—were involved in Jan's report of the current activities of the Alex Kahn Foundation. Carol, caught up in the Vietnam talk, was silent, but absorbed in every word that was said.

AS THE END of the school year approached, Carol confronted her father and Debbie about being allowed to spend the summer working with them in the civil-rights movement.

"David works with you every summer. Why can't I?"

"She's right, Freddie," Debbie said. "She's nineteen and intelligent. She's been brought up to have a social conscience. Just because she was born female doesn't mean she has to sit on the sidelines."

When school closed, Carol flew south to join her father, stepmother, and brother in working with a student group fighting for civil rights. She wasn't sure what she would be doing, but she felt confident it would be something useful. Her father not only worked with the civil-rights group but was trying to organize free medical clinics.

As she gazed out the airplane window at fanciful puffs of white clouds, Carol reran in her mind a late-night discussion in her dorm room with several of her classmates, all of whom felt guilty and self-conscious about their affluence.

"I don't think it's enough to just talk about it," Carol had said.

"Well, I think it's stupid," her roommate said. "I got arrested in Greenwich Village for marching against the cops that time they tried to stop the kids from hanging around the fountain and playing their guitars. That's enough."

Carol eyed her. "And what are you doing *this* summer?"

"You know." Her roommate was reproachful. "My mother rented this groovy house in Saint Tropez."

"Well, *I* won't be lying around in the sun in a bikini," Carol said. "I'll be doing something to help make the world a better place to live in."

The plane was preparing to land now. She fastened her seat belt. Across the aisle two middle-aged men were talking about the fighting in Vietnam.

"When American soldiers are killed in Vietnam, we're fighting a war," one said. "And when we send a battle group of eighteen hundred U.S. marines, I tell my wife I'm damn glad our two children are girls."

"Some of those in Washington are predicting Kennedy will ask for authorization to call up a hundred to two hundred thousand reservists before the end of the year. That means my kid, who fought in Korea."

Carol felt a coldness close in around her. Would David go to Vietnam? He still had another year in medical school. She remembered her father's years of horror in the Pacific. Hadn't the world seen enough of war in this century? Weren't two world wars and Korea enough?

As summer drew to an end, Carol fought with her father and Debbie about returning to college in September. She'd felt so *useful* working this summer. But Freddie and Debbie insisted she return to Barnard or not be allowed to work with them again the following summer. Reluctantly, she capitulated.

Pride demanded that she earn excellent grades in school; but whenever she finished studying, she would go down to the West End Bar or a nearby pastry shop where she exchanged rebellious thoughts with other equally rebellious students. During the Thanksgiving holidays she flew to Phoenix on the company plane with her grandmother and Aunt Jan. Six days earlier Anne had given birth to a son, and Lilli had decreed that the three of them would represent the family at the infant's *briss*. While they were there, Lilli hired a chauffeured limousine to drive Carol and Jan up to Sedona for a brief look at her beloved Grey Creek Canyon.

The following summer Carol joined her father, Debbie, and David in Alabama. With the same reluctance as the previous summer—lightened by the knowledge that this was her senior year—she returned to Barnard in September of 1963. She was determined not to go on to graduate school.

On a Friday afternoon late in November, Carol returned to her dorm to discover a cluster of girls gathered about the television set. Some of them were crying.

"What happened?" she asked.

"President Kennedy..." a student sobbed. "He's been shot! It's bad!"

Dazed, the students huddled before the television set long after the newscaster had announced that John Fitzgerald Kennedy, president of the United States, was dead. For Carol and many of her contemporaries, it was a personal tragedy.

THREE MONTHS LATER, Carol met Michael Graves, a graduate student at Columbia, in the Salters Bookstore on Broadway across from Columbia. After he'd retrieved a hard-to-reach book for her, it seemed natural to go with him for coffee and cake at a pastry shop favored by Columbia and Barnard students. Right away Carol knew that she and Michael cherished the same ideals. He was eloquent about civil rights, had spent the past three summers working, like herself, with a civil-rights group. The only subject they disagreed on was Vietnam. Carol shared her family's conviction that American forces did not belong in Vietnam.

"My older brother, Jason, is a correspondent in Vietnam," Michael said somberly. "He hints that what we're reading in American magazines and newspapers about what's happening over there is far from the truth. The war is just not working for our side."

Before she knew it, Carol was spending every free moment with Michael. She began inventing excuses not to go to her grandmother's Friday dinners. Instead, she and Michael sat around with other students at the West End Bar or East Village coffee houses. Their romantic efforts were largely unsatisfying; Michael shared an apartment on West 105th Street with three other grad students, so the two of them had no place to be alone. Carol knew he wasn't ready for marriage, and he'd said he was "too square" to sleep with her unless they were married.

A few days before graduation, as they strolled arm in arm through Riverside Park in the early dusk, Michael told her that he had enlisted. Carol froze in shock.

"Michael, why?"

"I think this country has to help the Vietnamese fight communism. I grew up in a middle-class New England family that goes back a hundred and fifty years. I was brought up steeped in patriotism—whatever my country does is right."

"But it's wrong." *American soldiers were dying in Vietnam.*

"I have to do what I think is right. Carol, I don't know how long I'll be gone. But when I come back"—*If he comes back,* she thought in anguish—"I want to marry you. If you'll wait for me."

"Oh, Michael, I'll wait."

He kissed her. "You know, nobody's going to be at the apartment tonight."

"Then let's go there." Who knew what the future might hold?

They left Riverside Park. "Let's pick up some sandwiches and beer," he said as they headed south on Broadway. "For later."

THE FAMILY WAS STARTLED when Carol told them she planned to stay in New York this summer and apply for admission to a graduate program at Columbia. "I've decided on social work," she announced to the surprised faces around the table at this family dinner celebrating her graduation from Barnard. How could she leave New York when Michael would soon be headed for Vietnam? She had to be here to receive his letters. "Meanwhile, I'll take some courses during the summer."

Grandma looked like a toddler who had just had a double-scoop ice cream cone snatched away, Carol thought with a mixture of guilt and defiance. She had never *promised* to go into Princess Lilli, even though Grandma always talked about it. She had Vicky and Howie in the business. The whole family didn't have to be involved.

"You'll stay with me," Lilli said. "Your father and Debbie will be away all summer."

"I'd like to rent an apartment near the campus," Carol said casually, turning to her father and Debbie. *Why did they look so shocked?* When Vicky was trying to break into theater, she had her own apartment down in the East Village. "It'll be more convenient to classes."

CAROL FOUND a cozy one-bedroom apartment with high ceilings and a woodburning fireplace in an old graystone on Riverside Drive. Michael would love the fireplace and the view of the river, she told herself. And soon—please, God, *soon*—he would come home from that crazy war and they'd get married. They could live here together. They didn't need a large luxury apartment.

It felt strange that nobody in the family had ever met Michael. It was just that they'd had so little time together. All she knew of Michael's family was that they lived in a small town in Vermont and that his brother Jason was a correspondent in Vietnam.

Carol focused her attention on her classes while she waited for admission to the Columbia School of Social Work. Her roommate had returned to Virginia. Most of her friends were scattered for the summer. A few would return in the fall for graduate studies. She spent virtually all her time in the Columbia-Barnard area, visiting only those places where she and Michael used to go.

On August 2 General Westmoreland took over the fast-growing American forces in Vietnam, where the first land-based jets were stationed. The Seventh Fleet was patrolling international waters off North Vietnam. North Vietnamese PT boats were reported to have attacked the *Maddox*, a U.S. destroyer in the Gulf of Tonkin. Fighter planes from the U.S. carrier *Ticonderoga* rushed to the destroyer's defense. Three days later, U.S. planes bombed installations and naval craft in North Vietnam, to a loud international outcry. On August 7 the Senate and House passed a joint resolution approving this action. A week earlier they had passed a resolution giving President Johnson authority to take whatever measures were necessary to repel armed attack and to provide help to any SEATO nation requesting help in defense of its freedom. The United States was launched on a full-scale war.

The months dragged by with a chain of brief, unsatisfying letters from Michael. He was on the move, he wrote. He had run into Jason, who was staying in Saigon on his own now with hopes of selling articles to magazines back home. "Things are not quite what I had expected," he wrote, and Carol surmised that censorship prevented his being more explicit.

American newspapers wrote about the war with an optimism that was not reflected by many of the young in the country. Americans were dying in Vietnam. How could the government refer to the 23,000 American soldiers in Vietnam as "advisers"?

On March 8 and 9, more than 3,500 U.S. marines landed in South Vietnam—the first acknowledged combat troops sent there. Two weeks later American spokesmen in Saigon conceded that the South Vietnamese forces were being supplied with a nonlethal type of tear gas by the United States. Members of Congress joined in the outcry against this action.

In May another 4,000 marines landed in Vietnam. With no mail from Michael in almost two months, Carol was distraught. When would this insane war be over?

48

LILLI LEFT HER OFFICE to take the elevator to the executive dining room where she would have lunch with Vicky and Howie. They were trying to settle on a model for long-term advertising for the Red Rock Country line. Lilli had not yet seen a model who fitted her image of the "Red Rock Country girl."

In the elevator, Lilli thought again about Helena Rubinstein's death last month. The newspapers had given her age as ninety-four, but some in the business were convinced she had been ninety-nine. A smile touched her lips. Compared to Rubinstein, Vicky had told her, she was an ingenue. Yet it was disconcerting that one of the "big three" cosmetic queens was forever gone from the scene.

Vicky and Howie were already seated at her favorite table by the window, shuffling through a batch of glossies—black-and-white photos submitted to Howie by a top modeling agency. Revson—who had moved on from Suzy Parker to Candy Bergen—felt it was of prime importance to use a model that personified a line, and Lilli agreed.

Lilli considered the photographs lying on the table. "Not one of them is right. With the money we spend on advertising, the girl has got to be perfect for the line." She paused. "I keep coming back to one girl."

"Who?" Vicky looked startled. "I thought we'd rejected all the other submissions."

"Carol." She refused to admit that this was a devious effort to draw her granddaughter into the business. "She's very young, clean-cut, lovely. I don't have to tell you how well she photographs.''

Howie stared at her. "Lilli, you're a genius. It synchronizes perfectly with Princess Lilli. Lilli Laval graces every Princess Lilli package. Carol Laval, carrying on the tradition of her grandmother's beauty, will be the image on every package of Red Rock Country. It'll make great copy!''

"Someone will have to persuade Carol to do this," Lilli said. "She's all wrapped up right now in social work." She paused. "On the rare occasions I've seen her these last months, she has looked unhappy. Oh, she smiles a lot and tries to pretend all's right with her world. But it isn't." She looked from Vicky to Howie. "Any idea what's bothering her?''

They exchanged glances. "None," Vicky said. "Should I try to talk to her?''

"No. I don't think we should press her." Lilli thought a moment. "Freddie and Debbie will be back from Alabama any day." They'd been there since Martin Luther King, Jr., led the five-day, fifty-four-mile march of 3,200 from Selma to Montgomery. "Maybe Carol will talk to them. But in the meantime, tell her we need her for the new Red Rock Country campaign. Stress that we *need* her."

WITH THE SCHOOL YEAR at an end, Carol was acutely conscious of the passage of time. She had not heard from Michael for close to three months. The newspapers kept talking about the low casualty figures of Americans in Vietnam—*but Americans were dying*.

Taking summer classes again to fill her time, Carol tried to locate Michael's family in Vermont. They lived in a small town, he'd said—she'd never heard of it. Finally she tracked down the phone number through Information, sat in indecision before the phone for ten minutes, then braced herself to dial. Her heart pounding, she heard the phone ringing at the other end. How could she come out and say, "Michael and I are in love—we plan to be married"?

"Hello?" It had to be Michael's mother.

"Hello. I'm a friend of Michael's." Her voice was strained with the effort to sound casual. "Several of us were talking about Michael last night. We're all out of touch since he went to Vietnam, and we wondered what you hear from him."

She heard a sharp gasp. "My son gave his life for his country." The phone slammed down.

Carol sat immobilized with shock. *Michael was dead*. He would never walk through that door. He would never live here with her. They would never marry and have children. He was twenty-three years old, and his life was over.

She sat in the living room while night descended on the city. Not bothering to switch on a lamp, ignoring the phone calls that interrupted the silence in the course of the evening, she tried to remember every moment she and Michael had spent together.

In the morning she wrote a brief note to her father and stepmother, to be delivered to their house in New York, and another to her grandmother. She'd decided to drop out of summer school, she told them. She was flying out to Arizona for a brief vacation.

She remembered her grandmother's infatuation with Sedona, that little town above Phoenix. She would rent a small house and be alone with the "red rock" cliffs until she could face the world again.

She went to the bank, withdrew a substantial amount of money, put most of it into traveler's checks, and took the next flight to Phoenix. When she arrived, she rented a car and drove to Sedona. She was able to rent a tiny cottage set in the shadows of Oak Creek Canyon. The locals were warm, but they left her alone. They assumed she was an artist, drawn by the splendor of the red rock country.

Slowly, through the summer, Carol came to accept Michael's death. She knew she must go on living, but the years ahead seemed long and empty. She sat for hours each day on the deck of her cottage, gazing in awe at the brilliant reds, pinks, and buffs of the cliffs that towered above her on every side, proclaiming the timelessness of nature. She took "Pink

Jeep Tours" through Oak Creek Canyon and lost herself in the beauty of the trails.

There was no phone in her cottage. She wrote to her father and Debbie and to her grandmother to say she needed some time alone because someone close to her had died in Vietnam. Her grandmother wrote back to say that the Kahn Foundation was siphoning substantial funds into a group that was demanding U.S. withdrawal from Vietnam. In a way, she told herself, her grandmother was providing a memorial to Michael.

ON HER RETURN to New York, Carol went on an apartment-painting binge. She decided to do it herself because she needed the therapy of physical activity. She was astonished when her grandmother and Howie asked her to become the "Red Rock Country girl."

"Carol, it's wonderful for our advertising," Lilli said at a meeting set up only a few days after her return from Sedona. "It's a marvelous continuation through the generations. And it's important to Vicky and Howie," she added. "After all, this is their line. But it's taking longer to push into high volume than some of the stockholders like. It's not as though we were a personally owned firm now, like Elizabeth Arden and Estée Lauder."

"If it's so important to you, I'll do it," Carol said. "Though I'll probably be awful."

Lilli smiled brilliantly. "It won't take up a lot of time. You could go back to school."

"No." Carol was firm. "I'm going to work with a group at Columbia that's setting up demonstrations against the war in Vietnam. That's more important right now."

The day before the scheduled October demonstrations against the United States' participation in the Vietnam War—to be held in cities across the nation—Carol came home to find a young man standing outside the door of her apartment.

"I was beginning to think I ought to ask for a lease." He had a warm smile. Did she know him? He seemed familiar somehow. "You're Carol, aren't you?"

"Yes." She reached into her purse for her key and paused. "I'm sorry. Should I know you?"

"Not really. Though I recognized you from snapshots. I'm Jason Graves."

White with shock, Carol dropped the books she cradled in one arm. "You were with Michael in Vietnam, weren't you?"

"We spent several hours together on three occasions." Suddenly he looked drained. He bent to retrieve her books while Carol struggled to unlock the door. "He told me about you."

Together they went into the apartment. "Would you like some coffee?"

"Great."

While she prepared coffee, Jason talked to her about Michael. "You know why he enlisted," Jason said. "His feelings of 'my country, right or wrong.' But that changed, Carol. Oh, he was still American all the way, but he was asking a lot of questions."

For three hours Carol and Jason talked about Michael and about Vietnam. Now she understood Mrs. Graves's abrupt reaction on the telephone. "Mom received word from the War Department about Michael just two hours before you phoned," he explained. "She thought it was someone with a lousy sense of humor."

Jason was going back to Vermont to write a book. He would take part in the demonstrations against U.S. involvement in the war. When he left, Carol felt she had found her purpose in life. To fight for peace would give her own life meaning.

Now Carol divided her time between the anti-Vietnam movement and modeling for Princess Lilli. She allowed herself little socializing except with family. She shied away from any romantic overtures. The hurt of Michael's death was still too painful.

The steady escalating participation of the United States in the war brought about International Days of protest the following March. In May 10,000 picketed the White House, but the war continued to gain momentum. In June at Amherst College, twenty of the 270 graduating seniors walked out of commencement exercises when Secretary of Defense Robert McNamara was presented with an honorary degree. Graduating seniors and faculty at New York University and Brandeis also protested the war.

In June it was announced that another 18,000 men would be in Vietnam within forty-five days, bringing the American total to 285,000. In August demonstrations were held across the country on the anniversary of the bombing of Hiroshima.

America continued its commitment to Vietnam the following year. In April Carol was one of a crowd estimated at being somewhere between 10,000 and 400,000 that marched from Central Park to the U.N. to protest the war. On the same day 50,000 marched in San Francisco. In July it was announced that American troops in Vietnam would be increased to 525,000 by the end of the year.

Shortly after Christmas of 1967, Lilli called a family business meeting at the Gramercy Park house on a Sunday afternoon. The past April she had arrived at her eightieth birthday. She knew the business upheaval that had followed Elizabeth Arden's death the previous year. She was determined that her own affairs be in order and that every adult family member understood them.

"Not that I'm preparing to step down," she said. "I may be eighty, but I feel half of that. But I want you all to know what's happening with Princess Lilli. Our advertising and promotion—and that's a huge part of the battle—is still young and aggressive. Revlon is losing ground, but Estée and Faberge are gaining a lot of counter space. We've got a three-pronged operation—Princess Lilli for the prestige trade, Mademoiselle Lilli for mass market, and Red Rock Country for the young—and I mean for us to be at the top in all three lines."

"Mother, you shouldn't drive yourself the way you do," Freddie said gently. "Lean more on Howie and Vicky."

"Those two are my right arm." Lilli smiled fondly at them. "But we must all be aware of a serious situation. I own slightly more than forty-nine percent of Princess Lilli stock now. I hold another three percent in proxies. But these are old ladies, and they're dying off. If their stock came on the market, I'd buy it up. But there's a conglomerate out there that's fighting to take over."

Howie looked shocked. "How did you learn about this?"

Lilli smiled. "My spies. The word has leaked through. It won't happen right away, but within the next eight to twelve months there's going to be a battle to take over Princess Lilli. Unless we can buy up enough stock to guarantee control, I could lose the company."

"What can we do?" Carol asked.

She was upset, Lilli thought with compassion. Carol—all of them—knew what Princess Lilli meant to her.

"We can approach everybody who holds shares and offer high prices," Scott said quietly. "Of course, that's going to shoot the stock price up. But if there's a conglomerate out for your scalp, Lilli, the price will shoot up anyway. That could account for the higher market prices these last weeks. It could be the moment for you to sell out for a staggering profit."

"Never, Scott." She knew Scott meant well. At her age, he was thinking, why should she fight? "I sold out once. Not again. I mean for Princess Lilli to be in business for the next three hundred years. It's my legacy to the family. I'm fighting for my company, and I won't give up."

IN APRIL 1968 the world was stunned by the assassination of Martin Luther King, Jr., in Memphis, Tennessee. A man of peace—just four years ago awarded the Nobel Peace Prize—had been brutally slaughtered. Carol flew with her father, Debbie, and David to Atlanta. They were among the 200,000 whites and blacks who followed behind the mules and the old farm wagon that creaked down the Atlanta streets with the body of Martin Luther King. Carol knew she would never forget the image of Coretta Scott King, beautiful in her grief, the mother figure in the tragedy that involved them all.

From Atlanta Carol flew to Phoenix, where her grandmother was visiting on business. Lilli's secretary had come down with the flu. Lilli was insisting on returning to New York, and at the same time insisting that her secretary remain in Phoenix to recuperate, so Carol was delegated to be her grandmother's companion. There was a secret family pact not to allow Lilli to travel alone, even on the company plane.

Carol lingered in Phoenix for two leisurely days, captivated by Greg and Anne's young son, Seth, while Lilli huddled with an elderly stockholder whose proxy she held. Carol was surprised when she was selected as a celebrity guest, the "Red Rock Country girl," at a reception to be held in Lilli's honor at the Arizona Biltmore.

"You handled yourself well," Lilli said with pleasure when they were en route to New York. "You have a feel for the business. I think you'll be able to take over some of the personal appearances for me."

"Grandma!"

"Just now and then. It's good training for you. After all, one day you'll own a lot of Princess Lilli stock."

Carol didn't want to argue with her right now. "How did your visit with the lady stockholder work out?"

Lilli sighed. "The woman is senile. So far there's no problem—her son is satisfied with Princess Lilli stock. And he should be. They all should be. Our sales and profit figures show steady growth and profitability. That's why it's so damnably hard for me to get my hands on the shares I need."

On the flight back to New York, Carol talked for the first time about Michael.

"I hurt for a long time. I don't think I'll ever be in love again."

Lilli smiled, patted her hand. "One day someone will come into your life and you'll change your mind. Your grandfather—may he rest in peace—killed my love. Oh, it took a lot of

years, and I was sure I'd never love another man. And then
Alex came into my life. He would have been a real grandfather
to you, darling. He was a real father to your dad. Someday,
Carol, I pray you'll meet a man like Alex. He's been gone almost twenty-three years, but sometimes I feel as though he's
still beside me."

Carol kissed her warm, soft cheek. "You were a lucky lady,
Grandma."

NOW CAROL WAS CAUGHT up in the presidential campaign of
Senator Eugene McCarthy. But along with the rest of the
world, she was stunned and shaken when, on June 5, Bobby
Kennedy was shot at the Ambassador Hotel in Los Angeles.
Roughly twenty-five hours later—about 5:00 A.M. eastern
time—Frank Mankiewicz, Kennedy's press secretary, made the
brief announcement to the press that Senator Robert F. Kennedy had died.

Carol had alternated between television set and radio
throughout the night, too shaken to consider sleep. When at last
word came that Bobby Kennedy was dead, she was too stunned
to cry. In her lifetime—*in the last five years*—three American
leaders had been assassinated.

Mayor Lindsay proclaimed Saturday as New York City's
official day of mourning, with only city departments vital to the
health and safety fully staffed on Friday. Movie theaters announced they would be closed on Saturday—the day of the funeral—until after 5:00 P.M. Governor Rockefeller ordered that
flags on all state buildings be flown at half-mast until after the
funeral. President Johnson declared Sunday the official day of
mourning and ordered that flags on federal buildings throughout the nation be flown at half-mast.

While Bobby Kennedy's body lay in state in St. Patrick's
Cathedral, 150,000 mourners lined up to pay their last respects. On Friday, Carol felt herself drawn to join the lines, yet
twice she left the apartment to head for St. Patrick's and twice
returned. Newscasters reported that at times the line, eight
abreast, stretched for twenty-four blocks. At last Carol willed

herself to go downtown in the blistering heat and join the hordes shown on television. Some of them waited as long as five hours.

The crowd was as diverse as America itself: Wall Street stockbrokers, suburban housewives, young couples with babies, mini-skirted teenagers, flower children, Harlem schoolboys in faded Levi's and sneakers. Occasionally Carol was conscious of a curious searching glance from a girl or woman who recognized her from the ads for Red Rock Country. She wished now that she had worn dark glasses, but that seemed so pretentious.

She tried to analyze her feelings while she waited, muscles aching from standing so long. She was here because she was angry and upset about what was happening to America—and to Americans: three assassinations; the race riots in Detroit, New York, and dozens of other cities across the country; police brutality.

At last those waiting moved into the tall Gothic cathedral, walking in two lines up the center aisle toward the mahogany coffin, unadorned this morning by flowers. The summer sun filtered through the stained-glass windows as the line moved silently past the closed coffin with its honor guard, the six amber tapers. A woman ahead of Carol reached to touch the casket. "It's closed," she murmured in disappointment. "We can't see him."

Out on the sidewalk again, Carol paused, not sure of her destination. She felt strangely reluctant to leave the crowd with whom she had shared this shattering experience.

"This is a day we'll always remember," a man's voice intruded, and Carol turned to the young man beside her. "We're living in such weird times."

"I can't believe that within three months and one day both Dr. King and Bobby Kennedy have been assassinated." Carol welcomed the chance to talk to someone.

"Would you like to walk for a while?" he asked. "Away from Fifth Avenue."

"Yes."

The dark-haired, brown-eyed young man beside her introduced himself as Peter Fiedler. He was two years out of Northwestern with a law degree. He'd come to New York straight from law school. His mother, who had died during his junior year at college, had been a New Yorker. His father, whom he had not seen since he was twelve, was on the faculty of a small midwestern college.

Even though they were tired from the long wait at the cathedral, they walked up to Central Park. On the way they passed a delicatessen and stopped to buy sandwiches and fruit juice.

They sat under a tree in the park and talked, grateful for the chance to share their thoughts.

"I don't want to work for some huge law firm," Peter said. "I was offered some great deals out in Chicago, but that's not why I broke my back getting through law school. I want to know that I'm working for something of value to humanity. Right now I'm working for Legal Aid."

"You sound like my father," Carol said softly.

"Tell me about him."

THOUGH SHE HAD BEEN CERTAIN it could never happen again, Carol knew within four weeks that she was in love with Peter Fiedler, and she suspected he was in love with her. But she was torn by conflicting emotions: exultation that she could feel love again, and fear of losing that love.

Late in July she phoned Peter to tell him she was going away for a few days. "I'll call you when I get back, Peter. I need time to sort some things out."

49

LILLI WAS PLEASED when Carol called early Friday morning to ask if she was going to Southampton for the weekend. During the summer, the traditional Friday-evening family dinners were suspended.

"Yes," she decided at that moment. "The beach always rejuvenates me." She was exhausted from the strain of these last three weeks. On the advice of both Scott and Howie, she had been stalling her response to the conglomerate's offer of $76 million for her shares of stock in the company. But her time was running out. She couldn't hold off a confrontation with the stockholders for more than another four or five months.

"May I hitch a ride?" Carol asked. "I'm too lazy to drive out myself."

"Sure. Let's leave early—you know what summer traffic is like on a Friday. We'll pick you up around noon. Can you be ready?"

"Of course. I'll be waiting in front of the house."

It would be a quiet weekend at the compound, Lilli thought with satisfaction. Lou and Marcia, Vicky and Howie, along with the children, had left two days ago for three weeks in Europe. For Vicky and Howie—now heading the international department of Princess Lilli—it was more business than pleasure.

Freddie and Debbie were in the Midwest campaigning for Gene McCarthy. After completing his surgical residency, David was off celebrating for a week with his girlfriend, a pretty young doctor whom Debbie was sure he'd marry. Jan and Scott were spending long weekends at Southampton until well into September.

The new Princess Lilli line—Natural Beauty—would be launched early in January with the usual expensive advertising-and-promotion campaign. Revson was all steamed up over fragrances this year—the hypoallergenic battle would be staged between Princess Lilli and Estée Lauder. It might take four or five years for Natural Beauty to move into the black, as it had with Red Rock Country, but her instincts told her the climate was right for a properly introduced hypoallergenic line.

At precisely noon Ralph parked at the curb in front of Carol's apartment house. As Lillie watched her slim and lovely granddaughter hurrying toward them, she noticed the faint shadows beneath her eyes. Carol had no idea that the Red Rock Country ads were already making her a minor celebrity. Howie was urging Lilli to use Carol for their next round of TV commercials.

"Did you see your father and Debbie before they left?" Lilli asked as Carol settled into the back seat.

"I came down for dinner the night before and slept over," Carol said. "And went in the car with them to the airport."

"Was David there?" Lilli knew she was being a busybody, but she couldn't resist.

"Yes. David and Eleanor." Carol smiled. "I think he's serious."

"It's time," Lilli nodded in pleasure. "He'll be thirty-one in November." She took pride in never forgetting a birthday.

"How's Red Rock Country doing?"

"It's moving up in sales. I'm pleased to accept the fact that I'm not immortal, but as long as I sit at the head of Princess Lilli, it won't become another cog in a conglomerate machine."

The question was, how long would she be able to remain in control? She had fought some desperate battles in her lifetime. She had fought with the conviction that she would win. For the first time, she wondered if this was a battle she couldn't win.

SHORTLY PAST SIX on Monday morning, Carol joined he
grandmother in the Rolls. Ralph was yawning behind the whee
Lilli was determined to be at the salon when it opened.

It had been a good weekend, Carol decided. Though sh
hadn't planned it, she had begun to talk to Grandma abou
Peter. Grandma had let her talk without pressing her. Only he
warm, approving smile told Carol that she liked what she wa
hearing about this young man. While they walked along th
beach at sunset, Grandma reminisced about her unfortunat
first marriage and her joy in the last. Could she and Peter shar
the same joy?

Back in her apartment, her heart pounding over her deci
sion, Carol phoned Peter at his office. "I'm back," she an
nounced. "What are you planning for this evening?" Th
weekend in Southampton had cleared her mind. She loved Pe
ter. She wouldn't fight that love.

Now Carol and Peter were together constantly. She was gla
that he didn't try to rush her into marriage, though he made i
clear that he anticipated spending the rest of his life with he
This wasn't like with Michael, she began to understand. Tha
had been young first love. She had known Michael for barel
three months. She wasn't quite twenty-one when she met him
Michael had been twenty-three.

Carol and Peter campaigned together for Gene McCarthy
and in late August they huddled together before the TV as the
watched the horrors of the Democratic convention in Ch
cago. Like many of the young antiwar protesters, they wer
depressed and bitter that neither Gene McCarthy nor Georg
McGovern had made any real impact on the voters, and the
were sickened by the brutality of police and National Guards
men, who beat hundreds of people—including bystanders an
newsmen—in full view of the TV cameras.

"Peter, what's happening?" Carol's voice broke. "It's lik
in Nazi Germany."

"It'll change," he said. "Because of people like us. Peopl
like your father."

"It's scary."

"Don't be scared. We're in this together."

ON THE FRIDAY following the Labor Day weekend, Lilli sat at the head of the conference table, flanked by Howie and Vicky, and listened to the lawyers and accountants explain the most recent crisis. Last week she had been forced to make a decision about Handler Drug's offer of $76 million for her Princess Lilli stock. She had rejected the conglomerate's offer. Now what she had feared for months was coming to a head.

"We have to be realistic," the senior member of the law firm was saying, his face troubled. "Handler knows now they can't bring off a clean take-over. They're setting the stage for a proxy battle—actually less expensive for them. At this point they've managed to buy up only eight point two percent of Princess Lilli shares in the last twelve months—at exorbitant prices. And that's shot the price way up on the market."

"It took me years to buy up twelve percent of the shares," Lilli said bitterly.

"And you were offering top money," the senior accountant said, "not insane prices, as Handler has done. You had the proxies—you knew you were all right." But her elderly ladies were dying off and the new shareholders were not so trusting.

"There are over seven thousand shareholders," Howie said. "Handler can't possibly know—"

"They've just latched on to the shareholder list," the accountant said.

Howie exploded. "How the hell did they get that?"

"The usual way," the accountant said. "Somebody greedy for a payoff. And they've got a sticky point on their side, Lilli. The word has leaked out about your new hypoallergenic line. Every time you introduce a new line, there are shareholders who turn green at the amount of money you're spending."

"What you're telling me"—Lilli struggled to remain calm— "is that Handler will go after proxies with a story that I'm about to bankrupt Princess Lilli with the new line."

"That's it." The accountant nodded grimly.

"The only way I can hang on to Princess Lilli is to buy up so much stock that Handler's eight point two percent—and whatever they can pick up in the meantime—will be too small to matter." Lilli paused. "I want to buy. *At any price.* I don't care if we have to hire a team of fifty people to go out and buy."

The lawyers and accountants looked at her in shock. "I'm not sure you can personally handle that kind of a campaign," the senior accountant said.

"Then I'd like a full breakdown of my assets," she said. "I'm willing to sell everything. The Princess Lilli Building, the factory building, all my real estate. Even the paintings and my jewelry. I want control of my company."

"You'd need close to seventy million," the lawyer said. "I'm afraid you'll fall short. You've put so much into the foundation—and trusts."

"Please give me a breakdown of my assets. I'll expect it by Monday morning. I'm not ready to abdicate."

LILLI WAS TREMBLING with rage and frustration when she returned to her office. She inspected the diamond-and-emerald-encrusted watch that Jan and Scott had given her for her eightieth birthday. The meeting had run longer than she had anticipated. She'd have to leave soon for the house. She made a point of dressing for the Friday dinners, even when only three sat down at the table.

A faint smile touched her mouth. Tonight Carol was bringing that young man. Which meant she was serious about him. Howie and Vicky would be there. Freddie and Debbie. Lou and Marcia and the children were down south visiting her family. Jan and Scott were coming. For a little while, in the bosom of her family, she would try to block out this crisis.

She was downstairs and waiting when Carol arrived with Peter. She liked him instantly. She noted, in the course of the next half-hour, that the others, too, were impressed with him. When Carol mentioned that Peter was on vacation for two weeks, Lilli urged her to take him out to the Southampton house. "I'm keeping the house open until late in October, and it's especially lovely out at the beach this time of year, when so many people have closed their houses for the season.''

Despite her resolution to avoid business talk, Princess Lilli intruded. Carol asked about a new moisturizer—packaged in an attractive globe-shaped bottle with a top in the form of a tiara—that was being test-marketed in the Southwest.

"It's taking off," Lilli said. "Expensive to manufacture, but the reception so far is terrific."

"Even the controller, who screamed when he saw the estimates, agrees it was a smart move," Vicky said.

Lilli could tell that Howie and Vicky were upset. They had put so much of themselves into the business. If there was a takeover, who knew if they would be able to stay on in their positions?

They had moved into the library for after-dinner coffee when Lilli received a phone call from Greg in Phoenix. "I just learned an hour ago," he said excitedly, "that Mrs. Ransome died several days ago. I called to offer my condolences. Maybe it was callous, but I brought up the question of her Princess Lilli stock. I hinted to her son that you'd be willing to pay well over market price."

"Call him again and make an appointment for me to see him late tomorrow afternoon."

"I can handle it for you," Greg said. "I just wanted your approval."

"No, I want to be there. I'll come out on the company plane tomorrow." She paused. "I'm sorry, Greg—I'm superstitious about this. Bear with me. Make the appointment." She would be back in New York on Monday, when the accountants came in with the list of her assets.

EARLY THE NEXT MORNING Lilli and her secretary, Glenda Arnold, boarded the plane for the flight to Phoenix. On their arrival Greg explained that Mr. Ransome had been unexpectedly summoned away from Phoenix but would return on Monday morning to discuss the purchase of the stock, Lilli fretted at the delay, but she was determined to clutch at whatever became available.

On Monday she conferred with Mr. Ransome. Arrangements were made for the purchase, but legal technicalities delayed this for another two days. Lilli called New York for a long, difficult discussion with the senior accountant. Item by item they went over her assets, estimating the market value of each piece of property.

"Everything goes up for sale," Lilli said. "Except the Gramercy Park house. Put this into motion right away. I should be back in New York within seventy-two hours at the latest."

Anne suggested that she and Lilli take Glenda for a drive to Sedona and Grey Creek Canyon. There was nothing else she could do but wait, Lilli fretted. They'd drive to Sedona for the day.

When they prepared to leave Phoenix on Thursday morning, Lilli was told that the plane had developed engine trouble.

"I'll go back on a commercial airline," Lilli said. "Glenda, make arrangements for two first-class seats."

Two hours later, Anne drove Lilli and Glenda to the Phoenix airport. While the three waited for the boarding announcement, they chatted with a friendly older woman and her son who were returning to New York after a visit to her parents. They were flying first-class, the woman confided, because she was recovering from a broken ankle and needed the extra legroom.

"Pardon me for staring," she said after a few minutes, "but aren't you Princess Lilli, the cosmetic lady?"

"The firm is Princess Lilli," Lilli said. "I was a princess—by marriage—very briefly."

"Wait till I tell my daughter that I met you at the Phoenix airport!" She beamed at her son. "My son's a detective. He meets all kinds of exciting people. But this is the most exciting thing that's ever happened to me." She reached for a tote bag, rummaged inside to bring out a bottle of the new moisturizer being test-marketed in Phoenix. "I bought this at your salon in town."

"I hope you enjoy it. Give me your name and address in New York," Lilli said. "I'll send you a bottle of our newest perfume—I think you'll like it."

While the woman carefully printed her name on a scrap of paper, they heard the boarding call. Lilli kissed Anne, asking her to bring Seth and Greg to New York for Hanukkah. Then she and Glenda joined the line to board the flight to New York.

Remembering that on the flight out Glenda had been fascinated by the cloud formations, Lilli insisted she take the window seat. The detective and his mother were seated directly across the aisle. Lilli suspected that his mother was not entirely comfortable flying. He kept up a stream of lively conversation as the plane rose into the air.

Moments after the seat-belt sign flashed off, a Hispanic-accented masculine voice from the rear of the plane demanded their attention.

"Everybody stay cool and nobody gets hurt," he said. "I got a grenade here under the handkerchief, and my sister's got a gun. Nobody move. Go on, Luisa. Talk to the pilot."

Lilli turned to Glenda, who was white with shock. Across the aisle the detective was guarded, understanding he could make no move that might cause harm to the passengers. His mother seemed fascinated by the action.

The stewardess walked ahead to the pilot's cabin and unlocked it. "Tell him we wanna go to Cuba," the hijacker yelled to the girl he called Luisa. He moved forward, a perspiring arm held above his head. A hand gripping the handkerchief-wrapped grenade.

The stewardess unlocked the door. Luisa ordered the pilot to change his destination.

"We'll have to stop in New Orleans to refuel," the captain said. "We don't carry enough to make it to Cuba."

Luisa called back the captain's request.

While Luisa relayed further exchange between hijacker and captain, Lilli focused on the object in the hijacker's hand. In his tension he gripped the handkerchief so tightly that it outlined the object beneath.

No grenade. A bottle of Princess Lilli's newest moisturizer. The tiara top poked against the soft material of the handkerchief.

Lilli turned to the detective, who kept his eyes on the girl. Lilli coughed lightly. The detective turned to her as though in rebuke. She held his eyes meaningfully, turned to stare at the so-called grenade, then with slow deliberateness turned her gaze to the tote bag at his mother's feet. She saw his sudden comprehension.

The detective was weighing the situation. It was clear the girl was unfamiliar with guns and too frightened to shoot. He tensed for action, then lowered his head in a slight nod.

As he lunged for the girl, Lilli called out, "That's not a grenade! It's a bottle of moisturizing lotion!"

The detective grabbed the gun. Three male passengers relieved the hijacker of his bottle of Princess Lilli's latest moisturizer.

IN NEW YORK the plane was met by police, the press, television cameras. Freddie and Carol stood in the crowd. Lilli and the detective were interviewed by TV news people. Lilli took full advantage of the situation to promote Princess Lilli's newest moisturizer over the networks.

At last Lilli and Glenda were swept off to her waiting Rolls-Royce by Freddie and Carol.

"Mother, you might have been killed," Freddie said when they were seated in the car.

"By a bottle of my own moisturizer?" Lilli clucked. The excitement of these last hours had been exhilarating.

Carol laughed. "Never mind, you two. The family's at the house, waiting to welcome you home."

There must have been news bulletins about the near-hijacking, Lilli supposed. The pilot had radioed ahead, of course. And the children, bless them, had rallied in alarm for her safety. But this experience—like the one fifty-one years ago in Paris, where she had come so close to being taken by the

Germans—once again made her face the harsh realities of this world.

She decided to sell to the conglomerate and use the years remaining to enjoy her loved ones. When Greg came east with his family, there would be four generations at the table. What more pleasure could she ask of life? The money from the conglomerate would go to Howie and Vicky to start a new cosmetic business. Her reign was over.

At the house she was welcomed with touching warmth.

"Mother, you're a heroine!" Vicky hugged her tightly.

"That was a great plug for the new moisturizer!" Howie said. "We couldn't buy that kind of advertising!"

"The family has something to say to you," Freddie said gently, exchanging a glance with Lou. "Let's go into the library."

Lilli sat in her favorite lounge chair. Lou was at the safe that had been installed in the library at Scott's insistence several years ago. He came forward now with a box piled high with documents. *Stock certificates.*

"We're all stockholders in Princess Lilli now," Freddie said. "While you were in Phoenix, we formed a team and approached stockholders. We offered them ten times market value for shares. Greg was in on it. His job was to keep you in Phoenix as long as possible."

"Ten times market value?" Lilli turned this over in her mind. *They must have all drained their trust funds.*

"Saturday morning, after the family conference, Peter and I went to the financial editors of all the newspapers," Carol said. "We went public with the whole story. It made the Sunday papers—a real scoop for them!"

"Including the introduction of your costly new line," Peter said with a grin. "And your own estimate that it might take five years to move into the black. When the team went out to buy, what we offered seemed great."

"Now nobody can ever take over Princess Lilli." Lou reached for his mother's hand and lifted it to his lips. "Long ve the queen."

Lilli's eyes swept about the gathering. Oh, she was blessed! "You did this for me." Never had she felt so loved, so happy with her world.

"It was a sensational business deal." Carol's smile was dazzling. "We're all your partners now. It's a family business, Grandma. We're all in it with you."

Her children and her grandchildren had sacrificed their trusts for her. They had that kind of faith in Princess Lilli. *They were a dynasty now.*